THE EYE
&
THE BLADE
TRILOGY

David Johns

POMEGRANATE PRESS

Published by Pomegranate Press,
South Chailey, Lewes, Sussex BN8 4QB
pomegranatepress@aol.com
www.pomegranate-press.co.uk

ISBN 978-0-9548975-3-6

The Frozen City was first published by George Allen & Unwin in 1984 and by
Unwin Paperbacks in 1985;
A Flight of Bright Birds was first published by George Allen & Unwin in 1985.

By the same authors:
Boyhunt [ISBN 978 0 9548975 2 9]

British Library Cataloguing-in-Publication Data.
A catalogue record for this book is available from the British Library.

Printed by 4Edge, Eldon Way, Hockley, Essex SS5 4AD

CONTENTS

The
Frozen
City

PART ONE

Arrival

1 Curfew

A group of men, five or six of them, their faces hidden within large hooded garments which fell over their shoulders, moved silently in the gathering dusk under the tall windowless wall. They said nothing. Tom hesitated, wanting to ask them where he should go, but there was something sinister about their silent progress and he stood still and watched them pass.

When he had entered the city through the large gateway only minutes before, he had been seized by feelings of hope and excitement. The guard, turned from the grille to laugh at a joke shared with a girl in the room behind, had not seen him slip inside.

It was the party following – a family pulling a handcart – which had caught the guard's attention, and even now Tom could hear the continuation of an argument, presumably about their identification papers. The voices were too distant to distinguish clearly. Nor was it possible to tell whether they spoke his own language.

Tom clutched at his coat and felt the picture safe in the pocket inside. It had been a long and a lonely journey. His shoes were battered and leaking, his trousers blotched with mud from endless hiking across fields. His skin had been flayed by the elements, so that it was brown and coarse and tough.

He felt uneasy now that he had arrived. The vision of the city had driven him on, but the reality was not as he had imagined. A thin mist swirled between the lights affixed to the high wall, and there was the sweet smell of woodsmoke adrift on the evening air. The group of men having passed on, there was a desolate emptiness in the narrow, twisting street, broken only by the sounds of a distant hammering and a muttered conversation at some hidden corner.

There were two paths he could take. One followed the high wall, running round the vast bulk of the metropolis, and seeming as if it would go on for ever. The other turned inwards, sloping down to an area enclosed by tall buildings. His feet led him along this route.

How hostile the city silence seemed! In the dark nights of his journey, sheltering in a hedge bottom or in the corner of a ruined barn while the moon skimmed the ashen clouds overhead, he had suffered from cold, damp and other discomforts. He had known fear when he was lost or when unseen wild creatures came snuffling close. He had been inexpressibly lonely, far from any human habitation. But never had he experienced the feeling of rejection which came over him in these narrow streets.

A volley of bells rang, sudden and loud, somewhere above his head. They seemed to echo on and on, further and further away, until he realised that there were other bells, countless, all of them pealing at the same time throughout the city. And at once there was new movement: doors opening and closing; a sprinting figure; somewhere a horse, its hooves clattering and skidding on a hard surface, as if it were being backed into a cart. Even as Tom stood indecisive, puzzled by the commotion, a bulky shadow materialised from the mist, passed on and then, pausing, half-turned back to him. A deep voice admonished him.

'Get along, young fellow. Do you want to be stranded at curfew?'

And then he was gone into the murk.

Tom was startled as much by the man's language as by what he said. It was his own tongue, though spoken differently, with a harsh accent. After weeks of wandering alone, without the sound of a human voice, it was like a blessing.

But the curfew! The bells rang on, and they seemed to grow more urgent by the second. Where could he go? Who would take him in?

The din ceased, momentarily, to be followed by the intoning of a solitary, more sombre, bell. From the direction in which he had come there was a metallic grating as the huge outer gates of the city were swung to and the heavy bolts thrust home. The light was failing, and the mist slipped down into the streets as if stalking any unfortunate who might still be abroad.

Tom shrank into a doorway, petrified. He wished himself miles away under a thorn bush, alone but not menaced. He had not examined his tattered clothing out there in the uncharted wilderness: now he looked down at his rags and felt weak and ashamed.

At last the monotonous tolling died away. In the silence he heard himself breathing, shallowly. Along the street dark curtains were pulled across the only windows he could see. No sounds came from within. The fog, enveloping the lights on the high walls so that they broke up into dim, fuzzy circles, dampened his jacket and began to seep through to his shirt.

And then, distant but growing closer, came the regular tattoo of marching feet. It rose from a light flutter to a distinct tramping, until Tom knew it was very close, behind the nearest buildings. There must be a dozen of them, the city guards. They came on and on, until – clearly no more than a few hundred yards away – on a sharp order (which Tom could hear) they halted. There was a shout, the scrabble of running feet. A man's voice called out, despairingly.

'No, no!' Tom heard. 'Misunderstanding! Lost!'

This was followed by a brief scuffle and a hideous cry. It seemed to have no ending, but to float on the dense mist, seeking him out where he cowered in the doorway.

The soldiers came on. The clack of their boots on the metalled surface grew sharper and louder, until they turned the corner – they were in two files, arms lightly swinging – and advanced towards him. They were so close that he could make out the design of their uniform, blue and green with gold epaulettes. The leader wore a large drooping moustache.

Tom was lifting his hands as if, impossibly, to hide himself from their view, when the door behind him swung open and, stumbling backwards, he collapsed in a heap on the floor.

2 The White Room

A hand dragged him inside and the door slammed shut. For several seconds his numbed senses were aware only of the closed door, its heavy metal knob. And then, slowly, he stood and turned round.

He was in a room, that was the fact of it, but the feel of it was very different. Green lights seemed to turn the warm air to liquid, and the faces that gazed upon him appeared to be fixed to bodies that swayed like seaweed in a gently swirling current. Indeed, the whole room began to sway, and Tom found himself unable to breathe. The green, underwater world faded until the faces became pale globes floating in darkness, these too ebbing, dissolving. He fell to the floor once more.

Sunlight flooding his senses. He was alone again, and in a different room, large but sparsely furnished. There was a bed, upon which he lay, two chairs and a writing desk. Opposite there was a large window, but the glass was frosted and it was set in a simple frame with no obvious means of opening it. The walls were white and interrupted by just one small painting, the subject of which was hard to determine under its cracked layers of darkened varnish.

Tom tried to move but his legs felt weak. The harshness of the light hurt his eyes and he rested his hand across his face, trying all the while to remember the events that had brought him here. There was a tangle of confusing images, but as he recalled the soldiers, the scream and the green room full of faces, his confusion turned to fear. What was he doing here? Who had brought him to this bed? Why did his legs refuse to move? Was the door to this room locked, and had he become a prisoner?

The last question was answered almost immediately, for the door in question swung open and a girl stepped inside carrying a tray. She smiled and set it down beside him.

'Mother thought you would like some breakfast.'

Tom could only stare at her, not quite able to believe his apparent good fortune.

'Fancy you being out after the curfew bell. Whatever possessed you?'

He remained silent. His mouth was dry, and the words that kept racing around his mind refused to fit themselves together to form a sentence. The girl sat on the end of the bed.

'You don't say much, do you? You really are ill, perhaps. We thought it was fright that made you faint.'

Now she spoke coaxingly.

'Have some of the breakfast, won't you? You're ever so thin.'

Tom looked at the tray, upon which rested a small jug of milk and a plate with bread and cold meat. He reached for the milk, drank a mouthful and felt himself able to speak.

'You're very kind . . . '

But once more he lapsed into silence, this time because the urgency of his hunger had suddenly taken control of him. He broke pieces from the bread and pushed them into his mouth. It was delicious bread, coarse and nutty, and the meat was salty and satisfying.

'Been here two days and nights, you have. Lying there shivering and muttering. Mother says you've churned up the elements for us: that misty weather lifted the night you came here and we're into the clear skies and frosts of the first winter.'

The girl, who must be about his own age, sat and watched him eat. What did she think of him? His clothes were worn and dirty. His hair was unkempt. He smelled a bit, he was sure.

'Would you like some more?'

Meeting his dazed expression she shook her head lightly and was gone again, downstairs.

For much of that day he slept, his slumber interrupted at intervals by the girl with his meals. He would try to rouse himself, allow her to push food between his lips, tilt a cup so that he could drink. Then he would fall back again, faint and indescribably drowsy. He felt, in the fitful moments when his brain cleared, that hour upon hour was passing. Only gradually did consciousness steal back.

Daylight was fading. As he lay still, staring at the darkened ceiling, he seemed to hear a sound rising from beneath him, an eerie sound as of distant voices raised in song. It was indistinct, yet when he shook his head from side to side the singing did not go away.

Then, from much closer, female voices rose on the air, one of them anxious and admonishing.

'He can't stay – you know that, don't you? He might endanger us.'

'He's too weak to go anywhere at present, mother. Give him a little time.'

'Why did it have to be our door – and during the meeting, too! Do you think he recognised anyone?'

'It was too dark, and he fainted almost straight away.'

'He can't stay. He'll have to go.'

Then the voices ceased, leaving on the air only the faint singing which lulled him once more into a deep sleep.

By the middle of the next day he was feeling much stronger, and with his strength came curiosity. What was the meaning of the green room and its occupants? Who was this mysterious girl who bent over him with such tenderness?

'Are you able to walk now?' she asked.

He levered himself to his feet. His legs were still weak but a few hesitant steps answered the girl's question. She looked at him, her eyes large and dark blue, and smiled sadly. It came upon him quite suddenly how pretty she was.

'I've brought you fresh clothes,' she said. 'There's a washroom next door you can use. Soon you must go from here.'

He sat on the bed, heavily. Tears began to fill his eyes.

'But where can I go?'

'That I can't answer.'

'Who are you?'

But she ignored the question, busying herself with the tray.

'Why do you care for me and then turn me away?'

'It has to be,' she said. 'I know nothing of you and you nothing of me.'

He reached forward and clutched at her arm.

'I remember a green room. When I arrived. You know what I am speaking of.'

'We can't talk of such things.'

'And last evening I heard singing – voices like a choir.'

She pulled herself way.

'If you have any regard for me,' she said in a strained voice, 'you will never ask me such questions or ever mention this house to another soul.'

Tom could only nod miserably.

For a while, after she had gone, he wandered around the room exercising his legs. Closer inspection of the picture revealed nothing: it was, perhaps, a portrait, as there seemed a paler oval at the centre. Was he imagining a strange resemblance to the picture that he carried in his pocket? At the thought of it Tom looked anxiously for his coat and found it draped over a chair. The picture was still there.

The frosted glass of the window prevented a view of the street below, although he judged that he was a long way up. The sky itself had turned from pale blue to sombre grey, and fluttering blurred white shapes beyond the glass suggested that it was snowing.

On the wall, below the window, he saw something scratched into the white plaster. It was a tiny inscription, and he peered closely to read it:

> *Wear me as your helmet*
> *falling masonry will break*
> *across my back*
> *Wear me as your spiked heel*
> *I will bite into ice for you.*
> *T.W.*

He did not fully understand the words, but the initials seemed to spring at him from the wall.

At first light next morning the girl appeared, carrying a black overcoat. Her eyes were red, as if she had been crying.

'You'll need this.'

It buttoned tightly across and reached down to his ankles. The buttons themselves were of a peculiar oval design, like a human eye.

The girl led the way down to the street, down to the door he had fallen through. Was this, then, the green room? Now it was not green or remarkable in any way. Confused, he stepped into the snowy street and, as he turned to say goodbye, she leaned forward and kissed his cheek. Then swiftly she was gone and the door was shut.

Tom stood in the gently falling snow, feeling desolate and perplexed. The disappearance of the green room was one mystery, but there was another. As he had followed the girl down the stairs they had passed a partly open door. There had been stairs that led down and down, and far in the distance he could see lights and, he fancied, movement. But most startling of all he could hear a distant sound, a sound that was lacking in these empty streets – the sound of a city going about its business.

3 Scarlet Daggers

Tracks in the snow revealed that he was not the first abroad in the early morning. Animal footprints passed close to the house, one of each set lighter than the rest as if the creature were limping on its way. Fainter, because now almost silted up, there were the marks of large boots, the strides between them impressively lengthy.

The sky was heavily muffled with drifts of snow yet to fall, so that the light was murky although the sun had been above the horizon for more than an hour. Was that why the city seemed so desolate?

No, there was another reason. The buildings against the street had turned their backs upon it. As he started on his way Tom observed not only curtains still drawn against the day, but doors sealed up or obliterated. In many cases coarse rubble had been piled in the opening and roughly cemented, as if the task had been carried out in haste. In others the old unused door remained but was heavily barred, with great sharp spikes driven into the ground before it. And where there was no side entrance, so that the front door was necessary, it was always immensely strong and pierced at eye-level by a Judas hole so that visitors could be closely scrutinised.

On his coat the flakes fell fat and white, lingering a moment before dissolving into a twinkling wetness. On the road the white carpet was already half an inch thick, and the roofs of houses – some lightly covered, others patched with dark areas of melted snow – revealed which parts of the buildings were inhabited. Always they were the parts furthest from the street.

And then he noticed a peculiar decoration. On each house, usually so high up as to be almost hidden under the eaves, there was a square black tablet. Painted on it was a single emblem – a scarlet dagger.

It was while he paused before one of these curious devices which was rather lower than most (so that he could make out the ornate hilt of the weapon and its wickedly sharp point) that Tom's attention was caught by a movement further along the street.

Turning, he saw on the other side, half-hidden by the massive porch which screened the doorway of one of the larger houses, the figure of a boy. He was staring intently at Tom, and the marks in the snow behind him suggested that he had been trailing behind for some distance. He was a fair-haired lad, slightly built, and about his own age. He wore a long, dull brown jacket and a pair of black boots which reached almost to his knees, the sombre effect of this offset by a scarf the colour of fresh leaves wound several times around his neck.

Tom raised an arm in greeting, but there was no reply. The other youth continued to stare. When Tom called out, his voice echoed strangely in the empty snow-blanketed street.

'Can you help me? Do you live here?'

Still the other gazed impassively ahead, almost as if he were blind and deaf. But blind he certainly was not, for when Tom began to cross the street the young lad turned and ran.

Tom gave chase keenly, stronger than for many weeks after the food and rest he had recently enjoyed. But the long coat hampered him. He felt himself losing ground to his quarry, who seemed to spring across the slithery surface with never a slip or check.

After they had run back along the street for a few hundred yards, the boy turned into a narrow alleyway Tom had not noticed before. It ran between the sides of houses – drawn curtains again, guarded doors – and into another street similar to the first. Tom saw the lad rounding a bend some way head, and then he was following footprints as his only guide.

Now there were sounds in the city, though muted and distant, but still there were no signs of any other living creature. He trod unbroken snow, always running alongside the tracks of the boy with the green scarf. These turned off the street to cross an area of waste land, where an immense pile of rubble was the only testimony to what must once have been an imposing building. He picked his way over the ruin, wondering at such complete destruction. The footprints plunged into a series of alleys.

The sounds were louder now: hammer-blows and what seemed to his ear to be the creaking of a winch and the scraping of metal on metal. And once (though he could not be sure, since the blood pounded in his ears from the running) he thought he heard a shout. And now there were other footprints entering this maze of closed-in passages – at first the tracks of individuals and then those of pairs and groups of three or four. It became increasingly difficult to follow the footprints of the boy who had watched him with such interest.

And then – still before he had seen a single person – he came to a meeting of ways where the snow had been trampled to a dirty pulp. The clues disappeared. Five paths radiated from the spot, each running between poor, ugly buildings as grey and closed as any he had passed. One of them had had all its snow compressed to water and was obviously used as the main thoroughfare of this district, and Tom followed it, now slowed to a walk, apprehensive of what he might discover.

Smoke, swirling into his eyes and open mouth, was his first introduction to the hidden life of the place. It billowed over a wall which protruded half across the path. On the other side of the wall was a courtyard, and to the rear of it a large furnace glimmered deep red with burning coals. The smoke lifted off it in great dusty clouds alive with sparks.

'Who's this, then? Who's our visitor?'

The words were spoken from the shadowed recess of the workshop by a man who emerged slowly into the dull light of day. He was a tall, thickset man, immensely broad across the shoulders. Despite the weather he wore nothing above his trousers but a stained leather waistcoat. He beckoned with a large and muscular hand.

'Come on, then. Let's be taking a look at you.'

Tom obeyed, meekly. Scared though he was, he thought the man's rough speech not necessarily hostile.

As he entered the workshop he saw a vast amount of equipment hanging on the walls – metalworking tools, hoops of iron, ornate grillwork and a host of other objects whose purpose he could not guess at. The heat of the great furnace swept across his face and he flinched from it.

'I was passing by,' Tom said.

The blacksmith (for such, clearly, he was) looked down on him from his considerable height and folded his arms, as if contemplating what he should do. His shaggy black eyebrows drew together in concentration.

'Passing by,' he repeated slowly.

And another voice, a lighter and a sneering voice rising from somewhere low down, joined in.

'Passing by, was he? Bad luck for him, I'd say. Doesn't do to pass by when workers are needed.'

Tom stepped back to look behind the furnace and discovered a thin, shabbily dressed man sitting on the floor with his legs splayed out unnaturally. In his fists he held the handles of a pair of stout bellows and, keeping his eyes fixed upon Tom, he now jerked himself into action, pumping air into the coals.

'Apprentice material, I should say.'

The remarks of this wizened creature seemed to galvanise the blacksmith into action. He strode forward and grasped Tom by the shoulders.

'How strong are your arms?' he demanded. 'What work have you done?'

'Very little,' Tom stammered. 'I don't want to be a blacksmith.'

'Neither did I, but I had no choice. Nobody has any choice.'

Miraculously there was a reprieve at that moment as two men entered the workshop. Tom noticed that, before speaking, they both half-turned towards one corner and gave a slight nod of the head, with a clenched hand against the forehead. It was done in a second, and as if from habit, and the men immediately began to engage the smith in conversation about iron gates. On the wall in the corner to which they had gestured was another plaque bearing the scarlet dagger emblem.

As the three men began to talk earnestly about prices Tom saw his chance of escape and began to edge gingerly towards the street, but he had moved only a few yards when the bellows-pumper sang out.

'Someone's trying to leave without permission.'

At this the blacksmith looked across, muttered something to his companions and grabbed Tom by the arm. Without a word he thrust him to the rear of the workshop, the force of it hurling Tom against the wall. He fancied he heard a snigger from behind the furnace.

No sooner had the two men left than the singsong voice began again.

'Some people have to be shown the way. Some people don't make things easy for themselves.'

And again this appeared to stir the smith to anger. He seized hold of Tom by the arm and dragged him close to the furnace.

'Off with that coat!' he demanded. 'Let's see what you're made of!'

Trembling, Tom did as he was ordered. He watched the coat hurled across the room, to land in a heap on a wooden bench. Beneath the new coat he still wore the old thin garment with which he had arrived in the city, for it held his precious picture, and, anxious that this should not be damaged, he quickly slipped it off and ran over to the bench with it.

'What eagerness!' mocked the bellowsman, pumping vigorously, and Tom – in his desperation – was almost glad that he had run so that they might be lenient with him.

'But a little more encouragement might make him more eager yet.'

The smith advanced with a heavy hammer in his hand. He was a fearful sight, his muscles picked out in the glare of the flames, his face gathered in a scowl.

'Get the rest off!' he commanded. 'It's a man's work you'll be doing.'

Stripped to the waist, Tom felt slight and puny against the blacksmith. The hammer that was pushed into his hand was heavy and unwieldy. The gases from the blazing coals choked him.

The blacksmith handed him a narrow bar of iron which immediately tilted away from him and hit the edge of the furnace with a sharp clang.

'Control the thing!' boomed the smith, putting a huge, muscular hand around Tom's. 'Lift it here.'

He manipulated the iron into position over the red coals and lifted the hand in which Tom held the hammer. He hurled the hammer down upon the iron so that pain shot up Tom's arm, and he would have released his hold had not his hand been trapped inside the other's far stronger one.

'We're making hinges,' the smith explained, less harshly. 'Like these.'

He picked a piece of shaped and flattened metal from the floor. Tom had seen many like it on doors he had passed – large and heavy like the doors themselves. It was difficult nonetheless to believe that they were created from such thick bars of solid iron. He lifted the hammer and dropped it upon the metal. It seemed to make no impression.

'Someone isn't trying,' taunted the voice from the floor. 'Someone needs coaxing.'

Tom raised the hammer again, his shoulder aching with the mere lifting of it, and brought it down on the iron bar. Again there seemed no result.

'You come and do it, then!' he cried in a sudden temper. 'If you're so clever, you can do it!'

A giggling laughter, which yet seemed totally without humour, was the only response.

'He can't,' muttered the blacksmith. 'His legs don't work.'

He pushed his thick fingers into the top of Tom's arms as if feeling for the sinews, causing him to cry out in pain.

'Someone isn't trying,' repeated the creature on the floor. 'Someone's being defiant.'

Now the blacksmith seemed to lose all patience. he shoved Tom violently in the back and again lifted his arm and dealt the metal a resounding blow. Tom's whole body shook with the force of it. The smith repeated the action, roughly and violently, and again and again. Sobs rose through Tom's tortured body, his breath escaping in short gasps between the blows. He could not cry for mercy. It felt as if he himself were being beaten against the metal on the furnace. His head swam and his eyes closed.

And then it stopped. A woman of middle-age had entered the workshop. Despite a clumsiness of gait and a dowdiness of clothing, which emphasised the shapelessness of her body, she clearly commanded respect. She seemed to pay no particular attention to the scene by the furnace, nor did she utter a single word of greeting. The smith released his grip on Tom to watch the newcomer cross the room towards a door in the far wall.

Before she reached it, however, she swung round to the bench on which Tom's clothes lay. Something had evidently caught her attention. She lifted the new overcoat and took one of the buttons between her fingers. After examining it closely she looked at Tom for the first time.

'Where did you get this?' she asked urgently.

Tom was unable to speak. The shock of his ill-treatment by the blacksmith seemed to have affected his vocal chords. And he was unsure of what he should say. He treasured the memory of his time in the white room as the one pleasant interlude in months of hardship and fear.

The woman signalled towards the pile of clothing.

'Fetch these and follow me,' she ordered.

The blacksmith stood passively by as Tom left his side, gathered his clothing and passed through the doorway. Even the bellows-pumper remained silent, as if overawed.

Beyond the door was a wood-panelled hallway, where the roar of the furnace was already dulled, and then a lighted corridor along which Tom followed the ungainly figure of his rescuer.

He was taken into a small room, with warm-coloured wainscoting and large, deep armchairs. Tom dressed himself while the woman busied herself in a cabinet, at last laying her hands upon a pair of spectacles. She put them on.

'Come now,' she said, recognising Tom's nervousness. 'Sit in that chair and stop your teeth chattering.'

'I'm sorry,' Tom replied, wondering what he should say. 'The blacksmith was forcing me to work in the forge.'

'That doesn't surprise me at all,' said his host in a matter-of-fact tone. 'You're easy prey, young lad. What are you doing here?'

'I was passing by.'

'And that is no answer at all, if I may say so.'

She pulled out a handkerchief to wipe her glasses. The room was warm and cosy. Tom's gaze passed from the oil paintings on the wall, to the large stone fireplace and to the heavy black curtains which reached to the floor. And then, with a start, he noticed, high on the wall to his left, the plaque with the scarlet dagger design. He was sure the woman had not nodded towards it.

'Passing by in order to end up where?'

Was it the release from the pain in the forge and the comfort of this lived-in room, or did this frumpy woman really have a kindly look about her? Tom had been looking for someone he could trust, and apart from the girl with blue eyes (who would not allow questions) he had found nobody.

'I don't know.'

'Don't know? Come now' – it was clearly a mannerism – 'come now, young man. Let us not have mysteries. You speak with a stranger's accent. You visit the dangerous parts of the city. What is your purpose?'

Tom hesitated for a moment, wavering. And then he decided to trust his intuition that she was honest. He reached into his inner pocket for the picture he had carried for countless miles and thrust it under her bespectacled eyes.

'Have you seen this man?' he pleaded.

4 Above the City

His hope faded almost as it was born. The woman frowned and pushed the picture back at him.

'What are you asking of me?' she demanded. 'Why do you show this to *me*?'

'But you don't understand,' began Tom. 'I'm . . . '

He stopped. He had meant to explain that he was alone, that the picture was of his father, that he was searching for his father. But she frowned at him uncomfortably. If she discovered that he belonged to no group, that the buttons on his coat signified nothing more than the kindness of a girl, would she then deliver him back to the smith? She averted her eyes from the picture.

'I can't help you, I'm sorry.'

It was then that Tom detected something different in the woman's voice – could it be an element of fear? Could she possibly be a little frightened of him or, rather, of whom she supposed him to be? Sensing an advantage, Tom addressed her with as much authority as he could muster.

'Who can help me, then? There must be somebody who can help me.'

The woman hesitated.

'I know of someone who might.'

Her voice was reluctant, but Tom's was eager.

'Where does he live? Is he near?'

'Not far. The smith will take you. But why did they send such a young boy?' (This last question was to herself and demanded no reply.) 'You'd better stay here till nightfall. You can go then.'

Tom wanted to ask about the curfew and soldiers, but he felt that his ignorance might expose him. Instead, an inspiration prompted him to feel each of his pockets and then to say: 'I've lost my papers. They must be in the smithy.'

The woman looked worried.

'I'll see,' she replied – and was gone.

Nightfall, and Tom stood ready, his coat buttoned tightly and, in his pocket, in addition to his precious picture, a complete set of newly forged papers. The smith entered dressed as in the morning, but now with the addition of a roughly woven cloak thrown about his huge shoulders. Tom could not suppress a shudder at the arrival of his former tormentor, but the smith's face showed no hostility, and his voice was friendly.

'It's a cold night little man, and icy underfoot. You must tread careful.'

He led the way through a door that opened onto an upward flight of stairs. Tom felt both dwarfed and comforted by the huge bulk of the man and followed readily, though puzzled that they should be climbing stairs when they were already on the ground floor. At the end of the first flight they turned a corner and were facing yet more stairs. Up and up they walked until Tom's legs ached, but he dared not pause for fear of being left behind by his giant companion.

Eventually they arrived at a steel door, and as the smith opened it Tom was forced back by a gust of cold air. The door had opened onto a narrow parapet which ran between a slanting roof and a low wall. On the other side of the wall the sheer drop was eventually swallowed by the blackness of the night. The air was full of fine snow, carried in eddies around the walls and chimneys by the wind.

The first part of this journey high above the city streets took them along the parapet for several hundred yards. Tom dared not look to his left for the wall was no higher than knee level, and where the stone was blown free of snow the surface was hard and slippery. But his fears were multiplied a hundredfold when he reached the end of the parapet, for there was a door in the wall of the next building which could be reached only by crossing a narrow bridge, a mere plank's width (though it seemed to be of metal) and, for support, a single handrail.

Tom hesitated before following the smith onto the bridge, but he knew that he must follow, and so forced himself forward. Looking down to his feet he saw the thin strip made pale by a dusting of snow and, below that, a vast black chasm. He held the rail with both hands and eased himself along, passing one hand over the other, but never letting go. The sensation was made more sickening by the vibrations that were created by the smith's heavy footfall, and the thin crust of ice that coated the bridge.

If my feet slip, thought Tom, *I shall plunge into that blackness* – and he shut his eyes.

'Hop across, little fellow.'

A giant hand lifted him inside the door. Another swung the door shut on the icy air. Once inside, Tom had to sit down: he was shaking and sobbing quietly. The smith stood patiently for a minute or two then, with a voice of amazing gentleness, encouraged him: 'It's all right, little man. You'll be all right. But it's best we were going in case they start the flares.'

Tom climbed to his feet and numbly followed. Who 'they' were and what the flares were seemed of no consequence.

Back in his home village Tom had once seen a play performed. The director, one of the few educated men in the area, could find no actors of talent among the villagers. He had, therefore, devised a play with a large cast, none of whom said more than a few lines. The play was interesting enough, but the plot was impossibly obscure. Tom's life since he had entered the city was beginning to feel very much like that play.

They walked along a corridor, roughly plastered and without doors, and then down several flights of stairs. The corridor and stairs were lit at intervals by lights set into the ceiling, but there was no sign of habitation in the building. Eventually they came to another door, and this led once more to the roofs, but now at a much lower level. The streets below them were visible, though dimly lit, small puddles of yellow light forming around street lamps.

'We must be careful now: we can be seen. We follow this ledge along to those chimneys. After that we have to edge our way along the ridge. It's a bit grim, but you'll be all right if you take care.'

After the bridge this prospect held little fear for Tom. True, if he fell from the roof he would probably be killed, but at least the ground was there, clearly visible. He followed the smith to the chimneys, which were a curious complex of brick stacks, arranged to afford steps to the ridge of the roof. Here they sat astride and edged their bodies along with their hands. As they neared the end of the ridge where the roof sloped down to meet another building, the smith turned to Tom and grinned.

'Nearly there, little man.'

Tom's relief was short-lived, for suddenly the darkness became as brilliant as midday. A white ball hung glowing in the sky above them and there were shouting voices: 'There – up there!'

Shots rang out, thin sharp barks in the cold air. The smith grunted. His huge body sagged forward and then slowly keeled over and slid down the slope of the roof and into the space beyond. Tom lay flat along the ridge. He heard a heavy thud as the smith hit the street, and then the flare faded and he was in darkness once more. With as much speed as he could manage he pulled himself along to the end of the ridge, slid down the roof to an adjoining wall and, easing himself along it, felt for a door. There were voices from below, one louder than the others.

'You've got one of them, but it's the other you want, the other. Try another flare.'

But before the instruction could be followed Tom had found his door, scuffled desperately with the catch and was inside. Pressed against the inside of the door in total darkness he gasped for breath, dizzy with fear. The shouting voice was one that he had recognised: it was, without doubt, the voice of the bellows-pumper.

He stood, hunched, inside the room, totally ignorant of his surroundings – whether he was in a confined space or a vast hall. He reached out with his arms, but met nothing. Pressed against the door, he fancied he heard faint sounds from the street below, but it might have been his fevered, his terrified imagination.

Minutes passed until, with a suddenness which caused him to jerk himself upright, a dim shaft of light appeared before him. It grew, escaping from behind a door which was slowly being pushed open. Two figures entered the darkness and, silently, came to him and grasped his arms. He offered no resistance. He was half dragged, half carried into a dimly lit corridor. Rough hands turned him to the wall, jostled his arms out of his coat and explored his inner clothing.

Presumably (his head reeled) it was the same hands which swung open an iron door and thrust him into a small windowless room, furnished with a low bed and a single hardbacked chair. In one corner there was a washbasin, on one wall there was a shelf of books, and stretched on the bed there was a gaunt man of about thirty with closely cropped hair and a line and agitated face.

5 The Prisoner

'Hey ho!' the man crooned in what at first seemed a jovial tone. 'A *lamb* to the slaughter this time, is it? Well, I never!'

It was when he cackled and his eyes remained frozen and hard that Tom realised this was no good-natured welcome. The door slammed shut.

'What have they got you for?' the other asked him, sitting up and swinging his legs to the floor. 'I hope you did a good deal of damage.'

'No,' Tom replied. 'I've done nothing.'

'Caught in the act, were you?'

Tom avoided replying by crossing the room to the wooden chair and dropping onto it. He felt close to collapse.

'No, you're quite right to say nothing,' said the thin man. 'That's the wise policy. They'll be listening to every word. If you've secrets, keep them to yourself.'

On an impulse he leapt to his feet and swung a kick at the wall. He then raised his fists and hammered on the plaster.

'I know you're there!' he yelled, his face screwed up in fury. 'I can feel you through the wall. Scum! Cockroaches!'

The fit passed, he sank onto the bed and turned once more to Tom.

'They'll torture you,' he said confidingly. 'Bastinado. You know what that is? They'll bare your feet and beat them like drums. Bruises first and then the bones crack.'

Tom covered his face with his hands and felt himself shiver.

'Perhaps they'll torture me, too,' the prisoner said in a careless tone, 'but that will only be for sport. They know everything about me already. I've no secrets.'

He lay back on the bed.

'Then they'll kill me,' he said lazily. 'That's all they can do. They've no choice whatsoever.'

Tom was shocked into speech by the man's casual attitude to his own death.

'Why must they kill you?' he asked.

This brought on a burst of mirthless laughter.

'Because if they don't, dear young fellow, I will most certainly wipe *them* out, every last one of them. I'll squash them into the ground!'

Here he sat up again and his body tautened. His eyes seemed to focus on some distant horizon. He stood up and began to pace the small room, restlessly.

'Only when every last one of them has been eliminated,' he declaimed, pounding a fist into the air, 'will the city be purified.'

Although the man spoke with great anger and bitterness, Tom strangely felt no fear of him. For all his hammering on the wall it seemed that his fury was expressed chiefly in the continual flow of words. And though he spoke confidingly to Tom, he never seemed to desire an answer. It was as if he were talking to himself *through* Tom.

'It's an evil world,' he proclaimed fervently, still stalking up and down the room, turning every few paces because of its smallness. 'And this is an evil city, overrun by vermin. We've got to stamp them out!'

He paused and leant down towards Tom.

'Are you with us?' he demanded in a hoarse whisper. 'Are you one of us?'

Since Tom had no knowledge of the conflict referred to by the prisoner he could not give an answer.

'Aren't you afraid to die?' he asked simply.

At this the man flung his arms in the air with a gesture of contempt.

'Afraid? It's an honour! To die for the cause!'

He pushed up the sleeve of his tunic to reveal his upper arm. Vividly pricked into it – the outline a rich blue, the centre vermilion – was the large tattoo of a dagger.

'Listen.' He moved closer to Tom and spoke in a low voice. 'If you ever get out of here, tell them that you met me. Tell them I won't let them down.'

'But who . . . '

'Marcus. That's my name. Just say Marcus. They'll know.'

He sat on the edge of the bed.

'That's if they let you go, which isn't likely. You'd know too much.'

'I know nothing,' protested Tom.

'Yes you do. You know me. You know my name. Perhaps you even know where we are.'

'I've no idea.'

'How did you get here?'

'I was led here,' said Tom. 'It was dark. I don't know the city.'

The prisoner shrugged.

'I was brought here unconscious,' he said. 'They know that once we discover any of their hideouts we'll find them all. Then there'll be some blood spilt.'

This was too much for Tom to stomach. In a blind panic he stood up, and – to occupy himself – took down a large book from the shelf. It shook in his grasp.

'Why must there be blood?' he asked numbly.

'Because there'll be no rest until the matter is finished,' his companion replied. 'We're too deep in the struggle to turn back. It's them or us.'

It was a book of maps, which fell open in his hands. His eyes, not focusing properly, were aware of towns and rivers and forests.

'You and I,' said the prisoner, 'we don't matter. Let them do what they like to us. It's the cause which matters.'

He lay back on the bed with his arms behind his head.

'I've been tortured before,' he said baldly.

There was an awful silence.

'What happened?' asked Tom, dreading the answer.

'Burns. They ran the flames over me. It was in the open and they lit a large fire. Of course I knew it was for me long before they told me. What a glorious blaze it was, red hot in the centre! Then they asked me for information which I had, and I refused. I'll always refuse.'

Tom returned to the chair, feeling sick. He could see the fire, and the men gathered round it, and the other one lying pinned to the ground.

'And then they brought the flames to me – at first not very close, but gradually nearer and nearer. You have to think of something else. There's a tip for you, young lad – absent yourself mentally when it happens. It eases the pain.'

He gazed calmly at the ceiling.

'But I could smell the burning.'

Tom leafed through the book, wildly fumbling the pages. They were thick and old, with broad margins. The maps were extremely detailed.

'I told them nothing,' the prisoner said proudly.

There was a map of an area he knew and, comforted by the discovery, Tom turned another page, and another, following a route he roughly recognised. Finally, and gratefully, he came to the map of his own home area. His fingers traced the familiar mountain range, moved in a curve along the road which ran along the foothills to the village.

To his amazement, he found that the page had been marked. The village – one among so many, among hundreds in these pages – had been ringed by two thick circles of ink.

'Stand by!'

The call, from the prisoner on the bed, was followed immediately by the opening of the heavy door, and two large men entered. They signalled to Tom, and he put down the book and let them take his arms.

'Don't cry out,' urged the prisoner. 'Whatever they do. Don't give them that pleasure.'

He heard the voice calling to him even as they took him outside and swung the door back into place.

'For the cause, remember. Don't cry out!'

Tom was aware of nothing but the dreadful image in his mind of the torture chamber, with a fire and irons and heavy objects to beat his feet, and the thought that they would never let him go.

6 Eagle's View

'Child, you seem ill!'

The man to whom he had been taken – a tall, silver-haired, grave man – was certainly no torturer. He looked down on him with a tender concern.

'Are you troubled?'

Tom was indeed troubled, the relief and the confusion issuing in hot tears which flooded his eyes and filled his throat. He bowed his head, ashamed.

'Come, be seated.'

It was another room without windows, but much larger and of a curious shape. On the wall facing him there was pinned a large map of the city, with green markers dotted about it. Through his tears they glowed like small beacons. The floor was thickly carpeted, and there were comfortable chairs grouped together facing the map as if the room were used for meetings. Turning his head, Tom counted eight walls, one of them largely obscured by thick draped curtains of a mustard colour.

There was a silence, during which his questioner studied him thoughtfully. He seemed to Tom a man of great dignity. He moved slowly, but easily – now he sat in a chair close to Tom – and when he spoke it was in slow, measured tones.

'I think perhaps apologies are called for. I am sorry you were treated rather roughly. We have to be a little cautious, you know.'

On a table to one side of them Tom saw his new coat, with the old and tattered one half-hidden beneath. Lying next to them was his picture and the forged papers. He found himself stammering.

'You're not going to, to . . . ' He could not say the word. 'You don't intend to harm me?'

A puzzled expression crossed the man's face.

'Harm you, child? Why, no indeed. And why should I?'

Tom felt that he should not explain his fear. He felt a queer loyalty to the prisoner in the small room. But at the same time – perhaps as a reaction from his terror – he found himself angry with the tall suave gentleman who remained so calm while other people suffered.

'You hurt the prisoner,' he accused pugnaciously. 'You tortured him.'

The words hung outrageously in the air.

'Poor child.' He turned away from Tom for a moment as if reflecting on what he should say. 'That man is a great danger to us, but we have not injured him in any way. Quite the reverse.'

'He said terrible things had been done to him.'

'And so they probably have. He is a man who is attracted by violence, and violence is doubtless sometimes done to him. But not by us.'

'What will you do with him?'

'That I cannot tell you. It is true that we cannot simply let him go.'

'Then you will not let me go!'

'Child, you do not understand.' Again he turned away. 'How could you? This man is evil. He would bring danger to a great many good people.'

It was true that Tom did not understand. When the prisoner had warned him of his captors he had believed they were wicked men. Now this man told him that the wickedness belonged to the prisoner.

'But enough of that,' the man continued, as if suddenly impatient of Tom's questions. 'I have some things to ask of *you*. These papers I recognise as being drawn up by us. By what name are you really known?'

After some hesitation Tom yielded up his first name, unwilling to reveal more than necessary as long as he remained undecided about his interrogator.

'Well, Tom, you must tell me a few things about yourself. You have come far?'

'I have travelled for weeks on end.'

'Alone?'

'Yes, quite alone.'

The man seemed, for some reason, embarrassed – or was it *moved*? – by this simple statement. He put his two hands against his cheeks as if for greater control.

'And where have you come from?'

Tom named his village and began to describe his journey – the cold nights, the hunger, the kindnesses and the rejections of the people he occasionally met. But he had not told the tenth of it when he was silenced by a wave of the hand.

'This picture,' the man asked, turning to the table. 'Why do you carry it?'

'It is of my father.'

His questioner stood up, abruptly for one who moved in so dignified a fashion, and turned to the map on the wall. But he did not seem to be studying it. Although his fingers toyed with the green markers there seemed no method in what he did. Tom thought it was as if he were fidgeting, which clearly could not be so.

'I am looking for my father,' he continued. 'I believe he may be in this city.'

'Ah.' It was almost a sigh. 'That's it, child.'

He turned.

'And why here?'

'I don't know. My mother believed it very strongly.'

Thoughts of home, not for the first time, began to infiltrate Tom's consciousness but, as before, he repelled them. He knew that if he remembered the sights and sounds of his village, pictured the people going about their business, he could not face the hardships which he had borne for so long and which he must continue to bear while his father remained lost to him.

'Tom, I will show you something. Fetch your coat.'

He followed, through the thick mustard curtains and a door beyond and up a narrow flight of winding stone stairs. The air struck suddenly chill. They emerged in a small, low, circular room which had openings at regular intervals all around it. Approaching one, Tom discovered that they were at the top of a high tower, with views across the city. The moon shone fiercely in a sky of dark velvet, the heavy clouds having retreated to the east, where they gathered densely, a menacing dingy grey. The roofs stretched away below them, sparkling white under the triumphant moon. How vast the city was, how immeasurable!

'You come at a time of anguish for us all,' his guide explained in a tired voice. 'Although some things must remain hidden, there are matters you should understand. If only' – he added quietly, almost to himself – 'so that you are to survive.'

So high above the city, Tom felt for a moment jubilantly free, as if he had only to open wide his arms and soar like an eagle, up and up towards the burning moon. He had a desire to fling himself through the opening, but when he put his hand against the stonework the coldness of it somehow reminded him of how earthbound he truly was and how, if he leapt for the inviting space beyond, he would plummet like a dead weight. This, in turn, reminded him of the terrible fate of the blacksmith, and he withdrew from the gap with a shudder.

'Here, Tom – look from this side. There below you, see? Do you recognise that tower and the great gate?'

It was the gate by which he had entered the city, and he was surprised to discover that he had not come very far. His eyes followed the narrow road round by the wall until he found the place at which he had turned off, down the slope, before he heard the guards marching. Where, then, was the house with the green and the white rooms, and the gentle girl with the blue eyes? It must surely be the tall white building with shutters across its windows – except for one high window, where a light shone behind a curtain. Who was in that room? he wondered. What was she doing? Did she remember his brief stay in the room with the white walls and the faded painting and the cryptic lines scratched into the plaster?

'All this area here,' the tall man explained, sweeping the flat of his hand in a broad arc, 'from that tower by the east gate to that other tower you see rising up from the wall in the distance, then back by that massive fortification you see through this window' – they moved round as he spoke – 'all this is under my command.'

He allowed himself a weary smile.

'Or it would be if we had control over the city,' he added. 'In fact I command a number of loyal people who hope that one day we shall live in happier times.'

'And then you will be in charge?'

'And then, for a while, I shall perhaps be the eastern commander in fact as well as in name. But we may have to wait for a long time yet.'

It was not late, and lights shone in the city below them, in some parts dimly and sparsely, in others in thick, bright clusters. In many buildings the lighted rooms were the high ones, leaving the lower areas along the street in darkness.

'Tom, I can help you find your father.'

His heart lurched. The hope rose up in him like a physical thing, lifting him. 'You know where he is?'

He had to restrain himself from seizing hold of the man's coat and shaking information from him.

'Where is he? Tell me!'

'I do not know myself, but if you are prepared to put yourself in our hands I shall make every effort so that you are guided towards him.'

Tom, overcome, did not know how to reply.

'You are right to hesitate,' said the commander, misinterpreting his silence. 'You know nothing of us, and you will be putting yourself in danger. Understand that we shall be using you for our own ends. I am not acting simply from kindness.'

They stood together, elbows on the stone, gazing out over the city.

'You are too young, Tom, to judge easily whom you may trust and whom you should fear. Later you will read the signs more expertly. But you must believe me when I tell you that this city is in the hands of a malevolent power. Men are forced to obey what they know is a manifestation of evil.

'It cannot last for ever, because there is more goodness than evil in ordinary men. Already we find that although the people will submit to force, their spirit remains free. When the call comes, they will respond.'

Tom saw that the man's hands shook against the stone sill as he spoke, and his eyes were bright with tears. A chill breeze stirred the grey hair at his temples.

'My father,' Tom broke the silence. 'How far away . . .'

'I cannot say. I imagine, very far. You see how the city stretches, beyond the eye. You may have all that way to go.'

'And is it all as it is here?'

'There are places less trouble, Tom, others even more cruelly suppressed. Weigh that in your mind before you decide.'

He turned, and they made their way to the staircase, Tom following the commander down.

'I shall not force you,' the slow, tired voice rose to him. 'If you wish, you may leave unharmed. The mission I would propose to you is not an easy one.'

'I am ready,' Tom replied.

7 The Mission

Lost in the depths of a huge armchair, roasted by a fire almost the equal of that at the blacksmith's forge and fed beyond his measure, Tom sat and waited for the commander's return. His life had never known such total comfort and he drifted into a deep sleep.

He felt himself to be a snow crystal gently falling from the black heavens, through the sky's midnight blue, turning and turning, caught by the light of the moon and the gentlest of breezes and wrapped in complete silence. He fell past roofs, he fell past windows, past faces he fell – the girl in the room, the blacksmith, the bellows-pumper, the prisoner, the commander, and finally the face of his long-lost father, now alive and smiling unlike the frozen image of the picture that he carried.

And then, through the silence, a voice calling his name. The voice grew louder and more insistent until Tom wakened, shaking his head and opening his eyes. He was awake and the voice continued, although it appeared to have no source. Opposite was an armchair identical to that in which he sat, but it was unoccupied. Tom looked round the room, which was of no great size, but that also seemed empty. The voice continued: 'Wake up, wake up! You've slept well, but there's work to be done!'

Tom turned to where he imagined the voice came from, and there in the shadows by the fire, and lit only by its flickering red light, stood a man. At least, the face was that of a man, while the body was more that of a small boy. He was the most complete dwarf that he had ever seen, and Tom's startled expression and the stare that followed it prompted the little man to further speech.

'Yes, I'm small, and I've reason enough to be glad of it, so stop gawping. We'll be seeing plenty of each other, you and I, so you might as well get used to me.'

He moved to the empty armchair, stood before it facing Tom and suddenly bounced upwards and backwards into it, seeming momentarily to disappear into the folds of leather. Re-emerging, he continued to speak.

'I understand from our commander that you've agreed to undertake a certain mission for us. Is that correct? A nod will do.'

Tom nodded.

'I also understand that you know very little of our situation here. Correct? A nod will do.'

Again he nodded.

'It is advisable, therefore, for you to appreciate something of the background before I explain this mission that you've undertaken.'

Tom nodded vigorously as if to prove that an invitation to do so was unnecessary. The dwarf scowled.

'Stop moving your head like that. It's unsettling. Now listen carefully' – and he sat back in the armchair, stared at the ceiling and began what seemed to be a carefully prepared speech.

'For many centuries our city was ruled over by a dynasty of city lords: princes, you might call them. At first these men ruled alone, having total power over the people, but as the centuries passed a system evolved in which the city lord shared power with an elected group known as the citizens' council. These citizens were chosen carefully to represent each group within the city. The rich, the poor, the tradesmen, the artisans, the professions – all were represented.

'It was a system that seemed ideal. The citizens could not assume too much power because there was always the city lord to answer to, and the city lord was restrained by the need to consult the citizens' council. There were times when members argued for the interests of individual groups with such fervour and at such great length that things did not get done, or were done too late.'

He paused and sat forward.

'You hear me, I trust. You're not falling asleep?'

'No, no,' answered Tom urgently. In truth the dwarf's strangeness and the fascination of his story were keeping him wide awake.

'Well then, this is how it was. There were times when corruption entered the council chambers, but generally they ruled fairly and with the interests of the city at heart. For a long time, indeed, the people were satisfied and the city flourished.

'But satisfaction is never permanent in human affairs. Groups began to murmur – "They're weak . . we need stronger government . . . we need people who will get things done . . . there must be more discipline . . ."

'So the murmurings grew, and from them there emerged a movement whose aim was to destroy the city lord and the citizens' council and to seize power by violence.' (Here the dwarf's voice dropped and was tinged with a mixture of sadness and anger.) 'And they succeeded. Their emblem is a blood-stained dagger. They call themselves the Red Blade and they rule from a grim fortress called the Citadel.

'Entering the chambers, they cruelly murdered the council members and, it was thought, the city lord himself. The people were stunned by the viciousness of their rule, and people began to disappear. You might think there was nothing surprising about that – I daresay the prisons were full enough; the graveyards, too. But some people disappeared so completely that it became clear that even the Red Blade didn't know where they were.

'It also emerged that the city lord had escaped the bloodshed in the chambers and that the Red Blade still sought him. Rumours spread that he ruled in secret in another city.'

The dwarf look closely at Tom, adding quietly: 'A city below this one.'

Yes, he looked closely. Did Tom's face betray anything? He could not be sure.

'But the rule of the Red Blade had anchored itself firmly and bloodily, and people forgot.'

As the story unfolded Tom found himself gripped by a strange and feverish excitement. Yes, frightened he certainly was at the prospect of being thrust once again into the dangerous streets of the city – terrified. But the mysteries of the vanished lord and the fabled underground city enthralled him.

'There are many of us who wish to restore the rightful government. We have control of the rooftops, but the streets are still under the tyranny of the Blade.'

'But why should you trust me?'

The dwarf shrugged.

'Why should you trust *us*? Let us call it intuition, Tom.'

Now he struggled out of the depths of the large chair.

'Your mission is nothing less than to find the underground city – if it exists. There is a room for you in the House of the Star: you will find it in the old quarter. You must leave tomorrow.

'We shall meet every so often, but you must not know me in public. If you make a mistake in that direction I shall not hesitate to betray you.'

He reached into a deep pocket and held his hand out towards Tom with the palm upturned.

'Take this,' he said.

Tom had to bend to make out the flat metal object that was presented to him. It was oval in shape and, peering closer, he saw that it was a representation of a human eye with a bright blue iris.

'Anyone who carries this,' explained the dwarf, 'is a friend. But remember that there will be more enemies than friends.'

'But why do you have faith in me,' Tom asked, 'if you yourselves have failed?'

'You aren't known in the city and you are young. It's a protection of sorts. Your only contact with the commander will be through me. It's safer for us all that way.'

Still Tom persisted.

'There is something you haven't told me,' he said. 'The commander mentioned my father. He said . . . '

'Very well. A few years ago a man came on a long journey looking for the underground city. He contacted us, but we could not help him. He disappeared. It is possible that if you find the city you will find the man.'

'The man. . .' Tom interrupted wildly.

'We believe he is the man in your picture.'

PART TWO

Quest

8 At the House of the Star

Ignoring the wild tumult of talking, laughing, backslapping, leaping up and down, singing and whistling in the large and crowded room behind him, Tom rubbed his hand against the window-glass and peered into the frosted world beyond. The snow lay deep and crisp. The buildings across the street were distorted by the thick ice clamped to the outside of the pane

For almost two weeks he had been a prisoner in the House of the Star, trapped by the bitter howling gales of what the people called the second winter. At night, in his small room on the floor above, he heard the wind career along the canyon of the street, dislodging loose tiles and wooden boards, jangling chains at the doors like a madman set loose in an ironmonger's shop. By day, as the snow silently swirled in fierce eddies, he sat reading in his room or came downstairs to where the lodgers were joined by local people and passing travellers in search of warmth and company.

It was the afternoon and the light was fading. The snow, at last, had stopped falling. Outside, an old lady so heavily wrapped against the weather as to appear scarcely human was struggling through a drift which reached to her knees.

'Dreaming of building a snowman, young Tom?'

The question, half-shouted in a jovial, attention-seeking manner, was put by a man whom a fortnight ago he would have shrunk from looking in the eye. He wore the blue tunic with green sash and gold epaulettes of the city guard. Half a dozen of them had taken to calling in at the hostelry for a drink and noisy conviviality, and as the weather worsened their visits had become longer and more frequent. They had almost adopted Tom as their mascot.

He smiled awkwardly. A few months ago he might, indeed, have played in the thick snow, but now it seemed a childishness.

'Here's a nose for it,' called another of the platoon, fishing a large cigar butt from an ashtray and laughing to show all his teeth.

His companions joined in the merriment. A shabbily dressed white-haired old man sitting alone on the fringe of their group and puffing on an ancient pipe had his hat lifted from his head for a moment and waved in the air.

'Got to keep a fellow warm!' chirped one of the young men, almost beside himself. 'He's already got the hair to match!'

The old man seemed unruffled by the attack and the hat was replaced. Smoke drifted from the battered bowls of his pipe and the aroma struck keenly at Tom's nostrils. The guards turned to a game of cards which, however, seemed to demand much the same volume of shouts and laughter.

There were some twenty tables dotted about the room, all of them occupied. A few were grouped round the large fire by the far wall, and at one of these was the man they called Old Weasel, an emaciated figure whose fingers plucked at the strings of an instrument Tom had never seen before, rather like a large mandolin. On his head was a black beret, pulled down hard to his ears. Occasionally he raised a thin voice to accompany the tune, but he received little attention from the people around him.

Above them, on the wall, was the grim insignia of the Red Blade. Tom had at first watched closely as visitors entered, imagining that he would be able to test the strength of their allegiance by their reaction to it, but this was not possible. Nobody more than nodded towards the plaque, and the guards, who were obviously loyal, sometimes swaggered in so full of themselves that they appeared to overlook it altogether. Good humoured as they seemed, however, Tom could not forget his arrival in the city and the chilling cries of the unseen man seized by the guards after curfew.

The glass had misted over again and he rubbed at it impatiently. He meant to go out. Day after day he had waited for a break in the weather so that now – although darkness was gathering and the snow was deep – he could not contain himself. And yet if he rose immediately he would be noticed and might be asked difficult questions. All eyes would be upon him. He remained seated and gazed around the room. Who was friend and who was foe? Who, if anyone, was entrusted with his secret? His room was paid for, but who knew why?

He had invented a story, should anyone ask what one so young was doing at such a place alone. He had come from a distant region following the death of both his parents and had thrown himself on the mercy of a relative. This man, being none too eager to help and having no room for him at his own house, paid for his lodging at this hostelry until a more permanent solution could be found. It was an alibi which would allow him to remain here for months, if necessary.

Somewhere out there – to the east it must be – lay the house with the white room which he must visit once again. Surely that glimpse of a subterranean world had been no dream. Surely it must be connected to the legend he was entrusted with exploring. Tom clung to this hope as fervently as he had believed, on his travels, that once inside the city gates he would immediately find his father.

'Can I persuade you to a hot toddy, whippersnapper?'

It was Clem, the man who ran the house, with a tray of steaming drinks. But Tom did not want to delay himself.

'I'm warm already, thank you,' he replied

'Is there no draught from that window?'

'None whatsoever. I'd be too warm by the fire.'

Clem smiled down upon him with a knowing expression Tom had noticed before but did not understand. It was impossible to fathom whether it meant that he knew of Tom's mission or that he was of the other side and suspected him. Perhaps it was only his peculiar manner.

'A fine luxury, that window,' he added, shaking his head and continuing on his rounds.

It was indeed a rarity in this city, the ground-floor window, but this was a strange building. It was tall, and yet Tom had never been able to find a way of climbing higher than the first floor where his own room was. The stairs mounted to a long corridor with bedrooms leading from it, but there seemed to be no way up. His own room somehow seemed larger outside than inside, so that he was always surprised by the snugness of it.

Clem had a large wife – both taller and broader than himself – who seldom mixed with the clientele but whose occasional weighty presence diminished the volume of their babble in an instant. She always wore black and she walked with menacing strides. Tom could not believe that Clem owned the hostelry: he had too much the air of the superior servant. But his wife, whom everyone called the Sphynx (when she was away) could have led an army.

'Holloa! Forfeit! Forfeit!'

The guards had finished their game of cards and were determined to have a little sport with their less exuberant neighbours. One of these, a man with large expressive eyes and a fearful stammer, was about to leave, and two of the guards, grinning hugely but rather menacingly, were blocking his way.

'Nobody leaves without a forfeit!' cried one of them.

'But wh-wh-what can I do?' pleaded the poor man, whom Tom knew well by sight. He was staying in the very next room to his. 'I c-c-can't recite anyth-th-thing.'

'Can't recite,' exclaimed another of the guards. 'What's he to do?'

'Play an instrument!'

'N-no. C-c-can't.'

In a desperate urge to make himself understood and to escape he flung his arms about in a ludicrous fashion.

'Let him dance.'

'N-n-no.'

'Dance! Dance! Dance!'

The call was taken up by others of the group and the victim had his hands and elbows manipulated by the strapping guardsmen, who began to jig him along on a tour of the tables.

Tom, embarrassed and dismayed, looked for someone to help, but no assistance was forthcoming. Some people looked away; others obviously enjoyed the spectacle. Old Weasel, on an order from one of the platoon, struck up a rhythm on his instrument. The guards began to clap, and this was picked up at other tables, the pathetic man being shuffled through the crowd, his eyes wide with fear and humiliation.

The mad procession came closer and Tom wanted to signal to the man how sorry he felt for him, but, tugged this way and that by his tormentors, he only looked wildly around the room and failed to notice Tom at all. Would this cruel baiting stop if Tom leapt to his feet and protested? He could not, however. The idea flashed across his brain, but his feet did not move.

One of the spectators was watching the scene closely, but with no show of emotion at all. Tom had often seen him drinking alone in a corner: he would be there when Tom went to bed, which suggested that he, too, was a lodger here. He was a man of about forty with closely cropped grizzly hair and a pair of gold-framed spectacles. He always dressed immaculately, the colours carefully matched. He spoke very little. Now his eyes followed the unhappy business, first resting on the stammerer, next on one of the guards, but it was impossible to judge what he made of it. His gaze met Tom's for a moment and quickly moved away.

'Enough! Enough!'

A member of the platoon, presumably of a gentler disposition than his comrades, let go of the unwilling dancer's arm and prevented the little troupe from advancing further. They stood back, laughing harshly.

'You've entertained us splendidly, sir, and we thank you. You're free to go.'

The group broke up and the released prisoner stumbled forward, blindly.

'Bravo!'

'A born dancer!'

'What energy!'

And now the unfortunate man, his large eyes watery with mingled relief and anguish, had to undergo a volley of backslapping and false bonhomie.

How Tom hated the city in that moment! He hated the commander every bit as much as he hated the odious Red Blade. He hated himself for being drawn into the struggle. He had no certain friends. It was not at all clear why he had been led to the House of the Star. Perhaps it was because there were people here who were loyal to the commander. But possibly – and just as likely – it was because here the enemy were at their strongest. He would be used in order to learn what he could about their organisation, and if he were discovered he would be simply another failed spy executed by the Blade.

In a spirit of wretched disillusionment Tom rose to his feet and collected his coat and his boots from where he had left them under the window. He had no choice but to continue with the mission. It provided the one opportunity of finding his father, although that hope rested only on a vague legend. His feet sank into the fur-lined boots. He would seek out the house with the white room – and perhaps run his head straight into a noose.

The white room! A pathway cleared through his depression at the thought of it. In his mind he was outside already, standing on the threshold, and the girl with blue eyes was greeting him. There was hope in her kindness. She understood.

He struggled with the catch of the large door, aware of an icy draught on his forehead from the narrow gap between door and wall. The second winter, they said, would persist for weeks to come. He had never known it so cold.

'Whither to, young Tom?'

A hand grasped his arm and tugged him back into the room. The guard with pearly teeth smiled down on him with a playfulness that failed to disguise the viciousness underneath.

'You haven't paid your forfeit yet, my lad.'

Perhaps if he had waited a few minutes more they would have been settled in their chairs intent on other business, but the excitement of their sport with the stammerer was still alive in them. They clustered around him, grinning unpleasantly. They would not be denied their fun with him.

'I was coming back,' he said helplessly.

'You'll be coming back,' said another, 'after you've gone. And you can't go until you've paid your forfeit.'

Tom looked around him desperately. He heard muted sympathetic noises, but nobody dared to outface the city guards.

'This is no time for venturing out,' said the tallest of the platoon, putting huge hands around Tom's ribs and lifting him in a swinging motion towards the centre of the room. He landed lightly. 'It's less than two hours to curfew.'

'He wants to make a snowman. That's it, eh Tom?'

They were being cheery with him, but to satisfy themselves rather than Tom. He knew they would not allow him to leave without a show.

'I don't care about going out,' he said.

'Oh, too late, too late,' he was told. 'You meant to go out and there's no changing your mind now. A forfeit's what's required, your worship.'

There was no enthusiasm for it outside the small circle of guardsmen, but they had worked themselves up to it. Off came his outdoor clothes. They cleared a space for him, backing away to give him room to perform while they struck ridiculous poses as if waiting for some famous artiste to appear.

'What's it to be?' demanded one of the platoon. 'Another dance?'

'No, no,' his companions protested. 'Not again. Let's have something different. Give us something stirring. We're bored fellows with great imaginations. Come on, come on!'

Standing helpless among them, Tom became suddenly defiant. He knew he could not escape, but the anger he had felt when the stammerer was made to dance surged up in him again.

'I'll give you a song from the country,' he declared aggressively. 'They're better than city song.'

It was a foolish remark, no doubt. It was meant to be insulting to the city. But the guards clapped their hands and hooted their approval.

'A country song, eh? It has a decent chorus, we hope?'

'Of course it has.'

The guardsmen seemed relieved not to have to bully him into submission. They sat on their chairs or lounged back against the tables.

'The chorus then, Tom. Let's learn the chorus.'

Even as he began singing, in the raucous fashion common in his own district, part of Tom slid away back along the tracks he had followed, through wilderness and forest, to the places his family had known for generations.

> *You reckless moon*
> *Mare with no rider*
> *Leaping the billows*
> *You reckless moon!*

He sang with eyes half-closed, but he was aware of a strange reaction from the white-haired old man who sat close by. As the first two lines came to a close his eyes took on a startled expression and the pipe fell from his lips. It was over in a moment – his hands fumbled for the pipe and trapped it on his chest – but Tom knew that he had not mistaken it. The man pushed his hat more firmly onto his head and looked at the floor.

'Bravo, Tom!' enthused pearly-teeth. 'An earthy peasant song. Haunting, wouldn't you say, fellows?'

'A fine chorus. Let's have it again!'

And again he sang it, and gradually more voices joined in. Old Weasel began to pick out the tune. There was a relaxation throughout the room because the guards were appeased; they would not humiliate him.

> *You reckless moon*
> *Mare with no rider*

One face remained frozen as the volume of singing increased around him.

The gentleman with gold-rimmed spectacles fixed a stare upon Tom, as he had earlier upon the dancing stammerer. His lips did not move with the others.

'It goes well, Tom. But what of the story? What's the song about?'

He spoke up enthusiastically now.

'It's a story of what the moon sees as she sails across the night sky. She looks down on the countryside and the people in their houses.'

'A pretty idea. Let's have it, then. Some applause for the maestro, please.'

And, to his confusion, there was a hurraying and a banging on the tables that must have been heard a street away. The forfeit was forgotten. They wanted the song.

He had not sung it – had not even thought of it – for years, and yet the words arrived in his mouth spontaneously. They spoke of labourers home from the fields, women with children, animals in the barns.

> *Bats leave the oak tree, flit in the darkness*
> *Low past the alders gurgles the brook*

He saw, at once, a particular oak tree, in a field corner where a path crossed, and under it – for it was a fine day in summer – a family party with friends. It was so finely pictured that a large fly hummed close, threatening his sandwich, and he flapped it away, protesting.

And all the while that he saw it so vividly the words continued to flow from him as if they were coins he tipped effortlessly from his pocket.

> *A light at the window, the flicker of flames,*
> *Heads by the fireside, a leatherbound book*

It was a scene which he knew as if the song were written precisely for him, although never before had he thought of it in relationship to himself. The family shared the large volume, the father reading a page, slowly and with great dignity, as the children stared into the coals and weaved additional thoughts around the words. And at the conclusion of the page the book was passed to the mother who took her turn – her reading of it faster and lighter, but suddenly dramatic where the text required it. He heard the voice, and he saw a head turn from the fireside to smile up at the mother, and he knew it was himself he saw turning.

When the chorus was repeated they all took it up, hands clapping out the rhythm, Old Weasel animatedly plucking his strings, the guardsmen thumping the table tops with their fists in time with the beat. But Tom, a sob in his throat and tears welling up in his eyes, only mouthed the words without a sound escaping, his hands held out before him as if conducting an orchestra.

> *Under the hedgerow the vagrant is sleeping*
> *The leaves for his pillow, his feet in the mire*

He found voice to continue and he saw the vagrant (a tinker who had called at the house on day when he was feeding the hens and who had startled him by rapping on the slatted henhouse roof with a pot), and he saw the hedges that ran by the lane that led from his house toward the flatlands that gave way, gradually, to the lower mountain slopes in the distance. And he was by the river again, floating boats (what were they: twigs from the alders?) and splashing his sisters. And with him always, although he could not now see her, was the presence of his mother and the echo of her voice, gentle and coaxing. And so as the music played and he blurted forth the song, he was home again and no city existed and he had not lost his father.

At the end of the song and the last chorus they all struck up again, unwilling to bring it to a close. Large hands hoisted him onto a table top and he stood above them in an ecstasy, blinded with tears.

> *Mare with no rider*
> *Leaping the billows*
> *You reckless moon!*

Then what a commotion of yells and applause. They lifted him down – not aware of his emotion; too full of their own pleasure – and tousled his hair. The guardsmen loved him again. They called him Tomkin and Mr Tom and Tomtiddledum. And then up again onto shoulders and he was borne towards the door.

'The best of the evening to you, young peasant swain!'

'Go forth under your reckless moon!'

Large hands fumbled with buttons as they helped him on with his coat, his boots, even with his gloves.

'And your hat. Where's your hat?'

'No, I don't need one.'

'You'll freeze your ears off, young Tomtit!'

And at last the door closing on their quips and their chuckles, their self-important noises.

A blank whiteness in the street. The silence made his head swim. The surface of the snow curled like the gentle waves of a flowing river, and as high. It had a thin frozen crust.

The cold burned his ears. His cheeks felt as if they bled. He blew gently and watched the plume of his breath disperse.

There was little time: he must return by curfew. He could not hope to do more than find his way to the house and then trudge back again. Nevertheless, fascinated by the dense beauty of the snow, he could not resist pausing to scoop the airy whiteness into his gloved hands. When he pressed upon it he heard it creak and shrivel into a tight ball.

Above the doorways the drifts hung, massively poised. He flung his missile and there was a silent explosion. Dislodged, a thick wedge of snow sliced in two and plummeted into the softness beneath.

He was playing after all. How peculiar it had been, the singing in the House of the Star. He had not meant to amuse them. When he thought of the poor man with large, damp eyes being tugged between the tables in a mock dance it seemed brutal and unfair.

But, although he had only to open the door and enter, it was a world away.

Here in the snow he could see and hear no one. The high walls of the buildings climbed towards a pitch sky in which a few stars glinted, frostily, and the new moon was a radiant sliver. The cold had already penetrated his thick coat, and he began to walk down the street, lifting his feet high over the piled snow.

Brighter than any star in the sky was the planet Venus. As a country lad, Tom knew the heavens: he had used the constellations to guide him towards the city, and now he took his bearings by them once again. Further to the east Jupiter was high above the horizon, and near it, smaller and smudgily red, was Mars, bringer of war.

He turned at the first corner. Against the wall an ancient waterpump wore what looked like an enormous white hat, precariously balanced upon it. Unable to resist the temptation, he bent once again to gather the freezing flakes into a ball. It was then that a flash of colour caught his eye.

Standing at the corner, half-screened by the enormous building which reared up towards the evening sky, was the lad with the long green scarf. He was gazing intently at Tom, who stood upright, feeling the snow melt into his glove. Surely he was rather younger than Tom. He had no expression on his face, not even curiosity.

When Tom moved, however, he showed himself to be extremely alert. He disappeared from view before Tom had taken two paces forward.

'Wait!' Tom called. 'I want to talk to you!'

But the other hurried away, scuffing the snow in a thousand directions.

9 The Monument

Tom floundered through the drifts in despair. He could not catch the boy with the green scarf. For a few minutes he struggled to keep up, but he knew that, as before, he would not succeed. They were, in any case, heading in the wrong direction. Although he had first seen the boy outside the house with the white room there was no reason to think that he was going there now.

Did he hear a distant laugh of triumph? He could not be sure. But, giving up the chase, he felt downcast and humiliated. Inside the hostelry he had been eager to begin his quest: now he felt the hopelessness of it.

Passing through a small square, he noticed what appeared to be the remains of a monument, half buried in the snow. It was obvious from its breadth that it had once been impressively large. All that survived some crude act of destruction was the fractured stump of the base.

Tom was puzzled by these signs of neglect in a city crowded with sturdy buildings, and he trod a laborious path across to it, his feet breaking through the crust of the snow and leaving a trail like pockmarked skin. Had there once been a statue here, perhaps? The dark stone now seemed to represent nothing more grand than a jagged, broken tooth.

He kicked a boot against it and thin shards of snow slid from the top. He stooped to look more closely. The stone was very hard and smooth. For a reason he did not understand, Tom looked round him, almost furtively, before squatting on his haunches by the wrecked monument.

There was no one. Only the pure white vistas of snow along the streets and capping the roofs; only the monstrous closed-in buildings reaching towards a sky sprinkled with faint stars.

Bending to the stone again, he rubbed at it with his gloved hand. He did not comprehend his own actions, what he hoped to find, but he felt a sudden unevenness beneath his fingers. Scrabbling in the snow he uncovered what seemed to be an inscription at the base. In fact, it could only be the end of an inscription, for as he swept the last of the powdery covering away he discovered the jagged remnant of another line at the very top of the broken masonry. He crouched to one side, allowing the pale light of the moon to pick out the words which remained.

He could not believe what he read. He looked round once more into the silent streets, empty and white, and felt his scalp tingle with a strange fear that had no name.

> *Wear me as your spiked heel*
> *I will bite into ice for you*

There was nothing under the lines, but Tom could not forget how shaken he had been when he had first met these words on the wall of the white room. For the initials beneath had been those of his father. The weirdness of finding the inscription repeated on this fragment discovered by chance in a city square filled him with an unease he could not explain to himself. He rose from his crouched position and felt horribly threatened, as if forces which he could not fathom were creeping up on him, ready to pounce.

And now these vague but potent fears became mixed with the horror of being caught in the streets after curfew, and although the first bells had not yet sounded he began in a panic to career through the piled snow towards the House of the Star. His legs would not move quickly enough. With each pace he felt as if his boots were being tugged back, preventing him.

His heart hammering, his breath catching and rasping, he reached the sanctuary of the inn at last and leant trembling and faint against the stout outer door.

10 Old Weasel

'Mind you don't say not word to a soul. That's my advice to you, my laddie.'

'I haven't. I won't.'

'Nor a signal of no kind. There's many a body who's been undone through a careless moment.'

They sat in the tiny room Old Weasel called his home, sipping strong tea from heavy mugs. It was the afternoon of another bitterly cold day, through the length of which the wind had swept the snow in shafts through the streets, preventing any journeying out. After lunch, when they were the only people left at the large wooden table downstairs, the old man had surprised him by a swift beckoning movement and his invitation.

'I've lost more friends through loose tongues than for every other reason put together.'

His old black beret hung on a hook over his bed. It was half an hour since he had taken it off, but Tom found his eyes still fixing themselves on the curious contours of the wizened old head that normally hid beneath it. It was a completely hairless head, blotched with a dozen shades of red, pink, blue and grey. The bones were thin but prominent. They enclosed hollows and formed brittle ridges. It was a landscape, an immensely varied landscape that invited detailed exploration. When he spoke there were tiny movements here and there, fascinating to behold.

'These are troubled times, but nobody my age has ever known anything else. I'm a survivor. I don't live well, as you see – but I live.'

The room was clean, but there was very little in it. If it contained all of Old Weasel's possessions then they were no more bulky than could be squeezed into the sturdy cupboard attached to the wall in one corner. His strange musical instrument leant against it and Tom, never having had a chance to study it before, noticed that endless loving polishings had given the wood a soft and glowing quality.

'Been with me fifty years,' said the old man, observing Tom's interest. He put down his mug and took the neck of the instrument in one hand. The fingers of the other hand alighted on the strings with the unconscious deftness of birds on a wire. The tune he plucked from it made Tome start.

'Let's say I wasn't kindly disposed towards you.' The music ceased abruptly. 'Let's say I was suspicious of this young wisp who'd arrived from nowhere. I'd listen very carefully to that song, now wouldn't I?'

'I don't understand,' said Tom fearfully. 'It's just a song from the country.'

'It is indeed. A song about the reckless moon and the gurgling brook. A fine tune I hadn't heard before.'

Tom stood in alarm, but the old man waved him down again.

'No, laddie, I'm not that suspicious chap myself. Don't fret over that. But I see things and I'm giving you a timely warning.'

The instrument was returned to its place by the wall.

'Don't give yourself away, that's what I have to say to you.'

'But I haven't,' protested Tom. 'I've hardly talked to anyone since I arrived here.'

'Ha!'

He wagged a finger towards Tom, accusingly.

'Lesson one, which you'd do well to heed. We give ourselves away as much by what we *don't* do as by what we do. Similarly by what we don't say. Speak by all means, my sparrow, but take care the tongue doesn't slip. That's what I mean to say.

'Why – I might ask, if I were suspicious – does this young lad arrive out of the blue at the House of the Star, a hostelry notorious for attracting the strangest clientele in his part of the city?'

'For a very good reason,' Tom spoke up boldly, his alibi well prepared. 'Because when my parents died . . .'

But Old Weasel waved him into silence.

'That you've a story I don't doubt, and it may be true or otherwise. But every rogue has proof of his innocence. In fact he usually has better proof than the virtuous man, which is another warning for you. The story doesn't matter.

'What our suspicious character asks himself is first, what wind has blown this young leaf into his path. He then asks himself where he might have come from. The accent tells him something, but perhaps not quite enough. And then – what luck! –the young chap sings a native song of his home village and the job's done for him.

'Now he examines this infant's behaviour. Look – he speaks to few people. Why's that? Is he shy? He doesn't appear particularly so. Has he something to hide? A possibility at the very least.'

Here old Weasel paused and cocked his head to one side.

'Why does our young friend look so wistfully from the window of an evening? Has he an errand he badly wishes to undertake?'

Tom did not know how to reply. The frail old man seemed to be offering advice but might be taunting him, hoping to find out more. Chill with fear, he felt that everything he said would be analysed: even things he did *not* say.

'For countless years,' said Old Weasel, changing tack suddenly, 'I was a messenger. That was my profession. There's no part of the whole country my feet haven't trod at one time of my life. A job for cunning is a messenger's.'

He rose and lifted the large teapot.

'Another, while it's still warm?'

'No, thank you.'

'You're wise, no doubt. There's more tea than blood in these old veins.'

He lifted the lid, stirred the contents with a spoon and poured himself another mug of the thick brown liquid.

'There's many who think messenger is another word for spy. Of all my colleagues from over the years in the service of a dozen different factions I don't know more than two or three who escaped with their lives. That's the mark of the troubles we've known. Leaders have been overthrown and the new rulers themselves toppled within a week.

'I tell you, my laddie, there were times when I carried a message to a distant town not knowing whether it would be friend or foe who greeted me at the gates. Now, you imagine dealing with a perplexity like that!'

'How did you?' asked Tom, forgetting his fear.

'Caution, deception. A wise head. Kept my own council, made my own rules. There were times for delivering messages and times for quietly destroying them.'

'But how did you know what the messages said?'

'Lord bless you, there's no man would take the job who couldn't unseal a note and reseal it without a trace. A very necessary skill. I remember one time I read a letter through – highly confidential it was – and, at the foot, it said "Dispose of the messenger". Dispose of me!

'As you can see, they didn't. And why not? Well, I knew a fellow who was desperately anxious to make himself known to the ruler of the town I'd been sent to. He had a favour to ask. I let drop a few hints, and before you could say "gullible" he was *bribing* me to let him deliver the message.'

'But then,' Tom broke in, horrified, 'he was killed instead.'

'Instead. I survived. Messengers have to be good survivors. That's the first virtue.'

Old Weasel bent forward.

'Don't be squeamish, laddie. These decisions are forced upon you. If the message hadn't been delivered I'd have been a hunted man for life. As it was, they thought me dead and I found myself a new employer.'

He took deep gulps from his mug of tea.

'Other times, when they trusted you, they'd send a message by word of mouth. It was for you to put it across the best way you could. Then you were like an ambassador, but with no protection whatsoever. There are vicious rulers who'll put the bearer of bad news to death as though he's responsible for it himself.

'You learn to watch people closely so that you can react in time – dodge the knife before it's thrown.'

Tom found his own reaction completely confused: he was excited by the story but disturbed by the cynical moral that accompanied it.

'Ha!'

Now the old man laughed at a memory, and the skin tautened on the frail cheek bones and quivered along the gaunt neck.

'On one occasion when I was working in the far west of the country I had to deliver a word-of-mouth message to the ruler of a nearby town. My task was to ask for military aid, men and arms. I was within five miles of the town when I met a long, straggling line of people, all of them exhausted, some of them wounded. The garrison had been overthrown. The town had been seized by a band of brigands.

'Now, it was impossible to judge how powerful these brigands were. If I returned home with the news I stood a fair-to-middling chance of being run through with a sharp sword. What to do, eh? Well, I waited a couple of days and then I strolled up to the main gate of the town, saying I had a message for the chieftain.

'A fearsome man he was, I can tell you. Crude and strong, and not well washed. But you have to keep your head as a messenger. I told him that my master congratulated him on his victory and wished an alliance with him. I know the words for that kind of thing.

'The next few days were uncomfortable. First I had to convince him that there was any reason my master should wish to make peace with him: if you can't talk fast and smart you're no good as a messenger. Then I had to hope he wouldn't send an envoy of his own so I would seem, to my master, to be untrustworthy. And then I had to wait upon events.

'It was a bloody time. Most of our times have been bloody. Within a few days an army was at the gates seeking to regain the town. I paced up and down, ready to turn either way. A wave of attacks surged right up to the walls and was then repulsed. The brigand chieftain sensed victory and then had it snatched away. A renewed attack breached the walls. Men poured through.

'Still I waited. The battle was open. But towards evening it became apparent that the brigands were losing. They retreated to the innermost tower. Now I acted. I raced to the dungeon, which had a solitary guard.'

Tom, caught up with the story, sat forward.

'You were armed?'

'No, no. Wouldn't know how to use a knife, save to cut up my meat. Wit is my only weapon, my laddie. No, I went down to the dungeon and I approached the guard drunk as a lord. I was swaying everywhere, falling down and slowly climbing to my feet, pushing and shoving him, singing in a slurred voice. Poor chap didn't know how to handle me.

'He pushed me away a few times, but when I tried to dance with him that really touched his temper. He buffeted me against the wall, unlocked the door and kicked me inside the dank hole where they put the prisoners. Very nasty it was, too.'

'But why?'

Old Weasel frowned disapprovingly.

'Come, come now. Can't you see it? You want a good deal more of cunning, my laddie. Consider what happens when the victorious army breaks in. The brigands are hanged or decapitated or whatever seems best for them. The prisoners are released.

'And there am I, the enemy of the brigands, cruelly mistreated, released to give my master's original message. All is well. Military aid is granted – and I survive.'

Well pleased with the memory, he took his mug once more to the teapot, but found it too far cooled.

'Survival has nothing to do with strength, Tom. It's all up here.'

And he tapped the top of his head with a bony finger.

'I ended my working life in this city,' he added, 'and there's no more testing place than this. It's vicious and brutish. It's treacherous. And what applies to the city as a whole applies to any one part of it and any one hostelry within it.'

Tom felt that he should be grateful for the warning, but it seemed that he had been told very little at all. He spoke quietly, though urgently.

'But who,' he asked, 'who should I fear?'

'Oh dear me, no. It won't do, laddie.' Old Weasel appeared offended by the question. 'Tell me, if I were a suspicious character, how would I react to your eagerness? Wouldn't I wonder why the young chappie was so anxious? It seems to me that you've learned nothing at all.'

But he relented a little and sat down next to Tom.

'No secrets, that's the rule. There's never a secret that can't be broken. Whisper a word and you'll find it painted six feet high on the wall when you turn the corner in the morning.

'Old Weasel's taken a liking to you and that's the beginning and the end of it. He's given you the warning. He watches and he listens and he knows what he sees and hears. But he doesn't tell.

'And why? Old Weasel's a survivor.'

11 Mazes

The next morning was serene and beautiful. The last grey clouds were gone, replaced by a sky of limpid blue whose brightness fell onto the snow and transformed it, the reflection lighting the city from below as the sun lit it from above. The buildings seemed almost to evaporate in this light. Tom stood at his window. The past few weeks became unreal, a dark dream people with shadows. The soldiers, their hapless victim, the boy with the scarf: had they really existed?

He was eager to be out to begin his search. He took his breakfast in the parlour downstairs, alone save for the landlady, whose brooding presence confirmed the reality of his situation. Compared with the food of his native village the breakfast seemed tasteless and was quickly finished. The woman in black – brusque and silent – gathered his empty plates. Tom put on his overcoat and stepped out into the morning.

For the first time since his arrival in the city he felt relaxed and happy walking these strange streets. Workers had been out early, clearing passages through the snow which now, discoloured and lumpy, rose even higher at the sides. The House of the Star was in an old quarter and the buildings here – now that he saw them in the light of day – seemed less threatening despite rare touches of the grotesque: a grimacing face carved on a door lintel and painted with violent and unlikely colours, red eyes, blue protruding tongue; a wall with a large painting of a burning man, his face defying the flames that enveloped his body by wearing a malevolent grin; another wall studded with the skulls of dead animals, each partly embedded in the roughcast surface.

Tom could barely suppress a shudder when he passed these things. They were no so very unpleasant in themselves perhaps, but what sort of people possessed the gruesome imagination to have created them?

The streets were narrow, the houses at times almost touching above his head, but to his surprise he came to one open space the size of several houses and filled with small trees. He gazed on them with a feeling of shock. It was, he realised, the first time he had seen growing things since he had entered the city gate. Leafless now, they nevertheless reminded him of the countryside that had hitherto seemed firmly locked out by the city walls. And there (he looked upon it in wonder), moving briskly between the bare branches, was a small brown bird.

People trudged along the streets wrapped in heavy winter coats, their faces muffled and difficult to see, for despite the bright sunshine it was still achingly cold. Tom travelled in the direction that he imagined the house with the white room to be. The streets grew broader and the buildings larger until they opened out onto a large market square. This provided Tom with his first sight of a large number of people engaged in normal activity. They pushed, argued, struck bargains in the way of all markets. He threaded his way between the crowded stalls, his eye taken by one which seemed devoted to displaying cult objects of the Red Blade: brooches and badges bearing the emblem, belts with dagger buckles, and plaster hands holding aloft imitation daggers painted with dripping blood. There were also various printed texts designed to be hung on walls, one of them bearing the legend 'Only one city – and that for the Blade' and another 'There is only corruption beneath the surface'. Tom wondered at the meaning of this.

At a stall selling fruit he bought a bag of large mottled apples. Biting into the juicy flesh brought back a flood of memories of orchards and late summer and sunshine. In my heart, he thought, I belong to the country and not to this strange city. But this thought could not displace an odd feeling that had been growing within him ever since his first entry through the city gate, and that feeling was that he did in some way belong here in these streets; that this was somehow real, and the village that he had grown up in was part of a dream that he was now waking from, even if the waking was, in part, dreamlike itself.

'Never have I seen someone so thoughtful about eating an apple. A very special apple, perhaps – or a very special someone.'

Surprised, Tom dropped what was left of the fruit and turned to face the speaker. He was surrounded by people, yet none appeared to be the owner of the voice that had addressed itself to him and which he half-recognised, until, looking down, he found the dwarf close by his side. He motioned Tom to follow him and began to move through the crowd towards the edge of the market. Tom found it difficult to keep pace with the little man, whose size gave him an advantage of movement and also made it easy for him to disappear behind people.

Before they were clear of the crowd Tom had lost him. Unsure what to do, he decided to wait by the corner of an alley that climbed in steps from the market square. The dark silence of the alley behind him contrasted oddly with the activity before him, and Tom was musing on this fact when he was disturbed by an object which came rattling down the steps and lay at his feet. It was a smooth round tone. Picking it up, Tom found on it the words: 'To remind you that I'm here'.

He turned and ran up the steps: the alley beyond was deserted, as he had known it would be. He returned to the message. What could it mean? Was it to encourage him, to reassure him, or did he detect a slightly menacing tone, a threat even?

For lack of any better plan he decided to carry on along the alley, believing it to lead in the general direction that the house with the white room lay. But it led him nowhere; or, rather, it led him into a maze of tight alleyways that eventually deposited him, thwarted, in the market square once again.

This became the pattern throughout the long hours of the morning. Roads which seemed wide and inviting would become narrower and would twist back upon themselves so that he made no progress and was continually being led back to places that he recognised as having already passed – the market, the small plantation of trees and, eventually, even the back of the House of the Star.

His legs ached, his stomach was pinched with hunger. Tom went to his room and wept, exhausted and dispirited.

Lunching on another apple, he decided that the city must have actually been designed to confound. A street plan would have simplified the task, but no such thing existed. Instead, he must attack the problem in a more systematic way. Sallying forth once more, he devised a new method. He would turn right at one junction, left at the next, right at the next, and so on until he reached the city walls, and then he would follow those round to the gate he had first entered by. From there it should be easy to retrace his steps to the house with the white room.

But this, too, was unsuccessful. He never reached the city walls. Instead he found himself back at the market which now, in the early afternoon, was almost deserted, with only a few stalls in evidence. He began again, starting with a left turn. It again led him in an enormous circle.

The frustration gripped his throat. His forehead burned, his temples throbbed. Tears were not far from his eyes. Should he stop someone and ask directions? But he was terrified of giving himself away. He averted his eyes from the faces of passers-by.

Once more he found himself in the square with the trees and the solitary bird. There were four streets leading from it: surely he had tried them all? There was no point in going further. Yet there must be a way. He set off again.

This time, by finding an alleyway he had not noticed before, he emerged at the square with the ruined monument. As if to emphasise its degradation, this was now hidden from view beneath a dirty pile of cleared snow. Heartened by the discover, he struck out along a broad thoroughfare, only to be led, as ever, into narrow streets which – resist it as he might – forced him back to the market square.

He would not give up. In a delirium almost, he paced the city streets. He lost consciousness of time. He passed and re-passed the familiar landmarks. His feet took him on, with a will of their own.

'Hey! Boy!'

He stopped. He looked behind him. It was several seconds before he realised that the woman who spoke to him was gazing at him with concern.

'Aren't you well?'

'Yes. Yes.' The sound of his own voice seemed to wake him up. 'I'm lost.'

'Oh, lost are you? Where are you heading?'

It was too late for second thoughts.

'I want to get to the city gate,' Tom said. 'The one to the east.'

He pointed, but the woman took no notice. She shouted across the street in an urgent voice.

'Dirk! Come now, quick! There's a boy asking his way to the east gate.'

Tom heard movement in the house across the way.

'I'm coming,' called a voice.

'I'll keep him!' yelled the woman. 'But you hurry, Dirk!'

Even now they could hear running footsteps from the side of the building, and it sounded as if there were at least two pairs of feet in motion.

'What's the matter?' asked Tom, fearfully. 'Why did you call?'

The woman grasped his forearm by way of reply.

'The east gate you want, is it?' she said through her teeth.

Tom did not wait to hear more. Tugging his arm free – and even as three burly men came running into the street – he held his coat tight about him and sprinted towards the entrance of an alley. He heard their heavy footsteps hammering along the paving, and he looked desperately for a place to hide.

He turned off the alley into another once, twice, three times, but still they pursued him. At first they had called after him, but now, saving their breath no doubt, they chased him in silence, save for the sound of their boots on the ground. He could hear them, but he did not dare look round. Were they close? Were they tiring?

Now he came to the market square once more. There was a large open space containing nothing but a few stalls and the old pile of rubbish. One of the stalls was draped with hessian and he flung himself beneath it, shrinking back from the sides, his body shaking.

His pursuers pounded into the square. He heard them talking urgently among themselves. They split up. He heard the footsteps in three directions. One man came towards the stall, but he was running and clearly had not considered that Tom might be hiding there. He passed so close that Tom saw one of his boots.

He remained there for a long time. When he emerged the sun was falling behind the buildings, rapidly sinking the streets into their former darkness. All the day's promise had vanished. He returned to his room, limp and bewildered.

Over supper Tom found his spirits reviving. He had slept for an hour after his return and now he sat in the warmth of the downstairs room, drinking thick soup and biting into grainy bread. The life of the inn ebbed and flowed around him. The city guard were in again, swaggering and roistering before the fire, and Tom sat alone in a pocket of silence.

Perplexed he was, but he began to be fascinated by a sense of intellectual challenge. Here was a puzzle to be solved. Two facts had emerged from his endless walking. One was that it was difficult to find that which he sought; the other was that it was difficult, if not impossible, to lose himself since he was forever turning back on himself.

The house, he knew, could not be far away: he had seen it from the tower. Was it possible that this part of the city was somehow sealed off from the surrounding area? Perhaps the whole city was divided into sections shut off by rings of buildings: that would certainly explain his circuitous routes. If that were the case, he would have to travel through a building in order to arrive at another part of the city. But which building? And how, with most doors firmly closed or blocked up?

The alternative, of course, was a route over the rooftops. Once more he found himself wrapped in confusion, faced with so many unanswered questions. How could he find his way to the roof of the House of the Star? Could the dwarf help him? If so, why had he not offered advice before? How, in any case, was it possible to find the dwarf?

Another question concerned the terrifying events of the afternoon, when he had been hunted by the three hefty men. Why had it been wrong to ask for the east gate? Was any travel outside this sector forbidden? And then a more disturbing thought entered his brain. Perhaps the woman had been so quick to seize him because she had been warned. Was someone perhaps looking for him? Could he have been betrayed already?

He looked around the large room. Who would suspect him? Clearly not the city guards. They regarded him almost as a pet, to be cosseted and occasionally mistreated. The one with the pearly teeth sat at a table playing a board game with the white-haired old gentleman, and he waved at Tom cheerily. The ancient pipe sat, dribbling smoke, on a corner of the table as its shabby owner leaned forward to study the game. The board was coloured green and red, and the pieces, of blue stone, were representations of weapons – knives, clubs, crossbows.

Each evening there were new faces, but Tom felt that the danger, if it existed, must come from one of the regular guests. Had he really divined something strange in the look of the proprietor, Clem? And why – he met his gaze now – did the man with gold-framed spectacles and crinkly hair pay such close attention to the people around him without ever betraying any emotion?

'M-m-may I sit here?'

Tom's thoughts were broken by the new arrival at the table.

'I'm a little l-l-late for s-supper.'

'Of course,' Tom said, pushing the large board piled with bread to his companion. 'The soup's very good this evening.'

He thought with embarrassment of the incident two nights before when the poor man had been paraded around the room by the guards. His large eyes, though no longer filled with tears, seemed to express a deep inner sadness, even when his conversation belied this.

'G-good, good! I've w-w-worked up an appetite!'

He ladled the soup into his dish and bent his head to scoop the liquid into his mouth, greedily. Although he and Tom had adjoining rooms they rarely met. When they did run into each other, however, he noticed that the man's stammer improved as the conversation continued. He seemed to relax.

'You're right,' he said. 'It' excellent s-soup.'

He wiped his mouth on a clean white handkerchief and, the sharpest pangs subdued, proceeded to drink in a more leisurely manner.

'Well, young man,' he began after an interval, 'and wh-what have you found to amuse you today?'

Tom picked at a piece of bread. The moment the question was asked he caught a glimpse of Old Weasel, plucking a tune by the fireside, and an answer dried in his throat.

'Have you b-been outs-side?'

'A short walk.'

He felt wretched. He felt sympathy for the man after his recent humiliation and therefore condemned himself the more strongly for his evasion. The remark was, surely, an innocent one.

'But it's been a f-fine day.'

'Still a little cold, though.'

Tom was surprised by his own resolution. It was as though the weeks of uncertainty and danger, the warnings of Old Weasel and the frustrations of the day had bred in him a new determination not to be downtrodden. His conscience told him that it was unfair, that the man was trying to be pleasant. But Tom knew that he would not give anything away.

'D-d-did you g-go to the market square?'

'Not today,' Tom said.

'That's a l-lively place to v-v-visit. You can b-buy yourself a cheap l-lunch there. Fruit, for instance. Very good a-a-apples.'

'I'll remember that.'

The man smiled and wiped his mouth once more with the handkerchief. He had suffering eyes.

'But watch out for r-r-rogues,' he said.

Climbing the stairs to his room after the meal, Tom again found himself wondering about the puzzle of the city streets, which seemed to form mazes within mazes. He passed along the thickly carpeted corridor, with doors to right and left. If there was a way out of this section he was determined to find it. A way up, perhaps.

As if in answer to his thoughts there suddenly came the clatter of footsteps from somewhere above his head. It ceased momentarily and then started again, but more faintly. Surely it was further along the passage. Running lightly forward, Tom strained his ears to hear the sound again.

12 The Great Invisible One

The footsteps were gone – but Tom's determination to discover the way up had been quickened. On this floor there were three connected corridors leading to seven doors. Tom's room lay behind one door, and he had once seen into his neighbour's room as the stammerer had entered: it was a small one similar to his own, similar to Old Weasel's. That left four doors, and behind one of these must surely be the flight of stairs leading upwards.

Most of the guests were downstairs. His own door could not be locked, and he now hoped that this was true of the others. In quick succession, his breath stopped in his throat, he tried each one of them. Each swung open easily. Each was unoccupied and similar in size and furnishings to the three that he already knew.

The operation was completed within minutes, and he was back in his room, shaking from the excitement of anticipating the welcome that might have greeted him had any of the rooms not been empty. And yet, how easy it had been. Why had it taken him so long to decide? A flatness overcame him: now that he had acted, it was in vain. He had discovered nothing.

Or perhaps he had: something was wrong. He looked round his own room and tried to estimate the size. Seven rooms the size of his could fit comfortably into the bar downstairs, and the corridors were not so very wide either. But the bar downstairs was only one of a whole complex of rooms. The outside of the building suggested that the first floor had the same area as the ground floor, so what had happened to the missing space? The walls could surely not be so very thick, and nor was this just one wing, for windows from the corridors looked out on all four sides of the building.

Pieces of the puzzle were beginning to fall into place; ideas were beginning to form. Each of the small rooms had a window like his own, and there were four windows in the corridors – eleven windows in all. And outside? Strangely agitated, he hurried down the stairs and through the crowded bar. His progress was slowed by the greetings that were called to him, by hands lightly touching his arms and shoulders, but – on the pretext of needing a breath of fresh air – he at last reached the door and stepped outside.

Even in the dark it was easy to count the windows on the first floor: four on the side immediately above the main door, floor on the side facing onto the alley, five at the back and five on the remaining side. He was right! As with the city itself, the house comprised sealed-off units interlocking in such a way that only the closest scrutiny would ever suggest the existence of anything more than was immediately apparent.

How, then, was he to get to the rooms between the rooms? Did two staircases lead up from the ground floor? He had only ever seen one, but another must exist. There must be a way, if only someone or something would show him. He felt totally helpless, and it must have been this despair which made him think of his mother and her faith in the old beliefs. How he envied her those certainties. He gazed up at the rooftops, white with frozen snow. She believed in a power beyond this mortal world.

And then an idea, a fine piece of trickery, stung his mind and brought a smile to his lips. It was just possible that it would work. He lifted the catch and re-entered the House of the Star.

The fire-flung shadows of a large semi-circle of men played on the furthest walls of the bar. They were in good humour this night, toasting themselves before the flames, the chill misery of another working day driven away by warmth, beer and entertainment. Tom smiled with them, laughed with them, nodded with them and shook his head with them, all the while waiting his chance.

There was, it soon emerged, a special reason for the guards to carouse, for one of the group – the tall, burly one who had hoisted him onto the table to sing – had been promoted to the rank of captain. His face was ruddy in the firelight and the glass in his hand seemed always to be full, although he drank from it continually. He touched it against those of his companions, waved it above the heads of the assembled company when he told a joke, raised it up and down to the rhythm of a tune played by Old Weasel.

He was, it appeared, a popular choice. The atmosphere was pleasant, relaxed. The guards mingled easily with the other guests. Even the immaculately dressed gentleman with the grizzled hair could be seen exchanging a word with his uniformed neighbour. Clem appeared from time to time, to proffer trays of drinks or to hurl huge logs into the fire, and always he was detained with some story or joke before picking his way through the throng back to the kitchens.

The evening grew long with their talk. The guards became light-headed, loose-tongued. One tipped his glass, laughing to watch the amber fluid pour into the lap of his companion. But the man with the drenched lap, who on another night might have flared into anger, only sympathised with the other's loss. One of the platoon even pretended to engage the landlord's wife in a dance, to be driven back by a scowl as the company hooted and cheered. And still Tom waited.

His chance came at last during a rare pause in the conversation, one of those moments when all fall silent and appear to drift into their own private musings, gazing vacantly at the fire or into their glasses. He spoke quietly and without emphasis, almost as if to himself.

'It's on nights like this that one would thank the Great Invisible One for being alive.'

There was a silence, broken by the sound of one of the guards choking on his beer. They looked at him in amazement. The one with pearly teeth seemed to speak for the others.

'Who is this Great Invisible One you would like to thank?' he asked, quickly glancing up at the dagger emblem on the wall. 'I'm sure that I know nothing of him.'

'Sounds treasonable to me,' put in another.

'Why, my mother told me of him when I was a child,' Tom answered. 'It was he who made us and who watches us.'

'Watches us?' demanded a third man, looking around apprehensively for a hidden pair of eyes. 'What do you mean, watches us?'

Before Tom could reply to his second question he was interrupted by the captain, who stood close to the fire and who now decided to give the congregation the benefit of his wisdom.

'Religion, that's what he's talking about.'

The captain's face was hot and flushed. He was rather drunk and his mood had become ponderous.

'Let me tell you a story and then you'll understand.'

He leaned heavily against the wall with his eyes closed and began to tell his tale slowly and deliberately, as if it were something he had once learned by heart and could not produce effortlessly, just as Tom had sung his song of the country without conscious thought. The story at first appeared to have little to do with their conversation, but his hearers were too polite, or too befuddled or, perhaps, some of them, too afraid to interrupt, and they listened intently.

'In the gathering dusk of an autumn evening a young man stood outside a city wall. The gates were closed and he was too late to enter; in any case, he had no permit and it was doubtful that he would be allowed in. The city rose from a coastal flat and there was no shelter for the young man from the wind that had begun to gust in from the sea. On his back he carried a knapsack. He walked to a freshly ploughed field, took the knapsack from his back and with his hands began to scoop a hollow in the ground large enough for him to lie in.

'Then from the knapsack he took two sheets of oilskin and carefully laid them in the hollow, one on top of the other. A low drystone wall provided large stones to anchor the edges and, that done, he crawled between the two sheets, wedging his knapsack near the edge to allow the access of air. The night's darkness was now complete and the space between the oilskins was utterly black, but warm and secure; for the young man knew that on this moonless night his shelter could be seen by no one. His day had been long and he was tired. Within minutes he was asleep.

'But this sleep was soon disturbed. The wind catching the edges of the oilskin caused it to flap and crack like a whip. As he lay cursing the noise above him he became aware of noise beneath him. He pressed his ear to the ground. He could hear hammering and, yes, voices far away. But surely they could not be beneath him. It must be an illusion. He lifted his head and listened: nothing.

'Pressing his ear once more to the ground, he again heard the faraway voices and the hammering. It was definitely coming from beneath him. Memories stirred of stories he had been told as a child, of the earth spirits, of the gods of the harvest and spring growth, stories that were laughed at and ignored by his friends as the mere pratings of ignorant peasants.

'The young man grew afraid. Had he not also scoffed at these spirits, and would they not wish revenge? He quaked with fear and, pressing his mouth close to the ground, he begged forgiveness of the spirits, and vowed to serve them for as long as they gave him life.

'The next day he refolded his sheets of oilskin, packed them into his knapsack once more and, without attempting to enter the city, set off home. Once back in his village he set about convincing people of the reality of the old earth spirits. At first they laughed at him and called him crazy. But as he repeated his story over and over they began to listen. He set up a shrine in the fields and each day performed strange rituals before it. These rituals attracted followers.'

Here the captain paused, and his eyes opened a crack, swiftly surveying his audience.

'On the following Midsummer day two events occurred: the young man recruited his hundredth follower and believer' – and now the captain grinned hugely – 'while, beneath the northern city plain, underground sewers that had been under excavation for the previous two years were finally completed.'

He pushed himself from the wall triumphantly. Had he not told his story well? Stooping forward, he patted Tom on the knee.

'That's religion, my boy, that's religion. A nonsense. No disrespect to your mother, mind you.'

Some of the other listeners, having been somewhat slow to understand the story, were beginning to laugh.

'Ha, that's a good one! He though the sewer-builders were spirits! That's rich, that is!'

But Tom frowned.

'No,' he said loudly and with great determination. 'That's not true. It's not like that.'

The captain stilled the others with a wave, addressing Tom in a fatherly tone. 'You tell us then, Tom. How is it?'

Tom left his chair and joined the captain at the fireside.

'At night,' he said, 'when you stand in the fields under the stars, you can feel him watching – not always, but sometimes. He's completely invisible, and completely good, and he completely surrounds you, and he's definitely there. Or sometimes, by the seashore, when the light of the sun bounces off the sea and seems to wrap you in itself, then he's there in that light.'

As he spoke these words Tom pictured his mother's face, for the words had been hers, and he knew that he had been just as uncomprehending as these people who watched him now.

'It's not superstition, or' (he grinned at the captain here) 'underground sewer-workers. It's real, and if you wished you could feel it for yourselves.'

But the captain shook his head.

'No, lad. I've lived for many years – some would say *too* many – and I've trudged the streets many a night after the curfew beneath the stars. I've felt nothing such as you describe. Imagination is what it is. Imagination, coupled with your mother's teaching.'

Tom, refusing to be put off, leaned forward and fixed the captain with his eye.

'But how could you expect to feel the Great Invisible One here in the streets, surrounded by houses and people?' (Here he threw up his hands and turned to the whole company.) 'No, it's no use. You'll never understand. Perhaps if you were to stand on the rooftops, up above everything, and look up at the stars, then you would feel him. Perhaps he would come to you then, perhaps . . . '

The speed with which the subsequent events occurred amazed him. The captain spoke abruptly.

'Right, men – we have a duty to this lad. On your feet!'

The guards stood up. One or two of them, unsure of their ability to do so, held onto chair backs or to the wall. The captain examined them quickly and singled out two of the steadiest.

'You and you,' he ordered. 'You too, Tom – come on.'

He found himself being marched out of the bar into a smaller room behind it, through another door, down a flight of steps into the cellars, between a row of barrels, grey and cobwebbed and standing one on top of another, beneath a low stone arch with a carved keystone, through a narrow passage to a spiral staircase which wound its way up and up. They climbed silently, the evening's celebrations now telling on the legs of the three guardsmen. Their pace grew slower and slower as they climbed higher and higher. At last they reached a door. Through the door, and Tom was there – on the roof, on a small railed platform, standing beneath the stars between the three tall men.

He stood trembling, partly from excitement and partly from the coldness of the night after the warmth of the downstairs bar. The captain looked down at him, smiling.

'What now lad, eh?'

They stood there, a little cluster of human beings, high above the streets of the city, silhouetted against a moon which had escaped from behind a cloud and now flooded them with sudden light.

'You must be very still and wait for him,' said Tom in a hushed voice.

For several minutes they stood still and silent. Along the snow-capped roofs they could see for miles in each direction. Nothing stirred. Finally the captain spoke.

'Well, my lads – do you feel anything?'

They shook their heads, impatient to be done with the business.

'And you, Tom? Do you feel anything?'

He shook his head dumbly and hung his head in the universal gesture of dejection.

'No. No, this time I don't. I can't explain it.'

The captain put his hand on Tom's shoulder and spoke almost tenderly.

'Don't take it so badly,' he said. 'You'll get over it. These fancies are just part of growing up. Better to face facts, especially here in the city: no time for country ways here. Come, I'll buy you a drink and we'll warm ourselves up again, eh?'

This suggestion noticeably cheered the guards, who had grown very cold standing on the exposed roof for no reason that they could well understand. They led the way down.

'I'm not meaning to be cruel, now,' the captain continued, following close behind him. 'You understand that.'

Tom was relieved that he did not have to show his face, for his heart sang with elation within him. Not only did he now know a way to the roof, albeit without yet having solved the mystery of the other floors, but also – while he had been standing out there in the cold air and the moonlight had poured itself over him – he had indeed felt, for the first time in his life, the presence of the

Great Invisible One, and he had been enveloped in the feeling of complete power and complete goodness that his mother had spoken of.

And at that moment he had looked towards the east and seen, clearly under the moon, the house with the longed-for white room.

'Nothing on the roof, young Tom? Better try putting your ear to the ground!'

'Give the boy a stiff drink, Clem. We can all see things after a few jugs of ale!'

Of course he had to endure a round of bluff, though good-natured joking when they returned. he did not mind it at all, but he tried nevertheless to play the part of disillusion and dejection slowly cheered by good company. It was a difficult part to play, for he felt jubilant and full of new hope. The evil that manifested itself everywhere that he looked in the city no longer seemed so overwhelming.

He glanced at Old Weasel who sat, eyes averted, plucking a sonorous melody from his burnished instrument. The firelight flickered on the glowing wood. Surely, if he knew, the old messenger would be proud of him, the cunning he had used. But then, he probably understood everything already. There was nothing that escaped him.

The company had never been so contented. A few of the guards were actually nodding in their chairs and the white-haired old gentleman was snoring throatily, his pipe happily keeping itself going for a while on the table. His belly heaved and fell under a stained and buttonless shirt. The old slippers on his feet had holes in the toes.

'A toast! I give you a toast!'

The captain, whose night it was, had not finished yet. He carried a jug among the guests, topping up their glasses.

'Let's salute a *future* captain of the city guard – the Great Invisible Tom!'

And tonight he did not mind their nonsense in the least, not even the tipsy heads thrust close to his own as they bumped glasses and yelled his name.

There was a way to the roof. There must be a route across the city skyline. His fears, his memories of the blacksmith, were submerged for the moment beneath his newfound hope. He must find his way to the railed platform once again and pick his way across the buildings by night.

Not this night, however. Even as he mused about the task before him his eyes began to close, and he had to force himself awake, shaking the encroaching sleep from his head as he prised himself from his chair. It had been a long and eventful day – the hours of walking through the city, the pursuit by the three men and the adventure of the evening – and his body ached for rest.

It was not to be granted immediately, however. When he reached his room and swung open the door he found that someone was there before him.

13 Angry Words

'That was a foolish mistake, to ask for the east gate.'

The rebuke, uttered in a harsh, high voice, was delivered even before he had shut the door behind him.

'It might have been the end of you – and it would have served you right!'

The dwarf sat perched on a chair, his knees drawn up to his chin. He had flung his coat on the bed and helped himself to one of Tom's books.

'I didn't mean to,' Tom said, lamely.

'Ho! That's a fine one! He didn't mean to. But he did. That's the inescapable fact. He did!'

Tom dropped into another chair. He was about to explain, to say that he had been tramping the streets for hours when the woman had surprised him, but he felt suddenly angry. It was not only his tiredness: he felt the injustice of the dwarf's attack.

'And he might have undone us all in the process.'

There was a silence, which seemed to surprise the dwarf. Perhaps he had been expecting an apology. He jumped down from the chair and stood before Tom with his arms folded in a challenging manner.

'I wouldn't have needed to ask,' Tom said, 'if I had been told in the first place.'

'Oh! He wanted to be told!'

'If someone had explained the city to me,' Tom persisted, 'I might have been on my way to accomplishing the mission by now.'

'Or on your way home!'

The dwarf stood immobile before him.

'Why, might I ask, did you want the east gate? Why do you need to leave this sector at all? A trifle suspicious, wouldn't you agree?'

Tom considered before replying. It seemed to him that the commander, and so the dwarf, was fighting against an evil force. He knew enough of the Red Blade and its cruelty to sympathise with their cause. But he remembered the words of Old Weasel and reflected that no good could come from telling what little he knew.

'I have investigations to make.'

'A-hah!' The dwarf cackled, mirthlessly. 'So he has investigations to make. He's a sleuth!'

Tom could abide this treatment no longer. He leapt to his feet and found himself shaking his fist in the little man's face.

'That's what you want me to do, isn't it? I'm supposed to be doing your dirty work for you, discovering things you haven't the wit to find out for yourself! And what help do you give me? You tell me nothing that I need to know, but come strutting in here as if I'm your servant!'

The outburst shook them both. They both sat down. The walls, fortunately, were thick.

'I'm not your servant,' Tom added, emphasising the point.

The atmosphere was uncomfortable, but fatigue and his anger had dulled his sensitivity. He did not care what the dwarf thought of his behaviour. As for the dwarf, he sat fidgeting his fingers, composing himself.

'Well now,' he said after some minutes. 'I think that perhaps we should start again, don't you?'

'If you like,' Tom replied.

'I do like. We both should like. Because unless we work together we can't possibly succeed.'

Tom said nothing.

'I will agree that you were told very little. There was a reason. We could not be sure of you. We had to watch. After all, you might have betrayed us at the first opportunity.'

'I didn't.'

'So we find. But, had you done so, you would have had few secrets to give away.'

'You could have explained about the city streets.'

Here the dwarf seemed to make a concession.

'Perhaps we should have done so,' he said. 'But – I'll be frank with you – we had no reason to imagine you would need to leave this sector. We believe that the answers are to be found at the House of the Star.'

Tom's temper began to rise again.

'And you have therefore risked my life by setting me down in the most dangerous area!'

'Of course.'

This time the dwarf was in no mood to compromise.

'Don't you want to find your father?'

'You know that's why I am in the city.'

'Then the dangerous way is the only way.' He perched forward in his chair. 'What have you discovered so far?'

'It's too soon,' Tom replied. 'I've nothing to tell you yet.'

'But weeks have passed!'

'The weather kept me in,' Tom countered.

'But "in" is where you need to be. Have you learned nothing of the people?'

'Nothing that helps.'

The dwarf frowned, but seemed to be making an effort to control his irritation.

'And the eastern gate,' he said. 'Why do you wish to go there?'

'It's not the gate itself.'

'The sector, then. Why does it interest you?'

'I can't say.'

'Ho!'

'No, I can't say. Not yet.'

The dwarf hopped from his chair again and began to pace the room.

'There is a five-letter word called Trust. There's a rune we learned at school – I wonder if you know it?' (He paused for a reply which never came.) 'The first T stands for truthfulness, the R for reliability, the U for unselfishness, the S for stability and the final T for tolerance.'

Still Tom said nothing.

'We need that trust between ourselves.'

The dwarf continued his progress around the room until it brought him to Tom, who looked him steadily in the eye.

'How do I reach the east gate?' he demanded.

The question deflated the little man in an instant. He turned his back on Tom and occupied himself for a while at the shelf of books above the bed.

'Of course there are routes through the buildings,' he said eventually, 'but they are very well guarded. You need passes. It's almost impossible.'

'But not quite impossible,' Tom insisted. 'We came here ourselves.'

'We have our own route, but it is open to very few. The risk is too great. I can come and go.'

'But I may not.'

'No – not at present.'

'At present?'

'It would need special sanction. From the very top. Perhaps it might be arranged.'

Tom spoke urgently.

'How long would it take to arrange?'

'I don't know. A week or two, perhaps. But perhaps not at all.'

'And the rooftops? There's a way across the roofs?'

The dwarf seemed to shudder. He shut his eyes and shook his head.

'It's perilous. Our people sometimes use that method, but only in an emergency. I can't' – the very thought seemed to injure him – 'I can't cope with those heights myself. I once . . . '

But he did not finish. The memory was obviously too dreadful.

'I'll try,' he said. 'I'll do what I can to get you the sanction.'

The hostility had passed. They spoke more quietly now.

'I will show my trust in you,' the dwarf went on, 'by letting you further into my confidence. Your work is more vital than you were aware. We face nothing less than the extinction of our organisation – the extinction of all hope.'

He began to dress himself for the bitter cold outside.

'We are weakening. Every day another of our leaders is seized. If we make no fight now the cause is lost – we have to make one great effort. Yet many of our comrades have lost heart. They lack the courage to take up arms and challenge the Blade on the streets. We need to inspire these people.'

'Is that possible?'

'There is one way,' replied the dwarf. 'The myth of the underground city is well known. If it exists, and if we can find it, our faint-hearts will be persuaded to stand firm – to fight alongside those good people underground. That is why your mission is of the greatest urgency.'

He paused, with his hand on the doorknob.

'Unless we risk everything now we shall all be destroyed – and the Blade will rule for a thousand years!'

14 Vertigo

Along the spine of the roof the thin snow had frozen to white ice. His fingers would not grip. Leaning forward, straddling the ridge, he was aware of his thighs slipping, twisting him over, however gingerly he edged forward. The roof fell away, glistening under the moon, with dark patches of slate where parcels of snow had shot down the steep slope and plummeted into the black abyss.

He could not look down the hundreds of feet to the ground. He saw only the pitch of the roof, inviting him to plunge into the spaces beyond. When he raised his eyes he found himself alone in a gaunt, silhouetted world of gables, parapets and chimneys.

Six more feet and there was nothing that he could see. The roof ended there. A breeze buffeted him, pushed him off balance, but the more tightly he rasped the masonry the more his fingers skidded on the polished snow.

Taut with fear, he inched forward. At the end there was a projecting strip of metal: a lightning conductor, perhaps. He reached out – carefully, tremblingly – and clutched it. He pulled himself close to it and shut his eyes.

There was no sound. The city was asleep. If he fell, nobody would know. His frozen body might lie, lost among the high roofs, never to be found.

He opened his eyes. Beneath him an icy slope gave access to a long flat area. Behind him – he turned, cautiously – crumpled snow revealed the route he had taken from the House of the Star, down a steel ladder, along a stone walkway to the precarious ridge on which he sat.

If he slid down the incline, a distance of perhaps ten feet, he could not possibly climb up again. Yet he knew that his nerves would not allow him to return the way he had come. Gripping the metal so tightly that it cut into his flesh, he manoeuvred himself to the top of the slope, cradled his knees in his free arm, and let go.

The impetus sent him slithering along the roof on his back, his feet ploughing through thick snow. His hair was flecked with it. He stood up and beat the flakes from his coat with stinging hands. The roof was wide, with no balustrade or ornamentation of any kind. To right and left the nearest buildings stood well back: he feared even to approach the edge and gaze across.

Ahead of him there was an adjoining roof, but much lower down. He knelt as near the brink as he dared and looked over. The wall fell sheer for twenty feet and there was not the slightest foothold.

Sick with desolation, he raised himself to his feet. The breeze mocked him. The moon sailed on, pitilessly. He was trapped, with no chance of being discovered. All around him the buildings rose dark and forbidding against the sky. Heavy grey clouds were building up in the west – clouds that his companions at the hostelry had told him marked the onset of further vicious storms.

He retraced his steps, knowing that it was hopeless. The slope could not be scaled unless it was dry. If only – it was a childish thought – if only he could leap from one building to another he could cross to the eastern sector in twenty bounds. He could not be sure where one sector gave way to another, and he was now too low to see the building with the white room, but he had studied the cityscape carefully before leaving the railed platform and he was sure that he knew how far to go and in which direction.

In a panic he returned to the edge where the wall dropped smoothly to the lower roof. Was there really no way down? Had he perhaps overlooked a snow-covered ladder that led to the safety of the next level? But it was a mere foolishness. The wall was flat and steep. Even a mountaineer would have shuddered at the prospect.

Now he cursed his own conceit. To have thought it would be so easy! To have congratulated himself on his trickery, without considering the consequences! Where was the Great Invisible One now? In his moment of triumph he had told himself that he felt the goodness and the power, but now he could not bring that feeling back. He stood stiff and straight, as if challenging the spirit to appear, but he was unable to receive it. He watched the clouds lifting out of the west, bringing more onslaughts of driving snow, and he shivered.

What of the sides of the building? It was in desperation rather than hope that he crouched to peer over. Here the drop was immense, broken hundreds of feet down by a narrow ledge which was itself high above the ground. There was no window to call at, no sign of human habitation at all. He kicked his way through the snow to the other side. The view was identical, the wall as sheer.

And then he noticed what at first seemed to be thin shadows at the corner nearest the lower roof. But they were not shadows. Hurrying across, he discovered that iron stakes had been hammered into the wall, descending. They were set irregularly and were spaced well apart, but it was obvious that they had been designed for people scaling the wall because, further down, they changed direction and took a lateral route towards the next building.

Tom flattened himself on the roof and edged himself into position. Once he was satisfied that his feet would find the first bar he gripped the stonework as firmly as he could and swung himself over. For a second he hung in the air, his fingers trembling with the effort, and then his boots touched the metal and he struggled into a standing position. He had to turn half sideways in order to keep his footing, since the stakes came straight out of the wall. Steadying himself, he craned his neck to look for a handhold. There was another iron bar to his left just above knee height, but when he stooped to reach it with his left hand he felt his right slipping away from the roof. Twice more he tried it. The iron way had been designed for men.

He flattened his body against the wall, his arms aching with the effort of supporting him. There was only one solution, and it horrified him. He must position himself as close to the stake as possible, skewed round with his left hand hovering, and then, for a brief moment, let go completely, falling onto the projecting iron.

He prepared himself and counted slowly to ten, but at the last his nerve gave way. He had to stand upright again. The second time he was sure he would go, but his right hand seemed frozen to the roof. Always he let his eyes look no further down than the section of wall he had to cross.

Something pressed uncomfortably against his chest. It was the picture that he always carried safe inside his coat. If his father could see him now! He thought of his father, perhaps – or was it a wild dream? – perhaps at this moment deep underneath the city while he was far above it. And, in the moment of reflection, he dropped and clutched the metal bar, bracing himself hard against the wall.

Now it was possible to lower his legs onto another support. He moved hands and feet alternately, picking his way down the face of the wall, which was smooth and glistening with tiny crystals of ice. The sky above the hard line of the roof was dark, invaded by the first of the dense snowclouds. Below – he looked for the first time and was almost undone. Unreal in the deep distance, a miniature street glimmered white through the shadows. He would fall and fall and roll and float before he ever reached it. His body felt as though it pulled him away from the wall, eager to plunge into space. His brain somersaulted. His hands gripped the stake violently. Their hold was too rigid: the iron would slip through. He would surely topple.

He could only press himself against the wall until the worst of the fit had passed. There was so little space between life and death, so great a divide between hope and achievement. He started down again, but clumsily, stiffly. His heart raced, his brow was covered in sweat, his hands ached with the strain of holding onto the iron.

After a while there were no more stakes beneath him. He stood on the last support above the chasm. A double row of spikes ran to his left, towards the low roof, the higher ones only just within his reach. He had to stretch his arms to hold on as his left leg swung in the air for a footing. Here, where the iron ladder changed direction, he discovered a marking on the wall. Leaning back a little to examine it, he found it to be the sign of the eye which the dwarf had shown him at their first meeting. He carried the metal disc in a safe pocket. There was no colouring on this etching, but it was unmistakably the same device.

Spurred on by this finding, Tom moved more easily across the face of the wall. He was able to reach the lower roof and haul himself onto a wide shelf which ran between two steep slopes. He sat for a while, his head in his arms, panting, his eyes closed. He had never imagined such terrors.

Now the way was easier for a time. he climbed a ladder, wickedly iced along the rungs but secure to the wall, and found himself on the first of a series of flat roofs. He could see for some distance ahead, and between the roofs there were wooden plank-bridges with rope supports for the hands on either side. Taking care to look only ahead, he began to cross the first of these bridges. The ropes swung a little as he held them, but he was able to keep his balance without difficulty. He breathed more freely.

He was on the fourth plank, crossing a gulf of some thirty yards between grim grey buildings, when he found that a section of rope to his right had broken away. He approached the spot nervously. The rope was strung on metal posts driven into the planking at intervals of about ten feet, and he saw that it had snapped in the centre. The two ends hung uselessly in the void. He wondered, with a shudder, whether the weight of a man had broken it.

He started across, holding the remaining rope with both hands. It was wet and in poor condition: the strands had begun to fray and separate. He was just beyond halfway, and leaning as heavily as he dared, when it snapped and he was flung forward. His fingers grappled furiously for a hold. His body slid across the planking, his head already out over the edge. He felt one leg lose its contact with the wood and his body turning over. His fingers found a crack in the worn surface of the bridge and he dug them in, frantically, but the other leg began to slip away. He could not prevent it. He was out over the edge, tugging at the one anchoring arm. There was not enough strength in it. He swayed, all but gone, his body twisting away from the plank and then returning.

Slowly, not to disturb the tenuous hold he had, he raised his free arm and groped to locate another purchase in the wood. His fingers dug into frozen snow, scrabbled wildly, and found, at last, what appeared to be the head of a large nail. He dangled, feeling his strength ebb.

He knew that his aching frame could manage only one mighty effort. If it failed he would hang suspended for a few seconds more before spinning off into the void below. He tensed his body for the attempt, took a quick, deep breath and hauled upwards, his muscles feeling as if they would tear out of his arms, his neck straining, his legs kicking fiercely. Halfway, and the agony was unbearable. He came up and forward; he reached a knee onto the planking; he rolled himself over; and he lay hunched and heaving and safe.

It was impossible for him to stand again. He dare not trust the rope. His feet might slip. Once his breath was back, he crawled forwards on all fours like an injured animal, his hands raw and numb. He crossed to the next roof and collapsed in a heap.

The worst was over. Soon he came to a properly constructed thoroughfare. Where there were steeply pitched roofs this pathway was built into the slope, with a parapet on the open side. He stumbled gratefully onward, his eyes clouded with tiredness.

When the route climbed to a high point he paused to take his bearings. At first he could not see the house with the white room. He looked into the middle distance with a growing despair. But when he turned towards the buildings nearer at hand he discovered with joy that the house he sought was now almost within reach. It was not accessible by the route he was taking – it lay at an acute angle from it – but it was clear that he must have already crossed into the eastern sector. He had only to find a way down.

The first door that he discovered would not open. It was under the eaves and approached by an iron staircase. He threw himself against it, but made no impression at all. Soon afterwards, however, he came across another, this time let into the pitch of the roof. The handle turned and the door swung open. Steps led down steeply, and the turning of a corner plunged him into complete blackness. His boots thumped heavily on the stone. He steadied himself against the wall with one hand, descending slowly.

After some minutes he began to feel uneasy. He was not lost, since it was possible to climb back again to the door in the roof, but the darkness was oppressive. Every so often the stairway changed direction, but always it led steeply down. He began to touch the walls to right and left for fear that he might pass a door unawares.

The door, when he found it, was in front of him. He collided with it. He fumbled for the handle and stepped into a murky light. High to his left there were small windows in the wall. The steps led straight down now, with not the slightest turn. Tom began to count them, reached five hundred, and tired of the exercise.

Some minutes later he was surprised to find, to his right, an archway leading to a corridor. It was deeply shadowed, but he imagined that it must lead to rooms. The air was chill, even so far from the roof, and the area clearly was unused. Another twenty steps down and he came upon an identical passage. There was an eeriness about the darkened entrance and he hurried on. He passed another three archways, all deserted, and then came up against a stout wooden door. This time the handle would not turn. He tried it this way and that. He leaned on it, pulled it and pushed it. The door was so heavy that when he tried to shake it there was no movement and no sound. It was only after some considerable time wrestling with it that he stood back and noticed a large square section in the centre. He touched it and immediately felt it yield. His fingers pushed against the top and it tilted away from him to reveal a sizeable opening.

On the other side, once he had swung the flap to, the opening was completely invisible. The door was panelled and decorated, giving no hint of its secret.

The windows were a little larger now and the air was warmer. And when he came upon another passage he was surprised to find a plant hanging in a pot from the arch. There was no sound, but he felt that there were people close by. He moved more stealthily, descending past several more corridors, until he reached a point at which the stairs made a sudden turn. At this moment, around the corner he heard footsteps and he drew himself up against the wall.

There was something he recognised about those steps – the steps of several people at a time, in unison. He had heard them before, and the memory was not pleasant. It was the sound of marching. The steps drew near, very near, and passed on, tramping.

The city guards! The crunching of their feet faded away. What were they doing here? He turned the corner and found the answer. He faced a door, the final door. Cold air swept through the cracks around it. He had reached his destination: the street lay beyond. Tearful with relief and tiredness, he sat propped against the wall and fell asleep.

He was awoken by new sounds from the street – the muted conversations of people up earlier than their neighbours. Then came the clatter and break of a horse and cart, passing at an easy pace.

From inside the building there was nothing. Tom rose, rubbed the sleep from his eyes, and quietly opened the door. A light wind was blowing large white flakes along the street. He stepped outside, his boots making fresh marks in the snow.

15 In the Night Cafe

'Where are you going, boy?'

The man seemed to have appeared from nowhere. He looked frail and slightly mad, with his intense eyes and his wild grey hair and knotted beard. The firmness of his grip on Tom's arm disposed of any lasting belief in his frailty, but his sanity remained open to question.

'Where are you going, I say?'

Tom flinched. Was the man some sort of official set to question strangers in these empty streets? He certainly looked nothing like one. His clothes barely held together, their raggedness was so complete, and the way that he shifted his starting eyes, looking first one way down the street and then the other, suggested that he was as fugitive as Tom himself.

'You look a bright sort of lad; the sort of lad who wants to know things, to understand things. You come with me, boy, and I'll show you wonders that will make your mind dance, that will set the constellation of your thoughts into movement. You come with me!'

Tom found himself tugged across the street, into an alley, and from there through the door of a low building. It was a night cafe, so well hidden that its custom must of necessity be drawn from those intimate with the area. The door swung to behind them. It was like entering a forest, the light of the streets giving way to a strangely greenish gloom. The only light came from a window which faced the narrow alley between tall buildings, and it was muted even before it fought its way through the grimy glass.

Tables stood in clusters, scrubbed and bare. At two or three of these sat breakfasters, silent, their heads remaining down even when Tom and his companion entered. There was a stench of stale wine and smoke mixed with the smell of food. But, despite the gloom and the unwelcome odours, Tom was attracted by the warmth and privacy of the place.

By the door was a small bar, and there stood the waiter, a cloth slung over his shoulder and a cup in his hand. He surveyed the two new arrivals carefully as they made their way to the furthest and darkest corner of the cafe, Tom in tow. Sitting down, the older man waved to the waiter who, until this moment, had scarcely moved – even the hand with the cup seemingly frozen into immobility. Now he set down the cup and approached the table.

'My young friend and I would each like a breakfast, if you please.'

The waiter turned to Tom to verify the order, and there was a sympathetic look in his eye. Tom nodded his head uncertainly, and the waiter shrugged and disappeared towards the kitchen. Once he was gone the old man leaned forward, speaking in a hoarse whisper.

'I know the secrets of the city, my boy. Would you like me to reveal them?'

The man's eyes had begun to burn with a sudden intensity that frightened him, and the tone of his voice was changed, too: the voice that had coaxed Tom into this cafe and ordered food from the waiter had become higher, faster and edged with malevolence.

'I was the keeper of the archives, all the archives. Before they burned them, that was. I had access to all of those documents before the flames snatched them away. Those ignorant pigs of soldiers, what wouldn't I pay to see them and their brutish faces vanish in the flames instead! Ha! They grinned, you know: they grinned! I escaped them, though. You can't fool a city archivist so easily. Oh no, I had the beating of them.'

He spoke with a dreadful fevered seriousness, his lips flecked with spittle. Tom felt himself mesmerised as the river of speech rolled relentlessly on and on.

'They thought they were dealing with a madman, you see. Can you believe that? The poor fools! Do I look it, eh? I had the beating of them all right, the beating of them!'

This monologue was cut short by the arrival of the breakfasts which, though short of being delightful, were at least more easily digested than the bearded man's speech, which left Tom completely mystified. The waiter again gave him a sympathetic look and made his way back to the bar. The old fellow pushed his food aside with a gesture of contempt and carried on talking as animatedly as before.

'Thought they'd captured everything, they did. But they hadn't. Oh no, they certainly hadn't! Ah, the archives – what a treasure house they were! My father kept them before me, you know. You knew that, did you? Yes, it's a family tradition – thirteen generation of city archivists. I'm the thirteenth, and the last, thanks to *them!*'

At this point his eyes welled with tears, and he took a fork and crudely thrust a mouthful of food between his lips as if in order to control himself. He consumed it messily, noisily. This done, he leaned forward and, prodding Tom with the end of his knife, said softly, 'But they didn't burn all of them, you see. This hand snatched some from the flames.'

Tom looked down at the hand and noticed, for the first time, the dreadful swollen scar tissue that covered one side. The man grinned, horribly, but the expression changed in a moment as he looked over Tom's shoulder towards the door.

Tom turned and witnessed the dramatic entry of a patrol of city guards. The man leapt to his feet, whimpering, but within seconds the soldiers had pushed their way across the cafe, scattering tables and chairs. The terrified creature threw his arms around the still seated Tom, as if to anchor himself and prevent arrest. The movement thrust Tom backwards and the chair overturned, throwing them both in a tangled heap on the floor. The poor wretch, meanwhile, was screaming and clutching at table legs, chairs, anything, in a futile attempt to prevent their carrying him off. The soldiers waded in roughly and yanked them to their feet, bundling them off towards the door. Tom, confused and afraid, made no effort to resist and his sudden exit from the cafe was prevented only by the waiter, who stepped forward and held up his hand.

'It's not the boy's fault – don't take him. This old fool is always grabbing people and dragging them in here. He's mad if you ask me, quite off his head, but the boy here's done nothing.'

The captain looked down at Tom, who was near to tears, and shoved him towards the waiter contemptuously.

'Take him, then. We've got who we came for.'

For several minutes the screams of the old man could be heard fading into the distance. The other breakfasters, who had observed the violent scuffling in silence, returned to their eating, each alone with his thoughts. Tom was badly shaken and sat with his head in his hands for some minutes. When at last he regained his composure and opened his eyes he found the scene unchanged – the customers chewing dumbly, the waiter with his cloth by the bar. The incident, which had been so short-lived, seemed never to have happened.

The waiter, who until now had said so little, came over and sat next to him.

'Have you somewhere to go, lad?'

Tom, surprised by the question, said nothing.

'You're a stranger round here, I know that, and strangers are rare in this sector. It's a guess, then, that you're running from someone. No, no – I'm merely thinking aloud. You needn't say anything. "No prying" is the motto of this place.'

Tom spoke slowly.

'I'm looking for someone,' he said.

At this the waiter glanced rapidly around the room. he stood up and cleared his throat.

'No names,' he said. 'It's our second motto. Now, you wait here a moment lad. Do you promise?'

'I promise.'
'I've a little idea. You just hang on.'

16 Strange Papers

As he sat waiting, Tom became aware of an unfamiliar weight in the pocket of his coat. Plunging his hand inside, he discovered a bundle of papers held by a knotted cord. They looked old and were charred at the edges. He stared at the bundle, remembering the shrill screams of the mad archivist.

The cord was difficult to untie, but his struggle with it seemed to go unnoticed in the darkened cafe. Eventually he was able to slip the papers out. He unrolled them, straining to make out the faded writing.

Document I (fragment: the edges charred)

> . . . the forest and facing the plain.
> Who could say that he had no fear?
> The sun pinning my shadow to the ground by day,
> scraping a hollow in the earth at night
> to escape from the wind,
> my mouth moistened by torn fingers.
> Who could say that I had . . .

> . . . plentiful as the stars
> that fill the night sky
> lie the graves upon the hillside
> now that the excavations are finished.
> A hundred years – men born to carry earth
> have died still carrying earth
> and men born to masonry have sat and waited,
> their hair turning white, their bodies wasting
> and they have died, still waiting.
> A mountain range has grown . . .

> . . . and a boy will enter the city.
> Through the gate, unwelcome he will creep
> like a tick entering the wool of the sheep
> he will come, and like a tick he will
> drink the blood of the city.
> But another will follow seeking a father.
> Secretly he will enter the city –
> like a steel comb he will enter the sheep's wool . . .

Document II (full sheet – hand written – tiny blocks of writing seemingly scattered at random across the page)

> I sing of a city with no night –
> do you remember the stars?
> I sing of a city with no clouds –

do you remember rain?
I sing of a city with no warrior –
do you remember his wounds?

No birds sing beneath
the city's vaults;
the eagle's wing cracks
against stone.
There are stairs
into the snow;
we will climb into
the freezing air of winter
and watch gulls engrave
white arcs onto a grey sky.

An eye of blue
vivid blue
that stares and never closes

Document III (clearly a section from an official document
relating to the payment of functionaries)

City keeper – 30 pieces
Street watcher – 20 pieces
Lampman – 20 pieces
Sanctuary guardian – 15 pieces
Watcher in the Tower – 40 pieces (plus associated
     rooms and robes)
Keeper of the Stairs – 50 pieces
Executioner – (post removed)
City poet – 10 pieces (plus associated room and
     pen allowance)
Keeper of the artificial birds – 15 pieces
Keeper of plants (city/real) – 15 pieces
Keeper of plants (city/artificial) – 15 pieces
Transporter of plants – 15 pieces
Garden maker – 25 pieces
Painter of stars – 25 pieces (plus 30 pieces for other
     maintenance of sky vault)
Moonmaker – honorary (unpaid)

Document IV (handwritten, the script increasingly loose
and erratic, as if written in a fevered state)

An account of the birth and death of the star machine

I Olegial in my 37th year decided to replace the peeling stars
of the sky ceiling with an illusion more convincing to my
fellow citizens, and I set about the construction of the star
machine whose clockwork mechanism unwound in such a
way as to allow a beam of light to pass through an ever-
changing grid, thus casting a multitude of small stars in
movement across the ceiling. At its first trial the machine

was received well and I was complimented for the birth of a new heaven. Astrologers once more turned their heads upward at a sky no longer static, and astronomers began to map my lights and plot their movements, commenting with excitement at any new light caused by a flaw in my machine. For two years I basked in the praise of the whole community. Sad the fate of man. Short the reign of praise. My machine developed a fault that sped the mechanism to destruction, first flinging the stars in wild confusion across the sky and then freezing them, hauntingly. Astrologers predicted the end of the city, causing great fear among the population. Astronomers tore up their carefully calculated charts in anger. Praise turned to abuse and my machine was smashed. I have lived these last thirty years shaven-headed among the remains of my machine. People have forgotten my moving sky, and each night I am rebuked by the golden stars that remain fixed and staring. Recently I have constructed a rainbow machine. Dare I test it? Dare I . . .

17 An Old Acquaintance

There was a movement in the shadows. He hurriedly thrust the papers into his pocket as the waiter returned to the table.

'Have you got work, lad?'

'No.'

'Would you like a job with us here, then? My Lucy says it's all right. There's not much money in it, I grant you, but there's a small room going with the job.'

'Thank you,' Tom replied, 'but . . . '

'It's not hard work. Mostly nights, but not every night. Not much money, but we can offer a room and food – and when you've got a roof above you and food inside you money counts for little enough.'

Tom was moved by the man's kindness.

'You're very generous,' he said, 'but I can't stay. I have to find the person I mentioned. It's important.'

The waiter stood back.

'You must choose,' he said. 'You're old enough to know your mind – though you're young enough to find trouble, in all conscience. Will you make me another promise?'

'What is it?'

'That you'll think about what I've said and not forget it. You'd find it a safe place here, lad. Not many outsiders get in here.'

'I won't forget,' Tom said, rising. 'I would stay . . . '

'I know, I know,' conceded the waiter, opening the door. 'Business is business, lad. Good luck to you.'

He escaped from the stifling fug of the cafe, and the crisp air seemed to buoy him up. He strode forward, feeling an elation which quite overcame his tiredness. Even the strange affair of the archivist's papers was for the moment forgotten. He knew he could not be far from the house by the east gate, with its longed-for white room in which he had been protected and nursed through his first days in the city. And as he passed along the silent streets, the walls of the buildings etched with hard dry snow, he was sure that already he recognised certain features – a doorway here, up there high on a wall an especially vicious example of the Red Blade insignia.

Then he came upon a huge pile of rubble which he instantly knew. He had scrambled frantically over the fallen stones on the morning he had left the house and the tearful girl. It was as mysterious now as it was then: a large building which had been utterly demolished. He remembered his despair on that cold early morning. He had been pursuing the boy with the green scarf . . .

Now there was a movement beyond the ruined building and, as in a dream, he caught sight yet again of the slender lad, one arm pulling the scarf tight across his throat. It was no dream. On catching Tom's eye he turned swiftly and skipped along a nearby passage, soon completely lost to view.

But Tom had not given chase. He was surprised to find that he had no impulse to catch the youngster. Was it that he felt the task beyond him? No: this morning he felt alert and full of enthusiasm. He fancied himself the taller and stronger of the two, but he was not drawn to follow.

Instead, he hurried along the now familiar streets. The snow had been cleared in the centre and he was able to make good progress, his cheeks and his forehead smarting from the smack of the chill early morning wind.

Somewhere he miscalculated and took the wrong path, but almost immediately he found himself under the high wall, close by the eastern entrance to the city. He stole close. A dim light flickered in the guardroom. There was a murmur of voices. The huge iron gates were heavily bolted, impenetrable.

Keeping to the shadows, he hurried down the hill just as he had done on his arrival in the city. The tall buildings were sullen, closed and dark. A little further along he saw where the road disappeared into a bend: from round that turn the city guards had marched that terrifying evening. On his left was the building he had looked for so anxiously – that he had gazed down upon from the tower when he talked with the commander; that he had seen like a distant beacon as he picked his treacherous way across the rooftops. He approached nervously and touched the wall with a hand. It was cold, but massive and real. And here (he reached his fingers into the gloom) here was the door through which he had tumbled into the room which swam with liquid green.

But there was no door!

He groped, disbelievingly, for the handle, but there was none. His eyes, becoming accustomed to the halflight, discovered nothing but flat wall. It was not even possible to see a join where a door had once been.

Smitten by despair and an unnameable fear, Tom crossed the street to look back at the building. He had not mistaken it. This was clearly the house with the white room. But now there seemed to be no way in at all.

He looked up at the windows. It was not credible. A whole line of them had disappeared, leaving no trace. The white room, so far as any observer could tell, had been entirely obliterated.

A harsh cough alerted him to the presence of another early morning frequenter of the city streets. A gaunt man with close-cropped hair, hunching himself against the cold, appeared from around the corner. He had not yet seen Tom, for he seemed intensely interested in the buildings on the far side of the street. He carried what appeared to be a notebook, and he paused to consult it – running a finger over the contents – before coming on again, his head still turned away. After hesitating a second time, he advanced to the very spot Tom had been standing only moments before. It was as if he, too, were seeking a way into the building. He looked in the book again and then upwards towards the rows of windows, all in darkness.

At that moment Tom recognised him. It was, without doubt, the prisoner Marcus whom he had last seen in the small cell before he met the commander. How well he remembered his chilling tales of torture! Tom's insides melted with fear. The man was a paid killer for the Red Blade – one, moreover, who enjoyed his foul profession.

The notebook was pushed into an inside pocket. Tom began to edge away, his heart racing. He dare not run. He walked silently towards the bend in the street, his feet gathering pace. Another twenty strides . . .

'Wait! Hello!'

The sounds echoed through the empty streets. Oh say they were not meant for him! He hurried on, not looking back. But he heard the running footsteps behind him, and even as he reached the corner a hand grasped him by the shoulder.

'Hey, wait young fellow! Don't we know one another?'

18 Dog-fight

'It's my little fellow-prisoner, is it not? And all in one piece!'

He took Tom's chin roughly between thumb and forefinger and tilted his head this way and that as if looking for scars and bruises.

'You escaped the swine, did you? How did you manage that?'

His lined face seemed always in motion, the eyes darting, the tongue playing along the lips. Tom remembered his restlessness in the cell, how he had flung himself against the wall.

'They've paid for meddling with me, they have!'

He set off down the street with a gesture to Tom he could not disobey. They turned into a narrow alley, flanked by high walls.

'Paid?' Tom asked nervously.

'The fools! They took the weapons from me and imagined that was enough. They forgot these!'

He paused for a moment and held his hands in the air, the fingers curled and grasping, the muscles straining. They were like talons.

'Amateurs!' he muttered scornfully, leading Tom into a network of mean passages. 'The ones I strangled were fortunate. The others have been hunted and destroyed like vermin.'

They came at last to a neglected house of two storeys. The paint had long since flaked from the woodwork and the sills were feathery with decay. Patches of plaster had broken away from the wall, which was stained with deep-seated damp. The door was rotten and yielded to a push. Inside, the house had a matching sense of degeneration. Low down on the walls Tom noticed an evil-looking black and green fungus, and there was a moist, earthy smell that was not pleasant. They passed through a kitchen area to a cavernous room containing two large and shabby chairs. He was motioned into one of them.

'Will you drink?'

'No. No, thank you.'

'I will.'

Marcus produced a bottle containing a colourless fluid and filled a large tumbler. He gulped a mouthful, coughed violently, and took another swig. The glass, Tom noticed, was long unwashed.

'That's where warmth comes from,' he said, putting the bottle by his feet as he sat down. 'There's no fire in here.'

There was a pause, during which he stared closely at Tom as if he were making up his mind about something.

'You escaped,' he said eventually. 'Tell me how.'

'How?'

'What happened when they took you away?'

Tom began to think quickly. It was suddenly clear to him that the gaunt man who sat so menacingly close to him perhaps regarded him as a sympathiser, a friend of the Blade. Of course he knew nothing. How, Tom wondered, would Old Weasel have dealt with such a situation?

'I was taken to a man they call the commander,' he said. 'A tall man. He asked me questions and threatened to kill me if I didn't answer them. I refused.'

'Ah – there's my cocksparrow! Refuse, did you?'

'I told him he would never wring a word from me.'

He was saved from becoming ridiculously dramatic by a tremendous growling sound from the other side of the wall. Marcus leapt to his feet.

'Silence, Fang!' he shouted, throwing open the door and disappearing into the room beyond.

The growling gave way to a series of ferocious barks. There was a metallic sound, as of a chain being taken from the wall, then a dull thud and a horrific yelping.

'Quiet, I say!'

Tom, who had covered his ears to shut out the noise, could not remain in his chair, but rushed through the door. He saw first Marcus, swinging a length of heavy chain, and then, cowering in a corner, a huge black dog, its teeth bared, its yellow eyes wild. Its unkempt hair stood out in an unruly shock, save for a strange area across the chest where it was flattened and sparse.

'A handsome brute,' said Marcus with a thin smile, waving the chain so that the poor creature pressed itself even more firmly against the back wall. 'But he must save his anger for when it's needed.'

Without explaining this remark he led the way back into the other room. Tom heard a continuous low growling from the dog, a prolonged grating sound from deep in its throat. They sat down again.

'So you told them nothing?'

'Nothing at all.'

'And you escaped.'

He laughed loudly and practised once more the grip with his fingers.

'No broken necks, I suppose?'

'He took me up to a tower. There was a view across the city. While he was gazing down below and threatening me with vile tortures I crept down the stairs. I reached the bottom before he raised the alarm.'

'And you found a way out?'

'It was easy. I'm small enough to hide in tight spaces. I'd seen a coil of rope in the tower and, when they'd gone, I climbed the steps again, tied it to the balustrade and let myself down.'

'You lowered yourself from the top of the tower?'

'Yes. I nearly let go the rope more than once, but it reached all the way down.'

'You've a head for heights, youngster?'

'They don't bother me,' Tom lied. 'It was better than remaining their prisoner.'

Marcus shook the liquid in his glass and sipped noisily.

'It wouldn't have mattered. Once I escaped they were doomed. You wouldn't recognise that commander today.'

He swirled the liquid again, enjoying the revelation, revelling in it.

'Not recognise?'

'Pieces are missing. An ear, for instance.'

Tom shrank into the worn back of his armchair.

'He'll talk eventually. They all do. We're about to rid the city of these scum once and for all.'

The low grumbling sound from the other room faltered and resumed more urgently.

'You're a likely lad, there's no mistake. Like to do some work for me, would you?'

Tom had no voice.

'Oh, you needn't be afraid I shall ask your business. Silence is the keyword, my mannikin. One unguarded word and you're a dead duck in this game. But we're on the one side, whatever your particular duties have been. We serve the same masters.'

Still clutching his glass, he stood and moved closer.

'Well?'

'Of course,' said Tom quickly. 'Tell me what I should do.'

Now the other's manner became manic. He paced the room with his fists clenched in front of him, his face twitching.

'Search and destroy!' he declaimed. 'That's what we'll do. Search and destroy. Until there's not a single one of them drawing breath!'

He crossed the room once and twice more and then flung himself into the chair, spilling the remains of his drink onto the floor. He closed his eyes and took deep shuddering breaths.

'Do you know the way out of this sector?' he asked at last, reaching down for the bottle. He filled the tumbler again.

'No,' Tom replied. 'There's no way through.'

'Of course there's a way through! How do you suppose the authorities pass about the city? You need the proper documents, that's all. You haven't got any, I take it.'

'No.'

'You shall. That's no problem. I have a spare pass for a trusty lieutenant. That's you. What do you say?'

Tom could say nothing. The excitement he felt was tempered by the fear that he might betray himself. To cover his confusion he reached out for the glass which Marcus seemed to be holding towards him, took it in both hands and drank. The liquor splashed into his mouth. It was like fire! His throat burned and ached, his eyes watered and a pain ran down his insides.

'We drink to it!' enthused his companion, taking a much larger gulp himself. He clapped Tom on the shoulder.

From outside in the street there came the sound of passers-by. Marcus went to the window, which had no curtain, and peered through the grime on the pane.

'It's time,' he said. He raised his voice. 'Ready, Fang!'

'Time for what?' asked Tom, his throat still stinging.

'He's got to earn his food. And mine. It's what I keep him for.'

Tom followed him into the next room, where the dog was on its haunches, trembling. It was impossible to tell whether the animal shivered from the excitement of going out or because it was in a state of terror. Marcus reached high on the wall for a stout leather muzzle which he thrust onto the vicious snout. He slipped the chain over its head, and then all three were outside in the narrow alley, which was rapidly filling with people.

The sun had risen and glimmered dimly through thin cloud. All along the street there was a bustle of people, mostly men, and all walked in the one direction. From time to time smaller paths joined the main thoroughfare and groups of people emerged to mingle with the throng.

'Where are we going?' Tom asked, wondering at the sudden flux where but minutes before there had been emptiness.

'Don't know,' said Marcus. 'Those at the front know the way and we follow. There's no fixed place for it.'

Tom decided to ask no further questions, but gazed instead at the people around him. Most were dressed very poorly, their heavy coats threadbare, the boots creased and down at heel. At first few words were spoken – Tom remembered the silence of the deserted streets by the east gate – but as they grew in number they seemed to lose their reserve and soon there was a babble of voices and a whirl of gesticulating arms.

All the time Fang pulled on in front, opening a wide path for them: nobody, having cast eyes on the wild-eyed brute, wished to be within range, despite the muzzle. It tried incessantly to open its teeth and a thin spittle dropped from its jaws. Tom saw people nudge their companions and point to the shaggy-haired beast, and there was a muttering and nervous laughter.

'That devil has *my* money,' he heard one of them whisper.

Marcus said nothing and looked neither to right or left. His lined face carried an expression of great concentration. Only when they reached a large waste area, where the crowd spilled out and began to form a large, jostling circle, did he show any interest in his surroundings. The ground was bare and hard, with patches of brittle snow in the hollows. It dipped towards the centre and the ragged flock stood back from this lower ground, creating a rough arena.

'Marcus, ho!'

A tall, bearded, athletic man pushed through the crowd towards them carrying a contraption of leather and steel in his hand. When he came closer, Tom saw that it was a harness. Now he understood the wasted hairs on Fang's chest: the harness had a thick leather breastplate, from which protruded a wicked metal spike. Tom recoiled in horror.

'Who do we fight?' asked Marcus, following the man towards the centre.

'An unknown beast,' he was answered. 'The people from the fourth precinct have put it up.'

'It has no chance,' said Marcus in a tone which forbade reply. 'What breed is it?'

'They're keeping silent about it.'

Marcus reached into a pocket and pulled out a wad of paper. He held it out to Tom.

'Money,' he said. 'A lot of it, so don't lose it. You see the men up by the big tree there? Put the money on Fang.'

It was difficult to fight his way through to the bookmakers. There was a busy throng around them and a great deal of cash was changing hands. When Tom at last squeezed his way to the front a fat little man bounced forward and took him by the shoulder.

'Here's a young punter of promise!' he cackled, capturing everyone's attention immediately. 'Learn the skills of betting early, my son, and you'll not want for anything in your old age.'

Behind him his colleagues were chalking prices on a blackboard. At a rickety table a young man scribbled on small pieces of paper.

'So let's see the colour of your money, young man. We're not proud here, we're not. The smallest coins accepted!'

Tom held out the thick pile of notes, conscious that all eyes were upon him. The bookie faltered for a second, seeing the sum he was offered, but quickly regained his composure.

'That's it!' he shouted, waving the notes in the air for all to see. 'Start as you mean to go on, my son. There's gambling in you, praise be!'

There was a murmur from the crowd, which edged forward excitedly.

'And where should the money go?'

He came closer and saw that Tom did not understand.

'Which cur takes your fancy?'

'Fang.'

Now there was a greater commotion and the bookie turned to his companions with a broad smile that suggested relief.

'So the world isn't of one mind, after all,' he said, still holding the money aloft. 'Here's a supporter of the old champion, my friends.'

Some of the onlookers shook their heads at Tom, while others waved their hands at him to catch his attention.

'Don't do it, lad! Change your bet! It hasn't a chance today!'

But Tom stood his ground.

'Here's a man who knows his mind,' rejoiced the bookie, turning to the young man at the desk. 'A thousand on Fang.'

'No, no! Wait a while! Give him a chance!'

'He's made his choice.'

'Take it back, boy! Change your bet!'

The fat man, enjoying the commotion, handed the notes to a colleague and passed Tom a slip of paper. There seemed to be nothing but squiggles on it.

'Might as well tear it up and throw it away,' he heard someone say as he made his way back to Marcus. 'Not a chance today.'

There was now a flow of people from the betting area towards the arena. Around the inside of this, at intervals of about twenty paces, stood a ring of men carrying stout spears. They wore metal protectors around their legs. Tom found Marcus and the man with the beard bent over the dog to fix the harness. The metal spoke thrust out evilly. The last strap was being adjusted when there was a stupendous roar from the crowd. It was a terrible sound, suggesting fear and passion and rage. Tom, who was not tall enough to see what had caused this spontaneous explosion, started back in alarm.

'What is it?' asked Marcus, testing the leather.

His companion, who had raised himself on his toes to look into the arena, said nothing for a moment. He seemed shaken.

'It's the other hound,' he said at last. 'It's a monster!'

'Huh!'

Marcus's expression was dismissive as he straightened up and led Fang towards the one opening through the crowed. Tom and the bearded man followed him through the ranks of spectators to the arena. Was it a pitiful glance each man seemed to give the shaggy brute?

Once in the arena, Tom understood the violent clamour. The other dog, held back by no fewer than three men, was truly of a monstrous size. It stood more than a head taller than Fang, and its body – contrastingly sleek and a light tan in colour – seemed to dance with muscle. It pawed the ground. Its eyes were a rich red. Its upper lip bared to reveal sharp and gleaming teeth.

Marcus, kneeling to release Fang's muzzle, showed no sign of concern, but Tom could not believe that he was not trembling inside. Fang, now that the business was about to begin, strained wildly to be at its adversary, snarling loudly, the ferocious eyes turning up in their sockets and almost lost to view.

There was a brief ceremony in the centre of the arena which Tom, sick with fear, hoped would last for ever, and then the two animals were released and careered towards their first bloody collision.

The commotion was unbearable. Tom found himself covering his ears and turning his eyes away, but the noise hammered through his hands. The crowd exulted, bayed, but even this heavy sound failed to extinguish the savage yelping of the two beasts, the barks of pain, the vicious growling.

He opened his eyes. The spectators surged forward, yelling wildly, as the animals flung themselves at one another, the terrible spikes always racing ahead of them. They rolled over and over, the ground crimson beneath them. As they lurched towards the front rank of spectators two of the men with the spears darted forward and struck them blows to force them back into the arena. Fang, one eye closed and swollen, found itself trapped beneath the heavy body of the other dog and writhed and snapped. The spike had missed its body, but now the huge animal heaved and trust down again and the sharp meal grazed Fang's flank and blood spurted in the air.

Tom turned away again, loathing it, and saw that Marcus's face glowed with a terrible enthusiasm. His mouth was open but speechless, his hands beat the air, he swayed to and fro with excitement. It was as if he wished to be out there in the arena, battling with the threshing, murderous dogs. Tom watched him, appalled. This was the man who could help him, whom he must seem to make an ally of. His eyes had a crazed expression, the thin lips drawn back in a gape of depraved exultation.

'Kill, Ripper, kill!'

The supporters of the larger creature urged it on and, indeed, its superior size seemed to be carrying the contest. The beasts were adept at dodging the advancing blades and there were repeated collisions of the shoulders, one of which sent Fang spinning to the ground where it was temporarily at the mercy of its rival. Twice the blade struck home and Fang staggered away, howling but still defiant.

But now it revealed its experience. It tore at the huge Ripper, made as if to strike and then, at the last moment, veered away. Surprised, the larger animal hesitated for a crucial second and found itself attacked from the side. Fang leapt upon the exposed flank, the sharp spoke burying deep. Its teeth bit into the flesh of its adversary again and again. They tumbled over, panting and snapping, and when at last they separated and struggled to their feet it was the other dog which limped away, badly torn, not relishing the fight. Its skin was laced with running streams of blood.

'Again, Fang! Take him now!'

'Turn, Ripper, turn!'

How could they enjoy so cruel a battle? Tom held his hand over his mouth for fear he would disgrace himself. He must not let his horror show. All around him the excited faces were turned upon the wrestling dogs, the grating voices raised to urge them to greater violence. Would he, too, react like this once he had lived among these people for a while longer?

But one other person did not share the general emotion. With a shock, Tom recognised a face from the House of the Star – that of the grizzled-haired man with gold-framed spectacles. He seemed to take no interest in the sport but bestowed his impassive gaze upon his fellow spectators. As at the inn, it was impossible to gauge what he felt. Tom only thought how strange it was that he should be here, in this sector and among such violence, and he turned away so that their eyes should not meet.

By now both dogs were close to exhaustion. They attacked, it seemed, merely from habit. Fang's matted fur, saturated with blood, stood up in spokes like black spearheads. Ripper's handsome brown coat was criss-crossed by broadening crimson rivers. Occasionally one would stumble and fall even when its opponent was some way off, but always the fear of the oncoming spiked harness put a new impulse into the weary legs, and the feinting, leaping and biting continued all over again.

The spectators, sensing that the end was near, grew more hysterical in their cries. There was money to be won and lost. The men with the spears pushed the crowd back with arms outstretched, though never taking their eyes from the thrashing animals.

Ripper, as the heavier of the two, began to gain the advantage of its weight, pinning Fang to the ground, where the two lay gasping, and taking sudden violent snaps with its vicious teeth. Tom saw no way in which the shaggy black creature could escape, but he had taken no account of its cunning. Its submissive posture must have been exaggerated to deceive its enemy, for it suddenly heaved and convulsed and was free. Even as Ripper struggled to its feet, Fang lunged forward, keeping the spike low down and slightly raised. The larger beast collapsed onto its back, feet pawing the air desperately. Fang, in a frenzy, struck again and again, suddenly sure of its triumph. Its wild eyes blazed as it thrust and thrust and thrust.

Tom could not watch, but heard from the noise of the crowd that the battle was over. There were groans, a few exclamations and then, for a few seconds, a strange silence, a terrible silence. From the dogs there was no sound at all. And then there was movement, a shuffling of feet and the rapid dispersal of the spectators, funnelling into the narrow alley whence they had come, leaving slips of torn paper on the ground behind them.

Marcus, having won a great deal, was in good spirits as they returned. They made slow progress because of the crippled condition of the poor lacerated animal that followed behind, but Marcus never gave a glance to the rear.

'They thought they'd surprise us,' he said scornfully. 'Who was surprised, young Tom?'

'He's badly hurt.'

'Of course he's badly hurt. He usually is. We won't fight him again for a while yet.'

The crowds had completely evaporated, so that the alleys through which they passed were once again empty and austere. Although the sun had broken through the thin clouds, the air was chill, painfully so.

'Six times he's been challenged,' gloated Marcus. 'Six times he's seen them off.'

'Is it always to the death?'

'Unless they run. And it's not possible to run.'

When they reached the house the dog struggled to its room and collapsed in a corner, too exhausted even to lick its wounds. Marcus paid it no attention at all, but poured two glasses of the colourless liquid Tom had tasted before. He sat back in his chair, a serene expression of self-satisfaction on his face.

'We taught them a lesson,' he said.

Tom wetted his lips with the drink but took none of it into his mouth. He sniffed at it, but could smell nothing.

'Here's to those,' said Marcus, raising his glass, 'who meddle.'

Tom raised his own glass, put it to his lips and dipped his tongue in the drink. It burned.

Outside there were faint sounds to indicate that the city went about its secretive business. A distant hammer clanged on iron. A saw bit into wood, rhythmically. There was a trundling noise, as if of machinery turning. After a while Marcus rose to recharge his glass and, instead of returning to his chair, he sat on the arm of Tom's.

'So you're ready to help the cause,' he said. 'To search and destroy.'

'Whenever you like,' Tom replied. 'I'm ready.'

'I can promise you excitement,' Marcus told him, 'and enjoyment. Especially enjoyment. There's nothing so pleasurable as destroying enemies of the cause.'

Tom played the lip of the glass around his mouth, pleased by the calmness he was able to display.

'And this time,' went on Marcus, smiling with his pleasure, 'we've an especially fine bird to bring down.'

'Bird?'

'In fact, two of them. Two of the fair sex, young Tom. That's who we're after. We'll pluck their feathers one by one. Are you game?'

Tom nodded vigorously.

'Do we know who they are?'

'Do we know? Why, of course we do! One, to be sure, is getting on in years and doesn't merit another thought. But the other, young Tom, is a speciality it'll be a delight to ensnare. It's quite lip-licking!'

His eyes were loose with excitement.

'Mother and daughter, they are, and the young one a most delightful creature. The loveliest flaxen hair, young Tom, and eyes of the most heavenly blue!'

19 Meditation

The picture, propped against a pile of books, stared steadfastly back at him through the gloomy light of the late afternoon. Tom, alone once again in his room at the House of the Star, watched it carefully as if at any moment it might twitch into life. Next to it lay the papers, charred at the edges, which the mad old man had pushed into his pocket.

Would his father be surprised if he knew how keenly Tom sought him? No, no: surely he would understand. Would he be horrified to know of the experiences he had so far endured? Again, he would understand.

The face in the picture was of a strong, warm-hearted man. Tom knew this by looking into the eyes. Of his flesh-and-blood father he had no memory at all: or, if he had, it was submerged beneath the character created by his mother's stories of the early years. The image was filtered through his mother's lost and yearning, so that it seemed to represent an ideal, godlike human being.

And yet, surely he could see that in the picture, too? There was a reassuring honesty in that weather-beaten face and a keen intelligence in the expression. Tom knew that this was a man worth following, wherever the journey took him: he would not be disappointed.

In the large room below, the evening's entertainment had begun. He could hear the rhythm of Old Weasel's instrument and the occasional shout rose, muffled, through the floor. For the inhabitants of the inn the days merged into one another almost unheeded, each a copy of the one preceding it, while for him there was incident and change and there might not be days enough.

The violence with seethed below the surface of city life had been apparent to him ever since he had arrived, but yesterday's meeting with the vicious Marcus and his involvement with the terrible fight between the two dogs had served to emphasise the danger he was in. Now he remembered not only the bloody tussle in the makeshift arena but his later journey home to the House of the Star. How tremblingly he had held out the pass Marcus had given him, with what relief he had hurried through the passages that led from one sector to the other, emerging at last from a door indistinguishable from all the others in the mean grey street.

He was ashamed of his trembling. He knew that he could not remain a prey to events, to other people's plans and schemings, and survive. He must act for himself. He must exercise cunning. Perhaps, in his own way, he must be ruthless too. But what would his father think of him then?

The eyes seemed to offer him reassurance. 'Do what you do for the best reasons,' they seemed to say, 'and all will be well.'

Yet he knew that this was too simple. The alliance with Marcus offered him a way to rediscover the girl with blue eyes and so, perhaps, would lead him to the fabled underground city. At the same time it was a dreadful threat: Marcus would not hesitate to act brutally towards him if his suspicions were aroused. How should he protect himself?

There were things that he had always considered evil. To kill was horrific. Suppose – just suppose – that to kill Marcus was the only way to reach the underground city. In his childhood days at home (how far off they seemed!) he had often played with his village friends at games of warrior gangs involving dire death and destruction. But they were only games. Was it ever right to kill a man, really?

'Do what you do for the best reasons.' Yet even Marcus believed his own cause was just. He blindly destroyed people in order that the Red Blade should rule the city. Tom saw the error of this quite clearly – Marcus wanted to create his ideal city, ignoring the price that would be paid. He schemed and killed for a controlled, well-ordered city but overlooked the fact that it would be a city in which murder and cruelty had become commonplace. It wasn't possible to ignore the actions that people took to achieve the results they wanted. These actions left their indelible imprints behind them.

Even so, could a death sometimes be justified? If – he reasoned desperately – if he *knew* that for Marcus to die would mean the triumph of good over evil? But that was no use. Of course he could never know it. We could never know for certain the ends of our actions.

Did that mean, then – he shuddered to imagine it – that if Marcus found the girl and intended to kill her, he, Tom, should do nothing to stop him? No, no, clearly this couldn't be right. Here there was a clear end to the action proposed. If he did nothing to prevent it, he would be guilty of allowing it to happen. It would be no use to say it was nothing to do with him. He would have the choice either to do nothing or to resist: it wasn't possible to escape the choice, to say the responsibility wasn't his. So if he had to kill Marcus to save the girl, surely then this was what he should do.

Tom gazed at the picture for strength, but he knew that the strength must come from inside himself. He had never before in his life had to tussle in this way with his conscience and his courage. How could he learn to be secretive, single-minded, even perhaps ruthless, without becoming warped and dishonest in the process? Must he *be* like Marcus in order to confront Marcus? The consoling thought came to him that his father had surely been afflicted with the very same doubts. He did not question that his father was a good man. Yet if he had survived, if he was really in the underground city alive, surely he, too, had had to use his strength and his wits. It must be possible to be both tough and honest.

So long had he been engaged in these difficult speculations that, on raising his head, he was surprised to see through the window that the daylight had now completely gone. He drew the curtain across, suddenly feeling extremely weary, and smiled sardonically at his own presumption. To think that he should have been so blithely considering Marcus's death when his own was so very much more likely. He was, in truth, in a precarious situation.

Further morbid thought on these lines, however, was prevented by a heavy knocking on the door. Tom quickly took the picture and the papers and slipped them under his pillow. The knocking grew even more vigorous and seemed to be accompanied by hefty kicks until, before he had reached it, the door gave and swung open.

20 The Hunted

The man who stepped inside and threw the door shut behind him did not, it was immediately apparent, have any violent intention. He stood heaving for breath, a finger pressed to his lips. It was the shabby old fellow who seemed to spend his entire life in the room downstairs. His battered hat was missing, revealing a thin matting of fine white hair which fell in a shock about his ears.

They faced each other in complete silence for what seemed a very long time. Tom noticed again the stained and crumpled trousers, and saw that the worn slippers gave loose covering to what were otherwise bare feet. Finally the old man tottered forward and subsided heavily onto the bed. He fumbled at a pocket and clumsily produced his familiar pipe. The smoke, thick and pungent, drifted slowly towards the ceiling.

'Safe,' he sighed tremulously, but still looking anxiously towards the door as if at any moment it might open. 'She's gone.'

'She?'

'The Sphynx. Terrible woman.'

Tom, whose imagination had prepared him for a more sinister explanation, almost laughed out loud.

'You're frightened of her?'

The smoker nodded, his eyes moist and grateful.

'Fearful woman. Fearful woman.'

Tom sat in his chair, fascinated. He had never passed more than a few words with his uninvited guest and yet, for a reason he did not understand, he found him strangely familiar and easy to talk to.

'But why should you fear her?' he asked. 'Has she threatened you?'

'She will. She will.'

The old man spoke slowly and fell into silence once more. He pulled on the pipe lovingly, the smoke rising thickly from the side of his mouth. He seemed to disappear for a while, his thoughts far away, until he suddenly sat upright and held out his hand.

'Clutt,' he said. 'That's my name, or one of them. That's what they call me downstairs. You're a good lad.'

Tom, who could not reach without standing, leaned forward to grasp his fingers.

'I'm Tom,' he said.

'Oh yes indeed,' said Clutt, as if clearing up a doubt that Tom had about his own identity. 'Quite right. We all know you, young Tom. You didn't hear anything outside just then, did you?'

'No. Nothing at all.'

'There aren't any locks, that's the trouble. It's difficult to hide.'

Ash from his pipe drifted onto his lap, but he appeared not to notice.

'It's the rent,' he said at last. 'I owe a month's money.'

'But she's not threatened you.'

'Ha! You've seen her eyes Tom, have you? They're a constant threat. True, isn't it? They're always coming at you, aren't they?. She doesn't need to speak, that one.'

Tom again had the feeling of familiarity with the old man, although he had certainly never met him before his stay at the House of the Star.

'Can't you find the money?' he asked.

'Oh, I'll find it,' answered Clutt. 'It's due to me. The delivery's held up again, that's all. Communications in the city aren't what they were, young Tom.'

'And can't you explain to her?'

'Explain! To that one!'

Clutt shook his head wonderingly and occupied himself again with his pipe, packing the tobacco with a horny finger and taking vigorous sucks at the stem.

'I suppose I may have to eventually. It's just that she panics me. Women always do, but she's the worst I ever met. Did you ever know one like her?'

'She's very fierce,' Tom admitted, smiling to himself.

'They have a way of unsettling you, women have,' Clutt went on, speaking in a slow, dreamlike manner. 'They've always got a plan, and they've always got a place for you in it. There's no leaving alone with them.

'I'm a man that likes to be let alone to think my thoughts and go about my business, with a bit of social chatter just every so often to pass the time of day. You follow me? I don't want all that here-ing and there-ing and how about this-ing. That's a woman's way.

'She's the worst of the whole lot.'

Tom sat back in his chair to watch his guest puffing at his pipe and declaring his simple philosophy. Clutt obviously felt no pressing need to talk, and between his random comments whole minutes passed during which he cradled his pipe and gazed into smoky space.

'It was a bossy woman who drove me away from home,' he said eventually, with a meaningful glance in Tom's direction. 'I couldn't see any escape from her if I stayed.'

Tom, who could think of no appropriate answer, only nodded solemnly.

'I shouldn't be surprised if she's still the terror of the place. A tall, boney, red-haired woman. I shouldn't be surprised if you'd met her yourself, Tom.'

'Me met her?'

'It wouldn't surprise me, I say. But if you had you wouldn't forget. She'd have her finger on your soul.'

Tom smiled politely, unsettled by the strangeness of Clutt's conversation.

'I don't think I can have known her,' he said.

'Well, perhaps not. Perhaps she's passed on by now. I'm not a young man, after all. But she had the fierce dominating personality of those women who come from our part of the world. Untameable.'

'*Our* part?'

'Well!' Clutt laughed. 'It can't be said that we own in in a legal sense. But don't we feel that it's all ours – those proud mountains and the deep pure streams?'

Now Tom realised with a start why the old man had seemed so familiar, why he had sat talking so easily with him. He had not been aware of the accent of his homeland, but it had spoken to him unconsciously.

'You, too – ' he began, but he quickly checked himself for fear of betraying his secrets.

'To be sure, yes! Have I lost so many of the ways that you couldn't tell all along? Ah, when you stood up on the table and sang that song it was as though you'd taken hold of my coat and spun me round in a circle. I'd forgotten it all, you see – it was so long ago.'

He toyed with his pipe again, fussing with the tobacco in the bowl. He sucked and sucked until a thin wisp of smoke crawled upwards once more and then, his cheeks collapsed inwards, attacked the business with a will until the miniature furnace was soundly kindled.

'I wasn't much more than twenty, you see. A farmer's son. Not much of a future, but I was contented enough with the way of the world. Then the lady in question began to lay snares for me and I upped and sought my fortune in the city.'

'And did you find it?'

'No, lad. No fortune. But the life has been good enough, good enough.'

They sat in silence, old man and young boy joined together by a wreath of grey smoke. Clutt closed his eyes and wriggled his feet out of his threadbare slippers. He seemed completely at rest.

'The strange thing is,' he said after some while, 'that the last time I heard that song was in this very house. "You reckless moon, mare with no rider . . ." A strange thing, that.'

'You heard it here?'

'I did. Sung in a proud and boisterous fashion by a fellow who stayed here for a night or two.'

'Who was he?'

'Don't know. I never enquired. He was from our parts, sure enough. Not a bad voice.'

Tom was out of his chair and perched on the bed close to the old man.

'What kind of man was he?' he demanded urgently, forgetting his caution. 'Could you describe him?'

'Oh, it was a long time ago, laddie. A great deal gets forgotten.'

He must not give his secret away. He must certainly not show his picture.

But he could not contain the excitement in his voice: 'Nothing at all? Can't you remember how he looked?'

'Let me think, then. Give me a moment.'

The moment stretched into a period and the period into a passage, until Tom thought the unkempt old fellow had nodded asleep. His chest rose and fell, and the pipe cooled and lost all signs of life.

'A poet, I think they said he was. Well known in his way, though that meant nothing to me. I don't read much. We never had time for reading in our family. A life on the land. They called him, I seem to remember, the Poet of the Wilderness. That was it. He left very soon.

'He was fairly tall. I have the picture of him standing there, singing that song. A robust man, the sort of man other people notice. I didn't speak to him, though. My life in those parts was long ago.'

Tom grasped him by the shoulder, helplessly.

'His eyes. How were they? Did they seem honest eyes?'

'What a question!' Clutt laughed wheezily. 'To be sure, I've no idea. Why do you ask me that?'

'I don't know.'

'Homesick, I dare say. That's only natural.'

His memories exhausted, Clutt slid off into his own mental world once more. The subject was closed. His body reclined on Tom's bed but his thoughts were far away. A contented smile moved his lips. Tom returned to his chair, his own thoughts in tumult. Who was that stranger at the House of the Star? Was it conceivable that it had been his father? If so, what was the meaning of the coincidence?

Down below, the usual rowdiness was in full swing. The floor seemed to throb with the sound. But now, as he imagined the scene downstairs, he found that the soldiers, the regular guests, Old Weasel, dwindled to mere shadowy presences hovering in the corners, while at the centre of the room stood a tall, imposing, handsome man who dominated the company; a man from from his own distant part of the country, mysterious, quickly disappearing. What had brought him to the House of the Star? Where had he gone?

'You're a good lad, Tom. A good lad. But it's time I was gone.'

Clutt, who had come out of his reverie, struggled to his feet but immediately hesitated.

'One more favour though, eh? Take a peek out of the door for me. Quietly, now.'

The corridor was empty. Tom beckoned to Clutt, who shuffled outside and stopped.

'The third door along, Tom,' he whispered nervously. 'Would you mind? A small favour.'

Tom led the way, once again smiling to himself. How strange for a grown man to be so afraid of a woman! They crept forward silently, and he pushed the door open.

He could not believe what he saw. All the furniture seemed to have been picked up and thrown around; drawers had been emptied; even the curtains had been tugged from their rail and hung in shreds. He felt Clutt push his way into the room beside him.

'My things,' he said brokenly, passing his pipe rapidly from one hand to the other and back again, left to right, right to left. 'My things.'

They stood side by side, shaken, until there was a sound in the corridor and, turning, Tom found Clem and his large wife coming up behind them.

'Clutt!' exclaimed the Sphynx loudly, raising her shoulders as if to take a swing at him. 'Been skulking, have you? Foolish man! There was no way you could have escaped *me!*'

21 Ransacked

Tom swung round angrily.

'Why did you do it?' he demanded. 'He's done you no harm.'

The Sphynx totally ignored the accusation and clamped a firm hand on Clutt's shoulder. Strangely, he seemed too overcome by the shock of what he had discovered to be terrified of the woman he had abjectly hidden from only minutes before. The tears formed in his eyes.

'We've no room here,' the forceful woman lectured him, 'for people who avoid paying their way. That's not very wise of you at all, Clutt.'

'The money's coming.'

'But the future tense is no use to me, Clutt. We have to live in the present.'

'By tomorrow. I promise it.'

Clem, who seemed rather uneasy about his wife's fierceness, eased his way past her into the room. When he came upon the disarray within he turned on Clutt with puzzlement in his eyes.

'What's this here, then? What's happened here?'

Clutt was unable to reply. He merely waved a hand towards his scattered belongings. But Tom felt the fury rage inside him.

'As if you don't know!' he shouted. 'You thought you would punish Clutt by breaking up everything he had. It's cruel, its inhumane!'

'Foolish boy.'

It was the Sphynx who spoke. She, too, now stood inside the room, surveying the chaos. She folded her arms and her large bosom swelled with a powerful emotion.

'Disgraceful!' she said simply.

There was a silence, during which Clutt shuffled forward into what had been his ordered little home. He bent to retrieve an object from beneath the bed. What it was the onlookers were unable to see. He knelt to the floor where a drawer lay tipped over, its contents spilled out in a heap. He lifted it up, fitted it back in the chest to which it belonged and placed the object inside. Then he closed the drawer. He had, all this while, the trance-like air of a sleepwalker.

Tom spoke quietly.

'You didn't know?' he asked.

'A stupid idea. Do you think we would wreck our own building?'

Now Tom felt not only perplexed but humiliated, too.

'Why should anyone do this?' he asked.

But the Sphynx ignored the question.

'Courage, Clutt!' she ordered. 'They've not touched *you*, man. I'll have someone here immediately to put the place to rights.'

With that she strode away and the atmosphere in the room lightened considerably. Clem put his hand on Clutt's arm and led him to the bed.

'Sit you down,' he said. 'We'll sort it out, old chap.'

There was not a thing in the room which had been left untouched. The few books Clutt possessed stood straddled on their open leaves as if each had been thoroughly shaken before being discarded. Two pictures had been taken from the wall and tossed into a corner where they lay among slivers of broken glass. The bedclothes had been stripped.

'Why?' Tom asked again.

Clem, who had begun to pick objects from the floor, seemed about to reply until, with a sharp cry, he stood rigid, staring at the wall. The colour in his face drained away. Just below the ceiling, the paint spattered in dabs and drips, was the emblem of the Red Blade.

'Even here,' he whispered hoarsely. 'Even here!'

The paint was still wet, for at that moment a large blob, which had obviously been gathering all the while, broke open and a scarlet stream ran down the wall like blood from a wound.

Clutt sat moaning on the bed, too far gone even to light his eternal comforter, which protruded awkwardly from a pocket, occasionally breathing specks of old burnt tobacco. Clem sat by him and shook his shoulder.

'There was nothing to find, was there?' he stated, demanding a negative answer. 'You were hiding nothing?'

'No.'

'You speak honestly now, Clutt. There was nothing?'

'Nothing.'

Tom began to push the furniture into position, glad of something to do. He could not bear to watch either the old man's brokenness or Clem's sudden terror. They made him feel menaced himself. Of course he was menaced. He thrust the chest of drawers against the wall, the edge of it digging into his shoulder.

'It's because you're a stranger, Clutt, that's why,' Clem said, reasoning to himself. 'In the bad times it's always the strangers they suspect.'

Clutt only whimpered by way of reply.

'Even though you have been here half a lifetime,' Clem added.

Tom lifted a small chair from the floor and swung it upright. He must escape. Now. Tonight. They would surely come for him next. Was it wise to run? He ignored the question: he understood too little of anything to judge the wisdom of running. He only knew that he felt his life hung on a thread.

'And worse times are coming,' Clem said ominously, carefully avoiding the young man's eyes. 'I wouldn't be a stranger for all the world.'

22 Friends

The light inside the cafe was so dim that Tom stood for some moments in the doorway before he made out the figure of the waiter, cloth on arm, standing by the bar. There were but three customers at various tables, eating in silence.

'You offered me work.'

The waiter came forward, smiling.

'Good lad. I had a feeling we'd see you again. When can you start?'

'This evening. Now.'

He was led through the door behind the bar, along a short corridor and into what was unmistakably the kitchen. Great clouds of steam swirled about their heads. There was the sound of bubbling liquid and a clatter of plates.

'Lucy – here's someone to help you. The lad I spoke to you of.'

The words seemed to be swept up into the encircling billows, never to be heard, but they in fact conjured up a gradually materialising human form, which took shape among the vapours. The drama of her ghostly emergence was enhanced by her appearance – a huge red woman, pouring with perspiration, stripped to the waist, her flesh hanging in folds, culminating in a face of greater width than length and split in two by a broad grin. The lower part of her body was clad in pyjama-like trousers made of white cotton, and her feet were bare.

'Is this 'ims gonna help? Bless you, boy!'

And with these words she threw her arms around him and hugged him, wrapping him in hot, wet flesh until he felt he would suffocate. But no sooner had she released him than she was sucked up by the belching steam once more, only her disembodied voice left behind.

'We needed someone. Bill's been working 'is legs off, 'aven't you, love?'

Bill nodded, pointlessly for she could not see him.

'Are you giving him Lugg's room?'

Bill nodded again and Lucy swam back into view.

'Nice little room is Lugg's. He liked it before he took off. Small, but nice. You show 'im, Bill.'

Tom was taken from the kitchen through a door that led to a narrow and steep staircase. Lugg's room was indeed small, a tiny box of a room containing little furniture and one round window high on the wall opposite the door. It was, nevertheless, as welcoming as Lucy had promised. It was clean and had a pleasant smell, and what little there was in it struck Tom as attractive and well matched.

He put what few possessions he had, including his precious picture, in a small cupboard by the bed. At this moment he suddenly became aware of the eery singing he had first sensed while in the white room. It seemed to well up from far below, and yet it appeared that his companion did not hear it.

'You make yourself at home, lad. Now I can't keep calling you lad, can I? Do you have a name?'

'Tom.'

They thrust out their hands and shook them solemnly and warmly.

'You make yourself at home, Tom, and when you're ready come down and join us. You're among friends here.'

And friends they very soon seemed, the more so because they were for a while marooned with only themselves for company. The next day, after a clear warm morning that held the promise of spring, it began to snow with an earnestness that made the winter's earlier offerings seem meagre indeed. Beginning with a few small crystals that spun lazily down, it turned by degrees into a swirling, blinding mass of large flakes that seemed to choke the very air. Windows filled with it, turning the rooms behind them into shadowy caverns. Doorways were sealed with its fragile cement. The rare city bird, returning to ledges that had disappeared, flew around confused, afraid of becoming part of the falling whiteness. The harsh outlines of the city grew softer and rounded as the streets gradually climbed the walls of the buildings and became impassable.

Tom stood in his apron by the cafe window and watched. His immediate problems were solved. Until this snow cleared – and still it fell and fell – he could do nothing but stay here, serving any customers local enough and hungry enough to force their way through the drifts. So far there had been none.

As afternoon turned imperceptibly to evening Tom settled down with Bill and Lucy at one of the tables and played a board game. Tom was unfamiliar with it. There appeared to be an extraordinary number of complex rules which formed the focus of a whole sequence of bantering arguments between Bill and Lucy, during which Tom simply gazed at the board, enchanted. It seemed possessed of a rare beauty, with its detailed drawings and diagrams interspersed with numbers and instructions, all crudely printed and hand-coloured. The various items represented included a migrating flock of birds, whose formations across the clouded sky created the likeness of a human face; a man from whose mouth flowed a galaxy of stars; and a rainbow which became fire at one extremity and ice at the other.

Bill and Lucy, who had suggested that he watch them play for a while – 'You'll soon pick it up' – had offered no clue as to the purpose of the game. Neither did the written instructions, which contained such items as 'Swords fall upon the dream of the insane king' and 'Take nine in consolation for the loss of a silver moonscape'.

Despite his ultimate failure to grasp the logic of the game, Tom could not but take pleasure from the first moments of good-natured and innocent entertainment he had known since his arrival in the city. And the sight of Lucy and Bill dissolving into laughter at their inability to agree over the rules was enough to infect Tom with similar convulsions which became so uncontrolled that they left him lying on the floor gasping for breath before they had run their course.

For a week nobody called. The three of them found small jobs to do in the daytime, talked and played in the evenings. It was warm inside, and intimate. In the cafe area their voices echoed, and the light from outside was an even more muted green than before. When at last the snow stopped falling and the drifts slowly collapsed and began to recede, one or two people kicked a path through to the cafe again.

To Tom's surprise one of the first to appear was a man he had seen both at the House of the Star and at the grim fight between the two dogs. It was the man with grizzled hair, gold-rimmed spectacles and impeccable dress. Today he wore, beneath his heavy top coat, a lilac shirt with a silk cravat of deep maroon and a jacket which seemed to reflect the colour of both.

What was even more surprising, however, was the deference Bill paid to this guest. He hurried to clear his plate away when he had finished eating, seemed anxious that the food, the drink, even the humble seating should be to his liking, and on one occasion actually addressed him as 'sir'.

Tom challenged Bill about this later in the day, when there was a pause in their work and they drank large mugs of hot soup in the kitchen.

'His name is Porlock,' Bill said. 'He's a real gentleman, Tom, that he is. A refined sort of man.'

'But you seemed to treat him differently,' Tom persisted. 'As if he were special.'

'Ah well, Tom, so he is. Special in a manner of speaking.'

He seemed unusually guarded, embarrassed too at not being his normal frank self.

'He's a business contact, you might say. Yes, that's what he is undoubtedly. And a real gentleman, too.'

This explanation might have closed the conversation, but Bill's strange manner disinclined Tom to let the matter drop.

'I've seen him before,' he said. 'Several times. Mostly at the House of the Star.'

'You know that place?'

There seemed some alarm in Bill's expression, and Tom was angry with himself for having let fall the unguarded remark.

'Yes, I've been staying there. That man, Porlock, is also often there.'

'Well, that's as maybe Tom, and to be sure I don't know a thing about it. No I don't. Let me tell you, Tom, that this city is a dangerous place, and I'd be very surprised if you knew the twentieth of it. The point is that we don't talk about much else but our own concerns and the weather we're having and the food we put into our stomachs. You like this soup, eh?'

'Delicious.'

'And you'll have noticed I'm sure, as you're an intelligent soul, that Lucy and me haven't asked you a thing about yourself. Nor will we, rest assured. You can tell us what you like and we'll listen – we'll listen with great interest, Tom. But that's for you to decide. We won't ever pry into your affairs, old fellow. You're among friends here, and friends don't ask questions.'

Later, while he was resting in his room, Tom had a visitor of his own. The dwarf appeared, wearing boots so high they almost throttled him but still only just high enough for the tops to be above the snow. He took off his wet outer clothing and sat in Tom's best chair, quite without his usual swagger. His face was pale and his hands shook.

'So you found you way to the east sector,' he said. 'May I ask how you managed it?'

Perhaps he meant to assume his usual inquisitorial manner, but the edge had gone from his voice.

'At first,' Tom replied, 'I came over the rooftops.'

'No. I don't believe that. You couldn't.'

'I did. There were spikes down the side of one of the buildings, with the sign that you gave me – the eye – on the wall. There were crossings between the buildings and then a door and a long steep flight of steps down into the street.'

The dwarf, convinced by the description, only shuddered.

'That sign,' Tom asked. 'What does it mean?'

'We don't know.'

'Don't know?'

'Of course we use it as an emblem to distinguish friends from enemies, but the meaning has been lost. We believe it was used by the masters of the underground city. There is much that we don't understand.'

They sat in silence for a while. Tom thought how much had happened since last he met the dwarf, and how that had changed their relationship. He felt now that he need keep nothing back, that they were indeed united against the evil that he had seen all around him.

'Afterwards,' he volunteered, 'I met a man called Marcus whom I first saw as a prisoner of the commander. He's an agent of the Red Blade and he thinks that I sympathise with him. He's given me a pass.'

Here the dwarf passed a hand over his face in a gesture of despair.

'I'm glad you have told me this, Tom,' he said. 'It proves your honesty. I know the man Marcus and I've seen you with him. We are in terrible trouble. The commander and many of our colleagues have been arrested by the Blade. They are being tortured: they cannot all hold out. You must tell me all you know.'

Tom began with his arrival in the city and his experiences in the house with the green and white rooms. He told the dwarf everything and found that the telling left him exhausted but strangely happy: sharing his problem had halved it. He mentioned his brief encounter with the mad archivist and the papers he had found in his pocket.

'Papers? Let me see!'

Tom brought them out from their hiding place. The dwarf unrolled them and began to scrutinise them, every so often reading a word or a phrase out loud.

'I must take these,' he said finally. 'I don't know what to make of them.'

'He was strange,' Tom said. 'The soldiers took him away.'

When he came to leave, the dwarf grasped Tom by the arm almost tenderly.

'Time is running out,' he said. 'Don't let us down, Tom.'

'I shan't,' he replied, with more confidence than he felt.

His main task was taking orders and scurrying back and forth with the trays. Although he felt happy with Bill and Lucy in the night cafe, he could not help comparing the gloom and hush of the place, the surliness of the customers, with the boisterous gatherings at the House of the Star. Here eyes were averted and little was said.

An hour before dawn on the morning after the dwarf's visit the man called Porlock came again. He ordered a large fish breakfast which he ate fastidiously, carefully dissecting the salted flesh and placing the slender bones in a neat row on his plate. Tom noticed that Lucy had selected the best she could find and had added an extra portion of marinated potatoes and dressing.

Melted snow from his boots must have trickled across the floor, for Tom had just delivered a steaming pot of coffee to the table and was turning away when his foot slipped on the polished surface and, in a bewildering instant, he was one his back, striking his head against a chair. Porlock, with little expression, leaned over to help him to his feet, and as Tom lay there, looking up at the face in the greenish gloom of the night cafe, he realised that he had been through this very experience before; that he had known this face before the House of the Star; that he had once before looked up at it washed in green light only, on that occasion, for it to fade into darkness and to be replaced, upon his waking, by the brightness of the white room.

He realised, too, that Porlock instantly divined his recognition. The hand that held his arm and helped him to stand retained its grip once he was standing. It forced him down to a chair.

'So.'

His voice was low and hoarse.

'What games are you playing, boy?'

Tom sat silently, not knowing how to answer, the grip biting into his arm. Porlock signalled with his free hand and Bill locked the door and lowered the blind. He looked perplexed, but obeyed another wag of the fingers and disappeared into the kitchen.

'Well?'

'No games,' Tom said breathlessly. 'I'm trying to find someone – in the underground city.'

At this Porlock released his arms and brought his bespectacled eyes close to Tom's.

'You *know*?'

Tom nodded.

'As I was leaving the house I heard sounds from below. At the time I didn't understand. Since then . . . '

'Well?'

'I have heard the stories and I believe the city exists. I want to go there.'

'You are in hideous danger.'

'I know that.'

'This man Marcus I have seen you with. What do you know of him?'

'That he is hired to kill by the Red Blade and that he is searching for the girl with blue eyes I met in the white room.'

'Sonia.'

'Ah.'

It was strange to hear a name attached to a girl he had thought of only in terms of her eyes and her hair and, above all, her kindness.

'He is looking for Sonia and her mother,' Tom continued, 'and I am hoping to find them, too.'

Porlock regarded him carefully.

'Hideous danger,' he said again. 'If you realised, child.'

'I'm not a child,' Tom protested boldly. 'I believe I understand the danger. It's the only way to find the underground city. Unless . . . '

The meaning of his unspoken sentence was surely obvious, but Porlock gave him no help at all.

'Unless you can take me there,' Tom concluded.

'No. That's not possible. Or shall we say, it's highly improbable.'

'Why?'

'Because very few are shown the way. Many would wish to go, but the risks of betrayal are too great.'

Porlock pulled a colourful handkerchief from a pocket and wiped his glasses, methodically.

'I, too, am looking for Sonia and her mother,' he said at length. 'I wish to take them to safety. You know that their usual route has been sealed off?'

'Yes. There's no way in.'

'Fortunately the soldiers found nothing. The entrance was well disguised. There are, of course, other routes but they're not known to the two ladies in question.'

There was another silence during which Porlock gazed into space with the expression Tom knew so well. It was impossible to tell what he thought. Tom had found the man rather sinister in the past, but at the moment he felt only a burning excitement.

'I well know,' Porlock continued eventually, 'that there are many people, good people, who would like to find the underground city. It cannot be. Not until certain prophecies are fulfilled. You must not breathe a word of what you know.'

Tom thought of the dwarf and said nothing. It was too late to unsay what he had revealed.

'You can help me if you will.'

'And then . . .'

'I can promise you nothing: it would be dishonest of me to do so. I shall do what I can and you must leave the matter there. Those are my terms. Will you help me find Sonia and her mother?'

Tom nodded.

'Marcus has many more people working for him than I have. You have told me that you understand the risks.'

'I must take them.'

'You realise that I have in turn risked my life in talking to you. I shall go further. I shall come regularly to this place during the next few days. If you intend to betray me I shall be waiting for whoever they send. Mine is but one life and you can threaten no others.

'Until that happens I shall continue to believe in you.'

The going was difficult, in parts even more difficult than he had anticipated. Combined with the problems of actually walking were the problems of finding the right house, for the snow had made the streets even more anonymous than before. But although fearing himself lost on several occasions, he eventually found the evil alley and the decaying house. The snow had not improved its appearance: indeed, against the shining whiteness of the ground the walls looked even shabbier and the door more rotten.

Tom felt his heart beating against the wall of his chest, yet knew that he must calm himself if Marcus was to suspect nothing. He tried to think himself into the role of assassin until, standing there in the snowy street, he felt his face assume the contours that he associated with hardness. Having thus steeled himself, he banged with his fist upon the door.

Fang's distant growl was accompanied after some seconds by a peculiar creaking and rumbling sound from within. The door opened slowly. The face that peered out into the dim dawn light was an unexpected one. Straddled on a strange wheeled contraption, his legs hanging uselessly on either side, was the bellows-pumper.

23 Enemies

A hand grasped him by the wrist and tugged him viciously inside, so that for the second time that morning he found himself flat on his back. This time, however, there was no offer of help. The bellows-pumper flung the door shut and, working a long lever backwards and forwards, manoeuvred his weird vehicle closer to Tom's spreadeagled body.

'Head over heels!' he crowed, leaning down with a lopsided leer on his face. 'So *you're* the young man who's wormed his way into Marcus's confidence. Now fancy that! What tricks life plays on us! What cruel luck for you, eh my mannikin?'

Tom said nothing, a numbing sense of hopelessness stealing over him.

'Such a pity,' continued his captor with familiar sarcasm, 'that we didn't have time to make a blacksmith of you. But you simply disappeared!'

The dog continued to growl thickly through the inner door until the bellows-pumper shouted a command. The noise ceased abruptly.

'As for your blacksmith friend, I'm afraid he isn't with us any more. He decided to take up flying but found himself a little too heavy. Such a waste!

'But then, you knew that didn't you, my cherub? Nearly took flight yourself. What a pity for you that you didn't – much less gruesome than what lies in store.'

Tom picked himself up, brushing dust and dog hairs from his coat.

'So sorry,' crooned the bellows-pumper tauntingly. 'What excruciating manners – I didn't offer you a chair. Please be seated. Put your feet up and enjoy yourself. Just there. That's right.'

To Tom it seemed colder inside the house than out. The wretched state of the room, with its cracked plaster, moss-grown walls, rotted window-frames, the unclean damp smell – this squalor echoed his own miserable situation.

'Where's Marcus?' he asked.

'Oh indeed, where's Marcus? Where's Marcus? Because when Marcus arrives he'll have a little sport, won't he? To think of being fooled by a young sprat with big innocent eyes. Marcus won't like that, not a bit. Marcus carries a long sharp knife, you know. Did you know that?'

'Where is he?'

The bellows-pumper only chuckled to himself and began to pilot his vehicle in a circle round Tom's chair. He thrust the lever back and forth with a manic energy until he was travelling at such speed that it made Tome dizzy to watch him.

'Not much good in the legs, I grant, but strong enough of arm! Like to test it, would you?'

Tom, ignoring the remark, received a sudden blow on the head which knocked him half out of his chair.

'Feel it, did you? That was a lazy one. I can do better!'

This time Tom was prepared and ducked beneath the clenched fist.

'Good, good! I like a challenge. Steady now!'

Round he came again, and Tom threw himself away from a blow that was never delivered. The bellows-pumper seemed beside himself with mirth, cackling deliriously, so that Tom was off guard when the fist was swung again. It caught him full on the nose and he felt the blood run down over his lip.

'Two-one!'

Tom, dazed, instinctively raised his own fists, but his tormentor seemed already to have tired of the entertainment, wheeling away out of reach and bringing his conveyance to a halt.

'Like some more games to wile away the time, eh?'

There were two doors, Tom reflected, assessing how he might possibly escape. The dog was behind one of them, while the bellows-pumper blocked his route to the outside world. Could he outpace the vehicle in a sudden dash? There was also the window. The individual panes were too small to allow him through, but if he threw himself against it the woodwork would surely splinter and collapse.

Perhaps it was a glance that gave him away, for the bellows-pumper rapidly wheeled himself to the inner door and pushed it open. Fang brushed past him and bounded into the centre of the room, barking loudly. Its fur, torn and still matted where the blood had run, gave evidence of the recent fight, but the beast's spirit seemed to have recovered completely.

'Hold, Fang!'

At the order the dog immediately stopped in its tracks, its yellow eyes aimed at poor Tom, who pressed himself back into his chair.

'A surprise visitor, Fang, but very welcome. Like the smell of him, do you? Think he might taste good?'

The bellows-pumper not only showed no fear of the animal himself but seemed to have an uncanny hold over it. Tom watched in wonder as a mere motion of the index finger bought Fang across to the chair, head cocked.

'A kiss, my pretty one?'

And as the bellows-pumper bent his head, Fang raised itself on its haunches and licked his face lavishly. He laughed all the while, contentedly.

'I need my sticks, Fang.'

The dog now disappeared for a moment into the other room and returned holding both of a pair of crutches in its huge jaws. The bellows-pumper took them and dropped them into slots clearly made for the purpose on his vehicle.

'Now I'm ready to leave,' he said.

'Leave?' exclaimed Tom with mingled amazement and undisguisable hope.

'There I go, treating my guest abominably again! My sincere apologies, lambkin. Excuse my uncouth manners. But I know you'd love to meet your friend Marcus again as soon as possible. I'll get him for you, that's a promise. Delivered in person.'

The bellows-pumper ferried himself to the street door, but at the last moment swung round.

'However,' he said, 'it would be thoughtless to leave you with no company at all. Shall I leave you the dog, perhaps?'

Tom said nothing but held tightly to his chair.

'On guard, Fang!'

The brute leapt forward, snarling, and lay on the ground not a yard from Tom's feet. From its throat came a prolonged and ominous growl.

'A dear pet, you'll find. Affectionate and faithful. Rather playful sometimes, it's true, but a real treasure.'

He paused in the doorway.

'You really should wipe that blood off your nose,' he said.

Tom, unthinkingly, reached for his handkerchief and, with an ugly roar, Fang leapt to its feet, the fur on its back erect, its teeth bared. This quite delighted the bellows-pumper, whose stuttering laughter could be heard for some time after he had slammed the door behind him and wheeled himself off down the street.

A silence fell upon the room. Tom desperately scoured his memory for the merest hint of how to deal with a savage dog. Fang rested with its snout on its extended front paws, to all appearances asleep yet patently not so. Experimentally, Tom made the slightest movement with his foot: the creature's ears instantly pricked and the eyes unfolded.

'Oh Great Invisible One,' he prayed silently, 'help me now.'

Surely the supreme spirit was not a frequenter only of rooftops under the moon. Surely it was possible to sense the power even in a miserable hovel such as this. Yet once again Tom found himself unable to open himself to the experience: his fear still mastered him.

Back in his own part of the country, he suddenly recalled, there was a strange old man who spent all his life out on the mountains. They said he 'communed with nature'. There were many stories about the life he led – foraging for his food and living alongside the creatures of the wild. Once, it was said, two young children had strayed from their home and, while wandering lost on the mountain slopes, had come face to face with a wolf. The old man appeared just as it was about to attack, and he called to the wolf with peculiar sounds. It turned away from the children, meekly slunk to the old man's feet and, after further admonishing noises, loped away never to be seen again.

'Good dog,' Tom whispered hopefully. 'You're a good dog, Fang.'

At this the beast became alert and a growling sound seemed to run up and down between its throat and its stomach. Tom tried a soothing sing-song effect.

'*Good* dog, *good* dog, *good* dog . . . '

But the growling only increased and Fang thumped its tail menacingly on the floor. Perhaps if he hummed a monotonous tune . . . Now the animal sprang to its feet and barked savagely.

There was clearly no way in which he could escape. The danger which he had confronted so bravely when it was an idea in his brain was almost impossible to bear when it grew close in the person of Marcus. Even now the bellows-pumper must be telling his story. Within moments they would be upon him, Marcus thirsty for revenge. He carried a long knife.

Like a prisoner languishing in the condemned cell, Tom found himself insanely fascinated by every detail in the room around him, the last objects he would ever see in this life. The very growth on the walls which he had found so repulsive now seemed precious to him as being part of the world he knew. These short feathery fronds would be here when he had gone. Why was human life so brief? The cracks in the plaster seemed to be speaking to him in words he could not understand. The smears on the window-glass: why had he not noticed their intricate patterns before? There was so much he had not noticed, had not appreciated, and now it was too late.

The hairs along Fang's back quivered and its head turned to one side. An ear lifted. A low growling started up again and then the dog was on its feet, though never moving an inch away from its prisoner. The door was kicked open, and in strode Marcus.

'Hello young Tom,' he said, approaching the chair.

Tom's senses reeled.

'What – no voice? Lost it in the snows, have you?'

He went to a cupboard, stooped to bring out a bottle and a tumbler. He filled this to the brim and gulped a mouthful down.

'Got a bloody nose, have you? Gave as good as you got, I hope. Here, Fang, out of the way!'

But the dog would not move. It stood hunched in front of Tom, its head lowered, one eye following Marcus around the room.

'Has there been anybody else here?' Marcus asked, dropping into one of the battered armchairs.

'Anybody else?'

'A man, Tom. Another man. I was expecting someone.'

Tom's body seemed to understand the situation before his brain had grasped it. He shook and all but fainted away.

'Are you unwell?'

'No, no. I banged my nose, that's all.'

'Ha!'

Marcus tipped the tumbler to his lips, all the time keeping his eyes on Fang.

'What's the matter with the dog?' he asked.

'Nothing.'

'Nothing, is it? Fang – to your bed!'

There was no movement save the lowering of the animal's tail.

'He doesn't go. You see that?'

He stood up and came closer.

'There's something wrong here. Why doesn't he obey me?'

Tom improvised wildly.

'It my fault, I think. I gave him some scraps to eat. I had some food with me. He wouldn't go away.'

Marcus squatted, looking into Fang's eyes, considering. Master and dog stared unblinkingly at one another for a long time.

'So that's it,' Marcus said at last, rising to his feet. 'Greedy are you, Fang? What I give you isn't enough, eh? I thought I'd beaten the bad habits out of you, but you've a few more lessons to learn, that's clear.'

It seemed that the dog knew what was about to happen even before it heard the chain being taken from the wall in the next room. It whined and fretted, its paws trembling, but still it did not move. Tom put his hands over his eyes, horrified and remorseful. How could he have brought about this cruelty? Yet he could not stop it.

The blows fell, three or four of them, before the dog retreated, whining and snapping uselessly at the flailing chain. It was driven back into the other room, Marcus cursing it even as he continued to whip the harsh metal down upon its body. It was some while before he had finished and had shut the door and come back into the room, taking up his drink again.

'They need bringing to heel,' he said simply.

Tom gratefully escaped from his chair and stalked up and down the room, free to move his arms and legs again.

'I would have come sooner,' he said, 'but I was snowed up.'

'So were we all. But your sense of timing is excellent. The time is ripe, Tom lad!'

He drained his glass, picked up the bottle and hesitated.

'Question is,' he said, 'do we wait for the fellow I told you of or do we strike while the iron is hot?'

'It's usually wise,' Tom suggested, 'not to delay.'

'Or, to put it another way, shall we have one more drink before we go, to give us strength for the work in hand?'

'What work?'

'Ah, now this will excite you, my little confederate. It's those two birdies I told you of – the mother and her succulent daughter. I think we've found them. A joyous moment this is going to be!'

He put the bottle on the floor and upended the tumbler upon it.

'Feeling a bit bloodthirsty are you, my young slasher? Like to see how the deed is done?'

Tom could only nod, weakly.

'Then as drinks can wait, and as people don't always keep appointments, I think it's best we set to our mouthwatering duties. Don't you agree?'

24 Across the Water

Marcus paused only to scribble a note, which he pushed underneath the bottle. Tom trailed after him through the door and into the alley, all the while glancing warily this way and that for any sign of the returning bellows-pumper. Did he hear the creaking of those wheels?

They set off along streets he had not entered before, all of them as mean and narrow as any he had yet seen in this inhospitable city, the snow piled up to either side. Marcus volunteered no information as to where they were going to meet their prey, nor under what circumstances, but his eagerness drove him at such a pace that Tom found himself breaking into a trot to keep level.

After some while his nostrils picked up a scent which was immediately familiar although he could not put a name to it. The smell was not of itself pleasant – in fact it seemed somehow unclean – and yet it stirred a strange excitement in him. He said nothing, however, only straining to keep up until, turning a corner, they found themselves confronted by water.

A wide river flowed sullenly past, carrying lumps of ice and assorted flotsam. Tom, amazed, watched spars of wood swirl by, a leaky barrel, lengths of discoloured cloth knotting and unwinding as they passed. Above his head an iron winch projected from a gaunt warehouse. There was a landing stage and a desolate stretch of quayside.

On the further shore, in the grey distance, the city continued as if without interruption – more grim buildings, narrow passageways. Some way upstream a monstrous bridge spanned the water. Marcus paced along the empty quay, his face clouded, and the evil exhilaration seemed to leave him for a moment.

'Where's the ferryman?' he snarled. 'This is his place. How does he expect us to reach the island?'

He waved his hand downstream and Tom saw a small hump of land rising out of the dingy water, scrubby vegetation behind a narrow grey beach. The wind ran chill across the river, painfully stabbing at their faces.

'Ah – he's left us a present!'

Marcus's unpleasant smile returned when he saw the ferryman's shallow boat tied close-by.

'If the fool's not here he won't miss it, will he? How's your rowing arm, Tom?'

Tom smiled.

'It used to be good.'

They descended steps cut into the quayside, moving carefully at the bottom where there was a carpeting of green weed. As they stepped into the boat Tom noticed that Marcus seemed less than confident, bending low and almost crawling along as the boat rocked to and fro. He nodded to Tom to sit in the centre and take the oars. Slowly, clumsily, he reached back to untie the rope, and Tom began to row with a confidence that betrayed a past familiarity with boats.

What memories he had of family excursions to their nearest river! How he had loved to take the oars and bear his shrieking sisters into the deepest waters, his mother trailing her fingers in the passing bubbles and laughing merrily at the fun. The oars were familiar in his grip. For a moment his relationship with Marcus seemed to have changed entirely – he confident, masterful, the other quiet, hunched, even frightened.

Marcus, facing him, made no effort to help. In fact he made no movement at all. He sat rigid at the back, clearly impressed by Tom's ability.

'You've a way with boats, lad,' he said. 'You've handled them before.'

Tom nodded.

'Well, it's not for me. I like dry land under my feet. I'm useless in the water. Couldn't swim to save my life.'

He gave a little laugh, as if to excuse himself the rare weakness.

'You need both feet anchored firmly to the ground when you thrust a knife between the shoulders, eh boy?'

They drew closer to the island. The water lapped around it, leaving a creamy scum behind each time it retreated. There was no sign of life, so that Tom was surprised to hear a faint shout on the air.

'What's that?' Marcus demanded urgently.

Tom, looking over his shoulder, could see nothing. When the cry was heard again, however, he realised that it came not from the island but from the land they had recently left. A figure waved frantically from the quayside, small in the distance but unmistakable because of the wheeled vehicle in which it sat.

'What is it?' Marcus asked again, not daring to swivel on the planking.

Tom shook his head.

'Don't know,' he said desperately.

The cry came again, and a word separated itself: 'Beware!'

Now Marcus, clutching the side with a grasp that whitened his knuckles, turned to look back. The bellows-pumper continued to wave his arms and shout. The word 'trust' carried across the water.

'Wait!' Marcus ordered.

Tom pulled on one oar, trembling. His companion strained to hear the words being shouted from the quayside.

'Turn back,' he said after a few moments. 'Head back to the shore.'

Tom stopped rowing and shipped his oars.

'Back, I say. Do you hear? Turn her!'

Marcus made the mistake of instinctively rising to his feet, swaying forward as he did so. Tom instantly shifted to one side, dipping one oar into the water and hauling on it as strongly as he knew how. As the boat rocked violently he grasped at Marcus as if to steady himself – yet knowing that it was not to steady himself – and, locked together, they tumbled into the icy water.

They sank beneath the surface for a moment, the breath dragged from their bodies by the coldness of the water. By the time they had resurfaced the current had swept the boat beyond their reach. Marcus clutched desperately, his open mouth sucking in air, but Tom shook off the grasp, kicked himself away. His coat was so heavy that at first he seemed not to move at all. He frantically struggled at the buttons, then the arms, fighting to be free of it. Three times he sank under and felt he had no strength to keep going, and yet each time he emerged, his chest heaving for air. At last the coat came away. He struck out for the shore.

An arm rose from the racing water, and then the head, for the last time. Marcus screamed, but although the wretchedness in that cry tortured Tom he continued to swim away, battling against the current. He swam painfully, heavily, until at the last an eddy carried him swiftly in and he stumbled onto his knees on the dirty sand. His body shook and ached with fatigue. The water slapped at his legs as if trying to reclaim him.

'Come on, mister. You're safe now. Come on, then.'

A man came running towards him. He was fat, and the running left him as breathless as Tom. He crouched down and peered at the wet boy through two large protruding eyes which, combined with a receding chin, gave his face such a carp-like appearance that Tom began to wonder whether he had indeed reached land or had slid to the depths and was being greeted by a creature of the river.

This fancy was dispersed when the man had regained his breath enough to speak. His voice was high and reedy and came in gasps.

'Not much . . . hope for Marcus . . . went under . . . no chance . . .'

'You know Marcus?'

'I've brought . . . the ladies . . . in the gardens . . . '

At this moment he, too, caught sight of the bellows-pumper at the far-off quayside. He answered the wild gesticulations with a broad two-armed wave of his own.

'Look,' he said. 'I must fetch him.'

Tom, feeling weak and ill, sat heavily on the ground, shivering.

'Stay,' he pleaded.

'Must go,' the man said. 'Back soon . . . must get him . . . you go to the gardens, see . . . dry off . . . or you'll die of the chill.'

Without waiting for any further stuttering conversation he lumbered along the strand and pulled a boat from out of the bushes. He shouldered it into the water, leapt into it and began to pull strongly for the shore.

Tom, his spirits low, struggled slowly to his feet. He had no idea what 'the gardens' could be, but his misery was too complete for him to care. Coldness left him numb, save for the aching in his arms and legs and the violent pumping of his heart and lungs. He walked leadenly to the fringe of low bushes and pushed his way through. He was surprised to come upon a high wall, with a small black door set into it.

The wall and the door seemed to sway before his eyes as he approached, and for a moment he felt as though he would fall. The door was of heavy iron, and although he turned the handle he could not at first push it open. He braced himself against it and, at last, inch by inch, it gave and he tottered inside, immediately collapsing from the effort. He lay for a while, eyes closed, head throbbing.

He opened his eyes upon a green world! Never had he seen such a place, nor could he have imagined one. Wide lawns led to dense shrubberies of luxuriant tropical growth. The air seemed scented and heavy and, even more astounding, it was warm: many degrees warmer than the air that scoured the city streets and blew across the river. And yet above was the same lowering grey sky, blocking out the winter sun.

Already the heat had penetrated his clothes so that his body, so recently frozen and wretched, became comfortable and relaxed. Steam began to rise from his clothes, until he was transformed into a column of mist. Standing, he moved on towards verdant shrubberies, feeling that it grew warmer still, until the heat became oppressive and sweat poured from his feverish brow. Between the tangled growth of shiny leaves and vines he could see a trellised path, and he was drawn to it, at the same time wondering and alarmed.

The air around him now buzzed and droned with the sound of insects, and perhaps it was the high-pitched sound combined with the torpid heat, but he suddenly seemed no longer alone. Were there voices, whispers? He began to move faster, glancing about him as he did so, and then broke into a trot. The greater activity combined with a mounting panic quickly enervated him and he fell to his knees, sweat pouring and head pounding. His eyes closed and salt stung his breath, coming in short gasps. He remained in this state for several minutes until slowly, stage by stage, his panic subsided and he climbed to his feet once more.

He was sure that he discerned movement in the thick undergrowth and he plunged in, scattering leaves and blossoms as he fought his way through. But the growth was so thick that he made little progress. A cavernous darkness,drove him back to the pathway. He determined to make his way back towards the grassed area where he was safe from ambush, and he set off once more along the path until it opened upon lawns.

The brightness of the open space contrasted strongly with the overhung path, and it was several seconds before he noticed the two women seated on the grass and looking intently at him, one rather old, the other about his own age. He was transfixed. Sonia smiled at him and he, to his constant shame henceforth, instead of rushing forward and greeting her, simply stood where he was and burst into tears. And there he remained standing until Sonia went to him and guided him back to where her mother sat.

He fell forward on the grass, semi-conscious – knowing where he was and knowing them to be there, but unable to think clearly and certainly unable to move. He felt them turn him over, and there was a cool feeling across his forehead. He lay with eyes closed, hearing the murmur of their voices without understanding what they said.

Slowly his spirits revived. He felt himself rested and breathing more easily. His mind began to stir. Yet, when he opened his eyes, he saw that the green world was still about him and he felt the air warm against his temples.

'Where are we?' he asked.

'Shhh.'

'I must know.'

'On an island. But say nothing. Rest.'

'What is this place? Why is it so warm?'

Sonia smiled down on him, but nervously.

'It's the vents.'

'No, Sonia. You must not speak so.'

'I'm sorry, mother.'

They fell into silence once again, but Tom fought against the desire to sleep. He thought of the man with the face like a fish rowing to pick up the bellows-pumper at the quayside.

'Were you watching me just now? When I was on the path?'

'Yes. We were hiding. We're waiting to meet a man called Marcus. He's coming to help us.'

'He's dead.'

'No – don't say it!'

'I was with him. He drowned. It's best for you that he did.'

Mother and daughter exchanged glances of combined bewilderment and horror.

'Listen,' Tom said. 'We haven't much time. You recognise me, don't you? You remember that you helped me?'

The mother shook her head, but Sonia said simply, 'I didn't think ever to see you again.'

'That Marcus was an agent of the Red Blade. You will have to believe me. He intended to kill you both. There is another man who even now will be in a boat on his way to the island with the same purpose. Are there any other boats here?'

'I don't know.'

They made their way from the gardens, Sonia with a determined expression on her face but her mother overcome with despair. She had to be led along, through the overhanging greenery to the iron door.

'Such a paradise,' Tom said wonderingly. 'Why is there nobody here?'

'They are afraid,' Sonia explained. 'There are stories about the place, superstitions.'

Outside, the air was again so chill that their hands and cheeks ached with it. Tom, without a coat now, felt the cold penetrate to his bones. The three of them pushed through the scrub to the shore and saw the bellows-pumper already halfway towards the island. They stumbled along, frantically searching for a means of escape. A humped shape on the mud sent a shudder of anticipation through Tom, but closer inspection revealed the rotting carcass of an upturned boat draped with wet sacking.

By now the oncoming boat was close enough for the bellows-pumper to yell taunts at them, and he rejoiced ecstatically in their impending doom. Tom unavailingly tried to shut out the shouted threats and abuse. They had no more than ten minutes. Coming to the end of the island, they soon traversed the width of it and began to hunt along the further shore.

'Porlock is seeking you,' Tom said, as he and Sonia searched, for a moment, in the same clump of vegetation.

'You know Porlock, too?'

'Do you trust me?'

Sonia paused as if to consider her reply and at that moment there was a cry of despair from her mother. She had sat herself down upon a large stone and covered her face with her hands. Sonia ran to her side, stroking her and imploring her to stand up and go with them.

And then Tom found the boat. It was old and green with slime, but there was no obvious sign of damage. He yelled to the others and heaved it onto the sand. At first there seemed to be no oars, but he kicked and scrabbled furiously among the bushes until he found them, side by side and serviceable. They pushed the boat to the water's edge and clambered in.

How far away were the bellows-pumper and his pilot? Even now they might be landing on the other side of the small island. Tom pulled strenuously on the oars, glancing briefly over his shoulder at the landing he must aim for. There were quays on this bank of the river, too, and he fancied that he saw people moving on them, perhaps going about their business.

Sonia sat with her arm around her mother's shoulders, which heaved with her continual sobbing, as Tom pulled nearer and nearer to land. He was well across the river when he saw the man with the fishy face come running along the shore of the island, look over to the boat with its three occupants and run back again to alert the bellows-pumper.

'We haven't long,' he said. 'Where do we go when we get to land?'

Sonia shook her head helplessly.

'I don't know the city,' she said.

'Don't know it?'

'Hardly at all.'

'And your mother?'

Sonia spoke quietly into her mother's ear and received a vigorous shake of the head in reply.

'It's been a long time since she travelled about,' Sonia explained. 'We've been . . . elsewhere.'

Tom, understanding, said nothing. The boat with their two pursuers now came round the head of the island and he pulled even harder on the oars.

'We had to leave the house you met us in,' Sonia said.

'I know,' he replied. 'I know all that, Sonia.'

She spoke almost brusquely.

'How is it that you know so much?' she demanded.

But now they were at the landing-stage and no reply was necessary. As he manoeuvred the small boat into position he saw, further along the quay, that men were working, carrying and loading. He tied the boat and they clambered onto the slippery quayside.

'Hey! Hold those three!'

The voice of the bellows-pumper carried across the water, and one or two of the men looked up from their work. Tom seized hold of Sonia and her mother and began to run towards the nearest alley.

'Hold them, I say. In the name of the Blade!'

25 Rats

They ran between large cavernous buildings, workshops and warehouses. There was the clattering sound of following footsteps which, however, soon died away. Tom, knowing that pursuit was inevitable, made abrupt changes of direction, never once pausing to look behind.

He would have pushed on even faster, but Sonia's mother was already gasping for breath and straining to be free of his grip.

'Stop, Tom,' the girl pleaded at last, shaking his arm. 'She can't. You'll kill her.'

So now, after a brief rest which seemed to him an age, they proceeded at walking pace, through dingy deserted thoroughfares. From within the buildings they occasionally heard sounds indicating that people were working, but there was a strange, an eery hush about an area that was so obviously designed to be thronging with labour.

Tom, catching Sonia's eye, found an expression on her face he could only describe as one of horror. Yet she had seemed so composed in the boat in the face of their great danger.

'We'll get away,' he said as cheerfully as he might. But she ignored his false optimism with an expressive frown, as if disturbed for quite other reasons.

'This place,' she said at last. 'To think that men made this.'

'I don't understand.'

'The city,' she asked. 'Is it all like this?'

'More or less.'

'So severe. So without – joy.'

They came to another meeting of ways and Tom, intent on choosing the best route, merely shrugged.

'It's a city,' he said. 'Men must have buildings to live and work in, after all. Beauty is quite another matter.'

He felt, as he said it, that it was a wise remark, but she only looked at him witheringly, as if in fact he were a child.

'You don't believe that, surely? That this is the best man can create?'

'I don't know,' Tom faltered, feeling at a disadvantage. 'It's the only city I've known. I come from the country.'

'Ah,' she said simply. 'If you but knew!'

After a while Tom encountered a familiar problem. Their repeated turns and backtrackings only brought them back to places they had visited before. They were in another self-contained sector of the city and had reached its limits.

'We must find somewhere to hide until nightfall,' he said.

The old lady, tears permanently in her eyes, nodded gratefully at the thought of resting her tottering legs.

'There's no escape,' she mumbled pathetically, and once having said it she repeated it over and over – 'no escape, there's no escape.'

'There, there, mother,' Sonia cajoled her as they led her inside a large hangar-like building. 'We'll do what we can.'

Tom again found himself admiring the girl's calmness and her realism: she made no attempt to pretend to her mother that their situation was anything but desperate, yet she refused to despair.

There was a ladder leading to a high, open loft on which were standing dozens of heavy crates. They helped the poor woman up – Sonia, who climbed first to show that it was possible, by repeated words of encouragement, Tom, standing a rung below her, by the reassuring pressure of his hands on her elbows. At the top it was dark and evil-smelling, and there was a heavy scuttling sound as they groped their way towards the inner wall. They all instinctively held back for a moment.

'It's nothing,' Tom said. 'I think I kicked a stone.'

But Sonia was as ruthlessly honest as before.

'Rats,' she said. 'They live here. But they won't hurt us.'

They found dry sacking and made as comfortable an area as they could in the corner. The mother lay down, an arm crooked over her face, shaking. Tom and Sonia sat in silence for a while.

'We can't remain here for long,' Sonia said eventually. 'They'll make a search.'

'Tonight we'll find a way out.'

She made no answer. No doubt she thought he was uttering meaningless phrases, mere words. He felt that she judged him unkindly.

'I've survived worse trouble,' he heard himself saying too loudly, his face flushing. 'At least I haven't been hiding myself away while other people were in danger.'

There was no reply. It was impossible to unsay what he had spoken. They sat in a silence much heavier than before.

'Why did you say that?' she asked eventually.

'I don't know. I'm sorry.'

She glanced at him, keenly.

'You think I've led a sheltered life.'

'You admitted yourself that you don't know the city. It frightens you.'

'It appals me. I had thought it was like that only by the east gate – the area I know.'

'You lived in that house where I met you – and in the underground city. There are many people who would like to find that city, good people. They are not permitted. Meanwhile their lives are threatened.'

He had not realised that Sonia's mother was listening, but now she whimpered and clutched at the girl's sleeve.

'Say nothing. You mustn't!'

'It's all right, mother. I know what I should not say.'

She leant towards Tom in the darkness.

'You must understand that I can't talk of those matters. But how do you think it is that my mother and I are in this wretched situation – if we lived a sheltered life, as you imagine?'

'I don't know. The entrance was sealed up. You were betrayed, perhaps.'

'Perhaps. We did not live cloistered in that house, you know, like members of a religious order. We were alongside those who took the risks. It was while we were in the eastern sector that the way was closed to us.'

'Who sealed the entrance?'

Sonia paused before replying and then continued in the same quiet tones.

'It had to be done quickly, according to a pre-arranged plan, at the first sign of danger. There was no time for mother and me to be told.'

'And you know no other way of finding the underground city. Porlock told me so.'

The mother's sniffling now turned into heavy sobs. Sonia lifted the trembling head onto her lap and gently stroked the dishevelled hairs at her temple.

'Tell me of your adventures, Tom.'

So he began, and spoke for a long time, explaining that he sought his father and describing the events that had occurred since he left the house with the white room. Sonia listened gravely, interrupting him only to clarify some point he had left obscure, occasionally lifting a hand silently over her mouth in a gesture of amazement or horror. When he came to the death of Marcus she shook her head wonderingly.

'We shouldn't be alive now,' she said, 'if you hadn't . . . '

She left the sentence incomplete.

'No,' Tom said quickly. 'I didn't kill him. He fell in. I turned the boat and we lost our balance. He couldn't swim.'

Yet he knew that this was not an honest remark. In fact he could not bear to think of those moments in the boat when he had acted on an impulse, not hesitating, tipping them both into the icy current. As if in consolation, Sonia reached out to squeeze his hand – and at that moment they heard voices in the street. She did not release her grip.

'We'll try this one,' they heard. 'You search the workshop the other side.'

The light was fading outside, so that even the large area downstairs was shadowy, its features indistinct. They heard the steps of three or four men, and then the sound of heavy objects being moved.

'I say they've flown.'

'There's nowhere they could go.'

'Slipped back to the river, maybe.'

'A lot of good that would do them. The guards are shoulder to shoulder along the quay.'

Sonia's mother, unable to hold back a terrified whimper, thrust her face into her daughter's lap. Her body shook convulsively. Tom held his breath, knowing that the searchers were growing closer, until the ladder suddenly rattled against the floor of the loft.

'Here's a likely place.'

'You going up?'

'I don't like heights. I'll hold it steady for you.'

'There's my hero! Hang on, then.'

Steel-tipped boots clanged against the iron rungs. The floor trembled. A head came over the edge, a dark shape in the gloom. Tom, crouching low in the corner, felt Sonia's hair fall across his forehead. He could see only that the man started in the other direction.

'Anything useful up there?'

'Lot of crates, that's all.'

'Valuables? We ought to get something for our trouble, don't you think?'

'Some hopes. I'll have a feel inside.'

There followed a furious scrabbling and a fearful scream. Something brushed past Tom's shoulder, gone in an instant.

'What's the matter, man?'

'My hand – the devil!'

'What is it?'

'I'm bitten. Help me down. A blasted rat.'

They heard the boots on the ladder again, moving much more quickly this time.

'I'm bleeding. Look! Vicious brute.'

'You found the nest, I'll be bound.'

'Vicious. Give me a cloth.'

The voices died away, leaving a silence which even the four-legged occupants of the loft forbore to break. The old lady, trembling still, sat up and looked about her.

'They've gone?' she asked. 'We're safe?'

'Safe, mother. Try to sleep.'

Sonia smoothed out the sacking and plumped up a makeshift pillow for her mother to rest on. Now that the immediate crisis was past she seemed to relax a little, and within a few moments she had fallen into a deep slumber. Sonia and Tom watched her with relief. For a long time they said nothing, only listening to the rhythmic breathing and feeling the bitter cold of the evening slowly infiltrate the recesses of the warehouse.

Tom considered what he could do. A return across the river was clearly impossible. The chances of sneaking down to the quayside unseen and finding a boat must be very small, and he had no doubt that the bridge he had seen was heavily guarded. He thought of Bill and Lucy in the all-night cafe and experienced a pang of what felt almost like homesickness.

The only hope was escape to the next sector of the city, yet they had been unable to find a way through. He had the pass. Had the bellows-pumper alerted every part of his organisation to watch for the three fugitives? Tom began to formulate the beginnings of a plan.

'Don't laugh at me,' Sonia said suddenly, still speaking in hushed tones, 'but when you first arrived at the house – when we looked after you – I thought of you as a little brother. I never had a brother, you see.'

'I shouldn't have thought,' Tom replied, 'that I'm an inch shorter than you.'

'No, no. It was because you were unwell, I think. Exhausted. You needed protection. I don't think of you at all in the way now.'

And how *did* she think of him now? Tom was surprised to find that it mattered to him that he should know. He could not ask the question, however, and, stifled with embarrassment, he pushed himself to his knees.

'We must go,' he said. 'It's dark now.'

'I'll wake mother.'

It seemed cruel to rouse the old lady, but Sonia did it kindly, shaking her hand and speaking softly close to her ear. Gradually the eyes opened and she sat up. In fact the sleep seemed to have calmed her, and she listened to their suggestions and prepared herself to leave. Tom first descended the ladder and spent some minutes in the alleys outside, ensuring that the way was clear. Then he returned, called up to them and helped them down to the ground.

'When we find someone in authority,' he explained carefully, 'I shall produce the pass. You must remain in hiding. I shall then try to get us all through.'

This sounded straightforward, and neither of them chose to question the simplicity of the operation. They advanced silently through the streets, Tom leading the way around each corner. The air, he noticed, though still raw (and especially to him, since he had lost his coat) seemed nevertheless a little less chill than for several weeks. The snow, still packed high at the sides of the thoroughfares, was dimpled along the surface where, during the day, patches had begun to thaw.

After some minutes there was a sound that he had heard more than once in the streets of the city, a sound which, because of past association, filled him with alarm. Yet it was what he wished to hear.

'The guards,' he said. 'If you wait in this alley I'll go forward to meet them.'

He asked the question Sonia had not answered before.

'Do you trust me?'

'We trust you.'

Sonia pressed her mother's hand and the old lady nodded, trying to smile but only bringing the tears to her eyes. The marching footsteps grew louder and Tom, not wishing to arouse suspicions, walked boldly in the middle of the street. As the guards – a platoon of eight – drew closer, he raised an arm in confident greeting.

'At last!' he called. 'You don't know what a search I've had for you.'

The platoon halted and the captain stepped forward. He looked Tom up and down carefully.

'Looking for us?'

'Well, I've a problem. I've a need to get through to the next sector, and although I've got a pass I'm blowed if I can remember the way through.'

'Been through before, have you?'

'Yes, of course. I'm always here and there about the city. But I don't know this sector as well as some.'

The captain continued to look thoughtfully at Tom. He turned to his men, as if to judge their reaction.

'Let's see your pass.'

Tom pulled it from his pocket. He and the captain turned to allow the light of the moon to shine upon it, and he discovered, with a lurching feeling at his heart, that his swim in the river had made the ink run so that the words were scarcely decipherable.

'What's this?'

'I had a tumble in the snow,' Tom said quickly. 'I was helping a colleague to make an arrest when the fellow grabbed me by the throat and rolled me over. I lost everything from my pockets.'

He swallowed hard and looked over at the guards, attempting a cynical smile.

'I'm pleased to say that he lost a lot more than that!'

One or two of them chuckled and the captain, though still hesitant, handed the document back to him.

'I don't know whether they'll accept it,' he said. 'Come this way.'

They were in fact only a couple of minutes from the corridor to the next sector. The captain rapped on a door which opened to reveal two heavily armed sentinels, one an elderly fellow with a lined, weather-beaten face, the other considerably younger and more lively. Tom told his story over again, and again waited in suspense as they examined the paper.

'Whose signature is this?'

'I don't know,' Tom replied. 'I work with a man called Marcus. He obtained the pass.'

'Marcus?' asked the younger one, interested. 'That the one with the dog?'

'Fang. Yes.'

'Look here,' said the other. 'That's his mark there.'

'So it is. A wild dog, that.'

'A champion,' Tom said. 'He's unbeaten.'

'More's the pity. I lost money on that creature. I was in the east sector when it fought the last time out.'

'And what a fight!' enthused Tom, taking advantage of the change in the conversation. 'That Ripper was a demon, wasn't it?'

'Size of a lion, I'd say.'

'And what teeth!'

'I didn't see how it could lose.'

'But Fang's got cunning, don't you agree?'

'Oh, he's smart all right.'

The captain, feeling rather out of the conversation, made a brief speech of farewell and marched his men away.

'He's smart,' the sentinel continued, 'but one day he'll meet his match. He'll get too old for it.'

His companion, apparently having no interest in dog-fights, handed Tom the pass.

'I should renew this,' he said. 'There's some as wouldn't allow it.'

'I'll do it in the morning,' Tom said. 'In the meantime I need your help.'

'In what way?'

'Well,' he continued, playing the actor's role with more confidence as the minutes passed, 'I've a couple of prisoners who don't know they're prisoners.'

They laughed.

'How's that, then?'

'They're two ladies who're wanted for interrogation. They don't suspect me at the moment, and I'm anxious that they come quietly as far as possible. If I bring them through, will you give them a smile and a nod?'

The young one nudged his colleague.

'At the very least,' he said. 'What have they done?'

Tom put a finger to his lips.

'Can't say,' he told them. 'But they could swing for it.'

'Fetch 'em, man. Let's be seeing these treacherous beauties!'

So he hurried along the street and led Sonia and her mother to the doorway and the passage through to the other sector.

'Say nothing,' he warned them.

The two sentinels, surprised at Sonia's youth and beauty, smiled even more broadly than Tom could have hoped for, bowed as well as nodded and waved extravagantly as the three made their way along the windowless passageway. He had a moment's panic when the sound of running footsteps was heard behind them, but it was only the younger man who, caught up in the sport, made it a point of chivalry to escort them past the guards at the other end. He waved again, and then they were for the moment free, alone under a moon which rode fast among its heaving clouds.

'Where now?' asked Sonia, her face showing relief and delight.

But Tom did not answer at once. To his astonishment he recognised some of the buildings they passed. He had been in this sector before. At first he could not say where he was, but soon they came across the delapidated monument he had discovered on an earlier journey through the city streets, the strange inscription on its base.

'I know this!' he called out, brushing away the snow. 'Look, Sonia – these words. They were also written on the wall of the white room. "Wear me as your spiked heel: I will bite into ice for you". What do they mean? Whose words are they?'

'They are part of a poem.'

'But why here? And why in that room?'

'It is a poem which is important for many people.' Sonia was reluctant to say more. 'I think those people must have erected the monument.'

'And who destroyed it?'

Sonia only shook her head, and her mother, who had now recovered much of her composure, said: 'There are things you must not ask. We cannot answer.'

Now they passed along streets he knew well. They came to the market square, and he remembered the long chase and how he had hidden under the cloth that covered the stall. Tall buildings rose on either side of the narrow thoroughfares, with scarcely a window to be seen.

'In a moment,' Tom said, 'we shall be at the place I told you of – the House of the Star. It's a place which holds great danger for us. I believe I was first sent there because it houses agents of the Blade. But I believe there may be friends there, too.

'I can't expect you to accept these dangers if you don't want to, but I know that for myself I must go in. It's the only chance I have.'

Now they turned a corner and saw the sign of the star swinging in the evening breeze. Sonia answered him immediately.

'We'll take the chance with you,' she said.

26 On Trial

Tom was totally unprepared for the scene within. First he found the door guarded by a sinister fellow in dark clothes and black beret who half-dragged them inside and motioned them to seats by a small table. Although the large room was crowded, he was immediately aware of a strange, brittle silence, so unlike the usual clamour of the place – a silence which was broken by an angry, declaiming voice, raised for all to hear.

'And who, I ask you, had a greater opportunity to betray our movement than this treacherous creature you see before you?'

The voice – it was scarcely credible – was that of the normally subdued Clem. But there was a greater shock in store, for the object of his accusation was none other than his own wife, the redoubtable Sphynx.

A long table was drawn up before the huge, glowing fire. At one end sat the Sphynx, bolt upright, her face expressing extreme distaste. Clem stood with his back to the flames, addressing his remarks to a cluster of hunched, predominantly elderly men Tom had never seen before and who were grouped at the other end of the table. Like the man at the door they were sombrely dressed and wore black berets. They seemed to Tom like flies on a carcass.

Now he looked around the room and saw, among the throng, many people he recognised. But this evening there was no thought of talking and joking with their neighbours. Most of them gazed at the floor, as if not wishing to be involved with the drama being played out before them.

'Look at her now – carefully. Is guilt not written across her features?'

Slumped in a comfortable chair near the centre of the room was his fellow-countryman Clutt. His head lolled on his chest, which rose and fell gently as in sleep, yet one hand still firmly clutched the inevitable pipe. Tom saw the stammerer and, on a low chair close to the fire, Old Weasel, his instrument between his knees and silent. He wore his customary black beret and was gaunt and old like the strangers, yet he seemed to Tom a different kind of creature. Was that only because he had befriended him?

'Oh, I studied her behaviour for a long time before I could believe in her infamy and was ready to report my findings to the local committee of the Red Blade.'

Tom caught the eye of the city guard with pearly teeth who on so many occasions had been the life and soul of the company. Now – although he must surely support the rough and ready court proceedings they were witnessing – his expression was curiously cold and distant. His fellow guards sat close by, heavy and mute.

'Three days ago she disappeared for one whole morning, and being suspicious . . . '

The words evaporated in Tom's brain as he saw, sitting alone with a glass and a decanter, the elegantly attired figure of Porlock. He maintained, as ever, his air of the disinterested spectator, fixing the proceedings with a steady gaze through his gold-rimmed spectacles. He was turned away from Tom, but must surely soon see him if he had not done so already. Tom glanced towards his two companions, who sat close to one another, clasping hands. They must given no sign that they recognised the one man who might yet save them.

Tom looked again at the group of strangers, menacing in their brooding attention. He trembled. This was no charade, no evening's entertainment. Beyond them, on the wall, was the dagger emblem with its dripping blood.

' . . . until I discovered evidence which links this woman with association of the enemy.'

Tom thought of his own helpless position – a stranger to the city who had run away from the House of the Star. The evidence surely pointed a crimson finger in his direction. But he found that the plight of Sonia and her mother prevented him from concentrating on his own danger. The old lady once again seemed on the point of collapse, her lowered head shaking, but he noticed how Sonia not only caressed her mother's hand reassuringly but forced herself to show a calmness she could not feel. She might have been a local girl dropped in for a warming nightcap rather than a fugitive hunted at this moment by agents of the Blade.

How he longed for happier times when he might wander the world with Sonia! He heard little of Clem's chilling betrayal for dreaming of ways in which they might escape, even imagining the first moments when they were free to talk, to share their thoughts. These sensations were so new to him as to seem suddenly absurd, with the consequence that he returned rudely to the present just as Clem wound up his denunciation.

' . . . and I ask you, therefore, to take her to the Citadel for the final judgement and sentencing.'

There was a leaden hush while the old men inclined their heads towards one another and muttered inaudibly. Clem avoided his wife's eye, turning towards the fire, which seemed to snap and snarl in his face. A few of his guests, who this evening seemed more like prisoners in the House of the Star, shifted in their seats and stole furtive glances at their neighbours, who studiously avoided them. Tom stretched his fingers to touch Sonia lightly on the arm, but he dared not say a word.

One of the old men signalled to Clem, who now bent his head among the black berets. This conspiratorial action was more than the Sphynx could bear, for she now rose to her feet and in her full and disdainful voice began to berate her husband.

'Oh you poor jack-rabbit, you! To tell such lies and incriminate your own wife! Who ever heard of such abject behaviour? The degradation that cowardice will drive a man to!'

But the hostelry was no longer hers. The voice that had been accustomed to striking terror in her clientele had no effect on the present masters of the place. She was waved back into her chair while the whispered consultation continued. She was defeated.

'So concludes the case for the prosecution,' announced Clem after a while. 'Who will speak in defence of this noble lady?'

For the first time the old men took an interest in the other inhabitants of the room. They turned lined, unforgiving faces upon the assembly, as if to challenge a champion of the Sphynx to stand forward. The silence was so absolute that the spitting of the logs upon the fire could be heard at the furthest point, like snakes in a pit.

Could the Sphynx indeed be an opponent of the Blade? Tom had felt all along that there must be friends as well as enemies at the inn. He thought back to the incident which had caused him to flee the building: the ransacking of Clutt's room. He remembered the Sphynx's anger, Clem's dread on seeing the dagger symbol on the wall.

'I-I-I'd like to say s-something.'

Incredibly the stammerer stood and made his way forward, approaching the large table.

'A counsel for the defence, eh?'

The stammerer, having made what must have been a supreme effort, now seemed unable to continue.

'What evidence have you to put before this tribunal?'

'E-e-evidence?'

'You're speaking for the lady. Let's hear what facts you have to defend her with.'

Watching the stammerer forlornly struggling for words, his face white and taut, Tom felt ashamed. He knew he could not will *his* legs to propel him forward, however just the cause. Yet this poor man had been humiliated once before. Tom remembered the pathetic procession around the room, the guards having their boisterous fun, and he remembered how then, too, he had done nothing, only felt anger and pity.

'I have n-n-no evidence. I m-merely want to say h-how g-g-good she's been to m-me since I've st-st-stayed at this pl-place.'

Here the old men looked at one another with raised eyebrows and Tom almost expected them to laugh out loud. That the brave man should have put himself in this position simply to speak for the Sphynx's kindness to him only increased Tom's admiration.

'Generous, was she?'

'Y-y-yes.'

'Generous to whom? That's the question. To the wrong kind of person, my friend. What's your station in life?'

'I'm a c-c-clerk. G-g-grade three.'

'A clerk? That covers a multitude of sins! For why was the lady so generous to you? That's what we'd like to know. Work in a sensitive area, do you?'

'N-no. S-s-sanitation.'

'Ah! Sewers and the like, eh? Escape routes for criminals. That's what you've been up to?'

'No.'

It was obvious that Clem taunted the stammerer for the sport of it rather than out of any belief in his guilt. It was equally obvious that, brave as the intervention had been, it had not helped the Sphynx at all: perhaps the reverse.

'There are severe penalties for people who waste the time of tribunals,' barked Clem, changing tack. 'Have you nothing more to say.'

'N-n-no.'

'Then sit down my friend before you're marked down for a trip to the Citadel yourself. Sit down!'

Tom watched the stammerer return to his chair and slowly lower himself onto it, stiff, in a state of shock. No one said a word to him. There was another conference at the table, and it was some time before Clem straightened up and addressed his remarks to the whole congregation.

'The tribunal will have more people to question. Nobody may leave until its business is finished. There will, however, be a short break in the proceedings and you are requested to enjoy yourselves.'

Seeing that there was no response whatsoever, he banged a fist on the table.

'Talk – you understand? Drink! Do what you would normally do!'

He swung round on Old Weasel, who sat immobile, nursing his instrument.

'Music! Come on – play! Enjoy yourselves, all of you!'

The first notes were plucked and people began to mumble incoherently to their neighbours. After the initial murmuring there was a sudden welter of sound, as if everyone raised his voice at the same moment in a great release of tension. There was a great deal of shoulder-slapping and punching among the city guards, and even a forced laugh or two.

'I don't think,' Sonia said wryly, 'that this was a good time to arrive.'

Tom again marvelled at her composure.

'Have you seen Porlock?'

'Yes.'

'Don't show that you know him.'

At this moment the gold-framed spectacles turned in their direction, but they did not pause. Porlock might never have seen them before in his life.

'Are you frightened?' Tom asked.

'Only as I was yesterday and the day before.'

The music, plangent behind the babble of voices, became suddenly, poignantly, familiar. Old Weasel's fingers plucked the tune he had sung in this room all that time ago, and the notes seemed to speak to him through the confusion and terror he felt, offering him reassurance. How thankful he was then to the old minstrel, the great survivor. He almost believed that his own survival was possible.

Not for long, however. Clem and the men in black berets began to turn their attention towards the imprisoned customers at the tables. The old men nodded and passed brief comments as Clem, standing behind them and leaning forward, singled out individuals with a pointed finger. That finger swung towards Tom and stopped. The questioning seemed to intensify, and one of the group took a glass from his pocket and held it to one eye, peering intently.

'Sonia,' Tom said quietly. 'Do you know these men? Will they know you?'

'No. I don't think so.'

'I wish I hadn't brought you here. You would have been safer by yourselves, the two of you. I've put your heads in a noose.'

'Don't speak like that.'

Old Weasel's tune changed again. Not for a second had he looked towards Tom as he played. He concentrated on the strings of his curious instrument, his spindly fingers rocking from one to the other without a pause. Nor did Porlock turn in his direction again: he examined the people at the long table with his usual careful scrutiny, apparently quite without concern, let alone fear. The Sphynx, for so long the dominating character of the inn, sat humbled in her chair, her eyes downcast. Despite Sonia's presence by his side, Tom felt horribly alone.

'Silence! Enough!'

Clem raised a hand and immediately, with the speed and finality of a guillotine, the low murmur snapped into a silence as deep and ominous as that which had seemed to hollow out the room before.

'The tribunal is reconvened. If your name is called, stand forward and answer respectfully.'

Now there was another awful moment while he once again consulted his superiors. Faces in the throng were drawn and white with fear, hands clutched for comfort at glasses, chairs, the edges of tables. Finally Clem took up his position once more.

'The lad Tom,' he said flatly.

His head swam. He rose, but could not feel his legs. He brushed past the seated customers heavily, clumsily – a glass toppled to the floor and shattered – but was unaware of making contact with them. The men with black berets were like malevolent monkeys. They seemed to jabber angrily.

'Where's your respect?' Clem demanded.

'Respect?'

Here one of the old men spoke for the first time, inclining a ravaged face towards Tom.

'You did not stoop before the sign,' he accused, his voice thin and cruel. 'It is not your practice, perhaps?'

'Stoop?'

'Bow the head!' broke in Clem in an exasperated manner, but the old man silenced him with a wave.

'Were you brought up to honour the Blade?'

'I come from far away,' Tom replied instantly. 'I had not known of the sign before I arrived in the city.'

'How long ago?'

'Just before the first winter.'

Now another of the tribunal intervened.

'What brought you here, boy?'

'My parents died. I came to stay with a relative.'

'Name?'

Tom faltered, ludicrously unprepared, but a loud voice saved him.

'Brach. Edward Brach. Fourth district. His uncle. No room in his own house.'

The words were uttered by the Sphynx so quickly and forcefully that nobody was able to stop her before she had provided Tom with his alibi.

'Silence!'

Clem glowered at his wife, then beckoned Tom round the table to stand before the glowing fire.

'So dear uncle Edward sent you here, did he?'

'Yes.'

'Oh, I'm sure that's what the records say, my young friend. *She* had charge of the records. But if she speaks up on your behalf there's not much hope for you, and that's a fact.'

'He paid for me to stay here. He had no room.'

'Poor fellow. Came visiting, did he?

'Once or twice.'

'Big fellow? Bewhiskered? Wore riding boots?'

'No.'

'Not that one. Let's think. Did he limp rather badly? Had a watch on a chain?'

'Neither.'

'Hm. A visitor for young Tom . . . Yes, I have it! A little chap, so high. A dwarf, no less. Oh yes, I've known a dwarf come seeking you out.'

'That wasn't my uncle.'

'Ah – not! Who was he?'

'A friend.'

'And what a friend!'

Clem whispered in the ears of the tribunal, who shook their heads solemnly.

'He's known to us, your friend. He's a marked man. How did you come to meet him?'

'He tumbled in the snow,' Tom replied quickly. 'I helped him up and brought him in to warm him.'

How had he learned to lie so effectively? Yet once would not be enough. It was as if he were on one of the toboggan runs of his childhood, clinging desperately to the careering sledge, skirting one hazard after another, no time for self-congratulation before the next protruding rock thrust up from under the snow.

'And the ladies you've brought with you. Your aunt and your cousin, no doubt.'

'No. Just acquaintances.'

He had meant to prevent Sonia and her mother suffering from the association with him, but as he spoke the words they sounded like a betrayal and he wished he could unsay them.

'Just acquaintances! On the contrary, I'm sure we shall find them most interesting. But that pleasure we'll delay for a little. Tell us first what you've found to do in this great city of ours since your arrival.'

He began to tell of the places he had visited, the sights he had seen, the people he had met – some of them genuine, others fictitious. He had been a tourist in the city, enjoying the cut and thrust of the market, admiring the architecture. As he spoke he looked about him and found that the eyes of the people he knew were averted from him, that there were sorrowful expressions on their faces. Did they know that his case was hopeless? Nevertheless he pressed on, forcing a manic cheerfulness into his voice.

'A lover of our city, it's evident! All credit to you! By which gate did you enter?'

'The east gate.'

'And how did you pass through to this sector?'

'I forget the route.'

'There is no open way.'

'My uncle had a pass.'

'Oh blessed uncle! Too bad he shouldn't be with us tonight. You know his address, of course?'

'He never told me. I've not been there.'

As he responded to this interrogation the outer door opened. In the silence between question and answer there came a familiar creaking sound, and the man guarding the door stepped back to admit a wheeled vehicle and its sinister occupant.

'We come now to your unexplained disappearance. A most suspicious circumstance.'

Tom, the panic immobilising him, offered no reply. The bellows-pumper made no immediate intervention in the proceedings, simply resting his chin upon folded arms and seeming content to survey the spectacle. More accurate, perhaps, to say that he savoured it. There was a thin smile on his lips and Tom saw that he bowed with mock graciousness towards Sonia and her mother.

'Why did you leave us so suddenly?'

'I followed your advice,' Tom said desperately. 'When one of the lodgers' rooms was ransacked you told me that strangers to the city were threatened. I was frightened.'

For the first time Clem seemed discomfited, as if Tom had touched on an incident he would rather forget.

'You had no advice from me!'

'I thought you meant me to run.'

'Then you're a fool!'

This outburst seemed to unsettle Clem, and he gave a nervous sideways glance towards the old men of the tribunal. One of them called him over, and there was more whispered conversation. Tom became aware that Old Weasel was attending to the great fire, throwing wood upon it, and when he took up the log basket to replenish it from the pile that was kept in a small room off the kitchen it seemed to Tom's overworked brain that a wisp of smoke followed him. Although most eyes were still turned towards the floor, he found that Porlock studied him as dispassionately as ever, while the bellows-pumper smiled jauntily, provokingly. The only person to answer his gaze was Sonia, whose dear face appeared the more beautiful because he felt that after this night he would never see it again.

'Like to visit the Citadel, would you?' Clem resumed eventually. 'Like to enjoy a taste of true justice?'

'I've no wish to.'

'I'm sure you haven't. But that's what's in store for you, my lad. That's the course of action I propose to the tribunal.'

He turned to his captive audience.

'Who'll speak for him? Who'll defend the indefensible?'

Again the old men swung round. This time, however, there was no brave champion to speak for the accused. The silence seemed to press in on Tom, as if it would crush him.

Slowly, the wheeled contraption rolled forward. The bellows-pumper began to snigger, a horrible sound that reverberated around the room. Working his lever back and forth, he grinned merrily at the people he passed until he brought himself close to the great table.

'Don't know who'll speak for him, but I'll damn him!'

A sussurus swept through the onlookers like the wind under a barn door.

'You know the agent Marcus – a bold man, loyal to the Blade in bad times as well as good? This creature' – he flung a contemptuous arm in Tom's direction – 'killed him.'

'No, no, I . . .'

'Drowned him. I saw it myself, but hours ago.'

The tribunal, unprepared for an indictment so specific, sat silent, hanging on the bellows-pumper's words.

'He's known to me from the eastern sector, where he escaped us over the rooftops. We fired the flares and brought down his companion – a treacherous blacksmith – but this one gave us the slip. When I met up with him again he was worming his way into Marcus's confidence.

'I followed them to the river. They were rowing to the Isle of Flowers, and when I called across the water this cockroach tipped the boat, wrestled Marcus overboard and swam to the shore.'

He worked the lever on his machine, manoeuvring it until he had his back to the men in their black berets, giving himself a view of the crowded room.

'But this one, your honours, murderer though he be, is nothing to our other captives. Take a good look at the two ladies at the table there. Innocent-looking, wouldn't you say?'

Heads turned to Sonia and her mother. Sonia's statuesque calm contrasted vividly with the old lady's pitiful demeanour. Tears coursed down her face, which crumpled with fear and anguish. A moaning sound escaped her lips.

'These are the two most wanted people in our city. Enemies of the Blade, indeed, but more than that – much more than that, your honours.'

The bellows-pumper rotated again, making the most of his revelation.

'They know the way to the city underground!'

Now there was, for the first time this evening, a spontaneous outburst from the whole assembly. The sudden commotion was a mingling of shock, of disbelief, of excitement, of wonder.

'It exists!'

'They know the way!'

'Didn't I say it was true?'

'Another city! There's another city . . .'

One of the tribunal pushed himself to his feet.

'It is forbidden to speak of that place. It's the Blade law. These rumours of some mythical city . . .'

But the bellows-pumper would not be silenced. As the babble increased all around him he raised his voice.

'We need no longer pretend, comrade. We have nothing to fear. The city exists, and we have the way to find it!'

The first wave of sound, even as it ebbed, regathered like the foaming oceans and seemed to tumble about their heads. But, dimly at first, Tom became aware that the nature of the sound was changing, that a new sensation began to flow through the room and that it was a sensation of panic. Then his nose picked up a smell which was at first indistinguishable from the smoke stench from the blazing logs nearby but which soon became more acrid.

'Fire! In the room beyond!'

'For mercy's sake – let us out!'

'Water! Where's water?'

Great folds of billowing smoke wafted in from the kitchen area. Tables were overturned, glasses smashed, as the nearest customers leapt to their feet, backing away towards the centre of the room. The old men of the tribunal, who had scarcely moved a muscle during the proceedings so far, scurried about like ants caught in a forest fire. It was Clem who took the decisive action.

'Guards to the door! Let no one leave the building!'

The doorway to the kitchen was now totally obscured by the pall of smoke, which rose to the ceiling and began to drift across it to the furthest side of the room. Clem, without hesitation, plunged into the swirling fog, which followed him in an instant.

One man who had made no move at all despite the general hubbub was Old Weasel. He sat with his instrument, his face expressionless – and, at once, Tom realised how the fire had started. He had not imagined the thin trail of smoke which had followed Old Weasel with the log basket. Why had he done it? The answer was at once obvious and unbelievable: to save Tom if it were at all possible. Yet surely the great survivor had broken his own lifelong rule – had risked his own life. He saw Tom's enquiring look and, raising a finger to the frail and bony skull which was the seat of all his cunning, was close enough to say simply: 'Old age has made a fool of me.'

The sooty figure of Clem, arms across his face for protection, staggered through the smoke.

'Five strong men!' he gasped. 'We can do it. The fire's not yet taken hold.'

Two men shuffled forward, but others shrank away so that Clem had to step in among the throng and seize them by the shirt fronts.

'Come on!' he yelled, abusing them for their reluctance. 'There's water through here.'

Finally he mustered a small party of pressed men who stripped off their jackets, held them over their mouths and charged headfirst through the smoke. Tom, unrestrained, hurried among the panic-stricken crowd to where Sonia and her mother still sat at their small table.

'Quickly! Follow me!'

There was no escape through the street door, which was now defended by members of the city guard. These were busy pushing away any frantic individuals who had completely lost their wits and were clamouring to be out in the night air. Nor, of course, was there a way to the rooftop, since that route was cut off by Old Weasel's conflagration. Tom led the way up the inner staircase to the bedroom area, elated to be free of his persecutors although he knew that it offered no way out of the building.

'Where are we going?' Sonia asked breathlessly.

He made no reply. How could he tell them that there was no escape? He led them forward, along the corridor towards his own room. Even as he reached for the handle, however, there was the sound of hurrying footsteps behind them and a brusque command.

'Stop! You won't get away through there!'

27 Steps

It was Porlock. The old lady threw herself onto his chest and clutched at him, sobbing with relief. With Sonia on the other side, he helped the weeping, almost senseless, figure along the corridor.

'This is my room,' he said, pushing a door open. 'We'll be safe in here for a few moments.'

Tom, trailing behind, found his brain almost choked with questions.

'The Sphynx,' he asked. 'Is she really an enemy of the Blade? Is she with you?'

'An enemy, yes. But she is one of those who still seek the underground city. She knows nothing of my position.'

'And Clem?'

'It is as you see. He is a dangerous man.'

They helped the poor shaking creature onto the bed, where she lay trembling, her eyes closed. Sonia sat at her head, stroking her cheek.

'It is not the time,' Porlock rebuked him gently, 'for *you* to be putting questions to *me*. There is much that I could discuss with you, Tom, but I will simplify matters by asking one thing.'

He reached into a pocket and withdrew an object that was instantly recognisable. It was the picture Tom had carried with him from his home village.

'Of course,' Porlock said, 'I searched your room at the all-night cafe. This is yours?'

'Yes.'

'Why do you carry it?'

'That is the reason I am in the city,' Tom replied. 'It's the man I am seeking – my father.'

Porlock appeared deeply shocked by this information. He studied Tom's face, then the picture, then Tom's face again.

'You are saying' – he spoke slowly, deliberately – 'that this is your father? You tell me this in all seriousness?'

'It's true.'

Porlock turned away from them for a moment, still examining the picture. Sonia's mother was now whimpering quietly, while from below the firefighting could be heard as a muffled commotion. Tom expected the door to burst open at any second.

'Come.'

Porlock crossed to a corner of the room, knelt down and lifted a small section of floorboard. He put his arm inside the gap. Tom heard a click and a large panel swung open in the wall.

'This is the way down.'

Tom felt his lips quiver, sudden tears burn his eyes.

'To the underground city? You're taking me?'

'I am taking you, Tom. But I am also taking these two ladies, and I think you might give some assistance.'

Through the wall there were steep steps and then, almost immediately, a passage with windows which looked down upon the darkened street. Porlock closed the panel behind them and they followed the passage along the length of the House of the Star. At the end was a door.

'Few have passed this way,' Porlock said, opening it.

Stone steps led down. As Tom waited his turn to begin the descent he looked from the window. A thaw had begun. The whiteness of the roofs was laced with thin black runnels of melted snow.

A movement at street level attracted his eye. Outside the inn, and gazing up it seemed to the very window at which he stood, was the boy with the green scarf. He appeared so small and pathetic from Tom's vantage point, so vulnerable. He raised an arm, a beckoning gesture. What innocent, childish world did he inhabit? What carefree hours did he spend playing about the city streets? He beckoned, and Tom felt the allure of those untroubled times of childhood, free of striving, free of responsibility.

He turned away and followed the others down the steps.

PART THREE

Revelations

28 Another World

Oh, but the descent was darkness – and anticipation of arrival was lost in the slow and dangerous progress through the tunnel. Each step was tested by a groping foot, and each steadied by a hand that was guided by the rough wall. And there was, alongside the darkness, silence, saving the soft padding sound of footfall on stone, for no one spoke for fear of confounding the senses. The smell was dampness, wet earth – the walls running in patches, the hand dragging through slime – and there seemed no end. Was the staircase slowly turning? It was impossible to be sure. Tom felt a numbness grip his mind He could hear Sonia's mother breathing, a slow rasping sound; Porlock had begun to mutter to himself . . .

And then there was a suggestion of light – not even so much as a glimmer at first, yet Tom found himself distinguishing the figures of his companions which seemed gradually to detach themselves from the clinging blackness.

Light after darkness is usually welcomed, but in this instance the sight of the staircase falling away steeply before him, with no obvious end, unnerved him. The gradual curve appeared now to have been illusory, for he was staring down a long straight shaft that cut diagonally through the rock of the earth's crust. Further down, the rock walls appeared to become glass, and it was through this glass that the light was flooding in. Tom knew that he must sit down before giddiness overcame him and sent him tumbling the remaining length of the staircase. The others seemed to understand and halted.

'Don't worry,' Porlock counselled him. 'It is always so the first time.'

They re-started, Tom now concentrating on the wall beside him. His eyes kept track of a rock-face growing smoother as they descended, until at last it took on the smoothness of glass, and instead of staring at a wall he found himself looking into seemingly endless space, at a vast domed ceiling supported by columns, between which were revealed further domes and columns, and then beyond, yet more, a huge honeycombed space, and below – the city!

Words . . . of what use are words? Words can only diminish what Tom experienced. Here was space after the confines of the tunnel, brightness after shadow; here was a tumble of buildings and pathways, styles heaped upon styles, long tiled roofs pierced by brick chimneys growing into white stone columns that sprouted balconies and walkways which, winding upwards, led to houses of glass than hung like lanterns from the cavern's ceiling. Brick walls became stone walls, became wooden walls, became glass walls; elegant façades grew into pleasing grotesqueries of contorted detail; picturesque cottages resolved themselves into sheer curtains of glass that plunged several storeys to become transparent pavilions; and, threading between these structures, there were streets, magical streets, lined with spherical lamps – the space on either side seeming to recede endlessly between columns – while below and below (was there a ground level?) these passageways skirted chasms that seemed to contain more windows, more walkways, sudden splashes of green vegetation, more roads, more chimneys, more bridges, more roofs . . .

Tom felt as a beetle must feel having crawled into the stonework of a Gothic cathedral, to emerge at the highest point of the transept arch: and, indeed, as the cathedral's ceiling would be bright with painted pattern, so too was this – gold stars faint against blue sky, clouds rolling past sunny skies, birds wheeling in formation, the skies of the upper world frozen in a luminous sheen of paint upon the roof of this subterranean world.

And then the streets themselves – warmth, the scents of summer flowers. So much he could sense already, but how? The people moving with purpose, calm, lacking the furtive shadow-creeping of the surface; a man cleaning a window, a slow regular comforting movement; another two talking on a corner, unaware of the world, happily engaged in their own private thoughts; the smiles, the greetings, the fresh complexions (why not paler in this underground world?) the delightful detail of the buildings that held the eye, preventing their enormous size from overwhelming and becoming oppressive; window boxes (could those really be plants? but they must be, for wasn't that an old lady, kind-faced, white-haired, poised with a watering can above the box, apparently lost in thought and smiling benignly at the street below?); walls with inlaid ceramic plaques and niches for sculpture, not the horrifying images of the surface city but images of grace and delicacy; everywhere variety, pleasure, ornate vents, bow windows, lamps glowing soft colours from shadowy corners – for one of the glories of this elfin place was the artificial light which created pools of colour and though never gloomy was nowhere either harsh or glaring, so that one seemed to float from soft green to pink light, or from cool blueness to apricot, while in the distance the lights twinkled deliciously as if one were moving through a gigantic jewel box.

Tom trembled with a pleasure he had never before known. If his life were to end at this moment, in these streets, it would have been fulfilled by the mere sight of such a place – though death would seem the crueller for snatching a life which lingered on the very threshold of delight.

Porlock halted before a door, plain save for a glass porthole at face height; and indeed, within a minute a face had appeared at the glass – a face which broke into a broad smile at the sight of the new visitors. The door was flung open and Porlock was engulfed in the arms of a huge man. Tom stared, disbelieving. The blacksmith had surely been killed, he had fallen so far . . . but who, then, was this? The smile broadened even more when he saw Tom.

'So you made it, little man! We both made it!'

He tousled Tom's hair and then clasped Porlock's shoulder once again.

'Thanks to this gentleman. Thanks to his compassion.'

Porlock shook him off, goodnaturedly but with a trace of embarrassment.

'Enough of this,' he protested, leading the way inside.

As Tom followed, he observed to his horror the misshapen bulk of the blacksmith's body, the painfully slow limping motion. The blacksmith, suddenly turning, read his mind and simply smiled.

'The main thing, little man,' he said, still rejoicing, 'is that we both made it!'

29 Evening Chorus

They sat in a delightfully cosy room, well fed and holding mugs of steaming punch. Since the conversation rarely touched upon things that concerned him, Tom found himself drifting into his own thoughts. There were so many things that he wanted to know, so many questions to ask, but he knew they would have to wait. For now the time belonged to old friends with news to exchange, and the lion's share of the conversation fell to the blacksmith and Porlock.

Beyond leaded windows he could hear the sounds of children playing and, with a shock, he realised how much of his own childhood had fallen away. He thought back to the boy who had first entered the surface city, and he seemed to be a different person. So much had happened in the outer circumstances of his life that the changes that had taken place within him had passed unnoticed.

As the evening wore on the light began to dim at the window. It would soon be dark, he mused – and the implication of that thought at once startled him back to attentiveness.

'But why is the light fading?' he asked. 'Why, down here?'

Sonia smiled across the room at him.

'Man needs sleep, and the darkness is for sleeping. It's almost time for the evening chorus.'

She went to the window and flung it wide. A few moments later, from the distance, a bell was heard and this became the signal for the people within the room to burst into song. At the window Sonia sang with a particularly strong and beautiful voice, and her voice and their voices became mingled with other voices as the whole city swelled with the singing of every citizen – one enormous crescendo of sweet sound that Tom found delightfully and unexpectedly familiar. It was – incredibly, it seemed to him – a song that his mother had sung (softly, bent over his bed) when as a young child he had been unable to sleep. He found his eyes filling with tears at the memory, and he began to sing the words that he knew so well. And as the singing progressed, so evening became night and the lights in the roof of the cavern diminished to stars and Tom joined Sonia at the window.

As the song ended and the voices faded away, a vast silence fell upon the city, which seemed more enchanted than ever.

'You know the song,' Sonia said, standing beside him in the darkness.

'Oh, so very well! It's a song of my home country!'

Now there was movement in the room. The blacksmith stopped in the door-way, wishing everyone a blessed good night, and Porlock rose too, pausing for a moment to smooth the creases from his finely tailored trousers. Having experienced the beauty of the city, Tom now understood Porlock's fastidiousness of dress, the carefully matched colouring in everything he wore.

'Sonia, don't keep the young man up too long. Show him to his room shortly, eh? Tomorrow is a busy day.'

Nodding, she closed the door behind him.

'That song,' she said. 'It's from your country, you say?'

'Yes.'

'How strange.'

'Why so?'

But she shook her head, as if unwilling to explain.

'We have sung it every evening for years past.'

And now Tom realised the nature of that ethereal singing which had tantalised him at various times while in the city above. It had been no figment of his overworked brain. He had been listening to the music of this beguiling place without ever knowing it.

30 The Doll

'At last you've arrived . . . the time is ripe for action . . . we've been waiting . . . '

Who was talking? Where did the voice come from? Tom rolled listlessly on the bed in the heat of the room.

'We've been waiting.'

'Why have you been waiting? What's expected of me? I came here to find my father – who are you?'

Tom sat up, open-eyed but only partially awake. He was alone in the darkened room, but still he could hear the voice: 'We've been waiting.' The walls whispered it; the air was full of it; it came from no person but still whispered loudly and insistently: 'We've been waiting.'

'What must I do?' he cried, this time aloud. But there was no answer and the voice seemed to die as he became more alert. Silence. He lay back on the bed; but sleep had deserted him. It was a dream, perhaps.

He walked to the window and, opening it, stepped out onto a small balcony. The stars glimmered high above him. He made out Orion with its studded belt; the Twins, Castor and Pollux; the scattered lights of the Great Bear; the lovely pale orange of Arcturus . . . and sensed, almost immediately, that they were adrift, inaccurately placed both in relation to one another and to the time of the year. Tom knew his night sky and how it looked as winter departed. Yet he was in no way disappointed by this dome of velvet with its glittering constellations. The city was at peace around him, bathing him in its tranquility. Nothing stirred. How he longed to be a part of it! But he felt – he could not say why – that this peace could not yet be his, that this was merely an interlude until . . .

What was it that was expected of him?

The balcony was a little way above the pavement. Tom climbed over and dropped softly to the path beneath. It led upwards between houses until the street ended with one of the dizzying chasms so characteristic of this strange place, and the path continued as a bridge whose low balustrades he kept well clear of. Beyond the chasm the pathway forked, one way leading narrowly down between glass-fronted buildings and the other climbing by means of a stairway to a wide square. Tom chose the stairway. Everywhere seemed deserted, although some windows were lit, and he sensed rather than observed the movements beyond the glass. The streets, lit at intervals with coloured lanterns, returned to Tom that feeling of total bliss he had experienced when he first arrived, and his restless sleep with its unanswered questions seemed never to have occurred.

It was a rhythmic chanting, only just heard, that led him to enter an archway which opened onto the square. Beyond was a courtyard where an old man knelt before a large yellow sphere that rested upon a low plinth. As he knelt he rocked slowly to and fro and chanted. His eyes remained fixed on the sphere and he either ignored Tom or was unaware of his presence. Tom, however, felt no sense of intrusion and stood and watched, first the white hair at the top of the man's head and then, as it reappeared from each deep bow, his face – a wise face, heavily lined and seemingly weather-beaten by decades of exposure to sun and wind.

The curious nature of this last fact escaped Tom at first and he continued to stare, almost hypnotised by the regular rhythm of the movement and chanting. The words he could not understand, but they seemed to him an ancient dialect of his own language. And then something curious did strike him: the old voice continued to chant its set phrases and at a certain point, and always at the same point, the voice clicked unnaturally.

'Excuse me.'

Tom decided to confirm a suspicion that was slowly forming in his mind. There was no answer. He knelt by the figure and rested his hand on the frail arm, immediately starting back – startled even by a discovery that he had expected to make. His hand had rested not upon warm flesh but upon a cold, hard surface that was clearly not human. The nodding, chanting figure was merely a doll, an automaton, whose mechanical vigil had been designed by earlier hands in earlier days.

It was uncanny. Tom was shaken. There was something eery about this lifelike puppet performing its mechanical rites beneath an artificial daylight and moonlight. How much more of the city was not as it seemed? How many of the figures that he had seen performing their comforting, routine jobs as he had walked through the streets, were but machines? The old lady watering the window box: had she paused in thought like that throughout centuries? The man cleaning the window? The people talking privately and unconcerned about the passers-by?

Tom left the courtyard, his feeling of euphoria replaced by a sickening uncertainty. He felt suddenly alone. He retraced his steps, crossing the bridge with scarcely a thought of the abyss beneath. Coloured orbs dappled the street in rich minglings of emerald, lemon, magenta, but he had no eye for them.

He was close to the house when he almost walked into an elderly lady carrying a lantern and emerging from a narrow opening between two buildings. She opened her eyes wide in surprise and then, lifting the light in order to see Tom's face clearly, she smiled a friendly greeting.

'You're about late, young man. Youth needs its sleep. You leave the night streets for old insomniacs like me. Blessings be with you! Goodnight!'

She was indeed real, and as Tom watched her shuffle away a new surge of confidence filled him. He climbed the balcony, entered his room, lay once more upon the bed, and this time fell into a deep, undisturbed sleep.

31 Prophecies

'Mirrors and machines,' Sonia laughed. 'Mirrors and machines.'

She led Tom through the city under the perfect copy of a glaring mid-morning sun. They passed between copses of trees whose delicate foliage cast a cool shadow on lush grass, while birds called among the branches.

'But what is reality? If, as you say, so much that we see is illusion – if distances and perspectives are deceptive – how do you know what is real?'

Sonia took him by the arm.

'It's *all* real, Tom. Why does it matter that it has been especially created? Isn't the beauty enough?'

Beyond the next buildings a river rippled through a far-off meadow and tumbled in a series of cascades over large rocks.

'It's very beautiful.'

They entered a square which was dominated by a large white circular building. Earlier, while they had been breakfasting, Porlock had appeared and asked with a peculiar insistence that Sonia bring Tom to the debating chamber. Now they entered the impressive carved stone entrance and mounted a flight of wide marbled stairs which curved to a first-floor balcony. Sonia pushed open a door and Tom found himself in a vast gallery which looked down upon the chamber itself.

The light was muted compared with the glare outside and he realised, as his eyes became accustomed to it, that it was tinged with green. On one wall, so large as to be seen from all part of the interior, was the painting of an eye, with a bright blue iris. He and Sonia were alone in the viewing gallery, but as he looked over the balustrade to the circular chamber below he saw that an assembly of several dozen people was already engaged in earnest discussion. Although there were men and women of all ages, there was a preponderance of elderly men, many of whom clutched large black books to their chests. One of these was speaking in a low voice – so low that Tom struggled to understand the words he spoke – while a few yards away the figure of Porlock stood impatiently, as if waiting the chance to intervene.

'The eye,' Tom whispered. 'What does it mean?'

'There is no single meaning. It stands for knowledge, for justice and truth.'

'It is also used by the people in the surface city who wish to overthrow the Red Blade,' he said. 'I was helped after I first met you because of the design on the buttons of the coat you gave me.'

Tom felt in his pocket for the metal disc the dwarf had given him.

'Look.'

'Yes, it's identical. The symbol of the all-seeing eye is ancient. It existed before this place was brought into being.'

'Members of the Blade bow to their scarlet dagger.'

'It's different with the eye,' Sonia said. 'The eye sees within. There is no need to bow before it.'

Down below Porlock had begun to speak. Tom peered over the balustrade to watch him. He had removed his gold-framed spectacles and held them in one hand as he answered the old man with the book.

'Why does he want me here?' Tom asked.

'I don't know. He wouldn't say.'

To Tom's surprise, Porlock spoke of the very people he himself had mentioned only moments before.

'There are people in the city above us,' he declaimed in a rather grand fashion, 'who need, who crave, our sustenance and support.'

'And why do they need it, pray?'

'You know as well as I. The Red Blade grows more powerful by the day. Leaders of these brave people are at this moment being tortured and killed in the infamous Citadel.'

'But is it a concern of ours?'

Several of the old men fussed at their books. It was obvious that Porlock faced a united opposition. A man with a long grey beard pushed himself to his feet, an outraged look in his eye.

'The ancient writings tell us that there are two worlds. The two worlds shall remain asunder.'

There were loud noises of agreement and a clamour of voices quoting lines from the large black books. Sonia shook her head sadly.

'The debate has been continuing in one form or another for weeks,' she said. 'Porlock has support, but there are many of the ancients who rely on the old texts and will not move.'

'Is Porlock powerful?'

'He has influence. Only in recent years have watchers been allowed in the surface city, and that was his doing.'

'Watchers?'

'Those of us – mother and I, Porlock himself, a few others – who have been trusted to live in the city and observe what passes there. But we may only watch. It is forbidden to intervene.'

'The rule here sounds rather strict.'

She smiled.

'How should a place like this exist without rules for the good of us all? The people here are no less human than those in the city above – as you may hear!' (The voices rose once more in a furious babble.) 'But we live by an inherited wisdom.'

'Bound up in those black books?

Now Sonia laughed.

'They are not the law. The law can be made and unmade. But many of the old ones treat them as the exact truth.'

New voices had joined the debate, urging various conflicting courses of action. It was some time before Porlock spoke again, and then he changed the direction of his argument.

'If my learned colleagues are satisfied that we have no duty to those who suffer in the city, let them consider our own survival. For that, my friends, is now at stake.'

This brought about a frightened commotion.

'Nonsense!'

'On what evidence?'

'Explain yourself!'

Porlock calmly wiped the glass of his spectacles before continuing.

'I have reported to this assembly more than once that the Red Blade grows more cunning as well as more powerful. It has a dozen agents in every sector. We have, within the past few days, had to close the way to the house by the east gate.'

Now a heavy silence fell upon the company. Porlock turned his gaze slowly round the hall.

'The way had been discovered. We closed it with minutes to spare. Minutes, my friends. Two of our number were almost lost because of it. The way can never be re-opened.'

'Who betrayed us?'

Porlock turned to his questioner.

'If we had a betrayer, my friend, we should be thankful. There would be a solution, would there not? But the matter is not so straightforward. The Blade has investigators everywhere. As they gain in strength so will they by chance – by pure chance, I say – so will they discover our secrets. This is why we cannot, we must not, ignore the horrors of the city above us.'

This time Porlock's words had more obvious effect. There was no eagerness to shout him down: the old men sat mute, shaking their heads enigmatically. A woman of about thirty stood up and began to question him briskly.

'What exactly are you proposing?'

'That we make contact with the forces for good and offer them our support.'

'When we number but a few hundred and have no weapons?'

'Yes.'

'And what good, what possible good, will that do either them or us?'

Porlock folded his arms.

'My friends, there is no point in suggesting that we have physical strength. What we possess is moral strength. The very knowledge of our existence and our support will invigorate those who stand against the Red Blade.'

Now the debate became more complicated. Some opposed the use of force in principle: the black books were consulted again. Others were of the opinion that moral strength would be of little avail in the violent city above. Speaker after speaker rose to make a contribution.

'A few hundred,' Tom repeated. 'Is that all there are of you?'

'And no weapons. We live in peace.'

He sat rigid, astounded. He had expected something different. Only half-listening to the debate, he found despair overcoming him. If the community was so small, why had he not yet been reunited with his father? If his father was not here, what chance had he now of finding him?

Porlock, having restoked the fires of the debate, sat back stroking a hand over his grizzled hair. He cast a quick glance up at the gallery and nodded towards Tom before turning away.

'Does he bring many people to the underground city?' Tom asked.

'Of course not. It's a rare honour. There are so many who would wish to come – who would give everything they have.'

'The blacksmith was brought here.'

'He was terribly injured. Porlock knew him to be a good and trustworthy man.'

They sat in silence for a while, their eyes turned to the gathering below. It was clear that Porlock's second intervention had swayed many people to his side, but there was still a seemingly immovable opposition by the old men. They had a text for every argument, always a story from times gone by to parallel anything that was happening today. Eventually Porlock rose to his feet once more.

'We have listened,' he said gravely, 'to detailed recitations from the ancient texts. Although they do not have the force of law, they demand great respect from us all, and it is only because others among us are more learned in this respect that I have not hitherto referred to them myself . . . '

He paused, and there was a silence during which, it seemed, his audience attempted to gauge whether he perhaps spoke with irony. Sonia, for her part, looked on with an expression of bewilderment.

'My distinguished friends will know well those writings which foretell the rise of the Red Blade. We are all aware, are we not, that this repulsive sect was initiated many years ago by a stranger to the city – "Like a tick entering the wool of the sheep" does it not read? "And like a tick he will drink the blood of the city." Aren't we all aware of those prophetic lines?'

There were nods of the head all round the chamber. Sonia, Tom noticed, seemed no less bewildered than before. Porlock's voice grew ever more ponderous as if to match the sanctity of the books from which he quoted.

'And do I need to remind you, my friends, of the passage which follows – another passage of prophecy? This one is, until now, unfulfilled. Until now . . . '

He again paused. One or two of the old men began to move their lips, soundlessly rehearsing the lines.

'"But another will follow seeking a father . . ."'

At this point several members of the assembly began to utter the words, softly, so that Porlock led a chorus. Tom clutched the balustrade so that his fingers ached.

> *Secretly he will enter the city –*
> *like a steel comb he will enter the sheep's wool*
> *rake out the clinging vermin . . .*

Porlock spoke challengingly.

'Do we not believe in prophecy? That each prophecy will in time be fulfilled?'

The man with the long grey beard stood slowly to face him.

'We do believe so, friend Porlock. But you must explain yourself.'

Porlock swung round and raised his arm to the gallery.

'The time is nigh. One has followed, seeking a father.'

Amid the commotion which followed Tom realised that he was being beckoned to descend to the chamber. Overwhelmed by what he had heard, he was scarcely aware of his progress down the wide marble stairs and into the auditorium. Faces swam at him in the greenish light, and he would surely have fainted away had not Porlock placed an arm around his shoulders and led him gently to the centre of the throng.

'One has followed,' Porlock repeated. 'I want you, Tom, to answer all the questions that I and these people ask you. Speak openly, for they are friends.'

Tom nodded, unsure whether words would come.

'You have come seeking your father. Tell these good people how you came here, and from where.'

He began, falteringly, with a description of his journey. He told of the cold, lonely nights, the days of wandering without food, his clothes torn and soiled. He explained why he had come, how life had been in his home villages, what he had expected of the city – and what he had found.

They listened, curious, even moved. When he had finished, though, he was aware of an air of puzzlement in the chamber. There were whisperings and shakings of heads.

'A fascinating story, friend Porlock,' one of the assembly commented at length. 'But why the fulfilment of prophecy?'

'Are you deaf that you cannot hear?' Porlock demanded. 'Or blind that you cannot see? You have heard the story. You have heard this young man tell you where he comes from.'

The bafflement of his audience had in no way diminished, but it seemed that Porlock relied on this perplexity for the effectiveness of his next move. For he now reached into a pocket and withdrew an object which Tom at once recognised.

'Is this, Tom, the picture of your father which you carried with you to the city?'

'Yes.'

'And is it not, my friends, a remarkable picture?'

He held it up and turned it slowly so that everyone should see it. There were sharp cries of surprise, howls even, an incredible cacophony of exclamations, a furious babble of excited voices. Tom felt Porlock's reassuring arm around his shoulders once more as the noise seemed to go on and on for ever. The picture was passed from hand to hand, each recipient grasping it eagerly and poring over it with attention to every detail.

Then they began to ask him questions. What kind of man was his father? What could he remember of his early years? Why had he decided to follow his father to the city? He answered as best he could, repeating some of his story, often having to shake his head and admit that he did not know. Eventually – the interrogation having abated somewhat but the interest of the assembly remaining as keen as ever – Porlock had a whispered conversation with a group of the old men and led him towards the door.

'Our thanks to you, Tom, for your clear and honest answers. The remainder of our debate must be in private.'

Sonia had come down to escort him to an antechamber. They dare not look one another in the eye for the awesomeness of what they had heard. He followed her into an iridescent cavern, where a fountain played into a shimmering pool lit from below and the further recesses seemed hung with gleaming ice, fold on fold of stalagtites, despite the bright shafts of sunlight which illuminated the place from some hidden grille. Sonia sat on a low bench by the fountain, her fingers trailing in the water.

He could not talk about what had happened. Indeed, he could scarcely think clearly about it. Was he therefore the fulfilment of a prophecy? He glanced towards Sonia and her eyes, which had been turned on him, quickly looked away. They were suddenly shy of one another, awkward.

'The light in the chamber,' he said at last, his voice echoing. 'It was green – as in that room I stumbled into. Why is that?'

'All our meetings are held under green light. It's the sacred colour.'

They fell into silence once more. He, too, sat by the fountain. The water was clear and very cold. He shook his fingers and beads of water sprang sparkling through the air.

'Victory!'

It was Porlock, who came striding towards them and unashamedly embraced them each in turn.

'Fine work, Tom. We've won the day. Now we've work to do.'

He turned to Sonia.

'Fresh clothes and the necessary papers for our young gentleman, if you please. We leave within the hour!'

32 Disillusion

But Tom's heady sense of destiny was not to last.

After swift preparation he had taken his leave of Sonia (whose tearfulness reminded him of their first farewell at the house with the white room) and followed Porlock through streets he had not travelled before. The stairway was a different one – wider, and with two cables of thick rope stretching up into the obliterating darkness. At intervals were strung large wicker baskets which must move up and down on a pulley system, but the lids were on and he could not see what they contained.

As they began to climb, Porlock looked over his shoulder and gave a short laugh.

'I'm sorry about all that prophesying nonsense this morning,' he said. 'The fact is, those old fogeys won't listen to reason. You have to pander to their fanciful notions. Nothing like a few of the ancient texts to fire their imaginations!'

Tom, taken aback, merely kept on climbing.

'You heard me appeal to their humanity: no concern whatsoever for the people in the city above! So I explained the dangers we ourselves face: they chose not to believe in them. Nothing for it but to make up fairy tales.'

'You mean,' Tom asked wildly, 'that you don't believe me?'

'Believe you? Of course I do! You're an honest fellow, Tom. I knew you'd not let me down.'

'But the picture . . .'

'Your father, that I don't doubt. The question is – who is he?'

'I don't understand.'

'The moment I discovered that picture I saw the resemblance to a certain man. I need say no more, I think – a mere resemblance. And your story fits neatly. Coincidences. But I know these old men with their thick black books.

They can't resist the suggestion of a mystery, the hint of prophecy. They swallowed the bait!'

Tom halted abruptly, his surprise turning to anger.

'You used me!' he accused. 'You've been dishonest with me!'

'I promised you nothing.'

'You led me to believe that I would find my father. You've deceived me. He isn't here.'

'I don't know where he is.'

Tom sat down heavily, his legs weak, a sick feeling in his stomach. He covered his head in his arms and wished he could cry, but he felt only a burning ache where the tears should be.

'For shame!' Porlock chided. 'All's not lost.'

But Tom would not hear, and the words floated away down the steep steps. Porlock made as if to proceed upwards, perhaps calculating that this would spur Tom into action, then came down again. Eventually he shook Tom's shoulder and spoke loudly and sternly.'

'My duty is to the many good people in this city and the city above. Am I to prefer their deaths to the disappointment of a boy who has undertaken an impossible mission? Find a lost father in a place so vast! Should I not seize the chance to save so many?'

Tom listened without answering. He remembered his own soul-searching at the House of the Star, when he had asked himself what actions were permissible to reach a desired end. Again there came the dreadful vision of the boat and Marcus drowning, and he knew that it was for the best and yet that he could not accept it, that he had killed a man.

'Stay here,' Porlock continued, 'and you're no better than the old men, with their antiquated texts and their fine words and their blindness to the perils of others. Stay here and you'll be forever stuck fast in your own selfishness.'

'The people here won't betray me as you have done.'

'Betray!'

'Sonia would not lie to me.'

Porlock sat on the step and his voice grew softer.

'Yes, I could have told you that your quest was hopeless. What good would that have done you? Didn't you want to reach the underground city? You talk of betrayal and lies. These are mere words. Life isn't so simple that a man can never tell a lie in the cause of justice.'

Tom, although he felt too bitter to reply, yet recognised the truth in these words. He opened his eyes and looked back down the tunnel. It would not take long to retrace his steps. Porlock rose to his feet.

'Without you,' he said, 'I am likely to fail. Why should the people in the surface city trust me? But you know them. You can vouch for me, for the underground city.'

His voice grew severe again.

'Submit to your feelings of anger and frustration if you will. By all means take your revenge on me. But recognise, Tom, that the decision is yours.'

He began to climb the steps, but slowly, as if he expected Tom to join him. And, indeed, without making any conscious decision to do so, Tom found himself on his feet and following. Their progress was steady, necessitating frequent rests during which they stood lightly panting, leaning against the damp wall. They had gone far beyond the light before Porlock spoke again.

'Don't think too badly of me,' he said. 'If this business goes well I shall help you all I can.'

How dense the blackness was! He dare not look behind, yet it was unnerving to stare ahead into the void. Occasionally he strayed too close to the wall and his shoulder brushed one of the baskets. At these moments the slight creak of the wickerwork seemed to flood his senses, which were completely starved of other stimulation.

'There are only three ways to the city,' Porlock revealed during one of their rests. 'The one by the east gate is closed, as you know – probably for ever. The route by which I took you underground has also been sealed off. I heard as we set out that the House of the Star was badly damaged by the fire we witnessed. This way is therefore the only one that remains open for us.'

It seemed that they would climb for ever. Tom could not believe that the journey down had been so long. His legs ached and he was stung by sweat.

'The lights!'

It was a few seconds before he realised that he was not imagining the flickers of illumination some way ahead. As they drew closer he found that they were set into the wall, waving a shaky light over the damp rock. He could make out the strands of rope, too, which here seemed to plunge downwards, away out of sight again. Or perhaps it was that they themselves were climbing more steeply and in another direction.

'The door,' Porlock panted. 'Somewhere here.'

They stood together, fumbling desperately as if the door might no longer be there, leaving them marooned in darkness.

'Yes, here!'

Porlock led him through. They emerged in a narrow staircase, lit by a high window. It was immediately familiar. Although at first he could not think where he was, he knew that he had been here before.

33 Handshake

A few steps and they were engulfed by swirling steam. They coughed and fought for breath. The kitchen of the all-night cafe! They stepped inside and there was Lucy, beaming broadly at Porlock and gathering Tom within one vast and motherly arm.

'Look at this! Bill, you come here! Visitors!'

Bill appeared, holding out his hand to Porlock, whom he treated with his customary respect, and nodding happily at Tom.

'Don't tell me, young Tom – you've come from down there!'

'That he has,' Porlock said severely, 'but it's better that the whole world doesn't know it.'

'Ah! I'm sorry. I got carried away. No one else here just now.'

They went into a back room, Tom marvelling that his old friends should know about the underground city.

'You've been down there?' he asked Bill in a whisper, afraid of Porlock's sharp tongue.

'One or twice, yes. But we live up here. We're needed.'

'Needed?'

'For the food, you see. You noticed those baskets on your way up? Nobody suspects a cafe for buying large quantities of food. We send most of it down.'

Porlock fluttered his hand in irritation.

'We've urgent business to attend to. We need to make contact with one of those who use the rooftops.'

'Do I know him?'

'He's been here before,' Tom said. 'A dwarf.'

Bill clapped him on the shoulder.

'You're in luck,' he said. 'He's often here asking for you. He sits in the corner, shrinking into the shadows.'

'Hunted,' Porlock said.

'You think so? Poor soul!'

'What does he say?' asked Tom.

'Nothing, save to ask if you've been seen. I just shake the head. Few words as possible, that's my motto. He sometimes takes a small meal but never finishes it.'

Porlock seemed satisfied.

'As soon as he arrives,' he said, 'bring him in here.'

The hours would have dragged had Tom not busied himself in the kitchen with Bill and Lucy. He left Porlock contentedly reading in the back room and spent his time carrying saucepans, adding salt and pepper to concoctions bubbling on the huge ranges, and helping to wash and dry a prodigious collection of utensils which seemed to be in constant use. It was strange to think that the food they were preparing would be sent down the long tunnel to be consumed by Sonia and the blacksmith and the other people he knew.

It was mid-evening when Bill waved Tom into the back room, following moments later with the dwarf in tow. Tom was shocked by his wretched condition. Not only did his clothes seem ragged and dirty, but he had the look of a fugitive, ill-fed and desperate. He eyed Porlock in a manner which suggested at once familiarity and wariness, and addressed Tom in a broken voice.

'I want words,' he said. 'Alone.'

'You can talk in front of Porlock,' Tom replied. 'He's a friend.'

'Alone, I say!'

Porlock complied immediately.

'Your caution is commendable,' he said, rising.

The dwarf followed towards the door, as if to ensure that Porlock would leave, swinging round urgently once it had closed.

'I'm in terrible trouble,' he blurted out. 'I can't evade them much longer. They're closing in.'

'I know,' said Tom. 'There's a man I call the bellows-pumper because of the circumstances in which I first met him. He is a man without the use of his legs.'

'That's the man! That's the man, Tom!'

'You know him?'

'Ha! You ask me that? That's a good question!'

Tom was accustomed to a strangeness in the dwarf's manner, but he had never before seen him in this wild, manic mood.

'Would you believe that he was a friend once? Can you see him as a friend to any man? But yes, he was. A friend!'

He paced up and down, with abrupt changes of direction.

'Even an enemy of the Red Blade, he was. Oh yes! Not that he ever hated the Blade as I did. Took against it more from a spirit of adventure, I'd say. He had his legs then, you see. A bold young man he was!'

'And what happened?'

The dwarf seemed reluctant to give a direct answer to this question. He continued his energetic parading around the room until, coming close to Tom, he stopped suddenly and thrust his face forward.

'He fell. Down and down. Smack!'

'An accident?'

'Of course, an accident. It was far from here – another part of the city. We were on the rooftops, devising a new route. And . . . we got into difficulties. No way back. We were on a ledge, a narrow ledge. There was a sheer drop . . . '

His eyes still stared towards Tom but they looked right through him. The dwarf was on the ledge gain, high above the city. Tom saw beads of sweat break out on his forehead and his hands clenching and unclenching.

'He fell?'

'I couldn't turn. He began to slip – called out to me. "I'm going," he said. "I'm going." I couldn't reach out. I had to hold on. He went over the edge and was gone. I heard it.'

There was a silence, during which the dwarf seemed to return by stages to the present.

'You've seen what happened. He lived, but his legs were gone. He blamed me for it – all of us. He joined the Blade and has pursued us ever since. Now he's in these parts and our people are being persecuted. Many are dead. Many are tortured.

'What have you learned that can help us?'

The question was put more as an accusation than as a plea. The eyes interrogated him.

'I've been to the underground city,' Tom said simply.

The dwarf laughed bitterly.

'So you choose to mock! Good may it do you! I hope you enjoy our suffering!'

'I've been there, I tell you. With Porlock. He is from the underground city. It exists. I've found it.'

Slowly it became apparent to the dwarf that Tom was in earnest. The effect was dramatic. His legs buckled beneath him and he collapsed full length on the floor. His eyes were not closed, but he seemed unable to move a muscle as Tom stooped over him and began to lift him up. Perhaps Porlock had been listening beyond the door, for at this moment he entered the room and helped Tom carry his burden to a chair.

'It's a wonderful place,' said Tom, seeing from the dwarf's expression that he could understand, although the shock had left him temporarily paralysed. 'There is colour and distance and beauty.'

The words tumbled from his lips, unordered but rich with praise for the new world he had found. He spoke of the sights he had seen, the people he had met. The dwarf listened for some minutes, a smile gradually playing along his lips.

'And there is water,' Tom said, 'cascading from nowhere into limpid pools, and there are birds up in the trees with songs and trills that you would never believe . . '

The dwarf sat up in the chair, his eyes brimming with tears.

'Oh, wonders!' he whispered hoarsely.

Porlock, as brisk as ever, drew up his own chair and, ignoring the dwarf's display of emotion, began to explain his mission.

'We have often met without knowing one another. Now we are united in a common aim – the overthrow of the Red Blade. I know you to be one of those who use the rooftops. Tom will vouch for me as a representative of those who live underground. Time, we both know, is short.'

The dwarf nodded.

'The people underground,' Porlock added, 'are ready to support you. I have been charged with offering that support.'

The dwarf continued to nod rhythmically, although for a while he said nothing. He stood up and began to pace the room again, at first uncertainly, then with the same quick movements as before.

'We can be ready within days,' he said in a low voice, half to himself. 'In some sectors the units are fully prepared. Elsewhere there's work to be done. A few have no spirit for it – though that may change.

'The messengers could be despatched immediately. That means the whole city could be alerted within hours. Speed is vital.'

Porlock interrupted.

'Your organisation,' he asked. 'Has it been infiltrated by agents of the Blade?'

'No. How can we tell? Certainly we have lost many valuable leaders – the eastern commander . . . Too many of our number are faint-hearted, but we are strong enough to strike them, with your help.'

He took to muttering to himself, planning the exercise that would be undertaken. He counted on his fingers, waved his arms, nodded his head vigorously, so that Tom was unable to prevent himself smiling at the performance. Finally he turned towards Porlock.

'How many men do you have under arms?' he asked.

'Under arms, none.'

'None! You mean . . . *none*?'

'We are not a warlike people.'

'Not warlike, is it!'

The dwarf began to shake with a sudden fury.

'You presume to offer your help when you have no fighting men?' he cried savagely. 'You lead me to believe you are ready to stand with us shoulder to shoulder – and then tell me that you are "not a warlike people"! What kind of fool's paradise do you inhabit?'

Porlock, stern of expression, made no reply.

'When men have been dying, persecuted by the Blade! They cry out, stretch out their hands for help – and are offered a bland smile. From a people who are "not warlike". That, my friend, is the kind of support we can do without!'

He looked up at Porlock, a bitter sneer on his lips.

'Or do you think we should preach truth and beauty to the Blade so that they throw down their weapons and submit? We are perhaps misguided in opposing force with force. We've misjudged the enemy. We've imagined the cruelties, the murders!'

Porlock allowed the thunder to pass, though the dark clouds on the dwarf's face certainly showed no sign of dispersing.

'I'm sorry,' he said. 'That kind of help we cannot give. What we do offer is genuine, however.'

'Genuine – but useless.'

'You must decide that for yourself.'

They were treated once more to a display of gesturing and mumbling as the dwarf argued the possibilities to himself. He had, for the moment, forgotten them. He paused, arm raised, lips silently moving, then swung round and marched along the length of the room, an urgent humming sound rising in his throat. He leant against the wall, shaking his head from side to side; ground a fist into the palm of the other hand; played his tongue reflectively over his lips.

'There is one way.'

'What's that?' Porlock asked.

'It's a plan we have considered. It requires only a few men at the outset – highly trained men, but only a few. To assault the Citadel.'

'That's impossible!'

'To enter the Citadel. You know that the Supreme Ruler lives on the top floor and is never seen? The top floor is shuttered. Nobody knows how well it is guarded, exactly where the Ruler is to be found. We have discussed the possibility of crossing to the roof of the Citadel and attempting to seize him. With the Blade demoralised, we would attack in force.

'I believe we could succeed, but it's obviously a perilous task and our leaders have been reluctant to attempt it.'

'What would make them change their minds?'

The dwarf screwed up his eyes and tilted his head to one side.

'The belief, perhaps, that the underground city exists and will give support. Especially if the nature of that support is not explained to them. Let's say they imagine a vast army stands by in readiness . . . You understand me? A little deception is excusable, don't you think?'

'In view of the urgency of the matter.'

'Indeed. The main thing is to act – and act soon.'

To Tom's amazement Porlock and the dwarf extended their hands and shook them, like comrades. He thought of Porlock's speech in the debating chamber, persuading the gathering by means that were less than honest, and he compared this with the dwarf's present intention of deceiving his own leaders. Both would argue that they were justified by the turn of events. Neither, it was clear, felt anything but satisfaction in their agreed course of action. This was apparent in the conspiratorial smiles with which they made their farewells.

34 Into the Citadel

The wind gusted across the flat expanse of roof so that the three of them – Tom, Porlock, the dwarf – found themselves huddling together for protection. Close by, a team of experienced climbers prepared for the assault. They wore black clothing for camouflage in the darkness, and had the paraphernalia of their trade slung about them: ropes, grappling hooks, knives. Across a wide and dizzy gulf, its roof slightly lower than the one on which they stood, lay the forbidding grey pile of the Citadel. The snow had melted, save in small pockets which never saw the sun by day, but there had been a light rain which made the surface glisten and this, combined with the swirling wind, promised to make a footing treacherous.

'See the top floor of the Citadel,' called the dwarf, cupping his hands around his mouth. 'It's always in darkness, with the shutters closed. It's lower down that the guards patrol.'

As if in response to this remark (though he had in fact been engaged in conversation with his colleagues) the leader of the group suddenly motioned everyone well back from the edge of the roof. He dropped to the ground and inched forward on his stomach to peer across the divide. The dwarf put his mouth to Tom's ear.

'There are guards on each floor,' he explained. 'They come and go at regular intervals. The crossing must be done within the space of a few minutes or we shall be seen.'

The leader stood and beckoned his team forward again. They worked speedily, apparently without fear of their precarious position. One sat with his feet out over the edge while he knotted rope, for all the world as though he were a mere foot or two from the ground. Tom had noticed that one of the men carried a crossbow: this was now taken to the edge and an arrow tied to a length of rope. It shot across the chasm and stuck fast. Two men now grasped the rope and hauled on it, testing it for strength.

'Down!'

A sentry had evidently appeared on another floor. Each man flattened himself on the roof, motionless, until a signal brought him back to his post. There followed a heated discussion, raised voices occasionally carried on the wind, but undecipherable. The leader detached himself from the group and approached the watching trio.

'It's the devil to get a decent hold. We've done the best we can, but it's uncertain. We need a light weight to go first.'

'Me!' exclaimed the dwarf in terror. 'You mean me? I can't! Not near the edge!'

'You only have to hold on,' the leader said carelessly. 'If the rope comes away at the far side you hang on and we'll haul you up. It's time we're up against. If one of us goes and it comes away we'll have to start over again.'

But the dwarf backed away, shaking.

'Can't! Not possible!'

Tom remembered that the dwarf had spoken before of a terrifying experience on the rooftops. He remembered, too, his own escape when the rope had snapped on the icy bridge between the House of the Star and the eastern sector. Yet he found himself stepping forward.

'I'll go. Tell me what I have to do.'

The leader nodded approvingly.

'Well, you're not so very small, my lad, but lighter than any of us, to be sure. Quickly, now.'

They stood around him, anxious to be at their task. He was shown how to grasp the rope; how to pass hand over hand; told what he must do when he reached the other side; how to react should the rope come away. There was no sentiment among these men – merely a sharp tap on the shoulder to tell him it was time to go.

He launched himself into space, feeling for a moment gloriously free as he swung forward and began to carry himself across. The awfulness of it struck him seconds later. A dash of wind rocked him sideways and the rope shook violently, vibrating under his fingers. He clung on, his shoulders already aching from the effort. He kept his head up, his eyes on the few starts that glinted among the clouds. Hand over hand he advanced, close to panic but knowing he was watched from the roof behind. Knowing, too, that if he failed the mission itself might come to nothing. The Citadel grew closer, but very slowly. His arms burned with the effort; he could not feel his hands. What if his numbed fingers lost their grip? What if the wind tore them from the rope?

He was near enough to the building to make out the small scarlet dagger on each of the shutters masking the windows on the topmost floor. No light escaped from between the slates. He wondered whether hidden eyes were watching his jerky progress across the gulf, hidden sentries waiting to seize him. Further down, light burned behind large windows, and anyone looking up could not fail to see him. He came close to the arrow which, buried in woodwork, was his only support. Was it possible that this alone kept him aloft, prevented him from plunging down and down to the distant street? It seemed so fragile: it shook in the wind. The leader of the assault party had been so matter-of-fact about the crossing, but if the arrow should shake free he would be swung down into the side of the building behind him, battered against the brickwork before plummeting to the ground.

The wind shook him and spun him round as he reached out a hand for the roof. He needed to pull himself up, away from the rope, but he froze between the two – propped awkwardly against the building but not daring to let go of the lifeline. The wind slapped him again, tugging his arm out into the void. His shoulder began to slip from the wall. He heard himself moan with the effort as he threw both hands towards a small projection and began to haul himself upwards.

Once safe on the roof he could not believe that he had come so far. The rope stretched away like a slender thread, and on the far roof the men who watched him seemed small, remote. He quickly took the end of the rope as he had been instructed, untied it and fastened it to a strong support. It was heavy in his fingers and wet from the drizzle which had started up again. Knotting it was difficult. When he looked up they had all gone: he could see no one. He stood alone on the roof, underneath him the very headquarters of the infamous organisation he had grown to fear and loathe. Suppose he were left here, stranded . . .

But they must have been avoiding another sentry, for he saw that now the first man had started forward, a coil of rope unwinding over one shoulder. He picked his way across the gap at incredible speed, body and limbs in perfect harmony. As he put a foot on the roof he gave the slightest of nods to Tom by way of acknowledgement, checked the knot he had made and fastened his own rope. The next man, too, brought a rope with him, so that the rest of the party – after another brief disappearance – swayed across on a makeshift bridge. The last to arrive was Porlock.

'Good man!' he said, shaking Tom by the hand.

'But where's the dwarf?'

'He couldn't. His nerve has gone. He'll wait for us.'

A rope-ladder was slung over the edge. The team went to work, each man carrying out his duties at great speed and in complete silence. One by one they disappeared from view. Finally a head and shoulders re-emerged and the waiting pair were gestured to follow.

The way in was through a pair of shutters which had been forced. The wood was soft and rotten, and as Tom brushed it with his shoulder one section broke off and fell away into the darkness. He saw it turning and turning, hitting the wall and spinning down and down until it was lost from view. A window had been broken – the rainy squalls must have disguised the sound – and he climbed through it.

A long corridor lay in heavy darkness. The assault party had clearly encountered not a soul during their entry. Along one side were the shuttered windows. On the other there seemed to be doors at regular intervals, and two of the group approached the first of these, while another pair took up positions close by. There was only a faint light from the broken window but it was enough to run along the blade of a long knife. Porlock motioned to Tom to keep well back and, needlessly, put a finger to his lips.

The door, surprisingly, was not locked. The men, on a signal, hurled themselves inside. It seemed but a second for the whole group to be in the room – and little more before they all came out. One of them, who Tom now saw carried a small light, shook his head wonderingly and they moved on down the corridor. Tom and Porlock, bringing up the rear, paused in the doorway. As their eyes adjusted to the gloom they were able to make out, dimly, rows of glass cases with specimens of some kind mounted in them – insects, perhaps, or spiders. There was an unpleasant smell of neglect and decay. Porlock drew Tom away.

The men in black regrouped around the second door. Their technique was identical, and again they hurried out and continued down the corridor. This room was completely empty. The third appeared to be some kind of shrine with a huge scarlet dagger emblem on the wall, glowing faintly in the darkness, but a shrine that had long since fallen into disuse. It was eery, unsettling, almost preposterous. They had expected guards, lights burning long into the night, perhaps, in some intelligence centre: instead they found silence, darkness, emptiness.

Every door opened easily, to reveal no sign of human habitation, yet still the group advanced stealthily, prepared at any moment to be surprised. They came at last to a door which clearly led to the floor below, but which had been efficiently sealed. There was no way of passing through it without arousing every sentry in the building.

Then how . . ? Tom saw the question on every man's face. How did the ruler of the Blade communicate with his underlings? Or was their information, perhaps, at fault? Did the ruler not inhabit the top floor, as everyone believed, but operate from elsewhere in the building?

There was one last door, at the very end of the corridor. The knives were once more held in readiness. Two men put their shoulders to the woodwork. Tom watched as they turned the handle and stepped swiftly inside. This time they did not immediately come out again. Tom and Porlock heard low exclamations.

They crept forward and peered inside. Darkness. A glass chandelier hung heavy from the ceiling. The floor was thickly carpeted. There were bookcases around the walls and, before a large shutterless window, a massive desk littered with objects it was impossible to distinguish. Tom started back. The moon, passing from behind a cloud, shed a fleeting illumination over the interior to reveal that the room had an occupant presiding over chandelier, bookcases and the cluttered desk. He sat in a leather chair under the window, grinning and gaping – a brittle human skeleton.

35 Life in Death

The hardened men who minutes before had risked their lives with scarcely a thought now shrank back, stricken expressions on their faces. Only Porlock retained his composure, taking the flickering light from the man who carried it and playing it on the bones, which gleamed a sickly white. Tom, notwithstanding the horror in the chair – which seemed to stare at him from its ghastly hollow sockets – edged close to his companion. The objects on the desk were now seen to consist largely of papers, and they stopped to read them.

Dust covered everything; time had starched the paper; sunlight had faded the writing. A spidery scrawl was now visible as a kind of faint echo of the original, so that they had to dwell on each cluster of signs to decipher the meaning. The script was in the fashion of an earlier time and the language, too, had an antiquated ring.

> He who discovers this has discovered the secret of the Red Blade.
> But he has discovered it too late.

Porlock lifted the sheet and the corner crumbled in his fingers.

> For here is a paradox. I am the Blade and I am no more. Yet the Blade
> lives for ever. Gaze on me and you look upon life in death.

Tom declined to obey the instruction and turn. He drew closer to Porlock and was not ashamed of his fear. Porlock himself seemed unsettled. The members of the assault party were shuffling out of the door, regrouping in the corridor outside.

Power is with a ghost, because the living wish it so.

These strange words completed the first page. Porlock, with great care, slid it gently to one side, but it instantly cracked in several places and the edges began to flake. The second sheet, not bleached by the sun, was rather more easy to scan.

I, a stranger, found a people needing strength. I offered them strength. They seized it. They worshipped the sign of the Red Blade.

Men are weak. They crave control. The Blade controls. The Blade will always control. I have ensured that it shall be so.

Gaze on me and you look upon life in death.

Porlock, moving aside this second sheet and blowing away the particles that broke from it, gave Tom a questioning glance as if to ask whether he wished to leave. He shook his head vigorously and bent it once more over the desk. The writing on the third sheet was more closely packed.

The chain of command is hidden from every eye. No member of the Blade knows the man whom he obeys. I have devised it so.

Each man communicates in code. The codes are elaborate and there is none but understands a mere fraction of them. Let a man ask advice; let him seek authorisation; let him give a command. He will not know who hears. He will not know who answers. He only knows that the Blade has spoken, the Blade has acted.

For each message is taken by one man and passed to a third, according to the code. The code commands. And none knows who rules him and whom he rules.

So it is, and ever shall be, that all men – even to the most powerful – pass orders one to the other and believe that they obey the Supreme Ruler. And they do obey the Supreme Ruler. He sits in this chair. He is beyond human hurt and his work cannot be undone.

I am the Blade. Gaze upon me and you look upon life in death.

Porlock drew the sheet aside impatiently.
'Madness,' he whispered. 'Surely this is madness!'
At this moment the light gave out. Only the moon, gliding among the clouds, offered a pale illumination within the room. Porlock took the next page in trembling hands and carried it to the window, Tom following closely.

Let enemies of the Blade weep bitter tears,' they read. 'The work cannot be undone. For I have set it in motion and the wheels will turn for ever. They turn slowly, but they will not stop.

'I leave this world but I control the city. Is this not admirable? Is it not
a thing of wonder? Gaze upon me and you look upon life in death.

This was all.

'Can this be true?'

Porlock, motionless, let the sheet fall from his fingers. It disintegrated as it
touched the floor.

'For how long . . ?'

The wind fussed at the panes. The moon passed behind a cloud. With a
sudden decisiveness Porlock began to gather papers from the top of the desk.
Tom saw his dark shadow sweeping them together and lifting them in a fragile
bundle. He followed Porlock to the door.

Had one of them touched the chair? As they passed into the corridor the
skeleton gave a jerk, slid swiftly downwards and collapsed in a shower of dust
and splintered bones.

36 Flight

'For so many years!' Porlock muttered as they hurried along the corridor. He
was talking to himself rather than to Tom. 'The leader of the Blade! It's
madness, very madness!'

They climbed through the window into the squalling wind and struggled,
swaying, up the rope ladder. Fragments of the old documents flaked off and
floated away into the darkness. Once on the roof Porlock began to question
himself all over again with a great intensity, but in tones so low that Tom could
not make out a word.

And then the night erupted. There was a terrible insistent braying sound
and the rooftops were suddenly as brilliant as day. It was only as the first
radiance dimmed that he was aware of the guttering embers of the flares
spiralling down to the ground. The howling sound, which seemed never to
cease, prevented him from thinking, from acting. He only felt a disabling fear.
New flares shot up into the sky above them, the glare revealing members of the
assault party already on their way back across their rope bridge, tiny black
spiders on a fragile web.

'Quickly! Off the roof!'

Porlock tugged him to the edge. They swung themselves over, already
gasping for breath. There were ropes for hands and feet, but in their haste they
rocked crazily from side to side. Their progress was achingly slow. Tom felt
something career past his head. They were as good as dead, he knew it. One of
the ropes, presumably hit by a missile, simply fell away into the void so that
one of his feet dangled in space and only the strength of his arms saved him.

There was such a distance to cross! Porlock, no athlete, concentrated
violently on keeping his body vertical and putting one foot in front of the other.
Ahead of them one of the party jerked away from the rope. He must have been
hit. He floundered in empty air and dropped and dropped away. Tom's despair
increased. He and Porlock moved slowly across the trembling, kicking bridge

and every moment he expected to be swept away, tossed into the deep blackness. The noise intensified.

They arrived and were hauled up. The dwarf was on the rooftop with the men in dark clothing grouped round him.

'Hurry!'

'Are we betrayed?' demanded Porlock, fastening a quick, stricken look upon the uncomprehending Tom.

'No. The first man across was seen by a sentry.' He paused. 'You don't have the individual we wanted.'

It was, in the dwarf's usual manner, an accusation.

'It wasn't possible. It's the devil to explain.'

'As we go.'

Flares burst above them, painful to the eyes. One of the team knelt by the edge of the roof and severed each rope with the swift motion of a sharp knife.

'Groups of three,' the dwarf explained. 'It's pre-arranged. You and the boy with me.'

From a pocket he pulled a length of thick black cloth.

'Tie this around my eyes,' he said. 'If you please.'

'I don't understand.'

'We have to cross the roofs and I can't look.'

'But if you should . . . '

Porlock evidently found it difficult to express the responsibility he felt.

'Nonsense! The way is not hazardous here. A few buildings and we shall descend. These other fellows will go on further where the way is narrower.'

His judgement of the route was sound. Tom, who had had adventures enough on the rooftops, was relieved to find that the parapets were wide and that, where difficult manoeuvres were necessary, iron hoops had been driven into the walls for support. The two of them helped the dwarf along, Porlock describing what they had found and adding interpretations which, when Tom chanced to overhear them above the noise, were pessimistic in the extreme.

'Nothing but a skeleton, and that ages old . . . documents, written by the Red Blade founder himself . . . there *is* no leader, has been no leader for years without number . . . '

The dwarf made no reply to any of this, but nodded his head time and again to show that he understood.

'A system so complicated that the organisation continues to function with no one in charge of it . . . '

They had approached, and the first men had already passed, a door set into the wall when Tom realised with a shock that he recognised it.

'But I've been here before!' he exclaimed. 'When I travelled from the House of the Star to the eastern sector. This is the route by which I went down.'

The dwarf raised his eye bandage and stared at the door for some seconds before replying.

'If that truly is the door,' he said, 'you took more risks than you knew.'

'The steps go down a long way,' Tom explained, 'with uninhabited passages leading from them. Then there is a hidden door and more steps past corridors where I imagined people were sleeping.'

The dwarf shook his head wonderingly.

'That is indeed the place. It is the chief dormitory of the Red Blade. The city guards and some of their most feared assassins live there.'

He replaced the shield over his eyes and indicated that they should proceed.

'At this moment I imagine that it is in ferment.'

'But why the secret door?' Tom asked.

'Many years ago,' the dwarf replied, 'that was the largest hostelry in the eastern sector. As the Blade grew more powerful they seized the important properties for themselves. They needed only the first few floors of that building and sealed the top floors off. Fortunately for us, one of our sympathisers was given the job of fixing that formidable door.'

'And he built that hidden opening?'

'You can imagine the advantage this will give us when the time is ripe for attack. We have never yet used the door for fear of alerting them.'

His voice hardened.

'You might have ruined everything.'

Tom resisted the temptation to remind the dwarf that his journey would have been unnecessary had he received more help in the first place.

'It was when I emerged from that building that I met the mad archivist from the underground city who took me to the night cafe.'

'The archivist!' Porlock started. 'You met poor Grimbald?'

'He passed old documents to me when he was arrested by the city guards.'

Now Porlock seized him by the shoulder.

'Documents, you say! What documents? Where are they?'

'We have them,' intervened the dwarf. 'And I must tell you, my good friend, that they have been an inspiration to my people.'

'What is in these documents?'

'Prophecies, the construction of the star machine. Nothing that affects your security. But for us they have been as holy writ.'

Porlock released his hold on Tom's shoulder.

'Poor Grimbald. He lost his mind long ago. He could not tolerate our artificial world so we brought him to the surface.'

'But surely,' Tom said, 'he is a danger to you.'

'Not so. He is ignorant of the routes down and speaks with no coherence. Who would believe anything he might say? His family were for generations our archivists, but Grimbald was never fit for the task. I didn't know that he possessed any documents.'

They had travelled beyond the flares and the worst of the din but, looking down to the streets, Tom saw that clusters of lights were moving away from the Citadel in the direction they were taking.

'The archivist had terrible burns,' he remembered.

'I know nothing of that,' Porlock replied. 'I am surprised that he has survived at all.'

With these sombre words they came upon another door, approached by an iron staircase, and again it was one that Tom recognised. He had tried it on that perilous journey but had been unable to open it. Now the assault party stopped at the foot of the stairway and the leader tapped the dwarf on the shoulder.

'Your route down, sir.'

The dwarf removed his bandage and took a key from his pocket.

'Gentlemen,' he said in portentous tones. 'You have served our cause with distinction. The fact will be recorded when our imminent victory has been won.'

The men, still with the bemused air of heroes who had prepared to fight a tiger only to find an empty cage, now moved off, leaving Tom and his companions to begin their descent. The way was steep, but thee were lights high on the wall every twenty feet or so and these gave a faint and welcome luminescence.

'Died, you understand,' said Porlock, doggedly resuming his jeremiad, 'before any of us was born. There's been no ruler since he died in that room all those years ago.'

The dwarf seemed hardly to be listening. Tom interpreted his expression and his movements as signifying acute concentration. A fist ground into the palm of the other hand. He took a few steps down at great speed, then paused for a few seconds nodding his head.

'Moreover,' Porlock went on heavily, 'the Blade has functioned very well without him all this time, has it not? It has, it seems, no need of a ruler. And without a leader to defeat, the organisation itself cannot be defeated.'

These mournful words hung in the air for some time. The trio descended in silence. At last the dwarf, who had been leading the way, stopped in his tracks and swung round on Porlock.

'My friend,' he said in superior tones. 'For a man of intelligence and breeding you are singularly lacking in judgement. What do you suppose the Red Blade guards at the Citadel are doing at this moment? Are they not breaking into the top floor to discover what has become of their leader?'

Porlock shook his head.

'But it is forbidden,' he replied. How else should the system work? Look here, at this sheet.'

He held it out and a corner broke off and crumbled into dust.

'Death – "a cruel death" it says – to any man who dares.'

The dwarf cackled derisively.

'Common sense, my man! Comes cheap enough, they say! Will they stand by and allow their leader to be taken? Being discovered out there on the rooftops was the best thing that could have happened to us!'

Porlock, unaccustomed to this rough treatment, puckered his brow painfully.

'Imagine their consternation,' added the dwarf, 'when they find an empty room. Splintered bones, you tell me? Think how many interpretations may be made of those! And you have all the documents – all of them?'

He laughed hoarsely.

'Utter confusion! They must believe that we have their leader, dead or alive. They will never be more ripe for attacking!'

He lowered his voice.

'Listen, my friend. What you have witnessed tonight is the beginning of the downfall of the Blade.'

They set off down the steps once more, Tom bringing up the rear.

'Some of your leaders have been taken prisoner,' he said. 'The eastern commander . . . '

'It's true, alas. He was captured and tortured – and eventually killed.'

The dwarf, speaking over his shoulder, could not see the horror in Tom's face.

'A very brave man. He told them nothing. Now we have a new commander. One whom you know yourself, I do believe, from your time at the House of the Star.'

'Who is he?'

'Who is *she* is more to the point.'

'The Sphynx!'

The dwarf inclined his head.

'So she was sometimes called.'

'But she was arrested. I saw it myself. They interrogated her. The night of the fire.'

'A savage fire, Tom. It took hold, you know. Amazing that no one was killed. That beast Clem was badly burned in it and few will be sorry. The old men of the tribunal and their allies fled into the night and the city guard spent all their time fetching water. Our leader escaped.'

'It was she who arranged for me to stay at the House of the Star?'

'Of course. She was our only member there.'

'I think Clem suspected me all along.'

'Quite possible,' the dwarf said airily. 'It was a tricky game to play.'

'And what of the others who stayed there – old Weasel, the musician . . . '

'Ah, an interesting case. I think he may be of use to us. Nothing definite, mind, but a suggestion that he supports our cause.'

'He wasn't arrested that night?'

'No, indeed! Why should he have been?'

Tom made no reply, happy to think that the great survivor had outfaced disaster once again. He followed his companions down the steps, the air growing warmer by the minute. At last the dwarf signalled them to stop.

'We're almost there,' he sad. 'When all is clear I shall leave. Allow some minutes to pass before you go.'

He held out his hand to Porlock.

'The revolution is at hand,' he said. 'I wish that you and your colleagues in the underground city could share it as we have long dreamed.'

Porlock shook the proffered hand.

'I am at this moment,' he said falteringly, as if reluctant to speak, 'engaged upon a mission . . .' (he hesitated, gazed at Tom, checked the words that first came to his lips) ' . . . a mission which, if it should succeed – though I think it unlikely, almost impossible – would give you greater hope than ever you can have wished for.'

He reached for his spectacles, wiped them tremblingly on a richly-hued silk handkerchief and said no more.

37 Hovels

They were barely in time. Even as they slipped through the door and ran across the street the first lights could be seen rounding a bend not a hundred yards away. The men in front of the mob were running and there was clamour of raised voices on the night air.

Porlock took him on an exhausting journey. It seemed that he knew every street in the city. They were soon well away from the Citadel and in another sector: they passed through with a curt exchange of passwords and kept pressing westward. It was long past the curfew hour and they had several times had to dodge into doorways and alleys to avoid platoons of the city guard.

Tom wondered at his companion's stamina. He never flagged for a moment though they had been walking for all of an hour and had passed through two more sectors of the city. The spoke not a word between them.

At length they came to an area which was poorer than any he had yet seen. There were no large faceless buildings here, only small hovels shoulder to shoulder in tortuous streets. They slowed as they walked on uneven cobbles, and Tom marvelled at the ingenuity of the builders, who seemed to have used any materials which had come to hand. One wall alone incorporated a rusted metal inn sign, fitted on its side, the discarded tailboard of a wooden cart and a wild assortment of ill-matching bricks. He assumed that the curfew must be in force here, but this did not prevent small, surreptitious movements on the darkened street.

Porlock led him forward until they could go no further. A long, low building with an unassuming turret at one end lay across the width of the thoroughfare. There were no lights inside, but Porlock did not check his stride. They passed through an arch and into a small courtyard. Steps led down to one side and the pair descended into a narrow corridor which, at last, had a few meagre flickering lamps along its wall. They passed a small, bare room in which Tom thought he saw, though he could not quite believe it, a man kneeling motionless. In another room a single candle burned unattended.

They entered a rather large space, dimly lit and rudely furnished with wooden tables and benches. Porlock sat down and motioned Tom to do the same. There was a smell which he did not know, a kind of austere fragrance. A plaque on the wall beside him was in a language that was strange to him.

'I'm sorry that I doubted you,' Porlock said in a low voice.

'Doubted me?'

'When we crossed from the Citadel. I could not help but wonder. I had planned the exercise as the final test.'

'Test of what?'

'Of you, Tom. Your trustworthiness. If you were treacherous you would surely have betrayed us then.'

Tom could not reply. He was not offended that his honesty should have been in doubt. It was rather that he could not fathom Porlock's deeper meaning. Why should he need to be tested?

'It has been a disturbing evening. Dreadful. I cannot come to terms with what we have learned about the Red Blade. That the leader should . . . '

His voice tailed away. Tom, who had had time enough to consider the meaning of what they had discovered, found himself speaking eagerly.

'But it's wonderful,' he said. 'Don't you realise that it makes people accountable for the things they do! In the past they have blamed the organisation, blamed the leader of the Blade. They can't do that any more. They must see that it is they themselves who have brought evil to the city.

'It seems to me that people live by dreams. They gain strength from their dreams, rather than from facing the truth. What did we find when we revealed everything to the dwarf? He was angry to find that we had no weapons and could provide no army. He and his friends had invented a false underground city. Because they are good people they had invented a city of goodness, but they were ill-prepared for the complete truth.

'And it's the same with the Red Blade – just the same. The Blade members believe in a supreme, violent, powerful ruler because that's the kind of ruler they wish to have. That is their dream – an evil dream. If they discovered the truth, if they saw those bones in the chair, they would feel cheated.

'Do members of the Blade carry out their vile deeds because they have a vile ruler? No. There is no ruler. That is their excuse. Their dream excuses them. What did that writing say: "Power is with a ghost, because the living wish it so."

'And the good people, who do nothing while they wait for deliverance underground. Will deliverance come? No. They must provide their own. The dream has prevented them from doing what they should have done. Always blame the dream.

'I long for the day when there are no dreams left!'

He found himself shaking from the intensity of the outburst. He had not planned any of it: the words had seemed to come of their own accord. Porlock had a queer, sleepwalker's expression on his face.

'No dreams,' he echoed, strangely. 'Away with dreams.'

Tom leant forward.

'Are you unwell?'

'No, not unwell. I was recalling a time, years ago, when the very same words were spoken to me . . . Let's be done with excuses. Answer for our own actions. No dreams, false dreams. An end to dreams.'

He spoke slowly, as if in a trance.

'Our lives are our own. We make our own decisions. None but ourselves to take the blame. Away with dreams. I believed it then . . . '

He closed his eyes and the silence seemed to fall all about them. Nobody came. The lights flickered on the walls, weakly.

'I am a rational man.'

Porlock opened his eyes and they had an intensity Tom had not seen before. His voice began to rise.

'Am I then to believe in portents and prophecies? What is this that is demanded of me? Should I now renounce the power of reason?'

Tom, astounded, started back.

'Is the world haunted? Are we ruled by magic, child's play?'

At this moment a figure passed swiftly along the corridor. It was gone in a moment but Tom recognised it, with a panic of incredulity, as the boy with the green scarf. He leapt to his feet.

'Wait!' he cried. 'I know you!'

But Porlock, who had also seen the boy, grabbed Tom by the arm and pulled him down.

'No. Not yet. Not until I have told you.'

'Told me?'

'The whole story. First you must hear me out and then you can decide what you will do.'

38 The Poet of the Wilderness

'Several years ago,' Porlock began, 'a man arrived in the city after a long, exhausting journey. He entered through the east gate and found lodgings in that sector.

'He was a poet. But, more than that, he was a man dedicated to the cause of truth and beauty and justice. Soon people began to know of him. They came to visit him, to hear his poems and to hear him talk – for he talked wonderfully – of the world as it was and the world as it might one day become.

'In those times the Red Blade, though powerful, had not yet strangled the city with its network of spies and hired killers. It was a while before news of this man reached the Citadel. Then the message went out to silence him.

'Aware of the threat to his life, he began to move about the city. Wherever he appeared there were many who thronged to hear him and to offer him what protection they could. In return he offered them hope. One notable poem has inspired thousands to keep a grasp of their courage: "Wear me as your spiked heel . . ."'

Tom, breaking in eagerly, picked up the quotation.

'I will bite into ice for you!'

'You know it?'

'I have read the words more than once. They are on a ruined monument not far from the House of the Star.'

Porlock nodded.

'This man was led to the underground city via the house you know by the east gate. But, although he was gone, the people had been inspired. They rose up. For a time certain parts of the city were seized from the Blade.

'Revenge, when it came, was terrible. Many were killed cruelly, barbarously. The statues and monuments which celebrated freedom were dismantled. The bastion of those who fought for liberty – a large building in the eastern sector – was razed to the ground. Only rubble remains. This was the time when the different sectors were sealed off from one another and the good people began to use the rooftops as the only area safe for them.'

'This man,' Tom asked. 'What did he call himself?'

'He gave no name. He said no man should bear a name until he was free. The people were not free. But his poems he signed with the initials TW. Whether because of this and the fact that he came from far off I am uncertain, but he became known as the Poet of the Wilderness.'

'Those initials,' Tom said, 'are my father's.'

'They are the initials of many people, my good friend. I am no romantic: no use to build a castle of theory on the sands of coincidence.'

'That is not all. There are things that you do not know.'

With a gesture that seemed more than weariness, almost a token of defeat, Porlock bent his head between his hands.

'Soon after I arrived in the city,' Tom said, 'I met the eastern commander, the man they killed. That was also the time when I first met the dwarf. In a small room which they used as a cell I found a book of maps with a mark against my own part of the country.'

'The wilderness is vast.'

'You don't understand,' Tom persisted. 'My very own village had been circled with ink. A place so small.'

Porlock only nodded.

'In the House of the Star I sang a song from my home village. An old man told me that, years before, the same song had been sung there by a stranger who was known as the Poet of the Wilderness.'

Porlock raised his head and gazed into the gloom, his mind seemingly far away.

'He was a singer of songs,' he said. 'He brought us many of them, wonderful songs. Our evening chorus was one of his gifts to us.'

Tom found himself clutching Porlock by the arm.

'How often,' he cried, 'was that song sung to me by my mother as a child!'

One of the lamps guttered and was spent. Porlock took out his handkerchief and dabbed it lightly against his brow.

'I shall tell you how it was. When he arrived underground we did not enjoy the harmony which you have witnessed among us. All communities have their times of growth, their times of decay. We were not happy then, and this man transformed our lives, revitalised us.

'You saw how the assembly greeted that picture in the debating chamber – the ecstasy! They thought it was the Wilderness Poet, whom they revere as a saint.

'He regenerated our love of beauty – beauty of the eye, beauty of the word, beauty of the way people may live together. He wrote us poems, he taught us songs, he gave us a renewed belief in ourselves . . . And then he left us.'

'Left you? Where did he go? Why?'

'The last lesson he taught us – those of us who would listen – is that the glory of our underground city is not sufficient. We said, "You would not take a name on the surface where evil reigns supreme. Let us give you a name underground." But he would not accept it. "When the city above is as the city beneath," he would say, "I will be known as who I am."

'He told us virtue was nothing more than a delightful device unless put to the test – an imitation sunburst in a cavern, he said. We had beauty, but a beauty tamed and protected. A beauty of dreams. You could not care for poor Grimbald underground, he told us, because he was not part of your beautiful dream. He would return to the surface city to discover whether beauty could . . .'

He paused, calling the words back from the past.

' . . . whether beauty could enter the flames and emerge glowing rich.'

Another lamp died. Although so close, Tom could not clearly make out Porlock's features in the murk.

'I was his disciple, you see. I learned all these things from him. This is why I have tried to bring together the underground city and the good people above. Only . . . ' – he faltered – ' . . . I found that I lacked the strength to do as he did.'

Tom rose to his feet.

'You talk,' he said fiercely, 'but you don't tell me what I need to know. All along you have thwarted me. You have used me and refused to acknowledge that the man you speak of is my father. Deny that if you can!'

'I won't. I can't. Of course I have recognised all along that you might be the son of this man. Of course it is possible. Possible. You came in from the east. You speak with the accent, the man Clutt assured me of that.'

'All those coincidences.'

'Yes, yes. Coincidences. The picture and so forth. I agree. But, you see, I have hoped desperately from the start that the Poet is *not* your father. I have put your credentials and your good faith to the test as often as I could. I have done this partly for your own good, but especially for the city as a whole. It will seem harsh of me to say so, but I sincerely hope that you are disappointed in your quest.'

Tom, dumbfounded, sat down again.

'I don't understand.'

'Allow me to continue with my story. From the first I realised that the Poet was an exceptional man. I owed him everything, even my very life. I shall never repay that debt. But we differed in one respect. I believed in the rule of reason, of logic if you like. He taught the power of mystery, of prophecy, of hidden influences.

'I fear those influences, Tom. I fear that they may be used by evil people as well as good. I am a rational man.'

The repetition of this phrase seemed somehow to mesmerise him. He sat motionless for a while.

'Go on,' Tom said.

'When the Poet returned to the surface city he was a hunted man. He lived a fugitive life. But his very presence in the place inspired the people. They wanted to make him their city lord, in name if not in reality. He said the time was not ripe. He taught that the time of their release would come, according to prophecy.'

'How?'

'There is a double prediction. Perhaps you know it. A boy like a tick entering the wool of the sheep, drinking the blood of the city. Another, following, seeking a father . . . I told him he was a fool to set store by it.'

'The first boy,' Tom said, 'was the Red Blade founder. Isn't that the story?'

'It was what he believed then. And he believed – why I don't know – that the second boy would be his own son. "Find him for me," he said. "Swear you will find him." I am a rational man. I counted the prophecy as so much nonsense. I doubted the son would ever arrive from such a distance. I made the vow.'

He paused and the pause extended. His breathing, grown tremulous, sounded deafening in the darkness. When he spoke it was in a whisper.

'Eventually a lad entered the eastern gate looking for his father. I questioned him a little and took him to the Poet . . . He was not the son. In reality he had not travelled a journey and was not looking for a father. He was an innocent waif, a simpleton if the truth be told, cynically manipulated by the Red Blade. A decoy. Such, you see, is the deviousness of prophecy. They captured the Poet.'

Here he removed his spectacles, tossed them onto the table and pressed his fists against his temples. Tom forced himself to ask the question.

'Killed him?'

'No. Not killed him. Not that.'

'Then what?'

A sound of grief held in Porlock's throat. For a while he could not speak. Then he forced himself into an upright posture and in the process his spectacles were swept to the floor. The glass smashed, tinkling.

'A monumental jest,' he said bitterly. 'The symbol of truth is an ever-open eye, and so . . . '

'They . . . '

'They deprived . . . they took out his eyes.'

He bent to the floor to gather the pieces of his spectacles, his face hidden. Tom shivered. They had taken out his eyes. It was not warm in the room but he had been unaware of the cold until now. And the darkness. They had taken out his eyes! Minutes passed before Porlock spoke again.

'They released him into the city as an example to others who might oppose the Blade. Fools! Those who live by violence can judge the world only in terms of pain. His influence was undiminished.

'Afterwards he told me that his suffering was pre-ordained. He meant it as a kindness to me, as if it would lighten the burden. That I should be the tool of prophecy, the destined cause of that agony! Can you wonder that I despise prophecies? Do you understand why I doubt you all I can?'

'But if you really don't believe . . . '

'Ha! You think the matter so simple? The strongest of us have weak moments, times when we think the world may indeed be governed by these weird forces. The world has yet to discover the complete sceptic.'

'Where did the Poet go?' Tom asked urgently.

'A sect of poor and humble priests took him in,' Porlock replied. 'A safe place. His only companion is the weak-minded lad who led the Blade's agents to him. He is a messenger, watcher, even son to him until his own son shall arrive.'

'The second boy,' Tom said.

'The very nub of the matter. The fulfilment of prophecy. Let's say I'm entirely rational and rule these fancies out. Which I do. They're insane. Nevertheless there are many who do believe them – many who will act upon them and many who fear them.'

'But why should they?'

'Because when that second prophecy is fulfilled – when it seems to have been fulfilled with the arrival of his son – the Poet will call on the people to rise up. Your dwarf thinks he has sufficient support, but his forces and the Blade are evenly matched, believe me. The Poet speaks and the city is aflame with revolution.'

'A just revolution which you surely support!'

'I support a revolution, but not at any price. There are linked prophecies which may come to pass simply because they seem inevitable. "Like a steel comb he will enter the sheep's wool, rake out the clinging vermin, and" – mark this well, Tom – "mastery shall be restored to the virtuous and the sons of the virtuous, and the city will be ruled as in former times". '

'I don't follow this. Surely it foretells a reign of peace and justice.'

'You have said the word yourself: a *reign*. Are we to return to the old ways when one man ruled the city? Do you not see the Poet established as sole city lord?'

'But a good man. You have said so.'

'Are we to return to the control of a dictator, however benign? Hasn't history taught us the danger of that? The power passed down from father to son' – here he gave a tug on Tom's arm – 'and in time abused, turned against the people. Can anyone truly say he knows how he will act with such power at his command. Can you?

'I have long sought a liaison between our underground city, which has no dictator, and the people of the rooftops who seek a return to the people's rule of the days before the Red Blade.

'Now you arrive and I am bounden by my vow. But I ask you, in all seriousness, whether it is better to turn now while there is time and go back from where you came. I have heard you speak passionately about dreams and responsibility and the myth of leadership. Turn back before you inherit a whole city.'

They heard a sound from within the building. The last two lamps failed at the same moment. Tom thought not only of his father but of Sonia in the underground city.

'I can't return,' he said simply.

'Then wait. I have done my duty.'

He touched Tom lightly on the shoulder and slipped away. The darkness seemed to thicken. It gathered round him. The sound came again: a door. There were footsteps. He was gradually aware of a faint glow from the corridor.

It was a candle. The boy with the green scarf held it high so as better to see him. But his companion, a large man whose beard glinted silver in the dancing light, was not troubled by the gloom. He stepped forward, his arms stretched wide, and Tom leapt towards him, his own eyes blurred with tears.

A Flight
of
Bright Birds

1 Hidden Eyes

' . . . for temptations unresisted, sins of the flesh and of the imagination.'

Whispered supplications, washing against the unyielding silence. The gilding on the icons glowed faintly through the gloom. The flames of the candles on the altar table trembled in unison, sweet odours of wax and incense mingling in his nostrils. Walter, alone yet sensing still that he was watched, raised himself from his knees and stood uncertainly in the darkened chapel. He made the sign of the cross over his chest.

'In the name of the Father . . . Amen.'

He passed slowly into the shadowed cloisters, where oil lamps widely spaced were tiny beacons in the dusk. A breeze fragrant with spring foliage played about his face. He heard only the tread of his own sandalled feet, a comfortable creaking and shuffling.

Worn flagstones, scoured by the perambulations of centuries. The cloisters enclosed three sides of a square, ending at a short flight of steps. He climbed slowly, pausing at the top, listening but not turning to look behind; then pushed open the heavy door.

The room faced west and he was drawn to the large open window which framed a glorious dayfall. The sinking sun scattered rags of flawed orange across the clouded darkness of the sky and he stood in wonderment, studying the richness of it. Below him the monastery garden was a pool of blackness, submerging the plot of medicinal herbs, the rows of sprouting beans, the lines of twigs which would train the emerging peas. Beyond, the shadowed landscape stretched to far hills which merged into the lowest clouds so that it was impossible to know where earth ended and sky began.

'Why do you follow me, brother Mark?'

Some seconds passed before the cowled figure of an elderly man limped into the room.

'Not follow, Walter. That has a sinister ring.'

'So be it, brother Mark. Not follow. Why do you watch me so closely? All day I've felt your eyes on me.'

The old monk, advancing painfully, joined him at the window, standing for some time in silence.

'Tomorrow,' he said at last, 'is your birthday.'

'My birthday? We never celebrate birthdays here.'

'You will be fifteen.'

Walter, perplexed, turned from the opening.

'Why does this matter? How would you know my age? I don't know it myself.'

The old man frowned and lowered his gaze. When at last he spoke there was a throb in his voice, and he gathered a fold of his habit and dabbed at his eyes.

'I remember the day that you were brought here. Just a baby, a helpless baby – laughing, despite everything. A covering of black hair even then! And that mark, which I fancied in my odd way as a kind of entry visa.'

Walter raised a hand and felt the small mottled area on his right cheek.

'And I've watched you grow, and grow among us, and I imagined that you would stay with us for ever.'

Here he broke off suddenly, either from discretion or from emotion, for he leant out over the sill with his hands pressing against the hood of his garment so that it completely shielded his face.

'But I don't understand you!' Walter exclaimed. 'What does this mean? You speak as if I were about to go from here. I've no wish to do that.'

The old monk eventually withdrew from the window and took Walter's arm in a shaking grip.

'I'm a foolish old creature who talks when he shouldn't. You'll learn everything soon enough – in the morning. Forgive me.'

He hurried away, one leg dragging, one sandal flapping busily on the flagstones.

2 Capture

Swirls of steam flecked with smudgy currants of soot lifted over the high iron railings and fell upon the crowds in the station concourse. There were three trains in, two just arrived and one about to leave, so that there was a flurry in all directions – latecomers running clumsily with bags in each hands and tickets protruding comically from their lips; whining children being tugged along by impatient parents; couples fondly embracing; uniformed porters manoeuvring carts piled high with luggage, wheeling deftly among the throng.

On the fringe of all this activity, in the shadows away from the flaring gas lanterns, a young lad edged cautiously towards the platforms as if afraid of being seen. He darted from one darkened area to another, every so often looking nervously over his shoulder.

Doors were slamming busily on the train soon to depart. The figure in the shadows peered through the railings, watching the last-minute leave-takings, the bundling of hefty packages in the guard's van, and one group in particular seemed to hold his attention.

A large, pot-bellied man, his head hairless save for wild bushes of grey over his ears, his body clothed in a strange suit of orange and yellow, stood behind a pile of luggage ticking off items on a large sheet of paper. Every so often he would pause to give an ineffectual push to one or other of his companions, all of whom were talking animatedly and with extravagant gestures (and all, it seemed, at the same time) and none of whom showed the slightest inclination to board the train. Among the luggage were several trunks, one of which carried the words, in large flame-orange letters, TUSKER'S TRAVELLING THEATRE.

Little by little the luggage was loaded on to the train and, at last and with apparent reluctance to leave the open expanse of the platform for the confines of the carriage, the group began to climb aboard. Each one of them was of a striking appearance. The last two lingered in the doorway – a short man with a swarthy complexion and enormous shaggy black eyebrows, and a woman encased in layer on layer of bright silken material – and the fat man with the list waved at them impatiently.

Anyone watching the wraith in the shadows would have seen it emerge into the busy area leading to the platforms and hurl itself into the path of an elegant couple who were too intent on catching their train to notice how they came to be trampling over a human form.

'What's this!' exclaimed the gentleman, stooping from a considerable height to reach out a helping hand.

'Oh, the poor dear,' lamented his companion. 'You've trodden on him. Are you all right, boy?'

They lifted him to his feet and examined him for cuts and bruises. What they saw was a shock of black hair and a face whose only remarkable characteristic – apart from an expression of alarm and anxiety – was a mottled area of skin on the right cheek.

'The train!' he wailed, as if in deep distress. 'I shall miss it!'

'Bless you, boy, so shall we all!'

They hurried him forward to the gate, where a station official stood sombrely checking the passengers. Even as the tall gentleman showed his tickets the lad began to cry out, with a catch of helplessness in his voice.

'Lost it! It was in my hand. Perhaps when you knocked me over. Can't travel without it!'

'There, there,' coaxed the lady. 'We'll look after you. Don't worry.'

'He's with us,' announced his new-found guardian in a lordly voice. 'If he doesn't find his ticket we'll pay for him at the other end.'

'Very well, sir.'

Once through the gate, however, the kindly couple were to be surprised. Their protégé was no sooner clear of the ticket collector than he was sprinting along the platform towards the round man who, even now, had not quite accounted for all his luggage.

'Mr Tusker! Wait! It's me!'

'Well, bless my soul!'

The young lad slithered to a halt beside the large black trunk.

'I told you I'd come.'

'Bless me, I didn't believe it.'

'Come to join you.'

'Well, well. Very good. Which is to say . . . perhaps *not* very good.'

'You'll take me? I'll work like a . . . '

But here he broke off. Two men, each wearing flat caps and tight-fitting tweed suits, had passed through the barrier and, having spotted him, were hurrying nearer waving their arms.

'I do believe,' said Mr Tusker, 'that this could be troublesome.'

The quarry was already gone, running the length of the train as the two men came dashing in pursuit.

'Stop, master Jack! Stop!'

He would not wait, although there was nowhere to hide but in the train. He lay flat under a seat, knowing that he was not well concealed, hearing them approaching closer and closer. At last they entered the carriage and hauled him from his hideaway, though without undue roughness.

'A real chase you've led us this time, master Jack.'

'Nearly got clean away. That's the furthest you've been.'

The trio, all panting for breath, returned slowly along the platform with the resigned air of people who had been through the same business several times in the past.

'Couldn't you have slowed the horses?' asked the dejected lad in hurt tones. 'Another five minutes!'

'And would our lives have been worth living then?'

As they passed the ticket collector, who gazed severely upon the miscreant, there was a squealing of metal on metal and a huge volcano of steam. The great wheels of the locomotive began to turn.

Outside in the yard the trap was waiting, just as he had known it would be. They climbed aboard and jolted back and forth as the horses began to pull them over the cobbles.

'In truth, master Jack, your parents are mighty hurt at you going like this.'

'Parents! They're not my parents!'

'Anyway, they're more than a bit put out. What with it being your birthday in the morning and all. They say it's an extra special day tomorrow.'

Jack put his hands over his ears and watched the city go by, house after house, street after street.

3 The Abbot's Letter

A perfect morning, the valley filled with the warmth of spring. The monastery itself seemed to have opened like an early flower, every corner, every recess touched with light. So he felt, early prayers over, as he padded along the corridors towards the abbot's chamber.

Spring, however, had not yet penetrated there: winter still held sway. A cold, grey, forbidding room, its windows were hidden high between the vaults of the ceiling. The abbot, opening the door to him, seemed to shrink from the brightness outside. A man not enamoured of earthly pleasure, he stood now poised on his toes as if wishing to detach himself from the earth completely and ascend towards and beyond the walls above him. This precarious posture caused his lean figure to sway to and fro as he spoke, and Walter was discomfited by the thought that he might lost his balance completely and topple forward on top of him.

'I have something . . . something of substance . . . that I wish to tell you, Walter.'

He spoke to the gloom above Walter's head, pausing often as if weighing each phrase, each word, in the balance.

'No, not wish . . . rather, something instructed, or requested. Something that I promised, a long time ago . . . a long, long time ago . . . almost fifteen years ago.'

There was an agony of indecision, of inner struggle.

'It hurts me in some ways, Walter . . . hurts me . . . But a promise, you will understand . . . a promise is . . . '

'I know.'

' . . . a promise . . . and you, like a . . . well, like a . . . a son . . . to me, I've always thought of you as . . . like a son. That is . . . yes, as I might my own son . . . if I had one.'

Walter nodded, as if to help the words along. And indeed he knew truly that if the abbot had a son he would have been treated with the same total detachment as Walter and every other human contact had experienced. It was not that the abbot was unkind: on the contrary, he laboured after kindness, but his kindness, like his speech, seemed directed more to the air above people than to the people themselves.

'You see, when I came here . . . When was it? Thirty years? . . . Forty years? Time means so little, Walter, in a place . . . a place like this . . .' – he closed his eyes as if engaged in a genuine calculation – ' . . . sixty-three years, I think it was . . . when I came here. Sixty-three years, when I chose to . . . well, not so much chose. But I was . . . a party to the decision. Or, at least, I knew about the decision, understood . . . understood, that is, what had been decided. I could have said . . . no . . . '

He puckered his brow as though the thought of his refusing to enter the monastery had just occurred to him, a dreadful thought that must bring with it no tinge of belated regret.

'I could not, or I would not have said no . . or, that is, I could have said no, but duty . . . duty would have prevented it, would have forbidden it. Duty, Walter. Duty. That is a . . . persuasive word. Duty. I am sure that you are beginning to understand.'

Of course he understood duty, but little else could he fathom, and he waited for the meaning to disentangle itself from the abbot's hesitations and repetitions.

'With me, then, choice. Choice dictated by duty. But with you . . . Well, you were a little young to choose . . . rather too young. I am sure that had you been able to speak, to make your wishes known, then . . . you would have said yes . . . Indeed, had you been able to walk I believe that still you would have wished to stay. I believe that, Walter, I believe it . . . The infants understands duty. Yes. It is so. And soon you must choose . . . to stay, to become a novice or . . . or . . . well, I cannot answer that, Walter. You have been an excellent scholar, a fine example to the other boys. Brother Mark has described you as . . .' – and here he paused before almost whispering the word – 'saintly . . . a fitting word, Walter. Fitting. You know where duty lies. But I . . . I made a promise. And a promise is meant . . . it has to be kept.'

That they were back to the promise, Walter was relieved to hear. His impatience overcame him.

'What is the promise?' he asked. 'To whom?'

'Ah.'

The abbot closed his eyes and wrung his hands. He seemed to make several efforts to speak before the words escaped his lips again.

'A promise does not wither for having lain dormant for fifteen years, but . . . neither does it mature. Mature like good wine. No . . . no, this has turned to vinegar, I suspect, Walter. Vinegar for me, if not . . . for you. Perhaps too for you . . . A promise, made all that time ago, given to the person who brought you here . . . to give you this on your fifteenth birthday.'

Here the abbot produced from the folds of his habit an envelope, old, brown and sealed with a splendid rosette of scarlet wax that held in its centre the image of an eye. The abbot, having discharged his painful duty, gave Walter no time to reply or to open the envelope, but ushered him back into the sunshine with a kindly smile that, as usual, missed its target and addressed itself to a passing bird.

4 New Vistas

A reluctant dawn, with colourless light seeping into cold, grey mist. A footpath stretching away, soon swallowed in darkness under the blurred presence of tall trees. Here the indistinct shape of a low building, a gate, an orange bracket holding an oil lamp which spilled a pool of yellow light like melted butter on a sign that read STATION.

It was, in fact, nothing grander than a country halt. The building was wooden and in need of attention. It was, moreover, locked. There were, surprisingly, two people waiting separately on the humble platform – an old peasant lady whose short, round body emerged from a collection of bulging bags as if it were merely another bag (a little larger, rather more shapeless) and Walter.

The old lady stood by the building, deriving what comfort she could from its meagre shelter, whereas Walter stood at the far end of the platform, a grey ghost in the grey air, with no luggage, a cloak wrapped around his winter tunic, and an expression which betrayed none of the confusion that lay within. He could distinguish little of the old lady's face, but from where he stood it had a dark and fierce appearance, and it was to her that he silently rehearsed the lines that should have been spoken to the abbot and now never would be.

'There are duties and duties, master abbot. My years at the monastery have been happy ones. You and the brothers have shown me every kindness and I have learned much. But your promise has become a duty for me which I do not myself understand . . . '

Here his imaginary speech halted as he saw the hurt faces of the brothers when they discovered his room to be empty. Why he had left like that: silently, furtively, in the middle of the night? Why had he repaid their concern in such a way? Had they not deserved more?

He would not have known how to answer them, how to explain the strange emotions that ran through him on discovering the contents of the envelope: a railway ticket to the coastal town of O—, an address scrawled on a piece of paper and a shard of glazed pottery. He had turned this object over and over in his palm without satisfying himself as to its purpose. The incomplete design on one side suggested that it might be part of an ornament of some kind: on the reverse, however, there was no hint of a clasp and letters had been scratched, seemingly at random, in the clay. He wondered, too – indeed, it was the question that bothered him the most – how a recently issued railway ticket had found its way into an envelope apparently sealed fifteen years earlier.

How could he explain to the brothers that this envelope and its prosaic contents made a demand of him? Absurd as it might seem, he felt his very destiny bound up with this enigmatic inheritance. He did not know whose address he had begun to travel towards, but he had no doubt that he must make the journey.

The old lady was beckoning. Walter look around him, half expecting somebody to materialise from the mist and answer the insistent gesture. What did she want of him? Had she seen him looking at her and taken offence? Was she about to beg for money? Perhaps if he ignored her she would stop . . . But no, she would not stop, and he found himself moving along the platform towards her. As he approached, her face, which seemed to be made of the same cracked leather as her festooning bags, took on an alarming smile that advertised a row of blackened teeth.

'You're not very sociable, my sonny. What you doing up there, all by yourself? I don't smell or nothing.'

This observation was not quite true, but Walter was nevertheless relieved to find her manner friendly.

'Train'll be here in a minute or two, and I can't carry all these by myself, now can I?'

Immediately she held her head to one side and raised a forefinger.

'Yes, there it is now. Dead on time.'

Walter, hearing nothing, marvelled at her certainty.

'You take those two, my sonny – they're not too heavy – and I'll take these.'

They lifted the bags and moved to the edge of the platform. Walter was amazed by her strength if hers were truly heavier than his, especially as she seemed to swing them about easily enough.

When the promised train arrived, labouring slowly up a slight incline, Walter helped the old lady aboard and climbed in behind her, and as they had shared the lonely platform so now they shared the same lonely carriage. She settled her large bulk upon the centre of a seat and lined her bags up on either side of her. Walter sat opposite. Before offering any further conversation she fished inside her shawl and produced a clay pipe which she lit with great ceremony, and it was from the ensuing black cloud that her voice eventually came.

'The day's very young. What's a nice lad like you doing travelling alone?'

Walter invented a story as improbable as it was hastily assembled. But if the old lady disbelieved him she gave no indication of it, and as the morning progressed and a new day revealed itself about a passing landscape of high peaks and lakes, populated largely by sheep and small herds of hardy cattle, she talked happily of her life and journeyings.

She was a widow with a number of sons and daughters, all of whom had left home to be married or to work in various corners of the country, and her life was spent travelling from one member of her scattered family to another. At each home she would spend two, perhaps three, weeks before moving on. She never tired of this, enjoying the nomadic life far more than she had her earlier fixed existence. As to expense . . . Here she touched the side of her nose and winked at Walter.

The mystery of her financial arrangements was compounded when from time to time during the day's long journey they were accosted by railway officials. The train would draw into a station and a small army of uniformed men would step forward, each man to a separate carriage. Without entering the train, they would request that the window be lowered and, standing with their heels together, they would clip the tickets that were given to them, handing them back with a small courteous bow. At these inspections Walter readily complied, but the old lady merely affected a blank expression and sat staring into space. Each time the inspectors ignored her – indeed, pretended not to have seen her. Walter was too polite to question her about this, and she offered no explanation, but as the train left the station her blank expression would crease into a huge pleased grin and her round body would quiver with suppressed laughter.

The carriage was not warm. It was a day on which the sky had failed to clear, and a continuous draught ran in at the edges of the windows. Each station, each halt, provided its own peculiar aromas as vendors moved from carriage to carriage, one with hot pies, another with spiced cakes, yet another with cabbage leaves wrapped around hot, moist potato. The old lady watched distress etch itself with ever more distinct lines in the face of her young companion.

'You're hungry.'

'No, no.'

'Have you any money?'

'I'm fine, really. I don't eat much anyway. I've very little appetite.'

But this story the old lady did not accept, and at the next station she called from the carriage until a ragged urchin ran up to her with a tray containing cold roasted meats and bread. Dropping some coins on to the tray, she took two portions of bread and enough meat to fill them and handed half of her purchase to Walter.

'You've got to eat, my sonny.'

'Thank you, but . . . '

'You can think of it as payment for toting my bags. If that makes it easier.'

Beyond the carriage windows the mountains had given way to the wide coastal plain. Walter knew it as a patch of dull brown in his atlas, and the reality was even duller and more brown. Ploughed fields raced away towards a horizon that could have been drawn with a ruler. Here and there villages clustered around churches that poked blunt steeples into the sky.

Not only was the landscape new to him, but the buildings were made of different materials: none of the dark stone to which he was accustomed, but a mixture of brick and flint. Presently they came to a river, and one such as he had never known – not a rippling brook, tumbling its clear, icy waters over a broken staircase of rocks, but a broad, sluggishly flowing thoroughfare, busy with boats of every description.

'Look!' he cried involuntarily, and the old lady smiled and puffed at her pipe.

'Smelly old river,' she said with a chuckle.

For Walter, however, it was magically exciting. He watched the barges, the small cargo boats, the gaily bedecked pleasure boats, and he rejoiced at a diversity of human activity he had never before witnessed. Everywhere there was movement: people pulling on ropes, pushing barrels, shovelling coal, hanging out washing on improvised lines . . . Away from the confines of the monastery he suddenly felt an exhilarating sense of communion with the whole human race. A lad like himself walked along the river-bank with a bag slung over his shoulder, and he looked up and waved his hand at the passing train. Walter returned the wave, jubilant, marvelling that he was part of such a world and convinced that everything in it was conspiring to lead him to the fulfilment of his destiny.

'How good life is!' he exclaimed, and the old lady, surprised, nodded through her smoke.

'Well, it's good enough. Leastways, it's a mite better than the alternative.'

'So much wonderful . . . variety!'

He could find no words for an experience which to his fellow traveller must be commonplace. She had already turned her gaze from the window. Thoughts of the goodness of life brought her back to her family, and she began a detailed report of her children's progress – the business success of one son, the military aspirations of another, the marriage prospects of a plain but intelligent daughter – a lecture so long and involved that Walter found his mind slipping off elsewhere until, with a start, he realised that the voice had ceased. She was sound asleep.

Moods of euphoria do not last for ever. Perhaps it was a growing fatigue, perhaps the influence of the weather – the leaden sky squatting on the land like a tired animal, the wind gusty, sometimes smearing a layer of fine rain across the carriage windows. Doubts began to trouble him. He had left the monastery armed only with the contents of the envelope. He owned nothing else. The monastery had been his provider throughout the years and he had needed no money. What if the people at the address he sought knew nothing of him? Suppose they were hostile towards him? The excitement that had sustained him earlier in the venture began to die and to be replaced by a hard knot of anxiety.

And then, as afternoon was darkening towards evening, he saw O—, its towers punctuating the distant skyline. Beyond them somewhere was the sea. There would be ships in a port. A dozen images slipped through his mind in an instant. What would happen to him at O—?

The old lady had long been asleep, her head lolling forward, rocking with the movement of the train. Now Walter inadvertently nudged her as he peered into the distance, and one eye opened guardedly.

'We must be nearly there.'

Her reaction was sudden and startling. Both eyes opened wide and she leapt to the window with greater speed and agility than her age and proportions should have allowed. Having looked out, she subsided once more onto the seat.

'Thank heavens!' she gasped. 'Just in time! Well done, my sonny. Where would I be without you?'

Walter, puzzled by her reaction, her effusive gratitude, was even more surprised when they drew into a small halt on the outskirts of town and his companion prepared herself to leave the train. He could see only a platform and a handful of poor cottages.

'Your son lives here?' he asked.

'Goodness, no. In a hole like this? He lives in O—.'

'But then, why . . . '

Her finger once more alighted on the side of her nose.

'Walking's cheaper than a ticket. There's never anyone at this place, and the town's not too far from here – not when you're used to it.'

Walter, shocked, looked at the old lady, surveyed her collection of bags, and, without further consideration, thrust his ticket into her hand. At first it seemed as if she would refuse, but he was already on his feet and half out of the door when the carriage jerked to a stop. Leaning from the window, she uttered a stream of country endearments his ears had never before met with, blessed him for his saintliness and pushed a small silver coin into his fingers.

'It's a longish walk and you'll need something to power your limbs.'

Before he could return the money the train began to move. He stood motionless, the evening gathering around him, and watched the old lady carried away into the darkness.

5 Freedom

Jack hung over the railings of the paddle steamer, watching the waters boil and churn below him. The wind was in his hair, there was a good meal in his belly and he was travelling further and further from home. He couldn't believe his luck.

When he had been brought back in the trap to the big house there had been a curt dismissal to his room, but no shouting and no beating. In the morning, his birthday, there were smiles and presents as if nothing untoward had passed. And then there was the envelope.

Bemused by the lack of harsh recriminations, he had not listened to the beginnings of what was about to become a speech by his guardian. There was a reference to his hidden origins, a subject he supposed he ought to be interested in but which the old couple had so taken over for themselves – giving them a power over him which he deeply resented – that he turned his back on it, longing for the moment when he could leave this house and his past along with it.

He had opened the envelope in their presence, coming first upon the paper carrying an address in O— and then the ceramic fragment. It seemed to him so much nonsense, but they read the address over several times, speculating about the sort of district it would be in, and held the clay biscuit up to the light, discussing what it might be and becoming quite overheated about the haphazard letters on the back.

'These are instructions,' explained his guardian with heavy seriousness. 'You must follow them carefully.'

'I don't understand what this is all about.'

'A message from your past,' said the woman (he could not call them mother and father) 'that we promised to give you on your fifteenth birthday.'

For a few moments he failed to understand what this faded envelope and its contents could mean for him. He watched the excited pair fussing over them and felt only a bitter dislike.

Had they been unduly harsh with him? It was natural to punish boys who misbehaved and disobeyed and did not always answer honestly. Other children suffered much more severely than he. But Jack could not accept them, let alone love them. They had been old even at the time he could first remember them. Was that the reason? They seemed to think differently about everything. His thoughts and actions were always the wrong ones. He was never good enough. How could he call them mother and father, as they wished?

'This address in O—. You must go to it.'

'I must . . . '

'Clearly. It is your duty.'

He did not care for duty, but his spirits bounded within him. He must go! Away from here, to freedom! He fought to control the jubilation which shook him until he trembled.

'There is very little, Jack, that we can tell you of your origins. You know that we adopted you long ago, became your parents . . . '

'When shall I go?'

' . . . and have attempted to raise you as natural parents would. It has not always been easy, for any of us.'

Surely he could keep himself in check for a few minutes more. He dug the fingers of one hand into the palm of the other until it stung with pain. He bent his head so that they should not read the exultation in his eyes.

'We always knew that this moment would come. We have tried to prepare you for it, to fit you for the world. So often you have not responded as we would have wished.'

He shook his head wildly, as if in penitence, the hair tossing over his forehead.

'You have so often disappointed us. And yet the time has come as we knew it would – and you must go.'

At the end of the lecture he had answered as meekly as he could, had agreed that certainly he must seek out the address on the paper, had quietly left the room – and had leapt up the stairs three at a time, his arms swinging, his mouth volleying a series of silent hallelujahs.

That excitement had not for one second diminished. The next morning they had accompanied him through the city to the river landing-stage and had waved him away, trustingly, downstream, down towards the sea and O—. The boat passed among the wharves, an area he loved, where great winches swung bundles and packages and crates from ships that had travelled the world, piling the cargo on busy quaysides. He enjoyed the details – the coils of tarred rope, the tally-boards on the walls, the flights of stone steps lapped by a yellowish scum.

Now, the city left far behind, he hung over the rails watching the waters lash and the bubbles and flecks of foam race out in the wake of the paddle steamer, and he felt at peace for the first time that he could remember. Of course, he would not go to O—. He liked the place well enough, especially the port with its big ships (he had been taken there once when his guardian had business in the town) but he had no intention of playing silly games with bits of paper and pottery. Not when Tusker's Travelling Theatre was performing many miles away and would take him on. He was sure they would! They were touring small town far to the west: he had read the name of their first destination on a label stuck to the big trunk at the city station.

The countryside was flat here and, after the bustle of the city, the scene had little to interest him. It was, moreover, chilly on the deck, and a spattering of rain swept into his face. This depressed him not a bit. A little further downstream there was a stopping point where new passengers would come on board: already he could see buildings on either bank. At least one passenger would be getting off.

He thought of the old couple once again. Why had they taken him into their home all those years ago? Not, certainly, for the money: his guardian was extremely well-to-do. Nor had there been an obligation: it had been made clear to him that they knew little more of his parentage than he did himself. The thought that they might have longed for a son he dismissed as soon as it occurred to him, and that brought an abrupt end to his speculations about the past.

Even as the boat nudged its moorings, before the crew had tethered it securely to the bollards, he slung his bag over his shoulder and jumped to the ground.

'You'll break your neck, boy!'

But he ignored the reprimand completely. He was free! Within a few miles he would reach a broad road going west. A few miles more and there was a railway junction. It was easier than ever he could have imagined. He crossed a wooden footbridge and began to follow the towpath upstream.

A train came chugging along a raised track which ran beside the river. It was on its way to O— and, from mingled relief, triumph and defiance, Jack waved a hand as it passed. He laughed out loud and joyfully kicked at a clump of little yellow flowers growing by the path.

For a while he walked on at a brisk pace until suddenly, having glanced over his shoulder a few times, he began to limp severely. To the innocent onlooker he would have appeared to be in considerable pain and, indeed, a minute later a deep voice called out from a coalbarge which was steaming upriver close by the bank.

'You hurt, mister?'

Jack looked across helplessly.

'My leg.'

'How far you going?'

'A few miles, if I can. But I'm almost done.'

A large fellow in a hooped vest came across to the side of the barge. He had a long pole in his hand.

'Manage to jump, can you?'

'I think so.'

'We'll be out in deeper water if you don't hurry.'

Miraculously overcoming his pain, Jack leapt into the barge and hobbled to an area of flat planking. He sat watching the world drift by, the smell of coal-dust in his nostrils, an outrageous smile lighting up his face.

6   Lights

Even in the remotest suburbs, such as the one by which Walter entered O—, night had already fled before the street lamps, and nearer the centre all was light, noise and movement. Nothing in his books had prepared him for this.

Once he strayed from the pavement and a hissing, crackling, sparkling apparition swept past him, the movement of air almost knocking him from his feet. He saw faces pressed to the windows of the tram, saw rows of coloured lights along its length, saw sparks dancing from the top of the long pole above it, heard that eery whistling sound above his head, and then it was gone along its rails, as if he had imagined it.

He walked the crowded streets both frightened and exhilarated by the crush of people and traffic. Sometimes he climbed steps where the pavement took leave of the road and from its railinged height was able to look on to the roofs of passings trams and carriages and on pedestrians who had taken the lower path.

Everything was strikingly different here. People wore clothes the like of which he had never seen before. A lady lifting the corner of her dress to avoid its dragging through a puddle revealed a stocking upon which was embroidered a flock of black birds, startled and flying up into the dark warmth of her skirts. Walter lowered his eyes: the village girls would have hesitated long before revealing even the smallest fraction of a leg encased in thickly knitted wool.

'Duty.' The word echoed through his brain. What would the abbot make of such a place? There were stories told in the monastery of thronging towns and cities, human whirlpools with parks and palaces dedicated to pleasures of the flesh. He had heard them often, and even the imagining had sent his senses reeling. These stories always ended in destruction, outpouring tides of lava, crumbling buildings, murderous hails of fire and ash, of floods and violent earthquakes.

'Move aside, boy, that's no place to stand!'

He felt himself pushed against a wall, and a braggart of a man, stripe-suited and moustached, swaggered past with a woman hanging on his arm. She turned towards Walter as they passed, revealing a face so completely painted as virtually to deny a role to nature in its composition. The scarlet lips parted in a half-smile – in sympathy with his distress? Walter could not tell. The parted lips were the only clue in that animated mask, the eyes having been caged within lashes of prodigious length.

He walked on, tired and intimidated, and the lips seemed to move on before him, always just out of reach. Was it the effect of fatigue and the endless lights and the noise and bustle upon his brain? As if in a fever, his eyes refused to focus on the world around him, and for a time he saw only a ghost of his imagining, a pair of lips half-open in a smile, luring him onwards, haunting him. Was this what it meant to be damned? The lips swam towards him, floated beyond reach, mocked him, enticed him – and finally faded and faded away.

Emerging from the trance, he fumbled in his pocket for the scrap of paper. In truth it was unnecessary for him to read it for the address had sung in his ears throughout the day's journey, yet simply holding it in his hand gave him the confidence to approach passers-by. For the most part they were reluctant to stop, perhaps taking him for a beggar in his dusty clothes and with his tired, forlorn face, but finally an austere-looking man carrying a silver-topped cane eyed him severely and asked what was desired of him. He took the proffered piece of paper and, holding it close to his eyes, scrutinised it carefully before handing it back.

'It's in the old quarter, young man. Take the next road to your left and follow it through. That'll bring you to the right area. I trust there's no mischief in your mission?'

Walter shook his head emphatically, wondering what sort of mischief he had in mind, but the man simply gave a curt bow of the head and set off once more, tap-tapping his cane upon the pavement.

The road was long. For a while it climbed steeply and he suddenly had a view of what was surely the harbour below. Those shadowy forms – were they not large ships with small lights on their decks? Beyond these were two larger lights, one red and one green, and then unbroken darkness. They must be the guide-lights at the harbour entrance, and the darkness must be the vast mass of the open sea.

He began to descend and soon found himself entering the old quarter. Here the wide, busy boulevards gave way to narrow alleys and courtyards, light gave way to shadows and noise gave way to silence. The houses hugged each other as if to keep warm in the chilly night air, and Walter's first impression was of a cosy quaintness – bowed windows and polished brass, hung lanterns and jettied walls. Above him the houses seemed to lean forward, almost touching those across the way, obscuring from view all but a thin ribbon of sky.

Twice more he asked the way, the directions leading him to ever more humble, even squalid, parts of the town until, turning a corner, he found the street name on a wooden post. Now he felt ill and weak with anticipation and unease, and he paused a moment, looking along the terrace of small ill-kept houses, some of them with boards nailed across the windows. A strange sound, welling up and dimming, seemed to hover in the air, but in his feverishness he paid little heed to it.

The house he sought was number 46, and he found himself advancing more slowly as he drew towards it. Most of the buildings appeared mere hovels, several of them uninhabited and all in darkness. The occasional muttered conversation or wild, unnatural laugh was all that indicated any human occupation of this neglected area.

As he passed down the street the sound he had been vaguely aware of became louder, more insistent. The thoroughfare ahead seemed at once to be filled with people who came jostling towards him, then veered off and disappeared from view. The row of houses, he soon discovered, came to an abrupt end. The far wall of the last house had attached to it the remains of its one-time neighbour, now torn down – strengthening joists, the portion of a fireplace absurdly isolated halfway up, the protruding stump of a blackened beam. The number of this last house, the painted figures faded on its front door, was 44. He stared at it with a dazed incomprehension.

Across the area of wasteland where further houses had once been, groups of chattering people now made their way to a much larger space in which crowds were milling about to a purpose which was not immediately clear to him. There were machines of some kind and movement everywhere, and everywhere noise and lights and more movement. Walter, who had never seen a fairground in his life, stood and wondered, trembling from mingled frustration and fascination and fear.

The entrance to the fairground was through a pavilion which, announcing

THE PLEASURE PALACE, was like the overwrought dream of an eclectic architect. He passed inside. It combined in brightly painted and varnished piles almost every known style of building: Egyptian temple columns supported Byzantine domes, classical friezes skirted gothic vaults and romanesque arches, and the whole was interwoven with a sort of manic baroque decoration. Unlike the small birds which seemed to have been kept unnaturally awake by the noise and light and were even singing on their perches, Walter's eyes could find no foothold on this structure and simply tumbled from detail to detail.

It was, he thought (and wondered whether the thought were wrong) the most splendid confection, inviting him to taste the delights beyond, and there was something deliciously, disturbingly alluring about the two half-dressed caryatids at either side of the main gateway, their pink bodies emerging from falling draperies.

He had no money, but he needed none. The pleasures were in the eye and the ear. Simply moving between kiosks and sideshows gave his reeling brain indescribable pleasure. He came upon the source of the plangent music: a huge, garishly painted organ ground out its tunes – tunes he had never before heard – powered by an engine that blew gobbets of steam into the air, sucking and blowing, violently shaking, while the music rolled on and on, penetrating his very being. Disembodied cries fell out of the sky. And were these human faces that swam through the lurid light, now green, now red, now blue . . . ?

The world spun before his eyes, rising and falling, turning, turning – and resolving itself in an extravagant roundabout. A fat woman with porcine features sat astride one of a rank of revolving gilded pigs. Leaning across, and rising and falling with the motion of the merry-go-round, a ruddy-cheeked man put an arm around her shoulders and alternately whispered in her ear and pressed kisses against the pink swell of her cheeks. Could he be proposing to her? From nowhere the thought came into Walter's head: 'What sort of swine proposes astride a pig?' He was vaguely shocked with himself for having the thought but laughed out loud at it – heard himself laugh – and walked on between the booths, a pleased grin spread over his face.

Had he turned he would have seen the man take an apple from his pocket and place it in the mouth of the fat lady who, having secured it between her jaws, was forced to leave it there while she rebalanced herself, an excessive amount of flesh having shifted to one side during the transaction and threatening to topple her completely.

His attention was next taken by two large eyes that stared from the beautiful porcelain face of a girl dressed in white silk pyjamas. She stood before a tent, very still and holding a board advertising THE SECRET ATTRACTIONS OF THE HAREM. Walter paused. Surely such stillness was unnatural: a wax figure, perhaps. But no, the eyes looked to the ground when she became aware of his attention, and he felt compelled to speak.

'How much is it?'

There was no answer. She simply lifted her mournful eyes and shook her head.

'It's no good speaking to her. She's a deaf-mute and not quite all there into the bargain.'

The speaker was a man who had stepped from the shadows of the entrance.

'Inside, on the other hand, they're more than all there, if you take my meaning.'

He leered, and his face seemed to Walter the very essence of evil, a white puffy face whose loose flesh seemed to have been powdered and across which two scarlet lips parted like an open wound. As the man's hand moved out to take his elbow and guide him into the hidden treasures of the tent Walter pulled himself free and moved swiftly on, shaking his head, his lips downturned, his brow furrowed.

But later, without knowing why, he returned to watch the girl from the dark space between the two booths opposite. For much of the time she remained unnoticed, as a pasteboard figure might, but what attention she did attract was of a jeering and unpleasant nature. A drunkard put an arm around her waist and kissed her lips: urged on by the owner of the booth, he was then taken by the arm and led inside. A group of youths stood around her, jostling her, resting their hands upon the silk-covered body and calling obscenities into the silence of her ears. Others simply pushed past her or brushed against her, never pausing to apologise but sometimes turning to grin. During these incidents the girl made no protest, remaining as still as her tormentors allowed her to, her eyes searching the ground.

Walter watched the passing world revel in this girl's defencelessness and he knew that he was witnessing a great evil, one that had been spoken of but had remained an abstraction during his years in the monastery. For the first time in his life he felt profoundly ashamed of being human: hatred and spite were almost virtues beside the casualness of this mocking cruelty. He clenched his fists in anger, his fingernails biting into his palms, and he found himself without regard of the consequences stepping from the shadows that had hidden him, walking across to the girl and taking her by the hand. She looked into his eyes as if she understood his feelings and she offered no resistance as he led her away. The board that she held fell to the ground.

A cry went up behind them. Walter began to run as fast as was possible with a girl in tow. At the edge of the fairground he was able to dodge into the darkness that fringed it, stumbling across the waste ground until the grass beneath their feet had turned to stone and he knew them to be in the streets again.

What was this madness that had seized him? He kept a firm grip of the girl's hand and she hurried with him away from the dancing lights into the enveloping darkness. What would she tell him if she could speak?

7 First Night

'O ravens of revenge, descend and tear out the eyes of my oppressors who have brought me to this wretched plight!'

A female form, encased in luminous gossamer apparel, fell to its knees in the centre of the stage, while an audience of perhaps forty souls chuckled and nudged and even conversed in low tones, quite declining to be moved with grief or anger.

Jack, having slipped into the darkened hall towards the end of the performance and having stood by the wall watching, now bent low and made his way forward. He fumbled with the side curtain, became enmeshed in it for a moment and struggled through to the other side.

A lean, almost emaciated man, whose every pocket seemed to be crammed with small tools and other objects whose function it was impossible to guess at, perched on a high stool, his long legs twined around the wooden ones. When he saw Jack he at first gave a delighted smile, then anxiously raised a finger to his lips. Jack nodded.

'Take pity on a poor maiden, ill-used by the world!'

It was a sight which always thrilled him. High up on the walls, flickering tapers lit the stage, that magical space which was one moment a battlefield, the next a desert or a drawing room, a space in which all things, all possible and impossible things, might come to be.

'Will nobody save me?'

There was a call from the audience, the sense of which did not carry as far as the wings but could be guessed at from the cheery laughter which followed it. The man on the stool bent low and took from the floor a large stick with a padded ball at the end. He swung round and struck a heavy brass gong which Jack had overlooked in the folds of the curtain. The sound reverberated loud and long.

'You!'

Standing on tiptoe, Jack could see on to the stage. Belle, the leading lady, knelt on the ground, her gaudy costume billowing around her, eyes astare with horror. She was in some sort of palace and through the door upstage left strutted Luigi, the features of his swarthy face all but lost to view in the uncertain light, his lack of height emphasised by the resplendent uniform he wore, his military bearing scarcely improved by those aggressively sprouting eyebrows.

'My delicious Fatima! I come to take you away!'

'No! Never!'

'The horses are saddled. I will not be denied.'

'No! Rather death than such a fate!'

The audience was beginning to get out of hand. Cries of encouragement were given to both parties, and although most of the interrupters took a chivalrous line, a few urged the soldier to have his will with the hapless girl and be done with. Nor was order restored when another actor made his appearance, leaping athletically to centre-stage and actually turning a cartwheel before advancing on the villain with fine disdain, twirling a curly and patently false moustache.

'Leave her be!'

'My saviour!'

'Foiled!'

'Let's try your skill with the blade!'

'Oh, help!'

A fight to the death took place in an atmosphere redolent of a prize-fight. Great cheers went up each time a blow was struck, technical advice was given freely and in raucous tones and, towards the close, missiles began to be hurled at the participants. Eventually the evil soldier was run through and the brave rescuer led the unfortunate lady to safety. Jack helped lower the curtain to the genuine applause of an audience which had thoroughly enjoyed itself.

8 Backstage

Afterwards there was a subdued spirit among the troupe.

'A tentative initiation,' was Mr Tusker's verdict, delivered in the grandiloquent manner of the showman. 'Tentative and equivocal – but the season is launched.'

They were in a cramped room at the back of the hall. A large and somewhat ragged orange curtain hung from wall to wall at one end, and behind this Belle was changing clothes and removing her make-up.

'A waste of time coming to a hole like this,' she called over the barrier in superior tones. 'No taste whatsoever those people. Culture's wasted upon them.'

Jack sat on a low bench, watching the transformation of sinister soldier back into Luigi and handsome rescuer into Amazing or, to give him his full name, The Amazing India-Rubber Man. Ma Tusker, waddling from one side of the curtain to the other, patrolled the room like a dumpy law officer with a suspicious mind, every so often pouncing on a pile of costumes or prodding at the contents of one of the trunks which spilled over with props or clothing.

'It's humiliating,' Belle went on, a quaver in her voice, 'for an artiste to suffer the indignity of an audience like that. Or perhaps you don't regard us as artistes.'

'Of course I do.'

Mr Tusker sat himself solidly beside Jack and spoke to the curtain.

'Every year the first night depresses you, Belle. Every year without fail. Try to think of it as a dress rehearsal, that's all.'

'We could do a rehearsal in *here*. Without the indignity.'

Luigi dabbed a cloth at his cheeks.

'To throw things like that! Incredible, eh? "Hit him!" they were shouting. "Use the flat edge, man!" I've known worse, mind. They enjoyed the fight, certainly.'

'Oh they enjoyed the fight,' rejoined Belle in a mocking voice. 'Why don't we bring on a dancing bear next time?'

Amazing, giggling like a girl, tugged the moustache from his lip.

'They clapped us,' he said in a pleased manner. 'That's what counts, isn't it? I quite enjoyed myself.'

'A little too much,' was Belle's reply from her closet.

'And what do you mean by that?'

There was a short silence, after which her face appeared around the curtain.

'Leaping about is what I mean. Cartwheeling. You've left the circus now.'

'I may go back.'

'Oh, may you! And I suppose you'll make speeches when you should be tumbling.'

'People like a spectacle.'

'Soldiers and romantic heroes don't do head-over-heels on the stage. Not on any I've seen. What do you say, Mr Tusker?'

The manager, relaxing, with his his hands on his knees, his large belly rhythmically rising and falling, shook his head.

'A little eccentric perhaps, Amazing. I think Belle may have a point. Fewer calisthenics, if you please.'

'Free expression is what you promised me.'

'As part of the company, Amazing. There'll be plenty of opportunity for tumbling. We'll find parts for you. But it has to fit in.'

'I can't just stand around.'

The dashing rescuer of the earlier performance now assumed a dejected expression. He sat looking at his discarded moustache, which lay jauntily on the floor until Ma Tusker swooped upon it and threw it on a pile of wigs and false beards. Luigi closed one eye in an expressive wink.

'All good seasons begin doubtfully,' he pronounced sagely, with the air of one who had been through seasons beyond number.

Belle emerged from her hiding place, the gaudy theatrical costume replaced by a dress of such rich, multicoloured splendour that Jack wondered she had bothered to change at all. Ma Tusker began to take down the curtain.

'Doesn't it matter to you,' Belle demanded, 'that those people laughed at us? While we performed for them, wrung our emotions for them?'

Mr Tusker waved her down.

'Not laughed *at* us, Belle. Never that. It was a kind of appreciation . . .'

'Ha!'

'Laughter is an outpouring of goodwill, never to be despised.'

'In a tragedy!'

Mr Tusker, apparently having no satisfactory reply to hand, closed his eyes and folded his arms upon his stomach. This air of contentment seemed to affect the whole company, so that even the leading lady concluded her outburst with a fine toss of the head and fell to brushing her hair with bold sweeping movement.

'I can remember,' said Luigi, knotting his tie, 'when I was chased out of a town. Fled for my life! Really, if we hadn't run . . .'

He smiled broadly at the memory.

'A small band of minstrels we were. I played the fiddle, and not very well. We made the mistake of trying the patience of a farming community at a time of poor harvest. But how should we know? Bowled into the place, we did, full of swagger and started up our music in the market square. I remember looking about me as I played and noticing that nobody smiled, but not thinking very much about it. Stupid I suppose we were, not to realise. We played on at quite a lick, proud of our quick fingering and our harmonies, and it wasn't until the fellow went round with the hat that the trouble started. They threw him in the air.

'Well, it was every man for himself then. My legs were pretty nimble in those days and of course I only had the fiddle. Pity our poor bass player! I never stopped until I could hide myself under the grasses in a ditch.'

Amazing giggled again, his lips quivering with pleasure.

'Now *that*,' concluded Luigi, 'was what I call a bad reception.'

The door opened, to admit the remaining member of the company, whose array of tools clattered in his pockets. He looked cheerily down at Jack.

'So you're back with us, then. Eager to work, are you?'

Jack nodded, but cautiously said nothing.

'Like to finish the dismantling with me, would you?'

Again he nodded, aware of the uneasy silence around him. Everyone seemed suddenly on edge.

'What's this? Is Jack not welcome? What does this mean?'

Mr Tusker cleared his throat.

'The boy is welcome, Oz. Of course he is. Welcome you are, Jack.'

He patted him on the knee, but warily.

'Are you legal, however?'

'What?'

'You've run away, have you? Are we to expect knocks upon the door?'

'No. Not this time. I'm allowed to be gone.'

'I have your word?'

'Yes, truthfully.'

Oz sat on his other side and held out a greasy hand in greeting. But before Jack could respond Mr Tusker intervened.

'It's not so straightforward, Oz, and you should know it.'

'But the boy's sound. He'll help me well.'

'Don't doubt it, not at all. But it's not the point. Ma – how do you see it?'

His wife peered over an armful of costumes and spoke with an air of grim finality.

'No profit, no pay.'

'Ah, well that's it, you see,' went on the manager. 'Question of money, Jack, when you get down to it. You heard what Ma said just now – couldn't have expressed it more eloquently myself. How was it, Ma?'

'No profit, no pay,' repeated the good lady doggedly.

'We're not a wealthy company,' Mr Tusker went on. 'That's the sharp truth of it. What's the balance at this moment, Ma?'

'Drawing on savings.'

'A minus quantity in other words. We are in sorry debt.'

Jack, never one to wait on events, spoke up bravely.

'I have some money,' he said. 'Enough for a while. I can buy my own food.'

Mr Tusker began to pace the room, scrutinising the faces of his players as if seeking a consensus of opinion on the matter. Ma busied herself at her work once more. Oz, who had been toying with a small hammer, leapt to his feet, brandishing it in his agitation.

'Aren't you paying *us*?' he demanded angrily. 'Is there no money for *us*?'

'Of course, my dear Oz. You know there is.'

'Then what's this about "No profit, no pay"?'

Mr Tusker, calling upon all his powers of compromise and gentle persuasion, approached Oz with his hands apart in a gesture of conciliation.

'An abbreviation,' he soothed. 'Ma has the gift of brevity. Her meaning, as I take it, is that the company must earn its keep.'

He smiled and stroked the bushes of hair on either side of his bald pate.

'I would love to take Jack with us. Wouldn't we all? But imagine that awesome eventuality, an unsuccessful run. Imagine us many miles away and destitute. What would happen to poor Jack then?'

'He should share my food,' replied Oz fiercely.

'If food there were.'

This confrontation between optimism and pessimism, or between sweet reason and obstinacy, seemed to offer no middle way. Luigi, however, taking the space on the bench vacated by Mr Tusker, spoke consolingly to Jack.

'No season makes a profit,' he explained, 'until some weeks have passed. We begin in small places like this where the audiences are small. If they don't like us it doesn't matter much. We pack up after one or two performances and move on.

'But we learn all the time. Why did they throw things tonight? Perhaps . . . '

'Because they're savages!' interrupted Belle, still preening her hair. 'Without souls.'

'Perhaps because the pace was too slow. or because we were too flamboyant. It's possible. Or it may be nothing to do with us at all. The young men here are bored, perhaps. They drank too much before they arrived . . .

'So we learn, and by the time we reach the bigger places – towns where we stay for a week or two – we are performing well. Then we make the money and the profits are shared. But it's a risky business, and first there have to be profits.'

This intervention, while it was interesting for Jack, failed to end the dispute.

'Risk!' exclaimed Oz, the hammer again swinging through the air. 'We always make a profit at the end. We live well enough. I'm the one who does all the heavy work with precious little help. There's still the scenery to come down out there.'

'And we'll all help,' replied Mr Tusker gently. 'Don't we always help?'

'When most of the work is done.'

Seeing that there was no easy victory in the offing, the manager changed his approach.

'In this company,' he said, turning to Jack, 'there's no such thing as a specialist. Everyone has to be adaptable. Oz here is a fine man backstage – scenery, effects and everything – but even he puts on the greasepaint from time to time. And Ma, too. She looks after . . . well, how shall we put it, Ma? What do you regard as your province?'

She took up two burnished helmets and tossed them into a chest containing articles of war.

'The necessaries.'

'Quite so. Ma looks after the necessaries. But she'll sell tickets and she'll learn the lines and tread the boards when circumstances demand it. We don't carry passengers.'

Amazing, with a nervous smirk, his eyes averted, piped up: 'And Belle?'

This apparently innocent question had remarkable consequences. Mr Tusker's brow corrugated and he fought for words which would calm the sudden rage which seized his leading lady. Palliatives came too late, however, and a hairbrush flew through the air and hit the one-time tumbler full on the chest.

'Go back to your circus!' screamed Belle. 'It's all you're worth! Go and join the dancing dogs and the clowns with their baggy trousers! Whoever heard of a theatre troupe without a star? It's not an acrobat they come to see!'

Amazing's lips continued to twitch, but Jack guessed this was now from terror.

'Don't you understand that I have to nourish my feelings? Come, Mr Tusker – don't I have to nourish my feelings?'

'Of course, Belle. Of course. Nourish . . . '

'Or would you rather I swept the floor? Forget sensitivity – I'll sweep the floor!'

And she grasped a broom which leant against the wall and charged full tilt at Amazing who, reacting just in time, sprang to one side, tugged open the door and fled. Jack, alarmed, was reassured by another large wink from Luigi.

'Don't take on,' urged Mr Tusker. 'Calm yourself, Belle.'

'Employing tumblers!'

'We'll train him. You'll see. Don't take on.'

Belle, who seemed to possess the ability to change moods in a moment, tossed the broom into a corner, picked up her brush and continued with her grooming. Mr Tusker disappeared in search of Amazing. Oz and Luigi set about dismantling the remaining scenery. Jack felt for a while that he had been forgotten. Eventually, however, the manager returned with Oz in tow and sat himself on the bench.

'What we'll agree to is this,' he said. 'The next few performances don't take us very far. You can stay with us till we're ready to travel longer distances. Then we'll make a fresh assessment. No promises.'

Jack nodded violently, the excitement temporarily depriving him of speech, and he shook and shook the greasy hand which Oz once more held out to him.

9 Wanderers

A keen wind whipped between the loose boards of the upturned rowing boat and, chilling his exposed face, woke him up. He rolled from under the sacking and raised the edge of the boat. His eyes took in first the shaking grasses, then the strip of bare earth by the fence. Beyond, piles of rope and tackle, skeins of drying nets, advertised the fishermen's wharf. He struggled out, raised himself to his knees and, facing the brighter part of the sky, flattened his palms together and began to pray.

As he finished he heard the girl begin to stir. She emerged and a ray of light seemed to focus upon her smile. He thought: *If she could only speak my name, say 'Walter' as she woke* . . . Together they watched the rising sun skip across the waters.

Already the waterfront was busy. The fishing boats were home, and light shimmered and danced upon the myriad red and silver scales of the dawn catch. Further along, a brazier burned and people stood around it, toasting their hands and chewing food that had been warmed over the coals. Away from the water there was more activity still, as if the town had never gone to sleep. Shops were already open and a window-cleaner, whistling merrily high on his ladder, sent a shower of suds about their heads.

As the morning progressed the life of the city unfolded itself ever more colourfully and Walter, holding his companion tightly by the hand, grew more excited with each new sight, each new discovery. He longed to ask her questions, but when he turned to the girl she would only smile and watch him with eyes that seemed to contain even more secrets and wonders than O—

itself. They walked wide avenues, narrow passageways, crowded streets, deserted alleys. The shops and markets were athrong, the docks teemed with boisterous life, the streets clattered and sparked with the electric trams which were a wonder to him. Hawkers sold breakfasts – hot rolls which the customers took steaming from heated trays and ate while walking, as if not to miss a minute of industry.

Remembering the old lady's coin, Walter fished it from his pocket and proffered it to a breakfast-man. It was too little, but seeing the disappointment on Walter's face and wondering at his silk-clad friend, the man nevertheless offered him a roll, which he immediately broke in two, passing half to the girl. The soft white bread beneath the crust held a layer of spiced meat that contrasted sharply with the plain fare of the monastery and transformed even this simple meal into a transport of delight.

It was several hours before fashionable O— was abroad, and amid the vagaries of dress evident in the sunny streets the austere cut of Walter's black clothes and the contrasting flow of the silk pyjamas was less noticeable. Sometimes Walter led, pulling his companion along; sometimes she led, skipping between the people in the manner of a playful young animal, several times leaving Walter red-faced and wrapped around an angry or amused pedestrian in his attempt to remain attached to her.

The aimlessness of their progress was so alien to his training as to cause a pleasant lightheadedness, a feeling of abandon, and, at the same time, an underlying unease. An awareness began to grow in him of the precariousness of his position. He had no money and no immediate prospect of getting any. And, far worse it seemed, he had no plan. Accustomed to ordering his life by the tolling of a bell, he felt a giddiness overcoming him in their career through the busy streets.

'If only . . . ' he began to say, and realised at once that she could not hear him. If only the house had not been destroyed. Perhaps he would have learned nothing of consequence, but now it seemed that he was never to know. He had come here from a sense of duty, from a feeling that his destiny was in some way bound up with the strange package left at the monastery from his early days. What was he to do?

He took the girl's hand and began to tug her away from the market stall at which she gazed with rapt attention. Was it not possible that he might yet discover something of importance by returning to the place? She followed complaisantly, uncomprehending, until they approached the fairground and then she began to pull away, stabbing a finger towards the scene of her humiliation.

'No, no,' urged Walter. 'I must. I must.'

He brought his face close to hers and pronounced the words clearly so that she could read the movement of his lips.

'I must.'

But she, for her reasons, must not and, he pulling and she resisting, they fought their first battle of wills. No doubt muscle would in the end have prevailed, but while they were engaged in their struggle they were surprised by the very man she sought to escape. His pale, bloated face leered down at them.

'Acting like man and wife already, I see!' he sneered.

'Leave her alone,' said Walter, stoutly.

'Oh, I don't want her,' was the unexpected reply. 'Trouble was all she was. Never played up to the customers. Not even a wink. I've found someone better, I have.'

The girl, covering her face and pressing herself close to Walter for protection, shivered from fear.

'Little half-caste wench. Most alluring. Smiles when the gentlemen stroke her.'

'I don't want to know,' Walter replied

'But perhaps you've had a better response from this one. Found the way to tease her to life, have you?'

'Go away!'

Walter took the girl's hand and began to lead her off. She opened fearful eyes and watched with amazement as her oppressor, with a final salacious remark, strode off in the other direction.

They stood by the last house in the row, an emaciated black dog sniffing at their feet. Who had lived in the missing number 46? Why had it been pulled down? The fairground was silent. Few people passed this way during the day, and most of those who came by were itinerants from the booths or vagrants who knew a place only by its pickings. Only one man offered any help at all, and that was meagre.

'Gone years ago,' he said. 'It's been like this for a long time.'

'But why?'

'Don't rightly know. Fell down, maybe. It's the Count's land, this is.'

'The Count?'

'Surely. But he has so much that I don't suppose he remembers it's his. Not a good place to hang around, lad.'

By mid-afternoon they were tired and hungry. Walter, moved by the girl's obvious boredom and discomfort, led her back into the centre of town. They sat for a while in a plaza. A street led from it with arcades on either side, reminding him of the cloisters that he had so recently walked through, dreaming of O—. These cloisters, however, lacked the elegance of those at the monastery: the arches were wide and plastered, and rested upon broad, squat columns. On either side, between the columns, were the shops, their abundance of goods tumbling from the shaded recesses of the interiors onto a covered walkway where the proprietors stood talking and eyeing the passers-by with a mixture of welcome and guardedness. Outside, men sat at tables playing chess. The street between the arcades at either side was bright with sunshine, and a beggar who stood with hands outstretched at the pavement's edge appeared even thinner as the surrounding light etched yet more flesh away from his already starved body.

How could these shopkeepers stand guard over their rich stores of food and face a hungry man? The monastic ideal of sharing for the common good was all that Walter had known and this alien ethic of the trader disturbed him. Those large and glowing oranges, for example. They grew on trees thanks to Providence alone and here were people demanding money for them. He vowed on the instant that he would never allow the girl and himself to starve in the midst of plenty. Trained to apply the powers of the mind to questions of truth and virtue and justice, he swiftly decided the ethics of the case. That which was not offered in open charity would simply have to be taken.

He took a step forward, his heart pounding . . .

10 Prison Walls

The cell was not uncomfortable, though bare enough: he was used to that. The police had not been cruel, simply indifferent; the meal had been substantial, if tasteless; and there had been ample time to eat and digest it. What really made Walter miserable was his separation from the girl. Where was she? Where had they taken her? Her eyes had turned imploringly towards him as they had led her away, and he felt that he had betrayed her.

'How long must I stay here?' he had asked the guard who sat at a desk between the rows of cells.

'Long enough,' was the answer. 'Thems as takes the goods must take the consequences.'

'But where's my friend?'

'In similar accommodation to yours, I dare say. She's a rum one. How'd you come to pick up with her, I wonder, an educated lad like yourself? Well, no affair of mine. Shut up now, there's a good fellow, and let's get some kip.'

And sliding his peaked cap forward over his eyes he allowed his round body to relax back into his chair and very quickly fell asleep.

Through a small window high in his cell Walter watched the sky turn by degrees from pale to dark blue and then from dark blue to purple until finally it became the star-filled blackness of night. He had time enough to consider the incompetence of his thieving. Having no experience of surreptitious behaviour, he had simply taken an orange in each hand and run. The girl had kept pace with him, but the way was crowded and arms, legs, baskets impeded them at every turn. However strenuously they pushed at the obstructions they could not possibly run fast enough . . .

Sleep did not come easily. It was fitful, and disturbed by dreams even more dreadful than the reality which he kept waking to. Eventually, however, and as the first light of morning was bleaching the small square of sky above him, he drifted into a deeper unconsciousness, from which he was woken only by vigorous shaking and a shouting in his ear. He opened his eyes to find the police officer staring at him.

'Wake up, son. You're in luck.'

Walter sat up, blinking in the brightness.

'What do you mean, luck?'

'Someone must be looking after you, that's what I mean. The shopkeeper isn't pressing charges. You're free.'

'Free!'

'Seemed a sensible sort of fellow when he brought you in. Don't usually change their minds. Somebody put in a good word for you maybe. Slipped a coin or two, I shouldn't wonder. Either that or you were born lucky. Anyway – whatever the whys and wherefores of it – you're free.'

Walter was led from the cells into the main room of the police station. The officer in charge, feet up on a large desk, asked him to sign a document and indicated that he should leave.

'But the girl!' Walter cried. 'I can't leave without the girl.'

'They didn't say anything about her.'

'Where is she?'

'You are to go,' said the officer woodenly. 'That's all it says here.'

'But, then . . . '

'This piece of paper,' the officer went on doggedly, 'is my instructions.'

'I can't, I *won't*, go without her.'

The officer's face clouded.

'Resisting the instructions of an officer of the law,' he said sombrely. 'You want to stay inside, do you?'

'No, no . . . Please!'

The officer shrugged.

'I'll go and check. If the answer's "no" you'll have two minutes to get off the premises.'

It was some time before Walter heard two sets of footsteps coming along the corridor.

'All right,' said the officer grudgingly. 'She can go, too. It's all the same to me. She's more trouble than she's worth, anyway. Can't get anything out of her.'

He reached for a slip of paper on the desk top and pushed it towards Walter.

'She'll have to sign this first, though. And I need a name. There.'

'A name?'

'Unless you want them to suspect me of locking up a ghost – then letting it go with an appropriate warning. A name is what I need, even if she won't speak up for herself.'

Walter took the pen. After a moment's deliberation he wrote, in a clear hand, 'Sarah'.

'And don't let them catch you next time!'

The reunion sealed the bond that had grown between them. The girl, her face tear-stained, simply held out her hand to Walter who, taking it, led her from the police station into a new day.

Yet it was the girl – Sarah as she must henceforth be – who led Walter into a new way of life. For the moment, leaving the police station, he felt only the triple joys of freedom and the spring morning and fond companionship. He did not, immediately, reflect on the fact that their problems had in no way changed. She, however, pressed on with great determination until they reached the main market square.

The traders were setting out their stalls for a new day's business. She stopped in an open space and proceeded to measure out an area of pavement with her outstretched arms. Walter watched in amazement, totally bewildered by her actions and the resolution that accompanied them. What could she be planning to do? They had nothing to sell. But then, as the first customers drifted into the market square, she began – and Walter watched open-mouthed as she twisted her body into barely imaginable positions. She arched backwards until her hands touched the ground behind her, and then, after thrusting her legs into the air, proceeded to fold herself gently downwards until her body, wrapped as neatly as a parcel, was held by her arms just above the pavement. She began to rotate, at first using two hands and then transferring the whole of her weight to one and performing the motion in a series of hops. From his position she suddenly sprang apart into a high star-jump, which was the beginning of a sequence of somersaults and back-flips delivered at such speed that Walter became dizzy from watching. Indeed, he was so taken by the performance that he failed to notice the other onlookers and became aware of them only when, at the final leap followed by a deep bow, they burst into a round of applause, the more appreciative throwing coins onto the ground in front of her. She stooped to gather them and handed them to Walter, who took them red-faced and alarmed at his new role of theatrical manager.

The first performance paid for their breakfast, and further sessions during the day not only fed them but left them a little over to carry back to the upturned boat at the fishermen's wharf.

The problem, Walter mused, had been solved. Sarah slept exhausted beside him as he stared at the blackness of the boards, his thoughts gyrating just as her limbs had done in the market square. The problem had been solved, but in a way that he hated. What had he been able to contribute? He had stood beside her, watching her share herself with passing strangers, and he had collected the money in the role of protector and exploiter.

He hated it, but as yet he had no alternative to offer.

11 An Invitation

'Deuced if I know, boy. You ask who lived in a house that isn't here? Why should it matter to you?'

'That I don't know.'

'What! Are you crazy, boy?'

Walter found himself drawn, day after day, to the wasteland where the missing house had been, yet however much he asked he could discover nothing of importance about it. He had even knocked on the doors of the mean buildings that remained, but the pitiful wrecks of people who answered his knock or pressed their faces to the grimy windows either would not speak or knew nothing of the past.

This afternoon he had left Sarah alone in the market place while he came to stand at the familiar spot, waiting in case anyone should approach him. The temperature had dropped suddenly during the previous night, as it sometimes does when spring has an apparently irreversible hold upon the world – as if to remind the unwary that winter is not so long dead that it cannot achieve a brief resurrection. Snow was forecast and the market place had become a place of bleak torment for Walter and his friend. Between morning performances he had wrapped Sarah in his heavy cloak and had near frozen, marching up and down and banging his arms around his body. Now he had left it behind with her and his bones ached with the cold.

'Excuse me, sir. Do you know this part of the town?'

'Tolerable well, I suppose.'

'Can you remember how it was here fifteen years ago? When there was a house here?'

'Fifteen years! I lived way out west, then. Been here three years come midsummer day.'

And so it went on. Yet he was determined not to give in. He had left the monastery, where he had known a sense of vocation, only because it was, mysteriously, demanded of him. He had even overcome his original distaste for the life he now lived. In a world which used money was it not foolish to turn one's back upon it? And was it not as honourable to earn money by a form of dancing as by locking people in prison cells? The world was strange to him, but he would try to understand it before he condemned it out of hand.

Today, however, he could stand the chill no more. Stamping his feet, rubbing his arms for warmth, he began to retrace his steps. Although he had left Sarah alone, she was not among strangers. They had swiftly become established in their part of the market. Walter had thought that the stallholders might object to their continued presence, but the opposite was the case: the unusual performance drew people to their quarter and the traders found their sales increasing. Not that this popularity brought them much money. There was little surplus at the end of the day, but they ate well, joining with the market traders in the eating houses that surrounded the square.

The traders were friendly and included Walter in the loose weave of their social life, and he for his part tried to reciprocate their friendship although finding it difficult. He shared nothing of their background and values, and he resented their patronising attitude towards Sarah and the curiosity shown in their relationship, yet he smiled when he could and learned how to banter in their good-natured fashion.

She was performing as he returned to the square. A large crowd was gathered – folk attracted by the roasted meats and hot pies on sale at various stalls – and it was some time before he managed to push his way through and stand by her side. She smiled up at him, but never for a moment faltered in her lithe, elastic movements.

When she had finished she offered him the cloak. They shared it, he trembling with cold, she warm from her exertions, and it was while they were crouched in this makeshift tent that a man stepped out of the crowd. He was a tall aristocratic figure, a man warmly and fashionably dressed and encompassed around by a scented cloud, from which a thin, reptilian voice descended.

'Just the sort of thing the Count would love,' it said.

Walter looked up into the powdered face.

'I beg your pardon? Were you addressing me?'

'Oh, and educated too! How splendid! Would you and your friend come to the Count's residence tonight, do you think?'

'To perform?' asked Walter, thinking with a twinge of shame of the fee he might demand.

'But as guests, dear boy, as guests. Perhaps a little performance if the occasion offers itself – all is fluid and the Count does enjoy diversions it's true. But no, consider yourselves as guests. And don't worry about dress: you both look splendid as you are – very colourful.'

At this he produced a card from his pocket, ornately printed in gold on purple. He handed it to Walter with a flourish and a bow, whispering in his ear at the same time, 'The food will be awfully good, too.'

Totally nonplussed Walter stood gazing at the invitation for some time.

> SNOW WATCHING PARTY
>
> a Japanese fancy
>
> * * *
>
> an invitation
> to the palace
> Rue de Rêve
> tonight towards dusk

When he looked up, the man had stepped back into the market crowds and was threading his way towards a carriage that waited at the edge of the square. The encounter had not been lost on one of the neighbouring stallholders, who nudged Walter with his elbow in a friendly way.

'You're all right there, boy. The Count's got plenty to spare – money, that is, not sense. Perhaps a bit'll come you way. You go, old son, you won't get many opportunities like that.'

12 The Snow Party

Walter and Sarah were shown into a large room permeated with the pink light of dying day. It was remarkable both for the plainness of its interior (it was unfurnished save for cushions scattered across the floor, and everything, walls, ceiling, carpet, cushions, was of a uniform silvery grey) and for the size of its windows, which comprised a complete wall. These windows were held by an intricate lacework of lead and supported by mullions of cast iron, gilded and fashioned into a row of palm trees whose branches met at the top to form a series of arches. Much of the glass was pure white, but some sections of tinted green and pink glass had been inserted, and these seemed to sing a delicate but emphatic melody against the monochromatic interior.

It was before these windows that the guests assembled, and Walter was comforted by the extraordinary variations in their dress. Some stood and some reclined on cushions, silent and watching. The gardens were already finely dusted with snow, a frozen white powder that sparkled in the fading light, but as they watched the sky began to fill with large flakes that floated down as silently as prayers. When darkness was complete a host of servants entered the gardens and lit coloured lanterns that were suspended from the branches of trees. They carefully avoided walking across the lawns and spoiling the snow that already lay like a freshly laundered white napkin. Instead they emerged from thickets that edged the grass, spirits from another world carrying their own small, protected flames. And now the falling snow was transformed, taking to itself one hue and then another as it floated past the various lights.

Still the guests remained silent and watching. Sarah stood beside Walter, her body as motionless as it had been at that first sight of her at the fairground but her warmth reminding him of the reality of her presence. He found himself seeing the falling powder as if for the first time, for although the mountain valley in which he had spent most of his life was often buried in snow and remained so for three months of every year, and although the high peaks that surrounded the monastery were continually covered in it, he had never stood still and watched like this, had never seen snow in this way. It had been a thing whose arrival had been greeted with delirious joy by the monastery boys, who welcomed this intrusion into dull routine and, out of sight of the brothers, would throw themselves into the drifts and pelt one another with snowballs until the novelty faded (as it did each year), until the cold, wet feet, chapped hands and burning faces demanded more attention that the frozen pleasures it brought.

Never had it occurred to him that the primary pleasure of snow was to be found in this process of transforming the workaday world into a place of perfection, filling corners, rounding off surfaces, covering dirt and decay and dereliction – and all of this silently, by stealth. He recalled part of the liturgy chanted each morning by the brothers, where they spoke of the masking of evil, of sin wrapped in chaste garments, and he found it imaged in this smothering snow. Pressing Sarah's hand more tightly within his own, he was at the same time aware of a stirring among the other guests. The Japanese Fancy had evidently run its course: it was time for other, less delicate, pleasures.

In the next room the chandeliers were being lit and the guests were ushered in by an army of lackeys. This room contrasted greatly with the one they had left. As that was simple, so this was ornate and heavily furnished. A huge fire roared beneath a fireplace elaborately carved with biblical scenes, although Walter noticed that the sculptor had concentrated unduly upon those that depicted the less virtuous side of humanity: indeed, had one's introduction to the Bible been solely through this fireplace one might have imagined this to be a more ancient Decameron. What would the brothers have made of this vivid representation of Eve sporting the serpent so wholeheartedly? What man would not be reduced to ineffectual weakness by this Delilah? And the wicked Jezebel, centrally placed, her open mouth receiving Naboth's grapes – who could fail to succumb to her blandishments? The sculptor's skill had so transformed the cold, hard marble as to give it the properties of living flesh, and Walter felt tempted to reach up and stroke it, press it. He was prevented only by Sarah's warm hand pulling him towards the table, where two seats were reserved for them at the banquet, hinting irresistibly at another biblical story.

The table was long and at is head sat the tall man who had presented Walter with the invitation, though he gave no hint of recognition. Walter leaned to the lady on his left and asked which was the Count. The lady, whose long pale neck supported an equally long face divided by a splendidly curved nose, the whole of which emerged from a mountain of sequined black taffeta like an early sun-starved plant, pressed her painted lips against Walter's ear in such a way that he received her reply both through whispered sound and felt movement: 'The Count never eats with his guests. He will be here for the dancing. You will know him when you see him. Such a man . . . '

She was interrupted by the arrival of a waiter bearing a lacquered tray.

What did they eat? They had no way of telling, so unfamiliar was it in appearance from anything they had ever previously consumed. And the taste – would that not provide a clue? Unlikely, for each natural flavour had been so overlaid by scented spices as to be totally unrecognisable. As for enjoyment, suffice it to say that they ate enough not to stand accused of ingratitude.

The guests, as they finished, left the table, not pausing to bid farewell to their neighbours. In fact the whole meal was taken with little interflow of conversation, the earlier flirtation with silence seeming to have thrust them into a more reflective mood that made them ponder each mouthful of food as dreamily as they had the falling snow.

And then the dancing! He had expected the ballroom to be perhaps grand in the manner of the dining room or elegantly simple in the manner of the viewing room, but it was neither. Here was rather a huge round area ceilinged with a lanterned dome. The surface of the walls and dome was of an unreflective black studded by thousands of small round mirrors which snatched the candles' light and thrust it back in a constant flutter of bright flashes. The impression was one of stepping into the heavens at night, and so cleverly contrived that for a moment Walter found himself looking at his feet to verify that the floor remained beneath them. But the glories of this were soon eclipsed by the arrival of the Count himself – a gilded bird, face and hair dusted with gold, jerkin and tights fully sequined, and golden wings that sprang from his shoulders and swept to the floor in a vast arc. He looked for the world like the Archangel Michael stepped from an icon, and when he smiled his parted golden lips revealed teeth enamelled with gold, beyond which the scarlet recesses of his mouth took on a richness of hue so that his words seemed to flow from torn satin. As he spoke, bidding a hidden orchestra to begin its playing, he stroked his chin with hands transformed into feathered talons, and as he walked his wings rustled and gently swept the floor. An archangel . . . had he been sober.

The silence of the snow-watching, the reticence of the meal, gave way now to an eruption of excited noise as the music began and the guests hunted for partners to drag to the dance-floor. Walter clung to Sarah lest he should lose her in the mêlée and she silently led him into a dance, guiding his body through the unfamiliar movements in a way that Walter could only wonder at, knowing her to be locked within her own total silence, for her rhythm was faultless. How? Was she able to feel the pulse of music through the vibrations of the floor? Did she take her clues from the other dancers? He simply followed, happy to be led.

And with the dancing, the wine began to flow. What had been adequate at the meal was now supplemented by filled goblets urged upon the dancers by persuasive servants, clearly bidden by their master to make sure that enough was drunk to ensure a lively affair. Sarah's deafness protected her against such persuasion, but Walter, with no such defence, submitted again and again. It seemed that whenever they paused for breath a glass was pressed into his hand, and he tossed back the contents before plunging into the fray once more.

His mind grew hazier and hazier. The drink numbed his brain; the music was a drug of another kind. He was aware of Sarah being snatched from him and whisked off into a wild dance, and then he found two arms embracing him and carrying him to the dark centre of the ballroom. He was dimly conscious of the long face with the curved nose, the lips this time pressing against his lips. Lips and murmurings. But partners changed; he felt himself moved from person to person, men and women alike, swaying and reeling, being twirled to the music, until he found himself enfolded in the gilded wings of the Count himself. Looking into the exotic face Walter divined an expression of distress that seemed to cloud the shining visage.

'Oh dear, I think I must go to the garden. Help me, dear boy.'

And he found himself supporting the stricken bird through doors held wide by footmen and into the snow-laden garden. The sudden coldness sobered Walter sufficiently for him to focus on the Count, golden beneath a silver moon, throwing up into the pale blue snow of the lanterned garden.

As the Count surfaced for air he turned a sad face towards Walter and murmured quietly but distinctly, 'Such a dear boy, a dear, dear boy' – then slid gracefully to the ground, totally unconscious.

Walter, leaving him to the attention of his servants, made his uncertain way back into the ballroom where he found a distressed Sarah surrounded by drunken guests imploring her to perform. She seemed so lost, so desolate, that Walter felt the pain keenly through his stupor. He took her firmly by the hand and led her from the party.

Walking back through the empty streets of O— towards the boat, Sarah sobbed gently and Walter, sick from too much wine and the memory of his own behaviour, clung to her, resolving that his weakness – his newly discovered weakness – should never again cause her misery.

What was the meaning of this life he now lived? Why had he been enticed to O— with its manifold temptations? Who was he supposed to meet at the missing house by the fairground?

13 A Picnic

His face, save for the unchanging blotch on his right cheek, had turned ruddy brown in the space of a few days. The brief cold spell had been followed by the balmiest of weather and Jack – always awake before the rest of the company – had gloried in the fresh country air from first light every morning. Happily engaged in helping Oz with the scene-painting, the construction of stageflats and other backstage work, he had nonetheless escaped into the open whenever possible, willingly going on shopping and other errands if they were merely hinted at.

So it was that he had discovered what the others would never have been aware of – a large lake, blue under the clear sky with grassy slopes where you approached it from the village and a wooded farther shore which demanded to be explored. Over recent days (a perpetual loading and unloading at small railway stations, a rushed building and dismantling of sets, a learning and revising of lines) they had performed for a number of small communities, to meagre audiences which nevertheless constituted the bulk of the population. This place was rather bigger and they would be staying one night more. Today, therefore, they could relax a little – though it seemed that the intense discussions about their craft never ceased – and Jack, by wheedling and pestering, had coaxed them into taking their lunch by the lakeside.

Now that they all sat eating grainy bread and drinking thick goat's milk which seemed to leave a lining on the palate he unfolded the second part of his scheme.

'We should take a boat out,' he enthused. 'We could row to the other side.'

'Boat?' queried Oz. 'Can't say I've seen one.'

'But I have!' Jack said quickly. 'There are several further along the bank. The men fish in the early morning.'

Luigi took a flagon of the dark local wine from the picnic hamper and filled the chunky glasses that were held out to him.

'I like boats,' he said. 'My grandfather was a sea captain. Schooners.'

'Splendid!' responded Belle dreamily. 'Find us a four-master, Jack, and we'll follow you beyond the horizon.'

Jack laughed and jumped to his feet. He knew to act while they were happily disposed towards the idea.

'A rowing boat will have to do,' he said, 'but I'll find a good one.'

He hurried along the bank, brushing through low bushes, until he came to a small wooden jetty. Some half dozen boats had been pulled up on to the shore, and alongside one of them the figure of a lean and elderly man lay stretched on the grass in the sun. His arms were folded over his face and his chest rose and fell rhythmically.

'Excuse me.'

There was no response. Jack repeated the phrase more loudly, with the same result: the old man might have been in a coma. The next ploy was to whistle, tunelessly, at a distance of about six feet, but he might as well have played sweetly on a harp. While he could certainly have aroused the sleeper by shaking his shoulder, Jack judged that a hasty awakening of that sort was unlikely to suit his cause. He pondered for some minutes until, stooping to the ground, he picked up a stone and tossed it up in the air and into the still water of the lake.

The liquid explosion was certainly far gentler than anything that had gone before but the old man, his ear trained for the surfacing of fish, was alert in an instant, propped on one elbow with a flat palm shielding his eyes from the glare.

'What want, boy?' he asked tersely.

'Looking at the boats. They're very fine.'

'Long as you only look.'

He examined Jack carefully, having all the time in the world.

'Where you from, then?'

'From the theatre. Tusker's. Did you watch us last night?'

'No sir.'

'Tonight then?'

'No sir. Not the theatre. No time for it.'

Jack, feeling at a disadvantage, nevertheless pressed on.

'We had a good audience last night. They called the actors back three times.'

The old man stretched himself out once more, but this time with his hands behind his head.

'The more fool them,' he said bluntly.

'But don't you like a good story – with plenty of action?'

'A good story, eh? No I do not. Airy-fairy nonsense. Plenty of good stories I could tell. And as for action . . . '

Jack grew closer and sat on his haunches.

'We've a play about the siege of Troy,' he said. 'And another's called Romeo and Juliet. It's a romance.'

'Ha!'

'But not a soppy romance. Really! There's poisoning and lots of fighting.'

His companion said nothing for some time, only made a discontinuous humming sound deep in his throat which might have signified derision, contentment or a dozen other emotions.

'All that fancy's for women,' he remarked eventually. 'Women and whipper-snappers. Amusing enough for them, I don't doubt.'

The conversation having taken an unpromising turn, Jack took to plopping more stones into the water. Since the old man was his only hope, however, he tried again.

'You've seen plenty of real action, I suppose,' he said encouragingly. 'That's why you've no time for the theatre.'

'True enough.'

The eyes closed and Jack expected that at any moment he would drop off to sleep again. Minutes passed in silence. Then the fisherman began to speak in a drowsy, distant manner that at first seemed rather eery.

'I've heard the noise of battle, boy. Once you've heard that there's no joy in bringing it back for play. The real thing's bad enough, believe me.'

'Back some years, mind. I was pretty young then, and innocent too. They rounded us up and led us off to war. You go down on your knees and pray that you never see war in your time, boy. Seems to have gone out of fashion, maybe, but it'll be back.'

An eye opened and winced in the glare of the sun.

'We'd never been five miles from home, most of us. Imagine how we felt, pushed into waggons and taken to the ends of the earth. That's how it felt. The ends . . . And then to fight . . . '

He looked Jack fiercely in the eye.

'Ever fired a musket, have you?'

'No. Never.'

'Nasty business.'

The voice ceased and Jack found himself breaking in urgently.

'Tell me about the battles! Where were you?'

'Ah, the battles. Grim, boy . . . '

He had not hesitated, but he seemed to respond to the questioning by becoming ever more vague and far away.

'Which battles?'

It was a while before the old man resumed, in little more than a whisper.

'Horses with tossing manes . . . Banners fluttering bravely in the breeze . . . The sound of gunfire, cannonshot. Blood. Men with terrible wounds . . . . A captain kneeling by a dying subaltern . . . '

The manner of the old man's speech had become so strange, and the description was so like that of a hundred paintings of battle scenes, that Jack had a sensation which slowly transformed itself into the thought that the story might be pure invention. Yet the man had scorned the fancy of the players' art.

'Who did you serve under?' he asked, wondering whether his doubt showed. 'Was he a great leader?'

'A fine man, my lad. Upright and honest. We lost him in our second attack on the hill . . . Shot clean through.'

'What was his name?'

'We buried him with full honours. The trumpets sounded. There were tears in the eyes of strong men when we lowered him into the ground . . . The thud of turves on the coffin lid . . . '

Jack, more than ever sure that his intuition was correct, nevertheless refrained from further interrogations. He let the story drift on (the remnants of the proud army winning a battle against all the odds; medals for the leaders; a rough back-slapping from the general for the other ranks) until it reached a natural conclusion and the old man smiled happily at the thought of travails bravely borne. More minutes passed before he spoke again, and now it was in his normal tones once more.

'And what are you after?' he asked sharply.

'I was hoping,' Jack replied, 'to hire your boat.'

'Oh, you were!'

He sat up, suddenly alert.

'How much?'

'I don't know,' said Jack, off guard. 'I'm not sure.'

'Two hundred.'

'Too much!'

'Lad like you could damage her. Two hundred.'

'I've adults with me. Fifty!'

Man and boy seemed suddenly in their element. Jack, used to practising his sharp wits on the streets of his native city, threw himself into the bargaining with a feverish expertise. The old man, amused, played him like a fish on a line – impressed to find him no easy catch.

'The more people, the more wear and tear. But I'll offer you 180.'

'Look at the boat. It's old. Those along there are bigger and newer. We might manage 90 between us.'

'I could make that in an hour's work on the water.'

'When you're working. But the boat's idle now. It's all profit to you.'

'Then 150.'

'A hundred's my top.'

The eventual result of their haggling was a compromise at 120. Jack, returning to his friends at a spring, swiftly calculated the charge per head if he were to make a small profit on the deal, deciding with equal rapidity that the risk of discovery was too great. As it happened, he found that not everyone was keen to go.

'Never did take to water,' apologised Oz, whittling away at a stick with his penknife. 'Washing's bad enough.'

Nor would Ma Tusker be persuaded. She patrolled the picnic area, whisking discarded plates from under startled noses, making a pile of used cotton napkins, and she shook her head to all of her husband's entreaties.

'Needs guarding,' she proclaimed, as though robber bands were about to leap from hiding and rifle the hamper.

'It won't be the same without you, Ma,' cajoled her husband, who today gaily sported one of his orange outfits that almost outstared the sun. 'The breezes will bring roses to your cheeks.'

'Needs guarding.'

These words were final. The rest of the party followed Jack along the lakeshore to the jetty. The fisherman had already manoeuvred the boat to the water's edge, but he produced the oars only after twice counting the money which Mr Tusker held out to him. Jack, helping to push the oars into the rowlocks, noticed that he limped badly, as if one leg were shorter than the other, and when his shirt fell open he saw broad and ugly scars criss-crossing his chest.

'Treat her well!' he called, pushing them out into the lake.

It was a large boat so that Jack, sitting at the prow next to the ample form of Mr Tusker, had plenty of room to move, twisting round to watch their progress towards the opposite shore. This progress was not steady, however, for Luigi and Amazing had elected to row and were not well matched. Amazing, for all his muscular control and balance, was not framed for heavy pulling and made violent stabs at the water while Luigi, bending heavy shoulders to the task, dug deeply and strongly. As a result their craft made strange tacking movements, much to the amusement of Belle who sat in the best seat, trailing her fingers in the rippling water, the flounces of her lacy dress waving in the light breeze.

'You'll be landing us a trout before you know it,' she teased Amazing, but without a trace of malice.

The party was in splendid spirits. Mr Tusker entertained them to a brief and colourful account of famous sea voyages through the ages, all of which he compared unfavourably with the epic journey they now undertook, finding a literary allusion for every one. Had not Odysseus required to be tied to the mast in order to resist the tempting voices of the sirens on the shore? Yet this band of sailors could view the greater sight of Ma and Oz on the grassy bank and pass them by with a wave! Columbus, discovering a new continent, had so far underestimated his distance as to believe his first sighting of land to be the Indian shore. These adventurers, on the other hand, had been impeccable in their navigation, however erratic ('athwart, behind and stray' he quoted obscurely) however unpredictable their course had been.

Belle, intoxicated by the gentle zephyrs and the limpid water, was unceasing in her praise of the natural world – a world which she normally shunned, spending her evenings in the theatre and the daytime indoors, resting and 'rekindling the creative fires'. As they floated into deeper waters, the ripples clucking at the oars, she exclaimed ecstatically at the patterns of the sunlight, the dancing droplets on the surface, the shades of green luminescence penetrating the depths.

Caught between these two forms of eloquence and preoccupied with their herculean labours, the two oarsmen nevertheless contrived to throw in the occasional remark. Amazing had become the company's jester. Jack had noticed over the days how his foolishness had become necessary to them all. Although Belle still abused him from time to time for his untheatrical behaviour, she more often chaffed him in an affectionate way. Whenever there was tension among the troupe Amazing's simplicity would offer scope for laughter and he himself, rather than take offence, would giggle weakly, quite unharmed.

'Pull harder, man!' Belle now admonished him, and his lips trembled merrily as spray from his oar dampened her hair.

Jack sat silent as the noisy badinage swept back and forth. He envied Amazing his position in the company, even though he would have hated to be the butt of general ridicule. At least the one-time tumbler had been accepted: his own position was far from certain. After tonight's performance the theatre said goodbye to the villages and travelled to the larger towns miles away. Would he be taken with them? He had been useful, he knew that, but hardly necessary. They seemed to like him, despite the occasional devilment which he seemed unable to resist. He could not bear to think that they would reject him.

These sombre speculations were interrupted, however, by a vigorous clap on his shoulder from Mr Tusker.

'Come on Jack, my boy. Time we showed these fellows how to row!'

So they clambered into the centre of the boat, grabbing hold of Luigi and Amazing as they passed, swaying tipsily, finally sitting side by side, each with a dripping oar. Mr Tusker certainly had more weight, but he very soon fell to panting wheezily. Sweat poured from his forehead and he stripped off his jacket, removed his cufflinks and rolled up his shirtsleeves. Jack, already lightly dressed, closed his eyes and felt the sun beat down upon his face and arms. They pulled for the shore as if their lives depended upon it.

'Now tell us, Belle,' gasped Mr Tusker between his exertions. 'Which pair has the finer style?'

She laughed, a loud and melodious chuckle.

'That's like asking which is the better dancer – an elephant or a camel.'

'A calumny!'

But the impresario had no further energy for talking. His face had reddened and the colour quickly spread to the bald area between the grey bushes over his ears. Jack, rather alarmed, pulled less enthusiastically, so that they advanced sedately but more or less in a straight line.

'By good fortune,' said Luigi as they reached the bank, 'I brought another bottle of this rather fine local wine with me. We can continue our picnic under the trees.'

Jack jumped from the boat and helped drag it up on the grass. The others seemed content to escape from the frying sun, flopping with gasps of relief in the shade. He, however, wanted only to explore. The trees came almost to the water's edge. Between them there was dappled light. He climbed a slight incline and came to a path which ran parallel to the shore. A rabbit, accustomed to having the place to itself, took a moment to register the human intrusion and scampered into the undergrowth. Birds sang among the foliage. One, a flash of gold along its wing, its face daubed crimson, flew down to a low branch in front of him: a city boy, he had no idea what it might be. Foolishly, he reached out a hand and it was gone, skimming above the ground in an uneven flight and losing itself in the greenery further along the path.

After a while he came across a majestic oak tree with branches which seemed designed for climbing. Up he went, hauling himself higher and higher until he emerged at the very top, way above the world. He could see the lake, silver under the sun, and two figures which he took to be Ma and Oz on the other side. The wood was extensive. Behind, there were hills and dusty roads and a church spire made of wooden shingles. Further still, far beyond his vision, were towns where the troupe would perform to large, appreciative audiences . . .

When, at last, he returned to his companions they appeared not to have moved an inch since leaving the boat and collapsing on to the ground under the trees. Belle had commandeered everyone's discarded clothing and was propped comfortably surveying the peaceful scene. Mr Tusker, his face redder than ever, snored gently in an unblemished sleep. Luigi, who gave a conspiratorial wink, nursed the bottle of wine, occasionally tilting it to his lips. Amazing's fingers played with grasses and tiny flowers which he shredded absent-mindedly as he stared vacantly into space.

'A tipple?' offered Luigi, holding the bottle towards Jack.

'No thank you.'

'It's time we were going. Your fisherman will be demanding an extra fee.'

Amazing, tugging at a clump of grass, said: 'I hope not. We paid too much as it was.'

Jack felt stung to retaliate. Had he not been a wily bargainer?

'It was a fair price,' he said.

'We could almost have *bought* a boat for that much,' replied Amazing casually, unaware of his resentment.

'I talked him down. He wanted much more.'

'Oh, I'm sure he did, Jack. But you have to be tough with these people. Use your noddle.'

'Use . . .'

He felt the frustration mounting inside him.

'Not a lad's work, Jack. Experience of the world is what's needed. Something you'll acquire.'

But Luigi had already become aware of Jack's anger, and with a quick joke and a general bustling about he urged the party to its feet and brought the conversation to a close. Mr Tusker, in truth, required a good deal of shaking before he was in a state to join them, but eventually they made their way together back to the boat in a spirit of renewed zest and jollity. Jack, however, still felt irritated. He knew it meant nothing, but his pride was hurt – and this led to a most unhappy incident.

They had climbed into the boat and pushed off from the shore, Luigi sitting at one oar and Amazing, on his feet, about to take the other. Perhaps he was encouraged by Belle's gentle taunting of the fellow, but as Amazing stooped to grasp the handle Jack seized the blade of the oar and tugged it to one side. His victim was completely off balance and had he been any other of the company would have plunged straight into the water. His strength, however, saved him for an immediate ducking. Even as he toppled over the side he hung on with both hands and swung his body knees-to-chin in a horizontal position just above the water. The effect of this was to tip the boat violently to one side so that they all slipped and rolled towards the edge.

Water came over the side, lapping Belle's dress in a chilly tide. Mr Tusker bounced out of the boat and was submerged from the waist down. Amazing, finally tilted under the surface, released his hold and floundered about, completely soaked. The boat kicked crazily and came to rest. Luigi wiped at his bespattered face with a handkerchief. Only Jack had escaped unscathed.

There was a silence. Nobody smiled. Mr Tusker and Amazing tugged the boat back to the bank. They all helped to tip it up until the water came gushing out. There was a wringing of sodden clothing, though to little avail. Amazing sat shivering on the grass despite the heat of the day: the lake water still held the coldness of winter.

'I'm sorry!' Jack blurted wildly. 'I didn't mean to do that!'

The journey back was excruciating. Conversation started up again – there were even mild jokes about what had happened – but he experienced a feeling completely new to him. Often, in the city with the old couple, he had been rebuked and worse for some misdemeanour. It had never meant anything to him. He had never felt guilty. Now, for the first time, he saw how his actions had hurts people he knew and respected. He thought bitterly of his stupidity and wished it undone.

There was, of course, another reason for his anguish which intensified when, after they had returned the boat, Mr Tusker called to him over his shoulder.

'You'll remember the terms of our bargain, Jack. We'll have words after tonight's performance.'

14 Stand-In

'That wasn't exactly bright of you, young Jack,' reflected Oz as they hammered together a piece of scenery. The sound echoed along the high roof of the barn. 'Not the wisest move you've made, I'd say.'

'It happened so quickly. I didn't intend that everyone should get a soaking.'

'Ha!'

The performance was still much more than an hour away but the work was almost completed. The play demanded an unusually large cast, so that Oz himself would be appearing (in two roles, in fact) and would soon need to prepare himself.

'Like to manage the curtains tonight, would you?'

'Yes please!'

'Well, I don't suppose Ma will mind. She'll be busy enough with the tickets and then with organising things backstage. I should put a bit of grease along the rail.'

Jack lifted the ladder into position, took the tub of grease and quickly climbed aloft. Finding that he had left the cloth behind, he simply dug his fingers in the slime as a more than adequate substitute. He was in this happy state when Amazing came slowly through one of the side doors and sat heavily on the makeshift stage. He crossed his arms over his chest, held each shoulder with the opposite hand and seemed to shake.

'What's up?' asked Oz, a nail between his lips.

'Feverish. I feel awful.'

He closed his eyes. Sweat sprang from his forehead, where the hair lay lank and wet. Oz put down the hammer and sat by his side.

'You should be in bed, man.'

Jack began to descend the ladder, horrified.

'A chill,' muttered Amazing. 'Hot and cold. It'll pass.'

'Not for a while, it won't. We must get you to bed.'

'The performance . . . '

Oz waved the suggestion away.

'Not tonight, my friend. You can't possibly.'

'But I must.'

'Better miss you for one night than let you act yourself into the grave. Don't think twice about it – we'll write your part out of the play.'

'No . . . '

'No, we can't. We've already written half a dozen parts out as it is. We'll double up the parts . . . No, that too . . . '

Jack approached with a timidity born of guilt.

'I'll stand in for you,' he said. 'I could do it.'

Amazing was too far gone to make any protest other than a helpless shaking of the head. He covered his face with his hands and gave a low moaning sound.

'You know the part, Jack?' Oz asked urgently.

'Yes. Well enough. I could do it.'

Oz found a heavy curtain and draped it around Amazing's trembling shoulders.

'Then this is what we'll do,' he said. 'You take Amazing to his bed while I tell Mr Tusker. Make sure you find someone to stay by him.'

After Oz had gone, Amazing allowed himself to be led slowly from the barn, across the yard and into the house in which they had their humble lodgings. The poor man was so ill that Jack was for the moment too woebegone to feel the excitement of the occasion. He helped him into the bed, where he continued to shiver despite the covering of the blankets, and arranged for the farmer's wife to keep a watch on him.

Only as he made his way back to the barn did he begin to look forward with relish to the evening's show – and even then the feeling was tinged with fear. Why had he not taken to heart Luigi's advice that he should learn every part of every play in case he should be required to perform it? Instead he had concentrated on a few of the grander speeches and paid little heed to the rest. The story of each play he knew well enough, the development, but the words . . .

As he sat upright in the chair to have the make-up applied he was offered generous advice by the rest of the company. Why did they not reproach him for being the cause of Amazing's absence? They must have known, yet they were concerned only with preparing him for his initiation.

'There's not a soul out there,' said Mr Tusker, 'who knows that it's your first time. You must make-believe to yourself that it's the fiftieth.'

'Yes. I will.'

Ma had smeared his face with grease, the stubby fingers moving expertly over his skin, rubbing firmly but painlessly. Now Belle came forward and, although herself not yet ready to go on, took the paints and began to make bold strokes across his face.

'A bit of a rogue,' she smiled. 'Give you a rascally look, shall we?'

'How do I look?'

'Fiendish!'

How he loved this spirit of camaraderie! It was as if everything which led up to this performance was a drab passing of time until real life began. In a few moments they would pass through the green curtain on to the stage and the world would be recreated, so that it was colourful, dramatic, meaningful. He loved the smell of the paint, the frantic last-minute adjustments to costume, the final back-slapping that told him they wanted him to succeed.

And then the nerves. They struck him moments before he was to pass through the curtain. The play had begun. He could hear Belle declaiming powerfully. His head swam. An ache came to his throat and he knew he could not speak. He felt frail, insubstantial. He would walk on to the stage and no one would notice him. The lines – what were his opening lines?

Luigi, standing by his side, put a hand on his shoulder.

'You feel bad?'

He nodded, wanting to run, to be allowed to forget the whole business.

'That's how you should feel. That's good. And your speeches?'

He whispered hoarsely: 'No. I can't. I've forgotten. Don't know them properly.'

'All right, all right!'

Luigi's assurance was absurd. How could he know how unprepared and inadequate he felt?

'You follow my lead Jack, eh? I'll keep near you. The words don't matter. Just get the idea across.'

And then he was gone, making a splendid entrance no doubt. Into Jack's mind came a picture of poor, trembling Amazing in his bed and he thought how, yes, he would gladly change places and be tossing and turning in a fever rather than undergo this torture. He felt feverish as it was. Perhaps he was unwell! His head throbbed and he could scarcely feel his legs.

'Now.'

He became aware of Ma, perched on a stool in the wings, the prompt book on her lap. She was making a flapping motion with the back of her hand. It seemed that she was waving to *him*.

'You're on!'

Of course. Belle's laugh. The dropping of the cup. He heard it smash and fumbled with the curtain. It prevented him. He tugged at it, felt it move. What must he say? There was nothing in his brain. He gave Ma a desperate glance.

'Rowdy behaviour,' she whispered.

That was it. Rowdy behaviour. He pushed through the curtain. Lord, where was he? The lights on the walls seemed painfully bright after the backstage gloom. Two people stood gazing at him. Belle and Luigi it must be: he could not focus upon them. And beyond, a menacing darkness, a gloom in which there were small movements. The audience. He was at the centre of the universe, threatened, pressed in upon, the victim. He was alone, completely – at the eye of a whirlpool, sucked down.

'Rowdy behaviour!'

The words came out, but weakly. He heard them as if they were not his own. They would not have carried beyond the second row. Luigi stepped towards him, rescued the situation in an instant.

'You call it rowdy behaviour, my friend,' he improvised for the benefit of those at the back. 'It was a mere accident.'

Accident. A mere accident. It was a familiar phrase but the reply would not come into his head. Something to do with the standards of the establishment.

'I suppose,' said Luigi, 'that you will tell me that accidents are not allowed to happen in his establishment. You believe the standards are too high.'

He paused briefly, unsuccessfully inviting Jack to interrupt.

'I suppose you will then begin to threaten me.'

Jack felt, helplessly, that the whole performance might continue without him saying a word – all his speeches being anticipated by Luigi. But at the mention of the threat he recalled a gesture which Amazing had used while rehearsing the part (a highly stylised shaking of the fist) and with this memory came the words of the script.

'I could have you thrown out!' he almost shouted with relief.

He stepped forward as he spoke and saw, for the first time, an individual face in the audience. She was about his own age and his sudden violence must have taken her by surprise for she started back, wide-eyed. How wonderful this was! He was so taken by this new-found power that the frailty seemed to leave him in an instant, no matter that the reason for it all so palpably remained.

Belle knelt on the ground collecting together the pieces of broken crockery.

'You'd put us on the street, would you?' she challenged.

Luigi, his back to the audience, whispered the one word 'mercy' and Jack – though he could not remember a jot of his script at this point – felt confident enough to invent a suitable speech.

'I could very well put you on the street,' he boomed (the girl in the audience put a hand to her mouth) 'and it would be the fruits of your folly' (this was, he realised as he spoke it, a phrase from later in the play and should be delivered by another character) 'but I will show mercy' (he softened his tone and the girl's lips formed a small smile of gratitude) 'and give you one last chance.'

He was in his element, and the very precariousness of his control, the real possibility that at any moment he might stand mouth agape, lost for words, gave his performance a wild intensity.

The play was no masterpiece but there was a good deal of action, a regular coming and going of actors. A murder had been committed at a small hotel. Jack was the owner – a cunning fellow whose one joy in life was extracting as much money as possible from his guests. It was not a major role and yet he made frequent entrances, his own schemings providing the author with a means of manipulating the rest of his characters. Oz in one guise was the law officer charged with solving the murder. Belle and Luigi were a couple of obscure origins. Mr Tusker was a sinister cleric. Oz, in his second manifestation, was a porter. Luigi also made a second quick-change appearance as 'a distant relative of the deceased'.

The audience was appreciative, and laughed and clapped at the least provocation: it was years since an entertainment had come this way. Jack spent his evening alternately being hissed instructions and cues by his colleagues and bestriding the stage with an increasing cocksureness. At times he extended his speeches even when he remembered them, raising gasps or bursts of laughter from the darkened auditorium, and such was the relief of Belle, Luigi and the others that the show had gone on and had prospered that he received nothing but encouraging signs and expressions, however outrageously he indulged himself.

Not that he was the only one with less than complete mastery of his part. He noticed that Mr Tusker always took up a position to one side of the stage and rather far back, sticking firmly to this position whatever the action. His voice was strong enough to carry to the furthest corners of the barn but Jack regarded this immovability as eccentric until, approaching the portly cleric to serve him a glass of fortified wine, he discovered the reason for it: the key elements of several speeches had been copied in large letters on long sheets of paper which hung on nails from the wall.

The play ended with the unmasking of the murderer – none other than the portly cleric himself. As Oz the detective swung on him with an accusing finger there were cries of surprise from the audience. Belle made a stirring exit, uttering profound thoughts about evil and retribution; Luigi assailed the injustice of accusing strangers and overlooking the vices of those in high and respected positions; and Mr Tusker, wringing his hands, made a full and fine confession. It was left to Jack, as the neutral observer of so much folly, to bring the play to a fitting conclusion, and he tackled the task with relish. The final speech he knew well, and but for a few asides he felt it needed little embellishing, but he had the power of the muse within him.

'Such is the way of the world that *honest* folk like me' (he so overstressed the improbable adjective that the audience howled in protest and amusement) 'respectable folk like me have nothing to show for their virtue . . . '

He passed from the mock lament to the mock heroic (how he and the common people at his hotel had fought bravely against villainy) and thence to the well-worn moral of the play. He stood centre-stage, arms outstretched, proclaiming that 'crime, my friends, does not pay!' – and the audience actually rose to its feet, clapping tumultuously, the sound hammering in his ears, that beautiful sound, and Belle, Luigi, Oz and Mr Tusker came from behind the curtain to take their bow and they stood, arm in arm, as the noise actually increased and seemed to go on for ever and ever and ever.

He could not sleep that night for the joy of it. Backstage, after the performance, Mr Tusker had uncorked a bottle of champagne and carried the first glass to him, laughing. He was a member of the company: he knew it before Mr Tusker told him so.

'A fine actor in the making, Jack my boy. Raw but resourceful.'

'New blood's what we need,' Luigi had thrown in, and they had all cheered and clinked their glasses. He had carried his own from person to person, threatening to shatter it with his exuberance.

'First of many,' Ma had said warmly, though whether referring to the acting success or the glass of champagne it was impossible for anyone to know. 'First of many.'

Now he sat on his bed, the applause still in his ears. In the next room Amazing lay in a deep slumber, feverish but (the village doctor said) on the mend and in no danger. Outside the window the stars glimmered in a clear sky.

Where might he not go with Tusker's Travelling Theatre? To think how many audiences there were to conquer!

It was in this sleepless and restless mood that, running his fingers aimlessly through his pockets, he came across the pottery fragment and the paper with the address in O—. It brought back to him the thought of the city and the old couple who would be horrified, angry, if they knew where he was. He liked the broken shard – though why he could not say – and he returned it to his pocket. But the writing on the paper was a summons he would never obey, and he tore the sheet into a dozen tiny pieces.

15 At the Crippled Rabbit

Tonight on the smooth waters
of the lake small boats seem to
hang in the sky . . .

In the cafe's darkness the white hand of the speaker described in a smooth arc the lake's dimpled surface. He sat perched on the back of a chair, his less eloquent hand clutching a wine bottle, and addressed an audience of upturned faces.

Their lovers embrace between stars,
thin blossoms of mist rise,
moths circle the hung lanterns.

Tonight there is no time,
we are suspended in eternity,
words are frozen to the roof of the mouth.

'Bravo, Celestin!'

'Splendid, splendid!'

The shouting was augmented by a banging of glasses upon the table tops while the speaker, descending unsteadily from his vantage point, clumsily tipped the bottle's remaining contents into the lap of his seated companion. She, a young woman whose coarse features were framed by a huge tumble of red curls, roared with laughter at her discomfiture and threw her arms around him. This sudden movement took him entirely off-balance and they fell to the floor in a flourish of arms and legs. Now the applause increased, and the sound of breaking glass suggested that the appreciation had become over-enthusiastic.

Amid this turmoil only Walter and Sarah were still. They had entered during the recital of the poem and stood together near the door. Walter scanned faces which were lit fitfully by candles on the small tables. There was no sign of the Count. He thought of the chess players in the park – the people were besotted with chess – and wondered whether he had himself made an intelligent or a foolhardy move.

'More, Celestin! Another!'

But the poet lay on the floor, laughing helplessly, his face smothered by red curls.

Perhaps he was mistaken, but Walter had a growing intuition that the Count was somehow involved with his mysterious summons to O—. Was it of significance that the Count had owned the missing house he sought? Or that he and Sarah had been invited to the snow-watching party? He could not know. But in recent days he had sensed that he was being watched and once, while waiting vainly by the derelict houses near the fairground, he had turned quickly and seen the Count's messenger hurrying away.

Why should so wealthy, so influential a man be so hard to find? Walter had pursued him unavailingly. Now he hoped, from hints that had been dropped, to locate him at the Cabaret of the Crippled Rabbit. It was not to be.

'A turn from you, Adele!'

'Send her up!'

A woman of about thirty, dressed like a man and with a long cigarette-holder between her lips, skipped to the centre of the room. She pushed chairs and tables aside to clear a space and, all the while making extravagant gestures, began to recite a monologue which soon had the place in a tempest of laughter.

Walter, not understanding what the merriment was about, looked down at Sarah and received a rich smile of reassurance. How was it that she understood so much? Daily he marvelled the more at her sensitivity. In the first days he had thought her deafness an impenetrable barrier, but she had shown such an ability to communicate with him that he began to wonder that people used words at all. Her face could express a thousand emotions. Her fingers made signs that he was quickly learning to interpret and which had a complexity he would never have believed possible. He was learning to speak in a new way, could reply in the language she had taught him.

'Bravo!'

As the performer, waving, made her way back to her seat Walter took Sarah by the hand and stepped forward. He had prepared everything in advance. For the first time in weeks he was able to look on his academic education as a source of strength rather than confusion. The speech was clear in his head, well rehearsed.

'Some of us, my friends, are gifted with the tongue's music,' he began, glancing across at the poet. 'Others translate their experience into the music of form and colour. In a few minutes you will witness the performance of one who, having no tongue, not even the whispering tongue of a muted flute, nor the means whereby she might make or mould with her hands, has developed the music of the body. Each movement a poem, her only speech. Each movement an essay in sculpture . . . '

'Shut up and let her get on with it!'

He halted abruptly, shocked by the interruption. His voice had been gaining an assurance that could have kept the speech flowing for several minutes but this, presumably, was what the interrupter had divined. His large, round, bearded face scowled at Walter, who could only look forlornly at the rest of his audience until one of them leaned forward and said in a kindly manner: 'They were fine words, young man, pretty conceits. Take no offence at my impatient friend here. It's simply that he is an artist, a very fine sculptor, and he is anxious to see the young lady's performance.

The sculptor nodded at this and raised his hand in a small gesture that might be taken as signifying apology. Walter bowed and stepped back, leaving the stage to Sarah.

She had never moved so beautifully. Her limbs seemed as made of liquid, the magical effect enhanced by the flickering play of candle-light upon her silken pyjamas. Walter looked on with pride, from time to time stealing glances at the appreciative audience and observing that the surly sculptor watched the performance more avidly than anyone. When she finished there was a commotion to match anything he had yet heard, and more glasses were shattered in the acclaim.

'Worth a dozen of my poems,' Celestin announced, his eyes brightly fixed on the dancer, and Walter, noticing storm clouds grow in the redheaded girl's face, quickly pulled Sarah away.

'Bring her here!'

The sculptor motioned for them to sit at his table. A waiter brought two clean glasses and their new host reached for one of the cluster of bottles around his chair.

'She's good, you know. Very good.'

'I know.'

'You do, eh?'

The sculptor emptied his own glass and filled all three. He sat staring at Sarah for what seemed an eternity.

'Would you model for me, my pretty? Would she?'

Walter nodded, but the sculptor's eyes had not moved from Sarah.

'Have to stand still, mind you. Would she do it?'

'Yes, I'm sure.'

It was, he knew, uncertain. It might even be perilous. Had he the right to put Sarah at risk? Yes (he reasoned swiftly) it was surely no more precarious than their present situation. Accustomed to living as part of a community, he found it strange to be acting as an individual. He would not consciously put the girl in danger, but he was determined that he should lose no possible opportunity of finding the Count.

'Be there tomorrow' – a powerful hand thrust a printed address card at Walter – 'and we'll come to terms.'

The sculptor rose unsteadily and held out his hand for Walter to shake, but before Walter could reciprocate he staggered to the wall and covered his head in his arms.

'Wine's a bit heavy tonight,' he muttered barely audibly. 'Better take a bit of fresh air.'

Clearly, Walter reflected, the Count's problem afflicted many people here at O—. This time he allowed the sufferer to make his own lurching way outside, where he could be heard coughing and heaving and groaning.

16 A Deal

The stairs were surprisingly dark and modest in size when compared with the white marble grandeur of the façade. They wound up past closed doors, reaching their culmination at the door of the studio itself. This one, wider and more ornamented than the others, made up in part for the visual poverty of the staircase. But it was the studio itself that was to leave Walter breathless.

His first glimpse of it was beyond the head of the sculptor, who after a lengthy interval, had answered his knock. He seemed to be standing at the mouth of a huge cavern, the height of several rooms and contained by walls each of which seemed longer than the extent of the building's external facade. To Walter it could be compared in its lofty grandeur only with the chapel of the monastery. Perhaps to a person of broader experience a museum might have seemed a more apt comparison, particularly as its main furniture comprised sculpted stone and plaster, forming a silent community of still, white figures.

The sculptor, wearing a smock that was thick with the white dust that lay upon everything in the place, stepped back to allow them inside. He seemed, Walter thought, less formidable than he had the night before. There, in the darkened recesses of the cafe, he had seemed a heavy, muscular man, but here he was dwarfed by the figures he had created. Indeed, standing beneath the huge bulk of an ancient warrior, who held in one hand a sword and in the other a severed head, he looked positively vulnerable. His speech was less brusque and confident, too. He seemed almost to grope for words, and when they did finally form upon his lips they were hesitant, the voice weak.

'Last night, wasn't it? I'd forgotten. Too much wine. Good, good. Did we agree something? I can't think well this morning. Do sit down.'

He indicated a sofa among the several spread around the room, his eyes immediately taken by Sarah, who seemed completely at home among the ghostly statues. The sculptor's words now began to flow more smoothly.

'Ah, yes! Of course, I remember now. Remarkable. Remarkable! You'll model for me? Can you hold yourself still?'

He spoke to Sarah, but Walter replied

'She can't speak. I speak for her. And, yes, she can remain quite still.'

'Is she your sister?'

'A friend. I look after her.'

The sculptor regarded the two faces for a moment.

'And who looks after *you?*'

'Nobody. We're alone.'

An expression of mild surprise.

'So you're her agent, my man. Did we agree terms? I don't suppose we did. She'll get the going rate if she can model well. Could she move around the room a little, slowly, using her arms and body as well as her legs?'

If Walter had been proud of his silent communication with Sarah, he was properly humbled now. To his great embarrassment, he realised that he had no way of expressing the sculptor's wishes save by example. He got to his feet and began the sinuous movement he assumed the sculptor to want, but self-consciousness stiffened his limbs and reddened his face until he resembled nothing so much as an automaton slowly running down, a sort of manic uncoordinated clown. He continued for perhaps half a minute before he dared to raise his eyes. To his surprise and irritation Sarah was gripped by a silent convulsion of laughter, her arms held across her stomach as she rocked to and fro. He turned to the sculptor who was clearly trying to contain his own mirth in order to preserve the lad's dignity – though his words could not help but take to themselves a softly mocking character.

'Do you think that your friend understood sufficiently? I should hate too accurate an imitation.'

But Sarah was already getting to her feet, her face more composed, though still lit with the amusement that she had felt. She began to glide, and Walter's clumsy jerks were translated into smooth hypnotic sequences of movement that held both the sculptor and himself entranced, quite dissolving any rancour that might have followed the sculptor's words. As she moved, the sculptor rose and, taking a piece of clay, began to shape it between his hands, pressing with his thumbs, drawing out with his fingers, moulding a figure in movement without once taking his eyes from the girl. And then, the process complete, he set that figure down gently and picked up another piece of clay.

'She's amazing. Where did you meet her?'

Walter was nonplussed by the question, innocent though it seemed. Should he trust this man whom he hardly knew? But, as with the chess players in the park, risks sometimes had to be taken for later advantage. The sculptor surely knew the Count. Perhaps he would even offer his help. So Walter began, telling first of their meeting at the fairground and then working backwards and forwards from it until the whole story was told.

Clabber did not interrupt, indeed seemed not to listen, so involved was he in his modelling, and the silence that followed Walter's revelations hardly encouraged him to expect much help. But then the sculptor indicated that Sarah should rest and, seating himself, reached in a pocket for a long cheroot. Having made a business of getting this going, he fumbled under his chair for a bottle, which he tipped to his lips, swallowing thirstily.

'Enough work for now,' he said, and it seemed to Walter that his voice was once more assuming the assurance of the previous night.

'So it's the Count you're after, if I'm to believe your story – though there's no reason why I shouldn't, I suppose. You've no cause to lie that I can see of. Tell me what happens if you get to meet the Count again. Do I lose myself a model?'

Walter did not answer and the sculptor again fell into thoughtful silence. He sucked the cheroot and then drank deeply once more, the liquid running down his chin.

'What if I offer you a more permanent arrangement?'

'Permanent?'

'Well, no, no. Nothing's permanent in this life, my grandee. No. But you could do with a roof over your heads, the two of you.'

'Here?'

'I don't live here, you see. Nobody does. It's just one room. Suit you very well, I'd have thought. Compared to a rowing boat, leastways.'

'But the doors on the way up . . . '

'False.'

'If you open them?'

'You're face to face with stone.'

The sculptor laughed.

'The ground floor's solid – it couldn't take the weight of all this otherwise. Old Hercules here would be in the basement in no time flat. It's just one huge room with a staircase.'

'But why?'

'Appearances, that's why. Never despise appearances, the pleasures of the eye. The street has grand self-important buildings and the man who had this put up wasn't content with less. It's absurd, you may be thinking – I can tell that's what you're thinking – but you can take it from me that it's far less absurd than half the dealings of men.'

He caught the smoke from his cheroot in the act of forming a shape that he liked and he half rose, blowing softly at the edges to add a finishing touch.

'This is where I work and where my clients come, but I live elsewhere. I like my privacy. What I need is someone to be here when I'm not. A caretaker, but with as much freedom as you like.

'You get free board and a small sum for food and other necessaries. I get a model of genius . . . Well?'

Did the nodding of his head, Walter wondered, seem a trifle too eager?

It grew dark. The sculptor had gone, and they watched shadows spread across the floor of the studio, the final shafts of dusty sunlight allowed in by a grimy and entirely redundant window in the south wall – redundant because the north wall was all glass and there was, in addition, a huge sloping fanlight that seemed to raise the ceiling's height to the evening sky itself.

Walter had already created within this cavernous interior a corner that could be regarded as a home for Sarah and himself. Certainly it lacked the snug intimacy of the upturned boat, but he had manoeuvred some of the plaster figures to form a wall behind which he had set two sofas and a table, adding to this a small stove which the sculptor used for melting wax.

One sofa had had to be moved when he discovered that, lying upon it, he was stared at by the severed head whose baleful expression could hardly have been designed to induce pleasant dreams, nor to commend itself as the first sight of a dawning day. The sofa's new position brought him face to face with a huge fish, whose melancholy eyes at least fixed themselves upon him with a little more sympathy. Part of an incomplete fountain, it held its mouth open, and into this space – one day to gush water into the sunlight of a city square – Walter placed his stump of candle.

Sarah, he noticed, simply moved around the room gazing at the figures, pausing to run her fingers across a marble cheek as if to wipe frozen tears away, pressing her fingers into the outstretched hand of a Roman slave, stroking the mane of a horse whose rider remained eternally at the point of death, struck through by a spear. Then she began to walk to and fro across one area of the floor, staring down at her feet, a concentrated expression upon her face. She paused, reached down to touch the floor, and resumed her careful patrol. Was she planning a new, problematical dance sequence?

'What are you doing?'

But of course it was useless to ask. Walter, about to prepare food that he had bought earlier that day in the market square, stood watching her, wondering what thoughts went through the head of his close but so distant friend of his. He could not help but be disquieted. What depths lay beneath his companion's silent surface? What mysteries were there yet to be revealed? Sarah's origins were becoming as great a source of wonder to him as his own.

17 Models

'When I was your age, Walter, I'd done nothing, knew nothing.'

The sculptor was completing a lifesize model in a beautiful pearl-like stone, and the steady chipping rhythm of his mallet and chisel relaxed him and made him more expansive. In but a few days the man and boy had developed a mutual trust, Sarah being for the sculptor little more than an extension of Walter, through whom their only contact was made. Now, as he worked, she sat serenely still, lovely in the clear light.

'I had the most secure of backgrounds. No mystery there. Good, solid, respectable, comfortable, utterly boring and unbearable. My father ran a chain of shops and small factories. He manufactured and he sold; no middle-men, all profits back to my father. He was shrewd and careful. Not, mind, that his employees suffered too much. He was a man of integrity and he looked after them even when they became ill or too old to work. A sense of duty. And so he was well respected – not much liked, but well respected – and I was expected to follow him, to enter the business, carry on building the family fortune. I had no brothers, you see, only six sisters.

'At your age I would lie in bed of a night staring at the ceiling, all too aware of who my father was and what future awaited me. Trouble is, I'm not much of a thinker, Walter. I can only think with these' – he paused to display his hands – 'and they're no good in business.'

He had reached an awkward fold in the sleeve. He concentrated silently for some minutes, then stood back, eyeing his workmanship.

'And so I ran away.'

Whether the pleased expression related to the memory of his escape or denoted satisfaction with the completed fold Walter was unable to gauge. Whatever the reason, his voice became noticeably more animated as he described the subsequent events.

'I was sorry to go in some ways. I worried about my mother, and two of my sisters had been particularly good to me. I left them notes of course: "Don't worry, I'll be all right, must find my own way in the world, dum-de-dah . . . " You know the sort of thing.'

Walter remembered, with a pang of guilt, that he had written no letter at all.

'As for my father, well I wasn't too concerned about him. He had plenty of sons-in-law to carry on the business and they could do it better than I could. Indeed, they still do. D'you see this mallet, "Clabber & Sons"? That's them, though I'm the only son Clabber ever had.'

He leant forward and chipped delicately at the stone.

'It would be nice to say that I became a sculptor entirely through the merits of my own talent and that I made my way in the world unaided, but it wouldn't be the truth. I found the early days very tough after my soft upbringing. Nothing of the monastery about my home, Walter – all cushions and overfeeding. I contrived to let one of my sisters discover where I was, and the money began to flow in my direction. Not much, but enough to keep me from starving or dying of exposure. I suppose they must have worked on my father, and I was enrolled at the art school and then apprenticed out to a sculptor.

'The rest is reasonably straightforward. I had more talent than anyone, including myself, had anticipated and so I gradually became successful. Well, a bit faster than gradually, in fact. As for my father, I never saw him again, although my mother and the two sisters followed my progress and we met from time to time.

'He's dead now, so there'll never be a reconciliation.'

He stepped back to consider the progress of his work, beckoning Sarah to rest as he did so. A cheroot and a glass of wine accompanied the next part of his conversation.

'You're probably as well off knowing nothing about the past, Walter, but I don't suppose I can persuade you of that. You think the Count can help you, eh?'

'It's just a feeling. That's enough when there's nothing else.'

'More than enough is what you may end up finding it.'

'What do you mean? How well do you know the Count?'

Before answering, the sculptor drank deeply and recharged his glass.

'The Count, my young friend, is something of a mystery. I know him as well as most, I suppose, but that amounts to very little knowing. He's not your run-of-the-mill aristo. What motivates him? I don't really know. Where does he spend most of his time? I don't know. Who does he mix with when he's away? I just don't know.

'What I do know is that he's a good customer when it comes to sculpture. Plenty of money, and he knows exactly what he's looking for. He's no fool, the Count. He's the sort of patron artists dream about, a man who really appreciates the stuff and can afford it.'

'The palace we went to . . . '

'One of several. Palace, hunting lodges, apartments – he moves around. But even so, if you tried to find him at all the known addresses you'd probably fail. He seems to disappear, you see. He'll turn up at the cabaret once in a while. If there's a party going he's likely to appear. Otherwise . . . '

He shrugged his shoulders and then leant forward, his voice quieter, more conspiratorial.

'But I should be careful, Walter. What I know of the Count, as I've said, is very little, and he's good to me. But I wouldn't trust him, Walter, I wouldn't trust him. If he does know something about you there may be a reason for his silence and you could be sailing into rough waters.'

He tossed the stub of the cheroot into a corner and got to his feet, but waved a hand at Sarah when she made to resume her earlier posture. Instead, he signalled Walter to sit by her in the good light and picked up a tablet of moist clay.

'Will you mind playing a minor role in my composition?' he asked.

'No, of course not.'

The strong fingers shaped the pliable material with surprising delicacy.

'This is for the Count,' the sculptor explained. 'It's the most ambitious thing I've ever done. You see how my stone Sarah is coming along here. She's the centrepiece. Not much of Sarah in her, to be sure – I've been working on her for months. But I've the head to finish yet.'

'And where do I come in?'

'Oh, one of the supporting cast, I'm afraid. Not too flattering, if the truth be told. Something half-human, half-beast.'

'Thank you!'

'You've a tail already, and scaley feet with large nails on the toes. I only need your face.'

Walter grinned broadly and unthinkingly moved his head.

'Not a born model, I think,' the sculptor smiled, waiting patiently for him to take up his earlier position. 'What we'll have here is one of the Count's stranger fancies. He invents his own mythologies. Sarah here' – he indicated the glossy stone – 'represents a beautiful maiden taming the creatures of the Dark. The whole group will stand in the garden at the Rue de Rêve.'

'When will it be ready?' Walter asked urgently.

'Soon. Quite soon. These are my last two heads.'

'So that the Count will have to come to see them!'

The sculptor stopped his modelling and put the clay on his worktable.

'Now that's a thought,' he said. 'That's certainly ponderable. The first answer is no, the Count may not come in person. He may prefer to see them in position before passing a verdict and parting with his cash. But there is a precedent . . . '

He brushed at his smock, and white dust sprang out of it and hovered in the air about him.

'An unveiling party. He did come to one once – loves a party, the Count. What do you say to that, Walter?'

Walter could only beam.

'It'll take me a little time to finish the work, mind. A few weeks. But it might just flush him out. As long' – he said with a mock-serious wag of the finger – 'as you don't take my prize model away from me.'

He took up his chisel and returned to the stone.

'Remember though, Walter,' he added in earnest tones. 'Origins are interesting enough, but where you come from matters far less than where you're going.'

18 Star Quality

Playing the towns was a completely different experience. Even the smells were new. Working in real theatres they had room for bold scenic and dramatic effects, and always in his nostrils was the heavy cloying sweetness of the size which they plastered over the canvases for strength before painting on the beauties of mountain scenery, the homeliness of a fireside, the splendour of a waterfall. Mingled with this was the smell (almost the taste) of gas, for the rushlights, candles and oil lamps of their village settings now gave way to modern mantles. There were gelatine slides, too, in numerous colours so that the lighting – in rows of battens high up – could evolve in a moment from the full glare of day to the violet shadow of evening, the rosiness of a luminous dawn.

They were a small company, but now they found local people to play walk-on parts – often well-known characters of the town who might be applauded or hooted as they strode on-stage, swords flashing in the flurry of battle perhaps or voice raised in a raucous crowd scene. Jack would often be among their number and occasionally was even allowed a minor comic role. His lesson taken to heart, he began to learn a range of parts, though always from watching rather than reading: there was rarely time to read.

'And not only the words,' Luigi advised him. 'You take notice of all the business, Jack – the timing, who stands where, what they do with the props. If you don't get that right you'll end up in a pretty fix.'

Now he understood the necessity of touring the villages first. These audiences were more demanding and, while they could hardly be termed sophisticated, would not tolerate a creaking performance. Moreover, the company was playing at each theatre for at least two weeks, so that healthy ticket sales depended upon a successful first night. He observed the others with awe. They had a repertoire of about a dozen plays, they never arranged proper rehearsals, yet everyone seemed to know thoroughly what should be done at any one point in a play. This applied even to Amazing whose time with the company was not very much longer than his own.

'Concentration,' was Luigi's explanation. 'It's the answer to everything, Jack.'

'But he was in the circus. It's completely different.'

'No, it's not. It's entertainment, and to do it properly you have to know what's required by the audience and how to bring it about. That's where the concentration comes in. Discipline.'

Jack, who had never held this quality in high regard, was so impressed by the advice and so keen to do well that he determined to discipline himself forthwith. If his efforts were not entirely successful his new seriousness was obvious to them all and, indeed, he sometimes caught himself in the act of taking mental notes of a performance.

The greatest experience was yet to come. When they arrived in their third town Jack accompanied Mr Tusker to the printer's to collect their advertising literature. This was on a scale he had never seen before. The posters for the billboards were large, brilliantly designed in the familiar orange colour and carried the proud embellishment in their heading: 'Tusker's TWENTIETH CENTURY Travelling Theatre'. In even bolder letters, under the title of the melodrama they were to perform, was the name JASON BULL. Jack, curious, read the name aloud.

'World-renowned titan of the stage,' read the actor-manager in turn, adding for the benefit of the man who stood behind the counter, a hopeful expression beneath his green eyeshade: 'All spelt correctly, I'm pleased to say. We had a little, ah, contretemps at the last place.'

'We aim to please, sir.'

Who this Jason Bull was Jack felt that it would be unwise to ask, revealing a shameful ignorance. But as they stumbled along the street, weighed down with heavy bundles of posters and leaflets, Mr Tusker admitted to a minor deception.

'"World-renowned" may be a venial case of decorating the particulars,' he confessed. 'But he's had a great success in Australia.'

'And he's acting with us?'

Mr Tusker laughed.

'I fancy we shall be acting with *him*,' he replied. 'With a man of that stature we rather play second fiddle. But it's very good for business.'

He broke the seal on one of the packages and began to hand leaflets to people as they passed, though never checking his conversational flow.

'Jason Bull lives not so very far from here and has a great reputation in the area. A stage presence, Jack my boy. Power. A natural leading man. We shall pack the house for a month, you see.'

'And Luigi . . . '

He did not know how to phrase his query, but Mr Tusker understood at once.

'No trouble at all,' he said. 'A true professional is Luigi. He's our own leading man, but he'll always step down when I hire a star. Everyone steps down a peg in turn, you see. That's the nature of the enterprise. Mind you' – he smiled and thrust another leaflet into surprised fingers – 'I never take on a female attraction. My nerves would not be guaranteed to withstand the consequences, if you follow me.'

Jason Bull turned out to be every bit as impressive as this introduction suggested. He was tall and heavily handsome. He moved with a physical self-assurance. His voice was deep and sonorous. If he seemed more than a shade disdainful of his companions, this to Jack was only fitting.

He had never experienced hero-worship before, but now he would sit in the wings, chin in his fists, captivated by Jason Bull's easy dominance of the stage. The audiences, as Mr Tusker had forecast, flocked in droves to see him. He could encourage them to roar merely by raising his voice a fraction. Another faint gesture and a hush would fall, awaiting the flicker of his eyelid. Tears flowed freely every night.

In the green room backstage, when they sat perspiring after the show, the star would say little. The general conversation passed him by. There were sometimes small criticisms of his fellow actors who had perhaps failed to respond promptly to a cue or had by some action detracted from his performance. He would send out for a drink of his choice rather than share what the rest of the company was taking. Very soon he would be gone, without a word of farewell. Jack sensed a growing resentment over this behaviour and felt ashamed on the star's behalf. Was he not entitled to special treatment? Could he not expect that the others would strive to match his own artistry? Jack felt how much grander Jason Bull was than the rest of them: even Belle, however much she preened and fluttered against her new lead, lacked his stature. When he himself emerged upon the stage he would be like that – strong, masterful, arrogant.

And then, incredibly, this paragon of the footlights showed an interest in *him*. At first this took the form of sending him on small errands which he was very pleased to undertake. Oz would perhaps ask for his help and then the deep voice would overrule him: there was no hesitating over which call to answer. Jack would fetch what the great man required, deliver it to his plush throne of a chair and return to his own lowly seat without a word. On one occasion, however, he was called back and asked what he had thought of the performance ('an honest appraisal, young scruff!') and thereafter they would often have a brief tête-à-tête on the subject. Jack, soon recovering his lively spirits despite being in awe of the man, would ask questions about the places in which he had acted before, the roles he had played, and Jason Bull seemed amused by his interest and pleased to give him an answer.

An observer would have seen the company gradually divided, an invisible line drawn between the aloof star with his willing pupil and the remainder of the cast. But Jack was oblivious of this. He no longer studied the details of the play, Luigi's 'business', but only the manner in which the leading man wrought his magical effects upon the audience.

One afternoon Jack was invited on a shopping expedition ('I shall need a bearer') and he noticed with pride how people in the street would point out his companion to their friends and, if they were bolder than most, would nod to him and smile self-consciously. Jason Bull took all this in his stride, rarely acknowledging the salute but certainly not seeming hurt by the attention. Eventually he disappeared into a draper's to buy a pair of white kid gloves, and while he was gone Jack strolled along the pavement looking in the windows. The shops were not, in general, as varied and as well stocked as those he knew in his home city, but one in particular captivated him. It sold chess sets in every imaginable material – stone, bronze, ebony, onyx – and surely in every possible hue. He gazed with wonder at what seemed to him a treasure trove.

'Do you play, my man?'

Jason Bull had returned and was pulling one of his new acquisitions over strong, spread-eagled fingers.

'No. I've never learned.'

'Would you like to?'

Was it not terribly complicated? he wondered. Apparently it was not. His mentor ushered him into the shop and bought a set in dark, glowing wood.

'Beat me once,' he announced, 'and it's yours.'

After that came the instruction in the actor's hotel room. In the best hotel in town! Jack's joy knew no bounds. It was a grand room with heavy chintz furniture, a glittering chandelier at the centre, thick, richly patterned carpets on the floor, french windows opening onto a verandah. Jason Bull seemed to take this space over as effortlessly as he imposed himself upon his audiences. A gown would be thrown carelessly over a chair and the chair would seem incomplete without it. He had brought a collection of photographs with him, and these now hung on the walls: Jason Bull with the famous theatrical impresario; as Othello in the great tragedy; dressed for the camera in a sheeny top hat and twirling (though not really twirling, for the picture was not blurred) an ivory cane.

On one table now sat the chess set, and Jack eagerly learned the moves. He had a nimble brain and was soon proficient in sending each piece in the proper direction. Winning a game was, however, another matter. At times he would sense himself sneaking in for the kill, quite sure that his intentions were obscure, only for his opponent to wipe out the danger with a single swift, unexpected capture.

'Vision, my foolhardy fellow!' he would laugh, his dark brown voice carrying into the corridor beyond. 'You must see the battle from the general's point of view.'

Jack, who would have followed Jason Bull into the thickest skirmish, acknowledged each rebuke and attempted to learn from his mistakes. He began to appreciate the various possible strategies, the potential of each piece in any one position, and he listened with rapt attention to the advice he was given. Nor, as time passed, was this advice limited to the game of chess. They began to talk more of the theatre, and Jack thrilled to the anecdotes. Had he been in any doubt of Jason Bull's stature these stories would soon have convinced him. The actor had appeared in every theatre of note, knew everybody of any consequence and had played all the important roles there were.

'How did you start?' Jack asked on one occasion when the recalling of a particularly thrilling triumph seemed to suggest boyhood stardom.

'At the top,' was the emphatic reply. 'Began with a leading role and never looked back.'

'But how? When you were unknown?'

'Unknown? Can't remember the time, my rapscallion! But I'll tell you how it was. A cousin of mine fancied himself as an actor and had been hired to play at a little theatre somewhere. I went along to watch him rehearse.'

He chuckled loudly and shook his head.

'Dreadful. He was quite dreadful! I watched him for as long as it was humanly possible to bear and then climbed on to the stage myself. Not like *that*, I said to him. Like *this*! And I proceeded to demonstrate how to get the most out of the part. Rather open-mouthed they were.'

'And they gave you his part?'

'What! No, that was nothing. A bit part, that was all. Hardly worth the improving. No, they put me in the lead role without a moment's hesitation. Begged me to do it. Well, it seemed amusing so I agreed to help them out for a couple of weeks . . . We ended by touring half of Europe.'

It was a wonder, that Jack acknowledged, and it both exhilarated him and gave him a feeling of restlessness. His own moment of stardom, that performance in the village barn, was nothing compared with Jason Bull's debut. And there had been no similar consequences.

'Did you never paint scenery?' he asked, almost pleading. 'They say it's invaluable to do the backstage work first.'

The great man laughed, a bellow.

'*Who* says? Eh? Those who've spent years of their life drudging say that, my lad! A mite of consolation to them, I dare say. Their work may be invaluable, I'll grant you that, but only in so far as it enables the real actors to weave their spells.'

'But Luigi . . . '

'Never undersell youself. That's a good motto for life in general, and it applies to the theatre in particular. If you want to be a star, think like a star and act like a star. Don't get dragged down with the also-rans.'

Jack, who did indeed dream of himself as a star, began to think deeply on this advice. He had been blissfully happy with the company, had wanted nothing but to travel with them, but he knew that Mr Tusker, Luigi, even Belle, would never attain the heights from which Jason Bull looked proudly down. Would he not be held back by their influence, the drudgery he must undergo? He began to withdraw from the humble tasks he had such a short time ago vowed to throw himself into. He obeyed when called, but he would not be found always at the side of Oz, attending to the scenery, repairing the props. Jason Bull's parts he knew by heart but he made no effort to learn the others, let alone to notice those elements of timing and positioning which Luigi had encouraged him to perfect.

Occasionally he would catch their glances and it would seem that they looked on him with concern. But he shrugged this off. It must be that they envied him. He would increasingly absent himself from the company to be with his hero, to play games of chess (still he was not allowed to win), to join him on trips around town. It must be that the others realised that he would soon be beyond them, on a higher plane. They did not care for Jason Bull, he could tell: doubtless he reminded them of their own inadequacies. He comforted himself with the thought that the great actor clearly was not impressed by his present colleagues.

'Quite full of airs and graces,' he once dismissed Belle's performance. 'As if she can dim my flame against a blaze of bright silk.'

And Luigi he scorned by refusing to discuss his playing at all.

'A supporting cast is a necessity,' is all he would say.

The melodrama had run with great success for almost two weeks. Jack had not dared to ask what Jason Bull thought of his own efforts as an obsequious butler, a drunken sailor and one of a crowd at a hanging. Indeed, since no comment was offered he had feared the worst. It was to seem, however, as if this were a gross misjudgement. They had taken their bow and retired to the green room, where Mr Tusker began to outline his plans for the tragedy that was to open the following week. He had assigned the various roles and was already discussing the dramatic effects they would be using (there was to be a volcano, a violent thunderstorm and a shipwreck) when Jason Bull interrupted, his powerful voice bringing the actor-manager to an abrupt halt.

'Not quite the casting I would favour,' he declared.

'In what regard, pray?'

'This young man' – he indicated Jack with a nod of the head – 'has more promise than you seem to allow. I'd like to see him as the Prince.'

There was a silence, during which Jack's face reddened with pride. The role of the Prince was a substantial one: Mr Tusker had already decided that it should be played by Luigi as the second male lead. If he were to change . . .

'A trifle difficult, that,' said the manager awkwardly, running his eye around the room. 'I think not, in all the circumstances.'

'I think you misunderstand me,' Jason Bull countered forcefully. 'The circumstances are that I shall pack my bags unless you agree to it.'

'Ah, well – I see!'

Mr Tusker, lost for meaningful words, wrung his hands and forced the semblance of a smile to his lips.

'A packing of bags. Surely not . . . '

'Surely so, my friend.'

Jack watched the others closely. They all appeared tense. Each looked at the floor or the wall. He knew they would not like the suggestion because it came from Jason Bull. And because it meant a downgrading for all the men. Luigi would have to move down to Amazing's role to accommodate him. Amazing would take Oz's lowly role, while Oz would play walk-on parts which required hardly a line of dialogue. How could they be so selfish?

'Shall we,' suggested Mr Tusker in a conciliatory manner, 'perhaps go outside to discuss the matter in private?'

'I'm perfectly comfortable as I am,' replied the star. 'The others may leave if they wish.'

Without a word and at the same second – as if after long rehearsal – they stood up and filed through the door. Jack brought up the rear. The door shut behind them.

'Insufferable,' he thought he heard Belle whisper, but otherwise there were only glances exchanged between them – between all of them but Jack. He felt uncomfortable but angry, too. Was it ridiculous that he should play the Prince? If Jason Bull recognised his talent, why could not they?

Eventually the door opened and a weary-looking Mr Tusker beckoned them in. Jason Bull still sat in his chair, appearing not to have moved a muscle.

'In the event,' began the manager forlornly, 'taking everything into account, perhaps it's best that we make a change. Variety. Best to encourage the young. We can but try new permutations. Quite see the point . . . '

He had little time to prepare for the part, but Jack threw himself into learning his lines with feverish dedication. Surprisingly, although the games of chess continued (and with the same result) Jason Bull never once raised the matter of Jack's promotion, and when the new prince himself broached the subject he seemed disinclined to say much about it. Even when Jack asked specific questions the star lead answered with airy generalisations which he illustrated with further stories of his own experiences on the stage.

'When I first come on,' Jack asked, 'should I appear bold? Should I swagger, do you think?'

'As you like, completely as you like. It's how you feel. I can remember how in one role I decided to make no preparations at all. I make very few as it is. As soon as I stepped on to the stage I knew precisely how to play the part and it brought the house down.'

Jack persisted.

'That scene where I find the old man lying injured on the ground. I'm not sure how I manage to bend over him with those opening words and yet finish the speech over by the fountain. When should I get up, do you think?'

Jason Bull shrugged.

'Somewhere in the middle, maybe. See how it works out. But one thing' – he leaned forward, suddenly involved – 'be at the fountain in good time. There must be no movement from your side of the stage when I make my entrance. We want no distractions, my larrikin.'

And he slid his castle along the back row to complete a devastating checkmate.

They had packed audiences once again for the new play, and in the warm summer evenings the theatre was a kaleidoscope of colourful dresses before the lights went down, heavy with the smell of humanity by the time the curtain fell to sustained applause. Jack felt himself carried along as in a dream. The early nerves soon passed, and now he discovered the demands of the craft for the first time. He spoke too fast, allowing himself too short a space in which to capture the audience's attention. He seemed always one step behind the others, remembering at the very last second that he must change his position, take off his hat, assume an expression of rage or bewilderment.

During his earlier experience as the hotel proprietor he had been rescued time and again by Luigi, but now he was on his own. Certainly Jason Bull was far too preoccupied with his own performance (and properly, he reasoned, for he was the cause of their success) to offer any help or encouragement to the novice, and there were few opportunities for anyone else to intervene.

Each evening, after he had creamed the greasepaint from his face and put his workday clothes back on, he would either saunter alone through the streets of the town cutting, he thought, a fine figure, or he would accompany Jason Bull to a restaurant and thence to the familiar hotel room for a nightcap. His contact with the rest of the company was now limited to the short period either side of a performance, and although they continued to greet him in a friendly fashion he felt that they had resigned themselves to his elevation to higher, greater things. He seldom had real conversations with them any more and once, when Luigi offered him advice, he bridled proudly.

'A pause,' Luigi suggested simply, 'is sometimes as effective as a speech, Jack. You've plenty of energy, and that's good. The part's coming along well, But if you could hold back sometimes . . . '

Jack reddened and kicked at a box of nails, which went careering across the floor.

'You'd like to see me quieter, less noticed,' he shouted. 'You don't want me to succeed. You don't like it that I'm playing a large role.'

He wrenched open the door. Oz was on one knee, returning nails to the box, and he gave Jack a look almost of pity, but he knew that could not be. They all resented his achievement, he was sure of that.

It was about this time that he conceived the plan of leaving Tusker's theatre and throwing in his lot with Jason Bull. What a splendid yet simple idea! The celebrated actor had engagements for many months ahead. He spoke, he said, several languages so that there were few places in which he could not perform. There was even talk of an Indian tour. If he had singled Jack out for special advancement here, surely he would be overjoyed to have an aspiring young actor to take with him on his travels.

The initial notion spread in his mind, catching colour and heat, until it became a glorious vision. He saw himself on distant stages alongside Jason Bull – if the shameful truth be told, as the equal of Jason Bull. They would become known as a team, parading their talents from Europe to Asia to the Americas! The apprenticeship was over and he was feted, idolised for his histrionic brilliance.

This burning vision shimmered behind everything he thought or did for several days. Often, when walking in town with his famous deliverer (for that was how he saw him now) or when he bent over the chess board, seemingly intent on leading his pieces to that first victory, he would be on the point of blurting out his thoughts and launching the unstoppable train of events which would see them triumph together throughout the world. Always some instinct prevented him. Perhaps he was afraid that the secret could not be kept until the end of the current run and that the envy of his fellow players would become unbearable. Perhaps he knew that his plan, however sound, was richly coloured by fantasy. But he never doubted that it would come to pass. He counted off the days, smiling to himself when he anticipated Jason Bull's growl of pleasure on learning what he proposed.

He would have made his announcement immediately after the last performance, but he found himself stupidly prevented. A bubbling Mr Tusker invited them to a celebratory party (clearly money had been made) and he accepted enthusiastically before discovering that Jason Bull would not be there. The star had changed out of his costume and was gone in a moment, to the evident relief of those he left behind.

'Here's a toast to our rising star,' smiled Luigi, raising his glass, and Jack was too downcast by the absence of his hero to recognise the generosity.

'You've done very well, my lad,' beamed Mr Tusker. 'A difficult time for you – for all of us, you might say. But well done! You've survived!'

Survived! Was that all they could say? He would show them.

'Not,' added Mr Tusker, 'that we can promise you the prestigious roles all the time, you understand. Rather a special circumstance, eh? But let's look on the brighter side, shall we? We'll remember what you can do, Jack. You'll not have to prop the rest of us up for ever.'

Not for ever. Not for another day. He thought of escaping now, dropping his glass and running, but he was surrounded.

'As long as a prince can also fix a bit of stage scenery,' grinned Oz from his great height. Jack felt as if they were all relieved that they had cut him down to size again. 'I've missed your help these past weeks.'

'Those lines took some learning, though,' threw in Mr Tusker kindly. 'Never much good at learning them myself, if I'm honest.'

'All prompts,' chuckled Ma, passing by on her rounds. 'Entirely prompts.'

Even Amazing, who might feel that he had been twice wronged, clinked his glass with Jack's and, giggling, recalled some minor accidents in his own performance. And Belle, while saying little, tweaked his nose and smiled, as if to say that all was forgiven. As if there were anything for them to forgive!

It was not until late that evening that he was able to get away. He hurried into the street. The lights at the hotel were still ablaze: peopled who stayed at the best hotel in town never went to bed early. His face was by now well known to the desk porter, but this gentleman frowned with surprise when he entered the lobby.

'Didn't think we should see you again,' he said.

'Why ever not?'

'With Mr Bull having left, I mean.'

'He's gone!'

'Why, yes. More than an hour ago. Packed everything up.'

'Gone for good?'

The porter laughed.

'Well, I hope not. He grants us the favour of his custom once or twice a year. I dare say we shall see him again.'

Jack felt a hollowness at the centre of his being and he felt that it spread and spread within him.

'Did he leave a message?'

'I'm afraid not.'

'Upstairs, perhaps?'

A shaking head and then the presentation of a key.

'Look, I shouldn't, but I know you. Run up there and have a quick look. But I'm sure he'd have left it at the desk.'

He tripped up the stairs twice in his hurry, though knowing that it could not be, that he would find nothing. The key rattled in the lock; he pushed the door open. The sheets were pulled back from the bed, the pictures had been taken from the wall, the gown had finally left its chair. It was an empty hotel room, sumptuous but without character. There was no letter.

Then he saw, on the table, the chess set. The pieces were as he remembered them from the last move, save that in packing Jason Bull had evidently touched against the board, knocking a knight and a bishop on their sides, toppling a lonely pawn to the carpet. The set was the only thing that had been left, but Jack could not approach it. He had not won a game rightfully to claim it, but that was not what prevented him. It was the carelessness with which it had been left, discarded. It was an unwanted encumbrance, useful for a time but now abandoned. It was no gift.

He stared at it for some moments then, in a spasm, leapt forward and swept the pieces in a shower to the floor.

19 The Party

The studio had been completely transformed for the party. Thick, heavy ropes on pulleys had transplanted most of the larger items to one end – all save those that formed part of the sculptor's ambitious commission. These were grouped at the centre of the room so that the visitors, as they mingled, would find themselves constantly reminded of the craftsman's skill.

Walter and Sarah had spent hours prettying the place. It could not be decorated in any conventional sense and yet the cold white company that occupied it hardly looked festive enough as they were. The sculptor had been generous with the money he allowed them, and they had bought colourful things – huge gourds in reds and yellows; sheaves of dried reeds and grasses dyed purple, bright green, vermilion; cloth hangings that blazed in the daylight and would glow warmly when illumined by lamps and candles.

There were lengths of patterned paper, too, which they experimented with, sometimes unsuccessfully. The severed head certainly appeared no less doleful when a confection in pink crepe adorned the hand which grasped its hair. Walter stood back to admire his handiwork, looking for all the world like the sculptor at his labours. He began to move the smaller, manouevrable figures into more sociable groupings, thus rendering he open-mouthed fish constantly amazed at what a nymph whispered in its ear, while a knight stood immodestly close to a maiden he might otherwise be imagined to be rescuing.

Whereas this cold, silent gathering could party on nothing, their warmer counterparts would need food and drink, and soon Walter was dispatched with lists supplied by the sculptor, returning to await the delivery of a quantity which, he reflected, would have satisfied the monastery for a full year. A brewer's dray arrived heavy with barrels that were taken from it single-handed by a huge shaven-headed drayman and carried upon his shoulder up to the studio to be set at intervals around the room. A slender wine merchant stood as overseer while three young men, little older than Walter, transported their goods more gently from the street.

'Fine wines need gentle handling, sir. Hey! You clumsy fool – set those bottles down carefully!'

Hams, spiced meats, crystallised fruits, nuts, assorted berries (selected more for colour than taste, he suspected) all arrived in their turn. Walter supervised their placing on the trestles that he had arranged. The sculptor, meanwhile, had retired to a corner as if oblivious of the arrangements going on all around him and was making rough drawings for a new work.

As the hour of the party approached, Walter began to grow anxious about the invitations. How many had been sent? How many accepted? The sculptor had not been forthcoming when asked: indeed, once he had made the decision and written the lists he seemed to lose interest. Now Walter tried again and this time, seeing the anxiety on the lad's face, he relented.

'Fact is, Walter, I've no idea how many will turn up. I've put the word out and people will start coming tonight and keep coming until the food and drink run out. Could go on for days. Knew a party once went on for three weeks. Don't worry.'

'Have you asked the Count?'

'I should think not! He would certainly refuse. Doesn't like his movements known, you see. Haven't you tried to trace him these past few weeks? But I've put the word out and he's sure to get wind of it. He always does, you know. I just hope . . . '

Here he tailed off and took up his charcoal again.

'You hope what?' pressed Walter.

But the sculptor shrugged the further question away and Walter returned to checking things he had checked several times already: the white wine lay in buckets of cold water; the hams were napkin-wrapped, each with its sharp knife for the guests to carve themselves slices; the meats were set out between dishes of pickles. Had Walter an appetite at that moment he could have eaten with rare prodigality. As it was, he had none whatsoever. His mouth seemed filled with dust, his stomach was tight with nerves and he paced and paced about the tables impatient for the first arrival.

At last the sculptor rolled up his paper, took off his smock and, with a final insistence that they be of good cheer, set off home to prepare himself for his eventual triumphant entry. Walter and Sarah, though they had precious little wardrobe, would not disgrace their landlord. Over the weeks they had earned enough to garb themselves in clothes that were unremarkable on the streets of the town, even if Sarah's liking for loose-fitting silks combined with her beauty to turn a good many eyes. Walter's hair had grown and had been cut in the modern fashion, and his face – that mottled area apart – had turned ruddy-brown under the hot summer sun. They no longer had the appearance of forlorn waifs to be pitied by all they met.

Walter stood at the window, the dusk gathering about him. The colour drained gradually from the decorations. When would the first guest arrive? For now, the encroaching darkness was the only visitor they had.

Later they lit the candles, the lamps and the lanterns and their hearts lifted momentarily to be in this enchanted cavern where colours burned at every turn. Surely a shimmering rainbow lifted through the fanlight into the night sky!

Much later, when the sculptor reappeared, making his entry with trimmed beard and flamboyant clothes in place of his dusty white working apparel, it was an audience of two that greeted him. Walter and Sarah sat side by side, their dejection the more expressive and poignant for the surrounding trappings of carnival. The sculptor scowled.

'Nobody?'

'Nobody,' Walter echoed.

The sculptor lifted an opened wine bottle to his lips and the colour that drained from it seemed to re-establish itself upon his face until, finally, he banged the empty bottle back on to the table.

'Damn the Count!' were his only words before leaving.

20 Fear

Two days passed and the sculptor did not appear. Walter's suspicions were confirmed by the poet Celestin, the main point of whose mission seemed to be that of gazing adoringly upon Sarah once more.

'Truth is, old Clabber's probably flat out in the gutter somewhere right now. Always turns to Our Lady of the Soothing Waters when trouble looms. Unless you can find him and get him back he'll end up behind bars again. He gets to fighting, you see. Last time he nearly killed a man and got six months to sober up in.'

Even as he spoke these grim words he was smiling at Sarah, teasing a turn of the lips in response.

'She really is amazing. No wonder Clabber's so taken with her.'

Walter, who felt resentment at the poet's attentions to Sarah, attempted to show him the door with as much politeness as he could muster, but Celestin was not so easily deterred. His eyes came to rest on the unopened bottles.

'Clabber wouldn't begrudge me a tipple or two,' he announced and, ignoring Walter's feeble farewells, he made himself comfortable on a sofa, tilting a bottle of white wine to his mouth.

Sarah, to Walter's unease, seemed to find nothing menacing in Celestin's behaviour. It was as if she recognised in the poet a simple and unaffected love of beauty and life. As if, the perfect citizen of gaudy O—, his was a butterfly spirit, flitting prettily around, alighting on this flower and that, attractive and essentially harmless.

'Where might he be?' Walter asked

'Anywhere,' was the simple reply. 'Try the docks.'

Walter signalled to Sarah that they should leave, but Celestin reached out and held her arm.

'Stay with me, my pretty,' he urged. 'He doesn't need you to help him. Not in the sort of places he's likely to find old Clabber.'

Sarah, however, lightly disengaged herself and, still smiling at the abandoned poet, followed Walter down the stairs.

The docklands were extensive and their progress was all the slower because Walter repeatedly stopped to stare at the huge ships which lay alongside. The masts were so high that he could not believe the seamen could climb them and not lose their senses, yet he saw lads of his own age up in the rigging, clambering up and down at great speed and with no apparent thought for their safety.

Huge chests, bales of thick cloth, piles of foodstuff littered the wharves, and he and Sarah made their way among them hand in hand. A black dog, thin and hungry-looking, attached itself to them. There were narrow alleyways running between warehouses and they peered into them in the hope of finding the sculptor. Sometimes they came upon small taverns, loud with the songs and curses of men far gone in liquor, and they would wait outside to watch people come and go.

Eventually they found him inadvertently. Stepping backwards into a dark alley to avoid a passing handcart, they fell over a recumbent form and became the objects of a torrent of imaginative abuse which died only after they had identified themselves. The sculptor's aggression turned momentarily to tears of self-pity as they helped him to his feet and supported his staggering career back to the studio.

Celestin lay on the sofa exactly as they had left him. He did not rise for the sculptor's entrance which – from the head gripped between the hands and the groans that were emitted – might have been that of a tragic actor on to the stage.

'Ha!' the poet gurgled merrily. 'And do we have here Ernest Clabber or the great Jason Bull?'

'Rot you!'

'The audience has been waiting a long time, maestro.'

'Drinking my wine. Where were you the other night?'

'In mourning.'

'Mourning?'

The sculptor shrugged uncomprehendingly and took up a glass.

'Here,' he ordered Celestin. 'Just what I need to steady myself. Pour a glass.'

'No, please,' started Walter, but he was silenced by a roaring from the sculptor, whose aggressiveness had suddenly resurfaced.

'It's my studio! It's my drink! Who are you to deny me my own drink in my own studio? Eh? If you don't like it you can get out!'

Walter immediately took Sarah by the hand to leave, but Celestin intervened.

'It's all right. He doesn't mean it. He always gets like this. Sit down and ignore him. It'll pass.'

Clabber tossed back the drink.

'What do you mean, in mourning?' he demanded.

He took the bottle from Celestin's hand and filled the glass again.

'Here,' the poet replied, passing him a newspaper cutting that had been crumpled in his pocket. 'A jest, I dare say. Someone's humour.'

Clabber took it. The newspaper was a week old and a headline announced: TRAGIC DEATH OF A FINE SCULPTOR. A single paragraph recorded his own passing.

> The body of Ernest Clabber, one of O—'s leading artists, has been discovered in his studio. His death appears to have been the result of a dreadful accident.
>
> The renowned sculptor was working on a set of large stone statues when one of them toppled and crushed him. His distressed assistant reported that Mr Clabber was about to hold a party to unveil his latest work. This would have been held in the very studio in which the unhappy fatality occurred.

Clabber sat down abruptly and the glass fell from his grasp.

'No joke,' he said hoarsely. 'That's no joke.'

'Sure it is, man,' consoled the poet. 'Don't take it badly.'

'Wasn't it obvious who had kept people away?' the sculptor asked. 'Didn't I know it all along? Nobody else would have the power to do that. But an obituary – like a death warrant . . .'

'You're alive, my friend!' Celestin encouraged him. 'No harm's done. Only a party.'

'And why did he stop it? You tell me.'

'Don't know. A jest.'

'The Count playing a joke? Is that what you believe? And why didn't you come, Celestin? You knew I wasn't dead.'

'Business.'

'Ha! You knew, my friend. You knew that was the Count's doing. That's why you didn't come. It's all up with me. I'm lost – and I don't know why.'

Celestin rose uncertainly to his feet. He put a hand on Clabber's shoulder but seemed to find no words of consolation. After some moments he said quietly: 'Madeleine's here.'

The effect on the sculptor was dramatic. If he was white and shaken to begin with, now he stared at his friend with wide, frightened eyes.

'Where?'

'Here in O—. Lornquist saw her yesterday. He pretended not to know where you worked or lived, but it's only a matter of time.'

Clabber sunk his head between his hands once more and groaned hollowly.

'Who's Madeleine?' Walter whispered to Celestin, but it was the sculptor who answered.

'She's my wife.'

'But what a wife!' chuckled Celestin.

'Must escape,' Clabber mumbled. 'Get away. Whole world's closing in on me.'

Celestin now shook the sculptor's shoulder.

'Come on, man. I'll take you away.'

Inspiration seemed suddenly to have struck him, for his eyes shone and he began to pace the studio with an eager stride.

'Into the mountains! How would that suit you, Clabber? We'll all go' – he threw a fond glance at Sarah – 'and give the world the slip. Lock this place up. Let your Madeleine find a copy of that newspaper and believe she's a widow!'

The poet's way with problems seemed to Walter remarkably direct, if not naive, but the plan seemed like a lifeline to poor Clabber. He smiled for the first time and brought his palms together in a slow-motion clap.

'Your genius, Celestin!' he enthused. 'An escape!'

Celestin sat beside him, lowering his voice as if unfriendly ears might hear.

'As it happens, I'm in a spot of bother myself. It's all rather uncomfortable. This will suit me very well.' He nudged his companion heartily. 'There's a lady I know, beautiful and very well-to-do, who'll welcome me with open arms. A fine house on an estate in the mountains. She'll insist that we stay for a month!'

Their preparations were made in no time at all and with such feverish excitement that Walter found it impossible to resist. He and Sarah were, willy-nilly, part of the plan. And, in truth, as they closed the door behind them and set off on their journey he was aware of his own sense of relief. He knew, moreover, from what it stemmed.

That newspaper article had been careful to mention Clabber's assistant, a detail that was surely unnecessary. If the writing was indeed the work of the Count, and if it was something more sinister than a practical joke, perhaps it was Walter rather than the sculptor who had reason to fear.

21 The Grand Tour

There can have been few less likely candidates for a walking tour than the small party which set off from the station that evening. Only the sculptor had in any way dressed for the occasion – booted, wearing a leather satchel over his shoulder and sporting a thick walking stick, he would have looked the complete professional had all his accoutrements not been so shiningly unused. Celestin, in contrast, carried nothing and stood casually hands in pocket, wearing his usual urban rig.

'Aren't you taking anything?' Walter asked, feeling inadequately prepared himself.

'Man was born free, unencumbered,' the poet laughed, pointing in the air, though without an upward glance. 'What do you see up there? The open sky and the freely flying birds. And what do they carry, Walter? Nothing!'

Now he allowed his eyes to carry skywards, only to share with Walter a view of blackened station girders. This caused him to burst into laughter, and putting his arm round Walter's shoulders, he spoke to him as in confidence.

'The truth is, my young friend, that I've precious few changes of clothes and I can't go back to my room to pack anything because of old Carrot Locks being there. She'll either tear me apart or insist on coming with us.'

From that moment Walter liked Celestin, despite having reservations about the reasons for his flight. Surely, he thought to himself, the two men should face their women rather than run away. The Count, of course, was a different matter.

They travelled late into the night, putting up at a small hotel. The following morning Walter was up from habit soon after sunrise, saying his devotions. He could hear Sarah moving in the next room, too, but the men were not out of their beds until much later. It was almost midday before they were ready to begin their walk into the hills.

Walter strode forward with a zest he had not expected. For the first time he realised that he had missed the mountains. Though these were not his own, the distant sight of high peaks fired a profound sense of longing. Unthinking, he began to whistle a tune that he had heard in the village by the monastery, a song that the country folk sang each spring to celebrate the passing of the snow from their high valley.

In truth, it was not a well-favoured expedition. Celestin's well-to-do lady was not at home. The house was boarded up: the family was, apparently, taking a holiday by the sea. They stumbled along ill-defined tracks, the two men increasingly irritable in the unremitting heat, strangely helpless away from the familiar landmarks.

The first night they found humble lodgings in a precipitous village; the second they wandered for hours in the murk before finding an inn whose owner allowed them space on his floor; the third they spent in the hayloft of a remote barn. It could not go on.

The fourth day was to be the last in the fresh mountain air. The path that the travellers walked led between large boulders green with moss. On one side a forest climbed the mountain, its shady coolness offering ample contrast to the sunwashed meadow that tumbled to the valley far below on the other. They had walked throughout the day, morning vapours slowly giving way to the heady warmth of noon, but now, with the evening approaching, the mists were beginning to gather again and the valley was filling with a milky light that promised to mask their view of the town that sat within. The rooftops were losing their distinctness, becoming a soft mosaic of pinks and ochres.

Of the four it was the sculptor who looked the worst for wear, and it was he who now halted, resting against a rock with the pretence of admiring the view. He was undeniably beginning to think the outdoor life a poor alternative to facing his wife. Celestin, on the other hand – his spirits raised by the sight of streets and roofs – skipped along as lightly as a chamois, his hands still thrust into his pockets.

'Planning a sculpture?' he chided gently. 'If you stay there we'll never get down before nightfall.'

His tired companion grudgingly relinquished his resting place and started down. The other two walked steadily hand in hand, Sarah drinking to the full the splendour of these surroundings and Walter replenishing his town-soiled spirit. The path descended steeply and was hard on their feet, but presently the rough stone turned to regular cobble and they found themselves entering the outskirts of the valley town. Lamps fixed to the walls of closely huddled houses lit their way in the gathering dusk and they came at last to the town centre. It was, Walter thought, impressive – a large square with a fountain; a gothic town hall whose layered splendour was matched by a large rococo church; the sweeping facade of a grand hotel; and a prettily painted theatre.

'A spa,' Celestin announced, though whether from knowledge or guesswork the others could not tell. All that interested the sculptor was the hotel.

'Civilisation at last. No more stretching in the hay like animals. No more damn chalets stuck halfway up a mountain. No more lumpy beds. Come on.'

His tired legs seemed to regain their strength as he marched up the steps of the hotel and into the foyer. The desk clerk, a well-scrubbed young man, looked at the arrivals askance: their shabby dust-laden clothes contrasted sadly with the elegance of their surroundings. A lady seated at the entrance to the lounge lowered the lorgnettte she read with to view them the more clearly and, shuddering, returned to her book. The sculptor was insensitive to the impression created by his appearance, and he sounded almost threatening as he demanded a suite of the very best rooms.

Perhaps it was this tone of voice that persuaded the clerk to comply, though he added rather tartly that dinner was to be served within the hour and that only properly attired guests were allowed into the dining room. But the sculptor was a match for this.

'Keep your dining room. It's a bath I want, and a soft bed. We'll find somewhere else to eat.'

As they walked the streets of the town Clabber and Celestin were united in their profound satisfaction at having escaped the wilderness. They rejoiced to see the large buildings, the windows stuffed with merchandise. The sculptor paused by a large equestrian statue which was not, it was obvious, a masterpiece, and he patted it lovingly, running his hand over the mottled bronze.

'Who needs chasms and thorn bushes and jagged flints?' he asked rhetorically.

'True, Clabber, true,' nodded his friend. 'Only the artificial is true beauty.'

Yet even this part of their adventure was to have its disappointments. The town, unlike O—, had no casino. The theatre, though it still boasted colourful posters outside, was closed: the travelling company had moved on a few days before. There was no cabaret to match the Crippled Rabbit.

'A quiet place,' decided Clabber.

'Regal,' added Celestin. 'Faded pomp. But no . . . no . . . '

'No soul,' concluded the sculptor, leading them unerringly to a sizeable tavern.

Here, Walter knew, they were destined to remain for a long time. Clabber, evidently happy to throw his money around from sheer relief, bought elaborate cocktails which he insisted Walter and Sarah take, too. But while the young pair sipped at their drinks so that they lasted for almost an hour, Clabber and Celestin downed one after the other and became more and more gregarious. Walter himself enjoyed the taste of the fruity cocktail and could feel its early effects, but he remembered his behaviour at the Count's palace and refused to give way to the temptation. He sat watching two old men playing chess at the next table until one of them, seeing him for the first time, promptly took up his walking stick and thrust it at Walter's chest.

'You tell your people,' he said gruffly, 'that they still owe me for carting the scenery.' Then he returned to his game.

Walter, perplexed, turned to Celestin, who only put a finger to his temple to indicate his idea of the man's sanity. Clabber was debating Michelangelo's control of form with an earnest young man who was, it seemed, the leading local art critic.

'Exquisite line" Walter heard the critic say.

'Power of the forearm,' was Clabber's pragmatic reply, accompanied by a baring of his own. 'See there. That's where you need strength, my lad.'

It was after midnight before they set off – Clabber staggering, Celestin dancing – through the darkened streets back to their hotel. A good evening was the verdict, but not a place to stay long in. Clabber enquired of a passer-by whether the town had a station, and the affirmative answer pleased him greatly.

'Tomorrow, my friends, it' s O— for me. If you wish to continue the tour you're welcome.'

The suite at the hotel was magnificent. In the centre of the main room a spreading chandelier hung from the ceiling. There was heavy chintz furniture and lush, patterned carpets. But they were almost too tired to notice. They slept soundly, rose late and departed as soon as possible for the station.

On the long journey home Walter marvelled at the ease with which the poet and the sculptor could forget their troubles. Surely not much would have changed in the few days they had been away, and yet they joked and sang and recited as if it were the dawning of a new age.

They entered O— in the early evening, a light breeze stirring the warm summer air. When the time came for Celestin to go his own way he exchanged brotherly hugs with Clabber, saluted Walter, brushed Sarah's hand with his lips, the while making loving eyes at her – and marched happily to whatever fate awaited him.

Clabber, too, walked rapidly, as if he were returning from a year's absence. He bounded up the last steps well ahead of the other two, unlocked the door and disappeared inside. Before they had reached the threshold, however, he re-emerged, a terrible pallor to his face, the breath rasping in his throat.

'Whatever's the matter?' shouted Walter, supporting him.

The sculptor fought for words.

'I've seen it,' he gasped, a floundering arm waving in the direction of a partly opened window. 'Seen it. The Count's monkey!'

22 Promotion

Jack stood in the wings, waiting to go on. Round the edge of the curtain he could see part of the first few rows. The people there were the refined sort, impeccably dressed, loud in their talk before the curtain went up and throughout the interval, but undemonstrative during the performance. The women wore long, frilly dresses and their hair was curled and piled.

How much he preferred the audience at the back! Ordinary folk, he called them. Not much money, but warm in their appreciation when they liked a play and rowdily indignant when they didn't. He felt that they were his sort of people. Those at the front reminded him of his guardians, of strictness and rules and harsh correction. They came to the theatre, but they would not mix with the likes of actors and actresses in the world outside.

'Married already, you jackanapes!'

It was Belle in a rare comic role, hitting a young suitor (Amazing) over the head with a cucumber and evoking an outburst of laughter which Jack's ears picked out as titters and polite giggles from the front, guffaws from the back.

He watched the leading lady going through her rehearsed routine and felt a warmth of pleasure soak through him. He loved these people as he had never loved anyone in his life. After the disgraceful episode with Jason Bull not a word of anger or resentment had been spoken to him. When he had tried, agonisingly, to apologise he had been met only with smiles and gentle nods of the head. They understood and they forgave. He was part of their family.

And he had worked so hard to compensate for his foolishness that it seemed, even to him, something of the far distant past. He had thrown himself once again into learning the techniques of the trade, and though he occasionally fell from grace (once stealing off, for instance, to join some local lads who were fishing in the river when he should have been repairing scenery with Oz), he always bounced straight back with an enthusiasm that affected them all.

Now, picking up his cue, he strode on to the stage dressed in a splendour which the plot was soon to reveal as a complete sham.

'Your rich cousin returns,' he declaimed confidently, at the same time expertly tripping over himself so that he collapsed at Belle's feet. The laughter washed over him, bathed him luxuriantly.

'Rich?'

He leapt to his feet and put a hand in his pocket.

'Many more where these came from,' he said, and pulled out, instead of bank notes, a wad of chicken feathers. The sports at the back howled.

He had learned a lot so quickly. Now he could look at an audience and see faces, not a pink blur. He followed Luigi's advice and early in any performance would find three stereotypes – the person who would readily respond to anything; the dour character who was a hostile forced to be wooed and won; and the bored spectator who would fall asleep unless roused.

'The first for confidence,' Luigi advised, 'the others as critics.'

Tonight, however, the battles were all won. The actors had the mood upon them and could arouse laughter even where the script had not intended any. When Jack made his exit he stood by the curtain, smiling for their triumph and watching the others at their business.

They were not stars like Jason Bull, but over the weeks he had come to appreciate the skills with which they created wonderful effects from few resources and limited talents. They worked for everything they earned. Belle, he recognised, had a narrow range (melodrama was her forte), but she never missed a line, she never forgot where she should be on the stage and she had developed a vast range of gestures and intonations of the voice to compensate for the fact that she found it difficult totally to become another character. Luigi understood more about the craft than anyone, but even those occasionals, Oz and Ma, were so well versed in basic theatre knowledge that they played their roles with no sense of unsuitability. It was a team achievement, and Jack more and more admired the genius of Mr Tusker in orchestrating these diverse talents in performances which were greeted enthusiastically everywhere they went.

Tonight the applause was particularly loud. Jack linked arms with Oz and Amazing as they went on-stage to take their bow. Oz, who had played a drunkard, staggered towards the footlights. Jack tripped over himself and fell to his knees, waving. Amazing, who had fainted dramatically at a key point in the comedy, keeled over, hit the floor, rolled and leapt to his feet again in one incredible movement. How the audience clapped and yelled! Even the grim-visaged man Jack had chosen for his examplar of dourness showed his teeth in a broad smile.

When the curtain had come down for the last time Jack felt a tug at his arm.

'Precious close to delirium,' Mr Tusker enthused, brushing his hands over the proud bushes of grey hair. 'Prodigious success!'

'It's wonderful.'

Mr Tusker led him backstage.

'I think your time has come, Jack my lad,' he said. 'You feel ready for it?'

'For what?'

'Your first decent role. At our next town. If you think you're ready for it.'

'Ready . . . '

'Just the role for you. You'll share the lead with Luigi.'

Jack, excited beyond the limits of self-control, leapt at Oz and beat the surprised fellow on the chest with a boisterous tattoo. He was far too thrilled by his elevation to ask where they were going.

23 The Count's Monkey

'Calm yourself! Please . . . '

Walter helped the trembling sculptor back into his studio, where he fell, ashen, upon a sofa. Sarah splashed drink into a glass and tipped it to his lips.

'The monkey!' the poor man gasped again. 'Here!'

On a workbench beneath the open window pieces of charcoal and sheets of drawing paper had been disturbed, and a crayon showed signs of having been chewed at one end.

'What does this mean?' Walter demanded. 'Even if it was a monkey . . . '

'*Was*, I tell you! The Count's. Up there. It swung out as I came in.'

'Where's the harm in a monkey?'

But there was no answer for minutes more. The sculptor lay back, shuddering, his tongue loose and heavy in his mouth. Walter feared that he was about to suffer a seizure of the heart. Sarah, the bottle put by, now leant over him with a damp cloth, pressing it against his brow, his temples and at his palpitating neck.

'An omen,' he whispered at last, his eyes rolling up in their sockets. 'Those who have seen the Count's monkey . . . '

There was a sob in his throat.

'If the Count's monkey was here,' Walter said reasonably, attempting to calm Clabber's fevered brain, 'it may be because it escaped. It signifies nothing that it came to this studio. Mere chance.'

'No! What do you know of it? Who are you to say?'

Clabber's anger could find no reinforcing energy. He reached for the bottle and swigged noisily.

'No accident,' he said. 'That creature lives at the palace. Pampered.

Worshipped, almost. It has no need of its freedom. Yet, once in a while, it visits a house in the town . . . and it brings a curse with it. Men I have known, powerful, happy, prosperous, that when the Count's monkey called were crushed and ruined.'

'This is superstition,' Walter protested, all his training rebelling against it. 'A monkey can bring no curse.'

'Mere superstition, eh? That's what you think? Well, that it might be. A supernatural power. There's many who believe it, and some of them, my young friend, who've been a little longer in the world than you. Who are we to say what powers move the world, for evil as well as good?

'But there's another explanation which is every bit as sinister to me, even if there's no magic in it.'

He took out a large spotted handkerchief and wiped it across his forehead.

'The Count sends the monkey,' he said quaveringly. 'It's his warning to a man. The curse is the Count's!'

At this moment, as Walter remembered the newspaper report and the fear that it was he himself who was threatened, there was a rap on the door and an envelope was pushed beneath it. Footsteps retreated, descended the stairs. Sarah, while hearing nothing, had seen the direction of their glances and she ran to collect the package. Walter took it. Seeing the splendid insignia in one corner, he held it out to Clabber.

'Open it,' the sculptor said.

'It's addressed to you.'

'From the Count. I can't read it.'

Walter tore the envelope open and withdrew a single sheet of paper.

'Tell me!'

'It's all right. The sculptures will be collected tomorrow. Payment will be made once they are installed. That's all it says.'

'All?'

'Nothing more. Look – it's a business letter.'

Clabber seized the paper and read the message several times over. He lay back on the sofa, his breathing coming more easily.

'Collected tomorrow,' he laughed crazily with a gush of relief. 'Payment on delivery. Old Clabber's not an outcast after all! The Count wants my sculptures. Ha! What do you say to that, Walter? It's not a benighted Clabber, it seems!'

He stood up, grabbed a bottle, his hand still shaking, and put his other fist round the stems of three glasses. These he filled with celebratory wine, insisting that his young companions share his joy. The glasses were clinked together.

As Walter tipped the wine to his lips Clabber's smile vanished for a second and the tone of his voice was at once sombre and questioning.

'But I did see the Count's monkey,' he said.

24 Pursuit

A ruddy sun slipped down to the horizon, flecking the waves with fierce orange daubs. Walter had spent the afternoon alone at O—'s fashionable waterfront, and now he took the route home, skirting the harbour arm and making for the dock area which offered him a short cut.

If he had imagined that his brief jaunt in the mountains would make the crowded streets less bearable, he had quickly learned his lesson. The town had begun to seep into him, to take him to itself. The thrust and parry of discussion and argument was honing his wit to perfection. To be Truth's honest broker in the monastery had been no challenge: there Truth was the general currency. But here, in the artifice and amorality of O—, Truth had to stand its ground against style and sensation.

How he had enjoyed his hours strolling among the pleasure-seekers of O—! At first it had felt strange to be by himself, Sarah having stayed behind to model for Clabber's latest commission, but soon he had succumbed to the spirit of ease and contentment under the blazing summer sun. Never before had he seen people discard so many of their clothes in a public place, and he found himself comparing limbs and torsos with those whiter ones fashioned by the sculptor in his studio. A powerfully built man who lay, eyes closed, on the sand might even, if his facial features were ignored, be taken as the model for one of the group which had, two days before, been transported to the Count's palace.

Walter felt the pleasures a sincere but susceptible puritan might feel in the courtyards of hell. He was attracted by what he saw, but constantly on his guard. Was pleasure an evil? No, the brothers had never taught him that harsh doctrine. But pleasure should not be selfish. It must be a by-product of doing good, acting wisely. Then how should he react to the simple pleasure of the hot sun beating against his face?

He remembered how Celestin's skipping progress though the mountains had caught his imagination. The brothers had ever taught simple reliance upon Providence while themselves relying rather upon thoughtful, careful preparation in all their doings. They were men of finely tuned moral judgment, beside whom Celestin seemed the slightest of creatures, his ephemeral thoughts translated into ephemeral actions. And yet it was *his* actions and not those of the brothers that accorded most with their teaching. Here was a fine puzzle to accompany him along the plage and through the dusty streets.

It was at once darker in the docklands. The sun had become a hot coal that painted the rooftops with a liquid fire as it sank behind them. In contrast the streets were a puddle of deep violet shadows, punctuated only by the yellow glow of windows and lamps. Work was over, and when he passed by the wharves there was a silence which seemed louder than the babbling, laughing voices he had heard in his ears throughout the afternoon.

Was it this sudden plunging from light into gloom that prompted the fear that he was being followed? At first he comforted himself with this explanation, while quickening his pace. He had felt watched before. What more natural than that the eeriness of the evening docks should excite his imagination? But it was no fancy.

When he paused he could hear, for a moment, his pursuer shuffling behind. Then stillness. He waited in silence, peering into the murk. Nothing. Walking again and abruptly stopping . . . those footsteps followed, and stopped.

Walter began to panic. He knew the way well enough, but he had a sudden terror that in the darkness he would take a wrong turning. Flotsam chocked at the quayside as he passed, and far out beyond the harbour and out to sea a ship sounded its hooter. He walked rapidly, the sweat irritating his collar.

In one area there were a few mean houses with people gathered outside, the adults talking desultorily, the children scampering about in play. The buildings bore the scars of dereliction, but his heart lifted and he slowed his pace.

'Lost?' asked an old man who was sitting on a pile of tarred rope.

'No. No, thank you,' Walter stammered, and could think of no conversation that would detain him here, keeping his pursuer at bay. He cast a quick glance behind him and saw a man's figure slide into the utter blackness of a shadowed doorway.

'Not a good place for a young fellow to be,' the old man remarked in a kindly manner as he passed.

He turned a corner and now he began to run, blindly. He did not notice what wharves he crossed. Once he slipped on a patch of oil and skidded along on his back. He rose to his feet, failed to make out a pile of iron bars stacked against a wall and cracked his shins, agonisingly. Out of breath, sobbing with pain and fear, he hobbled forward, through a gate, along a jetty.

There was no way forward. He came to the water's edge. A row of bollards awaited the arrival of a cargo vessel which was as yet far away, perhaps hundreds of miles away, where Walter at this moment wished himself. Had he been able to swim he would have thrown himself into the lapping scum and struck out wildly away from land.

He sat on his haunches for a period, catching his breath, listening. He had run fast and had, it seemed, outdistanced his follower. With stealthy movements he returned to the gate, recrossed the wharf. A little more composed now, he recognised the feeble gas lamp which stood in the narrow passageway beyond. That was the route he must take – past the lamp and up the hill through the old quarter. He closed his eyes and listened once more. There came that shuffling again, he thought, but then no more. Had he heard it? There was a profound silence.

The gaslight flickered and glowed. He crept closer, his shoulder brushing the wharf's perimeter wall. A pause: he dare not step forward into the alley, exposed. He turned an ear in the direction he had first come from. Silence.

At last he gathered his courage and sprinted forward, his eyes on the street beyond the lamp. At this moment a figure stepped from the shadows and the two collided heavily and fell in a heap to the ground.

25 Pleadings

'Brother Mark!'

The old monk, although he lay flat on his back, seemed much more concerned for Walter than himself.

'Are you hurt?' he asked, reaching out a hand. 'I didn't hear you coming.'

'No. I'm all right. Let me help you.'

They stood under the lamp, each wary of the other.

'You were following me,' Walter said.

'Watching. I was watching you.'

'You've been a long time in the town?'

'No. A day only. I arrived last night. I first saw you this afternoon.'

They began to climb the hill to the old quarter, brother Mark trailing a little behind, limping.

'I have special dispensation from the abbot,' he said, as if justifying himself. 'To come and fetch you back. If you wish to come.'

Walter made no reply.

'Truly, it's a terrible place,' the old fellow said in a lamenting tone. 'The vice apparent for all to see. Frivolity. Licentiousness. Human folly. Don't you just want to run from it?'

'I haven't finished the business I came on. It's too soon to make a decision.'

'But you've been here an age, Walter' his companion remonstrated, pulling at his sleeve. 'If you knew the loss that's felt by your absence! What keeps you here?'

'I don't know,' Walter said. 'The address I came to find doesn't exist any more. But I can't leave yet. I have a feeling that there are things I shall learn if I am patient.'

'Ah, patience. You always had patience.'

They walked in silence for a time. Walter was surprised to find that his initial relief in discovering that he was pursued by no dangerous villain had quickly turned to irritation. The shuffling sound of brother Mark's sandals was like a whisper of admonition. The humility of his simple garb condemned the colour and vanity of O—.

'When you left, without a word, there was a desolation in the monastery, Walter. Not to have prepared us . . . We worried. Always we expected to receive news of you, a brief letter perhaps.'

'I couldn't.'

'You having spent all your life between those walls and then cast among the devilries of a place such as this! Not only the noise and the vulgarity, but the evil. Monstrous practices.'

Walter swung round.

'Why do you condemn so?' he demanded. 'What can you know of the place if you've freshly arrived?'

He added, more quietly: 'It is not as you describe it.'

They passed through the streets of the old quarter, and as they reached the cobbled entrance of an inn yard two men stumbled across their path, much the worse for drink.

'A sorcerer!' exclaimed one, flapping a arm towards the becowled brother Mark. 'Magician!'

The other stood barring their way, his fists raised like a prize-fighter.

'I'm the man to teach a wizard a lesson,' he growled. 'Wallop a weakling wizard. Whip a wizened . . . '

Walter seized brother Mark by the arm and ran. The drunkard lunged at him but had no control over his movements. He fell to one knee and yelled inventive curses at them as they escaped. They ran, Walter tugging and tugging.

The sun had gone and a new moon glimmered in a velvet sky. Panting for breath, they came to a public square and fell on to a wooden bench.

'An evil place,' brother Mark gasped. 'Intemperance, profanities, violence . . . '

'Yes, yes,' Walter replied helplessly. He could not explain that there was so much more to the town, that (shamefully, it must be) he even found the waywardness of the inhabitants invigorating.

'A den . . . ' the old man began, pausing to throw the hood back from his overheated face.

'Of iniquity,' completed Walter, with scarcely a pause. 'I know the town, brother Mark. I have been safe in it.'

'Safe?'

Of course it was not true. He had known fear. His future was uncertain here.

'Come back with me, Walter. I plead with you. Rejoin your friends. We have prayed for you. I bring the loving greetings of the brothers and the father abbot!'

'Not yet!'

The old monk stood up, shaking his head with frustration.

'Very well. So be it. So you won't come!'

'Not yet!'

The cowl was pulled back over the venerable head.

'So be it. But I shan't leave you alone here, Walter.'

'Go, brother Mark!'

'I shan't be in your way, don't fear. A foolish old man you think me. I'll keep my distance.'

Even now he began to retreat, calling back over his shoulder.

'I'll be watching, Walter. And I shall ask you once more before I return. Once and once only.'

Walter, making his way home, felt uncomfortably discomposed. He had pushed all thoughts of returning to the monastery out of his mind. Doubtless – it was a silent assumption – he would return. But now his meeting with brother Mark and his refusal to go with him had raised the other possibility. Had he been hiding from himself a growing desire to stay in O— with its pleasures? Had he slipped into an easy acceptance of shallow living, moral looseness? And what were his duties to the monks? Should their wish to have him back – the wish of several – outweigh his own individual choice?

At the studio he was surprised to find Sarah alone. This surprise turned to anger when, from her signals, he learned what had happened in his absence. Clabber, it transpired, had received an invitation to the Count's palace on the Rue de Rêve for a celebration to unveil his sculptures. As was the Count's wont, this invitation had been a last-minute affair: the event was this very evening and would now be in full swing.

The anger arose from the fact that Clabber had made no attempt to include Walter, although he knew full well how much he wanted to meet the Count again. Yet – the whole thing was so typical – he had set off arm in arm with Celestin! The poet had arrived for his daily adoration of Sarah, had attached himself to his friend's invitation and had implored the girl to go with them. On his knees, to judge from Sarah's eloquent gesture. She had resisted.

'It's so unjust!' Walter fulminated. 'Why couldn't they have waited?'

He gazed from the large window for some time, looking across in the direction of the palace though he could make out nothing in the darkness. Later, tired and depressed, he made ready for bed. Before climbing into hers Sarah, understanding his mood, padded across to him and gently stroked his cheek, her large eyes consoling, soothing.

Walter's dreams, when they came, were not pleasant. As is often the way when exhaustion seems to invite only oblivion, a restlessness forced its way in. He found himself reliving the pleasures of the day, but no longer as pleasures: seen through the distorting mirror of a fatigued mind they ran before his eyes like a grotesque parody of themselves. The warmth of the sun became sticky and uncomfortable. The bathers were deformed, boneless, shuffling awkwardly through sand and water. A man who had raised his boater when passing him on the promenade, a mere pleasantry, repeated the action over and over again, his rubbery face leering ever yet more closely, the eyes now menacing, the tongue that had earlier bidden him good day now lolling from a wet and open mouth.

Beyond, the sea's sweet murmur had become an insistent throb upon the beach. Brother Mark's face swam under water, blurred. Woven into the fabric of these dreams was an awareness of the moonlit studio in which figures seemed to move, shades between the white statues, and a monkey, black, spider-like, swung across the beams of the ceiling.

Walter turned and turned, his restless mind as tumbled as the sheets that lay beside him. The man in the boater had become the monkey, a furry face with slate eyes emerging from behind the doffed hat, its human voice dropping from its mouth words that immediately lost all meaning and lay like stones at his feet. The sea was lapping against the feet of the ancient warrior, racing across the studio floor carrying its white surf, engulfing the board with its incoming tide. The heat grew stronger, more oppressive . . .

An acrid smell penetrated his dreams and he coughed himself awake. Visions of heat became the reality of fire. Instantly he was on his feet and dragging Sarah into consciousness. The smoke came curling whitely, densely around the stone and plaster figures. The farther end of the studio was no longer visible.

'The door!' he gasped, bending low under the thickening swirls and pulling Sarah after him.

The floor was their map. Nothing else could be seen. He recognised the foot of a statue, an indentation where a huge piece of stone had once fallen. His hands found the bottom of the door.

He wrestled helplessly with the handle for precious seconds before he realised the awful truth. The door had been locked from the outside.

26   A Likeness

Jack had thought their assignment a strange one when he had thought about it at all – his next night's starring debut at the town's theatre occupied much more of his mind – but the evening was to prove more bizarre and disturbing than he could ever have imagined.

To begin with there was the palace itself, colourfully lit from within so that whoever approached it must believe himself in the land of faerie. Each room glowed with a pastel incandescence which revealed rich glories within. And then, as they followed the drive past this magical place, there was the garden, acres of tamed greenery, scented shrubs, graceful trees where tiny lanterns burned in the encroaching dusk.

Mr Tusker led them forward on to the first of a series of lawns, this one already peopled by as eccentric a crowd as Jack had ever seen. Although Belle wore her most shimmering apparel, although Mr Tusker besported the brightest of his orange suits, they were among the more soberly dressed at this gathering. The women wore hats which seemed to have lives of their own, so separately, extravagantly and vibrantly did they perch upon the coiffured locks. Dresses in costly damasked materials flowed to the grass and seemed to ripple away from their owners in a brilliant flood. The men, not to be outshone, wore costumes that Jack might have taken for fancy dress, except that they referred to nothing but their creators' virtuosity. Colourful eye patches seemed to be in fashion. There were spurs at the heels of men who had surely never mounted a horse. Twirling canes threatened to loosen unwary eyes from their sockets.

'This way, this way,' urged the theatre manager, bustling forward and parting the throng before him. 'Over here.'

Costume apart, it was their dogged progress across the law which marked out the little troupe from the rest. Elsewhere yawning ease was the chosen manner, a posing insouciance.

'We're somewhat early.'

They had been summoned to the palace by an elegant gentleman who reeked of perfume and who looked down upon all but Oz from a considerable height. Could they perform a masque for the Count and his guests? It would, he thought, be 'rather droll' and amuse the company no end.

So they were here, far too early, costumes under their arms, prepared to improvise from a script hastily patched together by Luigi and Mr Tusker. Jack, bringing up the rear, saw that they had come to a place where large white statues were arranged on the lawn. A few of the guests were strolling among them, gesticulating and making knowledgeable noises. As the light failed, so the sculptures seemed to glimmer more brightly.

Ma Tusker, carrying out a speedy inspection, stumped away and sat herself on the grass.

'Not decent,' she declared emphatically.

The others, however, took more time over their judgement. Amazing's method was to approach stealthily, as if at any moment the figure might flee, and then to reach out caressing fingers to the stone. Mr Tusker stood back, arms folded, pondering, while Belle circled and circled, her eyes discovering new perspectives. Oz spent little time on each sculpture but, reaching the last one, he stared intently for some moments, brought his face closer and finally turned to Jack with a grin which seemed to combine surprise, amusement and – could it be? – a trace of fear.

'Come here,' he called. 'It's incredible!'

They gathered round the representation of some kind of mythical creature, with a tail, a reptilian body and a human face. The eyes which stared back at them were set in features familiar in every particular.

'More like Jack's nose than his own,' laughed Luigi, wonderingly.

'And the ears,' added Belle, seizing one of Jack's and giving it a gentle tweak. 'See how one is slightly higher than the other. Just a little.'

A little it was, and exactly as if he had modelled for the sculpture himself. The mouth, the line of the chin, the set of the head – everything was just so. But what made them shuffle hauntedly, what caused the hairs to stand on his neck, was the right cheek. Jack could not believe what he seemed to see. He raised a hand and touched the cold stone. A small patch had been roughly scored with the chisel to reproduce the blemish he had carried with him from birth.

'A jest,' said Mr Tusker bravely. 'A poor joke. Something of that kind.'

'But this,' began Luigi, seeming at once to regret that he had spoken, 'this is the work of Ernest Clabber. A celebrated craftsman. What can it mean?'

'A coincidence,' offered Oz, a hand on Jack's shoulder shepherding him away, and Amazing even managed a nervous giggle.

'The feet aren't quite right,' he said. 'Too many scales.'

They dispelled their unease by pointing out to one another, with ill-concealed merriment, the more outlandish of the costumes which mingled on the lawns. These must now be admired under the coloured lanterns sprinkled among the trees, for daylight had completely gone. New guests continued to arrive, and the warm night air was full of their babble.

At last it was time for the troupe to prepare for the performance. As they passed through the shrubbery towards the summerhouse which had been allotted to them as a changing-room, Luigi nudged Jack and pointed towards two men who passed arm in arm, laughing uproariously, each holding a bottle and seeming to stagger.

'The one this side is Ernest Clabber,' he whispered. 'It's a night of celebration for him.'

27 Conflagration

The smoke was thickening, opaque billows which briefly eddied to give glimpses of orange flame licking the drapes which swathed the sculptor's work-in-progress. The large window was inaccessible, the small south window too high and too secure.

Walter threw himself at the door. It would not give. He whirled round, desperate for some means to fight the crackling, choking fire, but knowing that its grip was already complete.

And then Sarah was tugging at his sleeve, pulling him towards the centre of the studio and pointing to the floor. At first he did not understand. She fell to her knees, banging and pulling at the boards. It was, of course, the spot which had held her attention on their first night at the studio. Had she sensed something? An opening? He joined her, trying to dig his fingers beneath the floorboards. Splinters speared him but he scarcely felt them. The boards would not move! He rose, gasping, plunged into the rolling smoke, collided with the bench he sought. He groped blindly for a chisel, reeled back towards Sarah, careering into her.

He attempted to lever the boards upwards. The task was hopeless. The smoke was choking them, the heat increasing. Still he struggled, as if the activity itself would prolong their lives. And then a board sprang loose and a cool rush of damp air revived them sufficiently to realise that they were poised above a shaft.

Flames darted out of the hugging smoke, illuminating a circular stone wall plunging into total blackness, and hard against the wall – oh, blessing of blessings! – an iron pipe held by brackets. They snatched at escape without pause, save for Walter's holding back for Sarah to lead the way down. As he followed he heard a crashing which heralded the collapse of the studio roof. Something struck him on the shoulder. Flames ran towards the shaft from all sides.

They descended, clinging to the pipe, and the stench of smoke gave way to the dankness of damp stone. Indeed, the wall soon became wet and slimy so that the pipe was difficult to grip. Walter's fingers, wrists and arms burned with the effort of holding on, the pain intensifying, until his feet hit something solid and he realised that they were at the bottom. Above them, through the torn boards of the floor, the studio had become a blazing furnace, its brightness flickering around the walls of the shaft and playing on their uplifted faces, painting horror and white fear with scarlet.

An updraught of air kept the shaft free of smoke and revealed in the fire's glow an old cistern still half filled with scummy water. From this cistern, and through what appeared to be the rusting remains of an old pump, pipes led upwards to the studio and horizontally into a tunnel, the mouth of which was a narrow circular hole that stared from the wall like the socket of an empty eye.

It did not invite entry and its width barely allowed it, yet falling debris was already entering the shaft, raining its hot ashes on their heads. Dropping to hands and knees, Walter led them into the wet darkness.

They had struggled several minutes along the tunnel when the sounds of the disintegrating studio behind were replaced by those of running water ahead. For Walter the sounds were vastly more comforting than the dense silence he had expected. Sarah could not share this comfort and the tunnel did not allow him room to turn and touch her hand as he would have liked.

It was cold. They crawled through a shallow, wet slipperiness the nature of which they could only guess at in the total absence of light. The sound of water grew louder as they crawled, and Walter imagined that his eyes picked out something that was not quite black in the impenetrable blackness. A grey dot, it seemed, of such a dimness that it must be an hallucination. But no: it grew more definite, a circle of grey whose circumference increased as they travelled towards it.

Then they arrived, and Walter found himself emerging into a culvert through which a small river was flowing. The tunnel they had crawled through met the walls of this culvert at right angles and about two feet above the water, whose depth Walter could not gauge but which, from the shape of its channel, he guessed to be fairly shallow. Unable to manoeuvre himself into a position from which he could let himself fall comfortably, he had to wriggle forwards and flop hands first into the water. In the event his dignity suffered more than his person, and he stood up to find the water flowing at knee level. Sarah's head now emerged from the tunnel and he was able to let her down more gently.

The roof of the culvert arched high above their heads, and the feeling of space was wonderful even in such gloomy surroundings. They began to wade in the direction of the water's flow, feeling its coldness lap their legs. The light that Walter had detected so far back in the tunnel grew more definite until they found themselves beneath a grating so overhung with ferns and crusted with dirt that even the space immediately below it remained in perpetual dusk. Although they could not reach up to it, and the curved wall of the culvert would not allow them to climb to it, it spoke of a street lamp directly above, for how else could light enter in the depth of night?

And it spoke of hope, for they could only be a little way beneath the streets.

28 Lamentations

Jack, pulling on a pair of vivid green tights, reflected that the costume he had dreaded wearing when Ma Tusker fished it from one of the trunks that morning would cause little stir here in the palace grounds. He doubted, in fact, that many of the sophisticated guests would bother to watch their little show. The troupe were nothing more than a minor diversion. He slipped the mask over his eyes and followed the others through the shrubbery.

The many visitors, such a short time ago scattered wide throughout the grounds, were now gathered in a large circle around the sculptures. The tall, perfumed gentleman seemed to be giving a languid lecture on talent, on art, on inspired patronage, while the sculptor himself lurked awkwardly behind one of his creations, from time to time tipping a bottle to his lips.

'Honour the artist,' concluded the speaker, inclining his wrist in the direction he imagined Clabber to be, 'but, my friends – revere the patron.'

At this moment a pile of black cloth which only the observant would have spotted in the shadow of the largest stone figure, shook and parted and disgorged a crimson jelly. This is turn revealed itself as a human form wrapped in a fiery costume which rode up and down its wearer's body as if made of a thousand sprung coils.

'The Count! It's the Count!'

And the murmur became warm applause at the ingenuity of the thing, the Count smiling with delight and exercising himself so as to show off his garb to best advantage. Jack for his part, struck by the absurdity of the performance, found tears of uncontrollable laughter starting behind his mask and running down his cheeks.

The Count had little to say, and that delivered in so aristocratic a drawl as to be almost incomprehensible. He mumbled a final compliment to the sculptor and bounced and concertina'd away, mightily pleased with himself. The nods and grins of his guests suggested that his act had been well up to standard.

Clabber was now pushed before the public gaze where he stood, seemingly stupefied, speechless. They began to call out to him, teasingly, inviting him to explain his art and, confused, he half turned towards the sculptures and, too loudly, said that he had used the best stone available. Then he clenched his fist and showed the muscles of his arm and said a sculptor needed strength.

'And liquor!' called a wag, and there was a welter of laughter, for the most part good-natured.

The baiting was ended, however, when Clabber's companion stepped forward and waved them all to silence. A single gesture swept across the sculptures and up into the summer sky where a crescent moon burned white.

> 'You are stone, yet you breathe,
> we see you shiver, the flesh palpate,
> we see the sinews flex and strain,
> sense the blood that courses.
>
> Stone when man was not created,
> you take the imprint of his spirit,
> you shiver with his weakness
> and are glorified.'

From the commotion which followed Jack learned that the poet had a popular following and that his name was Celestin. More he had no time to discover, for Mr Tusker was fussing them into position and giving his last-minute instructions. All of them were to be involved in the entertainment. Luigi, apart from acting, was to play a small recorder. Belle was to sing. The action was artificial, the players speaking mainly in stilted verse. There was some dancing.

Many of the guests drifted away as the troupe began, but enough remained to make a respectable audience. From the remarks he could hear, Jack divined that they had as little interest in the sense of the piece as he had himself, being more taken with the singing and the dancing. Unfortunately their critical eyes and ears were not totally approving, and he was more than once aware of disdainful titters where the response should have been delight.

He was standing by the sculpture which so resembled himself, waiting his turn to skip across the grass, when a young lad came running by, his cheeks red, his wind all but gone. He approached Clabber and Celestin, who sat mutely drinking, and the words came panting from his mouth.

'Your studio,' Jack heard him say. 'Quickly!'

'Eh?'

'It's afire, sir.'

Clabber waved a bottle, his own speech coming slowly and heavily.

'It's a studio, blast you!'

'No, sir. I mean it's blazing . . . The sky's all red . . . and they've got the firemen out . . . and the buckets and all.'

It was the poet who took the matter in hand, reaching into his pocket to give the lad a coin and attempting to hoist Clabber to his feet. The sculptor, however, resisted in a surly manner.

'Let go of my arm, damn you, or I'll break yours in two. Look at these muscles – they'll easily crush a skeleton like you. Lift a block of marble, they could. Much as you could do to lift a dictionary . . . '

At this moment the recorder started up and Jack raised his arms and went tripping forward in the brave imitation of a sprite. He was relieved, when next he looked, to see that Celestin had persuaded his friend to make his way home, but the incident, not affecting him personally, soon faded from his mind.

Later they were invited into the palace, and he marvelled at the wonders within it. Wealth he was used to, but of a limited and strictly unostentatious kind. The attention lavished on these grand rooms made his senses reel. Light was reflected and reflected again to confuse the brain into a suspension of judgement over distance and colour and form. And this bewilderment, he was aware, led to a suspension of other judgements besides. They came to an elaborately carved fireplace with sensuous carvings – perhaps of mythological scenes, but he had not the learning to know – whose impulse was unmistakable.

'Early Clabber,' said Luigi, appearing at his shoulder. 'Fine work, even so.'

In another room people were dancing. There was heavy perfume in the air and tinkling laughter in every corner. Belle revelled in this opulence, raising her glass to everyone who passed, her self-satisfied smile suggesting that it was the ambience to which she was accustomed.

'I should like to visit his studio,' added Luigi as he moved away.

The rest of the troupe stuck together, as if for protection. Oz and Amazing looked about them, passing occasional behind-the-hand comments to one another, fascinated and half afraid by what they saw. Ma Tusker, who had declined every offer of drink as if a proposition from the devil, stood against a wall, glaring about her in a manner which suggested that someone would be in trouble soon. Her husband, perhaps suspecting that he might be that victim, beamed continuously, his eyes far away.

Jack had seen their host threading among the throng from time to time but he froze with alarm when, on the next occasion he happened to pass, the Count stopped abruptly and stared hard in his direction. The crimson costume ceased to bounce for several seconds, and then the owner of all these glories stepped towards him, a perplexed expression on his face.

'Dear boy,' he simpered. 'I had no idea. You were quite disguised behind that mask.'

Jack could only gawp.

'Discarded your lady friend, have you?'

There was a silence during which Jack shook his head from side to side out of sheer incomprehension and embarrassment. The Count regarded him for a moment, frowned and turned on his heel.

'Lady friend, Jack?' whispered Oz. 'What's all this, then?'

'I don't know. It was as if he knew me.'

'Takes a shine to you, perhaps,' giggled Amazing. 'See how he's pointing you out.'

And, indeed, the Count was now talking earnestly to the tall powdered gentleman, both of them gazing intently at poor Jack.

'A useful man to have as an admirer,' added Amazing, prodding him conspiratorially.

But it was Ma who had the last word on the Count.

'More money than sense,' she said.

At midnight, with the party still in full swing, they prepared to leave. Oz, who had become Jack's unofficial guardian, ensuring that he ate and drank in moderation, evidently judged that tiredness would render his charge insensible before alcohol did. As for the others, they had seen enough to keep their imaginations fed for some time to come, and they trooped happily out of the palace and along the drive.

It was a fine, clear night with bright stars studding the heavens. Jack, allowing his companions' conversation to wash over him, found his thoughts turning to their new production and his own leading role in it. He heard the speeches in his head. He heard the applause of the audience as he took his bow. Certainly he was unaware of how far into town they had come until the smell of smoke brought him sharply back to the present.

'A fire!'

It was Oz who first saw the building in front of them, its upper portion black, broken and open to the sky. Dark smoke sparkling with red embers still poured from within and, although the fire had obviously taken hold long since and was now all but spent, a murmuring crowed remained outside. Jack knew what the building was even before they drew close enough to see how eerily the charred beams framed large and impassive human figures, sole survivors of the inferno.

Ernest Clabber sat on the pavement with his head between his hands. The poet Celestin stood by the side of an official with a notebook – a law officer, it must be – who was questioning the bystanders. Jack, creeping closer, heard one of them relay how an old lady, an inhabitant of the streets, had, at about the time the fire started, seen a black dwarf fleeing across the rooftops. The man with the notebook checked his scribbling and heavily crossed through what he had written. You could rely on the addle-brained, his expression seemed to say, for a bit of amusing colour.

'Come on,' said Oz. 'It's late.'

Clabber had not moved and Celestin's shaking of his shoulder seemed to have no effect at all. Jack watched, appalled. Having heard the news of the fire delivered, he felt somehow implicated, part of the story. The law officer touched the sculptor's other shoulder.

'Has he recovered a bit now, do you think?' he asked. 'You say he doesn't live here, so you'd best take him home. We can sort it all out tomorrow. He may have sobered up by then.'

Clabber slowly raised his head.

'The boy and the girl,' he said.

'No. I've told you.'

'In there. Did nobody come out?'

The officer turned to Celestin, exasperated.

'Haven't I told him? Nobody said anything about there being people inside. Just a studio, they said. Queer sort of place, perched up there – bottom floor seems to be solid.

'If there *was* anyone in there, they've had it. They couldn't survive that lot. Just look at it!'

Jack felt himself tugged impatiently by Oz. The rest of the troupe, sombre now, were already on the way to their lodgings. As he followed he saw Clabber rub away tears at his eyes and he heard him moaning pitifully.

'So young. They were so young, and she was so pretty.'

29 A Welcome from the Girls

It was ironic that in a room so full of the softly scented folds of naked flesh Walter's eyes should at first fix themselves upon the plain wooden leg of a small table as he emerged from the underworld. The noise of the moving grille had already startled the room's occupants, but when this was followed by Walter's face, blackened by the dual effects of soot and dust and topped by a mat of wet hair smeared with green mossy slime, it was altogether too much for their nerves to bear without the release of a sequence of squeals and shrieks which, in turn, startled the startler.

The world beyond the silent stability of the table leg seemed to have gone mad. Nobody rushed to help his progress through the narrow entrance. They had, rather, pressed themselves against the walls as distant from him as it was possible to be within the confines of the room.

'Help me!'

More squeals.

'I'm stuck!'

More shrieks.

'For heaven's sake!'

'It's only a boy!'

Yelps of laughter replacing those of alarm.

Walter, reduced by now to helpless silence, remained wedged by the shoulders, half in and half out of this new unfathomable world. Thus he remained for a full two minutes like a grotesque piece of furniture while the girls, who seemed to number around a dozen, slowly closed on him with shrill jokes ad laughter at his expense and while Sarah, still knee-high in the flowing stream in the darkness below, supported his feet in their hold on a narrow ledge. The hands that finally dragged his slimy body and delivered it wholly into the light were many and gentle, and the warm closeness of the powdered bodies suggested an arrival into paradise itself. He was lying on thick carpet recovering his senses when one of the girls, whose curiosity had compelled her to peer into the womb-like cavity from which he had appeared, cried out shrilly.

'Here! There's another one down there . . . and it looks like a girl!'

Sarah's appearance created an even greater amazement than Walter's.

'I've known clients come in odd ways,' chaffed one of the clamouring sprites, 'but I've never heard of one who brought his own girl before.'

The gathered watchers circled Walter and Sarah as they sat silently on the floor.

'What will Madam say when she sees them?'

'Who are you, then? What do you want?'

Walter, who was trying to convince himself that these girls were the invention of his distracted wits and would disappear with his reclaimed sanity, struggled for words to answer the question.

'There's a river,' he began, but then paused, aware that this was rather poor as an explanation.

'There's a river, he says. There's a river. We *know* there's a river – we add our bit at times through the grille. What we want to know is what you and your friend were doing in the river.'

He shook his head helplessly.

'Weren't spying on us poor creatures, were you?'

'If we call Madam you'll be out on your ears.'

'Oh, don't call Madam – he's nice! I bet he knows a trick or two, coming in unexpected like that.'

Several girls giggled, and they seemed to gaze on him sympathetically.

'We escaped a fire,' he began. 'We found a tunnel and it led to the river.'

All eyes were on him as he pieced the story together. His own eyes wandered from body to body but, from embarrassment, were unable to settle. He told how they had followed the river for a long time before they at last found the grille high in the wall. Now that they were safe, nothing would suit them better than to be on their way.

'Oh, you can't go yet, can he?'

'Customers'll be upstairs. They can't see you like that. Anyways, you need cleaning up before you go out. And drying out.'

The room was large and warm, the heat provided by a tiled stove which stood majestically against one wall. Stairs led up to a single door, and the fact that there was no window suggested that they were still below ground level.

'Give us your clothes and we'll get them done for you.'

'Paint your friend up a bit, too. She's not in the trade, I suppose? No, I thought not. Pity. She'd make a bit with her face – and I get the impression she wouldn't argue with the customers neither.'

Throughout these exchanges Sarah had remained still, her face registering total calm and acceptance of this new turn in their fortunes. She seemed to share none of Walter's confusion. It was as if she had understood the nature of the establishment the moment she had first seen it.

'Come on. No need to be shy with us.'

He was too bemused for shyness. In the warmth his clothes began to steam. His brain reeled from tiredness and strain, and the perfumed air wafted his consciousness half to sleep. They rolled him over. He was aware that they loosened buttons, that the sleeves were drawn off his arms. He saw clothes – his own and Sarah's – being dipped in clear water, squeezed, wrung out, hung above the stove. Then they stooped to lift him. He was aware of his nakedness but strangely unabashed by it. They lowered him into warm befoamed water, soaped his limbs and his body until, deeply soothed, he all but passed out in a delirium of heat and scent and weariness.

'Dolores!'

A voice falsetto and affectedly refined sounded at the door, which clicked open resonantly. The girls reacted first, crowding round the two baths to hide the pair from view. Walter himself, realising with a start that danger threatened, saw fingers – fat fingers tortured into a multitude of gold and gem-studded rings – clinging to the edge of the door. He ducked low above the soft water. He saw, between an arm and a shoulder, a head peer in, the wrinkles of the face filled with thick, encrusted powder.

'His lordship is here. Hurry, my dear.'

Dolores hurried, up the stairs and through the door. One of the girls whispered in mock-refined tones: 'Hurry, my dear. His lordship can hear me so I'm talking mighty posh.'

They all giggled conspiratorially, splashed the soap of his body and lifted him on to a sofa strewn with towels. He saw Sarah similarly borne to a luxurious resting place. More scent, cloying, a warmth that sapped his energy, a murmur of voices which seemed to recede and recede. He drifted into a profound slumber.

30 A Familiar Voice

If it was morning when Walter awoke he had no way of knowing it in the windowless room. A single lamp burning low revealed the sleeping forms of his rescuers, sprawled in a disarray of limbs that suggested more than anything else a scattering of fallen clothes. The climb to full consciousness was slow: he sat up, rubbing his eyes. The girls? Yes, the girls were real enough, their pink bodies rising and falling in the gentle susurration of sleep. The grille with the river beyond? That also must have been real to explain his presence in this place. And yet there was a moment of near panic when his own identity seemed lost and he struggled for meaning within the strangeness of these things.

Taking his clothes, dried and warm, from the stove he felt his identity reclaim him. With it came a tinge of shame when he thought of what he had undergone. How could he have failed to realise the kind of place he was in? True, he had been tired to the point of exhaustion, overcome by the peculiarities of the experience, but now he very clearly understood everything. He felt in his pocket for the pottery fragment and the paper that had brought him to O—, and their survival was a reassurance to him.

Sarah slept on and none of the girls stirred at his activity. Indeed, in the dim light their very separateness disappeared and they seemed to coalesce, to become as one not only with each other but with the furniture that they sprawled upon. Climbing the stairs, he opened the door and stepped cautiously into the greater gloom of the corridor, anticipating swift capture. Nobody was there.

The corridor was long and straight. No doors led from it, but it was punctuated on either side by latticed panels. As he drew level with the first of these he found that he could see into a room beyond, a room as sparsely furnished as a monastery cell, if not more so: the cell that he had regarded until so recently as his home at least boasted a bed, a table and a chair, an icon on the wall, whereas this one had no table or chair and, as if to deny even the tangibility of walls, had instead large areas of hinged mirrors.

Passing on to the next lattice he found it identical, and likewise the length of the corridor. None of these cells was inhabited, however, and there was an air of desertion about the whole place – enough to give him the confidence to turn the corner at the corridor's end to explore further. Truly a strange monastery this, and he smiled as he thought of the girls. He could not but loathe their trade, and yet he was mindful that these sisters had selflessly rescued and protected him; had cared for his needs without expectation of reward; were indeed models of the charity that he had been taught to value. And Sarah, whose instinct was unerring, had accepted them with smiling ease.

At the end of the corridor hung a heavy brocade curtain, golden threads glinting in its shadowed folds. Even as Walter's hand reached for the fabric there came the suggestion of voices beyond. He could hardly be sure, so muffled and obscure a sound was it, but he paused, listening. Silence. Caution gave way once more to curiosity and he gently eased the curtain aside.

He first saw, a distance away, a solitary green parrot that appeared to be in a state of torpor upon its perch. This parrot was the sole occupant of a room so large and ornate that Walter's breath was quite taken away. Even the Count's palace could hardly have prepared him for the vulgar sumptuousness of this place. The room (the word seemed, somehow, inappropriate) spread out before him, its vast floor stretching to walls that were so draped and encrusted with ornament as to resemble the loose and folded flesh of Madam with her jewellery, an illusion furthered by the ceiling of hung damask gathered into radiating pleats and held by lacquered bosses. The only furnishing consisted of randomly placed velvet ottomans, standing lamps, their varied and sinuous stands topped with globes of tinted milky glass, and, as if to establish a true centre within this formlessness, a mosaiced star set into the carpets of the floor, its eight points spreading from a sunken octagonal pool in which a fountain played. This fountain, Walter assumed, was what he had taken for the murmur of speech.

He stepped fully into the room, wary of the sleeping parrot for (he had read as much in the schoolroom) startled parrots screeched, and he was at pains to remain undiscovered if only for the sake of the girls who had offered Sarah and himself protection. And then he heard the voices again, more distinctly this time and unmistakably human. They appeared to emerge from yet another latticed panel, set this time into the wall at the far end of the room. Silent progress through this Turkish wonderland was no problem, so thick was the carpet, and he quickly drew closer.

He could make out the figure of a woman. She faced him, but the greater brightness of the small room that she occupied gave him protection. It was Madam. He saw the hands weighed down with jewels. Her voice, however, was different, the affected falsetto of the previous night dropped in favour of a lower, coarser delivery.

'You don't expect me to give away my secrets,' she was saying. 'It's enough to know that I do what's necessary.'

'I don't normally ask.'

The reply was from a man Walter could not see. He sat in an armchair whose high back hid him from view.

'And you ask now because you're too much involved, old friend. No room for sentimentality here, as well you should know. The important thing is that he's done for. Out of the way.'

'But who did it, Brunhilda?'

This question was asked in an urgent whisper. Walter, unable to place the voice, nevertheless felt that it was familiar to him. Madam gave a theatrical sigh.

'All right. Since it matters to you I can tell you that it wasn't me. I'm not a fire-raiser by trade. I don't know who started that blaze.'

'It might not have been necessary.'

Walter, stunned by what he seemed to hear discussed, took a step back.

'Possibly. But there was always the danger that he'd find out. If the other one turned up.'

'He may not.'

From where did he know that voice?

'You were never one to take chances in the old days,' Madam continued. 'Have you lost your ruthlessness because it's a boy? Weren't we taught to ignore treacherous feelings?'

'I do. I usually do.'

'The boy is dead, old comrade. Burnt to a cinder. I for one welcome last night's little drama. And so, if it's right for the cause, should you.'

She took a drink from a low table and, tilting her head back, swallowed a viscous amber liquid. Snorting, she replaced the glass with a decisiveness clearly designed to underline her no-nonsense attitude.

'You're not going soft on us?' she queried.

'You know better.'

She approached the chair and leant over him.

'Yes, I know better. No one has worked longer for the cause than you. And you watched the boy all that time. You've been as responsible for his death as anyone.'

There was a silence after this, as if the man were reflecting upon this judgement. At last he spoke in a lighter tone, turning the conversation in another direction altogether.

'Business is good, Bruny?'

'Ah, yes!' she laughed. 'Business is very good. Some excellent girls. Lots of sparkle.'

She touched her nose and Walter was close enough to see her wink.

'You must try one or two.'

'At my age?'

He knew he had heard the voice, surely many times, and although he could not yet identify it he felt that something jarred, as if he should not hear the voice in these surroundings.

'You're never too old. Why, they have to carry some of the clients in.'

'I'll bet they carry a few more out.'

Madam laughed, a process which set her body quivering in an alarming way.

'You wicked old devil, you.'

The figure in the chair rose and turned sideways. The shock gripped Walter's stomach and weakened his legs. It was brother Mark. Oh, horrible discovery! He reeled back, staggered across the exotic carpet.

'I'll call again, Bruny, before I leave town.'

In his blundering haste Walter caught his foot against the base of the parrot's stand, jerking the bird into life. With a frantic flapping of wings it leapt into the air. Its flight curbed by a chain around its foot, it let out a fearsome shriek, followed by a flow of rich obscenities. Madam's response was equally strident.

'I'll strangle that wretched creature!' she bawled.

Walter dived through the curtain. If he returned the way he had come there was no likelihood of a hiding place. He turned the corner and ran along the corridor. He came to what looked like a waiting room – comfortable chairs, low tables littered with magazines, pictures on the walls. There was a heavy curtain across a window from ceiling to floor and he slid behind it, panting.

'Shut your noise, stupid bird!'

There was a sudden squawk, suggesting that Madam had used physical force on the hapless parrot.

'Another shriek and you're tonight's dinner.'

'Poor beggar.'

This last comment was unmistakably from the parrot itself and was uttered in suitably glum tones.

From behind the curtain Walter could see an area of wall and a picture that hung on it a little above his eye level. It was of a lewd nature and he quickly averted his gaze to the text it presumably illustrated. He was surprised to read words that took him back to early childhood:

> I had a little nut tree
> And nothing would it bear
> But a silver nutmeg
> And a golden pear.

He had seen precious few children's books at the monastery, so that those which had come his way – secondhand, from the village – had been etched all the more vividly on his brain. But what was this visual corruption of the simple words?

> The King of Spain's daughter
> Came to visit me,
> And all for the sake
> Of my little nut tree.

He hid his face in the thick material, feeling sick and betrayed. It was if his whole being were mocked, as if there were nothing that could be trusted, safe from attack and cruel derision.

'We've done well so far, old friend. It remains to find the other one – and dispose of him, too.'

'What must be done must be done.'

The voices passed outside and continued along the corridor. He came out from his hiding place and crept to the door. Could it possibly be that he misjudged brother Mark, that he had misunderstood everything? He fervently prayed that it might be so. Certainly his brain would remain in this giddy turmoil until he could confront the old monk and demand to know.

There was another picture on the wall by the door. More vice: could there be no appreciation of beauty, of those things that delighted the senses, without perversion? Was his visit here simply the fitting culmination of his private journey through the pleasures of O—? The words under this picture he did not know, but he could only guess that they were another nursery rhyme:

> I had a little pony
> Its name was Dapple-Grey,
> I lent him to a lady
> To ride a mile away.
> She whipped him, she lashed him,
> She rode him through the mire:
> I would not lend my pony now
> For all a lady's hire.

He padded along the corridor. At the end it opened out and there was a spacious entrance hall with elegant ottomans by the walls and tall fronded plants in pots. Madam was opening the door to brother Mark, who pecked her cheek and limped out into the street. Walter bent low behind an ottoman, but Madam set off in the other direction, and he reached the door without being seen.

Outside, in bright sunshine, it was some seconds before his eyes adjusted to the light and he saw brother Mark disappearing round a corner. Walter began to run, but the way quickly became more crowded and he seemed to get no closer. Once or twice he had a fleeting glimpse of the cowled cleric shuffling along, but then he seemed to be gone from the face of the earth. Perhaps he had turned into a doorway or taken a flight of steps down to a lower level where the streets were no less busy. Walter hurried in all directions before admitting defeat, and it was then he realised that he was completely lost.

Having entered the house with the girls through a subterranean grille, and having left it in haste without a look about him, he had no way of knowing the way back to it. He could not even picture the building in his mind. He made a guess as to the general direction and began to comb the streets for a clue. Sarah would feel herself deserted, and this thought added pain and anxiety to his frustration. It failed to add inspiration, however, and the wandered about in a daze, totally confounded.

31 Improvisation

'The Count's in the audience,' Mr Tusker beamed, rubbing his hands together vigorously. 'First class! Excellent for business!'

'If he enjoys it,' threw in Jack, a victim of first night nerves.

'Especially if he enjoys it. But his presence is the important thing. I didn't expect it. Not for a company like ours.'

The curtain would go up within ten minutes. Jack was sharing a large dressing room with Luigi, Amazing and Mr Tusker though they could, had they wished, have spread themselves even more luxuriously. It was a splendid theatre. Belle, so often forced to change behind a curtain, was somewhere along the corridor in the star's dressing room, no doubt making a tour of the several large mirrors while Ma clucked at her heels, pins in her mouth.

'I worry,' said Amazing, rubbing colour into his cheeks, 'that they'll expect too much of us.'

Nobody made an immediate reply to his. O— had its own resident professional company which put on a wide range of productions most of the year. Tusker's Travelling Theatre was filling a blank week in the calendar.

'We've chosen a safe play,' Mr Tusker said eventually.

'But we're charging high prices,' Amazing came back quickly. 'More than anywhere we've been.'

Luigi, who had been engrossed in sewing a button on to stiff material, wagged a finger at him.

'This is O—,' he explained. 'They're used to high prices. We're asking much less than they'd normally pay.'

'And they're used to high quality,' persisted Amazing.

Jack, whose jumpiness was made worse by this conversation, stalked about the room anxious to get on stage. He dreaded his entry, but nothing could be worse than this anguished anticipation. Luigi, knowing how he felt, called out to him.

'They'll like us well enough, Jack. But don't expect a lot of noise.'

'Why not?'

'You saw all those people at the palace. Plenty of those types here. They'd come whatever was on. It's partly habit, partly a matter of wanting to be seen appreciating culture. All you'll get from them will be knowing frowns or smiles. Sophisticated.'

He pronounced this last word satirically.

'But there'll be enough who like good theatre, and that's what we're going to give them!'

Jack was allowing himself to be persuaded by this optimistic view when the door opened and Oz stepped inside.

'Five minutes,' he said. 'Are we all ready?'

'Perfectly,' said Mr Tusker. 'And outside?'

'Wonderful. It's filling up very well. I have a couple of fellows who say they're doing walk-on in the last act. What shall I do with them?'

'I'd forgotten,' confessed the manager. 'They know what they have to do. Send them round during the interval.'

It was as much as Jack could do to hold himself back while this low-key business went on. He wanted to rush backstage and peer through the curtains. Oz turned to him, smiling.

'You seem to have an admirer,' he said. 'You remember that dandified gent at the castle? The one who smelled of ladies' perfume? He was asking after you – wanted to know how long you'd been with us, whether it was just a few days.

'Of course I gave a glowing report of you. Such skills the work of a few days? This lad's a thorough professional, I said in hurt tones. Those talents have been developed during a full season on the road!'

They made their way along the corridor and up a flight of steps. A faint noise puzzled Jack until he realised that it was the murmuring of an audience larger than any he had yet known. He tweaked the curtain aside and met a sight which made him shake with wonderment, fear, with awe.

He had seen the theatre in the daytime and been impressed by its size and opulence, but now it was truly a magical place. Rose-coloured lights fluttered from high balconies and along the edges of boxes framed in gilt. The walls were of powder blue flecked with silver, and gleams of light struck through the air and were lost among the sparkling adornments of the gay, the talkative, the expectant throng.

'I can't,' he heard himself react with alarm but, as ever, Luigi was at hand with the consoling word.

'You mustn't let the grandeur frighten you,' he said. 'It falls on the actors just as it does the audience. Think yourself a foot taller when you go on stage, and so you will seem'

A foot taller! He felt he would need to be a giant in order to make any impression at all. He was vaguely aware of Belle arriving in her finery. Mr Tusker pulled a slip of paper from his pocket and muttered a few lines to himself. Oz took up position in the wings. Jack had a sudden, vivid memory of the first time that he ever stepped on to a stage, and he registered a subtle difference. Then he had thought only of his own role, of making a triumph. Now he worried that he should not let the others down. He swore that he would not.

'One minute,' whispered Oz, taking the cord in one hand and signalling to an unseen assistant with the other.

For the first time they had made no scenery themselves, having an incredibly varied stock to choose from. Permanent theatre staff were on hand to help with the scene changes. The lighting and general effects were taken care of. This was the theatre as Jason Bull must know it.

'Stand by.'

The lights dimmed out front, the effect apparent even in the backstage gloom. The babble sank in an instant, one or two persistent voices stridently isolated in the spreading silence. Jack breathed deeply. He felt a nudge in his back and he was on.

'A foul day and a foul night to come,' boomed Luigi.

It seemed so loud close to his ear, and yet he felt the words wilting on the air way back and back at the far reaches of the auditorium.

'Dirty weather.'

He must speak up!

'And we the most shamefully treated creatures in the world.'

Luigi had rewritten the first page of the script so that the first and the longer speeches were his own, and Jack knew that he had done this from kindness, from an understanding that his young partner would need time to adjust to the imposing surroundings.

'I'm exhausted.'

For the first time he looked up, tried to fix his eyes upon individuals in the audience, but they all outstared him and he fell, thankfully, to swinging the bundle from his shoulder and sitting down on it. He watched Luigi striding across the stage, realising that the very size of it enabled him to exaggerate his actions and indeed appear to stride despite the shortness of his legs.

It was a play of high passion, with a few bold effects. They were drenched by a thunderstorm and a ship was wrecked before their very eyes, the sails heaving and cracking in the gale. Belle stepped from it, as pale and haggard as the make-up could convey, and fell in a swoon at their feet.

'What pretty cargo is this!'

He heard gentle laughter, as if in appreciation of the conceit, and decided that they were not so frightening an audience after all. Perhaps, as Luigi had warned, they were not given to outbursts, but he felt that he could play to them. The early apprehension began to fall away.

Once he looked up and saw, clearly, the Count sitting in the best box in the house. He was peering through a lorgnette and Jack felt, although he was not directly involved in the action at that moment, that the lorgnette was trained on him. Did he imagine this? A light glared painfully in his eyes. The sun cut through the clouds and a spontaneous murmur greeted the appearance of a vivid rainbow.

When the interval came Mr Tusker was in a happy frame of mind, perhaps as much on account of remembering his lines as because he judged the response satisfactory.

'A discriminating clientele,' he decided. 'Discerning. Mutely appreciative.'

Luigi, unwilling to be drawn, rocked his hand in a gesture which suggested that success still hung in the balance.

'You're doing well,' he told Jack. 'Don't lose your concentration as you grow tired. We've a while to go yet.'

This caution proved well justified as the final act progressed. It became clear that the audience was nursing, however unconsciously, considerable reservations about either the play itself or its presentation. The release of these subdued feelings was triggered by the two walk-ons, both of whom seemed to have raucous friends in the cheaper seats.

They had reached a crucial murder trial towards the end of the play. Luigi was in the dock, Belle looked on tearfully, Amazing was the judge, and the scene was played in such a way as to suggest that the members of the audience were the spectators in the courtroom. The walk-ons were supposed to represent characters briefly discussing the likely outcome of the case before the proceedings got under way. No more was expected of them, but they obviously had other ideas. One of them, a swashbuckling young fellow who must be supposed to terrorise the streets of O— by night, pranced into the courtroom and began to berate the poor judge. His companion, a bespectacled and rather studious-looking type a few years older, was spurred by the cheers of the audience to have his say. He took the side of the judge and had the glasses swept off his face for his pains. The well-bred spectators exchanged merry grins; the groundlings roared for more.

Luigi, improvising swiftly, leapt from the dock and made an impassioned plea to be judged by the law without let or hindrance. Emphasising his innocence, he forcibly removed the chief offender and returned to submit himself once more to the mercies of the judicial system. Since the other walk-on had recovered his spectacles and stumbled into the wings, order seemed fully restored, but the two part-timers had obviously enjoyed their moments before the blushing limelights. Just as the judge began to pronounce the death sentence they came careering onto the stage and began their zany bickering all over again.

This time it was Jack's turn to repair the damage as best he could. He was due to make an eleventh-hour appearance with evidence which would save the condemned man. Now he first assailed the credentials of a court which would allow such a disturbance to take place, then (since he lacked the strength to remove them physically) attempted to argue the two interlopers into leaving. There was a growing demand from the audience for them to stand their ground, and they might have remained until the final curtain had not the younger one decided, for sport, to snatch the judge's quill pen and run off with it.

Apparently they were restrained in the wings, for the actors were allowed to complete their scene and proceed to an optimistic denouement which was greeted with great humour by the audience. The applause was generous There was an encore, for which the walk-ons, beaming with sheepish pride, joined the rest of the company (this, it transpired, was the bribe offered by Oz for their compliance) and the lights went up with the majority well pleased.

Afterwards Mr Tusker was uncertain how to react. He was first verbally flailed by Belle, who pronounced herself disgusted, disgraced and totally disaffected, and who threatened never to perform again. But since she was soon ensconced in her own dressing room, the others were allowed their reflections in a calmer atmosphere.

'Largely creditable,' suggested Mr Tusker. 'On the one hand we have excellent takings, on the other a slight disturbance.'

'How,' asked Amazing, still visibly in a state of shock, 'should we recognise a *considerable* disturbance?'

Luigi seemed only relieved. He put an arm round Jack's shoulders.

'You're a fighter,' he said, smiling. 'That was a real test, Jack. You kept your head and we won through.'

'Belle doesn't think so.'

'Belle's a perfectionist. Didn't they enjoy themselves tonight? Of course they did! Different shows for different rows, we always used to say. Every performance is unique. Without those clowns we should just have scraped through, I think. They liked us well enough. As it was – well, we might have had a disaster but we ended with an ovation.'

'But a close-run thing,' said Mr Tusker.

They were halfway through changing when Oz put his head round the door and beckoned the actor-manager outside. He was gone for but a couple of minutes, and when he returned there was an expression of apprehensive pleasure on his face.

'The Count's man came to see me,' he explained, brushing at the tufts of hair above his ears. 'A message from the Count himself.'

'He liked the play?' asked Amazing.

'Didn't say. That wasn't the point of it. The Count' – he paused as if to check an untrustworthy memory– 'the Count wants to play one of the walk-ons tomorrow night.'

32 The Eyes of a Stranger

And so that evening Mr Tusker, confidently predicting a prosperous week, entertained them to a splendid meal at a stylish restaurant.

'Can't fail now,' he declared, pulling on a large cigar which had a frustrating tendency to gutter unless sucked furiously every few seconds. 'There'll be a full house to watch the Count, and the publicity will do the rest.'

He waved at the waiter to bring more wine.

'It's been a good season,' he went on garrulously. 'We shall all eat through the months to come. Even young Jack here!'

Oz, looking rather strange out of his overalls, raised his glass triumphantly.

'Especially Jack,' he said. 'Hasn't he proved himself beyond question?'

'Indeed he has,' agreed Mr Tusker.

'A professional already,' said Luigi.

They all fussed him and clinked glasses with him, and he knew he had never felt happier at any moment in his life.

'But those men were odious,' added Belle, her sense of theatrical propriety still offended. 'Drunken louts.'

'High spirits,' defended the actor-manager, more than willing to forgive.

'And tomorrow,' said Amazing, a silent giggle moulding his lips at the thought, 'it's the Count's turn.'

Luigi leant towards Jack and said quietly: 'A test for you and me. We'll rehearse a few possibilities.'

Their jollity went on for a long time. It was late when they eventually pushed back their chairs, loudly sang the praises of the chef and wandered along the streets back to their lodgings. The town was still alive. They were on a tram route, and a car came swinging along, studded with tiny coloured lamps. Jack and Oz had small rooms in the attic of a tavern. As they approached they saw that the gas mantles still flared within, and they could hear the playing of a fiddle and a few voices raised in song.

They had said goodnight to their colleagues and had begun to push open the door when Oz gave an exclamation and swivelled around.

'My jacket,' he said. 'I left it at the restaurant. There's cash in the pocket. I must go back.'

'I'll come with you,' Jack offered.

'No, no. You're tired. You go to bed. I'll see you in the morning.'

Jack, watching him go, realised that he did feel very tired indeed. But before he could enter the tavern he felt a pair of hands pulling gently at his arm. Turning, he met the gaze of a girl about his own age. She wore a glistening trousered costume, perhaps of satin, but what struck him most was the face and, in particular, the eyes. They were large, round, expressive and, unaccountably, filled with tears.

'What is it? What do you want?'

She only looked at him, it seemed pleadingly, and continued to tug at his arm. Disturbed, he allowed himself to be led along the street.

'Is someone ill? Is that the problem?'

It appeared, however, that she did not even hear him. Once she turned and, fleetingly, gave a little smile as if to coax one from him in return, but the tears soon came flooding back. Later she paused again and took the cloth of his jacket between her fingers, giving him a quizzical look. At the first corner he halted and resisted for the first time.

'No. I won't come with you unless you explain.'

At this, rather than speak she shook her hands free of the billowing sleeves and began to make gestures that utterly confounded him. Her fingers moved, now singly, now in unison, against her wrists, her eyes, her forehead, through the air. All this was done quickly, deftly, with what seemed a confidence that he would understand, and when he only shook his head, wonderingly, her eyes once more glistened with welling tears.

'All right. All right, I'll come.'

She walked rapidly. Every so often she glanced at him, shyly it seemed, as if there was something in his attitude she did not understand, whereas surely it was he who had every reason to be bewildered.

A thin mist obscured the stars and turned the moon to an indistinct patch of luminosity that spread its pale glow throughout the sky. Silhouetted against this sky, Walter sat upon the keel of the upturned boat and stared at the flat waters of the bay through wet eyelashes. Frustrations and misery. Hours of wandering, hope fading with the day's fading light, and he had arrived at this once familiar spot. His feet had determined his destination, had set themselves along the path to the fishermen's wharf, and he had followed their prompting, his mind numbed, aching, unable to argue.

Sarah was lost to him, perhaps in danger. The darkness closed around him. He put his head in his hands and tears stung his eyes. Desolation. There came into his brain the lines of a poem:

> *Its flame extinguished,*
> *my lamp ceases to be*

It was his mood, no doubt, that called the words back from somewhere in the past. From the recent past. He remembered that they were Celestin's. The poet had spoken them laughingly as they tripped through the mountains, but now they came to Walter with the resonance of a prophetic utterance.

> *my world ceases to be,*
> *and you; and with your ceasing*
> *I cease . . .*

He heard himself – heady melodrama – repeat the line aloud with a shudder of despair: 'And with your ceasing, I cease!'

Where was he being led? Jack's uneasiness grew with each new turning into ever meaner, ever more menacing, roads and alleyways. Filtered through shadows, the moonlight was gathered and then flung from the folds of his strange companion's costume, turning her into the semblance of a stage ghost, this combining with her silence further to unnerve him. She led him by the hand, and his own hand, at first reluctant to join itself with hers, now clung tightly in the desperate hope that she would not abandon him in this dark underside of O—.

And then an alley, narrower, darker than any previous, pressed on either side by high frowning warehouses, their pulleys and chains hanging like gallows in the gloom, ended in the sudden broad airiness of the sea. The sight must have gladdened Jack's heart had it not coincided with a sudden and forlorn cry.

'I cease!'

They stopped at the same instant. Someone sat hunched on the dark shape of an upturned boat.

'A drunk,' Jack muttered nervously. 'That's all.'

But if this last phrase was intended as comfort it was entirely wasted, for the girl pulled her hand from his and scampered towards the silhouetted figure.

Jack followed haltingly, watching as one might watch the sequence of a ballet. Her moving was masterly, each gesture filled with grace, with expression: the touch upon the sleeve of the solitary mourner, the hand caressing his face, the head thrown upon his shoulder. The power and the pathos! He felt the clumsiness, the amateurishness of his own movements as he crossed the space that lay between him and this moonlit masque.

As he approached, their faces turned towards him – one, that of the girl, tear-stained but now smiling and full of wonderment, the other . . . his own.

33 Mirror-Images

Our lives are shifting mirrors, the configurations of our circumstances blurred, distorted, random, chaotic. Our fond dreams swim in shadowed distances, our surreptitious wishes catch the light, are thrown forward, sharply delineated. How memory, desire, apprehension hallucinate the senses! We peer at the glass, rub with a sleeve, searching for patterns, deceived by a kaleidoscopic jumble of fractured images.

That fugitive, Self, plays peekaboo among the debris, now doused in shadow; now leaping into the foreground glare but brightly out of focus; now offering a face which the broken light casts into a thousand masks in an instant – hero, villain, traitor, friend, clown, sage, waif, dissembler.

Thwarted, we create our own illusions, imagine we perceive a plan in the disorder. Do these colours not appear to match (or fail, at least, to jar?) Is this distinctive shape not etched over there (though on a different plane?) The contours shift and change, yet we resist their waywardness, their incoherence. If, we say, if we could only see – we strain to see – then we should find confusion meld to one entire though many-faceted reality.

So men dream dreams of wholeness, burn candles to it, kneel before it, craving deliverance from formlessness and flux. So men seize the world and twist it, subjugate it, mould it, tempering it with the heat of their will, their unifying and all-embracing will. And all the time the steadfast mirror reflects the dizzying and appalling truth, illuminates the naked lie, mottles the vainglory with subtle shifting maculations, reveals the wavering certainties. Who am I? How can we know? How trace the constant line among the web, the true colour beyond the prism? Treacherous apparitions!

But surely (we wonder, despairing) if we were to take up a different, constant position, were to hold the mirror still, to let the eye run deep into the picture . . . Is there no irreducible Self lurking where lines of perspective meet? Our last and fleeting hope. The glass is foxed, a crack distorts the view. The foreground is too busy.

We listen to voices. Let others tell us, for we wish to believe. How we cherish those who identify us, who show us what we might, perhaps, be! They become our teachers; we create them as our creators; we exist through their vision. We love those who declare our desirable oneness. They deliver us from oblivion. Until, still doubting, our eye strays to the mirror, betraying the fragmentation, and our Selves are shattered and scattered again.

Unless – O, rare and wondrous occurrence – unless we find the shadow of our Self which comes to meet us, as if the part of us we lack which once slid from us is joined to us again and makes us whole. Then every feature has its answering echo, no part of us can fly into the void but meets it partner and must cling. Then we become accomplished.

34   A Puzzle

GRYNNES 193

They lay on the hot sand surveying the legend upon the broken pottery. The long hours of the night spent in talking, the telling of life stories, they had slept through until the sun was almost directly overhead. Now they had come down to the edge of the water in the area frequented by the local fashion, but nobody seemed to pay any heed to a pair of twins and their girl companion.

'That's all it can be,' Jack said, frustrated. 'Grynnes 193. The letters and figures won't go any other way. But it's meaningless.'

Walter turned the two pieces over. Together they formed the shape of a human eye.

'It has to mean everything,' he said.

Sarah sat a little apart, tactfully. Of course they meant to include her. They smiled at her from time to time and communicated through gestures. But the magical aura which had settled about them the night before had not entirely evaporated. She had seen them, trance-like, as if moved by an intelligence that was controlled by neither of them but was rather a product of their being together. They were different people with different backgrounds, but she nevertheless saw that they were, incomprehensibly, one person and she was in awe of the phenomenon.

'I've come across the word before,' Walter stated. 'I don't know where.'

Jack shook his head.

'I'm hungry,' he said. 'Let's eat first. This can wait.'

'No. I must think. I've seen the word.'

It was as if Jack well knew the response he would get, for even as Walter began to reply he rolled his eyes comically and rubbed ruefully at his stomach. Sarah's reaction was immediate. Evidently she was hungry too, for she leapt to her feet and signalled that she would bring food. Jack, laughing, thrust coins into her hand and watched her glide away towards the promenade, a gaunt black dog fussing at her heels. Would that all audiences caught on so quickly!

'Such an unusual word,' Walter said, persisting.

'The whole thing's rather more than unusual,' Jack replied briskly. 'All the mystery, pieces of broken pottery, meeting places that don't exist. It seems like a stupid game to me.'

'But we can't know. That's to criticise without knowing the facts.'

Jack nodded, smiling but unrepentant.

'Yes,' he said. 'Quite so. You're absolutely right.'

The two lads were quite agreed in their disagreement.

Sarah came back with hot rolls which they took gratefully. For a while nothing could be heard save the sound of their eating. Then Walter beckoned to Sarah and pointed to the letters inscribed in the oval. She had not looked at it closely before. He traced the sequence of letters and numbers with a finger.

'What does it mean?'

She inclined her head, gave a slight shrug to suggest that the answer was obvious, and at once mimed eloquently with her hands – one of them flat as if holding something down, the forefinger of the other flicking repeatedly as if lifting the corners of sheets of paper.

'Of course!'

'What is it?'

'The bank!'

Walter, jumping to his feet, almost shouted the words, so that an elegantly dressed couple sitting under a parasol further along the strand turned alarmed heads sharply in their direction.

'Grynne's is the bank in the main street. I must have passed it dozens of times. Come on!'

'And when we get there?'

But Walter was leading them firmly away, allowing no time for reflection.

'Then we shall see.'

Jack lagged a little behind the others. The wonderment of their mutual discovery had not left him (he felt that it would never leave him), but he found himself irritated by the anonymous attempt to manipulate their fate. Had he not escaped it once before by running away to the theatre and destroying the address he had been given? Was he now to be sucked into a tiresome intrigue? There were his friends to think of. Oz, on waking that morning, would have found him gone and might even now be scouring the streets looking for him.

And then, as if to magnify his worries, he saw the familiar poster, freshly pasted on a wall: 'Tusker's Twentieth Century . . .' it began grandly, and he paused, signalling to the others. His own name, in squat lettering, sat opposite Luigi's higher than it had ever been. He stabbed at it with a finger.

'There I am,' he said redundantly.

But Walter only nodded with a faint smile, as if humouring his self-esteem.

He had other things on his mind. Jack was stung by this indifference, his eyes blazing with anger and humiliation.

'That's where I belong,' he blurted out. 'Not at Grynne's Bank on a fool's errand!'

His truculent mood was, however, dispelled by Sarah's behaviour. She studied the poster with great interest, then turned to Jack, pointing first at the name and then at him. They were the same? Then she was very pleased. She smiled on him as if welcoming a fellow performer.

'All right,' he conceded as they set off once more, the three falling into step as they resumed their quest. 'But afterwards I must see my friends.'

Grynne's! If Jack had carelessly imagined it would be a small, faceless bank justifying Walter's forgetfulness the illusion was quickly dispelled. Not only was it in the grandest street, clearly the commercial hub about which O— turned, but of all the buildings that towered above its busy pavement none dominated so much as Grynne's Bank. The name flashed in gold lettering across the broad facade. Its message was emphatic: for the merchants of O— it was the very centre of the universe, its huge granite steps drawing them up towards portals which, for more than a century (the date was on the wall) had seen the coming and going of both great and small, the factory owner and the market stallholder, each in turn awaiting the yea or nay of Grynne's – magnificent dreams shattered at the shake of a head, modest proposals encouraged to new heights of expectancy by an approving nod. Upon the steps that Walter, Jack and Sarah now found themselves climbing, the casual observer might at any single moment witness faces lit up with elation or clouded with gloom and despair.

Marble pillars, a tessellated floor. A phalanx of clerks sat behind high desks on either side of the entrance hall. Beyond, a broad, carpeted staircase promised a continuation of their ascent, but further progress could not be made without recourse to one of these sombre, dark-suited sentinels. The nearest, who seemed preoccupied only with specks of dust in the air above him, was thin, pallid, with transparent skin stretching across high cheekbones, his lips colourless. As they approached he looked down at the ledger before him and began to write, silencing the words that started in Walter's throat with an impatient wave of the pen, as if disturbed by the intrusion. For a full two minutes he kept up the pretence of labouring at his figures until, putting down the pen, he raised his reptilian head and let his eyes dart among the trio.

'Well?'

Walter, overawed by the pretentiousness of the place, wondered why Jack felt so calm. Jack, from his upbringing accustomed to the trappings of high finance, was disturbed by Walter's agitation.

'State your business.'

'It's difficult,' stammered Walter, who was slightly in front of the other two and felt it beholden upon him to speak. 'We're not sure of our business.'

'Then I don't see how I can help you. Good day.'

He turned once more to the ledger. The fingers of his free hand rattled in a slow rhythm on the desk top.

'We believe we have business here,' Walter tried again, 'but the nature of it is difficult to explain.'

The clerk looked up once more. His mouth, the merest pencil line across his face, was drawn into a supercilious smile.

'Try,' was all he said.

'Then . . . the number 193. Is there anything significant about it?'

'Of course.'

Walter drew breath deeply.

'What, then . . . is . . . its significance?'

'It's a prime number.'

'Prime?'

The gaunt clerk furrowed his brow like an irascible schoolmaster addressing a particularly dim pupil.

'A prime number, sir, is one that may not be evenly divided by another. You cannot, however hard you try, divide 193 by three or four or five or any number you care to mention. By all means experiment. It's an impossibility. That is the significance of 193.'

Walter, defeated, stood back. He felt humbled, dispirited, exhausted. The clerk coughed, needlessly, and half turned away.

Now Jack stepped forward, certain of his skill.

'Enough of this nonsense! We've put you to the test and you've failed it!'

He took the pieces of pottery from Walter's hand and placed them on the desk.

'It's this particular piece of the Count's affairs we've come about,' he improvised. 'Here's the 193 we refer to. The Count knows very well what 193 means and so, I wager, does your master!'

The phrases were clumsy enough but delivered with such blustering conviction that the arrogant clerk became immediately defensive.

'The Count! But why didn't you say? Who would you wish to see?'

'Mr Grynne himself, of course!' roared Jack, praying that such a gentleman existed.

The clerk's skin tautened yet further.

'Mr Grynne,' he muttered nervously. 'Mr Grynne. But then, if it's the Count's business' – and he leaned backwards on his chair and clicked his fingers to summon an elderly messenger who stood against the wall. The old man moved across as fast as his ageing legs would allow and raised his hand to his cropped grey hair in a salute to the clerk who, regaining his composure, swiftly rebuked him.

'Look alive, boy, these fine people are waiting. Are they to be kept hanging about all day because you see fit to dawdle? They are to see Mr Grynne. Take them at once. Be quick about it. Hurry!'

The old man saluted once more, straightened his uniform, bowed to Walter, Jack and Sarah and led them sedately across the floor, up the carpeted staircase and along a short corridor to a room proudly emblazoned with the name of the bank's founder, although the present occupant must be several generations removed.

A single gentle knock sufficed, and the door was opened by a uniformed attendant – peaked cap, braid, epaulettes – to reveal a vast, domed office lined with bookcases and littered with comfortable leather chairs, with a generously proportioned mahogany desk at the far end and, behind it, an even more generously proportioned man.

'Count's business,' the messenger whispered to the attendant, who scurried across the office to Mr Grynne and announced more audibly: 'Count's business, sir.'

'Show them in, if you please.'

Mr Grynne's voice was surprisingly breezy for so heavy a figure.

'That's it, that's it. In you come. Sit yourselves down. Count's business, eh? Of what kind, pray?'

The three stood facing him, close together for comfort.

'Like a parlour game, eh? Guess the Count's business. *Do* sit down, please!'

They sat, sinking into the chairs, feeling overpowered.

'So I'll begin, shall I, by guessing that it's not the Count's business at all. Am I right? Ah, I see that I am. Clue number one was that you're rather young to be trusted with such weighty matters. Clue number two – I shook the Count's hand in this very room not half an hour ago.'

The two lads looked at one another, uncertain whether to trust Mr Grynne's apparent affability or to suspect that it was but a cover for something more sinister. At last Jack leaned forward conspiratorially.

'It's like this, sir. We have a puzzle – a parlour game, if you like. And for all we know it may indeed concern the Count. Please observe these two pieces of pottery and how, once joined, they form the name of your bank.'

He rose, reached across the wide desk and fitted the two parts together. The corners of Mr Grynne's mouth had twitched slightly as Jack made his little speech, but now he produced an eye-glass and, his movements not helped by his corpulence, bent to examine the exhibit. After some moments he leaned back and stared at his visitors.

'So you're 193, are you? Well, bless my soul! 193!'

He rose from his chair and, with unexpected agility, circumnavigated the desk and shook their hands.

'Well, well! 193! If you'll just wait I shan't be long. Shan't be long at all.'

And summoning his attendant to follow, he waddled and rocked from the room and , still uttering exclamations, disappeared along the corridor.

35 Origins

'Perhaps it's money,' Jack said, once they were left alone. 'That must be it. At a bank.'

He had never fantasised about wealth. Had he stayed with the old couple he could have had an encumbering clutter of possessions. Money then had meant large, dark rooms, heavy furniture, fob watches, starched collars, servants, soberness, dull responsibility . . .

'No,' said Walter. 'I don't think so.'

Would he have left the security and contentment of the monastery following cryptic clues had he believed that his destiny was something so crude as a pile of coins?

'You mean,' challenged Jack teasingly, 'that you wouldn't know how to spend it if you had it.'

'No doubt,' laughed Walter. 'I'd never handled money until I came here. I have no need of it.'

He told of the simplicities of the monastic life. He explained how they grew their own food, how they kept goats for milk. He spoke of keen pleasures: walking in the large garden with its views of the mountains; tipping cold water, fresh from the well, over his head and neck in the summer heat; singing in the choir, their anthems rising into the high chapel vault.

'But I could use money quite easily,' Jack countered. 'Travel. Building up the theatre. I could even start my own!'

These nascent dreams were smothered at birth, however, with the opening of the door. Mr Grynne was followed by his attendant carrying a heavy black box. This was deposited on the desk, and Mr Grynne, panting from his exertions, placed a key on top of it.

'193,' he explained. 'It is yours to open.'

They stood staring at it. Whatever lay within had a power over them, might change their lives. It frightened them. They fought to delay opening it.

'When was it brought here?' Jack asked desperately.

'Oh, many years ago,' said Mr Grynne, stooping to examine a tag attached to the handle. 'Close on fifteen years ago. It's been awaiting this moment.'

'What do you know of it?' asked Walter. 'Who brought it here?'

'This,' replied Mr Grynne gravely, 'is a bank of standing, gentlemen. We ask no questions of our clients. A secret remains such with us. I can truthfully say that I am totally ignorant of what you may find in that deed-box.

'I know – how shall I say? – I know the broad context of the situation in which it was delivered here, but it is certainly not for me to utter a single word about that.'

He paused, smiling.

'However, the circumstances of its arrival cannot, I think, be regarded as in any way confidential, and I can tell you that I remember them as clearly now as I experienced them then. I returned to my office – to this room here – and was not a little alarmed to hear unusual sounds from within. I put my ear to the door' – he mimed, humorously – 'and realised that someone was making music in the very inner sanctum of Grynne's.

'Thrusting open the door I came upon a frail old fellow in a black beret who was plucking at as strange an instrument as I had ever seen – or have since, for that matter. How he had talked his way past the clerks downstairs I never quite discovered. The music, now that I heard it close to, was very fine – a good melody and a vigorous, stirring rhythm. Eastern, I'd say. The package he had brought with him sat on the desk exactly where that box is now.

'He finished his tune, gestured towards the package and informed me that I was honoured to be its chosen guardian. And I'll be deuc'd if he didn't more than half convince me of that by the time he'd finished. Often enough in all these years I've wondered about the fate of 193.'

He waved an arm in the direction of a tasselled bell-pull behind the desk.

'We shall retire,' he said. 'Please ring when you have concluded your deliberations. I shall have one further duty to perform.'

Mr Grynne and his attendant left the room, clicking the door shut behind them. The sound echoed in the large room. The box sat squat on the desk.

'We'd better open it,' Walter said.

'Yes.'

They approached the desk, towing Sarah along with them, then stood gazing, as if expecting the lid to fly open of its own accord. The key was large and unused. How much of their transaction Sarah understood they could not gauge, but now she put her hand on Walter's and guided it towards the key. He took it up and opened the box.

It contained three documents wrapped in protective oilskin. Jack reached his arm in and lifted them out. The first two were maps, perhaps pages torn from an atlas. One was dominated by a large city, and a red cross had been marked near the western end. The other showed a range of mountains, and two thick circles of ink had been drawn round a small village with a river running through it.

The third document was a letter, several sheets thick.

> My dear sons

They both averted their eyes as if from a painful glare. It was no easier to read the letter than it had been to open the box. Oh, it was far harder! Jack fell into a chair.

'You read it,' he said weakly. 'You're the scholar.'

Walter sat in Mr Grynne's large chair, making room for Sarah to perch beside him. He spread the pages out on the desktop and she scanned them as he began, slowly, to read the words out loud.

> So I call you now as I look down upon you and as, in my imagination, I see you all those years later, those travails and sufferings later, when you hold this paper in your hands.

It shook in Walter's. He flattened it on the desk and peered closer. The words were written erratically, sudden javelin-darts of the pen striking out for the margins. One line would be clearly legible, the next a tangle of haywire letters.

> This is a time of great danger. It is the middle of the night – we speed across a moonlit landscape fearful of surprise. A cold wind brings in the pungent smell of firs. A smell of my own country and one day I hope of your country. I cannot know if what I do is for the best. Forgive me!

Walter's voice rose little above a whisper.

> I pray to meet you fifteen years from now, when you are an age to understand. But if I am not there, if you read this, you must assume that I am gone – that I am dead. Hear my story. I pray that you will not condemn.

So ended the first page. Walter slid the second across the desktop.

> My dear sons. You are a joy and a grief to me. The life of your mother, my dear Sonia, was given in bringing you into the world.

There was nothing else on this sheet. The blank paper was a testimony to unspeakable remorse. Walter laid it aside. Jack, slumped in his chair, had a hand shielding his face.

> When I was young, even younger than you, I began a journey to find my own father. I left my home village, my mother and my sisters, and travelled many miles to a large city. I shall enclose maps.

> The city was vicious – ruled by an organisation which calls itself the Red Blade. The good people of this place had retreated behind their stout doors. Some had formed a resistance group which controlled the city rooftops. Their symbol is the eye you see on your poor mother's brooch. These people told me that the man I sought had been seen years before and might perhaps live in a rumoured city underground. Many doubted its existence, but I was determined to find it.

> And there truly was a city underground. A perfect creation, untouched by vice and corruption. But my father was not there. What a prodigy of a man! He had found the underground city, but he said that it was unreal. Its beauty was not tested. Virtue must survive on the surface, he taught. It had to triumph over evil, not escape from it. He returned, was captured, was tortured

Here the words broke off halfway through the line. Walter felt Sarah's fingers on his arm, reassuring. He took up the fourth sheet.

> My father, your grandfather, was a poet, a seer, a visionary. Before discovering the underground city he had won the hearts and minds of thousands – of tens of thousands. Afterwards he retreated into a community of humble priests in the western sector, awaiting the fulfilment of prophecy. He believed that I was that fulfilment.

> According to the revered old writings, a reign of peace and virtue would be heralded by the secret arrival in the city of a boy – 'like a steel comb he will enter the sheep's wool, rake out the clinging vermin'. My father awaited my arrival. Then he would stir the people up into a rebellion.

> And yet so many of the good folk wished it otherwise. They wanted a revolution, but not led by a single man. In the days before the Red Blade the city lord had been chosen by representatives of all the people. There was no dictator. These good folk feared that a victory under my father would lead to another dictatorship. They pleaded with me not to go to him.

> But how could I not?

It was doubtless the rocking of the carriage which had given this last sentence its particularly large and bold lettering, but Walter could not help but read into it an anguish of uncertainty. He reached for another page.

> The battles were long and bloody. I cannot describe them. The city was won, but at so great a cost. How many death justify the removal of oppression? What man can take upon himself

Here there was a break in mid-sentence and a gap on the page before the writing began again.

> Five years it took to force the Red Blade from the city. Then the people turned to my father, lauded him, demanded that he be their leader. A pure and inspired man! they raised statues to him, his poems were on every lip.
>
> He refused. He was long in years, he said. But he believed in prophecy. 'Mastery shall be restored to the virtuous', it said. Virtue was embodied in the boy who had journeyed to the city. That was what he believed and therefore what the people came to believe.
>
> I inherited the city.

Jack dropped the hand from his face. The two brothers, their faces expressionless, exchanged a deep glance.

> I became the new city lord. We enjoyed peace and prosperity. It was a happy time. But I knew that many still had doubts – in truth I had doubts myself – and after my father died I stood aside and arranged for my successor to be chosen by the people.
>
> Should I have gone then? Should I have returned home? I ask this to the night sky as much as to you. We can never know all the results of our actions. I decided to stay because the love and honour the people felt for my father had been transferred to me and, if bad times were to return, I might be needed once again. Some urged me to go. I had done my duty. I had served my purpose. They had eternal gratitude. And much more of the same. But I stayed.
>
> And now the bad times have returned. You cannot obliterate evil. The Eye and the Blade will be enemies until the end of time. The eastern sector fell yesterday and we may face years more of bloody fighting. I prepare to put on the heavy mantle once again.

A clock on the wall sounded the hour, each hammered note reverberating around the room. Walter waited for the last echo to fade away.

> This mission is painful to me. My two babies sent away to lives I may never know of. But present perils demand it. While that myth of leadership remains, first passed from my father to me, there will be evil men who wish you harm. While you live, the people will have hope.
>
> Understand the reasons for my actions! Do not curse me for an act of betrayal! I ask you to think well and long on what you should do. I came to find a father and found myself. The responsibilities I did not seek but were thrust upon me. You must not hope to find a father. Your task, if you will pursue it, is far nobler – to revive a people.
>
> You will have the maps. My home village, which I have never again seen – would that some day you could travel there and tell of what has passed! – and the city. The red cross marks the place where you will find the priests who cared for my father. They have other documents they will give to you.

My dear sons, I ask only that you act nobly.

There was but one page left. It contained only a short poem, and it was obvious that the writer had been at great pains to control his pen.

Wear me as your helmet
falling masonry will break
across my back.
Wear me as your spiked heel
I will bite into ice for you.

Sarah gathered the pages together. The two brothers could not bring themselves to speak for a long time. When Jack at last broke the silence he made no direct reference to the letter at all.

'We're in danger,' he said. 'Now that we're together.'

'I *was* being watched,' Walter replied. 'I always thought so. But perhaps, until there were two of us . . . '

He stared into space, calculating. Although both felt themselves deeply affected by what they had found in the box, they were silently agreed not to discuss it in haste.

'Brother Mark believes I am dead,' said Walter. 'The Count must believe so too.'

'And the Count knows I have been with the theatre all these months,' added Jack. 'The important thing is not to be seen together. Then they may not guess.'

He went to the wall and tugged at the bell-pull.

'Let's hope Mr Grynne is as discreet as he promises.'

'Sarah and I will sleep under the boat,' said Walter. 'Will you come after sunrise tomorrow?'

Jack shook his head.

'Let's say midday,' he offered. 'Theatre folk aren't much good in the mornings.'

Mr Grynne could not have been far away, for it was a matter of a mere half-minute before the door opened and his corpulent figure swayed towards them.

'Everything to your satisfaction, gentlemen?'

They nodded, unable as well as unwilling to explain.

'Good, good. Then my final duty is to make available to you a certain sum of money in the pursuance of objectives which I understand are now clear to you. You do follow me?'

'Yes, indeed,' Walter managed.

'Objectives, you understand, of which I know nothing. It's not a fortune. Very far from it. But sufficient to allow for travel and concomitant expenses. Do you wish to take this sum here and now?'

He saw the confusion on their faces.

'No hurry, eh? Quite understandable. There is absolutely no need to make an instant decision, 193. The bank will not be moving away. Come and see me again as soon as you have made up your minds.'

He held out a fleshy hand to each of the lads in turn and then, perhaps convincing himself that the immediate business had been properly concluded, allowed himself the luxury of putting an arm round Sarah as he ushered them to the door.

36 Count's Business

'Take this fellow away in chains!'

Luigi was dragged across the stage, fulminating. Jack stood to one side, looking defiant. The interval – the time he dreaded – would all too soon be upon them.

'He's innocent,' he proclaimed, flinging wide his arms.

Ah, but 'never mind the gestures' had been Luigi's advice before the week's run began. Gestures, apparently, tended to dictate themselves. Lungs were the thing. He was to swell them out, to take the air in deep, to speak from his stomach. Only, he could not concentrate tonight.

'We'll give him a fair trial,' came the reply (Mr Tusker, evilly turned out in black and with a piratical eye-patch). 'And then a beheading.'

How difficult it had been rejoining the troupe late that afternoon. Of course, they had been looking for him everywhere, expecting the worst. And he could not explain! He had been called away to talk to someone, he said, someone from his past. he had been unable to let them know. He was truly sorry, *very* sorry. It was all so weak, so unconvincing. ('Tall tale,' Ma had said.) Their initial anger did not last, but he caught Oz's concerned glances and shrank from shame. And yet he could not have done otherwise.

'Mercy!' cried Belle, an arm across her eyes in the most extravagant gesture yet seen this evening.

Down came the curtain. Moderate applause. But they knew the Count was to make an appearance. Everything before that was padding.

Jack followed the men to their dressing room. They were tense from having to fight for every reaction. They were tired. Yet he and Luigi had perhaps their most difficult work yet to do. They remained some time in contemplative silence. Mr Tusker muttered lines to himself. Then there was a knock on the door and the Count marched straight in.

'My fellow thespians!' he cooed in a delighted voice.

Mr Tusker's reaction was comical to behold. He ran towards their titled walk-on, brushing furiously at his (dyed) clumps of hair, and fell to one knee.

'Most gracious benefaction,' he mumbled into his heaving belly. 'Unprecedented. Much appreciated.'

The Count for his part only laughed goodnaturedly and turned towards Jack.

'I'm perfectly sure it will be a pleasure,' he pronounced prettily. 'But you, young fellow, are on stage with me, are you not? Perhaps you would just drop by my dressing room and remind me of what I have to do.'

'You haven't had the script?' intervened Mr Tusker. 'Sir?'

'My man has the script,' replied the Count loftily, and leading the way out so that Jack could not but follow. 'I require personal coaching.'

He was wearing a costume of midnight blue comprising dozens of individual strips of material so that, as he moved, vents opened to reveal brief glimpses of a multi-coloured garment underneath. Following behind, Jack registered red, orange, cerise, brilliant blue, two shades of green. Evidently he had no thought of changing it, for once they had entered the dressing room he pointed Jack to a chair and quickly sat down alongside him.

'You play well,' he said. 'Been performing all season, eh?'

'Yes, sir.'

'Oh sir, sir, sir. Let's have none of that. "Count" if you like. Or nothing. I don't need all that flummery, don't you know.'

Jack, determinedly on his guard, sat stock still.

'Was there nothing else to bring you to O—?'

'No.'

'No appointment of any kind?'

'No.'

But his very taciturnity would give him away!

'I don't think so, Count. What did you have in mind?'

There was a brief pause and Jack moved swiftly on to the attack. He could not help but entertain a chess image – the Count as the black knight, himself as perhaps the white rook.

'You wanted to know about the script.'

'Ah, yes. In a moment. I was interested in yourself, young man.'

The knight's moves, though limited, have a way of making opponents uneasy. It was not possible for him to insist in view of the Count's more direct approach.

'Where to you hail from?'

He named the city, attempting to sound relaxed, unsuspecting.

'And you have brothers or sisters?'

'No. I was brought up alone.'

Why did he say it like that?

'I'm an only child.'

Too obvious an adjustment. He began to sweat.

'And if I were to advise you otherwise?' the Count suddenly surprised him.

A bell sounded outside.

'Five minutes,' said Jack. 'Shouldn't I prepare you?'

'Oh, never mind that. I'm quite adept at ad-libbing, believe me.'

Now there was a rap on the door and Oz looked in. He was surprised to see the two together.

'Five minutes,' he said, bowing his head a little to the Count. He was about to leave when Jack kept him back.

'The trial scene,' he said. 'I'm worried that the Count and his man may not have been informed where they will need to enter.'

'But it's clear on the script.'

Jack was already half way across the dressing room.

'I don't think it's clear enough. I think we should check it out – with the Count's permission.'

Now it was his turn to use the knight. The Count, smiling to himself, shrugged and followed him from the room.

'Most touching,' he breathed, 'your concern for me. Let us by all means see your script.'

And, in the wings, Jack made a great play of pointing out this detail and that while the powdered gentleman who was to be the other walk-on observed their behaviour with a quizzical expression on his face.

'Pellucid,' drawled the Count at the conclusion of this instruction. 'So very much obliged.'

He lowered his head towards Jack's ear.

'Perhaps, if you've the time after the show, we might continue our little conversation?'

There was no time to reply. The curtain went up and they were immediately into the drama. The Count, when he came on, seemed at first somewhat subdued, but it required only a few audible remarks from the boxes for him to show all his usual flamboyance. He decided that he would make the best trial judge, and Amazing was stripped of his robes to accommodate him. His companion was to be, of all things, a hat-stand, and the Count insisted that they all remove their coverings and place them on his outstretched hands.

Jack could think of nothing to save this unforeseen situation but Luigi, as ever, was equal to it. He made no attempt to dislodge the Count from the bench but, by hoarse commanding whispers with his back to the audience, actually browbeat him into keeping to the plot. Jack was startled both by the method and its success. The Count clearly felt that fidelity to the story-line was a small price to pay for the sport of outrageously hamming it up on stage before a devotedly appreciative audience.

As the play came to an close and there were howls of pleasure and encores and more laughter still, since the Count continued to prance about by the footlights, Jack knew what he was going to do. He did not intend to be waylaid.

The curtain fell for the last time. He ran to his dressing room, tearing off his costume as he went. He grabbed his clothes, putting on only what he needed for decency, carrying the rest as a bundle in his arms. Along the corridor, and he was at the stage door, panting, alone and unseen.

But his escape was to be thwarted. Even as he opened the door he heard a great commotion from the street, and as he stepped outside a wildly running man careered into him, fell, leapt to his feet and was instantly engulfed by a crowd of pursuers wielding heavy wooden sticks.

37   Brutality

'Vive l'anarchie!'

The fierce eyes and consumptive face were the more startling for the artificial light that made of the cheeks dark caverns in green flesh. The police seemed to be everywhere, a frantic movement the still centre of which was the hunted man, now pinioned and being beaten into silence by flailing truncheons. But silence was not easily achieved, and the voice, heroically defiant, seemed to continue with a momentum of its own long after the body had slackened and become limp in its captors' arms.

'Vive l'anarchie . . . Vive l'anarchie . . . Vive l'anarchie . . . '

Jack, his escape cut off by a drama outdoing anything that had been fabricated within the theatre, felt the Count's hand close upon his arm as he stood on the steps of the stage door watching the arrest. His dismay was the greater for the sickening brutality of the scene before him: still the truncheons fell upon the defenceless head and still the voice cried, though with a gradual weakening until the flow of words was drowned by a flow of blood.

And then, when it seemed to be over, the man opened his eyes one last time and gazed around him. They were burning coals that scorched their mark upon all they surveyed – the police, the pressing crowd, all treated to the same scorn, the same hatred. Then these eyes turned towards Jack and the Count. Was there the trace of a smile upon the mouth as it forced itself into one final cry before oblivion?

'Vive . . . l'anarchie!'

The grip tightened on his arm. Looking up, he saw the Count's face lit by a feverish excitement. His cheeks were flushed, his eyes bright with a covert elation, as if he were tasting forbidden fruit.

'Here! he breathed tremulously.

There was both fear and relish in it during those few seconds in which he dropped his guard. Then the languid mask fell back into place.

'Unfortunate,' he spoke into Jack's ear. 'Unpleasant. All that blood, and such a young man. Waste! Terrible waste!' – and he shook his head balefully while a policeman, recognising him, humbly apologised for the inconvenience.

'But you'll understand, sir, a man in your position. We can't leave scum like that on the streets or they wouldn't be safe for respectable folk.'

'No, indeed. Unsafe, ungovernable. Well done, my man, and here's a little something for you and your colleagues to reward you for your courage.'

With that the Count removed an extravagant ruby ring from his finger and presented it to the officer who, with a confused shaking and nodding of his head, left to share the experience with his accomplices.

'Courage!' Jack protested boldly. 'Was that courage? Hundreds of them against one man!'

'Never exaggerate, dear boy. Merely a score or so. No real match for a free spirit.'

Jack, feeling there was something in the Count's manner he did not understand, watched the police drag the remains of the free spirit to a waiting wagon. The Count began to talk once more in a quiet, confidential tone.

'But we aristocrats have to stick together, eh?'

Jack laughed, feigning ignorance of his drift.

'Aristocrat! I'm just a struggling actor'

'An aristocrat of the theatre, dear boy. The aristocracy of art, the only true aristocracy. Is that not so? Was it different where you came from? I shouldn't be surprised if art ran through your family. Painters, perhaps? Poets?'

The crowd was beginning to thin. If he was to escape, this was the moment.

'Free spirits,' he smiled, as if about to reveal all – and then, as the grasp on his arm slackened, he tugged vigorously and was free himself. He sprinted away, not looking behind but knowing that the Count would not demean himself by running.

His swift departure was almost his downfall. A bystander, taking his haste as evidence of complicity with the hapless anarchist, gave chase and raised the alarm. Jack found himself followed by a crowd of men all waving their arms and shouting excitedly. Should he stop and reason? That would be hopeless: he would be beaten to the ground before his first words were uttered.

Salvation came in the shape of a dark alley that led between two high-walled buildings. He knew his only chance lay in flight combined with subterfuge. He dodged into the alley and ran its length, aware that the gang was closing upon him. He emerged into another busy thoroughfare and here he instantly changed his pace to a shambling walk, turned his collar up and stooped his shoulders. He coughed wheezily. His pursuers, emerging from the alley, saw no sign of the fleeing youth – only a street full of late revellers and a feeble old man. They split into two groups and went pounding away, shouting.

The streets of O— on a summer's night were truly the ether through which a free spirit could drift with maximum ease. Certain now of his safety, he straightened up, turned down the collar of his coat and, feeling more than a little pleased with himself, began to whistle. There was a dry warmth clinging to the streets, orphan of the day's departed sun, and the stars were beggared by the abundant lights, strung from cables that hung in swags between posts, blossoming like giant electric wisteria. Jack's tune wove thinly upwards, counterpointing the accumulation of noise below, and birds, freshly flown from the silent blackness of O—'s surrounding countryside and perhaps believing the dawn chorus already to have begun, joined in, adding a complex though barely heard piping fugue to the street's music.

And then the explosions began.

38 Snatch

Walter heard them while meandering through the old quarter with Sarah. She, lithe and graceful, threaded among the throng much more deftly than he, flitting well ahead of him in her glistening costume.

It was a place for bright costumes. The people, casually happy, looked to be moving from party to party: but, then, the streets might be the party and they thistledown blown along by the mysterious promise of pleasure that O— seemed constantly to whisper. If only the twins had inherited *this* place, what a rich gift that would have been! And Walter shuddered at the image of the grey provincial city their father's letter seemed to evoke.

The explosions alarmed him, although he could not know what they were, but she of course heard nothing, and when he at last caught her eye she only gave him a quick and merry wave and moved on again, tantalisingly out of reach.

He must reach her! He was aware of the consternation of the people around him. He noticed how they began to hurry, to move as if suddenly making for destinations, to disappear down side streets, and yet she continued to elude him, like a quick bright fish that flicked its tail and darted away and that he could not catch however much he thrashed and floundered. The breath caught in his throat; he seemed to have no air in his lungs; he was drowning.

There was smoke. People began to run, calling out to one another. Panic disarranged their senses. And so it was that nobody saw the swift villainy that snatched a boy from their midst, threw a blanket over his head and shoulders and bundled him into a waiting carriage, his muffled cries drowned by the cries of the frightened citizens and the clatter of hoofbeats as the horses were whipped into a clumsy canter.

39 The Attack on O—

At first Jack thought them fireworks – sharp cracking sounds, radiating splinters of light, that came from all parts of the city's central area. The reality became apparent when, a short distance away, an anonymous facade detached itself from its building, showering the street in bricks and glass and dust, and leaving the interior suddenly naked and exposed to the common view.

Then another, even closer. Jack was thrown to the ground by the blast and lay for seconds bruised and shocked. Regaining his feet, he dashed across to see what he could do for the victims of the attack.

The music of O— had become a screaming chorus, the dream-like promenading of its inhabitants transformed into frenzied, though equally purposeless, movement. It was Jack's fortune, and that of his neighbours, that the bombed building was secretive enough to boast little glass, so that the ensuing injuries were fewer, and less ghastly, than might otherwise have been the case.

Since the first living creature to emerge was a green parrot, squawking violently, its hovering flight hampered by a dangling length of chain, Jack's disordered brain fancied the place to be some sort of menagerie. Exactly which sort became clear when it was followed by young ladies of an even more exotic nature and ageing men in various stages of undress, choking and cursing. None seemed too much hurt, for the bomb had been thrown in at the door and the damage restricted to the front of the building.

As the dust settled it revealed an interior of shredded carpet and a litter of ottomans from which the stuffing had erupted. Small fires had started where lamps had tipped over, spilling their oil, and the ceiling was garlanded with hanging ribbons of fabric. Standing amid this ruination and destruction, like the very incarnation of the devil, stood a raging woman, her flesh-hung body quivering with fury as she waved her fists and railed: 'I'll kill them, I'll kill them! The swine won't get away with this! I'll kill them!'

Jack stepped forward to help, but even as he did so the police arrived and began to push everyone away from the building, waving truncheons at any bystander who was slow to obey. More girls filed through the smoke and stood in a group not far from him, but they were too distracted to pay any attention to the people around them. The last to emerge unaccountably sleep-walked towards Jack, her fingers twisting and twisting around one another in mindless terror, and she rubbed against him for a moment, moaning 'It's terrible, terrible' before sliding away to join her companions. Buckets of water were arriving, and great gouts of steam rose from the smouldering interior.

'Where's the engine?' someone demanded.

'They're busy in the centre,' came the reply. 'There are bombs everywhere.'

Jack, dazed, wandered away. All around him, it seemed, the city was a confusion of explosions and wailings, of hurrying, frantic people. He reached central O— and found the violence yet more intense. The bombing continued: sporadic explosions constantly rekindled the panic of the populace. Banks, offices and factories were burning – the town's very commercial foundations – and not least Grynne's Bank, which had sustained one of the fiercest attacks, with several bombs thrown through its basement windows and the whole facade in danger of imminent collapse.

The authorities were floundering, impotent. The handful of men responsible for the action easily evaded capture in the mêlée of policemen, firemen and distraught pedestrians. Their colleague caught and beaten by the police earlier in the evening had been the least fortunate: his eyes and ears sealed, he could not now enjoy the fruits of their long evenings spent planning and preparing in smoke-filled cellars.

Jack, having nowhere to go – he dare not return to his rooms for fear of the Count – joined a raggle-taggle band of survivors in a halted tram that sat in the centre of O—'s widest avenue. They crouched down or lay flat on the boards. In truth, it offered little protection, but there was a comfort in the company of others.

He was particularly comforted by a woman approaching her middle years who smothered him in the silky folds of her voluminous evening gown. Did she seek to shelter him as a mother might a son, or was it rather she who sought shelter from his youthful yet masculine arms? No matter: whatever her motives, Jack luxuriated in the attention as they lay on the tram's floor, their dark privacy occasionally interrupted by a sudden brightness that enabled them to see one another as a reversed after-image so that Jack imagined himself embracing a dusky queen of the harem.

Eventually, the supply of bombs no doubt exhausted, the terrorists became part of the night and the silence that surrounded central O—. The police and firemen began to take control of the situation, though there were fires which still simmered, threatening to erupt. Jack found himself part of a group of men and women who formed a water chain, passing buckets, hastily commandeered from a nearby shop, from hand to hand between a street fountain and a fire.

It was a gesture more than any real help, for the volume of water could in no way halt the rising flames. Jack's arms ached, and he complained loudly to all within earshot, but inside he felt strangely exhilarated.

40 Locked Up

He spent a long time in the carriage. There were short periods when it was in motion and he rolled this way and that on the floor, long periods during which it was at rest – any shaking being caused, he presumed, by the impatience of the horses. If he raised his head to listen or simply to change his position he was immediately pushed down again to the accompaniment of words he knew were coarse and foul though he had never heard them in his life before.

At last hands grasped him and lifted him up, and a blindfold was tightened over his eyes. He was marched from the carriage into the night air and then inside a building. The smell of smoke was heavy in his nostrils: it was not the scented woodsmoke of the monastery fires. He was propelled forward, shoved down a short flight of steps and thrown on to what felt like a bed. The blindfold was removed. When he opened his eyes, two heavy men were already on their way up the steps and out of the door. It was dark. A single lamp flickered shadows across the walls.

He knew where he was immediately – in the small underground room which he and Sarah had entered from the grille above the river. This shock was followed by the sight of Madam at the top of the stairs.

'Spit image!' she called over her shoulder.

Then she laughed.

'Same past, same future.'

The person she addressed – he had already guessed it – was brother Mark. He limped to the top of the stairs and gazed at Walter silently.

'Welcome to our little home,' smiled Madam, rejoicing. 'What's left of it,' she added more sombrely.

Brother Mark still said not a word.

'Anything we can get you,' continued Madam robustly, 'young Jack?'

She spoke the name with a relish of false intimacy.

'A bite to eat, maybe? A little drink? One of my lovely girls?'

Walter closed his eyes.

'Bit of sleep, then. An excellent idea. The sleep of the just. Oh, it's too bad!'

With this mock lamentation she turned on her heel and would have closed the door behind her, but brother Mark moved forward and started down the steps.

'Oh come now, my old friend,' urged Madam loudly. 'You're not going to sentimentalise, I trust?'

'No, no,' replied the old man hoarsely. 'But just a moment. The likeness is so . . . extreme.'

'And you'd have put paid to the other one just the same, and don't you deny it.'

Brother Mark, ignoring this remark, sat on the couch nearest the door and stared at Walter, who returned the gaze from between half-closed lashes. Madam, with a final sound of exasperation, slammed the door behind her and her footsteps receded along the corridor.

Several minutes passed in silence. The elderly sentinel scarcely blinked during this interval, his eyes fixed firmly upon Walter's face. When, eventually, he did speak it was hesitantly, in a low voice.

'I knew your brother,' he said.

Walter slowly raised himself into a sitting position but made no reply.

'Your brother. You . . . had a brother.'

Why was this necessary? Why did he tell him this?

'What happened to him?'

'An accident,' brother Mark came back quickly. 'Nothing to do with . . . Nothing to do with me. He met his death in a fire.'

There was another silence. It lengthened.

'I think,' Walter said deliberately, 'that you betrayed him.'

'No!'

Brother Mark rose to his feet and began to patrol the room, back and forth. He muttered to himself. Flap, flap went the sandal.

'Whatever you know, it is not enough,' he said. 'I have no obligation to tell you, but I wish to. It is right to do so.'

'You speak of morality?'

'And should a monk not do so?'

'A monk,' replied Walter, 'does not normally concern himself with matters such as this. I am to be murdered, I've no doubt of that.'

He was reminded of debates in the monastery, logic and theology closely married.

'Don't ask me,' said brother Mark hurriedly. 'That's not my business. Do you think I kill people? Me? With these hands? That's not my business.'

'But help others to do it?'

'It's not my province . . . those details. That is not what I concern myself with. More . . . the philosophy. Do you understand?'

'Not at all.'

The old cleric sat down once again, this time at the other end of Walter's couch. His expression was one of entreaty, as if he were imploring Walter to understand. He seemed to be rehearsing his thoughts with soundless movements of his lips, and he made several false starts before launching on his explanation.

'Many years ago,' he began, 'I lived in a city far to the east. I was not at that time in holy orders. I worked in a government department. It was a fine city, well ordered. I believe in order, control, discipline. So it was. But there were disruptive elements, too.

'In O— tonight the anarchists have been at their foul work. Indiscriminate bombings. It's their first attack but they will come again. They believe in the destruction of all governments. No man is free, they say, if he is governed. Foolish, dangerous talk!

'In that city, too, there were kindred spirits. They were not strictly anarchists, perhaps, but their aim was to make government less strong. Therefore they were dangerous. They spoke of democracy or syndicalism or fraternalism – all cant words!

'And so I decided to support the only organisation which would ensure firm government, law and order. It was called the Red Blade. I did little enough, I should say – I was, and am, a bookish man – but I was an organiser at a certain level. I did my duty. There were many who valued the service I gave.'

He made this assertion not as a boast but, rather, with humility, as if he were honoured by the approval of others.

'Later I left the city and entered a monastery to live a life of study and devotion. My work for the Blade, I believed, had come to an end. But I was mistaken. A personal tragedy was to re-establish the ties.'

'A tragedy?'

'My own nephew, my brother's son, was killed for the cause. A fine young man who was named after me. Marcus – that was my name before I took the vows. I had not seen him for many years, but I had followed his career through the family. I heard that he was doing good work, useful work, in the city.

'And then the awful news that he was dead. Drowned, they said, while carrying out Blade duties. I never learned the details, but it brought a great sadness to me.'

He stood once more and began, limping, to patrol the room, side to side, his hands crossed over his chest.

'One day a baby was brought to the monastery. Such a tiny thing! A refugee from trouble. He was to be in our charge, brought up in our ways.

'But this was no ordinary baby. He was, through his birth, a boy who might one day threaten the security of the city. I contacted the organisation at once. I had no hesitation. I had the pain of Marcus's death in my heart.'

'My brother.'

'Your brother. Don't ask me to repent of it. Of course, I have tortured the matter in my mind times without number. But how could I know?'

'Know?'

'That he should grow dear to me – a fine young man. A veritable saint. So he was, I assure you. If I had known . . . well, I can't say how I should have acted.

'As it was, my instructions were simple, undemanding. I was to watch the child, to report any contacts from outside as he grew older. I watched. There were none. So, in my foolish way, I imagined that it would last for ever.

'Until, one day only months ago – it seems a passage of years! – I learned from the abbot that he was to be given an envelope. Inside was information which, almost certainly, would lead him away from the monastery, probably never to return.'

'You informed the Red Blade.'

'No. No, I did not do that. Not immediately. I hoped he would not go. And when he did go – when I came into his room and the bed was unslept in and a terrible absence took the colour off everything I saw – then I told the Blade what I knew and said I would pursue him and bring him back to the monastery. It was time I wanted. Time to persuade. He would not come! I knew the danger he was in.

'And then, not the Blade but a fire took him!'

The old monk sank on to a couch, openly weeping. Walter could not but be moved by his suffering. His impulse was to comfort, even to throw his arms around his old teacher and tell him everything. He resisted it.

'And me?' he asked coldly. 'You'll happily sacrifice me to your friends?'

Brother Mark shook his head.

'That's no business of mine. I don't ask. They work for the best, for law and order. I don't involve myself with details.'

'You're a party to murder!'

Walter leapt to his feet, his emotion issuing in a vehemence which surprised him. He found himself trembling, the anger welling up in him.

'What's the value of your law and order if you have to kill people for it? The world you create is more evil than the one you leave behind. But you shut your eyes to it. You think you can remain innocent while your friends commit atrocities on your behalf.'

Brother Mark waved a hand in the air, as if fending off a buzzing, venomous insect.

'Man is evil,' he said. 'He must be controlled.'

'By other men?'

It was, indeed, like a monastic debate, but they had never disputed with such intensity. Brother Mark dabbed at his face with a sleeve. He wept silently for several minutes. Eventually he lifted his head, his face damp and ravaged, and spoke in calm tones.

'Where I have sinned, may God forgive me. What has passed is now beyond repair. What is to happen is, believe me, beyond my control. May God forgive me.

'I wished to tell you that I loved your brother and that I never wished him harm.'

Even as he finished speaking the door swung open and the two men reappeared carrying the dead weight of an unconscious body. They staggered down the steps and dropped their burden on to a couch. Brother Mark gathered his habit about him and, silently, departed. The two men followed him out.

'It'll be a few hours before he's in the world again,' one of them remarked. The door slammed shut and a key turned in the lock.

Walter approached the motionless form. His fellow prisoner was tall and, judging from his stertorous breathing, had been heavily drugged. The light was not far away, and Walter strained to make out the man's features when it flared across his face.

It was the Count.

41 Aftermath

The glow from the fires was being overtaken by the brightening of the world's eastern rim when Jack and his companions drifted from their labours. As the new day grew lighter, the sun glimmering behind a veil of cloud, he expected to see central O— reduced to rubble, but it was not so. By night it had seemed that the flames enveloped everything, but now it was clear that the destruction was isolated and selective – here a blackened gap in a row of shops, still hot and smouldering, there the shattered walls of a factory.

He had slept not at all, though there were times when he had found himself passing on a bucket that he could not remember taking hold of, moments when it seemed to him that the world had stood still for long minutes at a time. Now, as he wandered alone through the deserted streets, his head throbbed, his arms and shoulders were stiffening painfully, a heavy dullness overtook his spirits.

Grynne's remained standing, he discovered, thanks to an army of hastily contracted workmen who even now were shoring it up with wood and iron. Its impressiveness was for the time diminished. There were scorch marks on the walls around the market square, where, Walter had told him, Sarah had danced to earn money, but the damage was slight. Further on in his walk, however, he met a sight for which he was totally unprepared. The theatre had been hit by a powerful bomb and the front of it was reduced to a pile of brick and stone.

Sick at heart, Jack climbed over the crumbled wall. A fire had raged within. The interior was all burned away save, bizarrely, for one single seat at the front which offered the benighted spectator a view of charred curtains, gaping scenery, a blackened stage yet breathing wisps of dingy smoke. He groped forward and fell into the seat. Above his head the boxes for the well-to-do were streaked with soot but otherwise untouched by the devastation. The gilding along their rims was a pathetic irrelevance.

He nodded and dozed and, when he awoke, started with horror as if he surfaced from a dream to find himself in a living nightmare. He leapt to his feet and ran from the place, stumbling over the scattered bricks as he regained the street. There was nobody about. The air was oppressive this morning, a bank of denser cloud approaching from the west. He wandered on until he came to a large cafe where, in a daze, he ordered a coffee and sank down at a table with no thought of drinking it, his eyes closing.

'They want tearing limb from limb!'

He jerked back into consciousness to find a man at his table, looking at him over a newspaper.

'Anarchist scum!'

Had he been asleep for a second or hours? His hand found his coffee cup. It was still warm.

'Ought to round the lot of them up along with their sympathisers. Ship 'em out to sea and sink the boat. None of this pussy-footing. The authorities are too soft on 'em.'

Jack pulled the saucer towards him and cradled the cup in his hands.

'Why did they do it?' he asked.

'Because it's all they know, the lice. They gripe about the people with authority, but who do they bomb? Us! I'll bet not a judge suffered last night, nor an army officer, nor a police chief. You wait until they print the list, then you'll see – factory hands, fishermen, clerks and their girls out for a spree to forget the misery of work. "We'll free you from the bondage of work," they say, "we'll free you from the chains of authority." Oh yes, they'll free us! I'll bet they freed a few last night. There's no slavery when you're under a pile of bricks!'

'Lackey!'

Another face appeared over the shoulder of the first man. The newcomer placed his tray on the table and sat with them.

'It's sheep like you who cause the problem.'

Pausing only to dig a fork into his food and push it into his mouth, he continued to berate the first speaker, chewing between the phrases.

'Yes sir, yes sir, anything to please you sir! Oh, was I sitting in the wrong place? Of course I'll get up and move to please you, sir. Am I ugly to look at? Then I'll hide myself from view, sir. Does my work distress you? I'll do it as quietly so as not to disturb you, sir. Does the air I breathe belong to you, sir? Oh, but I'm sorry, sir, forgive me, I promise I won't breathe again, sir.'

If Jack expected the first man to react violently to this attack upon his beliefs he was mistaken. He simply moved along to accommodate the new arrival and then turned to him, poking the folded newspaper into his chest as if to emphasise the words of his reply.

'What, my friend, does throwing a bomb through a window achieve? Tell me that. Do you feel any more free of oppression this morning for the activities of your compatriots last night? Well, let me tell you, *I'm* freer – I'm free of a job because they bombed the factory last night. I'm free to starve.'

The second man seemed to regard this personal revelation as unfair and shifted his attack to an even more abstract plane.

'That tree outside,' he said, not taking his eyes from his plate. 'Did that tree ask permission to grow? Is that tree there courtesy of the king or the count or the priest or the overseer? No, the tree grew there freely, unsupervised. It didn't need someone to tell it how to grow, and I don't need someone to tell *me* how to grow. If I wish to spread my branches in one direction I shall, and if I wish to spread them in another direction I shall. I'm as free as that tree. And so could you be if it weren't for your lackey mentality.'

'It's not so much freedom you need,' said the first man, hitting the table-top triumphantly with his newspaper, 'as a pair of glasses. They cut down that twisted bush of yours last week.'

At this the other peered through the window and, roaring with good-natured laughter, threw an arm round his companion's shoulder.

'Never mind, old friend, and I'm sorry about your job. But by what right does any man tell another what to do?'

It was Jack's turn now, although he had not himself known that he was about to speak: 'But if the man is good, if the man is just? Does that not give him the right?'

'No. In fact the better a man is the more dangerous he is. Issues get blurred, people accept things that they shouldn't, power accrues, and then . . . Yes, then the good man dies and another takes his place and the power stays with him, if not the goodness and justice. All authority, however benign the wielders be, robs another of his birthright.

'I spit on leaders and despise the led, but at least a bad leader is easy to hate. The good leader . . . '

'The good leader is a strong leader.'

The first man said these words with a finality that closed the conversation, even though the other remained unconvinced and shook his head as he turned to his coffee.

A sound at the window was followed by thin rivulets trickling down the panes. The sky was dark, rolling layers of cloud heaped one upon the other and painted the savage purple of an ancient warrior, and the rain, once it started, gathered in intensity and hammered on to the street and dashed at the glass. Within a few minutes the water was high in the gutters, carrying the detritus of the preceding dry days and of the past night's chaos to the cascading drains. Jack watched people covering their heads and racing for the nearest shelter, and he was aware that several had taken refuge in the cafe, for the babble about him increased. His chin fell upon his chest.

When next he was awoken it was to find that the argumentative pair had gone. His shoulder was grasped by a powerful hand that was shaking him, shaking him. His eyes focused slowly on a face he recognised but for a moment could not place.

'Walter!'

It was a face whose expression combined wonderment and a tender delight. Now each of his shoulders was gripped and he felt himself lifted from his seat.

'Walter! Not dead! He's here, my Walter!'

Clabber set him down upon the table and took a step back, as if appraising one of his models.

'Escaped the fire!'

Jack, overcome by the warmth of attention, could only nod, seemingly in agreement. Clabber lifted him again, set his feet down on the floor, put a firm arm around him and led him to the door. All the time he exclaimed to himself, but in a voice so loud that all eyes were upon them.

'Thought him lost, but he escaped! And wandering in a state of shock, I shouldn't wonder. Shocked, were you, Walter? And didn't know where to find me.'

The rain had thinned but they splashed through deep puddles. Jack had no need to say a word, and yet the longer he allowed the misunderstanding to go uncorrected, the harder it was to explain. He found himself acquiescing, succumbing, agreeing to become Walter, even – when at last he spoke – adapting his speech so that, slightly slower and more deliberate than his own, it sounded more like his brother's.

'I was frightened. I thought the Count had started the fire.'

'The Count! That was no doing of his, my lad. So you hid away, did you, for fear of the Count? No, that was a lady's work, if so she may be called. My dear wife. Remember? We escaped her into the mountains, but she wouldn't give up. She thought me with someone else in the studio when it was you and Sarah, and she set the place alight. A mad woman!'

He stopped abruptly, whisking Jack round.

'And Sarah. Where is she? Unharmed?'

'Yes, she's unharmed.'

They continued up the street as before, he propelled along by the sculptor's strong arm, Clabber talking and talking, not caring what stares he attracted from the passers-by.

'I'm at Celestin's place now, for the time being. And won't he be glad to see you!'

He was piloted into the old quarter, along cobbled thoroughfares until they came to a small square that was full of life. Although it still rained, spitting against their faces, people were bustling about in the open, shopkeepers displayed their wares on large tables outside and everywhere, it seemed, there were hands waved by people who knew the sculptor.

'Good morning! Here's Walter – you know Walter? An old friend of mine. I'd thought him lost!'

Under a striped canopy, up a flight of steps, Clabber calling out to his poet friend. Jack knew he had not the heart to reveal his identity.

'Celestin! Come and see who I've brought you! Celestin! Get up, you lazy dog!'

They entered a large whitewashed room which was a celebration of disorder. Just inside the door there was a desk piled high with books, any free space being littered with sheaves of paper, most of it scribbled on. The walls were liberally hung with paintings, most unmistakably of a high quality though unframed and simply pinned to the plaster. In the two far corners were unmade single beds, while between them stone sculptures stood among a scree of chippings. As he advanced into this maelstrom Jack became aware of empty bottles and unwashed plates, the remains of ancient food stuck fast to the rims. The stubs of spent cheroots were scattered everywhere.

'Not here,' said Clabber, long after the statement was necessary.

Jack lifted a sheet of paper from the desk and read the lines which sprawled across it.

catherine wheels of orange flame –
the world revolves; nothing is the same.
faces explode, no feature bears a name

'I need more room, but this suits us well,' Clabber went on. 'I've new commissions already. He writes when the mood takes him. Rhyme's the latest thing. A return to form he's preaching, before most of them have even begun to experiment.'

He looked over Jack's shoulder.

'Affected him strangely, last night's business. He couldn't sleep. I suppose he's taken himself off to see the damage.'

'He condemns it?'

'He's an artist, Walter. Sit down, sit down.' Jack perched on the edge of one of the beds and saw from the window how the clouds tumbled head over heels through the sky. 'An artist doesn't judge, he observes and creates.'

'But surely . . . '

'Oh, of course, when the reality affects him directly. Then he's got to react some way, to decide what he should do. Even, I suppose, what he *ought* to do, though God forbid. But an artist doesn't think that way as a rule, not from choice. That part of life is separate from him.

'It was the power of it that affected Celestin last night. And the beauty of the explosions, I suppose. Opening like flowers, he said.'

'Catherine wheels,' added Jack, still holding the paper.

Clabber had been rummaging on the floor among the clutter, and now he came forward with an uncorked bottle and a couple of glasses which Jack decided not to inspect too closely. Before he had reached the bed, however, Clabber pulled himself up and stared hard.

'Amazing,' he said.

'What's that?'

Clabber set the glasses down and stood to one side, studying Jack's head against the light.

'Extraordinary. A nuance I can't explain. The light, perhaps? Though hardly. What you've been through? But that wouldn't explain it, not in the space of a few days.'

'I don't understand.'

'No, it's a sculptor's problem, nothing more. Wait there.'

He began to flick through a pile of charcoal drawings, making irritated noises to himself, until – with a gesture that suggested impatience with his own forgetfulness – he went to the wall and took down a head-and-shoulders study. He held this in the air and compared it with the head he saw before him.

'Losing my eye, maybe,' he said. 'A subtle difference only one man in a thousand would notice. Turn your head. The other way.'

But he soon admitted defeat, took the glasses again, filled them and insisted on a toast to homecoming – 'home being anywhere that true friends meet'. Then he took Jack by the elbow, led him down the stairs and told him they would seek Celestin in the public gardens.

There was no sign of the poet, but they sat on a bench near a playing fountain, watching ducks on a pond, and Jack, relaxed, felt a pleasant drowsiness enwrapping him. The rain had stopped, and though the sky remained overcast, the atmosphere was warm and muggy. The chess tables had been brought out again and several games were already in progress. Clabber rehearsed the woes he had undergone after the fire, partly financial but chiefly on account of Walter's supposed fate.

Jack was nodding, listening but taking little in, when he heard himself hailed loudly by name.

'Hey, Jack! Where have you been Jack!'

A figure came running towards them. It was Oz, whose long legs carried him swiftly across the grass.

42 Identities

'Who's this?' demanded Clabber aggressively. 'Who's he talking to?'

'We thought . . . the worst,' said Oz, shaking his head in the exasperated fashion Jack knew so well. 'If only you'd told us.'

'Who are *you?*' demanded Clabber again.

'The others asked me to find you, Jack.'

'He's not Jack. He's Walter.'

Oz looked at Clabber for the first time. He was by some way the taller, but he lacked the sculptor's obvious strength and no onlooker would have put money on him if it came to a brawl.

'Are you coming with me, Jack?' he asked bravely.

Poor Jack found that the words, for once, would not flow.

'I don't know what your game is,' Clabber growled menacingly, 'but if you mean Walter any harm you'd better think twice about it. He's had a narrow escape from a fire, and he's staying with me at my studio – as he has done for weeks past.'

'A fire?' questioned Oz, stooping to look the bemused Jack in the eye. 'Was that last night in the bombings?'

'It was *not* last night,' Clabber began to shout, his face reddening, 'and I can't see that it's anything to do with you. Will you be off?'

Oz drew himself up to his full height and seemed at that moment to recognise the sculptor from the evening in the Count's garden.

'Jack in your studio?' he said. 'For weeks past? Well, that can't be. He's been in the theatre with me for several months.'

'Theatre? Are you mad? Walter, do you know this fellow?'

Jack shook his head from utter perplexity, and found that he was denying a friendship. He tried to speak, but unintelligible sounds were all that came to his lips.

'That's enough for me,' bristled Clabber. 'You'd do well to make yourself scarce.'

Oz took a step backwards.

'You won't expect me to understand you, Jack,' he said quietly. 'I won't ask you anything further. I just want you to know that we shall be on our way in a couple of days. The theatre's burnt down and some of our equipment with it. But I shan't bother you more.'

'Theatre?' asked Clabber. 'What's this theatre you speak of?'

'In the centre. The big one. It was hit by a bomb.'

'Was it now? And what's your connection with it?'

'Tusker's Travelling Theatre,' replied Oz defiantly. 'We were to have played the town for a week. We put on two performances – and Jack here played the lead.'

'Now I've heard everything,' Clabber exclaimed. 'Become an actor, have you Walter?'

He turned to Oz.

'And does young Sarah star in this performance?'

'Who's Sarah?'

'Ha! Who's Sarah, indeed! Who's Sarah, eh Walter?'

He leant forward and pushed at Oz's chest with both hands so that the lanky handyman tottered back, almost losing his balance.

'Away with you!' he commanded. 'Find someone else to pester!'

The rain began to spatter on their heads again and, not far distant, thunder rumbled heavily. Oz, with a final rueful glance towards Jack, turned on his heel and walked away, head down. In the silence which followed Jack was sure that he heard the clink of metal tools in the deep pockets, bringing back to him with a searing vividness those many moments in the early days when they had worked together backstage, making and repairing the scenery they took around the villages.

By the strange chemistry of the brain, the single faint sound was instantly translated into a taste, a texture, an indivisible yet inexpressible image which fixed and celebrated a rich complex of experience.

'Oz!' he cried, beginning to run. 'Oz! Don't go!'

43 Dog

The dog – thin, black, little more than an articulated black line – loped behind the silent girl. Its nostrils, still swamped by the smell of scorched brick, sniffed the air that passed around her body. Expecting what solace? Her tears had been liquid silver by the moon, were now opaque silvery pearls in the murky light of emerging day. She was the silver girl.

Dream-like she moved towards the edge of O—, where the town spilled into the sea and the vastness beyond. To the upturned boat and the wharf, where the dog prodded its nose into the sand to disinter the dried bone of a fish. Gulls had stripped it of anything edible. It resembled nothing so much as a stinking comb.

But richer pickings at the market square: a heavier bone, late of a cow, to which shreds of red meat still clung. The dog tore at the firmly anchored flesh. Its darting eyes tracked the girl, who wandered to and fro across the huge open stage that was the deserted square, like an actress robbed of lines. Until she headed for one of the narrow streets that led to the cafe quarter, and then it bounded across and came to heel just as she entered the smoky shadows. Now it was rendered almost invisible save for the two yellow eyes.

Why did she stay here, gazing at the shuttered windows? The dog wove eccentric patterns in the space round her motionless figure. It raised a leg by the cabaret wall. The streets were no longer empty, but a buzz of animated chatter. She moved on and it tagged on after. Now to a ruin open to the sky, where it bounded up the steps behind her. But this was not freshly burned. It was cold and sour to the taste.

Dawn was somewhere behind the dark cloud that hung over O—. She picked her way through the charred remains of the studio. She bent to gather a black fragment. The dog sniffed eagerly at her hand, losing interest when the object offered nothing to quicken its senses.

The rain came later, when it was fully light and they were back at the area where the smell of burning was sharp in the nostrils. The girl sought no shelter, allowing the rain to wash across her face like the silver tears of the previous night.

A long time. The dog nuzzled against her. After the first rain there was a lull and then the noise of thunder and a deluge even heavier, on and on. She had stepped under a broken overhanging wall. The dog lay at her feet, whining, rubbing its snout against her until, at last, it fell asleep.

And later there were more legs, no longer passing but gathered around. They were the smooth perfumed legs of girls. A hand reached down and stroked the dog's head. It looked up eagerly, but it was not the silver girl. She was lying on the ground.

It whined again and pressed itself against the pyjama'd leg – until the green parrot attacked it and, yelping, it found shelter in the narrow recess of the shattered wall.

44 Darkness

Walter guessed that it must be well towards midday. The previous evening an insubstantial meal had been pushed towards him and the lamp had been renewed. It was now almost spent.

He had slept deeply, but not half as deeply as the Count who was, at last, showing signs of regaining consciousness. Walter sat on the couch by his head. The breath had ceased to rasp in his throat, and behind closed lids his eyes began to move.

Outside, there was no sound whatsoever. From time to time he had pressed his ear to the door, but if the girls were in the place they were far quieter than he had known them. The thought that he might escape through the grille was a solace to him, but two things held him back. The first was the fear that once down below he could not easily climb back again and yet might find no way out of the culvert. The second was the feeling that it would be dishonourable to desert the Count who, if he was not certainly an ally, was almost certainly his enemy's enemy.

'It's deuc'd gloomy.'

Low and languid, the voice took him by surprise.

'Positively Stygian.'

Walter bent over the Count, who returned his gaze from beneath hooded lids.

'We're prisoners. I was brought here before you.'

'Ho hum,' replied the Count with what Walter would have taken for jocular insouciance in other circumstances. There followed a luxuriant sigh, as if (as was perhaps the case) the semi-drugged state were a thoroughly pleasant one.

'I'm afraid, dear boy,' he suggested after an interval, 'that it would have been far better had you not spirited yourself away from the theatre in such outlandish haste.'

Walter, who could only guess at what had happened, nevertheless decided to force the issue.

'I thought you meant me harm,' he said.

'Ho decidedly hum, my angel.'

The Count folded his arms across his chest and enjoyed a further brief slumber. When, with a yawn, he awoke he reached out an arm and poked Walter with a bony finger.

'You know about your brother?'

'Yes.'

The eyes closed again. The Count breathed deeply. In his doped condition his speech came even more slurred than normally.

'It was my forlorn hope that you would not come, that it would not be necessary for me to intervene. One does so resist uncalled for complications in life, don't you find? Your brother was invited to one of my – ah – little evenings, but otherwise I acted only to protect him. I had him watched. I sprang him from gaol. I sabotaged . . . ' (here he allowed himself a smile) 'I sabotaged a party at which I thought undesirable people might be brought into close proximity with him. It was to no avail.'

'The fire.'

'The Red Blade, I presume. Not to be underrated. Our present hosts, as I'm sure you are aware.'

The lamp flickered and dimmed.

'But why you, Count? What harm have you done them?'

The reply was a high, quavering laughter which grew in volume and intensity, as if from hysteria, and which volleyed from wall to wall in their confined gaol. As it died away the flame guttered and was extinguished. The blackness was entire.

'I rather regret,' drawled the Count, 'my unpreparedness. I had not imagined that they would take so bold a step. Hubris on my part, I dare hazard. The blind pride of power. An irony there, if you will. The pride of power.

'But to answer your question, my bonny swain – it concerns a place far from here to the east. A city you may know of.'

'I do.'

'Then there is little more I need to add, surely. And I am so very weary.'

Walter heard him turning on the couch. Then a silence followed by gentle snores. He could only wonder at his companion's casualness. People who would seize the most powerful citizen of O— would surely let nothing hamper their designs. His own life was nothing to them. He reached out in the darkness, found a shoulder and shook it.

'And where do you imagine,' asked the Count, as if he were continuing an uninterrupted conversation, 'we might be?'

'We're in a . . . bordello. I don't know where exactly. There's a parrot in a cage and a waiting room with nursery rhymes on the wall, and pictures.'

'Oh, *that* bordello,' replied with Count, with what sounded like an affectionate chuckle. 'Mimi, Salome, sweet Dolores . . . I thought the aroma familiar.'

He continued to make little satisfied noises in his throat and the words 'sweet Dolores' were repeated to the accompaniment of a soft and panting laughter.

'I know a way out of here.'

Walter's interruption had the effect of stemming the flow of appreciative gurglings, but without prompting a direct response.

'It's that vixen Brunhilda,' the Count said in a manner which combined surprise with admiration. 'Never thought of that! Remiss of me to be sure. It is, after all, quite believable. Rum, I grant, but believable. Bruny's the Red Blade agent.'

'I know a way out of here,' Walter repeated.

A hand smacked against his chest.

'Help me up, old fellow, there's a dear.'

The Count struggled into a sitting position and kept hold of Walter's hands, perhaps because he could not keep his balance without them.

'Windows, none,' he said, as if ticking off a list. 'One lamp, but extinguished. A door . . . '

Here he made the supreme effort, pulling himself to his feet, and Walter heard him tottering across the floor and, after a scrabbling interlude, up the short flight of steps. From the ensuing sound it was evident that he had fallen against the door.

' . . . and that solid. Won't open.'

He said it almost with satisfaction.

'I have indeed,' he continued, 'been somewhat puzzled by the geography of this building, but puzzlement offers no solutions . . . Who said that, my love? Sounds a wise remark. Quotable. Puzzlement offers . . . '

'Over here,' broke in Walter, beginning to grope his way in the pressing darkness towards the wall with the grille in it. 'I came once before from down below, where the river runs.'

'A veritable troglodyte,' mused the Count.

'We could drop down there and escape. Or, at least, *I* could. It's rather small.'

'Distinctly disagreeable,' opined his companion. 'I'll take my chances with Brunhilda, if it's all the same with you, dear boy.'

Now he was at the grille, tugging at it, shaking it. But even as it came away he heard a terrible sound. It was the roaring sound of a river in full spate, echoing in its deep chamber. He could not believe the ferocity of it. It churned and swept along and it seemed, moreover, ridiculously close – as close as if the swelling tide should threaten their very prison room.

His worst fears were confirmed when he put his arm though the gap. His hand was immediately dashed with spray and, as he reached down, the foamy rush beat at his elbow.

45 Rescue Party

'Didn't I tell you?' Mr Tusker beamed triumphantly from within a garish pile of salvaged props and costumes. 'Did I not tell you that the boy's a survivor? I did. And he is!'

Jack, Oz and Clabber stood together, hair plastered to their foreheads, water dripping in puddles at their feet. They had first gone to the fishermen's wharf, where Jack had been greatly disturbed to find that the boat – turned right way up and littered with tackle – had clearly not been used by Walter and Sarah the night before. Now, dashing from doorway to awning in the thunderstorm, they had come to the remains of the theatre where, in the part that had been backstage, the members of the troupe were rescuing what they could from the ruin. The roof remained intact here, but squalls of wind brought in random volleys of stinging rain, and all the time there was a heavy and remorseless drumming above their heads.

'Take no notice, I said, of weak-headed old simpletons in clerical garb. The world is overrun with them and they never did a spot of good to a soul.'

The theatre manager stepped forward and took Jack's right hand between both of his and pumped it up and down as if expecting water to gush from the lad's mouth.

'And good day to you, sir,' he went on breezily, his spirits apparently unaffected by the violent turn of events. 'I seem to know the face.'

'Ernest Clabber. Sculptor.'

Luigi, whose head had been swathed in the folds of a tunic he was examining for signs of damage, extricated himself and came forward smartly.

'A great honour,' he said, without any trace of flattery. 'I was admiring your work at the Count's palace. Quite outstanding.'

But Clabber only nodded.

'At least,' Mr Tusker boomed, watching Belle toss a charred crimson gown into a corner, 'you had the luck to be untouched by this bomb-throwing business.'

Ma, constantly on the watch, seized the gown and added it to a large pile of discarded clothing.

'Stone, I imagine, can look after itself.'

Clabber only looked damply mournful and gazed on Jack as if for support.

'Simple-minded clerics,' Jack said urgently. 'What did you mean by that?'

'Oh, an old fool who tried to persuade us that you were in dire danger. A deranged monk. You had been captured, he said, by' – he enunciated the words comically – 'vicious felons. He was gibbering, shaking, rheumy-eyed.'

'And did he say more?'

Mr Tusker turned his back and began to sort through costumes with his leading lady.

'Very little, and that delivered in a feverish manner. Too confused to make a decent script. This one will serve, Belle – once a good wash has taken the smell of burning away.'

'And then?'

'Fortunately,' the impresario continued without pause, 'most of our props are in store. Just imagine if all our own scenery had gone up in smoke!'

He would, doubtless, have rolled on in this vein for some time had not the sculptor taken an arm in his firm grip and spun him round. Mr Tusker seemed at first alarmed, then hurt, finally submissive.

'I saw him off. You can't trust these holy people with their irrational passions. Consumed by the notion of guilt. You'd think they carried the sins of the world on their shoulders.'

'It's important,' Jack explained.

Mr Tusker tried to think.

'He said that you'd be killed by these vicious felons because, I seemed to remember him saying, of an accident of birth. Very strange stuff it was. Some of the others, I'm amused to recalls, were more than half-convinced. Then he told us where you were supposed to be incarcerated – but I really can't recall that detail. The poor fellow was rambling.'

'Please!'

It was Amazing who supplied the information, his face emerging from the fabric leaves of a stage tree that had turned autumnal during the fire.

'A ruined bordello,' he said. 'Blown up last night. That was it. But he didn't give the name.'

He giggled: 'A ruined bordello and a wild priest. I thought how ruined priests and wild bordellos go better together!'

Jack, not knowing where he was going, scarce knowing what he was doing, moved blindly towards the street.

'Must find it!' his own desperate voice sounded in his ears.

The sculptor started to life.

'But I know the place! There was only one bordello bombed last night. It's not far from here.'

Jack felt the strong arm on his shoulders and was aware of the troupe gathering round. If he had ever doubted that they had taken him into their family, those doubts were utterly dispelled now. Ignoring the driving rain, they hurried from the wrecked theatre while Jack, battling with the gusting wind, attempted to explain that he and his brother had come to O—, separately, each ignorant of the other's existence, and that, because of something that had happened far away and long ago, they had fallen into danger.

Had the weather allowed the usual gregariousness on the streets the small group would have caused heads to turn even in flamboyant O—. Such had been their haste to leave that they still had about them bits and pieces of the costumes they had been sorting through and trying on. Mr Tusker, who had left clutching a Roman helmet, pushed it onto his head against the rain. Belle, scurrying behind, was hampered by the flowing robes of ancient Greece. Ma held the chin end of a trailing white beard.

As they approached their destination, Clabber pointed out the girls of the house gathered hopelessly before the remains of their former place of employment. His eyes moved anxiously this way and that. Most of the frontage of the house had gone, and the girls seemed reluctant to do anything but stand in a small huddle outside, like freed circus animals unable to take advantage of their liberty and with no idea of fending for themselves.

'Ha! There she is!'

Jack saw the joy on his face, the tears starting in his eyes. Sarah was among the girls, but on the ground, as if she had been freshly awoken from a deep sleep.

'Ah, my beauty,' stumbled Clabber in a broken voice. 'A face I had feared not to look on again.'

He reached his arms out to her. As he did so, the green parrot – another of the dispossessed – swooped down to attack a thin black dog that lay by her side. The dog yelped and, tail between its legs, sought refuge in a gap in the shattered wall that ran down the side of the building.

46 Confrontation

The air inside the office still swam with dust and smoke, but brother Mark's eyes owed their redness to something else.

'You fool!' Brunhilda was berating him. 'Have those years in the monastery robbed you of your manhood? Look at you – fit to spit on!'

'It's only,' he stammered, 'only . . . '

The desk was piled high with papers which Madam must be clearing out prior to flight. It was impossible to stay here now.

'To let them go might be to our advantage. If we should be apprehended . . . '

'Let them go! Do you think I went to all the effort of capturing them only to unlock the door and wish them on their way? What sort of fool do you take me for?'

'The boy, then . . . '

'Ah, the boy. The darling boy! I could see you going soft on him. And what of the cause, dear Marcus? Were we not taught that for the good of the cause some must die?'

'But an innocent.'

'Yes, innocents too! Or have you forgotten your training?'

She took up a pile of papers and rammed them into a leather case. The rest she swept to the floor.

'We'll burn them,' she said. 'After we've dealt with our last two clients. What a pity they haven't been able to enjoy the luxuries of the house!'

Brother Mark, shaking uncontrollably, leant over the desk.

'I remember our training,' he trembled. 'I never questioned it before, Bruny. I never had to. Even now, I hate myself for what I have done.'

'And what *have* you done?'

'I've told others that the boy is here.'

Madam raised herself to her full, commanding height. She held her heavily ringed fingers in front of her as if she intended to strangle her frail accomplice.

'Told others!'

He backed away, whimpering.

'Well then, my friend, the job had better be done quickly before these others of yours turn up. I'm sure our two strong associates will love to get on with their work.'

She moved towards the door but, pathetically inadequate to the task, he attempted to bar the way. Pressing his hands against the jambs of the door he pushed outwards, his thin old body adopting the pose of Samson in Gaza. His eyes closed and he muttered a terse prayer – and at that moment the dog entered the wall.

47 Above and Below

The dog entered the wall. Terrified of its bright adversary, it raced forward into the confined space of its refuge, dislodging a brick and jarring its shoulder. Just as the slightest pebble careering down a mountainside can cause an avalanche, so the removal of a single brick from an unstable building can bring it to its destruction. The dog's shoulder dislodged the cornerstone of a pillar upon which rested a beam which, in turn, supported the upper floors of the ruined bordello. The result was a spectacular infolding of the building, at first curiously silent, then emitting a thunderous roar, accompanied by an eruption of dust and debris that totally obscured the watchers outside and sent them choking to the far side of the street.

Jack felt his legs so weak as scarcely able to support him. His head throbbed. Clabber groaned, his face in his hands. Who could still be alive beneath that mountain of brick? Mr Tusker, though knowing none of the victims, gave one of his better performances in a distracted, grief-stricken role, actually reducing several of the girls to tears. The dust slowly settled upon the rubble.

Sarah, however, was not with the others. She had detached herself from the group and was pacing back and forth in the middle of the road, a puzzled expression on her face.

Beneath the ground Walter and the Count heard the building's collapse as a deep rumble that shook the walls of their prison. Already the water, splashing through the grille, covered the floor and lapped at their ankles.

'What was that?' Walter wailed, feeling self-control ebb away.

'It rather sounded like the collapse of Bruny's, dear boy. Which is interesting.'

'Interesting?'

'In that, remarkably don't you think, we are not crushed. I suppose you haven't guessed the reason for that?'

'No.'

Walter's brain could not think. He was aware only that they were in utter darkness, that the water rose up his legs and that, in the world outside, there was a chaos which would prevent their rescue.

'I surmise, my sweet, that it's because we're not, in fact, beneath the building. In the past I've often wondered about the length of corridor in these basements. Often needed to lie down when I arrived!'

He chuckled. Walter lifted his feet from the water and lay on the couch.

'Perhaps if we shout?' he asked.

'A little vulgar, I should say, and unlikely to do much good. What do you think?'

Walter, taking the question as a granting of permission, rose on all fours and, straining, began to shout, the sound echoing and re-echoing around the sightless chamber, and even as his own voice came volleying back at him so he filled his lungs and bellowed louder still.

It was Clabber who heard them. He had gone to Sarah's comfort, believing her strange behaviour to be the result of overpowering grief, and there beneath his feet the road itself seemed to cry for help in a thin and distant way. At first he thought it imaginary, an after-effect of the deafening crash. But no: it was louder the more he bent his ear to the ground.

Then he saw the drain and heard that the cries rose from the grating. He pulled it away with his large sculptor's hands, while the others gathered around him. The space was perhaps just large enough to take his frame, but less than three feet down a channel opened to the right and left, and he knew he could not squeeze himself sideways into the opening.

'Down there!' he gasped. 'But we need someone small.'

He eyed Jack, who peered down nervously. The downpour had eased, but water still cascaded along the channel.

'I could try,' he offered.

Oz loomed alongside him.

'He mustn't try it,' he declared protectively. 'He might get round into the pipe there, but he'd never have the strength to hold his head above the water.'

'You and I can't,' replied Clabber obstinately.

'He'd drown himself,' Oz said.

Ma, stalking to the edge of the drain, nodded her head in decisive support.

'Certain death,' she ruled.

The cries continued, indecipherable but unmistakably desperate. Jack was willing himself to volunteer when a figure brushed past him and stopped to investigate the difficulties of the task.

'I can get in there.'

The relief among the onlookers was infectious. They exchanged optimistic smiles and pressed closer to the drain.

'Whether I can follow it along may be another matter,' Amazing continued. 'But I've a few inches breathing space if I brace myself against the sides.'

He was stripping off his outer clothing as he spoke, and seconds later he was lowering himself into the rushing water and twisting himself athletically into the channel. He arched his back, tightened the muscles of his arms and, rocking himself from side to side, disappeared into the darkness.

The others, their hopes entrusted to the absent india-rubber man, shuffled about in silence, averting their eyes from the ruin. The girls, used to deal with men chiefly in the protected opulence of the bordello, seemed ill at ease with them in the unscreened light of day, and silently moved apart.

At last Amazing's voice, drawing closer along the drain, called hollowly for tools to break through brickwork, and Jack – relieved to find an outlet for his tension – was despatched at a fast lick to fetch Clabber's hammer and chisels.

In the end, his voice weak from shouting, Walter fell to silence. The blackness was oppressive, the water at their waists. They waited for death, each preparing for its finality in his own way.

For Walter, the teaching of the brothers flooded back: this world a bridge that we pass over, but account must be given of the passing. And what sort of account could he give? Until his experiences in O— it would have been simple: he would have considered himself one of the blessed, innocent of the world's manipulations. But now? How much had his time in O— changed him? All the old certainties had left him. And yet he felt, somehow, as if here were a more complete person for his doubts. O— had made him a thinker, a questioner. Until O— he had merely stood in the wings, but here he had entered the stage of real life. Was that a thought he could die comforted by?

As for the Count, who can say what passed through his mind as the water rose higher and higher? The game was over. He had made his final move upon the chequered board. The reality that Walter had discovered, he had jettisoned years earlier: would he come fact to face with it again beyond death?

'I should enjoy a good *clean* bath,' he murmured inconsequentially.

And then they heard the tapping, the crumbling of old and damp brick that preceded the sudden glimmer of light, and they saw Amazing's head thrust absurdly into their dank tomb. Walter waded forward, conscious that the Count still had not moved. The hole was enlarged, chunks of masonry plopping into the water. Words were spoken – he did not take in a single one of them – and hands tugged him upwards.

A cramped, a delirious journey into daylight. They stood, their clothes dripping, their eyes blinking. The Count keeled over first, Walter immediately afterwards, coming out of his swoon to find the girls bent over him. Sarah, radiant among the throng, reached out her hand to him and, as he took it, he found himself at the same moment both smiling and bursting uncontrollably into tears.

They were lifted and carried away. As the procession moved off, the black dog nosed after an old peasant woman whose loaded multitude of bags promised all sorts of edible treasure. The air that passed around her body was perfumed differently from that which attended the silver girl, and there was another, pungent aroma from the pipe that she clenched in her teeth.

48 Celebrations

Celestin had a devil-may-care way of removing the chaos which littered his living-space. He had pushed, thrown or (a few precious items) carried his possessions to the corners of the room so that the party might be enjoyed by as many people as possible.

In truth, the celebrations had begun the moment he and Clabber had installed Walter and Sarah in the studio. Walter had been unable to raise himself from the bed, but the wine had begun to flow and more people than he realised he knew had put their heads in at the door to congratulate him on his escape and to rejoice with them all on the end of what Mr Tusker had termed, apparently quoting, 'a dire and unenviable transaction'.

That was yesterday. Today the festivities, though no more formal, were at least intentional. Walter was on his feet once more and as, from midmorning onwards, more and more revellers crammed into the studio he was reminded of that earlier occasion when he and Sarah had prepared for a party that had never been. This time there were no colourful drapes spread over the few figures Clabber had arranged at one end of the studio but, in contrast, there was noise, chatter, laughter, eating, drinking, singing.

'A charade! A charade!'

If the tipsy carousers were playing riotous games at midday, Jack wondered what state they would be in by the evening. There were many faces he did not know – Walter pointed out people from the cabaret and from O—'s bohemian art world – but in this atmosphere he was soon persuaded that he knew them very well indeed. He watched his theatre friends drawn into the merriment: even Ma, though drinking nothing stronger than a fruit punch, had a broad smile across her face.

And then, inevitably it seemed, there were the identity games. Celestin and the red-headed girl (now, to all appearances, blissfully reunited) led Jack and Walter away, dressed them in identical costumes and challenged the revellers to guess which was which. This was highly popular entertainment but was quickly deemed too straightforward. Now they disappeared again, returning singly for a wagering game. Each lad could lie about his identity if he wished, the interrogation eventually teasing out the truth. Meanwhile, large sums of money were changing hands.

'It's got to be Jack, describing scenery like that.'

'I'll put a hundred on it.'

'And what about Jason Bull? Did you ever meet him? What's he like? What sort of figure?'

'Tall,' guessed Walter. 'A powerful presence.'

'Two hundred!'

Although he was enjoying himself in this frolicsome company, Walter suffered moments when a sudden heavy gloom descended upon him. Partly it could be explained by his tiredness and the terror of the dark room and the rising water, but from his reaction to talk about the monastery knew it was also related to his dealings with brother Mark, to the sense of betrayal he felt and the horrible death of his former mentor.

'I'll double that!'

'What's the colour of the seats in our theatre?'

'They're . . . dark.'

'Ha! Dark is all he says! It's Walter!'

'The seats are dark now, my friend. Burnt to charcoal.'

'A thousand that it's Walter!'

With this sport at last over, and a series of recitations having begun, the two lads retired to a corner to take refreshment. They had scarcely slaked their thirst, however, when a familiar figure sidled up to them, travelling in a cloud of delicate perfume.

'My esteemed gentlemen,' purred the Count's man. 'I wonder if I might draw you away for a moment.'

He spoke in a low voice, with furtive glances to all sides as if not wishing to be noticed.

'My master regrets that he cannot be here, but he is most anxious that you join him at the palace for a short while. I have a carriage at hand.'

'With Sarah?' Walter asked.

'On this occasion, no. That is, if you will not mind. Only a brief interlude, you understand, but something only for the two of you.'

They exchanged glances.

'Very well,' said Jack. 'If it's important.'

'Oh, it is indeed.'

As they turned to go, Walter waved to Sarah who was separated from him by a jostling crowd. Knowing that he could not struggle through it, he made quick, deft movements with his fingers, using the language that he had learned from her to tell her where they were going. She nodded happily.

Jack and the Count's man were already outside, and he hurried after them. As they climbed into the carriage they heard the cacophony inside the studio subside and then Celestin's voice raised in an eloquent tribute to the people of O—, people (his lines said) in love with beauty and sensuous ease:

'their luminous visions,
dreams without words;
their gossamer dazzle –
a flight of bright birds . . . '

49 Signatures

Now that the stormy weather had completely passed away, the humid air of O— was heavy with the fragrance of the brilliant shrubs which trailed their scented blossoms over every archway, along every wall, across every shaded patio. The sky burned blue behind an overhanging ornamental tree as the carriage swept through the palace gates and up the drive. There was no breeze to stir the leaves. Furry bees droned about the open windows and sank, drowsy, into the gaping bells of vivid crimson and gold flowers, while the perfumed draughts on which they hung seemed to lull the brain to sleep. Large butterflies clumsily laboured through the dense atmosphere. A horse with padded hooves pulled a mowing machine, the dancing emerald spray suffusing the heady bouquet with the sweetness of cut grass.

They passed the Count by an abundant parterre, where he stood stooped in earnest conversation with a grizzle-haired elderly man sporting a suit of clothes as elegantly matched (violets, plums, muted yellows) as the blooms in the bed. Although the carriage drew up by the porticoed entrance, the two lads were led round the side of the building and through a less imposing door half-smothered by entwining honeysuckle. A short, white-painted corridor led to a flight of stairs down. At the foot there was another door, and then they found themselves in a large and luxurious room, richly carpeted and lit from windows set high in one wall. In a corner a narrow archway offered the glimpse of a passage beyond.

'If you would wait,' breathed the powdered gentleman, giving a light bow and retreating up the stairs.

The room was designed for cultivated ease: the eye could scarce take in the scattered ornaments, the objects for instruction and recreation. The walls were hung with rich oil paintings. Leatherbound volumes filled large bookcases to bursting. There was a chunky jade chess set – the pieces in play – on a low table of burnished mahogany; a globe atlas several feet in diameter; a gleaming orrery with its planets checked in their procession round the sun; a majestic pendulum clock on a marble plinth; a handsome roulette table of lustrous ebony; an oriental bubble-pipe fashioned in silver; a glass case displaying elephant tusks fantastically carved . . .

They were slowly wandering among these treasures when a sudden musical tinkling sang in their ears, filling the chamber with a volley of liquid notes and energetic trills. This was no human invention (though the mind could readily conceive of such a mechanical contrivance here) but the song of a beautiful bird encaged in bars of dull gold which its own plumage put to shame. Walter stood before it, wonderingly.

'Poor goldfinch,' he murmured. 'What do you find to sing about in this small prison?'

The bird cocked its head of black and white and crimson and it chirped and sang so insistently that Walter, remembering his own recent confinement, felt tears of sympathy start in his eyes.

'How you must long to fly out in the warm summer air.'

'I don't suppose it would thank you for its freedom,' Jack countered casually. 'It's better fed than in the wild. There are no hawks to take it here. It's better off by far in its cage.'

They passed beneath an archway and into the passage. It was but feebly lit. Two small bedrooms opened on to it, each simply furnished but comfortable and apparently in a state of preparedness. Further along there was a washroom and then a blank wall. There were no windows here. They returned to the large room with its manifold glories.

'My dear young things!'

The Count came in at the door, smiling a greeting. He was more soberly dressed than usual, in a suit of dark velvet, but on his arm, wearing a garish waistcoat of green and orange which its master might have envied was a bright-eyed capuchin monkey.

'I wished to congratulate you.'

He noticed the disturbed fascination with which Walter in particular gazed on the creature which clung to his sleeve, showing its teeth and working its jaws, but without making any sound whatsoever.

'You like my Mercury?' he asked, scratching the top of its head. 'The Count's monkey. A bad omen. Or that's what people like to believe.'

'I think they fear it,' Walter said quietly. 'Isn't it sent as a warning?'

'Oh, sweet fancy!' the Count laughed, fetching a peanut from his pocket and holding it at a distance so that the monkey had to stretch and scrabble for it. 'My little pet? And would a bright boy like you believe such nonsense?'

'I don't know.'

The Count sprawled into a leather armchair and perched the animal on his head. It leapt nimbly on to the back of the chair and cracked the nut between its teeth.

'Sometimes he escapes, my winged messenger, and he appears in the town. How should I know where he goes or why? But superstition – it's a relic of the past.'

He watched the two boys with an amused expression. They were still dressed in their identical costumes from the party, and he looked from one to the other as if to tease out any minute differences in their features.

'To congratulate you and to thank you,' he said, picking up his first topic. 'First to thank for his good company whichever of you endured that dungeon, and then to thank his brother for alerting the populace with such alacrity. I appreciate that you acted from common humanity and would flinch from something as vulgar as a reward. Nevertheless, I should like to offer you a gift.'

They shook their heads as the same instant.

'Quite so. Admirable! But perhaps if it were a gift entailing an obligation? I shall allow the thought to settle on your minds.'

He lolled towards the roulette table and set the wheel in spin. They heard the ball clattering on its contrariwise journey. 'Black,' they heard him murmur. Then – after he had spun the wheel again – 'red'. He made a disconsolate clicking with tongue and teeth.

'You knew we were coming to O—?' Walter asked, impatient to understand. 'You had us watched.'

'Ah yes, I knew. Long ago. Red!'

The metal ball raced around the scattered numbers, finding a new lodging place before the wheel had finished turning. The Count, muttering to himself, returned reluctantly to his chair, gesturing the boys on to a small leather sofa close by.

'I knew that you were destined to arrive here. Indeed, I knew – or thought I knew – exactly where you would meet. But that was all. Unlike the Red Blade I had no idea that one of you lived in a monastery. They had the advantage there.'

'And the missing house?' Walter persisted. 'Number 46. How did you know to watch there?'

'Ah!'

The restless Mercury having landed in his lap, he took it in both hands and tossed it towards a pile of damasked cushions in a corner.

'The story of my life is rather long to be told at this juncture, and doubtless more fascinating to me than to you. Don't we enjoy our own personal histories and dramas! You will have gathered that I have rather a lot of money and possessions. A ridiculous amount. I am, without question, filthily rich!

'My father was, not to beat about the bush, a tyrant. The genuine kind. Brutal, selfish, totally in control of everything, everyone, everyone's very soul. I scarcely exaggerate. He was universally feared, widely loathed. Our home life was cold. My mother he ignored. Materially, of course, she was well provided for, but he sought his solace elsewhere.

'As a child I could not approach him. I cowered in his shadow. And therefore he regarded me as unworthy, unmanly. I was weak. I was effeminate. I was artistic . . . It was simply bad luck for him that I was all he had.'

The Count evidently regarded this as the supreme irony, for he laughed long and loud with a touch of the hysteria Walter had witnessed once before.

'As a tyrant he had no time for liberal tendencies of any kind. How should he? They were a threat to him. By the time I reached young manhood and began to take an interest in such things – and found myself opposed to my father in every possible way – he had taken violent measures to repress any expression of free opinion. Public hangings. Mutilations. And since those who held such views were known to congregate in one part of the town, he simply had the whole area devastated. Pulled down inside a few days. Reduced to utter rubble.'

'By the fairground!' Walter exclaimed.

'The phoenix from the ashes, dear chuck. How I love fairgrounds! That was the place. And he had all but finished the destruction when, without any warning, he dropped down dead. One day wielding the sword, so to speak – in fact, literally wielding it – the next flat in his coffin. Everything came to a standstill then.

'Later I learned that those who conspired for freedom also supported the honest folk in that city of your father's. And because I sided with them, because all my adult life I have sought to further the cause of revolutionary freedom, I became party to certain confidences – and learned something of your destiny.'

'And yet,' said Walter, perplexed, 'you told me you had hoped we should not meet.'

'Ho hum,' reflected the Count, shaking his head. 'What we will say in extremity! A complicated matter, my pixie. Let us not labour the point. Let us talk about yourselves. What do you intend to do now that the crisis is past? I should be fascinated to know.'

They sat in silence for a while. They had exchanged no confidences about the matter. Neither, in fact, had thought it through.

'For myself,' said Jack after a while, 'if you had asked me the question several months ago I would have travelled east without a single regret. I like travelling. I like things to be different, exciting. But now that I've found friends at the theatre the decision isn't quite so easy to make.'

The Count nodded.

'And rightly,' he said warmly. 'What can it profit anyone for you to involve yourself in affairs you know nothing of?'

Jack could scarcely believe what he heard.

'You'd advise us not to go?'

'I would. I do.'

'Even though our father wished it?'

At this the Count merely shrugged.

'But that's something we can't simply ignore,' Jack said hotly. 'He wanted us to . . . help.'

'Out of the question!' came the brusque interruption. 'Help a city at war with itself merely through a line of descent? You think that at all likely?'

'*I* do,' rejoined Walter firmly. 'Our father left us a letter. There are many who would welcome us.'

'And many who would wish you harm. You have evidence of that from your short time in O—, my bonnie.'

'Exactly so. It's a dangerous place, but it's dangerous precisely because of that line of descent. I'm afraid I don't understand why you wish us not to journey there. If you were a supporter of our father.'

The Count, perhaps surprised by so reasonably obstinate a challenge, made no immediate reply. He closed his eyes and touched the tips of his long fingers together, as if in meditation. The bird began to sing again, a rich and lively carolling.

'If I were to tell you,' said the Count slowly, 'that your father was no longer in that city . . . '

'It is what we imagined,' replied Walter.

'We assumed that he was dead,' Jack agreed, 'because he wasn't there to meet us.'

'No. That is not the case. Your father is alive, but he is not in the city and he will never return there.'

They were unable to speak. He read the agitated anguish, hope and disbelief on their faces.

'I can prove this. If you were to journey to the city you would not find your father there. Does that not alter your perspectives?'

There was that in his manner which suggested that he pleaded with them, as if there were something painful to him in the thought that they should heed their father's request.

'Where is he?' demanded Jack.

The Count only wagged his finger.

'Not yet, my mannikin. Not yet. I ask you, does that not alter your thoughts on the matter?'

'Alive!' came the late echo from Walter's lips.

'It's strange,' Jack replied. 'It's wonderful, if he's alive. But there is the letter and what he asked of us.'

'Act nobly,' Walter quoted. 'I ask only that you act nobly. It wasn't for him or for ourselves that he wished us to go there, but as a duty for the good of others.'

'Good! You imagine the result will be beneficial? Folly upon folly! You'll bring ruin on them all!'

The Count, finding that he had, feverishly, declared his hand, stood up and drifted about the room, occasionally pausing to inspect one of the curios.

'Your father, my princelings, is a fine man. Himself noble. Unfortunately he is revered by the people. And in their devotion lie the bitter seeds of dictatorship – of an autocracy, if you will, like my father's.

'My own grandfather was a benevolent man. Ruthless where money was concerned, maybe, but decent in most of his dealings with men. He was human. But the people gave him godly robes and my father was the consequence.

'Of course, I don't say that you yourselves would be tyrants. There is no exact time-scale in these affairs. But you would revive the longing for leadership, for the smack of firm government. There is a prophecy in that city which many believe, and would readily believe referred to you – "mastery shall be restored to the virtuous and the sons of the virtuous and the city will be ruled as in former times". You would encourage the sheepishness in men, the follow-my-leader instinct.'

Now his voice rose stridently.

'That's an instinct of the past!'

He was at the roulette wheel again, but now he would not allow it to stop, whirring it into motion each time it began to slow.

'The future,' he breathed in a hoarse bespittled whisper, 'lies with our free spirits!'

And round and round rattled the silver ball, like the future itself in a perpetual state of near arrival yet always propelled further and further on.

'Free spirits,' challenged Jack, already afraid of his own temerity, 'like those . . . anarchists?'

'Ha! The vanguard, my friend. The breakers-open of prisons, the awakeners of dull conscience. How can a man not be stirred by them – even when they bring their eruptions here. Here! To O—, where there are freedoms you won't find anywhere else! Haven't you discovered that it's so? Come: tell me! Aren't the people here free?'

'In some ways free,' Walter replied thoughtfully. 'And yet some are wealthy while others beg on the streets.'

'Beggars, a few, yes,' the Count conceded. 'I don't deny beggars. Do you think I can work miracles within a few years? You don't know what I have achieved here. Modernisations. Some electricity. The trams for the people. Fancies without number! But freedom is what we were talking of, my young lawyer. A man's freedom to think as he likes and to live his own life unfettered by governments.'

'And police?' questioned Jack, tartly.

'Oh, you argue well! What fine disputants! Yes, the police we shall do away with, too, once we have progressed a little further. Give us time!'

He turned from the roulette table, trembling, his face towards them but his eyes far away. The foppishness had dropped from him entirely. He was transported.

'This twentieth century . . . ' he panted, as if in a trance. 'We stand on the threshold of a new age when men shall put away their struggles and their hatreds, their continual striving to do one another down. The time is passing when one man shall dominate another. In the society which we shall create each man will regard his neighbour as his brother. All will share equally what all equally have created. I see a century when evil is blown away, governments wither away . . . '

There were tears in his eyes as he spoke. When he had finished he remained gazing into eternity, quite oblivious of his companions. Only slowly did he return to the humble present, looking upon them as if they had suddenly materialised in front of him out of the air.

'And you won't renounce?' he asked truculently. 'You won't give up this dangerous quest?'

They shook their heads awkwardly. Their father's letter constrained them. They had made no decision and yet could not simply renounce. Whatever doubts they had entertained, they felt themselves bound. The Count approached the chess set, squatting on a satin pouffe to study the pieces.

'See here, my amorosos. Come closer. Which would you say held the advantage? The white, wouldn't you agree? A distinct superiority. You play the game?'

'A little,' both said at once.

'Then you shall be white – or, at least, the paler shade of green. And I shall allow, with an egregious generosity, that the move is yours. How will you attack?'

His rapid changes of mood were unsettling. He was alternately playful and severe; confiding and distant. They took it in turns to move the heavy jade pieces while the Count kept up an energetic commentary.

'Apparently wise. Who would not have counselled such a move? And yet, is it not based upon a miscalculation? What do you say? Note the castle on this square, the bishop on that. But no, no, there is no obvious criticism to be made surely. Only, if I advance my pawn here . . . '

It seemed for a while merely talk, empty babble, as their forces positioned themselves around his king. Gradually, however, it became clear that he had devised an adroit strategy which allowed them this appearance of being in command.

'The knight, you see. He is cunning, is he not? But a moment ago he seemed to be riding off into the distance, no stomach for the battle, yet here he is, lance held at the ready . . . '

He put their king in check, neatly extricated himself from a desperate counter-measure and immediately moved to mate. As he leant back, chuckling contentedly, the monkey sprang on to his shoulder and nibbled at his ear.

'A lesson in deception, my dears. A reminder that we may be at our weakest when we most think ourselves strong. Isn't that so?'

He rose, sauntered to the door, produced a large key, turned it in the lock and returned it to his pocket, which he patted theatrically.

'And now,' he said, 'we shall talk business.'

He held his waistcoated pet up to the birdcage and watched the goldfinch drop from its perch, making harsh sounds of alarm.

'Your father has been held prisoner for some time. Yesterday he was released. Perhaps you saw me talking with a gentleman when you arrived. That man's name is Porlock. He knows your father very well, as a friend. Your father is at this moment travelling to the west and will never return to that city we have spoken of. Nor will he ever visit O—. In effect, he has disappeared.'

'I don't believe it,' Jack said. 'Why should he do that?'

'Under certain pressures, my infant. Believing that, if he failed to comply . . . '

Walter understood at once.

'That we should be killed! You have threatened him with our deaths! You make fine speeches about freedom when you are prepared to murder!'

But the Count waved him down, a shifting smile on his lips.

'No, no, you do me a considerable injustice. I quite shudder at your imputation. You are safe, I swear, with me. Do you think I have bloodstained hands? Look – artist's fingers. Could I not have had you stifled long ago?

'Not violence, but deception. Your father believed himself taken by the Red Blade. Of them he could imagine anything. Had he known that Porlock was involved, that I was involved . . . well, deception was necessary. Once he was convinced that you were in enemy hands – and how obliging of you to sport such colourful distinguishing marks, the best kind of evidence! – he signed his authority away without further question. To save your innocent and tender lives. Does that not lift your spirits?

'To go and never return. That is the commitment. To sever all ties with that city. To allow the people their full freedom, so that they shall no longer look up to a glorious leader, a hero-saint.

'And indeed, your father *is* something like a saint. I honour him myself. He has visited that underground city which no one shall ever again find – that city frozen in goodness. He has witnessed those glories. Would that I could have discovered that place myself!'

With this lamentation he fell once more into the leather armchair. He found another nut in his pocket and tossed it across the carpet for the monkey to chase.

'The future, however, lies not with saints but with the liberated common man.'

'What of us?' Jack asked. 'You've locked the door.'

'And shall lock it again when I leave, my love, unless you contrive to see eye to eye with me. I do apologise in advance. It's not really a great deal that I ask of you, and I am prepared to make a substantial payment to you – the gift I spoke of, as thanks for my deliverance.'

'But you can't keep us prisoners here,' Jack began to shout. 'Below ground, with hardly any daylight.'

'Oh pooh-pooh! I offer you luxury accommodation for which I charge nothing at all. You'll eat better here than you would outside. You're safe from the cruel world's vicissitudes. Look on the bright side of things, do.'

'Explain what it is you want,' Walter said. 'A promise not to visit the city?'

'A little more than that, cherub, but only a little. You each sign a document, thoughtfully prepared in advance, forswearing any claim to leadership in that city now or at any time in the future. You are then taken late at night many miles westwards, to the very border of the country. You are spirited across that border. Farewell. Finito.'

He whinnied with pleasure, closed his eyes and lay back, content.

'This seems very trusting,' Walter replied. 'What can stop us returning? Who can prevent us or our father visiting that city?'

'Ah, a cynical view. Surprising in one so young. You think a vow easy to break?'

'Well . . . '

'You hesitate. You are your father's son. He is a man of honour and he will never return. I *know* it. I suspect that you will act likewise once your signatures are on that document. But at the very least there will be evidence against you in your own hands – vital evidence in a city which positively reveres the legalistic. Believe me, the times of strong, supernatural leaders are passing. We are witnessing the twilight of the gods . . . '

Walter thought of a ride through the dark countryside, Sarah left behind, perhaps lost to him for ever. He thought of a duty unfulfilled. Jack imagined the city and, beyond it, a small village where a family told tales of a vanished poet and the son who followed after him, nevermore heard of.

'If I were leading a Red Blade faction I should, of course, have you killed at once. You have not fallen into such hands. You have fallen, although in the circumstances you may be forgiven for doubting it, into the hands of friends. I genuinely wish you well.'

In the silence which followed a strange, magical thing happened. Jack and Walter, their thoughts concentrated by their predicament, found their minds fused into one. Was it a form of magnetism? Each felt it as a physical sensation. Each retained the power to think, but it had become a shared power. They thought the same; they knew together what they would do.

'We accept,' the said in unison.

The Count sprang from his chair with an unsuspected agility and took the two boys in a rough embrace.

'Ineffable moment! We shall celebrate. A bottle of something long-kept. Ineffable! A toast to our glorious twentieth century.'

He strode to a desk on which stood a wooden tantalus. He withdrew a cut-glass decanter, found three small goblets and filled them with a bronze-colour liquid.

'To the future!' he declared, as they tipped the drinks to their lips. 'To your future and mine, but most of all to that of the free spirit. May it rise up and rule!'

He slid a drawer open, took out two sheets of finely lettered paper and lay them on the flat surface. He brought out two pens and uncovered an ink-well sunk into the wood.

'Two copies,' he beamed, 'so that I may watch you sign at the same instant. A natural precaution, you will agree. But no hurry. Savour your drinks! Mine has a most pleasant taste. And yours?'

They put down their glasses and approached the desk. Each took up a pen. Each read the undertaking not to visit the city and never to show an interest in the governing thereof; the declaration that the city should be administered by the people for the people; the finely worded coda with its faith in the new world order soon to come into being.

'When you like,' sang the Count.

Each dipped and wrote, each knowing that as he signed his brother's name and so invalidated the document, unharnessing the future, the other was doing the same. And as the signatures crossed the pages (Jack's perhaps rather elaborate for a boy taught in the city schools, Walter's somewhat sketchy for one monastery trained) the Count, that cunning black knight, triumphantly smiled and smiled.

Shadows in Crimson Colours

PART ONE

Innocence

1 Easy Money

Up and along the thick drapes of the curtains sprang the escaped marmoset to shouts of surprise and encouragement from men who had sat long and leaden over their drinks, while the heavy rolling swell of the street organ faltered and the music slithered and died.

'The devil's loose!'

They banged on the tables as the manic creature, absurd in a scarlet waistcoat, a tasselled cap dislodged over one eye, picked at its head with the free hand, sucked greedily at the fingers, chattered and shrieked at the world below.

The poor organ grinder, a squat and swarthy fellow dressed in a matching scarlet costume, equally absurd now that he moved away from his hurdy-gurdy, gazed on the cleanly severed leather strap with incomprehension and advanced through the smoky club atmosphere, his arms raised in supplication.

'Fatima! Come, my Fatima!'

At this the foaming commotion quite boiled over.

'Ah, Fatima!' they echoed. 'Sweet Fatima! Come, my Fatima!'

'Return to the harem!'

'Come to Mahomet, my little one!'

Two employees of the place, themselves distinguished by uniforms of faded bottle-green, ran forward with an air of dutiful helplessness. One of them grasped a long brass window pole and began to wave it at the nimble fugitive.

'Come, Fatima. Come to your master.'

It grimaced at them, mocking the signs of jaded pomp its fierce bright eyes alighted on. The gilding had flaked patchily from the ceiling bosses and from the neo-classical pilasters; once-expensive flock-paper sagged wispily on the walls; the heavy armchairs were cracked and scuffed where once they had been a shining bronze. The men who sat in these chairs now perched forward, eyes raised, gesticulating and crying advice to the monkey's pursuers.

'Crack it one with the pole!'

'Here, use a bottle! Chuck a bottle at it!'

'See, it's swung away. Have the curtain down!'

Picking his way among them was a lad of about sixteen, selling tickets, who pressed on with his business seemingly oblivious of the furore. Each man he approached appeared to draw himself away from the tumult and to lean confidentially close before digging deep into his pockets.

The little monkey, agitated by the noise and the movement, retreated to the highest point and jabbered in a high-pitched voice at the fools below. When the pole swayed almost within reach, it pulled the cap from its head and dropped it neatly on the top so that the audience howled even louder.

'Bravo! Good shot!'

The second employee had fetched a ladder which he began to climb at a purposeful sprint, but as it was a yard too short the outcome was inevitable. He raised himself up on a rung as near the top as he dared and stretched out an arm while the marmoset spat squeaky obscenities at him. When the creature, using the folds of the curtain, suddenly swooped overhead his startled adversary almost overbalanced, his hands and arms a pantomime of panic until he managed to grasp the top of the ladder and, shaking, began to descend. The storm of laughter and cheering revealed that sympathy was now with the resourceful Fatima.

'What is it . . . exactly . . . that you are offering?' a heavily-jowled man whispered to the lad with the tickets. 'A little showing . . . '

'No, no, much more than a *little*,' the salesman smirked conspiratorially. 'A complete display. With participation if you should require.'

'Ah, with participation. So!'

'By negotiation. You see how they prepare.'

He nodded to where, beyond the clamour of those engaged in the chase, there was a small stage set back against the wall, masked all round by a railed curtain to a height of about six feet. The material shook from some hidden activity, and then a hand appeared and a lacy garment was hung tantalisingly over the rail.

'Participation,' the man repeated breathlessly.

'But it's after hours. You'll want a ticket to stay on.'

'Ticket, yes. How much?'

He fetched out the cash and handed it over, scarcely taking his eyes from the trembling curtain. The vendor moved on, and was at once assailed in a nasal sing-song by the single occupant of the next table, a man whose red and bloated face was topped by a carpet of close-cropped grey hair.

'Oh, you're a treasure, my Johnny! What a bright one you are, and that's no lie!'

'I don't need your lip,' the youth retorted quickly, noting the empty bottles grouped in one corner of the table.

'A true genius, and he knows that I mean it. Don't you, Johnny? Don't I admire your animal cunning?'

'I'd rather you watched the door.'

'Right in my line of sight, it is. Don't worry about the door. Or the proprietor. I've despatched him on a fool's errand. Or the waiters, who think our Sophie's meant for them. They'll be no trouble as long as you're quick about it.'

'Ten minutes and we're away.'

'A master, he is, at so tender an age! Did I tell you Mr Farg wants to see you when we're back in the city?'

The young man, who had begun to move away, swivelled rapidly when he heard this.

'You swine, Otto. You know you didn't.'

'Another admirer, I shouldn't wonder. Such deftness! So swift with the knife I never saw a thing!'

'But you don't tell me until now about Mr Farg.'

'For fear of spoiling your concentration, Johnny. What are we without concentration?'

A new tactic was being tried in the monkey-hunt. The organ grinder, at last persuading the hotheads that hysterical pursuit was counter-productive, scattered a handful of nuts on the floor and began to address his pet in noises never before heard from the lips of man. This was sufficient to rekindle the rumbustiousness of the onlookers, who made tortured sounds of their own and roared with pleasure as one of their number flung cashews at the discomfited marmoset, which tried in vain to catch them.

'No, please,' the organ grinder could be heard to intercede, in a thick accent. 'Love and understanding . . . '

The infectious merriment had dragged the sport on far longer than it was worth, and now the clientele became increasingly aware of the activity behind the low curtain. The laughter gave way to grunts and growls and low mutterings. As each man bought his ticket he forgot about the monkey and fixed his eyes on a performance which was the more suggestive for being hidden, unstated, imprecise. A slender and naked leg emerged from the folds of material, held itself poised in mid air for some seconds and was withdrawn.

'Here, my boy!'

He was tugged towards a whey-faced old gentleman whose tongue lolled uncontrolled from a fleshy mouth. Abandoned on a greasy plate were shreds of pickled cabbage and half a boiled sausage. A mug of beer stood in a glassy puddle.

'Give us a bit extra, can you?' he demanded softly, slobbering. 'Something different?'

'How different?'

The immediate reply was a frail hand which reached out and squeezed the young man's arm, not letting it go.

'You're a naughty boy, I shouldn't wonder. Not quite as good as you should be, eh? I can tell that. But too dark. I like a blond head. That becomes a lad.'

'I can provide what you want. But you'll have to pay double.'

'That's very good. Very good.'

Reluctantly, he released his grip and produced a plump purse. He counted out the money, adding an extra note at the end and winking.

'Blue eyes,' he hissed wetly. 'Make sure of that.'

The marmoset, ignored for some minutes, had decided to take advantage of the bait liberally sprinkled on the ground. It cracked the nuts loudly in its teeth, spitting out the shells. The organ grinder sidled closer, making his monkey noises. Perhaps he was over-eager and approached too rapidly, for his quarry leapt away at the last moment, enjoying its freedom. The chase was on afresh. The bottle-green uniforms felt obliged to scamper in pursuit all over again. This time, however, the little creature took a different route. It sprang between the nearest tables, to the hand-flapping consternation of their occupants, then sped towards the stage. With one elastic bound it reached the top of the curtain and, to utter pandemonium, disappeared.

'Johnny!'

He heard the cry of alarm over the din. A tall, expensively-dressed man had burst into the room and was marching forward with an evil expression on his face.

'He's come back!'

'Don't panic, Otto.'

He dashed past his still-seated confederate and seized the fuming proprietor by the sleeve.

'Thank God you've arrived, sir. It's the police.'

'Who the devil are you?'

'They're in the office. They say there are irregularities. They're ransacking the files.'

'The police! Heaven help us!'

Without pausing to reflect, he hurried distractedly away, muttering to himself.

Johnny and Otto, reaching the street door in seconds, turned to take in the scene. Several men were on their feet and edging closer to the stage. There were loud cries, many of them of a coarse nature. The two employees of the club, unable to control their prurient curiosity, tugged back the curtains.

The marmoset sat on a small table before an open window, a black silk stocking wound around its neck, a silver garter perched on its head like a coronet.

2 Strangers

The waggoner lifted his eyes to watch the flight of birds, their bright and easy progress to the south so much in contrast with his own lumbering movement in the opposite direction.

'That's the end of summer, I reckon.'

His words were addressed to a passenger crouched among the sacks on the back of his cart and so closely wrapped in an old-fashioned black cloak that one might have imagined it already the middle of winter. The cloak fluttered and folded. It settled. The waggoner, shrugging, resumed a tuneless whistling that was the near constant accompaniment to his horse's labours.

The track was deeply rutted, and weeks of dry weather had turned its uneven surface to stone, causing the vehicle to shudder and rock so violently that it seemed in danger of being rent apart. With each jolt he rolled easily about, his body accustomed to the punishment and as resilient as the waggon itself. But from behind there were fierce and strange mutterings which he could only assume to be curses: his passenger was a foreigner, a stranger to whom he had offered a lift in the vain hope of companionship.

'What we need is a bit of rain,' he tried again. 'Soften this road.'

Did some benevolent spirit hear the words? Even as he spoke, the first drops began to fall. He looked up once more, this time to discover a ragged black cloud directly overhead, outrider to a dense storm that would later follow. As it was, this first instalment was enough to drench them thoroughly and allow the autumn chill to penetrate their bones.

'Not far now,' he went on philosophically. 'Over the next hill and you'll see it.'

A shuddering of the cloak. The foreigner was withdrawn, immune from human contact, unapproachable. The cloak squatted in the back like an incubus. It had a terrible weight.

'There, civilisation!' announced the waggoner as they reached the high point and he saw in the distance the city that was their destination. It sprawled greyly across the landscape like a cancer. Above it hung a pall of smoke, and through the smoke flew an aeroplane that buzzed like a giant insect. This sound was immediately augmented by that of the waggoner's throat gathering phlegm, which he spat theatrically onto the track.

'Damned machines will bring us no good, you see. It's not natural, not right. They'll go upsetting everything, you mark my words.'

With this, he lapsed into a sullen silence matching that of his companion, a silence he did not break until they reached the smooth surface of the road that led into the city. Motor cars passed them in either direction, one speeding by so close that it startled the horse and earned a shake of his fist. The countryside by stages gave way to urban sprawl. The road became cobbles, once more jolting the waggon, but this time less violently.

'Not much of an entry for a gent like yourself, eh? Know where you want to go, do you? It's a big place.'

A black silence. No matter: he would simply deposit the cloak where he unloaded his sacks. He had asked for nothing, would doubtless receive nothing but had, by the same token, lost nothing. He felt the glow of a charitable man. They jogged on until, at last, he commanded the horse to a halt outside a large factory, a processor of foodstuffs which would render his produce unrecognisable and sell it at inflated prices.

'This is journey's end, my friend.'

But, turning round, he discovered that his words had been spoken to the air. There was no cloak, no stranger. Closer examination revealed one of the sacks split open, allowing apples to roll loose upon the wooden floor. He found two cores freshly stripped of their flesh.

'Foreigners!' he scowled, and again his throat summoned up an eloquent expression of his feelings at being so unjustly served.

Beyond the port-hole of the aeroplane the churning clouds loosening their burden of rain could be viewed with comfort, as one might regard the cold and alien world of fish through the glass of an aquarium, and Larooning puffed contentedly on his cigar between delicate sips of fine claret. Beneath them the countryside lay spread out, its pattern established throughout the centuries but only now seen for the first time by the common man.

Did the common man ever ascend in a balloon, Larooning wondered, and could Larooning ever be considered common? An unintentional smile crossed his lips at the thought, and as it did so an unfortunate bird flew into one of the propellers, spilling its brief life into the turbulent air. The hash of blood and feathers that rushed against the glass startled Larooning, so that the drink tipped into his lap. This incident, so minor, darkened his mood. The importance of his mission reinforced itself. He was once again the sombre man of destiny.

Looking into the distance, following the course of the wide road below, he fancied that he saw the city. The aerodrome's neatly ordered green rectangle was now clear to the eye, and instructions were being given in preparation for the landing. The stewardess hovered at his elbow. Larooning finished what remained of his claret, took one final, loving puff upon his cigar and settled back in the hope of a smooth landing.

Grim the place where the black cloak had journeyed. The accumulated slime of decades carpeted the stones of the courtyard, and each surrounding wall rose sheer – grey brick cliffs festooned with hung washing that was only slightly less grey. Through a dark and narrow arch. Open doorways led to stairs on all sides, and each doorway had beside it a roughly painted pattern of numbers. Inside, the stairwell held a stench that mingled urine with boiled cabbage. Up rose the black cloak, spiralling up the stairs to hover outside room 27. A knock that echoed. A voice gruff and suspicious: 'Say the words'.

'There is only corruption beneath the surface.'

The door opened, and closed. The garment was flung aside to reveal a tall and handsome young man whose pale complexion framed ice-blue eyes and scarlet lips, these parting in a huge and malevolent grin directed at his host. This older man, more coarse in dress and demeanour, returned an expression of guarded hostility: 'I didn't expect you yet.'

'A little cheer, in God's name!' came the reply. 'We're brothers, you and I, fixed in a common purpose. Isn't that so?'

The stranger slapped the other's arm heartily, but there was mockery in his voice and the gesture was a calculated declaration of power.

The silver tray placed before him held a stunning pyramid of cakes and pastries, but which to take? Larooning held the pastry fork, poised to indicate his choice, and the waiter stood patiently with his tongs ready to deliver that choice upon Larooning's plate. He chose one from the base of the pyramid and saw it deftly removed without visiting disaster upon the rest. So easy to remove one, barely noticeable as the waiter moved the tray away, and yet it had seemed impossible that it should be so.

Larooning toyed with the pastry, a confection chiefly composed of fresh cream and glacé fruits. Clumsily he prised a cherry from the side. Ah, he lacked the waiter's skill! Nevertheless, he reflected, skills could be acquired, and not only by waiters. He tackled the pastry with a newly-discovered enthusiasm.

'My bill!' he called after a while. Was this the correct idiom? It was not an easy language to master. 'And will you have coffee sent up to my room?'

The waiter gave a slight bow and held the glass door wide for his exit. Larooning, preoccupied with his destiny, walked into a potted palm tree as he crossed the foyer to the lift and completed the journey limping, to be helped into the cage by a uniformed boy.

'Room, sir?'

'A stupid place to put a tree.'

'Very stupid, sir. Room, sir?'

'Twenty seven. I think I may have broken my leg.'

'There is a doctor, sir.' (These last words as he slid the wrought iron door into place and pressed the button). 'Second floor.'

His broken leg served Larooning well enough to take him to his room, where he lay on the bed gazing at the ceiling's white plaster mouldings with their great and ornate star that radiated from the fixing of the hung chandelier.

'That's what it's all about,' he said aloud, though quite what he meant by this cryptic observation even he himself was not sure.

'But this is my place! I live here!'

'Did.'

'You can't throw me out!'

'And perhaps will again. But just for the present . . . '

'And if I won't?'

The scarlet lips were not grinning now. There was no warmth in the eyes of blue.

'If I refuse to go.'

'Oh, dear.'

A vicious knife. The stranger slipped it from his pocket and speared a morsel of cheese from the table, gently removing it from the blade with his teeth.

'I'll go. I'll go! But for how long?'

A laugh that ran into all the corners of the room and shivered down the spine of the older man.

'What's your name?'

'Rook.'

'Well, Rook, I shall have work for you to do. Now, however, I'm tired. Tired and impatient.'

'I'm going!'

A retreat, shaking. The stranger watched him go. He ate more cheese. He stood at the window and saw the bent figure shamble across the courtyard to the arch. Under each arm he held a paper bag that bulged with his hastily assembled possessions. A cap pulled over one eye and an upturned collar were scant protection from the heavy rain that had set in.

The observer laughed soundlessly. He knew all about journeying in the wet.

Larooning lay listening to the rain that flailed the dark window of his room, glassy rods that sped from the upper air down to the city's surfaces, exploding in a shower of crystal. The gathering waters raced through the gutters, picked up the detritus of summer and sent it plunging into the roaring drains – a used ticket for an open-air concert, a torn paper fan, cigarette packets, a scrap of paper upon which was scribbled a poem written by a discarded lover, he himself carried away as effectively by the waters of the canal . . .

Imagining greatly, Larooning thrust himself further down into the bed where a greater darkness enveloped him. The silk sheets were cool and slippery against his body, almost liquid. His senses began to flow beyond the banks of wakeful reason, to flood out across the meadows of sleep. A young face raised itself gasping from the waters, only to be dragged back under. A hand reached up, breaking the surface, but Larooning ignored it, refused it, and slowly it disappeared back into the depths.

3 Ambition

How clever Johnny was! What cunning schemes he devised to part people with their money!

It was the middle of the afternoon and Sophie stretched lazily on the bed, enjoying a brief interlude between clients, her fingers idly tracing out the pattern on the counterpane, all the time watching herself in the large mirror fixed to the wall beside her. She leaned across to pour a glass of schnapps, but discovered the bottle to be just beyond reach. Climbing from the bed, she filled her glass and crossed to the window where the net curtains had been turned to gold by the sun's first appearance of the day. Even as she moved, however, it retreated behind the massing clouds, and the curtains dulled once more to grey.

She drew them aside and looked out. Opposite, a 'house' boasted a *changement de proprietaire* on a painted board that swung above the door, the French madam clinging to her language in order to set her establishment apart from the others which surrounded it and gave the street its character. A girl smoked in the doorway beneath the sign, carpet slippers on her feet and a handbag under her arm, but there was little casual trade. The street was empty, save for Johnny and Otto who sat on the steps below the window throwing a pair of dice.

The girl watched the two rattle the bone cubes across the space between them, laughing and jeering and throwing up their hands in mock despair – there was clearly no money involved. But, then, Otto would know better than to play with Johnny for money, his age and experience being no match for the quick wits and ruthless cunning of his young companion.

Sophie gazed down on her brother with pride and wonder. It seemed such a short while since he had been a small dishevelled creature toddling between herself and Columbine, while they in turn played mother, nurse and tormentor to him. The streets then had been meaner than this one, and no room they had then known had been properly curtained, let alone carpeted. At this reflection she rubbed her bare foot into the soft pile beneath her. In truth it was a cheap cotton reproduction carpet, its Turkish design threadbare in parts, but Sophie would allow no detail like that to rob her of the sense of luxury which brought her so much comfort.

Not that Johnny saw it that way: 'A step on the road, Sis, that's all. It'll be real money soon, you see. Give me another year. I'll be looking after you then, and it'll be business in style.'

Sophie didn't doubt him. Four years previously he had boasted that in five years (he gave the precise date) he would see them out of the gutter and into wealth. She had laughed at him for being childish, and his eyes had narrowed with anger. But Columbine had listened, she had taken him seriously, and now Sophie took him seriously, too. Just think of that trick with the monkey! That took genius. How cool he was! And yet, for all her confidence in his abilities, the thought of Mr Farg made her uneasy. She knew the man only by reputation, but he surely swam in deeper waters than her brother had yet imagined.

She drained her glass and reached for the bottle, pausing only to consider 'house rules' before choosing once more to flout them. This time she filled the glass, taking pride in the steadiness of hand that allowed none to spill even when she danced a few steps, her bare feet heel-toeing the floor in a sudden *joie de vivre*, Mr Farg forgotten, the past forgotten, all forgotten except the glass in her hand and the soft carpet beneath her toes.

4 Master Class

'How can there be, I ask you to consider, an art as subtle, as consummate, as ours?'

Johnny leant back against the window sill. He had been offered a chair but had suspected that it would put him at a disadvantage, so now there was a line of pain across his kidneys.

'Let us take the fine arts,' continued Mr Farg, who had been talking relentlessly for a full ten minutes. 'To paint a picture requires a skill, there is no doubt of it. Let us praise our Titians and our Raphaels. Oh, indeed, and let us praise our Michelangelos, who can perform their tasks while suspended on their backs at great heights and in great discomfort beneath inconvenient domes!

'But the domes and the canvases, you will agree, do not move? Quite so. The skill is a limited one. Hand and eye, and a sense of colour. Once mastered, the art is somewhat dull and repetitive.'

When Johnny glanced from the window he had a view over the mean alleys, the overcrowded tenements of the area in which he lived. A thin morning rain flecked the panes. He knew the cold rooms, bare of any furniture but simple wooden beds, a table used for every family activity, the iron stove with its bubbling pot that was constantly on the go – a few potatoes, a filched cabbage or something animal tossed in when they came to hand. Then his eyes returned to this room, where the large, the awkwardly large, figure of Mr Farg sat dark-suited like a sober, honest citizen among his crazy ornamental clutter.

'And I would here include the plastic arts. Your sculptor has another dimension to master, I grant. And his relationship with the material is rather different. Is to chip away at stone to discover more of its properties than an artist learns of his canvas? I think it likely, don't you? But, again, the surprises come early. Later the sculptor knows his material through and through, and marble doesn't change. Similarly, the architect . . . '

Glowing Dresden figurines dominated the room. They were littered along every shelf, within every glass cabinet, on every polished table, on the arms of chairs, on the window sill, where Johnny's arm rocked a parasolled lady who blushed at the flirtings of a young man across a rustic stile. The blues, greens and pretty yellows danced everywhere, so that when he closed his eyes he seemed to see a rainbow breaking the darkness.

'It will seem monstrously uncultured of me to say so, but I have rather more admiration for our sportsmen. Your horseman, for instance, has not only his own strength and balance to attend to, but the capricious temperament of a powerful thoroughbred. Misjudge its mood and he'll be toppled and (who knows?) mortally trampled. Here we find kinetic art of a high order.

'But we can go further. The horse, at least, can be assumed complaisant so long as the rider treats it with respect. The two share the same ideal – to jump the fence or to sprint as fast as possible and win the race. Let us now proceed to the footballer.

'To flight the ball with accuracy over thirty yards and more requires an appreciation of the properties of the ball allied with supreme physical poise. We agree on that, surely? But there is far more to it than that. To play the game successfully he must overcome his obstinate, perhaps equally skilful opponents. Ah! Wit comes into play! No point in striking the ball at the goal if that part of the net is adequately defended.'

He had never before been summoned into Mr Farg's presence, had never exchanged a word with the great man, and he gazed on the signs of his wealth with admiration and envy. His face, however, betrayed neither of these emotions, nor the fact that he found the room's furnishings for the most part depressingly ugly. His expression was one of alert, stimulated concentration.

'Imagine the shock of a Tintoretto should one of his characters begin to slouch from the scene. Does he haul him back by force or win him over with fine arguments? "Don't leave, my good man, your handsome bearded visage is just what my composition demands. The blue of your cloak, over here by the fountain, is the perfect foil for the vermilion of that lady's dress. And, besides, I'm serving drinks on the hour."

'Could the painter cope with the human intrusion, do you think?'

'But your footballer has to confront an opposing team intent on bringing about his downfall all the while that he is putting his considerable skills into effect. That, I should like to submit, is a more comprehensive art.

'Its eminence, if you follow me, derives from its complexity, its human interplay we might perhaps term it. Skill and guile in combination. And yet, and yet . . . What guile is there, after all, in persuading someone that you intend to kick a ball *here* whereas, in fact, you will kick it *there*? It is, indeed, a severely restricted form of cunning. There are only so many tricks you may play within the rules of the game. I take my hat off to the adroit footballer, but is he of necessity a deep student of the human psyche? No. He may be a complete simpleton in such matters, possessed of little more than an acute physical instinct.

'So where must we look to find that superlative art which depends upon a profound understanding of our fellow man? Do I sense a QED in the offing?'

The question seemed rhetorical, but he paused for the very first time, inviting a reply.

'I never thought of it as art,' Johnny said directly.

'To your credit, I'm sure. Self-consciousness would ruin you. But an artist is what you are, young man – and what I am proud to call myself. Do we need physical strength, manual dexterity for our greatest works?'

Here he half rose from his chair and held before him his two bloated hands, the fingers swollen and twisted upon themselves with a far-gone arthritis.

'What use are these tree roots to me? And yet I seem to get by. Don't I?'

'You get by,' Johnny smiled at the understatement.

'I do, I do.'

The little joke brought them closer together. Johnny, relaxing, sat down in the chair he had been offered. Mr Farg, when he started up again, spoke more intimately.

'I have had you watched for some time. You show great promise.'

Johnny, knowing better than to comment, allowed a silence.

'You understand the world well for one so young. Who taught you?'

'Nobody. I taught myself.'

'Your parents . . . '

'Long gone. My father upped and left when I was eight or nine. He wasn't ever any good. My mother died later on. I had a couple of older brothers who drifted away. One of them's making a bit of money in the mines, the other I don't hear of. My sister has two children and lives badly.'

'So you have no ties?'

He shook his head. He knew he would hate the regular kind of life. He had become accustomed to seizing what chances arose. He was one of life's opportunists.

'I have it in mind,' said Mr Farg, 'to put some work your way. But it would curtail your freedom somewhat. You might find it took a lot of your time.'

'If it paid,' he replied swiftly.

'Ah yes, of course it would pay. Do you suggest something discreditable on my part? But I admire your straightforwardness, Johnny. Yes, it would pay enough, I assure you – and much more than enough should you pull it off.'

'Pull it off?'

Mr Farg turned away, leant towards a porcelain shepherd boy and rubbed at its glossiness with a sleeve. He gazed lovingly upon it, as if it grew more beautiful by the second.

'Don't you count yourself lucky,' he asked, 'to be born into times such as these? Ideal for talents like ours, wouldn't you say? Everywhere a lack of hope, a growing despair. Work not to be had. No faith in anything, human or divine. Not even the currency to be trusted! The people clutch at straws - hunt glow-worms in the dark in case they should be diamonds. And we are creators of glow-worms!

'Against stupidity the gods themselves struggle in vain. But we don't join the struggle. We positively encourage stupidity! In times like ours the strongest men lose their vigour while the loudest, the most aggressive, are in reality' – a giggle trembled in his throat – 'soft as a baby's bottom. Without question, soft as a baby's bottom.'

A wind had gathered outside. It drove the rain like pebbles at the glass. In the dull light the countless figurines seemed sometimes almost to move, a self-sufficient community, the high and the low born, the young and the old, the active and the contemplative. No need of this talkative gentleman in the heavy suit, the attentive lad in the chair.

'A certain organisation has approached me,' Mr Farg continued, 'asking for my help. For which, do I need to add, they are willing to pay. They are seeking a man who is believed to live in this city of ours. They know very little about him, but they want him very much.'

'Why?'

'Is a question I am not accustomed to asking in such circumstances. I rather imagine they are not friends of this man. It does not concern us. They want him.

'It may be that the task is impossible. I would not ask my established agents to undertake it. Their time is precious, they require certain rewards. In any case, an unknown face may be preferable. Who'll suspect a mere boy? The element of surprise!

'May I assume that you will not decline the offer?'

'Of course.'

It was important, he knew, to impress with his enthusiasm. He would have replied as emphatically even had he decided not to undertake it. There were ways of escaping obligations.

'Then I shall give you these.'

Mr Farg jerked open a drawer and, with a painful concentration, lifted a thin sheaf of papers between his crippled fingers.

'Take them. Come!'

He jumped to his feet. There were four sheets of paper. On the first there was a simple sketch, in charcoal, of a young man about his own age. The shading suggested that the hair was dark. The nose was proud. The jaw was firm. The lips had a downward droop, denoting perhaps a tendency to melancholia. But it was roughly drawn, as if dashed off at great speed.

'That,' explained Mr Farg, 'is the only visual evidence we have. What more can I vouchsafe to you? That the man you seek is now 25 years old. That he lived for some years in a country far to the east – and perhaps, therefore, he retains an accent, although this is nothing more than surmise and you will know with what caution one should address such uncertain possibilities. There is, I regret, little more I can tell you.

'If you find this man you must report to me at once. Finding him is not enough, however. There are items in his possession for which our friends will pay very well.'

'What kind of items?'

'No, no. Would *you* trust *me* so far? Let us first find the man and then proceed from there. Those' – he nodded to the other papers, which Johnny now began to examine – 'are apparently additional clues which you may or may not find useful.'

He saw the puzzlement on Johnny's face.

'And probably not,' he conceded.

The second sheet of paper, smaller than the others and with creases showing where it had once been folded in four, had red stains spattered over it. Inked in block capitals was the word BORSCH, and under it were the ingredients and simple instructions of a recipe.

> *Beetroot*
> *Onions*
>   *(half quantity)*
> *Potatoes*
>   *(half quantity)*
> *Chop the vegetables finely and boil*
>   *slowly for an hour in salted water.*
> *Add vinegar to offset sweetness*

A pencilled arrow speared at *salted* and a comment to one side read *not too much!*

Attached to the third sheet was a yellowed newspaper cutting. There was no headline, and the two paragraphs were clearly part of a longer report.

> *Among the successful gymnasia was the Huss Academy of Physical Education. All its entrants won their first-round bouts, two within the distance.*
>
> *Three Huss boxers won gold medals (results below) but there was not one who failed to enhance his club's reputation for bravery allied to neat skills.*

The second half of the last sentence was heavily underlined.

If the information on the first three papers was scanty, that offered by the fourth was more niggardly still. It consisted of two brief lines, type-written at the centre of the sheet:

stone dropped in well
clapper in bell

'And this,' Johnny asked, 'is all?'

'All. It means nothing whatsoever to me.'

'There's no name?'

'None that we know. He would have changed it on arriving here.'

He beamed with undisguised pleasure.

'As enigmatic,' he said, 'as a baby's bottom!'

5 The Huss Academy

Laid out upon the marble surface of the cafe table, the papers look every bit as insubstantial as the information they held. Johnny sipped his beer and scowled at them. The portrait was perhaps the most useful, but it was hardly to be trusted. How competent was the artist? How much had age changed the subject of the drawing? And, if the reference to boxing was a genuine clue, would that nose still be as proud?

A black fly settled on the table and began to walk across the sheets of paper. He watched its halting progress through the maze of letters. It paused on one of the red stains as if held by the promise of a meal prepared and enjoyed years earlier. The cafe stank of lentils and cheap coffee. He struck, and the red stain was covered by a darker smear from which radiated six twitching legs.

'My, what a fine figure of a young aristocrat!'

It was Otto, his pouchy face burnished by the cold air outside. He ran a hand across his thin matting of grey hair and fell onto a chair.

'Don't you look top drawer, indeed!'

'An investment,' Johnny countered, looking down at his well-cut clothes. They had cost far less than they were worth, thanks to a favour he was owed by the tailor, but it had hurt to part with the money nonetheless.

'We soon shan't know you,' Otto crooned, lifting a beer from the waiter's tray. 'I'm glad it's not me that has to play the milord.'

'You couldn't do it.'

'I couldn't, Johnny, I couldn't. And you'll do it to perfection, of that I'm monstrously confident. I am mere putty in your hands, my maestro. I don't even see why you need the likes of me at all.'

Johnny raised his eyes to the grimy window and looked across at the Huss Academy. It was a blustering red-brick building, desperate to express solidity and importance, but the architect had not been up to the task and his creation was like nothing so much as a factory with sculptural additions, the most impressive of which (in size rather than quality) surrounded the main door. If the athletes within performed with as little fluidity and grace as their carved counterparts it was a poor academy indeed.

'It's vital that you're with me,' he said. 'As long as you play the part as we've rehearsed it. None of that getting carried away you go in for.'

'I'm a willing learner, my Johnny. An ancient pupil put to school by a pup of genius.'

Johnny waved an irritated hand, then scooped up the papers and thrust them into his jacket pocket.

'It's time,' he said. 'Our doorman's just taken over.'

'The stupid one.'

'But the stronger one, Otto, remember. So let's play on his stupidity rather than his strength.'

'Lead on, my chieftain.'

They crossed the street and passed between the stone carvings. Even Johnny, whose training in things aesthetic was non-existent, recognised their feebleness and allowed himself a derisory grin as he entered. This derision, however, did not extend to the beefy hand instantly thrust a few inches from his nose, nor to the hulking, uniformed attendant who stood four-square an arm's length behind it.

'Business?' The voice was expressionless, robotic. 'Don't recognise you. Got business here?'

'Business?'

Johnny's voice expressed anger, resentment that his progress across the tiled entrance hall should be so boorishly impeded. Distantly they could hear the squeal of rubber footwear on wooden flooring, and a disembodied voice called encouragement to an unseen athlete.

'If I have business it would scarcely concern you. Step aside and let me pass.'

The voice wasn't bad, he told himself. A little unpolished in places, but good enough to convince a simple fellow that this young man was several stations in life above him.

'Droscher, my card!'

Otto obediently dug into a pocket and brought out a white calling card with gilt lettering. The doorman wavered. He let fall his hand. It was enough. Johnny had command of the situation.

'Is that the office?' He pointed towards a heavy oak door which had brass letters across its centre bar. 'Make it known that I wish to see someone of substance in this establishment.'

Beaten, the doorman retreated to the office and knocked his great fist gingerly on the door. There was no reply.

'For heaven's sake, man!'

Johnny marched forward and rapped loudly with his knuckles.

'Come in.'

The voice was muffled by the thickness of the door, but there was no mistaking the irritation in it. The doorman stood to one side and Johnny swept into the office with Otto in tow. He bowed. The speed and deftness with which imperiousness gave way to charm and diffidence was a measure of his talent.

'Forgive the intrusion.'

There were two desks. At one sat a middle-aged woman, grey-haired and hatchet-faced, at the other a thin dark-suited man whose bent frame, balding head and slipping spectacles bespoke a lifetime of offices. It was upon this desk that Johnny motioned Otto to deposit the card, watching the recipient of the favour lean forward to read the embossed gold letters – Baron Stramm, Schloss Altenberg. He spoke it out loud, and there was a meaningful pause.

'You don't quite look like a baron,' the woman ventured.

Johnny took back the stolen card. He allowed a moment's silence, during which he thrust it back at Otto, then studied his own appearance as if perplexed by this assertion. Finally, he laughed merrily.

'Ah, myself, my age, you mean. No, no! This card is my father's. I'll have to wait a bit longer for the title! I do beg your pardon.'

Was he overdoing it? The bespectacled man looked somewhat confused but prepared to believe. When he turned to the woman he saw that she simply stared at him, suspicion written all over her face.

'But to my mission . . . '

His face now became stern and aristocratic. He leant across the desk towards the more hospitable of the two, his voice carrying a note of confidentiality.

'My father is writing a book on the history of boxing. He was a considerable fighter himself when a young man, as you probably know – though perhaps not, as he usually went under an assumed name owing to his rank in society. Tiger Lenz. Does the name mean anything to you?'

The denizen of offices nodded eagerly: 'Ah, but yes! A doughty performer.' (*The value of a little research*, Johnny heard Mr Farg saying). 'So he was a baron, was he? Bless my soul! Who'd have thought it? No airs and graces at all. In the ring, that is. I mean no disrespect.'

'Droscher here was his coach, weren't you my man?'

'Yes, sir. And honoured to be so.'

The interest intensified.

'A boxer yourself then, once?'

'For many years,' Otto replied. 'Without the success of the baron, of course, but perhaps my coaching did have a little to do with that. I kept him at it, morning till night . . . '

'We are working for my father,' Johnny leapt in quickly to thwart a flight of fancy he could too easily imagine, 'as researchers. If you could give me a little time with your records I would be most obliged. After all, what history of boxing would be complete without some reference to the achievements of the Huss Academy?'

'I'm sure,' the man said, now fully losing his wariness, 'that Mr Huss would be delighted.'

'Except,' broke in the woman, 'that he's away. He won't be back for at least a month, I'm afraid.'

'Perhaps we could contact him?'

Johnny brought his smiling charm to bear upon his adversary, but found her unmoved.

'He's in Africa,' she stated, 'shooting lions – and other riffraff.'

'A telegram?'

'Hardly, I think. He'll be in remotest places, well away from life's annoying trivialities.'

Johnny shook his head and turned towards her companion.

'A great pity,' he said, 'but I'm afraid we shall have to move on. The material would have been interesting, but I daresay the book will survive without it.'

Now the man came to his rescue.

'I'm sure Mr Huss would greatly regret the academy being omitted from the history due to any reluctance on our part to comply with this young gentleman's – this young nobleman's – quite reasonable wishes.'

The woman snorted, but it was clear that his was the greater authority and she lapsed into a sullen silence, returning to the papers that littered her desk.

'Wonderful for lion-hunting, Africa,' Johnny tossed in knowledgeably for good measure.

6 Innocent Party

A half moon rose crisp in a sky of deep mauve and bloodied orange. A clear, cold night, trees and buildings pitch scarecrows against the simmering luminous drape.

Under the electric glare the young man's face was pallid but his lips were vermilion gashes. He pulled his cloak around him and stepped into the tram, journeying out from the brightly lit centre to leafy suburbs where the moon held sway.

The leaves were falling, falling. They were like dark spirits on some unspeakable visitation.

Dark shadows criss-crossed in a dark road, the shadows of the tall young man and the tree trunks and the gesticulating branches. The footsteps passed from darkness to darkness, but there was a light up ahead. It was only a glimmer, but it grew and grew.

There were people in the light, laughing. There was music, too. There was no moon and there were no shadows in the bright house where the people laughed and talked and danced. The black cloak was among them, the young man was listening.

He was moving among them and he was watching and listening.

The hours passed. The leaves beat at the windows. Still the people danced and mingled. Glasses met and clashed and sometimes broke. The laughter was louder than the moon was bright, out beyond the bright house.

Like a drifting leaf the black cloak fluttered. It settled and rose again. The eyes were blue and the lips were red but the cloak was black, and it beat against the laughter and the music.

Shadowed the porch when the young man departed. He slid from his pocket a wicked knife and fell upon the woodwork by the door.

7 Lyings

'You'd have been proud of me, Sis.'

He sat back and placed a cigar stolen from Mr Farg between his curled lips.

'At least you didn't involve me this time,' she replied with a laugh. 'You should have seen their faces – completely taken in. And that ridiculous monkey!'

His sister, taking advantage of an unexpected break between clients, crossed her silk stockinged legs and gulped at a glass of schnapps. The basement room that they shared wrapped them in a shabby cosiness. Yes, they were on the up and up: her 'tricks' were getting classier, and so were his.

'You're all right, Johnny,' she said, in a voice which betrayed affection and admiration.

He poked out his tongue as he blew smoke towards the ceiling but the rings wouldn't form. He would have to practise and practise.

'Those rotten ledgers,' he remembered. 'Covered in dust. Page after page of names. If I get anything out of this I'll have earned every penny in the Huss archives.'

'There are worse ways,' she replied knowingly.

'First to find an occasion when the Huss boxers won three gold medals. Can you imagine hunting through those tedious records for that? It happened just once. Then to find the names of those who lost their fights.'

'Why do that?' she asked, staring into a mirror and fussing with her eyelashes. He knew she wasn't concentrating.

'Because the man I'm after was proud of being described as brave and skilful. I've explained all this, Sis!'

'Sorry.'

'The best way to make sense of the newspaper cutting is to assume he was a boxer at the academy on the night they won three medals. But *he* didn't win one of them or he'd have kept the results, too. It says "results below". Instead he underlined this bit about "bravery allied to neat skills". Does that make sense?'

'If you like.'

'Presumably he likes borsch. We know his age, and we have his portrait. That's everything.'

'Let's have another look at that picture,' Sophie offered. 'I see a few faces in my game.'

Holding it towards the lamp, she studied it carefully for a few moments before admitting defeat.

'Not bad looking, is he? A bit too well-heeled to seek our company. The rich always get it for nothing – no morals in the upper classes.'

'Who says he's upper class?'

'It's the nose.'

He shrugged. His sister could afford to jump to conclusions. She didn't have to find the elusive one-time boxer.

'And these names you've written by the drawing,' she asked. 'Who are they?'

'You don't listen, Sis! I tell you how we're going to make our fortune and nothing goes in. I've found five names that fit the evidence, five losers on the night the Huss Academy won three gold medals. One of those is almost certainly the man who'll net us thousands of glinters if I can track him down. So now all I have to do is find them all and see which one matches the picture. Isn't that clear enough?'

She read them aloud: Martin Jolsen, Humbert Gold, Peter Ocklynge, Dirk Grimm, Eric Alph.

'Sorry, Johnny. None of them's in my book.'

He took the drawing and read through the names again and again. He would memorise them in case something should happen to the paper. *A little scientific methodology*, he heard Mr Farg saying, *fortifies the inspiration of art.*

'This Farg of yours,' Sophie said, as if reading his mind. 'Is he liable to turn up here?'

Johnny surveyed their room and grinned at the contrast it offered to Mr Farg's pleasure dome. Empty bottles were their only ornaments, and any accidental beauty that they might possess was buried under as much dust as the Huss records. Perhaps Mr Farg would polish them as he did his figurines.

'No, I hardly think so. But if he does, tell him how difficult it is bringing up your two children. It might be worth a gold piece or two. I don't suppose there's much charity in him, but it's worth a go.'

'What children?'

'The two I told him you had.'

His sister's mood changed to sudden indignation.

'What did you tell him that for? If that got around it wouldn't do my business any good. Men are funny about things like that.'

'He doesn't talk.'

'But it's a downright lie!'

Johnny showed the palms of his hands, defensively.

'One thing I've learned, Sis,' he said seriously, 'is never to be completely honest. The truth's an ace you have to keep up your sleeve for a real emergency. Fiction can always be twisted to suit your own purpose, whereas the truth's most often inconvenient. The only rule is never to forget your own stories. So you have two children as far as Mr Farg is concerned. That may be useful to me one day.'

His sister frowned: 'What would Mum say if she knew that you told lies about the family?'

'Mum's dead.'

This fiction obviously offended her far less than the earlier one and she burst into laughter.

'Oh, Johnny, you wicked little devil!'

An image of their mother's sour face reared before her like an admonishing witch.

'For all we see of her she might as well be dead,' she added quietly.

'We both make our living by lying, one way or the other,' was Johnny's last word on this subject.

They lapsed into silence, he studying the list of names, she regarding what little remained of the schnapps in her glass. Her face, heavily masked by cheap cosmetics, betrayed little emotion, but one might have imagined, with little effort, that a sadness had overtaken her. Her musings were interrupted by a knock at the door, followed by the face of a boy somewhat younger than Johnny, attempting to announce the arrival of a new client. The face, white and puffy, hung like a moon between floor and ceiling and the words seemed to catch somewhere at the back of the lad's throat, to become ensnared there, so that his facial muscles struggled in an exhausting attempt to throw them out into the world.

'He's a . . . ' (a straining and spluttering, followed by the rest of the sentence issuing in a furious babble) 'foreigner by the sound of it, Sophie.'

She regarded this moon in the way that an astronomer, engaged upon searching the heavens for new and distant stars and planets, might gaze upon its larger counterpart: its being there was a boring inevitability.

'Karl says . . . to hurry.'

'What's he look like? Fat, bald and fifty?'

'No. He looks like the . . . the devil.' The eye craters expanded. 'He's got a black . . . he's got a black . . . black . . . '

'Why do I ask?'

' . . . black . . . cloak.'

But before the final word had struggled into being she had left, passing him as he still hung around the door, his laboured lips moving in an agony of tortured sound.

8 Fisticuffs

Larooning entered at the same time as a milling crowd of high-spirited young men, which accounted for his freedom from victimisation by the doorman and for his immediate mistake. There were, after all, several doors he might have chosen. Was it his destiny always to make the wrong choice?

The hall was large and reeked of sweat. At one end there was a roped boxing ring with padded corners, and a pair of slender lads danced about one another with bulbous red gloves on their fists while a craggy man with a towel over one shoulder bent low and waved a hand, calling instructions to them.

'On your toes! Keep that left arm up! One, two – make it count!'

Larooning was so rapt by this performance that he quite overlooked the fact that several other young men were exercising in the hall. Another pair of boxers, bobbing and weaving, grunting and gasping, worked their way towards him, closer and closer. He changed direction, but still they came on. Now they were circling him, each man's eyes only on his opponent, the sweat running down their faces, their feet drumming on the wooden flooring. He stepped backwards, but anticipation had never been a strong point even when, as a portly schoolboy, he had been rather more agile than now. An elbow caught him in the side, so that he gasped and sank halfway to his knees.

'Sorry,' he heard himself mutter.

But they were oblivious of his presence. A foot stamped down on his toes as they skipped and shuffled away. Larooning snatched at his breath and stumbled to the wall. The place suddenly seemed very hot and very noisy. He was aware of echoing voices; of the heavy, dull sound of bodies landing on mats; of equipment being moved.

He began to rise and at once a heavy rope swung into view. He saw it too late to avoid it, feeling the coarse fibres rasp against his cheek. Behind him there were athletes swarming aloft like monkeys. Perhaps he might have apologised again, but he was totally ignored.

Was physical fitness a counterpart of mental alertness? Larooning wondered. Might he be better able to carry out his mission if he could run and jump like these people? Or was aggression sufficient? He would be aggressive.

He advanced, limping, on a stocky and well-muscled man who stood on a thick mat beneath a weighted bar which his glistening arms held high aloft.

'Excuse me.'

With a shuddering groan the strongman brought the weights to the ground in a single explosive movement. Larooning felt the displacement of air, he was so close.

'I'm looking for . . . '

But the man only stooped to the bar, tightened the weights and then, without a glance in his direction, swaggered away.

'Excuse me.'

Each athlete was in his own private world. The sounds he heard were his own breath, the throb of his own pulse, and the sights he saw were similarly limited – for the boxer, his opponent's jaw, chest and gloves; for the vaulter, the box over which he sprang; for the climber, the few inches of rope above his head. Were we not all in our own private worlds? Larooning mused, hobbling towards the door.

It was so near and yet so far. A group of young men with skipping ropes swung and clacked towards him, opened and swallowed him up. They skipped on the spot – thwack, thwack, thwack – and he stood immobile, the still centre of a whirlpool.

9 A Medical Opinion

'You're a new patient,' the young lady with the freckles observed, taking down the name he invented and instantly filing it.

Johnny nodded. He had been watching the people come and go, most of them obviously well-heeled, successful, but his eyes had returned time and again, fascinated, to the densely populated map of her face.

'Dr Jolsen will see you soon.'

He had taken the tram out from the city centre and found himself in a kind of paradise which nevertheless unnerved him. In his own narrow streets, labyrinthine though they were, every crossing had a dozen possible destinations, every landmark a dozen associations. They were the geography and history of his life. Out here, where tree-lined avenues wound into unknown territories, where isolated houses like this one had no relation to their neighbours in the separate plots along the way, he felt fearfully dislocated. There was no meaning in the place.

A bell rang from within and the freckled girl inclined her head at him and smiled: 'You're next.'

He opened the door on a large and comfortable room, prints on the walls, a thick carpet on the floor. The man who sat swivelling on a leather chair behind an expensive desk was, he noticed at once, dark haired, but Johnny put his age at rather more than thirty.

'Take a seat,' Martin Jolsen offered, scribbling on a pad.

Outside, in the lightly falling rain, a pair of misfits shuffled along the road. Johnny had passed them earlier – a blind beggar led he knew not where by a drooling simpleton, their route taking them into an area where they could not hope for succour. The blind man shook his tin while his companion grinned and called remarks at the passing clouds.

'What seems to be the problem?'

He let the pen drop and raised his eyes to Johnny's. It was not, at first glimpse, the face on the sheet of paper. The jawline was not dissimilar, allowing for the passage of time, but the nose appeared less prominent. And the lips? Johnny could not immediately decide.

'A pain,' he replied. 'Along here.' He ran a hand over his lower rib-cage. 'It won't go away.'

The doctor grunted and settled back in his chair: 'Since when?'

'At least a fortnight,' Johnny said. 'I can't sleep properly. It's there all the time.'

The pen scribbled again.

'And you can't think of any reason for it?' the doctor asked with an air of ill-suppressed boredom. 'No unusual activity?'

Johnny frowned.

'I'm afraid it may be my boxing,' he said in worried tones. 'I can't remember any particular blow, but I'm fighting all the time.'

'Are you, indeed?'

'Down at the Huss Academy. Do you know it? It's a good gymnasium they've got there.'

Dr Jolsen's listless expression was transformed in a moment. Smiling, he pulled open a drawer in his desk.

'You take a look at this,' he chuckled, sorting among a sheaf of papers until he found a photograph. He thrust it at Johnny.

'Recognise anyone there?'

It was a crude, unimaginative picture – two young boxers staring straight at the camera, their fists raise pugnaciously.

'That's you?' Johnny laughed, pointing.

This, surely, was not the man.

'At the Huss Academy!' exclaimed the doctor, excited now. 'Isn't that a coincidence? I was there for several years. Until a certain young lady came along and I got married.'

'And who's the other person?' Johnny asked, studying a tall, blond youth with a haughty demeanour.

'Would you believe that I can't even remember? It's another life for me now. A world away. But they were good times. Is old Emile still keeping the boys in order?'

'Retired,' Johnny said quickly, trusting that Emile was indeed old. 'So I'm told.'

'Is he, now? The place can't be the same.' He took back the photograph and dropped it into the drawer. 'You could have a cracked rib, I suppose. Take off your jacket.'

Johnny dutifully stripped to the waist and allowed the doctor's firm, cold fingers to explore his bones. The mouth was not right. And, close up, he saw that the line of the nose was different, too.

'Nothing there,' the doctor said.

'Something else occurs to me,' Johnny added with an embarrassed laugh. 'Before I first felt the pain I'd had two plates of borsch. I wonder if that could have upset me.'

'Borsch?'

'Two large plates.'

The doctor smiled openly: 'Well, if you will eat that foreign muck I'm not surprised that you feel out of sorts. But hardly for two weeks, I think. Still, I'll give you something for an unsettled gut, and if that doesn't do the trick you'd better come back again.'

'Thank you,' Johnny said, taking the slip of paper he was given and quickly dressing himself. No, this was not the man he sought.

'If you would pay my receptionist on the way out,' the doctor recited, already swivelling in his leather chair.

The befreckled young lady was sitting on a high stool as Johnny came through the door. Before she could accost him, however, he stabbed with a finger towards the surgery.

'Quick!' he called. 'He's having a fit!'

White and gasping, she dashed to the rescue, allowing Johnny to make a deft escape. He was outside in a moment, and he would already have been running down the drive had not something strange caught his eye.

The doctor's house was immaculately cared for within and without, the paintwork bright and glistening. But here in the porch one of the wooden supporting pillars had been violently gouged as if by a sharp implement, and the shape that had been dug out of it was itself – the short hilt, the tapering point – unmistakably that of a dagger.

10 Columbine

Evening, and the street lamps made of the platz a golden mosaic, each wet cobblestone holding upon its curved surface a crown of reflected light. Across this mosaic there was a constantly shifting pattern of motor cars, carriages and pedestrians, seemingly random but with its own inner logic, understood by the participants if not by the casual observer. It was the city's dance, choreographed by dusty men in dusty offices, but performed with all the magic of real life. Here limped a placarded beggar; there drifted a love-sick girl; in and out of the shadows skipped a scrawny child, oblivious of the world around.

Johnny, collar turned up against the fine rain, had at his lips a constant litany of abuse for the weather. Yet the truth was that he enjoyed walking in the rain. The cold rinsing of his face was exhilarating, invigorating, and the complaining was part of the pleasure. It reinforced his sense of alienation, confirmed the feeling that he owed the world nothing and could therefore dispense with the inconvenience of a conscience.

'Damn rain! What a night to be out!'

The limping beggar rattled a tin plate at him as he passed, but it was a feeble gesture and even as he made it he recognised its futility, pulling back the plate before it was knocked from his hand. Johnny cut diagonally across the square, weaving in and out among the moving vehicles with a dexterity which marked him as a true performer of the city's ballet. One car, in truth, had the impertinence to hoot, but he only sneered at the driver, whose face was lost in the shadowy world behind the windscreen, and continued on his way unperturbed.

At the far corner of the square stood a large church, its black bulk rising above the brightness of street level and climbing into the murky sky, its steeple disappearing into the wet mists. By day the dark grey stone dominated the square, its massive upward thrust contrasting with the urban elegance of the other buildings, but after dark it was far more an integral part of the scene and far more comforting for Johnny, who otherwise found his spirits oppressed by its looming presence. It was into this church that they had carried the body of his only brother after the accident and he could still visualise the cheap wooden coffin sitting incongruously among the Gothic stones.

His mother's face, as grey and stained as the carvings that surrounded them, had stared straight ahead blankly as if her life also had ceased, and so in a way it had. Was that the last time he had seen her sober? He supposed so, although he had been so young at the time, so full of discovering the world, that his mother's metamorphosis had simply complied with the rule of constant flux that governed all things. Perhaps that was why he was always confused when people spoke brazenly of truth, for truth implied an absolute that he had never experienced or had ever sought.

What he sought now was an alley that ran beside the church, a place of darkness and silence in total contrast to the platz. It descended by several short flights of steps, a hazard to the unknowing or unwary but not to him. This secretive place was his true element: here nothing existed beyond him or within him. He lingered.

The street, when he reached it, bustled with that life which is peculiar to clubs and bars, each vying with its neighbours in the amount of lurid experience on offer. Small, loosely knit gangs of men, most of them young, cruised the street shouting bawdy exchanges with the touts who stood by the doors. Girls with red lips and sullen expressions loitered beneath the lamps, waiting for company.

'Wake up, Colombine!'

It was to a girl standing dreamily beneath her lamp like a southern shepherdess beneath the moon that Johnny had journeyed. Taking her by the arm, he crossed the road with her and they entered a door. Dark stairs led to a basement and she led him into . . . a room? Hardly that. More a northern grotto, an icy cavern, a deep recess of the romantic imagination that was separated by huge distances of time and space from the street outside.

The walls dissolved into drapes of white chiffon, onto which were sewn sequins and silvered glass balls, metallic stars and snowflakes of white lace. A gap in this shimmering screen revealed a painted view of vast arctic wastes punctuated with dark firs gathered in whispering conspiracies, heavily cloaked in white and surmounted by a sky itself sequined with stars. Coloured rugs were scattered across the floor and these, together with several large embroidered cushions, seemed to constitute the only furnishing. From the starry ceiling hung a moon of wire and oiled paper which allowed a soft pink light to permeate the fairyland.

'Realms of bliss,' the girl stated in a peculiar, hauntingly brittle voice, pausing to stare at an area of drapes she must have seen a thousand times before. 'The world beyond.'

She dropped upon one of the cushions, her long legs thrown gracelessly across the floor with a carelessness he knew was reserved for the company of friends. Her face had been painted into the semblance of a doll, porcelain white with cheeks circled in rouge and a faint trace of pink on the tip of her nose. Her pose emphasised her resemblance to a broken marionette.

'I'm more concerned with the here and now,' Johnny replied, piling one cushion on another and perching high on top.

Was it a wonder that the few clients who penetrated his singular retreat should be dedicated to the strange girl who hovered like a moth close to the flame of madness? They knew, as she knew, that one day she would be consumed and achieve the ultimate escape. They felt half consumed in the mere sharing of her dreams.

It was no wonder to Johnny. In whatever circumstances he met this weird creature he could see only the friend of his and Sophie's childhood. No exchange of cosmetics for dirt, or black silk shift and French knickers for torn dress and unwashed cotton pants, could change her in his eyes, nor would he have wished it so. They had shared too much, the three of them, Sophie and Columbine as surrogate mothers, protecting him, amusing him, scolding him, but never excluding him.

'The Here,' she said, giving the words a meaningless in the strange way she echoed them, 'and the Now.'

As they had grown, so their roles had changed, the girls feigning a helplessness which life had denied them and luxuriating in his own pretence of masculine strength. Perhaps his life now was merely an extension of those earlier fantasies. Was his grip on reality any greater than Columbine's? He could not confidently say so. Sophie was the only one who had ceased playing games, and she – he had known it for some time just below the level of conscious perception and was gradually coming to admit it to himself – had begun to drink.

'Hans won't mind me taking your time?'

'Poor Hans.'

'He's fast with his fists.'

'But slow with his wits,' Columbine replied devastatingly. 'Like a malignant toad.'

'A powerful toad.'

'But toad-witted. As you are dragon-witted.'

'Dragon-witted?'

'A tongue that burns.'

Johnny shrugged. Columbine's conversations had always left him confused. Was it true, as rumour had it, that her father was a poet? For certain her mother had not been, though her flow of language had been at times prodigious.

'Has your friend come up with those names?' he asked.

She weaved shapes in the air with her fingers.

'My friend,' she said. 'My confrere. My associate. My man at the tax office. He is the master of the files.'

'Has he found anything?'

She gazed upwards as if trying to recollect and then removed a strip of paper from her garter. He took it.

'Good,' he said. 'Three of them already. Gold runs a factory over the river. Bits for tractors. Grimm's a solicitor with an office in the centre. Ocklynge has two addresses and is unlikely to be found at either.'

There was no response from the girl. Bits for tractors were not her world. She stared into a deep distance much further than he could see or would ever care to. He knew these moods of surface tranquility while her mind voyaged and dared. There would be no communion with Columbine this night. He rose to his feet, toppling the cushions.

'Your tax man will keep searching?'

Her eyes did not move. There was no change in her expression.

'If he wants to stay my special friend.'

'And if he doesn't?'

Her laugh was a dropped coin clattering down an iron staircase.

'I'll burn my eyes through his skull and melt his brains!'

11 An Awkward Moment

It was only a hunch which took him up the stairs of the large office block. He had seen a single light burning on the fourth floor, and the notice board in the entrance lobby announced that *D. Grimm. Solicitor* inhabited rooms on that level. Perhaps the gods were smiling on him.

There were no lights to illumine the stair well. He fumbled his way up and round, up and round, clinging to the handrail. Was this the fourth floor? He paused on the landing, peering into the gloom. But no: he heard a sound from somewhere up above. He climbed again, hurrying.

Once more that sound. Something rapping on the floor, maybe. It was intermittent. He strained to hear it again, and then saw the splash of light beneath a door along the corridor. He was creeping now, as if guilty of some unnamed crime. He drew closer.

'Oh yes, yes please.'

A voice almost whispering, yet urgent. He could not quite understand. The nameplate read *D. Grimm. Solicitor.*

'Please.'

He knocked lightly and, without waiting for an invitation, pushed open the door and stepped into the office. He almost tripped over two figures spreadeagled on the floor.

Who the woman was it was difficult to tell, for she was heavily veiled by an item of her own clothing, her face the only part of her person with any covering save for the crown of her head, which sported a felt hat of a curious and irregular shape. As for the man, his face contrived, somehow, to peer over the top of this hat so that he looked almost a part of it, his nose a red and glossy wax fruit decoration. Johnny stared at this montage for several long seconds, then found himself reaching out his hand.

'Mr Grimm?'

Nonplussed, it must be, the solicitor raised an arm and clasped Johnny's fingers in his own. Dirk Grimm had sandy hair, shaggy eyebrows and flared nostrils. The two shook hands firmly and solemnly. The woman, beneath, seemed to breathe with difficulty.

'Good evening,' Johnny added – rather lamely, he acknowledged to himself.

Slowly the eyebrows lowered and gathered, the nostrils dilated in a yet more pronounced fashion. The solicitor withdrew his hand. His face darkened, the expression gradually assuming equal parts of horror and anger. There was a terrible moment of silence while his fury gathered.

'Who the hell are you?' he roared.

Johnny stepped backwards, found the door and escaped. It was not until he was halfway down the stairs that a smile began to play upon his lips, and it was but fleeting. For the thought came to him that there might be a Mrs Grimm, and that her husband might offer much not to have his secrets revealed. Solicitors were a wealthy breed of men.

He reached the street door, but before he could open it he found it swung violently at him, knocking him back. A dark figure swept past him, blind to his presence, and began to climb the stairs at a swift pace. In the glimmer of light which bled from the street into the lobby he was aware of the fluttering of a cloak.

12   Three-Legged Cows

Larooning drew back the curtains of room 27 and viewed the weather with an audible sigh of regret. The continuing rain dictated that he review the day's itinerary. The Old Palace Gardens he deleted with a stroke of his silver propelling pencil, inserting St Ludo's Cathedral. Was that correct? Short for Ludovic, perhaps. His own writing was harder to read than any he knew.

Was the mausoleum of the Grand Dukes entirely suitable in the rain? How much shelter would it offer? He had dressed himself fastidiously. Since the guide book failed to provide the required information, discretion counselled another deletion: half an hour longer in the cathedral, perhaps. Then the shops.

The man of destiny had temporarily given way to the tourist. 'Time is not of the essence,' he said aloud, as if to assuage a conscience not quite as bruised as his body. On the way down he made several enquiries of the lift boy (who, with great politeness, asked after his broken leg) but the replies were vague in the extreme. Was he a man more easy to ignore than most? Larooning pondered.

St Luk's Cathedral, its vaults leaping in all directions about him, had a good section in his guide. Indeed, he was far too busy ploughing his way through the pages of close-set print to take much notice of the building itself. His feet mercifully avoided all obstacles as he lurched blindly around, the book before his eyes, but he did contrive to walk into a surly native whose paper bag fell to the floor, scatterings its meagre contents across stones worn uneven by centuries of pilgrims shuffling to the high altar on their knees – this picturesque detail supplied by the guide. It seemed, if he translated aright, that St Luk (or St Luck, as he was known locally, and incongruously) had been disembowelled at the very altar before which he now stood.

As Rook gathered his belongings together he filled the air with strange and obscure oaths, even threatening Larooning with a fist. In vain: Larooning was transfixed by the details of the saint's mutilation. The spilt blood had apparently (though here the language was particularly archaic and elliptical, so that a misunderstanding was forgivable) woven itself into the image of a cross born aloft by a three-legged cow. This unlikely occurrence proved the undoing of hundreds of cows throughout the centuries that followed, each St Luk's Day being celebrated by a procession through the streets of a crippled beast with a cross strapped to its back.

'Sorry,' Larooning said, faintly aware of a complaint from a fellow tourist.

Further custom had decreed that the animal should be slaughtered on completion of its journey, to be shared among the poor and needy, the recipients having to search their portion (he was sure this was how it read) for any relic of the saint which might have found its way miraculously into the meat. Whether anybody ever did find such a thing was not made clear, but thankfully the whole bizarre procedure was now prohibited on the grounds that the hobbling cow created a hazard for the city's traffic.

The journey from the cathedral to the Pleasure Mode store was short, and Larooning decided not to take a taxi. He trod with exaggerated carefulness to avoid splashing his smart grey spats with mud, but it was less his daintily lumbering progress than the expression of puzzlement on his face that would have caught the eye of a casual observer. His perplexity seemed to grow visibly by the minute, until the arrival at his destination uplifted him with new wonders.

As the uniformed doorman swung wide the glass doors, allowing him refuge from the weather, the full glories of the emporium lay all before him, the carpeted floors and discreetly whispering assistants creating a hush more profound than that of St Luk's. He summoned a page boy and demanded the china department. How rich it all was, and in a city where he had seen people queueing for food. Did they not work hard enough? Larooning asked himself. Was the interior of the Pleasure Mode store not a sufficient incentive for them?

He soon found himself surrounded by a frozen tableau of diminutive shepherdesses and their swains. It was the Dresden figurines that he particularly sought. Would they look so well in *his* room? He lifted one from its stand for a closer examination and, as he scrutinised it, so an assistant scrutinised him, as if his reputation had run before him. Larooning smiled comfortingly and replaced it, unruffled. He took up another.

It was at this moment that he caught, reflected in the glass cabinet, the malevolent stare of a wretched-looking man who stood clutching a torn paper bag to his chest. There was such loathing in his expression, and the loathing seemed so directly aimed at him, that Larooning replaced the figurine with nervous speed and stepped briskly away from the display – too quickly to notice that the figurine wobbled precariously and fell on its neighbour, with too much alarm to feel his shoulder rock the cabinet as he passed.

He hardly heard the series of crashes behind him, and certainly had no idea that it had anything to do with him. His eyes did betray a consternation, but this was because the problem which had troubled him before he entered the store had reasserted itself in his brain. He came to a sudden halt in the bedding department.

'But with only three legs,' he said aloud, 'surely they must have fallen over.'

13 A Riot

In the colourless light of dawn hosts of workers, their coats buttoned against the wind and rain, converged upon the factory district of the city, and Johnny took his place among them, the collar of his leather jerkin turned up and his cap pulled low over his eyes. He peered out in wonder at the mute infantrymen of this bedraggled army. What possessed them to pursue such drear lives? He despised them for their doggedness, their succumbing to the law and to the will of their masters. They had chosen Death while he had chosen . . . What? Well, at least each day began with fresh promise of quick and easy money, even if the promise was too rarely fulfilled, and for Johnny easy money equalled Life: it was the only equation the world had taught him. But these blank-faced creatures who shared the morning with him, what did they wake to? The certainty of toil, boredom, poverty.

A gaunt and crumpled man stood silently in the middle of the street, an island in the steady human stream. Around his neck hung a crudely lettered cardboard placard: DAY IS FADING AWAY. NOW IS EVENING COME TO ALL THINGS, EVEN TO THE BEST OF THINGS.

Johnny hawked into the gutter and watched the white spume flow and eddy and disappear into the blackness of a drain. Here he found himself one with the shuffling troops to either side. If but few revealed their hostility in quite so dramatic a manner, several dug at the lone sentinel with their elbows as they passed, while others called out crude and violent comments.

'Clear the path, God-guzzler!'

'Watch out, old fellow, or we'll dispatch you to the heavenly kingdom damn quick!'

What place was there for a prophet in times such as these? What fool could believe in fine ideals, sanctimonious morality? It was, Johnny thought, a kind of sickness to dream of better, distant worlds populated by the virtuous. People weren't virtuous. The world we knew was the only world. It was a bad place and you had to survive in it. And that was what his present companions thought, too.

'We'll put the police on you, Jeremiah, and then you'll call on mercy!'

For some reason the procession had come to a halt. A large group of workers had gathered in a knot at Gold's factory gate and had not entered. Perhaps they were early and the gates were not yet open, but he seemed to hear raised voices up ahead. There was a pushing and shoving. He found himself moved along again, and he became part of a backwash swirling around the edges of a large gathering of men – too many for him to make out what was happening at the gate beyond.

An angry murmuring began to fill the air around him, and others pushed in from behind, trapping him. He tried to raise himself so that he might discover the cause of the delay, using the broad shoulders of the man in front of him to assist the effort, but he saw only a plateau of heads, a human moraine that ended at the sheer cliff of soot-smeared wall which bounded the factory. He asked questions, but they were instantly lost, sucked up in the growing anger. He saw dead faces become disconcertingly alive and animated, some contorted with rage. The sound of their fury swelled and hammered at his ears.

'Dirty cheat!'

'He's taken our jobs!'

'Smash the place!'

It took but little time to realise what had happened. The factory had been closed and the workers locked out. Gold, anticipating a yet steeper dive in his declining profits, had grabbed what remained and departed to a warmer clime. Johnny, as understanding grew, felt himself no less a victim than all these others.

'The swine!' he thought. 'All this way and he's bunked it. I could still be in bed.'

He tried to force his way back, to detach himself from the crowd, but his slight body carried too little weight. He had no choice but to be jostled hither and thither as the mood of those around him grew uglier by the second. Something flew through the air. At the rear of the mob, men began to prise cobbles from the roadway and hurl them towards anything that would break. Gold's factory was too distant, but the lettered glass of a bar used by the workers shattered, exploded; the splintered frontage of a cobbler's shop spilled glass and leather onto the street; stuffy offices suddenly discovered the doubtful charms of fresh air.

And then the police were there, with an immediacy that seemed impossible, their batons swinging, their horses pressing in on the rioters, who scattered with their arms held protectively over their heads. But this scattering was only momentary, for the police had barricaded the streets and cut off their escape – they, unlike the workers, must have been forewarned of Gold's closure and had been waiting nearby to deal with the eruption they knew would follow.

Johnny found himself running with the others and regrouping with them, trying to ensure that he remained at the centre of each unit and away from the fighting edges. More people seemed to be arriving. Why did the police not allow them to disperse, he wondered, and who were these others with their black shirts, arm bands, shaven heads and studded leather flails? A glancing blow from a baton stunned his right arm and he fell to his knees, panic making him light-headed.

'Scum! Filthy trash!'

As the police were up on their horses and beating down at the heads of the workers, and as the flails lashed through the air at the same height, perhaps it was best to remain low down. He curled like a jockey thrown at a fence. The battle moved across him. He felt the trampling, bruising feet; something struck him on the back; he was thrown to one side. All around him there were loud clashes, wild shouts, and he constantly imagined a horse's hoof scattering his brains across the wet cobbles. At one stage someone hauled him half to his feet and tugged him along, so that he felt himself running despite himself. Then he was let go and tumbled over, his body banging painfully against something solid.

When he at last opened his eyes he found himself against the factory gate. The battle had drifted away. The rain fell steadily now. A large poster lay, sodden, at his feet. There was the caricature of a hook-nosed, heavily-jowled man with a skullcap and, in large black letters, the legend YOUR LABOUR – JEWISH GOLD.

A silence fell. He sat up. The police were removing the barricades, allowing the bloodied and defeated workers to drain from the scene like dirty water from a bath. A lesson had been given and perhaps learned. There would be more such lessons if necessary. The batons slid into their sheaths, the horses formed orderly lines as they left, chivvying the tattered remnants of the mob. The black-shirted men with the flails seemed simply to melt, smiling, into the misty curtain of rain.

He rose, surveying with jaundiced eye the carnage around him. Blood flowed between the cobbles, forming a red grid upon which were stationed, at random points, men in various states of suffering. Some lay unconscious, perhaps even dead; some sat helpless, dazed and sobbing; some writhed and groaned, holding together split flesh or supporting broken limbs.

Johnny retrieved his cap, flicking it against his leg to remove the excess rainwater, and he saw that the spray was pink. As he rolled it up and thrust it into his jacket pocket he noticed, a few yards away, an arm-band that must have been torn from one of the men with the flails, and he gathered it up and pushed it into the pocket with his cap.

A hand grasped at his ankle and, looking down, he saw the upturned face of a man whose blue and swollen jaw prevented him from begging the aid his eyes implored with a passionate eloquence. With a shudder, Johnny pulled his foot away and walked on.

He passed close to a man who stood silent and alone in the middle of the street, his placard sodden but miraculously intact: DAY IS FADING AWAY. NOW IS EVENING COME TO ALL THINGS, EVEN TO THE BEST OF THINGS.

14 Wounds

'You could have been killed,' Sophie protested, swabbing his back.

It was halfway through the afternoon and Johnny, lying face down and shirtless on the sofa, was still in pain. His neck ached, he could raise his right arm only a few inches, and there were cuts on his back which stung as his sister wielded the sponge.

'Cruel death of young innocent,' announced Columbine, who was crouched at a small table brushing bright flowers on an eggshell. 'Unjust fate strikes down youth of promise.'

The boy with the puffy moon face sat regarding the miniature art as if it were the work of a master. His tongue issued from his lips, and small sounds, evidently of pleasure and encouragement, came crackling from his throat.

'And you such a smart one at keeping out of trouble,' went on Sophie, taking up a towel and beginning to dab at his tender flesh. 'What came over you?'

Johnny laughed cheerlessly: 'Sticks and horses' hooves,' he said. 'And flails.'

'It's growing, this violence. You can feel it.'

'Some people,' Johnny said, flinching, 'can feel it a lot more than others.'

'In the air, I mean. People are getting rougher and wilder. There's a nastiness about.'

'A poison running in the blood,' Columbine started up in her mesmerical fashion, as if quoting. 'A curdling of the juices. Something bad is bubbling.'

They heard footsteps coming down from street level. The boy straightened with a start, his hands held together as if in prayer.

'I didn't see a single one of them, Sis. If I could put a face to them . . . '

This piece of vainglory was interrupted by the opening of the door. It was Otto. He carried a newspaper, which he began to wave in the air as a prelude to speech, but before he could open his mouth the moon-boy flung himself forward and all but toppled him.

'Steady on!' laughed Otto, with good humour and not a trace of surprise. He tossed the paper to the floor, close to where Johnny lay. 'Give a man a chance!'

Busy hands were hung about his neck, and he struggled forward with the lad dangling like a pendant. He fell onto the sofa by Johnny's feet. The boy's lips were working furiously and unavailingly, highpitched creaking noises being all that emerged, like an unoiled door on its hinges.

'Poor thing,' said Sophie with a sympathetic little smile. 'He's missed you.'

'And only a few days since I was here,' replied Otto, attempting to calm the onslaught with pats and fondlings. He reached into a pocket and brought out a bar of chocolate which the boy grasped in one hand, still using the other to claw wildly in manic affection.

'D . . . Daddy!' came the word from his lips after a prolonged and painful struggle.

'Bless him,' added Sophie, concluding her ministrations on Johnny's back. 'He's a good boy.'

'So you've been a good boy,' Otto encouraged, bouncing him a little on his knee for all that he was far beyond babyhood. 'Unlike our Johnny here, eh?'

'Rats,' Johnny said.

They could hear the rain beating into spreading puddles outside the window. The light was already fading. Columbine sat haloed in the brightness of a small lamp where she stabbed at her eggshell.

'The rats are gnawing at our entrails,' she declared, not taking her eyes from the petals of sky blue her brush created.

'He'll be all right,' Sophie pronounced.

'Says she,' replied Johnny at once. 'An arm that won't do its business. A neck that won't let the head turn.'

'But nothing wrong with the tongue, it's clear.'

The moon-boy had been pacified and now rested his head on Otto's shoulder, a smile of pure contentment on his face. Otto indicated the newspaper, which Johnny had begun to scan.

'They're blaming the Communists,' he said.

'They would.'

'Stirred up the workers, they're saying. Attacked the police.'

'And how,' Johnny asked, 'do you recognise a Communist? All these stupid labels – Socialists, Fascists, Nationalists. They're meaningless to me. And who were the men with the flails?'

'Flails?'

There was no mention in the article of a third force. Loyal and right-thinking members of the public, it said, had come to the aid of the beleaguered police.

'Here's an attack on Gold,' he said. 'They describe him as a leader of the Jewish-inspired international conspiracy to ruin the country's finances and destroy its moral fibre.'

'They would!' Otto laughed.

'And a photograph. He's certainly not our man.'

Sophie had begun to paint her nails.

'Isn't there something in that?' she queried. 'All these troubles we've got, and the foreigners make fools of us. Drive them out. Let it be *our* people who make the money.'

'Or the losses,' said Johnny.

'If our people make the money,' Otto threw in, 'it'll be just a few of them, you can be sure of that. The likes of us won't see much of it.'

'Not unless we fight for it,' Johnny agreed. 'Nobody gives you anything for the pleasure of it. You have to grab what you can. That's the way everyone behaves, even those who're fond of fine talk about things like peace and justice. Nobody I ever heard of put fine sentiments before money.'

With these deep thoughts he returned to the newspaper. A brief silence ensued, broken only by a strange and tuneless keening sound. Columbine was humming to herself as she worked. A wind gathered outside, shaking the windows and driving the rain heavily at the glass.

'Time's moving,' Sophie said at last, applying a bright red to her lips. 'You'd best be going or Hans will be asking questions.'

Columbine, making no immediate reply, put down her brush. She took up the egg and turned it slowly in her fingers. It was completely decorated with the pretty flowers. She held it to the light, put it briefly to her lips and then hurled it ferociously at the wall. It smashed and slithered – spattered yoke, shattered shell, slimy albumen – to the floor.

'Dear Hans,' she said.

Johnny was aware of none of this. His eyes had been caught by a headline in bold print on the front page: SOLICITOR AND MISTRESS CRUELLY SLAIN. He could scarcely believe the story that he read.

It was a typical, sensational report, of the kind he normally read with relish. Now a strange fear took hold of him, a fear he could not comprehend. It was, surely, a coincidence.

Columbine was already leaving, calling a farewell that went unheeded.

'Looking for his name in the paper,' Otto joked.

It must have happened soon after he had left the building. He remembered the swishing cloak ascending the staircase. Suppose that he himself had been seen! He pictured himself passing through the door to the street. Had he been spotted?

He continued reading: police officers were spending hours in the office, interviewing members of the staff and searching meticulously for clues, including fingerprints.

Could the police discover prints on a dead man's hand? he wondered desperately. Had he left anything behind?

'So you've some work for me tonight, my chieftain,' Otto said. 'Another man-hunt.'

He knew that he must reveal nothing to Otto. Since Grimm had not been the man he was seeking, the murder must surely be unconnected. He could not, however, prevent the thought from dwelling on his mind.

'Ocklynge,' he managed to say.

'In the city?'

'Maybe. Columbine's friend has been very clever. Only Alph has completely stumped him so far. But the two addresses we've got for Peter Ocklynge are both very old. He's probably not been at either for years. If you try one, I'll visit the other.'

'One of them's not a borsch factory, I suppose?'

Johnny barely registered the remark, but a vision of the recipe suddenly danced before his eyes and he saw the red blotches and shuddered.

15 Gone Away

It was a long night's work. The address had been easy enough to find – a warren of small workshops and traders' stalls under the arches of a railway –but tracking down his man had been another matter. Although the place teemed with life until well after most businesses had closed their doors, there seemed noone who had heard the name of Ocklynge.

At first he had found this frustrating, hurrying from one person to another and asking his question, but later it became a challenge. From the guarded replies, he soon began to suspect that there was a conspiracy of silence which a direct assault would have no chance of defeating. The only solution was an artful patience, and he spent some time simply enjoying the busy atmosphere, even buying a few simple items he would later find a use for.

His first breakthrough came soon after ten o'clock. He had bought a torch at one stall, and he took it to another at the far end of the mart, claiming that Peter Ocklynge had sold it to him and that it no longer worked. The vendor, looking sharply at him, protested that Ocklynge never sold torches and then, in some confusion, emphatically denied the very existence of anyone bearing that name.

'But I knew him,' Johnny insisted.

The man shook his head and turned away, muttering. He spoke behind his hand to the neighbouring traders, who stared at Johnny with a hostile distrust. Soon afterwards he saw that a young woman had become involved in this whispering. She, too, stared at him, but more from curiosity than fear, it seemed. She was about twenty-five years old, thin, her face drawn, and she held a shawl about her shoulders. He turned away, embarrassed.

Above the workshops, under the arches, there were a few small rooms, their semi-circular windows clouded with grime. There was a dark recess where stairs climbed to that level and, later on, he saw the woman nod to her friends and disappear into the blackness. A light came on above.

It was difficult to follow without being seen. He hovered at the stalls, drank a cup of strong coffee, listened to the ballads of a strident street singer. Always there seemed to be suspicious eyes upon him. Salvation came in the guise of a beggar, a well dressed and well spoken man of middle age who attempted to reason with his audience, explaining that he had a large family and had lost his job through no fault of his own. The response was antagonistic, and one or two young men began to push him about, telling him to be on his way. The beggar was offended and became belligerent in his turn. As the pushing and prodding grew more violent, Johnny slid away and climbed the stairs.

The woman, when she opened the door, looked at him for some time without saying a word.

'I'm looking for Peter Ocklynge,' he said.

The door began to close.

'He's come into some money. I need to find him.'

'Money?'

It opened a little. This time Johnny stepped back, confident that the bait had already been taken. He waited.

'What money?'

'Can I come in?'

It was a humble room, clean enough and adequate but with nothing other than life's essentials. They sat on uncomfortable hard-backed chairs. Now he saw how gaunt she was, and how tense.

'I get a bit of money,' she told him. 'Sometimes I do. But it's very little. It's not enough. I suppose he sends what he can.'

'Peter?'

She nodded: 'I don't expect he's got much himself. What's this money you're talking about?'

'A kind of legacy,' Johnny replied. 'I have to find him to tell him of it.'

'Leave it with me! Can't you do that? I'm his wife, after all – for what good it does me.'

'I couldn't!'

'I reckon I deserve a fair share of what's coming to him. How much is it?'

'Quite a lot. Enough to move you out of here.'

He saw that she was thinking hard. There was a shrewdness in her expression. She was down on her luck, but her brain was clear.

'Who's it from?'

'I can't say.'

'You can tell *me*.'

'No, it's the rules.'

'Rules be devilled!'

She was anxious to know, which meant that he held the best cards. At the very least he would play his hand the better. But she was holding out.

'I don't know where he is,' she said.

'Oh, surely.'

'No, he's disappeared. Long since. I used to wait for him, always thinking that the next month he would come, but I don't hope for that any more.'

'You've no idea where he is?'

She drew the shawl close about her.

'I know where he once was,' she replied. 'And haven't I thought of going there, only I know how he'd treat me for bothering him! But I don't know that I should tell you. The money's not likely to come my way.'

He said nothing, allowing her imagination to play with the thought that some of it might, indeed, come her way should Peter Ocklynge be found. He heard, faint on the night air, the ballad singer on his rounds. There were calls of 'goodnight' and 'sleep well!' from the traders below.

'I haven't told you this,' she said, glancing at the window. 'At the new spa, up in the mountains. He'll have changed his name, but you might find him there. That's where I heard he went, though it was a long time ago. I dread to think how long.'

She slid a ring from her finger, a circle of gold entwined by a scaled serpent.

'Give this to him,' she said, becoming fervent. 'Promise you'll do that. Promise!'

'I promise,' Johnny said easily.

'Tell him that I still love him and want him to come home. You'll do that?'

'Yes.'

'You promise?'

'Yes.'

She subsided. Johnny brought from his pocket the simple portrait.

'Could this be him,' he asked, 'when he was younger? I've no idea what he looks like.'

She studied it, tilting the paper as if to create an extra dimension.

'It could be,' she said. 'Perhaps. He's dark and very handsome. Tall . . . '

Here, though, there was a pounding of feet on the stairs and a hammering on the door. After a few seconds it was thrust open, and an athletic young man put his head into the room.

'I thought you'd sneaked up here,' he accused aggressively. 'Is he making a nuisance of himself, Marie?'

'No, no.'

'Asking questions?'

Johnny knew when the time for cunning had passed. He could tell that the young man was intent on violence whatever answers the woman gave. There was drink on his breath. His eyes were bright with excitement.

'About someone we've never heard of?'

Ducking low, Johnny sprinted for the door. A hand clutched at his shoulder but he shook it off, at the same time digging sharply with his elbow. Down the stairs and into the space under the arches. The place was deserted now, and there was noone to prevent him as he dashed away into the darkness, into a chilly drizzle which soon soaked his hair and worked under his shirt collar.

'Come back!'

He laughed. The call was distant, the young man was drunk. He would not be troubled by pursuers.

A dozen clocks chimed midnight as he made his way home. The streets were empty. His immediate mission over, he was increasingly aware of the ache in his arm and the stiffness of his neck from the adventures of the morning.

Perhaps it was his tiredness, but he fancied that he experienced an unnatural stillness as he took the stairs down to the basement room. He entered slowly, apprehensively. Sophie sat upright on a chair with a handkerchief to her face, her cheeks grotesquely smeared with make-up. Sprawled face down on the sofa was the boy, asleep but his body shuddering with the after-tremors of heavy sobbing. Brother and sister exchanged knowledge with their eyes.

'At the warehouse where you sent him,' Sophie stammered through her tears.

Otto was dead. The words were not necessary. Nor any details of the way he had died. He knew before she spoke.

'With a knife,' she said.

16 Of Good and Evil

'Moreover,' continued Mr Farg, by now well into his stride, 'it is often a mistake of the most crass kind to ask the question Why. For instance, Why is this planet of ours careering through the void like a runaway ball? Why must Man live but a few years on this runaway ball and then, inevitably, pass away? Why is human happiness but fleeting?

'Of course I do not deny that answers of a kind may be found to such questions. Has man not such ingenuity that he can invent a thousand speculative theories to meet every single scrap of fact? But what does such agitation of the brain produce? What does it serve? Does it issue in useful action?'

Johnny allowed this barrage to pass over his head. It was not required that he should answer. He sank further into his chair below a horizon of glistening Dresden figurines, and he heard, behind the interminable lecture, the sound of heavy rain hammering and clattering on the roof.

'And so it little avails to ask your question – why a man should kill brutally and apparently without any heed. It is simply one of the ineluctable facts of our existence. There are such men. Do we need to know why they behave as they do? We could, doubtless, make an investigation of early childhood, callousness in the home and so forth. But what would it serve? The man behaves as he does.'

He raised a swollen finger and stabbed it forward three, four times.

'Unless you acknowledge the otherness of people, that part of a man or woman you cannot ever reach but must accept as a fact of life, you will never be the true master of our craft. This man kills, perhaps for the enjoyment of it, on a whim. You and I are not like that, Johnny – our vices lie elsewhere – but this man is. Therefore ask no question Why.

'Another man acts from kindness, fair play, even a sense of decency. How foolish! you cry. What a simpleton! But so he behaves. You will seek the motive? Perhaps the craves the world's good favour, perhaps he fears divine retribution. No matter. You must understand that this is how he acts.'

Johnny had felt so low, so distressed, when he arrived that he had spoken unguardedly. It was not his habit to reveal his thoughts, let alone his emotions. Now he must pay the penalty.

'You have met such people?' Mr Farg asked directly.

'I've met hypocrites,' he replied bleakly. 'People with fine words. But I've never yet known one who put high ideals or fancy dreams above his own pocket.'

There was a dark brooding for some moments, a weighty silence.

'I still have high hopes of you, Johnny,' came the eventual pronouncement. 'You have undeniable potential, quite remarkable I think. Your wits are quick. You are a natural dissembler, slippery as a baby's bottom. But you have a great deal to learn.'

The criticism struck him painfully. He had been feeling depressed, irritated, resentful even, but he had fooled himself into believing that he was well regarded by this powerful man. Now he saw that he had been lax in his attention. The long discourse to which he had been subjected during the last half hour had been leading, all along, to this.

'I know,' he muttered abjectly.

'And perhaps little time in which to learn it.'

The fear plumed inside him. He saw again the cloak at the foot of the stairs. The recipe for borsch floated before his vision, its red stains spreading. Sophie's eyes announced Otto's death, which his imagination refused to picture.

'You knew . . . ' he began hesitantly, careful that it should not appear to be an accusation, 'you knew that I would be in danger?'

'Ah, what can we know for certain? Did I know it? No, in short. Did I suspect it? I can only ask, did you not yourself suspect it with all your worldly wisdom? Look at the rewards! Good money, eh? And that only to finance the search. There's much more should you succeed. Now, who would pay so much unless the mission were a troublesome one?

'The interesting question which now presents itself is whether you have the heart, the strength to match your guile. Most fascinated I shall be to learn it. The furnace is blowing hot, the coals are glowing red and you must be the anvil or the hammer. Which is it to be?'

Johnny, for the first time in his life, felt his natural artfulness desert him. He knew that he should answer promptly, confidently, but something prevented the pretence. Perhaps it was that he knew how expertly Mr Farg had judged him, so that the customary veneer was a futility. Perhaps it was the sheer profundity of the hopelessness he now experienced, his friend dead, the task not accomplished, a killer on the loose. He made no reply.

'Sursum corda, my man! Let us lift up our hearts! Are not these unhappy circumstances firm evidence that your investigations proceed well? You have made progress already, good progress. I don't doubt that you will succeed.'

Johnny nodded obediently. There was, after all, no escape from the bloody adventure he had involved himself in.

'You will kindly keep in touch with me throughout your travels. I have an insatiable curiosity.'

He turned away with a gesture which indicated that the audience was over, but as Johnny approached the door he called him back.

'Here,' he said, stooping to lift one of the Dresden figures in his crippled hands. 'A parting gift. I've seen you looking fondly at my pretty family.'

Johnny took it (a bonny lad with a blue suit and green, buckled shoes, nuring a lamb) and trusted that his distaste did not show.

'He has some value,' added his benefactor, 'but I'm sure that I can spare him. As long as I know that he will be cherished.'

Muttering his thanks, Johnny escaped. But Mr Farg had not quite finished. His voice came in pursuit down the stairs.

'Do help yourself to one of my cigars,' he called with fulsome generosity. 'And perhaps, if she would like it, one for your dear mother, too!'

PART TWO

Experience

17 Rite of Passage

Down the rough track through the trees they came, talking far more loudly than they needed, joshing one another mercilessly, the bags swung over their shoulders with an emphatic insouciance as if to say 'Look at us fine fellows down from the camp on Saturday night, just see how we'll liven the place up!' They kicked their boots at large stones and sent them spinning; they picked up sticks and hurled them, laughing, into the first row of conifers; they put back their heads and called raucously to an unseen audience of roisterous comrades and good-time girls, the exultant echoes driving them on, an affirmation, verifying them in their fierce yearnings.

A little way off there were stands of oak and ash, and the last leaves glowed upon them, burning reds, shades of incandescent orange, limpid yellows, the lovelier the more they were consumed. In the fading light, a thin mist wandering and rising among the grasses, they offered a reproach to the season, a quixotic reminder of warmer and more colourful times.

Johnny, hunched against the infiltrating cold, stalked silently among the jovial procession. The moment was coming. He had worked all week with these men on the say-so of Dorf, his ganger, but their employer, who knew nothing of this, might yet turn him away unpaid. An unpredictable character, they said: love you one day, knock you down the next.

They were passing small cottages, each with its garden plot wrested from the wilderness and defended by a low wooden fence. A leathery peasant stood glowering at them, an expression of contempt on his face. Only his eyes moved. A teenage girl appeared at a doorway and was immediately seized and tugged inside, to angry cries.

He had no pressing need of money, of course. Mr Farg had given him a handsome float. What he needed was acceptance. There was no room for the unattached at the Spa – he had learned that very quickly. It was designed as a playground for the rich, and unless you had a fortune to spend you had to be one of the workers. Casual drifters were hunted from the place like a deer fleeing the hounds.

'Come out, you swine!'

The shout brought them all up short. Johnny was alarmed to see Kristy, his fellow wielder of spade and axe, raising his fists towards one of the cottages. He rocked up and down on his heels with his young man's bristling energy. He was breathing heavily. How could this be? Kristy had seemed a good-natured creature, with a certain nervousness of temperament perhaps (a persistent twitch, a habit of turning away as he spoke and jerking his head to flick away the hair that fell over his brow) but with no signs of subterranean violence. Now he turned to his companions, his face darkening.

'Hit me with a stone,' he blustered. 'Someone in there's got a catapult. I'll pull his nose off!'

Dorf – big, slow, comfortable Dorf – put his hands on Kristy's shoulders as if preventing him from taking flight.

'Perhaps,' he reasoned, 'an accident.'

'Accident! With so much empty space to aim at?' Kristy indicated a reddened patch on his jaw. The skin was broken. 'Is that an accident?'

One of the cottage windows was open, but there was no sign of life within. A chicken came running busily across the grass as if answering a summons. The old peasant regarded the scene with no change of expression. He despised the workers and was content that they should know it.

'Hold, Kristy. Peace.'

The fourth member of their gang, the solitary and taciturn Venner, stood with hands in pockets, uninvolved, scarcely noticing. Behind him were men from other gangs who, following down the track, now loitered in the expectation of a fracas.

'Come on out!'

But it was only a gesture. It was obvious that nobody would obey the call, equally obvious that Kristy lacked the heart for a showdown. He allowed himself to be led away.

Johnny met the peasant's malignant stare. They both knew that a way of life was ending. Up by the camp a vast Palace of Mirth was being built. The gangs had laboured for a week, clearing the ground, but had made only a feeble impression on the area. Something prodigious would be created there. He and the peasant both knew what must follow – a proper road down to the Spa and then, in no time at all, new buildings clustering along the length of it. It was inevitable.

Yet he felt no sympathy. The world was ever changing: you had to change with it. These forest people, who in their pride refused to join the labour gangs, found even the short-term gain of decent wages passing them by. It was a crass narrowness. He saw the hatred in the man's eyes as a sign of boorish stupidity, and he turned away with a disparaging shrug and followed his companions down the slope.

Hours of undiluted pleasure! At the first sight of the Spa there was an involuntary slowing of their footsteps, as if they were in awe of the very thing they craved, frightened of their own passions. They tramped along in silence for a time, each man adjusting his private vision, nurtured throughout a week's hardships, to fit the rediscovered reality.

For Johnny it would be a fresh experience. He had arrived at dusk one evening, had barely noted the fine stone buildings near the centre with direction-signs pointing to casino, baths and hotels before being escorted up the hill to the camp. Now he was returning, to take advantage of the labourer's allowance – a fleeting taste of the rich man's dissipation.

'We'll sleep in clean sheets tonight!'

'Who'll have time for sleeping, my friend?'

Their banter started up again as they came down to the road that led into the Spa. They were a rough lot, uncouth, foul-mouthed, none too clean, but there was something childlike in their earnest desire to enjoy themselves. It made them vulnerable. They swung along the way, eager for sensation.

'Where's the young doxy who's been waiting all week to press her lips on mine?'

Their ribaldries went unanswered. The streets were empty. It was too early for serious pleasure, however much they attempted to invoke it. The rich had more patience.

At the near end of the street there was a large wooden building which the first of the men began to enter. The others followed them in, pushing and jostling. Johnny and his gang fought their way forward and found chairs by a long unvarnished table. It was a bar they were in, meagrely furnished and with sawdust on the floor, a place designed for the workers. A bored looking man stood behind the counter, quite unmoved by the fact that, despite the influx, not a single person had ordered a drink. He knew that they had no money. He was patient, like the rich.

Minutes passed, half an hour. The noise increased but the ears grew accustomed to it. Johnny, fatigued by his unprecedented labours, found his eyes beginning to close. What woke him was the sudden silence. A man had entered, tall, about thirty, with rich auburn hair and a drooping moustache to match. His skin, though, had none of the pallor common to redheads. It was a ruddy brown, so that his whole face seemed to glow with a smouldering fire.

'Kurt Cherfas,' Kristy said into Johnny's ear.

Their boss displayed an assumption of authority in the way he held his head, in the easy grace of his movements. He himself wore working clothes and he carried a large rucksack which he tossed onto one of the tables. The workers fell back, allowing him to take the most prominent chair. He began to unfasten the straps, all the while looking keenly about him, meeting the eyes of men who seemed somewhat abashed, apprehensive in his presence, and who quickly turned away. He was their master.

'We're barely on target,' he announced abruptly. 'You're in danger of falling behind.'

Nobody replied to this. It was obvious that noone dared. Yet Johnny, observing the man closely, read other signs in that mobile face: he was adept at such interpretations. Yes, there was certainly a ruthlessness there – you had to expect that from a man who had made himself a success while still young. But there was humour, too. Johnny read the lines. He knew the type. He was sensitive to the restlessness of character, the impatience, the need to prod people into responses either through criticism or the play of wit. All this he saw before Cherfas had yet spoken another word, while the various gangers came forward to accept the week's pay for their men.

'You, Carllson. Where are you working?'

'At the stream, sir.'

'The revetment? You're adrift on the schedule. That's money away.'

There was an agonised moment during which the poor man balanced the risk of arguing against the impossibility of leading a team for which he had made no fight.

'It was the recent rains, sir. They brought the bank down.'

'You reported that?'

'I thought it . . . obvious. Sir.'

'Aha!'

Cherfas came to life. He had no doubt made his accusation to emphasise his control over them but now, Johnny saw, he attacked for the pure challenge of it. A game was in progress.

'It was obvious, you say. Any man here would have known it. What do you all say?'

Nobody uttered a word. Cherfas stood and swept his eyes round the room. The bored barman was slumped over his counter, his head resting on his arms, his eyes closed. His time would come.

'Hey, you! Wake him up, someone!'

Dutiful hands shook the sleeper with an energy that made him start. He was motioned forward, stumbling between the tables until he stood, blinking, by the side of Carllson the ganger.

'When it rains,' Cherfas asked him enthusiastically, 'what happens to the river?'

'To the river?' repeated the barman, somnambulistically.

'No clues, gentlemen,' warned Cherfas, beginning to enjoy himself. 'Let this man answer impartially.'

'When it rains,' replied the barman slowly, 'the river rises.'

'And?'

'And runs more quickly and sometimes floods the banks.'

'Yes, yes. I admit it! Very good. Anything else?'

Cherfas looked from one man to another, a merry gleam in his eye. He was gratified by the silence.

'I think it's money away, Carllson,' he smiled.

The barman, too, glanced about him. Bewildered, he sought for some clue as to what he should say, but noone dared to prompt him.

'A good effort, nonetheless.'

Cherfas took an oilskin wrapper from the rucksack. He drew out a bundle of notes and tipped coins onto the table where they rattled and spun. Carefully, he took a few of the notes between finger and thumb and lifted them from the wad. He held them in the air, nodding at Carllson as if expecting him to sanction the deduction.

'On occasion,' faltered the barman, not understanding that he had been dismissed, 'it undermines its own banks and carries the soil away.'

Johnny knew what the reaction would be. He had judged his man and knew the judgement to be sound. The rest of the company, though, were tense with fear of retaliation. They watched Cherfas advance on the barman, seize his hands in his own and raise his arms aloft as if he were a champion boxer.

'Bravo!' he exclaimed. 'A victory in the very last round!'

He led the bemused fellow to a chair and helped him climb up on it. There he perched, trembling, perspiring, as the workers began to nudge one another and grin, realising that the worst would not happen.

'Well? Shall we have no applause for this knowledgeable man?' Cherfas admonished them. 'Where's your sense of fair play?'

He was in an obvious good humour, and now all the men clapped violently, some of them dragging the caps from their heads and waving them in the air.

'And your gang, Carllson,' he added. "Hasn't this man paid for a little extra wenching tonight? Do him the honour of bearing him back to his own domain.'

They obeyed the signs he made, each member of the gang bending to take a leg of the chair. They hoisted it into the air, the barman grasping desperately at their shoulders for support, and staggered across the room, depositing their burden behind the counter. Cherfas sat down again and, when they returned, pushed the whole amount across the table for Carllson to distribute.

'Next man,' he said flatly, forgetting the incident in a moment. That little joke was over. There was no more fun to be had from it. 'You, Berger.'

One by one the gangers were called forward. Johnny knew that Cherfas had seen him and had marked him out as a newcomer. Something would be made of it. He felt a gurgle of fear in his stomach and began, at the same time, to prepare himself. All the while the men who had taken their money were massing round the bar, thrusting out their fists and demanding to be served.

Dorf was the last to be summoned. An unflappable character, he was quite happy to sit musing until his turn came.

'We've a new man,' he said simply and without deference. 'He's worked all week. He's earned the rate.'

Cherfas was lightly combative.

'You've gone into the hiring business, eh?'

'It was agreed. I was a man short. Here's the note.'

This was waved away.

'And the name of your conscript?'

'He's Johnny.'

'A national?'

Johnny approached the table.

'Of course!' he said with mock indignation. 'From the city. I've a past we'll agree not to talk of if you'll pay me decent money for hard sweat.' He had to be bold, even slightly outrageous: Cherfas would respond to that. But if he went too far he would be squashed under the man's thumb. 'And I'm aching all over for doing your business.'

Cherfas laughed: 'I only take on men. Are you a man?'

'There's a few ladies who'd say so.'

'They would, eh! Very good. And you like a drink?'

'Not one by itself.'

His interrogator squinted appreciatively. He was pleased with the answers. The lad had spunk.

'We'll see what kind of man you are,' he offered. 'Convince me and you'll get your money. You reckon he can hold his drink, Dorf?'

'Maybe.'

'You've a full gang if he can. How do you like your liquor, Johnny – long or short?'

'Short.'

Was that a smart answer? There'd been no time to think the thing through. He was actually a beer drinker, but he doubted that his stomach would hold the quantities Cherfas had in mind. On the other hand, beer would have taken longer to sink. He must not lose control of the contest.

'Barman!'

Service was immediate. Moreover, all the workers seemed to divine, on the instant, that something was up. They watched the drinks being deposited on the counter, half a dozen glasses in a line. Schnapps. Johnny had a momentary vision of Sophie's face, the bright red lips with the glass tilted, the dulled eyes.

'Your health, my friend.'

Cherfas was drinking a cocktail. The ice clattered as they touched glasses. 'And yours.'

He sipped, smiling. He sipped slowly. That he disliked gin was irrelevant. The thing was to play for time. His tormentor's task was not to allow it. Johnny felt no resentment about this. The rules were clear. Why should he complain? He was rushed through his first three drinks, the dead glasses taken from his hand and replaced. He felt the effect already. He was weary and had eaten only bread and cheese for lunch. There were people about him, talking and joking, and the noise grew gradually louder.

'You're enjoying yourself?' Cherfas asked, exchanging glasses yet again.

'Who doesn't,' he replied as jauntily as he could manage, 'when someone else is paying?'

He contrived to dribble the liquor down his chin, but this trickery was spotted immediately and Cherfas, congratulating him on the failed ploy, replenished his glass with a flourish. Dorf sat close by, impassive. Kristy hovered, making little puckerings of his face which were no doubt meant to encourage, whereas they began to have a cumulative unnerving effect. Venner had gone.

The drinks kept on coming. After the first six they came three at a time. Nine was more than he had ever drunk in his life, but he was still on his feet, and he heard himself cracking jokes which seemed to make other people laugh. The laughter was surely excessive. Kristy's face loomed large, twitching.

'A secret life in the city,' he heard Cherfas saying. 'You have an unscrupulous past, Johnny?'

'I would perhaps agree with you,' he retorted heavily, 'if I could possibly pronounce the word.'

Cherfas guffawed and beat his hand down on Johnny's shoulder so that he staggered. But he propped himself against the counter, raised his hand and drained the glass.

'Encore!' he mouthed.

At the centre of his brain, it seemed, a clear straight path, brightly illuminated, ran between thick swirlings of fog. It was difficult to keep to that path and the fog kept drifting across it, but he had not quite lost his way. He knew there were things he should not say, and his consciousness remained alert to the danger even as its edges became clouded. He knew, too, that he must put on a show and, although he had no sure sense of how well he performed, he found himself able to raise his voice and chaff his companions.

The bar was full. He was not focusing well now, but occasionally he would make out a group of people at a table, their faces raised towards him, perhaps calling out to him, perhaps simply talking to one another. Kristy was up close to him, whispering in his ear, but he could not understand what was said. Dorf seemed not to have moved at all. Cherfas was always coming and going, slapping him on the back.

Ebb and flow. Sensation became tidal. Bright gleams and dim vision. Rolling, crashing waves of sound, receding and receding. His fingers on a glass, other hands on his shoulders, then a numbness, an airiness, a feeling that he was lifted and borne away, away into realms beyond words and thoughts, the encumbrances of mind . . .

18 Healing Waters

It was the chafing of the paper against his chin which woke him. He brought up his hand, his eyes still closed, and tugged the wad of notes from his top pocket. He had been paid. He was accepted. This he understood still without opening his eyes: banknotes felt like nothing else to his experienced fingers.

'Kristy?'

There was no reply. The large room echoed. He heard that it was large and empty. He had no recollection of coming here, of being brought here. His head felt too small to contain the throbbing inside it.

'Dorf? Venner?'

A pointless roll-call. He opened one eye. He lay on a wooden pallet, fully dressed apart from his boots which someone had charitably removed. His crumpled leather jerkin lent him the semblance of a dead cow. He was in a long dormitory, littered with the bags and caps and walking sticks of men who wished to leave their workaday trappings behind them.

'Blast you, Cherfas!' he muttered, but without venom.

It was already the afternoon. The sun was high and too bright for his condition. Nevertheless, he swung himself into a sitting position, fumbled his feet into his boots and hobbled to the window.

The Spa! He looked down on a scene which he at first believed to be the creation of his poisoned blood – he clamped a hand to his forehead to correct his focus. The images did not change. To the left, a tree-lined avenue wound sedately between solid stone buildings designed in a sober classical style. There were pediments above the windows, ribbed columns framing the entrances. Burgher respectability: the past. To the right (no, he did not hallucinate) all was manic, aggressive flux – at the agitated centre the New Casino (so it proclaimed itself in neon) whose swooping concrete forms and garish colour suggested a blancmange freshly emerged from its mould; clamouring all around it restless buildings which seemed to vie with their neighbours in bold, melodramatic display. Some boasted cubistic utility of form, not a curved line to be seen, all decoration shunned save for the occasional face daubed with a primary colour; others piled grotesquerie upon grotesquerie in an expressionistic hysteria, never allowing the eye to rest upon any surface: the present or, perhaps, the future. Here harmony, grace and tastefulness were evidently regarded as insipid weaknesses. It was a hymn to supercharged flamboyance. Calm was to be found only by contemplating the forest beyond where, above the ravages of the builders, the dark conifers guarded their silent and shadowy realm, inviolable, immemorial.

Where the old Spa met the new there were steps cut into the side of a mountain spur, and Johnny saw that they swarmed with people, a continuous procession down, a more intermittent, laboured straggle up the steep incline. What was their goal? Looking up, he could see trees encircling the summit and, rising among and above them, what seemed to be a huge dome of glass, flashing a molten white under the sun.

'What's your business? The light-fingered game, is it?'

He swung round to find a large, muscled woman brandishing the handle of a broom at him. She breathed heavily, seemingly eager for a skirmish.

'I'm staying here.'

'Not at this time of day you're not. Don't you know the rules? They're written up on the wall' – pointing to a yellowing sheet of paper which hung from a nail – 'for those who can read. Everybody out between the hours of ten and four. All this junk shouldn't be here, but it always is. They won't settle their bills until this evening, so they think they can leave a mess behind them. How am I supposed to clean the place?'

He muttered an apology and stumbled outside, pausing to lace his boots only when he was half way down the stairs. The sounds above his head suggested that his colleagues' personal effects were being hurled into the corners of the room. He escaped into the street and turned in the direction of the steps he had seen, addictively drawn to the bustle, the vibrant press of humanity.

It was no place for young men or, strangely, for women. He saw how a shuffling and panting column of weary souls laboured to the summit, the breath of these sufferers made all the shorter by their filling the air with vain curses. He tagged on the end. The sun struck warm against his face but he sensed, too, the underlying tang of autumn.

'You'd think they'd devise something mechanical to take us up,' one of his fellow climbers complained. 'In this day and age.'

'But then,' replied another, 'we'd doubtless undervalue the cure.'

'We'd be less in need of it!'

These were for the most part well-to-do folk, he could tell by the cut of their cloth, and it took him only moments to divine the purpose of their route-march. The glass dome covered the famed Palace of Waters. It was held together (he saw while still below the summit) by vast arcs of cast iron resembling the ribs of a stranded whale. Indeed, from the outside the whole building seemed stranded upon its platform of granite.

'A hundred and three,' gasped a tottering ancient, pausing at the top. 'Steps. I counted.'

'There'll be fewer going down.'

They entered. The huge tiled arena of the palace spread around them, furnished only with a quincunx of porcelain stoves (their delicate enamelled patterns contrasting absurdly with their cumbersome bulk) and clusters of the type of chairs more commonly seen on the decks of ocean liners. There was an unnatural, funereal quiet: conviviality was evidently bad for the health. Or perhaps, Johnny reflected, the climb had simply sapped their ailing powers.

He noticed, with his relentless eye, that each seated group represented a distinct social stratum. The highest orders, the fading aristocracy, gathered around the central stove, though spurning any show of luxury as if kind comfort might reduce the healing properties of the rust-coloured water they sipped from their metal breakers.

'A vile febrifuge.'

The sardonic comment was offered by a man seated close by and Johnny, turning, was amazed to see Venner among a group of artisans dressed in their Sunday best. His surprise had several sources. Venner was not one to mix with company; he was in his middle years, no doubt, but considerably younger than the general clientele; and he seemed the least likely of men to be caught up by a sudden fad.

'Tastes like piss and soda water.'

'Then why,' Johnny asked, clattering a chair into position, 'do you drink it?'

Venner looked vacantly into space for some time, and when he replied there was no trace of irony in his voice.

'Obedience to orders.'

Johnny laughed: 'I don't see you as the servile type. Whose orders?'

'Doctor's. Damn fool that he is. I never credited the cure from the beginning.'

'Then why . . ?'

Venner turned a thoughtful gaze upon him, as if considering whether he could be trusted with a confidence. When he spoke again, however, there was no immediate hint of personal revelations.

'Because I'm a believer in the buffeting of chance. Because I choose to be tossed by any wind that blows. Do you understand?'

Johnny shook his head. Venner swirled the contents of his mug, pulled a face and took a gulp. He sat silent for a considerable time.

'Once I was an ambitious young demon,' he said eventually. 'There was nothing I wasn't going to do. I was bright enough, useful with my hands, a winner at cards, a show-off with the ladies. A cocky young buck, if the truth be told. You know the sort – nothing original, but I was going to make a mark. That was the unwritten plan. You'd like a mug of this?'

Johnny waved the suggestion away.

'Rich in minerals,' Venner advertised unconvincingly. 'It'll bolster your blood.'

'No thank you.'

'Quite right. A sound judgement.'

He drank deeply and then, with a flourish, sent the empty mug sliding along the tiles beneath his chair.

'They called me up for the war. In the uniform I was even more cocky. But then came the trenches and the months of mud and rats, and then the gas . . . That's all that's wrong with me.'

He stared into Johnny's eyes.

'Yes, that's all. Just a few years of mud and rats with a light gassing thrown in. Educationally beneficial, I suppose, but not too good for the body. I don't work so well, as you may have noticed. Dorf carries me.'

'And so the waters of the Spa?'

'So, finally, this. It's a complete waste of energy.'

Distantly there were raised voices, the sound penetrating the glass dome, but indecipherably. Around the stoves the men sat still, save when shaky arms lifted mugs to lips.

'And the war – what did it do, Johnny? What has it done to us all?'

'We're defeated.'

'Yes, defeatist,' Venner agreed, perhaps wilfully misrepresenting him. 'No point in fighting your fate. There's nothing we can do. Man errs so long as he strives. Our businesses collapse, our currency loses its value by the week. The foreigners are at our gates. I've learned not to hope. For anything. More than that, I simply go where I'm pushed. It's as good a philosophy as any.

'I drift along as the spirit takes me. We're all moved by the same spirit in the end, so why resist it? The doctor says visit the Spa and I visit the Spa. Why protest? Aren't I as likely to improve here as anywhere? Or to die?

'And these sharks making a killing at the Spa – are we gullible fools for allowing it? You may speak for yourself, but I choose what I allow. I'm merely happier not caring a damn.'

As he finished these words there was a huge crashing sound followed by a prolonged and pretty tinkling of shattered glass. A great hole had appeared in one section of the dome, and an unmarshalled army of thickset men now advanced through it. They were peasants from the forest, short stocky types with long staves in their hands and uncompromising expressions on their faces. They must, Johnny reasoned, have approached along one of the tracks through the trees to the top of the spur.

'Where is she?'

The leader was a broad-chested man of about forty dressed in worn leather overalls. Raising his stick, he swept it through the air and brought it down softly to lie across the throat of the nearest seated drinker. He grasped both ends.

'This man's life for our Hildegard. Where is she?'

19 Cherchez la Femme

The man with the stave across his throat – a frail greybeard with watery eyes – dropped his mug and began to whimper.

'Who's got her?' his would-be executioner demanded. 'Who took our Hildegard?'

The thought that any of the assembled valetudinarians could woo a young maiden from her hearth and home, let alone take her by force, was so outrageous that Johnny had to stifle a laugh. He was obliged to treat matters rather more seriously, however, when the rest of the band followed their leader's example, each selecting a helpless invalid and forcing his head back onto his shoulders.

Venner spoke quietly in Johnny's ear: 'Cherfas has the girl.'

'Where?'

'Who knows? Perhaps at the Abode of Rest.'

He could say no more before they, too, were seized and half throttled. Johnny's windpipe ached, and he fought for breath.

'Don't doubt that we'll do for you all,' the leader went on in a sneering voice. 'There's not much life here as it is. Then we'll lay waste to the whole place. Burn it to the ground! You city scum have got it coming to you, desecrating our land with your palaces of filth!'

Johnny caught a look of deep, unfathomable spite in his captor's eye and Mr Farg's phrase repeated itself in his brain: the otherness of people. It would have been comforting to believe that these men would flinch from carrying out so violent a threat, one so out of proportion, surely, to whatever wrong had been done. At this moment, however, he knew that they were fully prepared for it.

'Wait!' he tried to say, but the pressure on his larynx only increased and he was reduced to weakly flapping his arms.

'There was peace in these forests,' the tirade continued, 'until you newcomers arrived with your trickery and your whoring and your fancy buildings. And what's that young vermin doing shaking his fist at me?'

He stomped forward and heaved Johnny from his seat. There was an odour of pine needles, onions and human sweat.

'You've something to say?'

'I think I've seen your Hildegard.'

'Ha!'

'If you'd describe her. . . . '

'Beautiful,' was the immediate response, 'and innocent. Blonde. Sixteen years and innocent. Where is she?'

'With a man who'll protect her.'

'Liar! There are none down there.'

'It's true,' Johnny protested. 'A man who took her in to guard her innocence.'

'And kept her for the night?' The belligerent face came close to his. 'She's been gone a night.'

Only an equal brusqueness would serve.

'You have no criminals in the forest?' he demanded. 'There are no thieves or seducers? Are you all to be condemned for the wicked few? There are good men at the Spa, too. This man will care for your Hildegard.'

The peasant was for a second nonplussed. He took a step back and eyed his confederates.

'Pick two men and I'll take them to her,' Johnny offered confidently. 'They'll fetch her back unharmed.'

The tension had already eased. The staves wavered.

'One hour,' the leader replied. 'Any longer and these friends of yours won't live to take another dose.'

He grabbed hold of a mug, sniffed its contents and, with a contemptuous gesture, tipped the liquid onto the ground.

'If she's touched, the place will burn!'

Johnny set off with two sullen foresters, who descended the hundred and three steps in complete silence. They were unhappy with their mission, he could tell. This was enemy territory they were entering. Their straightforwardness was out of place. They clutched their sticks and followed him, almost obediently, through the foreign streets.

Behind the New Casino was an edifice shaped like a corkscrew with, on the top, a glass-walled restaurant mimicking the neck of a bottle. Tucked between the two was the Abode of Rest, a low building with an ersatz eastern flavour – modern minarets, archways hinting at inner courtyards, flat roofs. Johnny stationed his two companions outside and ventured within. He first crossed a formal garden, where a fountain played, then found himself passing along a colonnade with water-lilied ponds at either side. At length he came to an entrance framed with drapes of purple cloth which extended inside a kind of vestibule. An elegantly dressed man sat behind a desk, smoking a fragrant shoot.

'Members only,' was his uncompromising welcome.

'Kurt Cherfas,' Johnny tried. 'It's urgent.'

A smoke ring formed over his head.

'Our clients are anonymous,' came a reply in indifferent tones. 'I'm unable to help you.'

'He won't forgive you if he's not called.'

'Rules, old thing. Sure you understand.'

It was not an occasion for subtlety. He skirted the desk and dashed through the vestibule, the langorous voice calling after him. There was a wide carpeted passage with framed prints on the walls. He heard music from behind a door, which he wrenched open to discover, on a velvet-covered dais in the centre of a large softly-furnished room, a string quartet playing something refined and classical. A visual shock, however – all four musicians, fiercely concentrated on their work, were pinkly and vulnerably naked. The audience, similarly unencumbered, sprawled in twos and threes on soft coverlets all around.

'Kurt Cherfas?'

His raucous intervention had no obvious effect on the pervading serenity. Cherfas, he could see, was not here. He tugged the door closed and ran on. He passed a trellised archway festooned with late flowers and saw, beyond, a small grassed area where couples dallied by a pool. Again, no sign of his man. He hurried on, his frustration gathering. Around a corner was another door: he pulled it open, to find himself enveloped in billowing steam. His first instinct was to escape, but as he backed into the passage he heard footsteps fast approaching. He took a pace inside and closed the door. Shadows moved beyond the thick veil of steam. The moisture settled on his lungs and he gasped for air. His clothes began to cling.

A short, squat and hairy man emerged from the vapour and gazed disbelievingly upon the apparition of Johnny in his soaking garb. He laughed, uproariously, and dragged him further inside, calling out to his unseen companions as he did so.

'Dag, Brigitte – come, look at this!'

They began to solidify all around him, until a group of five or six stood shaking their heads and smiling.

'You're bashful, eh? Don't wish us to see!'

'No, he has to leave early and wants to be ready!'

Johnny's face was too red from the heat to show any change of colour.

'I'm looking for Kurt Cherfas,' he said, as if that explained everything.

They howled in unison, their flesh trembling, but one of the women, sympathising, took the sleeve of his jacket between her fingers.

'He's not here,' she said. 'You'll find him in the Red Room.'

'But knock first,' grinned one of the others. 'If you know what's good for you.'

They shepherded him through the mist to the exit, hugely entertained. He was a visitor from an alien world, unadapted to the new environment. He shivered in the heat.

'Two doors along – a red door.'

'But knock first!'

They watched him for a moment, waving their encouragement, and then were gone. He had never felt so wet. The hair lay flat on his forehead. His arms and legs were sticky with damp. He reached the red door and knocked.

'Mr Cherfas?'

He knocked again.

'Go away, blast you!'

The resistance restored his spirits at once. Cherfas was inside: he must be persuaded to come out and play his prescribed part. Johnny beat his fist on the woodwork and waited. A count of ten? He had reached eight when the door was flung open and Cherfas, berobed, stood glowering before him.

'Oh, my . . .'

The anger passed instantly to incredulity and every bit as swiftly to hilarity.

'And didn't I say you'd need drying out!' He pulled Johnny towards him and ran a hand over his hair. 'A poor bedraggled creature . . .' His voice hardened. 'Why do you ruin my sport?'

'The girl Hildegard. You must give her up – return her.' He saw the anger surging. 'There'll be a riot otherwise.'

'They *all* want her, my young water vole? Is that the problem?'

'Her own people from the forest. They'll kill for her and wreck the Spa if they've the chance. Your projects, too. They're holding hostages at the Palace of Waters.'

'And your role?'

'I've talked them out of it so far. But they must believe my story.'

'Which is?'

Cherfas opened the door and drew him inside. The Red Room knew no other colour, but many shades. Soft drapes hung over a huge four-poster bed where the beautiful Hildegard lay, pouting, her body covered by the flimsiest of vermilion sheets.

'That you are protecting the innocence of an innocent girl,' Johnny replied.

Hildegard turned, and the covering slipped to reveal a slender calf and five delicate toes, the nails burning a violent crimson.

'Who needed protection from the vile intentions of the populace,' Cherfas experimented.

'And perhaps,' Johnny ventured, 'was discovered by you just in time to save her virtue but too late to return her home before nightfall.'

'Quite so. And this morning I've been showing her the sights.'

Hildegard sat up on the bed, holding the thin sheet provocatively to her throat. She seemed not to see Johnny at all, bizarre though his appearance was.

'Come on, Kurt,' she chided. 'Be good to me.'

Cherfas led Johnny into a small dressing-room and began to change. The threat to his business interests was evidently real to him. He asked a series of questions about the incident at the Palace of Waters and listened attentively while Johnny suggested the tactics most likely to succeed. Their story was preposterous and must therefore be promoted outrageously. Apologies were also in order, so long as they gave no hint of guilt.

'Our chief problem,' Cherfas said, 'is the girl.'

He put his head into the Red Room and ordered her brusquely to dress herself.

'If this works,' he told Johnny, 'I've a job that'll suit you more than labouring. I need a man who can pull wool over the eyes . . . Hurry, Hildegard – the party's over!'

20 A Confession

Another awakening. This time he knew where he was – up at the labourers'
sleeping quarters in the mountain. It was Monday morning. He was not
hung-over, but very tired. He took a few deep breaths: not even a hint of the
chill he had feared after his soaking.

Now yesterday floated back. The peasants and their threats. At the memory
a bird seemed to panic in the dome of his skull: he could feel its wings brush
against his face. No, that couldn't be right. A waft of perfume. He thought of
Hildegard. The lovely Hildegard. He almost raised his arms to embrace her.

Then the climb to the Palace of Waters with Cherfas and the girl . . . the
earnestly related story . . . Cherfas a man of the people, table-thumping and
smiling by turns . . . Hildegard fortunately too stupid to be amused by the
ironies of the situation, and therefore doggedly repeating her lines . . . the
cynical response of the foresters at last yielding to the reassurance they had
sought all along . . . handshakes and a new understanding, however temporary.

Again, the brushing against his cheeks. He moved his head and it persisted.
That perfume, strangely familiar. His eyelids were as reluctant to lift as broken
blinds. A blur. Patches of colour coalescing to form . . . it could not be! Fingers
touched his chin. A giggle.

'Columbine!'

There was a round of applause from the assembled workers who stood circling
him and the striking new arrival, fragile in a severe costume of lime green and
cerise which emphasised the length of her gawky limbs. She leaned forward
and kissed his cheek, her cool lips leaving a pink heart where they had touched.
More applause.

'So our Johnny really does have a past,' Dorf permitted himself to joke.

'What the hell are you doing here?'

She spoke in a whisper everyone could hear: 'It's Hans. That's why I've
come.'

The ringing of a bell prevented her revelations being broadcast to a general
audience. The men who had never stopped gawping at her now automatically
collected their napsacks and tools and began to drift away.

'You can't come here,' Johnny protested redundantly, sitting up and running
a hand through his hair. 'This isn't a place for women.'

'The world is no place for women,' she proclaimed. 'Male dominance, the
masculine principle, priapus, the machine. Pity us.'

'Quite so, Columbine.'

He gathered his possessions together, everything he had brought from the
city. Tonight he would be sleeping elsewhere. His wits had earned him a new
situation.

'Woman the receiver, Man the deceiver.'

He led the way outside into the cold morning air. The ground was hard with
the first heavy frost of the autumn, and he blinked in the sunshine. The men
were grouped around a small hut that served as a site office, and as each

foreman emerged with the day's duties his gang accompanied him along one of the tracks to their place of work.

'You're a complication,' Johnny told Columbine as he waited, 'but I don't suppose Hans will take long to sniff you out.'

'It's unlikely,' she replied with an undeniable triumph in her voice.

'Why?'

She put her head against Johnny's shoulder and began to laugh. Their bodies shook with it.

'Because I killed him.'

21 The Tower Room

Cherfas came striding from the hut, his auburn hair and proud moustache glinting under the bright, slanting rays of the sun.

'I see,' he grinned, 'that you're protecting the innocence of an innocent.'

'This is Columbine.'

'And you know, Columbine, that this young fraud has talked himself into a job?'

'She's just arrived.'

Cherfas set off at a rapid pace down a steep and twisting path, and they were obliged to follow.

'A personal assistant,' he continued, in buoyant mood. 'I've long been in need of someone to oil the wheels, as they say. There's a good deal of talking and bargaining to be done.'

They were already in sight of the bold new buildings below.

'See that lot!' he enthused. 'That's money you're looking at. Every brick, every paving stone, every barrel of concrete and pane of glass. I came here with practically nothing.'

Columbine, who perhaps had seen little of the place in her rush to find Johnny, shivered from a kind of wonder and came to a sudden halt.

'The contours of the Apocalypse,' she stated.

Cherfas looked strangely at her.

'I just build them,' he said with a shrug. 'I don't design them.'

Johnny, like most members of his class, tended towards conservatism in matters of taste: plush and gilt rather than chrome and glass.

'You couldn't *live* in those buildings,' he said.

'Ha!' Cherfas laughed aloud as he led them down. 'We'll see about that!'

As they walked through the streets of the Spa there were continual calls of respectful greeting to the man, who acknowledged them with casual waves of the hand. When they passed a building site, where the foundations of yet another architectural novelty rose above the surrounding clay and the labourers scurried to and fro with pickaxes and buckets, he ran his hand along the concrete, inspecting it. He called the ganger to him and, having introduced his new right-hand man, began to talk figures. Johnny, knowing a game when he saw one, nodded meaningfully. How much substance, he wondered, was there to Cherfas's expertise?

This business done, Cherfas took them into the heart of the new Spa, past the casino and the Abode of Rest to an array of austere, cubistic buildings connected by iron walkways painted a brilliant yellow. They climbed a ladder (yellow, too) and crossed a flat roof to where a door gave access to a square tower, stacked against the neighbouring blocks like a thumb against a clenched fist. Inside there was a single room oddly furnished with a number of faded velvet couches, purplish of hue and lavishly fringed, and an armchair with three legs which tilted haplessly in a corner like a drunken client at closing time.

'It's been used as a storeroom,' Cherfas explained as the other two progressed around the place in a kind of cushioned clamber, each lurching movement raising a cloud of dust from the horsehair stuffing. 'But it would serve you, I dare say? Space is short at the Spa.'

There was nothing above or below. There was no running water, no gas or electric lighting. Heating, yes: Johnny, peering out of one of the small windows, saw a ventilation shaft leading up from what seemed to be a boiler house, and he felt the warmth coming through the wall.

'I don't understand,' he said. 'What's the room for?'

Cherfas grinned: 'You don't expect good sense as well as design, surely,' he chided. 'That's not the way of it at all. This room's simply an accident. The outside walls happened to create it. These young architects are paid for their genius, not for their practicality.'

It was obvious that, as a down-to-earth builder, he found architectural pretensions ridiculous; equally obvious that he had no real quarrel with a profession which had helped to make him prosperous.

'I ask you to imagine the birth of this tower. Forget function. See our genius in his city studio proudly regarding his model. Children's play bricks! He leans his head this way and that, squinting and frowning. No. It won't do!'

He showed his teeth to Columbine, attempting to charm her.

'His cat rolls over and thrusts its legs out, horizontally. Everything is long and square and flat. It needs a new dynamic – but what? Then in trips his wife from the kitchen to announce a meal which, in the throes of his problem, he could well do without. He explains and laments; she sighs and nods, being used to his dilemmas. She lights a candle, prettifies the table at which they will eat – and returns to the oven, leaving a matchbox upright on the model's south wing.

'Ah, perfection! He calls her back, sweeps her appreciatively into his arms, and the dinner spoils.'

They laughed at his fancy and, gratified, he took his leave of them.

'But don't repeat a word of my nonsense,' he added, holding the door open. 'The actual designer of the place works for me here and has a share of the building. And he has no wife! He'll be along later to discuss details with you – if you think you'd like to use it. We can remove this rubbish and find something better.'

'We'll take it,' Johnny replied at once.

Alone, they finished exploring the room. He could tell that for Columbine it had an appealing flavour of fairy tale, of the towers of a thousand romances. She went to each window in turn, perhaps imagining herself a fair maiden imprisoned by a witch. She was happy.

Johnny unpacked his few possessions. There were the papers, the clues as mysterious as when he had first read them. He studied again the sketch of the dark-haired young man, and he wondered afresh at the significance of the two short rhyming lines:

stone dropped in well
clapper in bell

When he put Mr Farg's gift on a shelf, Columbine took it up and turned it in her fingers. She raised it until she and the shepherd boy stared into one another's eyes.

'It's ugly,' Johnny said.

'He is far from home,' the girl replied, 'yet close to his salvation.'

The serpent ring was on its way into a drawer with the papers when she seized it from him with a cry of delight.

'Divine!'

'No, Columbine, you can't. I need that ring.'

'See the forces from underground curling into human consciousness. Dangerous darkness. A fellow with a sting!'

'Please . . . ' But he shrugged and yielded. There would be a time for gentle persuasion. He knew the power of Columbine's moods and the need to accommodate himself to them. She would be softer.

He opened a cupboard door and an avalanche of old rags swept down upon him. Stooping to gather them, he found that on every one there were spots and stains of a dusky red. He stepped back, aghast. He closed his eyes and the redness spread like an incoming tide. What had happened here? Why so many? He had to force himself to raise the cloths in his arms and stuff them into the cupboard, slamming the door on them.

'Tell me about Hans.'

'Nothing.' She pursed her lips and blew lightly against his cheek. 'Nothing. Here and gone.'

'But why gone? How gone?'

'Moved into darkness. Better to move through darkness than allow darkness to move through you.'

They stood at a window. Down below a gleaming white Hispano-Suiza nosed along the street.

'Did he upset you? Is that why you killed him?'

'Killed who?'

'Hans!' The frustration registered in the pitch of his voice. Curse her elliptical answers, he thought, her enigmatic and elusive words! 'You killed Hans.'

'Yes, I suppose so. But he was already dead really. I just completed the circle.'

'With what?'

'A razor.'

Johnny grimaced. Minutes elapsed. Now a horseman passed along the verge, distanced, foreshortened, silent as a dream. Two birds fought in the grass.

'He opened like a flower. Blossomed. Pink petals unfurling . . .

There was a heavy knock on the door. Johnny, relieved, hurried to answer it. The man who stood before him was a stranger, but it was a face he had seen before. The blond hair, the scar etched into the right cheek: it took but seconds for the features to find their context – that photograph from the Huss Academy which Martin Jolsen kept in the drawer of his desk.

22 Buried Treasure

'I've missed Cherfas.'

It seemed neither statement nor question, delivered in a languid drawl that suggested no real interest in the matter.

'Yes, he's gone.'

He was tall, with a young man's arrogance (he was, perhaps, twenty-five) and he inclined his head in a superior fashion, as if to avert it from the contemptible world below. His eyes searched the room's interior. Columbine was kneeling on the floor, exposing a length of silky leg and a fraction of pink thigh, but the eyes never paused, scanning her as swiftly as they had the furnishings and returning to Johnny's face, where they fixed in a gaze so candid that he was discomfited.

'You like it?'

Johnny frowned: 'Like what?'

'The room. Do you like the room?'

'It's divine. A delight.'

The answer came from Columbine, who had emerged from the shadows and now stood behind Johnny, resting her head upon his shoulder.

'So . . . sensitively proportioned.'

'I'm glad you're pleased.' The architect never averted his eyes from Johnny's. 'It's such a necessary room and they've never really found a use for it.'

The absurdity of this observation passed Johnny by. He was unnerved by those eyes. He had an urge to back away into the room, but Columbine still clung.

'I knew someone would like it.'

'Yes, *we're* pleased with it. But *we* would like to know where to pee!'

Columbine launched her attack with such speed and venom that both men were silenced for several seconds, and before they could respond she had rediscovered her sweetness and charity and was inviting their visitor into his own room. He declined with a formal bow.

'Perhaps it is the wrong time. Perhaps some other time. When you have settled in, perhaps.'

But she seized his arm and pulled him inside.

'I've made a discovery,' she declared. 'Hidden treasure!'

'No, really. Really!' He handed Johnny a small white card. 'We must talk business, you and I. Alone. When it is convenient.'

'The room? To discuss the rent?'

'Yes, that's it, of course. Call on me.'

The card bore a single name: KUMANS. There were two addresses, one in the city, another at the Spa.

'Wealth underground!'

Columbine's exclamation at last caught the architect's attention. She was kneeling on the floor by an open trap-door. They drew closer. Below was a large, dark space containing, just out of reach, what seemed to be crates covered in tarpaulin.

'Dare!' said Columbine, echoing a call of their childhood.

It was a challenge Johnny could not resist. He clambered through the hole and dropped lightly onto the mystery cache.

'What do you think – forged money? Liquor?'

His voice bounced around the walls. Already she was with him, pulling the covering from one of the crates, making of the movement a ritual unrobing, as if performing a religious ceremony.

'And all shall be revealed,' she whispered urgently. 'All shall be revealed . . . '

Swathed in straw, like eggs in a rough, mossy nest, were several large brown bottles.

'Schnapps?' he hazarded, but she shook her head. She took one out and together they raised it to the light at the mouth of the hatch. On a dusty label was a row of letters and numbers, followed by three long and unpronounceable words.

'Chemicals!'

From above their heads there came a hard but prolonged laughter. The architect was amused. Peering out, they saw the stiff, embarrassed helplessness of one rarely given to expresssions of mirth. The eyes had a pleading look, as if asking to be spared this ignominy.

'You know what this is?' Johnny asked, depositing the bottle in the room. He cupped his hands into a stirrup and hoisted Columbine through the trap-door.

'Yes, I know. Chemicals!'

Still he laughed. Johnny, with some difficulty, clung to the woodwork, kicked his legs and heaved himself out of the hole.

'But you should not ask me. No, no, really. Do not ask. But if you like – smell the contents! I say nothing.'

Was the manner in which he spoke (lazy vowels, precise consonants) an affectation? Was there, perhaps, the trace of an accent in it? All he knew was that it set his teeth on edge.

'You knew before we went down there,' he accused.

Columbine had pulled out the stopper and was sniffing the contents with a wrinkled nose. It meant nothing to her. She invited Johnny to try.

'Yes, it's familiar to me.'

'From where?'

'I don't know. Recently. Here somewhere.'

This was too much for the architect, who raised an arm across his face to hide the shame of his merriment.

'Chemicals!' he said again.

Johnny closed his eyes and sniffed once more, trying to close his mind to all thought. He had an image of a glass dome; a sensation of chilliness; a vision of elderly faces.

'The Palace of Waters,' he said triumphantly. 'It's the smell of the natural water . . . '

Now he realised why the architect turned away, his shoulders shaking, unable to speak. He pictured again the quincunx of stoves, the tin mugs, Venner talking of his 'vile febrifuge'. The source was hidden! There was no-one to say how pure the water was, how fresh and sparkling from its mountain spring.

'That's very clever,' he added, admiringly. 'But what's the reason? The spring's contaminated?'

The architect put a finger to his lips.

'Dried up,' he revealed. 'Years ago. But say not a word. We are dead men else.'

'And the spa water?'

'Piped from below. But your silence, yes? Please?'

Johnny nodded.

'I tell you this little secret to make a friend of you. A confidant. We shall do business, shall we not? You will come? Boris Kumans is my name.'

'Yes, I'll come.'

'Good. Just the two of us. We shall like that, isn't it so? Good business!'

He bowed once more and was gone. Johnny turned to a Columbine whose knowing, impish smile riled him beyond words. Seeing his sudden anger she melted into laughter, continuing to tremble with it throughout the rain of powder-puff blows he dealt her.

23 Blood

The tent was illuminated by a single candle, and the whole of its light seemed to rest upon the object which the fortune teller held out before her. Sophie took it: a white icosahedron that appeared to be made of porcelain but which rested in her hands with a strange heaviness. She examined it, turning it to find each face identical and satisfyingly regular. It was, however, cold, the surface slightly waxy and repellent.

'Show me your nails.'

She held up a hand and the old crone leaned forward, peering at the carefully manicured points that completed each finger.

'They'll do. Scratch it.'

Sophie complied, presuming the object too hard for her action to have any consequence. It was *not* too hard: her nail gouged a thin groove from which welled droplets of liquid the colour and consistency of blood. She started back in horror, dropping the thing on the table. The impact further opened the wound, allowing the red liquid to flow more freely until it formed a dark pool around the geometric whiteness.

The candle flickered. The hunched clairvoyant sighed.

'Bad,' she said. 'An ill omen.'

'It's stupid! It's a trick!'

The old woman shrugged and held out her hand. Sophie flung two silver coins into it and fled. Trickery!

She hurried through the streets. A drink and a laugh and she would be fine again. She needed company. She heard herself cry out for Columbine even while little voiceless gasps of fear and frustration panted from her throat. Above her, scarlet leaves glowed in the sunset; virginia creeper, smouldering on the wall of a house, scorched her as she passed. Ah, no – not burning but bleeding! And the trees! And the sky! She stumbled on through a crimson haze.

Columbine was not in her room when she at last arrived, agitated and breathless – but Hans was . . .

24 Accostings

The place was full of strangers. For days now they had been flocking in, the effortlessly rich, the vulgarly rich, the unconsciously rich. What drew them, Cherfas explained, was the last fling of the season before the winter weather set in. A week of flamboyant money-changing, culminating in the Grand Gala when the stakes and the prizes would be at their highest.

Johnny sat on a half-formed wall at one of the buildings sites, overseeing the work. Learning the terms had been easy. He could trade jargon with the best of them, and being Cherfas's man gave him the edge of power. When he called for more speed, extra workmen were found; when he questioned a price, it had to be expertly justified or swiftly amended.

'Ah, the perfect pose! Wouldn't you say?'

'Redolent of ancient Greece.'

The accents were foreign. Two elderly men had paused alongside him, and Johnny was surprised and even a little indignant to discover that they referred to his own attitude on the wall – an elbow resting on a knee, chin propped on a fist. The one who had spoken first was, despite the flaccidity of old age, a strongly muscled man. His round face was cocooned in a large white beard and a cheroot perched on his lower lip. He put a heavy arm across his companion's shoulder and laughed aloud.

'But was that Greece or grease, old friend?'

They roared with abandon, clasped in a mutual embrace and seemingly oblivious of his feelings. The second man, slighter and fastidiously dressed in an out-of-date frenchified fashion – a dark striped suit with a tight-waisted jacket and flared trousers; a bright yellow cravat; an improbably blue carnation in his lapel – tapped him gently on the shoulder.

'An imitation, but what matter? To live life as a work of art is the noblest achievement accessible to man.'

Johnny jumped down from the wall and turned away, hearing their chatter and laughter recede as they sauntered towards the centre of the Spa. Their raillery stung him. He approached two men who were mixing concrete, and he eyed their work as if at any moment he would demand that they start all over again. He sensed their unease and enjoyed it.

'We'll have this finished before dark,' one of them said defensively.

That was Schmidt. Johnny knew all the names: it was part of his job. It was a method of asserting control. He had studied the lists of workers in the faint hope of finding Peter Ocklynge among them. Foiled in that quest, he had examined them more closely, memorising details which might be of use to him in his work for Cherfas.

'I should hope so,' he replied, yielding nothing.

If Ocklynge was here he had concealed himself under a new name and Johnny could think of no easy way of drawing him out. To reveal his interest would be a horrendous risk. Blood had already been spilt. A madman with a knife – Otto at the warehouse, Dirk Grimm on his office floor. He tried not to succumb to the lurid promptings of his imagination. He saw again the splashes of borsch. He saw the stained rags.

What he must do was visit the architect Kumans. He had been at the Huss Academy. Might he perhaps have known Ocklynge? It was obvious what he must do, but something had so far prevented him. What was it? He felt it as a distasteful physical sensation, like something crawling under his collar. There was a kind of threat in the man's warm and open approach. It was like an invasion – his instinct was to resist it. He wanted very much not to go to Kumans, but he knew that he must.

'You can work faster, I suppose,' Schmidt said.

Johnny heard the words some time after they were spoken and he could not be sure that they carried the meaning which seemed, nevertheless, all too apparent. Of course these workers hated him. He was young and cocksure and in the good favour of their employer. How could they not wish him ill? He didn't care at all what they thought. But they were generally like tigers in a circus, cowed by the whip which, in this case, was his power to have them removed from their jobs. Good – and like the accomplished trainer, he must only be careful not to lower his guard, not to appear weak, unnerved by their hidden ferocity. Had he heard a growl?

'I meant,' Schmidt added awkwardly, 'that you're the overseer because you've done it all yourself.'

Perhaps this did little to offset the effect of the first comment, for his companion felt the need to add his own reassuring remark: 'We'll have it done in the time, mister, or you can dock our pay to compensate.'

They nodded in unison, anxious to placate him.

'Don't worry,' he said contemptuously, walking away. 'I shall. And I think we'll bring the time forward to four o'clock. It's easy enough work, after all. I'll return to inspect it.'

There were far worse ways of earning a living, but these last few days he had felt the growing of an unbearable frustration. Time, which brought trouble closer, had delivered him nothing. Ah, that drawing closer! The threat seemed to settle on him, press down upon him, so that even that which he ought to do (the visit to the architect, the investigation of newcomers to the Spa) remained undone. It was not natural to him, this helplessness before events. He brooded – but still did nothing.

'Excuse me.'

A large, ungainly man, a suitcase in each hand, stumbled along the road. He was out of breath and sweating, his tie askew around his neck and flapping wildly. He fixed on Johnny a gaze so helpless and pleading that he was at once marked down as a victim. Such people were destined to be duped.

'Can you help me?'

The accent was foreign, the diction clumsy. He lifted one of the suitcases onto the wall and the catch immediately sprang open. The lid shot up and the contents spilled to the ground. There were expensive shirts, underclothes still shop-wrapped, white silk handkerchieves. Johnny, helping to recover them, picked up what seemed to be a net with a collapsible handle.

'In the event,' the stranger explained, 'of creatures in my hotel room. Bugs and cockroaches. Spiders. Do you think that likely? Or am I fated, as it sometimes seems, always to bring the wrong gadgets for the particular location?'

The suitcase fixed, he mopped his face with the end of his tie.

'That is, if I can find a hotel. I suppose they're all taken?'

Johnny pursed his lips, a picture of doubt.

'Not much available this week, sir. Full to the brim. The place is a termite hill.'

'Nowhere at all?'

He had no need of the money, but he had begun the game from habit and was unable to stop. Was it his fault if the man was so invitingly gullible?

'Just possibly, if you come with me. I know one or two of these folk, you see, and I might persuade them to do me a little favour.'

'I'd be sincerely grateful.'

Johnny took the more secure of the two cases, found it to be unexpectedly heavy and quickly switched to the other. He led the way forward.

'You may have to pay over the odds,' he warned.

The foreign gentleman would certainly pay over the odds. Johnny would take him to a place where he was known; would do a deal with the hotelier; would quote a higher price to the customer, pocketing the difference; and would probably get a tip into the bargain. His life had been a series of such ruses.

'Happily.'

It was a slow journey, his benefactor breathing heavily and making several stops to regain his equilibrium, but at last they arrived.

'You wait here,' Johnny said, 'and I'll fix it. What name shall I give?'

The visitor set down his case and it split open as if blown apart by a bomb. A prettily-coloured figurine jumped out of it, bounced once and smashed into several pieces.

'Larooning,' he said.

25 A Warning Shot

' . . . and indeed it may be,' the letter continued, 'that the exigencies of your Herculean investigative labours have nullified your intentions to communicate. The priority, after all, is the discovery of that certain person. And yet I am forced to question whether the composition of a brief missive has been beyond your remaining reserves of energy . . . '

Johnny raised his eyes from the typewritten page (the third of six) in order to rest his brain. Mr Farg's philosophisings were hard to assimilate when delivered face to face: even more effort was required with a literary version. He thought of the poor stenographer taking her dictation (those tuberous fingers could never cope with a pen) while the words were laboriously threaded into phrases and the interminable sentences ravelled and knotted. He did not understand it all in detail, but he could interpret the message well enough. He had disobeyed the instruction to keep in touch. This was regarded as a serious breach of trust. He must write. He *would* write. He read on, sensing the development of a different theme.

'Whether this dilatoriness betokens a mind otherwise but gainfully engaged or one simply not alert to the matter in hand I am, of course, unable to gauge. I reflect, however, not only that a useless life is an early death but that a lazy or unguarded mind may lay one open to the same conclusion, and in terms more real than figurative. Are we about to witness the enactment of this cruel truth?

'Shall we consider the *status quo ante*? One friend and one acquaintance dispatched shockingly early to that dark valhalla which will one day claim every soul among us. The poetic expression does not, I think, conceal the sombreness of their demise. And what do we infer from this unhappy circumstance? That the sands sift fast through their hourglass. That we are not alone pursuing our keen interest in that haunting riddle. That one ought to beware an unknown figure whose predations are vicious and somewhat random, as unpredictable as a baby's bottom.'

Here there was a partially erased query in the margin, as if the typist had doubted the written note.

'You will perhaps be tempted to scorn the advice of an ailing old man who sees little of the world save through the gap in his curtains. To which I might reply that there is not a man among us who is vouchsafed more than a glimpse of the clear light of truth. Let us celebrate what meagre knowledge we wrest from the grim clutch of ignorance! In this fraught area of human endeavour a little is far more than nothing at all.

'But I offer you instead the reflected light of rumour and advise you to regard its twilight glow as preferable to darkness. Ignore it if you will – and, who knows, you may be justified in your bland indifference. It may be those glow-worms we create! I permit myself to question, however, whether you are in a position to hazard such an interpretation. Suppose your doubts are mistaken. Suppose that pale light guides a tapering point to your bedside!

'Not that I gloat in any discomfort these considerations may cause you. My own self-interest, which I nurture with an assiduousness close to pampering, cries out for your success, and I shall be willing to forgive almost anything in the event of such an outcome. This is why I report the rumour, be it but a whisper along the alleys of conjecture, that dangerous elements move closer to you and will not long be denied . . . '

26 Visions

There was, as he entered the studio, a rustling of papers. They hung from the walls, long ribbons like bandages in a sterilisation chamber, each with a complex veining of blue lines which stood out sharply under the harsh electric lighting. From the other side of a huge drawing board, tilted to an almost vertical position, rose a plume of cigarette smoke. The architect's head appeared seconds later and hovered above the board's hard edge. Johnny shut the door and the rustling began again. Everything about the room fluttered in excited, agitated movement save for the still head, its lips smiling as if in anticipation of coming pleasure. Kumans stepped forward and shook Johnny's hand with an emphatic enthusiasm.

'Wonderful! This calls for a drink. What shall it be?'

He opened a cupboard to reveal an array of vividly coloured bottles and, observing the perplexity on his visitor's face, selected one a little bluer than turquoise and filled two small glasses. Johnny took a sip, regretting it as the syrupy bitterness filled his mouth.

'Chemicals!' laughed Kumans. 'Actually it's a potion I picked up in a bar in North Africa. The colour appealed. Can't remember any more. Something to do with camels.'

He sat on a high stool, regarding his visitor with a deep and unmoving gaze, and again Johnny experienced uneasiness and distaste. He felt squeamish. Kumans's otherness was one he recognised and positively disliked.

'I came to do business,' he said. 'You'll want rent for that room.'

'Nonsense! It's yours for as long as you want it.'

'But we discussed . . . That's why I came.'

'Oh, if you like. There has to be a reason, eh? In truth, I wanted to get you away from the young lady to see what friendly kind of a fellow you were.'

This frank and overbearing remark would have caused Johnny to turn on his heel had he been able to obey his instincts. But there was work to be done. He calculated what margin there was between a surface complaisance and a vile, unthinkable acquiescence. Certainly some initial resistance would do no harm and might even prove an advantage. He tilted his glass and it rolled its watery blue eye at him. He set it down with a flourish.

'Not so very friendly,' he warned. 'I like a man to be honest with me. I came only to talk business.'

He stood and began to examine one of the hung sheets, cocking his head to read a block of text. The handwriting was thin and effete, in direct contrast with the web of mechanical lines which accompanied it. The words meant nothing to him. Were they technical terms, outside his experience, or were they perhaps in another language?

'There you see the future.'

This was uttered with a defiance bordering on petulance, as if he expected to be challenged for his presumption. Johnny moved to another of the sheets.

'Star charts, are they? Run of the planets, that sort of thing? Could you tell my destiny from them?'

'No, no. I'm no astrologer. Our destiny is in our own hands. Those are designs for a future world, a blueprint for tomorrow.'

'It doesn't,' Johnny chanced, 'look all that comfortable.'

'Oh, but it is!' Kumans came to him, put an arm round his shoulder and then, with his free hand, took hold of Johnny's, gently squeezing it and guiding the forefinger towards a series of diagrams. 'Look. Do you need to make a short journey? Step on a moving pavement. Do you want to climb? Step on a moving stairway. Over here – is the street too cold? Then adjust the temperature. Pull the lever. Too warm? Turn it the other way. Too noisy in your room? Slide the glass insulating panels into place. Too quiet? Turn on the glass entertainment screen. You're hungry perhaps? Dial the automatic kitchen for a meal. Bored? Here's a machine that will beat you at chess!

'So there is comfort, my Johnny. *Only* comfort. And maybe, with a little more research from our doctors – eternity! Eternal bliss: think of it. Believe me, with a little more scientific knowledge it can be ours. No vague paradise promised you from a pulpit while you shiver or yawn in a pew. No dreams or wishful thinking. This is real!'

Johnny pulled himself away with the pretence of wanting to recover his drink, but he was closely pursued.

'It will come to pass,' Kumans pressed him, 'but it will need men of vision and courage. Ha! Only men of vision and courage need apply, eh? They're the only ones who'll deserve to live in my future. Supermen.'

He put out an arm, but Johnny kept him at bay by reaching for his glass and swinging round as if struck by a sudden thought.

'You can't sell dreams, surely. Even beggars have dreams – their own. They've no need of another's.'

'No dreams, I tell you. I'm not talking about dreams.' He swept his hand in an arc, indicating the hung papers. 'These aren't dreams but the stuff of science and technology. They need only vision and hard cash to bring them into being.'

Aware of the physical rebuff, he took the bottle by the neck and began to recharge his glass. He checked himself, however, before more than a few of the bright blue drops had fallen. His voice became softer, conciliatory.

'What we shall do,' he said, 'is this. With your agreement. We will go to a place I know, a good bar, and – yes, we shall talk business. How is that? Two businessmen talking serious matters over a few drinks. You agree?'

'If you like.'

It was not a long walk, but far too long for Johnny. Their route took them through a darkened park where the architect clearly relished the conferred intimacy. Their shoulders brushed. A ghostly moon hung like a Japanese lantern between the branches, and a soft breeze sighed among the foliage of the conspiratorial rowans.

'They fend off witches,' laughed Kumans, evidently referring to some piece of folklore, and snatching at a hang of blood-red leaves above his head. Johnny, sending up a little prayer to whatever kindly forces might be listening, quickened his pace and began to talk urgently about his work.

'And how's my friend Cherfas treating you?' the architect asked. 'He's the coming man, there's no doubt of it. We shall hear a lot of him. But vision – alas, no.'

'He's built most of the new Spa, hasn't he?'

'That's his nose for cash. Do you think he cares what he builds? Take a close look at some of those creations. Monstrosities! Nostalgia for the past or for some far-off clime. Do you know the Abode of Rest?'

'I've seen it.'

'Meretricious fake sentimentalism! And it's not the worst.'

This outburst and its aftermath kept Kumans fully occupied until they reached the bright lights of the entertainments area.

'Cherfas,' he was saying as they reached his chosen bar (he paused in the semi-darkness at the top of a steep flight of steps) 'listens without hearing. His mind's too busy with trifles – details of this and that, gutters, drains . . . which is one reason I'd like to talk a little business with you. If pleasure permits.'

The bar was a gloomy cavern, the murk punctuated by coloured lights on the walls. They sat at a table partitioned from its neighbours by glass screens upon which were etched reclining nudes. Or did they recline? Perhaps, Johnny mused, they were flying or floating: there was the hint of a diaphanous wing at each shoulder blade, though hardly of a size that would lift one of these healthy beauties from the ground. He wondered at the brilliance of technique which had allowed the artist to use the transparency of glass to show not only the shoulder blades and nicely rounded rumps of his subjects but also their heavy-breasted fronts. Beyond the screen two other customers – young, vital, immersed in one another's company – unwittingly became part of the illusion: their faces as they moved towards each other to join in a chaste kiss (which might reasonably be thought the herald of later and less chaste kisses) moved across the figured surface of the glass, so that with the merest inclination of the head Johnny could make their lips meet at the point of a delicately drawn nipple.

'Isn't that the way life should be?' Kumans demanded enthusiastically, grasping him by the arm. 'All the dross and drudgery gone. The machine as an ideal servant, doing exactly what you want, with no arguing.'

Johnny smiled, still taken with his pictorial fancies: 'And pretty poor company on a cold night!'

'No cold nights, remember! Just turn the lever a degree or two.'

Johnny sipped a dullish amber beer and took note of the people around him. If the Palace of Waters had suggested that the Spa was inhabited solely by the aged and infirm, this subterranean oasis signalled that it was a meeting place for the well-to-do younger generation, eager to spend a fast-depreciating currency. The bar was thronged with the expensively dressed and the smart-tongued, with the less-than-virtuous of all sexes. Johnny felt a hand fall upon his knee.

'A good place for enjoyment,' Kumans said, the scar on his face glaring a raw red under the lighting.

Johnny pushed the hand away: 'We have something to discuss, you say. Business. Let's hear it, my friend.'

The architect, temporarily defeated, began to talk once more of Cherfas and his growing influence. The builder, he said, had plenty of money to spend, but it was all too likely that he would spend it unwisely – successfully from a financial point of view, perhaps, but with no regard for the kind of visions Kumans wished to promote. This was a terrible waste. The architect's grand design allied to the developer's energy could revolutionise the face of the country in a decade. As it was . . .

'Don't misunderstand me,' Kumans went on, after tasting a tall, banded cocktail which had just been placed before him, 'I'm not after Cherfas's money. Not principally, at any rate. I have a good number of traditional clients who pay for my rather extravagant tastes. That isn't it at all.

'I'm looking for someone who'll share my belief in the future. I once had hopes of Cherfas. He has all the contacts, he attracts the investors and he's commissioned a few designs from me here. That Palace of Mirth they've begun up in the mountains is mine. We shall enjoy ourselves there one day! But he thinks the Spa is a mere sport. He won't see that it can show the way forward.'

'And my role in this?' Johnny asked.

'To open his eyes. You have his ear, haven't you? He speaks well of you. If you could make him see! I would pay you, of course. Ten per cent of any new contract – how would that suit you?'

'Plus expenses.'

'Anything you like. Only persuade him.'

The couple through the glass now clutched at one another as if each were pulling the other back from the edge of some dire chasm. One of the nude etchings floated above their heads, at once guardian angel and siren. Johnny toyed with the idea of mentioning the Huss Academy, but could find no credible reason for doing so.

'Better still,' Kumans continued, 'why not come and work for me full time? I'll be going back to the city in a week or two. You won't want to spend the cold months locked up here. It's a dreary place in the winter. Cherfas won't stay.'

'But he wants someone on site, he says. He's asked me to stay on.'

'You'll lose your mind in the silence and the snows. Come back to the city, Johnny! I'd only borrow you. Cherfas can have you back in the spring.'

'We'll see.'

He could think of no worse a fate, but there was no reason to suggest as much. On the contrary, he might need the architect rather badly. Had he known Ocklynge? Dare that question be asked? Johnny thought of Mr Farg's letter with its warning. He had a blurred and fleeting vision of Otto at the warehouse, Dirk Grimm on his office floor. In one palpitating moment his customary, self-preserving caution gave way.

'There's some business of mine you might be able to help with,' he began falteringly.

'For a very small consideration, I promise you.'

'I'm looking for a man.'

Kumans burbled uncontrollably, quite swept away by his own abruptly seething mirth, and the hand descended once more, roughly, upon the younger man's knee. Flustered by his ill-considered statement and this wild reaction to it, Johnny was about to blurt out Ocklynge's name when they were interrupted by the appearance of a familiar figure who came striding towards their table while throwing repeated nervous glances over his shoulder.

'Cherfas!' bawled the architect. 'Beware this depraved stripling. He may have designs on you.'

'The least of my worries,' the developer replied, bending to speak to Johnny, his voice low yet urgent. 'It's that wretched Hildegard. She's following me. She'll be here in an instant. You've got to get rid of her for me.'

'Where?'

'Anywhere to start with. Then back home before she starts a civil war.' He sank to his haunches and peered over the top of the table. 'That's her. I'll go this way. Give me five minutes to get clear.'

Keeping low, he waddled past the two practising lovers, tipped himself onto all fours and bounded, buttocks uppermost, into the shadows.

27 Hildegard's Story

'My people don't understand me.'

It seemed to Johnny, as he led Hildegard through the streets of the Spa, that her people probably understood her all too well. He was aware of how she looked about her with a greedy curiosity as if demanding that pleasure should come and sit her on its knee and fondle her. She tossed her blonde hair from her face and smiled pertly at every man who passed.

'I think that horrible Kurt is purposely avoiding me.'

She slid her arm through his and pressed close to him as they walked. He tried to ignore the waft of cheap perfume lavishly applied, the brushing of her coat collar against his cheek. It meant nothing. Besides, he dare not allow a single extra complication. It had been a relief to escape from Kumans' clutches, but there was a greater danger in this girl's more gentle importuning. She had guardians.

'You're trouble to him. Look what happened before.'

'It's worth it to have some fun. Why shouldn't I enjoy myself? I hate it in the forest.'

Perhaps Columbine could work her strange magic on the girl, he thought. She might better understand the determined waywardness, somehow talk her into returning home. He felt a tug on his arm, cajoling him to walk more slowly, and (telling himself that help was at hand) he allowed himself the luxury of a more comfortable stroll, Hildegard's head inclined to rest on his shoulder. They left the bright lights behind them, passing along the deserted late-night streets like two lovers under that fuzzy moon. The buildings were black cut-outs in a grey tinted frieze, the mountains a heavy, indistinct presence brooding mightily upon civilisation.

'A bit dull up there, is it?'

Her head snuggled more deeply into him and she pulled again at his arm so that they swayed along with a tipsy gait. He remembered how, only a short while before, he had been tempted to reveal too much to the architect, and now he fought to keep his wits clear with Hildegard. Nevertheless, it was pleasant to be alone in the dark streets with her, and there was no reason to hurry. It was too late to be making journeys out of the Spa.

'I suppose for a time I was happy with the pigs,' she began. 'If I think back far enough.'

'The pigs?'

'Of course we kept pigs, stupid. Everyone keeps pigs. Don't you?'

He smiled at her naivety but he could not despise her for it. It was another country she came from, even if they shared the same nationality.

'When I was tiny I used to feed the pigs, and I had a name for every one of them. They were all different. I suppose *you* think pigs are all the same!'

'Nonsense.'

'And they'd come running to me for their food. I remember that. Mostly they foraged under the trees, but I'd give them something every day and you never heard such squealing. "Quiet," I'd say, "there's enough for you all." But they always tussled for it.

'The first time they took the grown pigs and slaughtered them I bawled my eyes out. Didn't I think my father a brute of a man! They had to carry me away until it was all over and it was no use hollering any more. Then I got used to it.'

A sadness stole over her face, followed by a smile of such fragile wistfulness that his heart might have melted had he not steeled himself against it. No, it meant nothing. Her lovable helplessness was simply a routine performance.

'People have to eat,' he said doggedly.

'We were nine children in our family. The first was a girl – that was Inge – and the last was a girl, and that was me. All the others were boys. Well, Inge is so much older than me that I might as well have had two mothers. She really is old, you know! We don't understand each other at all. Inge is very peculiar. I always thought she was.

'So there was I, once I'd got bored with the pigs, with crowds of boys doing all those things which I'd never wanted to do, and nobody to care about me at all. I couldn't climb trees and make whistles out of hollow stems. I never wanted to roll in the bracken and get dirty fighting. That's what my brothers did all the time as far as I can remember. Practising to become men, I suppose. I'm mad about men, but I never wanted to be one.'

'What did you get up to?'

'Mischief!' She laughed self-indulgently and stroked the top of his head with tender fingers. 'I've always been a worry to everyone. I'm just bad, don't you think?'

Some way ahead he could see the harsh neon of the New Casino. It was not very far to go. He willed himself onward.

'There was never a time when I wasn't in trouble. They used to say I got the boys to do the wickedness for me, but I didn't have to ask them most times. They wanted to.

'Long days in the forest are very long, I can tell you. Just trees and squirrels. And as I got older all my brothers and their friends were off with the men, felling timber, and most of the girls were doing tomboy things or helping their mothers doing those tedious jobs indoors. At least I had Inge to do all that. I never got bothered with housework. They left me alone.

'What would you have done if you were me?'

Johnny shrugged: 'Run away,' he conceded.

'Oh, I did that soon enough. I decided one day that I'd have my breakfast and leave. Never ever go back again in all my life. I just walked off into the forest. But I was awfully young. I'd never been any distance from our village clearing. I was lost in half an hour.'

'And you sat and cried.'

'No I didn't. I made up my mind they were going to come and find me. It was their fault I'd run away in the first place, so they could come looking. Hours and hours went past. Nothing but trees and birds and boring squirrels.'

'But they're all different, Hildegard.'

'That's pigs, stupid.' She laughed at him, quite missing the irony. 'It started to grow dark. I sat on a stump, absolutely still, and I waited. I didn't care how long it might be. They were shouting through the trees, calling my name, but I didn't budge an inch. Let them come, I thought. They had to walk right up to me!

'They didn't know whether to hug me or beat me sore.'

She gave a low chuckle at the memory. They walked in silence for a while, comfortably interlocked. Their footfalls were the only sound on the night air but there was movement up ahead, the dark shapes of people at the casino entrance.

'After that I stayed in the forest for a long time and made them wish that they'd never come to find me, so I won in the end. They said I was a witch. I enchanted all the young men. When I said I wanted something they used to get it for me, even if they had to lie and steal. Pretty things. I've always liked jewellery and fine clothes.

'Then there were the fights! The boys all wanted to walk in the forest with me and they all wanted me to wear *their* earrings and little brooches. They'd go into a clearing somewhere and knock each other about for ages until they were all bloody and filthy. I used to watch sometimes, and if they saw me watching they'd leap on each other more violently than ever.

'A man called Larrup was thrown out of the village because of me. He was a real pesterer, that one. He was married. I didn't know then all the things you learn soon enough. He kept on, buying me clothes and perfume, until the village elders summoned him to the moot hall and told him he must never see me again, but when I crept up to his house one evening he couldn't resist me and that was the end of him. His wife wouldn't let him stay in the house and he had to go off to the city.

'I remember him trudging along the track, his wife and children by the gate just staring, and I decided he was going to wave goodbye to me before he went. It was a kind of challenge. I ran through the bushes and came out on the path in front of him. He stopped still for a bit and his eyes filled with tears. I gave a little wave, my hand up by my chin, and when he at last got going again he turned to me and raised his hand. A witch!

'The men in the forest are ghastly, really. They don't know anything except arm-wrestling and timber prices. I soon got tired of them all. That's when I began to leave the village again. They can't keep me up there.'

They had reached the casino. As they passed in front of it a party of gamblers came pushing out of the door and there was a fleeting glimpse of hooded lights over green baize tables. Hildegard wanted to loiter, but he dragged her on, suddenly in no danger at all. He hurried her to the ladder and pushed her up ahead of him, ignoring her pathetic protestations that she could not do it, that her shoes were inadequate for climbing, that she was sure she would fall.

Columbine was not alone in their room. She sat on one of the colourful tasselled couches with an elderly man on either side of her. Johnny recognised them as the two foreigners who had made fun of his stance on the building site wall. She turned to the frenchified one and patted his head, a smile of outrageous self-satisfaction on her lips.

'Meet my Daddy,' she said.

28 Lost and Found

'The Greek statue!' both men laughed delightedly, rising swiftly to greet him.

It was impossible to take hurt at their open and now clearly unmalicious humour. They held out their hands and all but embraced him as a long lost friend.

'Celestin,' added the one introduced, improbably, as Columbine's father, 'and this is my camarado, Clabber. Ernest Clabber, the famous sculptor.'

'Hound's teeth,' protested the other. 'Am I to wear labels on my shirt front wherever I go? This is Celestin, the renowned poet.'

'Of yesteryear, alas,' was the wan reply. 'I'm a dog who has had his day. Clabber's tail still wags.'

'The world's poor judgement, Celestin. You're a fine artist and any man who denies it will feel the strength of this.' He raised his arm and chuckled. 'And many a one has, eh old friend?'

These mutual artistic appreciations might perhaps have continued for ever had not Columbine put her head between those of her guests and fixed Hildegard with a quizzical gaze. Johnny, made the introductions ('A friend or, rather, an acquaintance . . . Kurt Cherfas's friend really.') sensing that Columbine immediately understood the situation from his own embarrassment and from Hildegard's sudden farouche dumbness, which contrasted strangely with the explicitness of her appearance.

'A surprise?'

She licked a forefinger and brought it down expressively through the air, a gesture of triumph from their childhood.

'One to me!' she added.

He looked from Columbine to Celestin and back again: 'You've just met?'

'For the first time since I was three years old.'

'And in the charge of an ogre of a woman, narrow and cantankerous,' threw in Celestin.

'My mother,' Columbine explained.

'And the dear girl was a distant guiding light to me ever after, veiled by heavy clouds but always a promise of dancing light where only the inner eye could see.'

'Beautiful!' Clabber exclaimed, as if he believed not a word of it. He fell back onto the couch and fished around under the tassels until he came up with a half empty bottle, which he tipped to his lips.

'Then at last I discovered her whereabouts,' Celestin continued. 'That she lived in a foreign city and that the said ogre was no more.'

'Swallowed by darkness,' Columbine agreed.

'And after some time calming my excited sensibilities . . . '

'He means,' boomed Clabber, slapping his knee, 'after several years of heedless depravity and dissipation!'

' . . . I vowed to haul my battered soul over the mountains . . . '

'Realised,' interpreted his friend, 'that there was good gaming to be had at the Spa.'

' . . . at once wrote to my angel . . . '

'Had a pen forced into my reluctant fingers by the tiresome Ernest Clabber.'

'. . . and arranged to meet as now we are.'

'But I thought,' Johnny began. He had thought that Columbine was here because of Hans. He could not, however, say such a thing. 'I thought you had come to see *me*.'

'Fate spins a complex web,' Columbine declared in her metallic voice. 'The strands cross and cling.'

Celestin, seemingly inspired by these words, flung a window open and began to declaim into the night:

Who is this victim
shaking in the gummed and treacherous web?
Who the trussed and bound
while the squat predator prances and spins?

'Darker,' Clabber commented, 'than he used to be. Experience oppresses us all. Every silver lining has a cloud.'

Hildegard sat close to Johnny, pressed to him for protection rather than with amorous intent. She was out of her depth. When Columbine looked at her she turned her head away, blushing. She stared at the two elderly men with a fearful incomprehension.

'When I was young and foolish,' began Celestin, joining the others in a comfortable huddle and putting a fragile arm around Columbine's shoulders, 'I never had children. But in my maturing years . . . '

'When he was middle-aged and foolish,' interpolated Clabber.

' . . . I pulled the trigger one time too many – and shot myself in the foot.'

'These are strange metaphors, old friend,' Clabber chided, 'and hardly flatter your sweet daughter. What's this I've found?'

With mock surprise he rolled another bottle from under the couch. He unscrewed the top, held the neck to the company in a kind of challenge and swiftly tipped the opening to his lips.

'A termagant, she was,' Celestin continued, 'with no understanding of the claims of art. The sort who elevates a kilo of cheese above a line of verse. Why did I ever show the slightest interest in her?'

'Do you need an answer?' chaffed Clabber, dribbling the drink down his chin.

'When she took the child and left there was never a happier man. Clabber will tell you. It was a time for celebration! Only later did I begin to wonder what had become of my little girl. Sentimentality is one of the afflictions of age. At last a friend of mine came across Columbine's mother, and I had only to wait.'

'For the darkness to enshroud her,' said Columbine. 'The black cloth winding and winding.'

'And now I've found her – and how wonderfully distinctive she is, how compellingly strange! A veritable work of art!'

Columbine was as Johnny had never seen her, no less bizarre but possessed of a quivering joy as if she looked down the shaft of a deep, dark well and saw a jewel gleaming there.

'You see,' she told him effervescently, tweaking his ear, 'I'm a child again now, with my Daddy! I've always wanted to be a little girl.'

She reached out for the other ear but was distracted, before she could seize it, by the sound of someone kicking the door. There was a brief pause after the first volley and then the assault was renewed with a rhythmical persistence.

29 Route March

The opened door revealed as unprepossessing a character as one was likely to meet at the Spa – a ragged, unshaven man clutching a large and lumpy paper bag with both hands.

'You Farg's boy?'

Johnny winced at the description but nodded nevertheless.

'Found somewhere to stay, have you? More than old Rook has. It'll be a park bench for me.'

'What do you want?'

A stale odour came off the man, who shuffled forward and gazed on the people inside the room. He raised a hand, as if to old friends, and his lips fell back over a broken battlement of carious teeth.

'Nobody cares what I want,' he stated, fixing the company with a blank unselfconsciousness.

Clabber, who had continued to drink prodigiously, leant back and toppled from the couch. Celestin and Columbine, whispering to one another with a fierce devotion, completely ignored the interloper. Only Hildegard returned the uncouth stare.

'Who are you?' Johnny tried again.

Rook carried his bag inside. He seemed to inspect the furniture in the way of a prospective tenant. He looked this way and that.

'My master's impatient,' he muttered, his eyes falling on Hildegard and staying there.

If he had been any ordinary vagrant wandering in from the street Johnny would have had him on his way already: he felt only contempt for the down and out. But this man's knowledge was sinister. How many people could be aware of Johnny's connection with Mr Farg? Very few. It was all the more frightening – he admitted to himself that he felt afraid – in that the possessor of this knowledge was a hopeless derelict.

'Oh, that's me, too!'

He became aware that Hildegard was talking. She chattered in an everyday conversational manner as if their visitor were a casual caller.

'Mother used to say impatience would be my undoing, you know. Hildy, she'd say – because she always called me Hildy – Hildy, you're too impatient by half. You'll take your cakes unbaked from the oven, you mark my words.'

Celestin, unable to resist the phrase, leaned away from Columbine for a moment.

'And do you?' he asked with wicked amusement.

None of this touched Rook at all. He turned at last, rustled in his bag until he came out with an envelope, and thrust it at Johnny. Inside was a sheet of thin paper folded several times more than the size of the envelope necessitated. Spidery letters looped and spluttered clumsily across the creased paper: *Time is running out. Write down all you have discovered and give it to the messenger. Farg.*

'Wait outside.'

Rook obeyed, shambling out of the door, hugging his parcel. Johnny turned to his companions, realising on the instant that there was no way they could help him. How could he explain? He was the recipient of a message that could not be genuine. Mr Farg would never write such a letter. It was, for one thing, a physical impossibility. More significantly, it was not remotely in his literary style. Someone, evidently, did not know this. But who?

He stepped outside, determined to force it out of the miserable wretch who had been sent to him. Rook was muttering and cursing in words half-formed, torn fragments of abuse directed at nothing in particular. He held a finger against one side of his nose, blowing noisily to clear the other nostril.

The scene that followed might have taken place in the flickering monochrome of the Electric Theater. A gang of desperadoes clattered up the rungs of the ladder, sweeping Rook and Johnny before them. Their coarse, bearded faces pressed forward to form a threatening screen of grimaces. The barrels of rifles waved before them. They were suddenly in the room, all of them, and all but Hildegard were lined up against a wall. There was a babble of voices as all the foresters spoke among themselves.

'Tell them, Hildegard,' Johnny tried to say, but a wooden stave was thrust at his chest and he fell silent.

'You've come!' Hildegard was wailing. 'At last! I was giving up all hope. They wouldn't let me leave. I wanted to come home, but they wouldn't let me.'

'They've hurt you, my precious?'

She seemed about to launch into a dramatic monologue, but she saw Johnny's consternation and checked herself: 'No, you were just in time.'

The leader, looking about the room with an avaricious eye, pounced on the figurine of the shepherd boy. He ran his calloused fingers over it and then – the ultimate test, no doubt – he sniffed it.

'It's valuable, eh?' he demanded and, taking silence for assent, dropped in into his pocket.

And then they were hustled roughly out of the door, down the ladder and through the streets, all confusion and pale protestation. More peasants emerged from darkened doorways until there were about twenty of them. Those few pedestrians about in the early morning streets ignored the scene, either because they were used to wandering groups of drunks or from an instinct of self-preservation. The makeshift army marched at last into the silent gloom of the surrounding forest.

Columbine clung to Celestin's hand all the while, seeking his fatherly protection, while Celestin – confused by his two new roles of father and kidnap victim – kept up a murmuration of obscure, disjointed lines of verse:

> *Carried, o the martyr was, carried off to roasting;*
> *Innocent the victim was, although his legs were toasting . . .*
> *A father's such a darling boy*
> *to every darling daughter . . .*

and

> *the axe across his shoulder laid,*
> *he stepped into the forest . . .*

Clabber, inclined to believe that these unlikely events were an illusion produced by too much wine and too little food, repeatedly enquired when they would reach their hotel room and why they kept such joyless, taciturn company.

'Who's *this*? he demanded, stabbing a finger into Rook's ribs – but Rook climbed silently with the others, apparently unperturbed, as if he might as well be here as anywhere. Only his fingers seemed to betray any emotion, picking at his bag so that shreds of paper fluttered in his wake.

Johnny, alone aware of the dire possibilities ahead, tried pleading with Hildegard but was silenced by a fist in his face. The forest track was difficult, with rocks and fallen branches hidden in the deep shadows. To the forest dwellers these presented no hazard, as their feet seemed instinctively to pick their way through, but their captives were used to smooth city streets and they stumbled and fell frequently until their legs were patterns of scratches and bruises. It was Clabber who fell the most and suffered the least, falling being an accepted part of his condition and the pine needle-strewn floor of the forest being kinder than the softest pavement.

'Remember a path like this years ago,' he slurred as he found his feet for the umpteenth time. 'D'you remember it, Celestin? We were younger then. Chasing women, over the hills and far away. Good days, eh?'

'Good days, indeed, but we were fleeing women, not pursuing them, as I recall.'

'Same thing. It all comes full circle. Why are we climbing now? Is this the way to our hotel?'

The fist that had silenced Johnny now swung at Clabber, but he held it back with a raised forearm the match for any woodman's.

'Steady on,' he warned. 'I've broken bigger turnips than you.'

The peasant grunted and stepped back, but Clabber stopped in his tracks, puzzled.

'No, that can't be right. What do I mean, Celestin? I don't mean turnips, do I?'

Celestin considered: 'Well, they have the rich smell of the earth clinging to them, as our friends here have. But perhaps something more of the wilderness would be better. Spindleberries, perhaps?'

'Brilliant!' Clabber caught up with his assailant and clapped him on the shoulder. 'Hey, I've broken bigger spindleberries than you!'

Briefly they left the treacherous path for a clearing bathed in moonlight. Far below them were the lights of the Spa. Somewhere down there Cherfas was at play, free of Hildegard, Johnny thought bitterly – but what were these primitives going to do to him and the others when they reached the end of their journey?

'I'm tired, Daddy.' It was Columbine, who spoke in a voice uncannily like that of a small child. 'I want to sit down.'

'Not now, my fairy. Just a little longer.'

She at once tugged her hand from his grip.

'Some father you turn out to be!' she stormed in her normal voice. 'All these years and you can't even give me a lousy rest. I'm sitting down, and just let these apes try to stop me.'

She sat, abruptly. The party halted. The peasant leader ordered her to her feet. She spat. He prodded her with the barrel of a rifle. She spat again. He tried pulling her up, but she buried her teeth into his hand and he let go with a howl of rage and pain. Several of his fellows immediately sprang forward, closing in menacingly.

The ugly scene might have grown far uglier had not Clabber chosen that moment to remove, with a flourish, a bottle from his jacket pocket.

'Who'll join me?'

It was a genuine invitation, for the sculptor was not reading the situation too well. The peasants paused and then relaxed, taking and passing the proffered refreshment. It went from hand to hand, each man greedily gulping before giving it to his neighbour and wiping his mouth with the back of his hand. Eventually it arrived back at Clabber, who threw back his head and drained the last few drops before returning the bottle affectionately to his pocket. And then, this universal rite over, it seemed decided by common and silent consent that Columbine should have her rest.

'We're almost there,' the leader conceded, 'and we can't disturb the village at this hour. Sweet Hildy must be taken home. A few of us will mount guard here until first light.'

He pointed his stick at the chosen men while all the prisoners save Rook grouped in a spot free of rocks and tried to make themselves comfortable, shuffling a futile dance to smooth the ground. Their captors stood grinning until the performance was over.

'You'll freeze. There's no shelter. Try the space between those rocks.'

And so the dispirited town dwellers went to the indicated place and curled up beneath an overhanging ledge, watched by half a dozen men with rifles. Only Rook kept apart. Doubtless accustomed to all kinds of bed, he simply rolled himself beneath the scant spread of a stunted bush and gave the impression of enjoying supreme comfort.

The main party of foresters had gone, but their voices still carried through the mountain air, and Johnny drifted into restless sleep with Hildegard's distant laughter in his ears. Columbine and Clabber soon followed him: only Celestin remained awake, gazing up at the stars with an expression of sublime contentment.

Dawn, and gauzy curtains of mist veiled the mountains, the morning sun showing only as a pale yellowish patch towards the east. Clabber yawned, groaned and clutched his head. Celestin sat resting his chin on his raised knees in monastic calm. A bird seemed to tear a brief hole in the vaporous air, which immediately healed as it passed. Clabber groaned again, irritated by Celestin's apparent lack of concern for his suffering. Johnny echoed the sound and turned in his sleep, muttering drowsy obscenities. Columbine slept like a child.

The sculptor rose to his feet and staggered around like a ham actor in a tragedy until Celestin was forced to acknowledge his wakened presence. Not so their captors, however, who sat several yards away watching the performance in silence with hooded eyes. Or were one or two of them actually sleeping? Celestin offered the suggestion that the noise might disturb them.

'Rot their leathery hides!' Clabber roared. 'But for those imbeciles we wouldn't be here now.'

Then, more quietly: 'Where in fact are we, old friend?'

'Half way up a mountain, on a path to the sky's azure plain. It's rather interesting. We're prisoners of some private war as far as I can gather. There may be a colourful finale – which would have its compensations. I've always dreaded dying of some boring disease, the sort that takes butchers and policemen.'

'Good God! Is it that serious?' Clabber pulled the bottle from his pocket and held it momentarily to his lips, then lifted it up, viewing through it a sky distorted by refraction. 'Empty!'

It was the shattering of glass that woke Johnny and Columbine. The flung bottle had exploded against a rock. Johnny crawled from the folds of his nightmare with difficulty and for a minute or two rested eerily between two unhappy states.

'Too much blood,' he said. 'Give me a cloth. The wrong avenue, it's not down here. The sky's too low . . . '

'Not so much that the sky's too low, more that we're too high. Mind your head when you stand.'

Celestin's kindly mockery effected the transition and Johnny remembered the previous night with a cruel clarity. He looked around to assess their present situation. The sullen faces of the mountain peasants left to guard them, and the way they sat with rifles across their knees, gave him all the information he needed.

'What do you think they've got in store for us?'

His question was addressed more to himself than to his fellow captives, who knew less than he did of the circumstances. He called across to one of the peasants, but there was no answer. Not one of them moved. The sun was up: why where these forest dwellers so still and silent. He called again, anger in his voice.

'Did you hear an echo?' Columbine asked. 'Do that again.'

But he was curious now. He walked over to one of the men, wary lest the rifle be lifted and aimed. Close, and no movement. Closer, and he could see the dried blood crusting the shirt front. And the next one. And the third. A neat wound, an opened throat.

'They're dead!'

This time he heard his words echo through the cool morning air, repeating and repeating between the walls of the mountains.

'Dead . . . dead . . . dead . . . '

Their throats had been cut, all of them. He fought back the urge to retch. His head swam. Celestin picked up a stick and prodded one of the corpses to make sure. It slowly folded over and toppled to the ground with a bump. Out of a pocket slid the glossy blue and green shepherd boy with his pure white lamb.

'I was awake all night and saw nothing. Heard nothing! A tricky performance, eh? Well executed, you might say.'

If this was a joke it was lost on Johnny.

'We must get away,' he said, shuddering. 'Quickly.'

Clabber was bending over another of the bodies: 'This is the spindleberry fellow,' he said. 'A surly character.'

Columbine walked backwards and forwards, hugging herself tightly, an inexplicably merry look in her eye, as if some monumental joke were struggling to be free. Johnny seized hold of her arm and was beginning to tug her along the path when he realised that the fifth member of their group was missing.

'Where's Rook?'

Nobody had seen him. The grass beneath the bush where he had lain stood tall and pearly with dew. A scrap of brown paper was the only evidence that he had ever been there.

'Did he carry a knife?' the sculptor asked.

No, it was unthinkable. That pitiable creature could never have accomplished so deft a piece of work. What kind of man was it who would kill the guards, leave their prisoners unharmed and disappear as silently as he had come? Johnny led a precipitate retreat down the mountain, following a trail of torn brown paper, his brain in turmoil. So many deaths, such a vortex of blood – Grimm, Otto, Hans, the peasants – while, at the still centre, he remained untouched.

But for how long?

30 Nerves

'A knife of your own! Is it a penetrator?'

Columbine reached out a finger to feel the blade, and he snatched it away. Yes, it was sharp, but why did he jump so? Why must he feel as if stricken by a fever?

'For self defence,' he said.

She was adjusting a filmy drape across one corner of the room, allowing it to fall from the ceiling and flow across several couches, creating a miniature range of snowy mountains. A constellation of tinsel stars already hung above and around them accompanied, incongruously, by a putrefying joint of beef, lately scrounged from a butcher and now suspended on a cord.

In the days since they had come down from the mountain he had lived in a trance, continually aware of another's presence, a flickering movement in the shadows behind him, a watchful eye across a crowded bar. He was forever moving on, eluding that hidden fate. He could not work. Relaxation was impossible. He had, quite simply, lost his nerve. Tonight Cherfas demanded he attend the Grand Gala, so he had bought the knife. He was prepared.

'We are,' stated Columbine icily, 'our own executioners.'

He paced what floor space the clustered couches allowed. Suppose he were to leave the Spa and return to the city: would Mr Farg be forgiving? He would certainly stop short of murder. But there could be no future in the city if the mastermind of organised crime took against him. He must have some reason for leaving the Spa other than pitiable, undisguised funk. Turning, he hit his head against the meat, which swung to and fro like a hanged man.

'It stinks!' he cried. 'Why clutter the place with this filth?'

Ignoring the outburst, she held his wrist and carefully removed the knife from his hand. She picked up a sheet of paper and, with a delighted smile, skewered it to the meat.

A Poem in the Modern Dream Style
by Columbine (& Father)

(This poem, like wine, sits politely
in the bottle – waiting to be poured)

I

> *Clouds rest like swabs on*
> *the open throat of the mountain*
> *while below philosophers in large cars*
> *reflected in the curvature of their chrome fittings*
> *have discovered geologies of human villainy –*
> *aeon upon aeon rich with deceit and trickery –*
> *behind curtains of light*
> *of bright birds of paradise they sing.*

II

> *The high flying rook*
> *far gone to the grim*
> *mountains where the light*
> *solar – O on in gleaming gold tumbles*
> *not to the moon*
> *but to sleep or locked doors*
> *where a watcher fascinated stands*
> *wrapt in his arctic imagination*
> *pitying the frozen.*

III

> *City – too hot to sleep in like a*
> *bad or faithless mistress –*
> *Look! he skips from wound to wound*
> *Like a drunken surgeon!*

IV

> *The father eyes his son –*
> *belong to the club, lad, express*
> *your love of society.*
> *What! Could a spartan mar*
> *cushions of silken comfort &*
> *still count himself an anarchist?*
> *a B a Z an X an A*
> *dumb letters of a dumb alphabet*
> *speak in riddles like a sphynx.*

(There, my wine is poured: examine well the sediment)

31 Fates

The dice clattered, hobbled and were still – three fours and a grinning six with its two rows of gleaming white teeth.

'To the glissade!' cried Cherfas. 'With a hanged man's finger nail in my baggage, if you please.'

A croupier obediently raked the large red counter to a new position on the table, placing an oval yellow disc on top of it.

'And a fresh journey behind the rainbow.'

He let a pile of chips fall from his hand and another counter was pushed to the violet arc indicated by his forefinger. Johnny saw how the rainbow stretched from leaping flames at one side of the table to a cavern of ice at the other. Beneath it and above it and superimposed upon it were extravagant scenes, the highly-coloured details punctuated by encircled numbers and interwoven with strange inscriptions.

'Roll!'

It was an immense, softly-lit room with a gallery which looked down upon the dramas unfolding at the many tables beneath. Johnny had been in other casinos and knew well the charged atmosphere, the tension between the suave, controlled behaviour and the rampaging greed. He understood the feverish pursuit of the almost possible, the flat despair of total loss. Here, though, was a new experience.

'Come, risk just a little of your hoarded wealth,' Cherfas badgered him between manoeuvres. 'A few crumpled notes at least.'

'I don't understand the game.'

'Ha! As if that made any difference! You're a canny and tightfisted lad who won't be drawn, and probably all the better for it.'

'I like to know the odds.'

The counters moved on, through spiralling smoke which became a tornado, beneath a flutter of bright birds which flocked to take the shape of a human face, among a galaxy of stars which issued from the mouth of a man entwined by serpents.

'Our own game,' Cherfas boasted. 'Where it comes from nobody knows, but it's the finest there is for the dedicated punter. There's nothing half as subtle. Inheritance, we call it. You can lay your money on one throw or carry the bet forward in a variety of ways. If you ever dare to hazard the journey to its end (risking everything, you understand) the ultimate reward is the ruler's sceptre – the bank, everything. Nobody's ever done it and I doubt they ever will.'

'Most people,' Johnny observed, 'seem to prefer something simpler.'

'Ah, but it's open house for the Grand Gala. The whole world may enter tonight, Johnny, and what do most of these simpletons know of such finesse? Let them enjoy their three-card tricks!' (His contemptuous gesture was actually directed to a roulette wheel, around which Johnny saw the concentrated faces of Venner, Kristy and Dorf). 'But as the evening wears on we shall attract some big money here.'

He brought yet a third counter into play and marshalled them with apparent expertise: every so often the croupier would silently guide a stack of chips towards him. Johnny wondered how long it might take to learn the rules of a game with such obscure instructions as *The magician's staff is a poison tree, Swords fall upon the dream of the insane king* and (disturbingly, so that his mind wandered for a moment) *The bucket in the well draws up blood.*

As Cherfas plotted and called and watched his winnings rise and fall he was joined at the table by a large, ungainly man who stood close to him, holding an open notebook into which he made frequent jottings. Johnny immediately recognised him as the foreigner with the exploding suitcases.

'From what I can understand . . . ' Larooning began, heavily. But Cherfas ignored him, fixed on his sport. He lost one counter, then a second. He laid more chips on his remaining voyager, cursed the dice and changed direction towards the House of Bones.

'The odds,' Larooning persisted, scribbling industriously, 'would seem to favour the bank the more the game progresses. But what is this baggage?'

Now the counter landed in the centre of a whirlpool, and Cherfas paced up and down in a display of irritation and indecision, twice brushing aside his interrogator. Finally he slid some more chips forward and motioned for the dice to be thrown.

'Oh dear,' commiserated Larooning, bending over the table. 'That can't be good, I think. It would seem to me . . . '

Cherfas, scowling, picked up his remaining chips and dropped them into a pocket.

'A close thing,' he commented, turning to Johnny. 'See how near I was to the Everglade. From there is was but a throw to the Chamber of Screams, a loading of gossamer and I was sure of doubling my stake.'

'Doubling?' queried Larooning earnestly. 'That's the effect of the gossamer, I assume. I don't quite follow how the baggage . . . '

At this, Cherfas swung round on his persecutor, fixing him with an incredulous and malevolent stare. He plucked the notebook out of one hand and the pen from the other, held them above his head for a few seconds and dropped them on the floor. Then he took hold of Larooning by the wrists and tugged him closer to the table.

'The way to learn,' he said in a blustering tone, 'is to play. You have money?'

'Yes, yes, of course. I only thought . . . '

Cherfas took the proffered notes, passed them to the croupier and signalled Larooning to begin. The dice were thrown, and the novice – sweating heavily, stooped over the table with avid eye, fussing horribly with his chips – set off in pursuit of his inheritance.

'Once lost my wife at a game of cards,' Clabber was recalling contentedly. He sat drinking with Celestin and Columbine in a small dimly-lit recess from where the business of the casino sounded like an eruption of nature: above the cataract of voices the thin stridulation of the roulette ball, the harsh chattering of the stacked chips. 'To a monk.'

'Having hidden the ace up your sleeve and left it there?' Celestin asked merrily.

'Oh, we were past caring what the stakes were. The lady was even less use to him than she was to me, but he played as if for the Holy Grail itself.'

Johnny perched on a chair, only half aware of their conversation. The nervousness had overtaken him again. He could not stop in one place for fear of presenting himself as a target. To whom? The dread stemmed largely from his inability to answer that question. He had taken on more than he could handle. Yes, he was smart, a deft schemer, an opportunist. He had few scruples to hobble him. But he was no secret agent, and he sensed that there were forces at work which demanded the experience of the trained and hardened operator. What did he know of the kind of grand scheming which led a man to kill with a knife? As for the blood, he had never objected to murder in principle (that would be an unbecoming weakness) yet he found the nearness of it so appalling that it seemed to threaten his very disintegration.

'The Holy Grail is a hole in your head,' Columbine declared authoritatively. 'Only the artist can enter the cavern.'

It was the last night of the season and every few minutes brought a new influx of gambling parties eager to retrieve all the losses of the past weeks and months in a single, ineffable moment. Stylish, bow-tied habitues of Europe's most renowned pleasure-houses mingled with the frail, respectable burghers who had come to the Spa for their health, with the common labourers allowed this one chance of a magical escape from their condition upon the throw of a dice, the turn of a card or the roll of a ball.

'The act of creation,' he heard Celestin say, 'is the apotheosis of Chance.'

'Too true, old friend,' Clabber replied with a laugh. 'A toss-up as to whether your patron will put his hand in his pocket or not!'

Columbine, unusually quiet, was drawing complex star patterns on a sheet of paper. Every so often she would lean towards her father and rest her head in a fragile fashion on his shoulder, as if to re-establish the essence of their relationship.

'Those precious few who *have* patrons.'

'A mixed blessing, believe me, Celestin. Imagine having your lines of verse ordered by the yard. "We'll have an antique stanza just there, my good fellow; over here a rhyming couplet with an animal theme; in the foreground a sonnet to the glorification of myself." Could you write a word under those conditions?'

'A word he'd understand too well!'

Now Columbine held up her work with the pride of a five-year-old fresh home from school. Having attracted the required smiles and nods of approbation she bent over the paper once more and began to write in the spaces between the stars.

'And yet,' added Celestin, 'the patron can force your work into a shape . . . '

'Like a whale-bone corset – and corsets are for unbuttoning.'

'All very well for you, amigo, but my vice is diversity. The whole world recognises a Clabber when it meets one. It has something quid-Clabber, eh? Your own essence.'

'Unwashed.'

'But my verses echo the mood of the moment. Where's their centre? Who, or what, is Celestin?'

'A question I have often asked myself in my cups.'

'Celestin, I will tell you, is a constellation of images and feelings with insufficient gravity to prevent them disappearing into the void. Put one of his poems against another and they might have been dashed off by different people. And people with little talent, at that.'

'Basta!' cried Clabber, rising. 'I won't abide this slander of my bosom friend. In art the best is good enough, and yours is the best of its kind I know. Let's to the tables!'

Along the gallery flowed a cloak, black against the shadows behind, blacker than the densest shadow. It fluttered and sank.

The light from below touched the face of the pale young man with bright blue eyes and vermilion lips. He was watching. He was seeking.

Down at the tables there was noise and movement and colour, but it was hushed and darkened where the young man stood. It was still. He pulled the cloak about him, watching.

Unknowing, the players at their games. They grasped their winnings and cursed their losings. They sweated at their painful pleasures. The young man was not sweating. He was cool in the gallery. Cold. He gazed on their frivolity with impassive eyes.

'Damn it, there's a devil riding on that ball!'

Kristy, with trembling fingers, placed a solitary chip on the table. He could not keep still. He seemed to hop from one foot to the other, his elbows jerking like a marionette, his head giving little sideways tugs against his shoulders. He willed the ball to stop where he chose, but it would not.

'What do I ask?' he wailed. 'Only that it's an even number. A fifty-fifty chance. It lands on the odd. So I switch to odds and it comes up evens! How many times can this happen?'

Dorf tugged at his sleeve.

'Stop now,' he coaxed. 'You've lost enough, Kristy. What will you have to take home from the mountains?'

'It's too late for that. Look, this is all.' He pulled a small pile of chips from his pocket. 'I have to win it back.'

'Impossible.'

'I *have* to, Dorf. I need it. They'll be expecting it.'

He laid another bet and watched through fingers clutched tight around his face as the ball spun and slowed. A broken growl deep in his throat was the only sound he made.

'You persuade him, Venner. He's got to stop.'

Venner shook his head: 'Why should I? He's a grown man.'

'But weak-willed. He has no self-control.'

'Then he's a man after my own heart, Dorf. What control do you think I exert over myself, eh? You think I sit here calculating?'

'You don't throw your money around.'

'Because I'm too lazy. Not like you – cautious and timid.' He said this in a matter-of-fact tone, clearly without any intent to wound. 'You count your money every five minutes like a nervous bank teller, but I'll stop when I'm bored or when I'm broke.'

'And what's the secret,' Kristy broke in, 'of your good fortune? You're ahead, Venner.'

'You're the secret, Kristy.'

'Me?'

'At breakfast this morning when I was drinking my coffee I told myself, Watch Kristy's face. Count the number of twitches before you put your mug down on the table. It was fifteen. So I place my bet always on the fifteen.'

Kristy considered this for some moments.

'It has to be fifteen? You won't change it?'

'Oh, I'd change it if I was implored to. It's of no concern to me. Staying with a number avoids the foolishness of making a personal choice, that's all. Would you like to suggest another one?'

Kristy brought his face up close to Johnny's, his eyelids fluttering: 'If I play the fifteen it will never win again. If I choose a new number for Venner it will win for him and lose for me.'

'Then stop,' reasoned Dorf, almost out of patience.

'Look,' said Venner. 'I'll back the odds and Dorf will back the evens. Then you can only ruin one of us.'

This offer brought a smile of relief to Kristy's troubled features.

'I'll follow you, Venner,' he said, laying one of his chips on the table.

The silver ball spun on its way, jumping nimbly, clattering loudly as the wheel slowed. Round and round it swung, comfortably settled in the zero. The croupier leaned forward and swept everything away for the bank.

'To be alone,' smiled Kumans, with not a hint of self-disparagement, 'is the fate of all great minds.'

He was, indeed, alone in that human maelstrom, at the still, concentrated (if not strictly geographical) centre where all that rush to turn the moment into eternity seemed a futile squandering of energy. Kumans was visioning. He had a pen and paper and was beyond the tawdry present with its toil and its conflict.

'There'll be time for gaming,' he said. 'I haven't the Cherfas stamina for it. How many hours has he been riding his luck?'

He bent to his work, suddenly oblivious of Johnny's presence. The scar on his cheek crumpled with concentration. It was some minutes before he spoke again.

'You've thought no more of joining me?' he asked, without raising his eyes. 'I pack tonight and leave in the morning. I can promise you decent money and an interesting life.' Now he looked up. 'But only as interesting as you wish it to be, I promise.'

He continued to sketch, reaching for a second sheet of paper with one hand while the other retained a frantic life of its own. He was somewhere in the future, out of reach. The thin writing hurried across the page. The nib moved to the margin and deftly sketched the outline of a building, scribbled something across one corner of it. Kumans stuck to his task even when a violent crashing sound reverberated throughout the place, seeming to shake the very walls.

'Revenge!'

At one moment the babble was sufficient to make the senses reel, the next there was a profound and unnatural silence. Into this vacuum strode a small posse of men, the shock of their abrupt entrance diminished somewhat for Johnny by a feeling of deja vu.

The peasants, silent and stocky, careless stubble on their faces, stood defiantly in the alien environment, glaring about them with stupefied aggression. They were the wilder for being ill at ease. And then Johnny saw three others, outriders of the group, who were altogether different. They were younger, their heads were shaven and they wore the armbands he had seen on the men with the flails outside Gold's factory in the city. He had one of those armbands himself, in his drawer in the tower room.

These men whispered sternly to the peasants, as if keeping their hostile spirits up. They were not overawed by the casino: they stared at the clientele in a scathing, morally disapproving manner, as if upon creatures which were less than human. One of the peasants, prodded into action, produced a sack from which he withdrew the bright, glistening shepherd boy figurine.

'Five deaths to avenge,' he uttered woodenly, in the manner of a ham actor uncertain of his lines. He let the ornament fall onto the Inheritance table and the head broke off and rolled away, following the arc of the rainbow.

Kumans, Johnny saw, continued to write, but all other eyes watched the interlopers carefully. Perhaps unnerved by so much rapt and silent attention, the spokesman now stepped back, and it was left to one of the cropheads to retain the initiative with a bitter speech which rapidly became a torrential harangue.

'These men want justice,' he declaimed. 'An eye for an eye. Who'd like to sacrifice himself to save the rest? Noone? But we want five! Five lives. That's what's owing to these men.'

He began to move among his unresponsive audience, tilting his chin to taut faces which were quickly averted.

'What a tin of maggots! Do I spy foreigners? The place is crawling with them. Bringers of disease – moral disease. Spreaders of infection. Putrefying lives, swarming with loathsome bacteria. This country of ours is being eaten alive.

'And what of the enemies within, our own countrymen smeared with this foreign slime? Look at you – mingling with these vermin, abetting the destruction of our culture. There'll be no mercy for you collaborators when we take control! You'll have something to answer for.'

The simple men from the forest looked fiercely about them, as if these were the very words they would have uttered had they the fluency. They stood more proudly, nourished by the energy of the diatribe.

'We'll round up the parasites, the leeches. They'll be sorry they ever drew breath. Oh, we've a plan for people like you!'

A protest was impossible. The men were armed. Nobody so much as glanced at his neighbour for fear that something should be read into the exchange. The whole company seemed to hold a collective breath as the hostile young man strode about the room denouncing vice and pampered ease and the impurity of foreigners. Finally he signalled to his confederates that the outpouring was at an end, shepherding them to the door and turning to state their terms.

'Five men delivered by midnight or the foresters will take their revenge.'

They trooped out, the door slamming behind them, and the liberated gamblers bleated nervously, patting one another on the arms, showing their teeth in trembling smiles, mumbling incoherently as they turned back to their sport. One or two, it was true, began to talk earnestly, as if addressing the imminent crisis, and Cherfas could be seen stirring employees of the casino into action, two of them hurrying out into the night without pausing to collect their overcoats. For the rest, however, the interruption might never have taken place: the ball was in motion once again and the dice rolled from the cups. The world outside swiftly faded and disappeared, the vital present moment with its revolutionary potential swelled to obliterate past and future, love and hatred, man and woman, right and wrong – everything but the endlessly renewing possibility of random events gathering to one ecstatic consummation.

'Mr Farg, I think, would have liked him.'

The foreigner Larooning stood cradling the beheaded figurine, the two parts pressed together as if love would heal the wound. His smile denoted self-satisfaction. He watched Johnny's face for a reaction and was evidently not disappointed.

'You wonder that I know your good friend Farg, perhaps? I have the advantage of you, I believe. I know you, but you don't know me! Isn't that right?'

He shuffled clumsily. His trousers were too long, the bottoms crumpled over his shoes and spilling onto the floor. He lowered his voice to a grating whisper.

'We are brothers, you and I. At least – forgive my poor grasp of your language. I do not wish to confuse you further. We are brothers in that we share a common purpose. We seek to solve the same great mystery.

'No words for me? I admire your prudence. Give nothing away! I operate in the same manner, my friend. I remain always inconspicuous. I merge into any crowd. Stealth! I have been practising these arts in recent months.

'Your Mr Farg, I think, would not be happy to see me here. Because I pay him to do some work for me, he wishes that I sit and wait for its completion. But is it my destiny always to remain on the outside of events? I say No. I pay him to pay you, and now I come along to see how my money is being spent. Is that unreasonable?'

He sneaked a series of quick glances around him.

'Are we close to success, my brother? Not even an eyebrow raised to tell me! We must be close or we shall be too late. Word has come that our enemies are hard behind us. Shall we not work together?'

He looked sadly upon Johnny's expressionless face, then lowered his gaze to the broken work of art. He held it close to him, silently grieving, perhaps finding it unbelievable that the damage should have been caused by hands other than his own.

Cherfas was playing the tables with a manic intensity. He moved from one game to another, impatient after a single win or loss, but he was drawn back time and again to Inheritance. Johnny saw him willing the dice to roll in his favour, slapping the chips down on the table, waving his arms in exasperation.

'Write a poem,' Columbine begged her father, 'for my furthest star.'

She handed him the paper. As it passed in front of Johnny he saw elaborate galaxies in a swirl of cosmic dust, with brief lines of verse afloat in the interstellar spaces.

'Not now, my little pigeon. My muse is asleep.'

Clabber roared his dissent and reached for the pencil, his arm heavily muscular: 'Let the muse go hang, Celestin! With the success we've had tonight even I can write verse.'

There was a tussle for the pencil.

'Do not profane the luminescence of the universe,' stated Columbine icily, holding on to her end.

Kristy was weeping. The tears washed his face and dripped from his twitching lips.

'You think I have no soul,' queried the sculptor, 'because I drink too much wine and win at cards? Don't I coax rough stone to sing?'

But he relinquished his hold and the pencil was thrust into Celestin's unwilling fingers. The poet, submitting, stared into distance far beyond the confines of the teeming casino, mumbling words experimentally to himself.

'Dark vacancies,' he tried. 'Unseeded wombs . . . '

Who could even guess at the amounts of money changing hands? Cash tumbled from pockets like raindrops from a heavy sky, the wash ebbing and flowing from the bank to the punters and back again. Still they were arriving, the ever-hopeful, the last-chancers, the long-addicted, and the press grew tighter and tighter, the mood more reckless, the stakes more high.

'Rot your bones, Johnny, you *shall* join me at the tables!'

Cherfas grasped his arm, playfully, dangerously aggressive as at their first meeting, but he froze even in the act of forcing him from his seat, his eyes elsewhere. He let go. He shouted, above the din, at Columbine.

'Where in God's name?'

Surprised, she raised a hand to her mouth, and Cherfas's gaze followed it. He reached out and took the tips of her fingers in his clutch, roughly. He drew her towards him, bringing the serpent ring close to his face.

'Where did you get this?'

She turned, involuntarily, towards Johnny, who nodded assent. Yes, it had come from him. He flinched before the brutal expression his employer cast upon him.

'Tell!'

There was alcohol on his breath. The teeth were white within the ruddiness of his face. He loomed closer still, insistent – and Johnny understood everything all at once. It was knowledge before it was thought. He saw, close to, the smudges of red on the collar; he observed the unusual complexion for one so red of hair; and he recalled the unhappy, abandoned woman in her small room above the railway arches.

'Marie,' he breathed.

'Yes!'

'She knew I was coming to the Spa. She thought I might meet you. If so . . . '

'Meet *me*? Meet Kurt Cherfas?'

There was an agony of perplexity and suspicion on his face. To one side Johnny saw Clabber lighting a cheroot. Beyond, there were only heads and faces and the fluttering of a cloak.

'No.'

'Who, then?'

Cherfas tightened his grip so that Johnny's arm burned. It was too dangerous to speak the name: it would be to deliver the man to whatever crazed killer was in pursuit. For this, no doubt of it, was Peter Ocklynge. He had fled to the Spa, dyed his hair and moustache as a disguise. The red was on his collar. Now Johnny remembered the stained rags in the cupboard in his room.

'I can't say.'

'You will!'

'But Marie asked me, if I found that person, to give a message . . . that she wants him to go back.'

'Ha! Go back!'

And yet (the realisation sickened him) Ocklynge was not the man he sought, could not be that man. However dark his hair might truly be, he was too old by several years. Moreover, the features were not right, neither the chin nor the nose. It was another failure – and there was only one chance left.

'Say the name!'

Cherfas had both hands around his throat and was shaking him. Johnny felt himself begin to choke. Blast it, if he could only get the words out he *would* tell. What reason did he have to protect this man? It had been a weakness to think of it. Before he could utter the merest squawk, however, something heavy fell in front of him and Cherfas was sent crashing to the floor.

'And that was only a gentle nudge,' smiled Clabber, who had evidently struck him a meaty blow. 'But one thing leads to another.'

Cherfas, dazed, groped for a support. His eyes were clouded. Blood ran from the corner of his mouth. Johnny, surprised at himself, knelt down to help him up.

'You're Peter Ocklynge,' he whispered. 'I know it. It doesn't matter how I know, but you must keep it hidden. You're in danger.'

'Never heard the name!' Cherfas replied belligerently. 'What kind of man is this Peter Ocklynge?'

How people enjoyed an incident! They were gathering round. Among their growing number he saw Larooning with the shepherd boy; the placid Dorf and his team; Kumans, still with a faraway look in his eye; two women he had last seen naked in the steam at the Abode of Rest; a frail old man who had raised his mug at the Palace of Waters.

'If you touch the lad again . . . ' he heard Clabber warn.

Cherfas was on his feet.

'Give me the ring,' he demanded, and Columbine meekly dropped it on his outstretched palm.

'Let's talk later,' Johnny suggested in as low a voice as could be heard above the commotion of the casino. 'Not now.'

Cherfas opened his mouth, saw the sculptor's fists tightening and wheeled away. He pushed among the throng, which opened and, most theatrically, closed – a black cloak like a stage curtain falling into place behind him.

'Poor Kurt,' said Kumans, quite without emotion.

Johnny turned towards him, his last, unpalatable, hope. He offered escape. He had known the Huss Academy. Even if he had never heard the name Eric Alph he was an excuse to return to the city, away from Cherfas-Ocklynge and whatever revenge that unmasked fugitive might intend. He provided an alibi for Mr Farg, that the search still continued, that Johnny had not yet failed.

'I've changed my mind. I'll come with you.'

The architect smiled and squeezed his shoulder. Behind him, Johnny could see Cherfas at the Inheritance table, watching the dice roll and then pacing back and forth until they should roll again. He was in a world of his own, brooding, yet he was watched, constantly watched.

'Creation's spindrift,' declaimed Celestin, beginning to write in the region of the distant star. Columbine clung to his free arm, her cheek rubbing gently against it, side to side, up and down. 'You drench us with eternity . . . '

Later, well after midnight, it was Johnny's arm Columbine clung to as they made their way back to the tower room. Neither spoke. The air was cold and still, the silence heavy after the ceaseless babble of the casino.

Above the darkened streets, clusters of stars glimmered in the mysterious heavens. All of life was a mystery, faint flickerings of light in a void. Foolish, as Mr Farg had said, to ask the question Why.

Dark and tree-covered, a scarcely distinguishable presence, the mountains were mysterious too, save where they were fitfully lit by what seemed the first rays of an early sun. Dawn, however, was hours away, and that leaping light was not in the east. It began to spread, hungrily, and was suddenly everywhere alive, to right and left, on all sides, running down the slopes towards the still slumbering streets.

The Spa was on fire.

PART THREE

Understanding

32 Modern Living

Kumans's house lay within the shadows of St Luk's Cathedral in a small maze of ancient streets that twisted themselves into tight protective knots, secure against the surrounding modernity of the city. The jettied walls of the houses lurched forward across the spaces which separated them, almost closing out the sky and creating below the roofs a permanent twilight – a netherworld inhabited only by students, by failed (or yet to fail) artists and by the very old and visionless.

Johnny sat inside the window, cap and overcoat by his side for the moment when his courage should be equal to his self-imposed task, and he wondered afresh why this ardent prophet of the future chose to live among what he so professed to hate. Perhaps he enjoyed the contrast, the single step over his threshold being a vast journey through time and thought and feeling. In which future epoch did he dwell at present? Johnny looked across the room: there he was, stooped at his life's work, among his cold chrome furnishings and fixtures. The walls which shone silver. Those slippery and uncomfortable chairs!

> *Pity - limping towards us –*
> *untouched by his absurdity –*
> *the idiot boy . . .*

Columbine moved about the room singing a crazy song of improvised words and melodies, strange, snatched phrases interspersed with trembling cataracts of sound that, modulated by her grotesquely mobile mouth and teeth, set the very air vibrating.

> *lost in the thick forest of his mind –*
> *rigid forest – held by ice –*
> *trellised by swags of snow –*
> *an ancient ruin moulders –*
> *broken arches of reason –*
> *his virtue's unroofed nave . . .*

A door opened and up came the silent and dull-witted workman from the cellar. His leather apron was moist and stained. Grimed hands clutched the inevitable buckets of earth which, without a glance about him, he carried outside. Johnny, rubbing his sleeve against the glass, waited for him to appear at his handcart by the front door. The afternoon light had almost gone. A persistent drizzle stuck a few tired and yellowing leaves to the pane. The buckets were tipped.

> *December nacht – see!*
> *he bears a gift of tinsel and glitter –*
> *lays it at the feet of his mother.*
> *She – said begetter of idiots – looks towards*

a permanent midnight – when animals talk –
when animals ta-a-a-a-alk . . .

'Oh, holy child! Spare me!'

This short and desperate refrain might almost have been part of the song. Kumans crouched unhappily over his drawing board, pen held in shaking hand. The two other members of her audience remained impassive, unmoved by this eery human equivalent of the *ondes martenot*. Johnny took up a newspaper while Sophie, at another window-seat, divided her time between polishing her nails and watching the life in the street outside.

'Please!' Kumans added.

Spare, O spare, O spa-a-a-a-are him . . .

rejoined Columbine, happy to incorporate fresh material. The workman returned, bringing a cold draught with him. Wordlessly he went below. Every day was the same. Each evening he left, trundling the filled handcart behind him, and each morning he reappeared with it empty. Kumans had never once referred to his labours, and now it seemed too late to ask.

Spare his holy hierophant –
keeper of tomorrow's mysteries.
Spare, O spare the ho-o-o-o-oly hierophant . . .

'Shut up, Columbine!'

This second, and less charitable, interruption came from Johnny, who had emerged from his newspaper with an expression of anger and resentment. He flapped the pages at his sister: 'They're going to get away with it!'

'Away with it,' Columbine echoed, her voice fluttering into silence as she sank cross-legged to the floor and allowed her features to relax into those of one rapt in meditative calm.

'It says here' – he stabbed a column of newsprint with his finger – 'it says it was an accident. Listen! "An oil lamp was inadvertently tipped during a drunken brawl among habituees of the casino. Despite the brave efforts of a group of Party members who happened at that moment to be passing, the casino was burnt to the ground and several of its staff and clientele perished in the inferno. The flames later spread to the whole of the Spa. A group of peasants vouched for the heroism of the young men, although one expressed anger that such nobility should be put at risk to rescue the degenerate". '

He threw the paper down: 'Who'll believe such rubbish!'

'Rather high-flown,' Kumans agreed, 'for the average peasant.'

'Confound the peasant!' Johnny choked. 'The whole thing's an invention!'

'Those young men have influence,' Kumans said with a shrug. 'I should hang on to that arm-band. It might serve you well, yet.'

Sophie leaned forward and poked at her brother's shoulder as if to test that he was the person she had taken him to be.

'Can it matter?' she asked. 'What's it to you, Johnny? Are you growing sentimental? It can't affect the likes of us here.'

Kumans's expression suggested offence at being, by inference, included in the likes of Sophie and Johnny. He sighed and returned his attention to the work in front of him but found himself unable to summon the concentration needed to guide his pen across the stretched white sheet of paper. How had he managed to surround himself with these people? That, clearly, was what he was asking himself. In welcoming Johnny into his house, he had failed to imagine Columbine's staying on too, nor had he foreseen the frequency of Sophie's visits. The studio in which they languished and he anguished had been a private place, a sanctuary, a source of dreams and hidden pleasures. Now it was an arena – its angular interior, its bright glass and tubular steel, had become the backdrop to a contest played out by mutual antagonists, Columbine's anarchic behaviour constantly threatening to tip his ordered world into an abyss of meaningless and chaos.

The likes of us . . .

she sang with a cracked smile,

Pity, O pity the likes of u-u-u-u-us . . .

No, of course it mattered not a jot to Johnny that lies were told about the firing of the Spa. On the contrary, the cunning was something to admire. There had been nothing in the papers for days, and then a cleverly orchestrated fiction in practically all of them. Why then did he roar his disapproval? Because his nerve had gone. Because the shouting kept his fear at bay. He had always controlled his environment, but now he failed to comprehend it. Who were the men with arm-bands who revelled in violence? Who was it that followed close behind him, wielding a stained knife? His senses seemed to swim, to flounder, in a welter of blood. Who – he looked upon her with a growing horror – was Columbine? Had she, too, plunged into this crimson tide, a razor in her hand?

'The weather's getting colder,' Sophie said, gazing into the street. She watched a boy with a long scarf wrapped tightly around his neck, the ends flapping in the wind like the wings of a manic green parrot. 'It'll soon be winter.'

'Winter.' Columbine no longer sang, but intoned the word solemnly as if it contained some terrible evil. 'Winter!'

Kumans continued to stare helplessly at his board, Sophie watched the scarfed boy's progress along the street and Columbine sat brooding upon the imminence of winter. Johnny put a hand on his coat. Did he dare?

'I can't work!' Kumans almost wept. 'I shall go and lie down.'

They heard him climbing the stairs. A shuddering sound advertised his collapse upon the wide mattress in the centre of his room. Comfort was not a priority here.

'Where are you going?' Sophie asked, and Johnny at once let the cap fall from his fingers. He was frightened of going, of what he might find, yet was restlessly eager to know. Desperate.

No comfort: by night he shared with Columbine a small windowless room, little more than a cupboard really and situated between floors at a bend in the stairs. This also housed a collection of dusty theatrical props and costumes and an ancient cat which Kumans had inherited with the house. They slept with the door ajar to allow themselves air, Johnny spread across a pile of costumes, a tumble of faded velvet, all that remained of a long forgotten and truly tragic Hamlet, and Columbine curled in a corner with the cat. A section of canvas backdrop, hung against the wall, depicted the interior of an oriental palace complete with fiercely coloured furnishings and a fountain, the crudely painted water of which suggested more a tuft of white grass. Columbine, whose own theatrical tastes in interior were mocked by this decaying collection, loathed it profoundly from the first.

'It smells of cheap imagination,' she had said.

'It smells of cat,' he had corrected, ready to chase the hapless creature out. But Columbine liked the animal: there was no question of an eviction.

Kumans's own room, which was above theirs, and from which he was nightly tempted and tortured by the sounds of their sleeping groans and fidgetings, was little bigger. His space, however, was clear of extraneous material and resembled nothing so much as a reflecting box, for walls, ceiling and floor were all tiled with mirrors, the only furniture being that mattress, upon which he would lie spreadeagled, able to watch himself recede into infinity in all directions, his pleasures and pains repeated and repeated over and over until sleep plucked him from the radiating star of his conscious self. Columbine, fascinated by the possibilities of sleeping in this room, had actually made advances which Kumans had rejected, thus further widening the gulf between them. Johnny, Kumans sadly noted, seemed to prefer his cupboard.

And yet the ambiguities of their relationships were as puzzling to the trio as they were to any visitor, particularly so to Kumans, who found himself with an attachment to Columbine that was as unexpected as it was unwelcome. By what magic was it that this attraction blossomed like a cancer within his psyche? He felt as one doomed: he had no means to express these new feelings and so merely grew more offhand with Columbine, more dogged in his vain pursuit of Johnny. Columbine pretended not to notice. Johnny failed to notice.

'I'm going for a walk,' he said, suddenly standing. 'There's someone I have to see.'

'A mystery?' Sophie asked mischievously. But she knew better than to invade her brother's privacies. 'You can take me home first. They'll be knocking on my door within the hour.'

There was a cold night in prospect. They closed the door behind them and huddled close as they walked, arm in arm. Pinpricks of rain jabbed at their faces. The air had a smoky bite, promising a frost.

'Columbine worries me,' Sophie said as they came out of the labyrinth onto one of the wide modern streets where black cars glided among the carts and carriages. The tyres hissed on the wet road. A beggar they had ignored shouted abuse at them. 'She's becoming more extreme.'

'Everything's more extreme,' he replied, feeling the touch, the embrace, of fear all over again.

Was he genuinely in danger or did he imagine it? He lowered his face and turned up his coat collar, as if to hide himself from it. No, he did not imagine the violence which the newspapers spoke of or that which he had seen with his own eyes. The times were brutal.

They passed under a lamppost and he looked at his sister with a sorrowful pride. She was dressed in the fashion as far as her purse would allow (a hat with a long silver pin, a coat with little strips of fur at the collar, dark stockings, shoes tilted on high heels) but she seemed to him horribly vulnerable. He felt unable to protect her.

'And you won't tell me where you're going?' she asked provocatively as she fished for her door key. 'And me your own flesh and blood.' *Flesh and blood*, he thought. *Flesh and blood.* 'Is it someone I know?'

Who did we know? he was tempted to reply. Did he understand Columbine after all these years? He had discovered otherwise. Could he really fathom the thoughts of his own sister, know what made her miserable and then, Schnapps apart, sustained her against that misery? But he only shook his head and retraced his footsteps.

Flesh and blood. He had endless visions of it, cloying nightmares sticky with deep red oozings. It had become an obsession. Victims of a knife: his friend Otto, five peasants on a mountain, a solicitor and his mistress on an office floor. And Hans. Was Hans dead? Had Columbine truly taken his life with a razor? It had begun to devour him, this death. Did he live side by side with a killer? If so, would there not be retribution? Of all his shadowy terrors this was the one which most oppressed him, yet it was the very one he might possibly dispel. If it should but turn out to be Columbine's strange fancy . . . Yet he could not speak to her of it, and he had flinched from asking Sophie what she knew.

His insecurity intensified as he weaved his way across the open spaces of the busy platz, and the church on the corner loomed more menacingly than ever. He pictured himself as he had once seen his brother, white faced, coffined and imprisoned by the waxen bars of candles – save that the smoke which curled upwards, flowing into the Gothic gloom, was redder in his imagining that he had actually seen it, and his mother no longer wept but smiled slyly as if to say: 'I told you so. Those who play with sharp blades cut themselves.'

This dismal reverie was brought to an abrupt halt by a sharp and painful flow dealt to his leg by a passing car. The city's dance! His former deftness had gone. Now he hopped around on one leg in the middle of the platz clutching the injured limb and raging and fulminating against his vanished persecutor.

'A moment, please.'

A policeman worked his way between the passing traffic and pedestrians, signalling to him. The arm wagged to and fro, puppet-like. Whether the purpose was to admonish or to help, Johnny did not wait to discover. He set off at a hobbling gallop.

'Come back!' The tone was suddenly vicious. 'Swine!'

The lights were soon left behind. Into a narrow alley, where he paused to listen for following footsteps. Silence. He had visited Hans only once before, and that was at night with Columbine, but he found the flight of greasy steps easily enough. At the top he paused and felt his leg again: an alarming stickiness caused his trousers to cling to him. Leaning against the wall he hammered his fist against the flaking paintwork of the door. As he had feared, there was no answer. Did he dare?

He tried the handle and the door swung open to reveal a dark passage that gaped like the empty socket of an eye. Was that stench from the darkness the foul odour of corruption or only the familiar breath of stale cooking and damp plaster? Gingerly he stepped inside, quite forgetting the pain in his leg. He opened a door to his left. It was a kitchen, its interior heavily shadowed. There was a wooden table with a plate of half-eaten food, the grease congealed into a white halo around cold brown gravy. He saw a cracked and stained sink, a scattering of unwashed saucepans, a spillage of salt, a dusty clump of hung herbs, all the evidence of neglect and squalor. But Hans?

The passage took a turn to the left. He had to feel his way through the gloom, his eyes at last making out two more doors. The first opened on a bedroom: tumbled sheets, brimming chamber-pot, ewer and bowl crusted with dried soap. He was standing in the doorway, gazing on the uninviting prospect, when there came a clatter from the direction of the kitchen. There was a shuffling movement, and then silence. Next a cough. Johnny felt a terror, a hot bewildering panic, such as he had never experienced before, and he rushed to the third door and flung himself inside.

A lurid green light from a neon sign somewhere outside in the street cast a sickly glow on a cluttered living room in which he made out the dark bulk of a sofa and the gleam of a glass table top as he rushed at the curtains and hid himself in their folds. The light snapped off. He felt his breathing as a tumult in his chest. The light came on again. Facing the window, he could see the room behind him dimly reflected in the glass. A late and fated fly hammered against the pane; somewhere a clock's regular ticking measured time; a thin black dog loped sure-footed across a roof in the dusk. The light went off, briefly, and then on. The shuffling started up again and began to come closer.

He pressed against the wall. The door, seemingly far distant in the poor reflection, began to open. At that moment, unable to keep his eyes on whatever horror should enter, he let his glance fall for the first time on a large armchair which sat in darkness against the wall. In the armchair was all that remained of Hans.

33 A Kind of Death

A hand reached into the room, fumbling on the wall, and a dim bulb began to glow from a cord in the centre of the densely cobwebbed ceiling. The eyes of the object in the chair were wide open but did not register the change. Now the dishevelled figure of Rook shambled forward, clutching something that rustled.

'Disgusting,' he wheezed, standing over the motionless body.

Slowly, as if sleepwalking, he shuffled to a table, carefully deposited the package and made his way back to the chair. He put out a finger and prodded, tentatively, as if unwilling to defile himself.

'For a woman,' coughed Rook, running a sleeve across his mouth. 'Disgusting. Not one of them's worth it.' Bolder, he pushed at the human wreckage so that it shifted in the chair, a foot swinging loose and crashing heavily into an array of empty spirit bottles which the darkness had concealed. 'What good did they ever do a man?'

Seemingly enraged by the lack of a response, Rook put out both hands, seized the tangled hair and began to rock the head back and forth, all the while muttering wildly: 'No good . . . what good did they ever . . .but old Rook'll do you good if you help him, eh . . . old Rook's the man to know . . . you'll be grateful to old Rook when you've got your brain back.'

From the lips of the abused head came a deep and prolonged groan. Another bottle toppled and rolled across the floor. Behind the curtain Johnny found himself shaking with relief and a feeling almost of merriment. O blessed groan! No razor blade! Big Hans looked as good as dead, his brutish frame collapsed in the chair, but he was in fact no more than dead drunk – pathetically, degradingly drunk. For all his cruel bravura he was finally brought to this, all his strength and violence reduced to a heap of pickled flesh. Where was the entourage which had formerly surrounded him, the girls who had played serf to his feudal lord: had they, like Columbine, deserted him? Was he dead for them, too?

'You,' Rook uttered savagely, 'disgust me. You deserve what you've got.'

Hans groaned again, like a mortally wounded animal. The light fell green upon his face. The room in which he morally decomposed was no more prepossessing than the others Johnny had seen, the cheap ordinariness of its fittings and furnishings suggesting a lack of interest and care. There were, it was true, a few sentimental and homely touches (the sepia photograph of a man and woman staring solemnly from their oval frame, a vase of withered flowers, a flute of some sort on the mantelpiece) but these seemed accidental intrusions in the general shoddiness. Little wonder that Columbine hated him.

'Old Rook can lead a helpful man to glinters.'

A bottle rolled along the floor and into the folds of the curtain. Johnny nudged it with his toe to help it on its way but succeeded only in sending it into a wobbling spin. Rook gazed at it thoughtfully for a few moments, his breathing noisily laboured, and then made a snatch at the curtain, tugging it away from the taut and trembling refugee.

'Ah!'

If there was an instant twitch of fear in Rook's expression, to find himself spied upon, it gave way at once to an inexplicable delineation of joy. His arms were held wide as if he wished to clasp the intruder in a malodorous embrace. His dancing eyes seemed years younger than the ravaged face that carried them. A chuckle rasped from his throat.

'I knew it,' he gloated. 'Didn't I know it?'

Johnny kept his distance: 'Knew what?'

'That Hans would find you for me. Yes, I knew the connection. The woman. Sooner or later . . . '

He picked up the bottle and tossed it towards the heap in the chair.

'And now I don't need him at all.'

Outside the window there came a prolonged, shrill screaming and then the sound of running footsteps. Shouts were exchanged. Someone pressed a car horn, repeatedly.

'You were looking for me?' Johnny asked.

'Oh yes! Yes, I was looking. Old Rook's good at looking.' He came up close. 'And now you're in the bag.'

Johnny flinched: 'Why do you want me?'

'Oh, it's not me that wants you,' Rook replied, with the air of an aristocrat caught fingering baubles at a cheapjack stall. 'It's someone else. *He* wants you.'

'What for? Tell me!'

But Rook only coughed into his sleeve and then spat wetly at his feet. He shuffled to a window, knocking against the chair so that the recumbent body shuddered and the head fell forward on the chest. Johnny remembered the night on the mountain and that grim dawn.

'At the Spa,' he said, 'after those peasants took us away, you disappeared. What happened?'

'It's dark,' Rook observed, his nose to the glass. 'I expect there'll be trouble.'

'Did you . . . Do you carry a knife?'

Rook laughed, the effort bringing on a paroxysm of coughing.

'Those men were murdered!' Johnny cried in despair. 'Someone slit their throats!'

The coughing at last subsided. Rook held on to the sill for support.

'That was him,' he panted. 'Fine gentleman in a cloak. A foreigner, he is, and nasty with it. But he pays. It's a very sharp knife.'

'Him?'

'He's the one who wants you, boy.'

He reached out a hand, but Johnny pushed it away and began to back towards the door. That green light was the colour of a nightmare.

'Don't follow me,' he ordered. 'I'm not stopping here.'

Rook showed his cracked teeth.

'You go on,' he said. 'You won't get away now I've found you.'

The corridor was utterly dark. He ran blind, hitting the wall, his hands waving before him. Where he was going only his legs seemed to know, out of the front door, down the steps where his feet skidded on the accumulated filth, along the alley and soon, without a pause, into a street which he recognised and up to a house which he wished he had never once seen.

34 Tainted Evidence

' . . . and it is without question a sojourn in purgatory,' pursued Mr Farg tirelessly, 'to become embroiled with the unprofessional, the more especially when so much hangs in the balance. While human lapses are regrettably unavoidable they are the harder to bear the more they impinge upon our well-being. A slack errand-boy is an irritation but has little power seriously to annoy. Likewise, one expects a percentage of hotel waiters to demonstrate a bumbling incompetence and finds it possible to shrug off the occasional smudge of soup on a table cloth. But we have, I would suggest, a right to demand rather more of someone who claims a degree of expertise and has, moreover, the power to destroy our reputation as well as his own . . . '

Johnny was close enough to see, to his consternation, that the Dresden shepherd boy who stood nursing his lamb on the desk top carried the mark of a crude repair which held head and shoulders together. He could not take his eyes from it.

'. . . our own reputation being in any case by far the greater. And what are we to make of the gaucheness of a man who contrives, albeit from the most generous of motives, to present as a gift that which has already been dispensed to another and then in an undeniably superior condition? Is it simply bad luck this fellow has or a pact with some lord of mischance?'

'It was taken from me,' Johnny said simply.

'Immaterial,' ruled Mr Farg, raising his swollen fingers in a gesture of impatience. 'Such a man finds a way of subverting the very geometry of the universe. Disorder is his milieu. I ask no tiresome questions about how he came in possession of it. It was, I aver, inevitable that he should unctuously proffer it to me, a smile of beatific smugness on his face. Part of his destiny. He cannot escape his uncomfortable fate, as I believe even he himself is close to acknowledging. But shall we be caught up in that fate, you and I?

'And yet, I hear you reply, he is the paymaster. Alas, true! Our Larooning is (as he so clumsily, so dangerously intimated to you) the man offering, on the authority of others we shall assume, these huge sums of money for the information he seeks. And a certain circumspection is due, therefore.

'I have, however, not hesitated to vouchsafe certain advice in terms I trust of sufficient forcefulness . . . '

Johnny showed no trace of surprise on learning of Larooning's role. He had come up the stairs trembling but, from a survivor's instinct, had entered the room in control of himself, as if he expected to be well received. Mr Farg was the only protector he had.

'The man's contrition issued in gushing revelations about the provenance of those pieces of paper I gave you at our first meeting, though I regret to say that your pleasure at such new information will be sorely overcast by the frustrations it brings in its train.

'In short, I feel we shall know less rather than more as a consequence of it.'

He brought his head down to the level of the figurine.

'Its value quite gone,' he said in lugubrious tones. 'The repair is worse than the fracture.'

It was impossible to hurry him along. Johnny waited, a sorrowful expression on his face out of respect for the stricken shepherd boy. Mr Farg closed his eyes and appeared to take a cat-nap.

'Several years ago,' he began slowly, the lids still lowered, 'Larooning's people made their first attempt to trace their prey. They deployed a veritable army of sleuths, it would seem, and at last one of their agents sent the longed-for message: he had found their man (or, more strictly, *boy* as he then was). Larooning himself arranged a suitably clandestine assignation with the agent but, traumatically one must suppose, arrived to be confronted only by a dead body. It was, an unkind observer would say, his destiny.'

His eyes opened and were smiling.

'In the agent's pocket were the papers I passed to you. Nothing more. The said prey had disappeared. Our poor Larooning then contrived to confide in a gentleman who proved to be of another persuasion entirely, by which time copies of these papers were presumably as thick as autumn leaves in the platz.'

He reached out with both hands and pawed the shepherd boy towards him. He nursed it against his jacket.

'The trail, however, had gone cold and, for a reason too obscure for me to fathom – or at least for my informant meaningfully to impart – no further interest was shown in finding this mystery figure until the present. Now he is desperately sought once again for certain documents he is thought to possess. We must assume, I think, that every other stranger we meet is in possession of a portrait, a newspaper cutting and a recipe for borsch – a veritable freemasonry of pursuers.'

He enjoyed his own humour, at the same time looking keenly at Johnny as if testing the quality of his reaction to the information they now shared.

'Are you saying that the portrait was found, with the other papers, in the agent's pocket? That was the first time anyone had seen it?'

'Bravo!' Mr Farg swung his hands close together in an exaggerated gesture of applause, stopping short of bringing his gnarled fingers into painful contact. 'You've hit upon it right away.'

'But that means . . . ' He was on his feet, agitated. 'It means that we don't know for certain that it's a portrait of the prey, as you call him, at all!'

'Quite so.'

Johnny began to pace the room but was prevented by the clutter of furniture. The glowing porcelain congregation gazed on him with a serene indifference.

'It means we have no idea what the man looks like. The portrait may be a false clue altogether.'

'Possibly. All the clues may be false.'

'So what's left that we know about him? His age. We know that.'

'Indeed. I confirmed as much with our friend Larooning. The man is, as we were first informed, twenty five years old. I fear that this is the sum total of our knowledge. We are reduced otherwise to proceeding by an inspired interpretation of unsatisfactory evidence. Let us trust that your inspiration has been sound.'

For the moment the fear had gone. Johnny was calculating. Mr Farg, lifting the figurine, held it to his cheek and began to croon, tunelessly.

'So we may have let someone slip through the net,' Johnny mused, 'by relying on the picture.' He began to calculate aloud: 'Forget the picture, only the age counts. The doctor, Martin Jolsen, was too old to be our man. So was Peter Ocklynge. Dirk Grimm? About right, but no – that newspaper article said he was twenty seven.'

'Good man!'

'That leaves Gold. I never met him.'

'But I have found time for a little homework. He must have been something of a veteran pugilist. The poor creature is in his forties.'

Pleased, they nodded and smiled like old cronies.

'Poor creature?' Johnny queried at length.

'Humbert Gold is a ruined man, his factory taken over and all his considerable assets seized. He escaped with very little. The authorities are on the *qui vive* for these foreigners beating a hasty retreat. They're all at the same game. They sense what's in the offing.'

Johnny remembered another foreigner: Rook's mentor with his cloak and his sharp blade. There could be no escape, Rook had said. The man would come. What did he want?

'I have pondered lengthily,' Mr Farg said, as if reading his mind, 'upon the motives and behaviour of the somewhat sinister fellow you have mentioned before – the butcher, shall we call him? It seems that he was ahead of you at the doctor's surgery, and we must therefore suppose something more than pure coincidence. Then your near confrontation in the solicitor's office: why should he visit the same people unless his evidence is similar? I suggest that he, too, visited the Huss Academy and busied himself with the files, coming to a similar conclusion.'

'He killed Dirk Grimm. In cold blood.'

'Which confirms my diagnosis. The man is, of course, a pathological killer, scarcely sane. He considered that Grimm was not his man. Had he been so, our butcher would have held back the knife (agonising though the constraint would have been for him) until the precious papers were found. As it was, he saw that the solicitor's visage and the portrait were quite dissimilar and so allowed himself a little sport. I have no doubt that he has been working to the same brief as you.'

'And now he's looking for me.'

'Oh yes, he's looking for you, Johnny. And will inevitably find you. Does that prompt you to an even greater urgency?'

He smiled, breathed upon the figurine, rubbed it with a sleeve and set it carefully on the desk top.

'However, we may perhaps steal a modicum of comfort from the supposition that he is, temporarily at least, a step behind you – though I dare say that I am more easily consoled than you in the circumstances. Remember his crude attempt to elicit information with that message purporting to issue from my pen. Refreshingly amateurish, wouldn't you agree? Certainly an admission of ignorance. He needs you alive at present.'

'Until I find Eric Alph. I have to carry on the search for Alph.'

'And hope that he turns out to be twenty five. Then, my young friend, it becomes a different game with different rules. Or with no rules at all. Who can guess what this erratic character's reaction will be then! Meanwhile, he flounders for a new clue. Your architect friend's connection with the Huss Academy is, you think, unknown to him? I am sure you will wish to keep it so for as long as possible.'

'But if Kumans leads us nowhere?' He had kept his pessimism to himself, but now the conspiratorial nature of their conversation encouraged a greater frankness. 'He's our very last chance.'

Mr Farg bent low over his desk, his eyes raised to Johnny's, unblinking.

'Can we ever know,' he pondered, 'what is the last instance of anything? This is my last cigarette says the man with his neck in a noose – and wakes to find that the rope has frayed. See my last enemy gone, rejoices the knight as he stands over the fallen on the battlefield – and his trusty old retainer promptly stabs him in the back.

'Let us regard life, rather, as offering a kaleidoscope of changing patterns, no first or last but a continuous flux, as volatile, as full of motion, I narrowly precede you in saying, as a baby's bottom . . . '

35 Frozen Music

The cat had woken with her and they both stood for a minute on the stairs in the evening gloom, stretching and blinking before going their separate ways, the cat in search of food, Columbine of company.

'Purrrrr,' her tongue fluttered against her palate.

She found Kumans in the studio surrounded by the paraphernalia of his profession and so lost in concentration that for a while he failed to notice her. When he did look up, however, it was not with the grimace of exasperation she had grown to expect but with a welcoming smile. Putting down his pen, he at once took her by the shoulders, whispered urgently that she should wait and disappeared into the kitchen, soon returning with two steaming breakfast cups of coffee.

'Splendid!' he beamed, raising the drink to his lips as he might a rare elixir and sipping with an animated expression of satisfaction.

Columbine, disarmed by this behaviour, remained silent, blowing patterns in the coffee froth until Kumans, unable to contain himself further, thrust his newly completed sheet of designs at her.

'There!' he cried, bursting with self-satisfaction.

But she could make nothing of the tangle of thin blue lines, turning it this way and that, bemused: 'I don't understand. Blue veins, wanderings of ice . . . '

'Of course, or course. I forget! It's the air filtering system.'

'Air?'

'For the city. They'll need air.'

She frowned, trance-like in her half-sleep. 'Why not open the windows? Panes of light, palpitating . . .'

Kumans laughed: 'There *are* no windows. There'd be nothing to look at if there were.'

'But why?'

'I thought you realised. It's all underground. Total control of the environment, you see. Imagine: no more weather! No more grey days, chill drizzle, piercing winds, icy roads . . .'

'Or sunshine? Or snow?'

'No, none of those things. Ah, I see a frightened look in your eyes! Well, sunshine's a bit of a problem from the health point of view, but I'm sure we can manufacture something equivalent. Something we can eat, perhaps? As for snow, I suppose we could arrange excursions to the surface. But, believe me, you'll not want all that when you discover the diversions we'll create – all of them tailored to suit your tastes and convenience. Look!'

And he unrolled more worksheets, all the while interpreting them with an earnestness which stage by laborious stage alienated Columbine even further. She prodded a finger into the coffee grounds and licked it; she took deep sniffs of the dark brown aroma; she rattled the cup in the saucer as if it were a musical instrument.

At last he grew angry, throwing down the sheets and standing over her.

'Don't you have any vision? Do you think we should carry on living like pigs grubbing around on the surface of the planet? Are we always to be subservient to nature? I say No! We must build a new world, forge for ourselves a new humanity . . . '

This fervent recitation of his creed was silenced by the abrupt flinging open of the door and the entrance of a representative of the decadent old humanity. Johnny shut the door behind him and leaned heavily against it, his breathing fast and shallow.

'No-one following me!' he gasped.

The short journey from Mr Farg's house had been a passage through hell. He could not dispel the image of a fluttering cloak parting to reveal a sharp silver knife. Now, safe again, he slowly reconstituted the scattered elements of his personality. He was aware of being stared at.

'Am I interrupting something?' he asked, in as jokey a fashion as he could muster.

Kumans bent to recover his designs.

'We were discussing the future,' he said. 'Columbine doesn't believe in it.'

'There is no future,' she replied, shaking her head, 'and no past. We are the present and there is only the present.'

'Ha! You lack imagination. My plans are already beyond today. See, Johnny – look!'

He began again and Johnny, content to have arrived home unmolested, allowed himself to be led along the blue lines, pretending to appreciate the glories they presaged.

'But these are only ideas,' he broke in after a while. 'Clever, I'm sure, but just as an artificial language is clever. You could make up all the words, but nobody would ever bother to speak it.'

'Esperanto! Yes, there is such a language, but it makes the mistake of borrowing from existing grammars and lexicons. Why should we sweat to master a language which seems just a pale echo of our own? It's not bold enough. You have to do away with all the cadences of the past. That's what we shall do in our architecture. New forms for the new Man that is to come.'

'How – a new Man?'

'Oh, it's so difficult to explain and yet so obvious . . . '

He seemed to tremble with the frustration of it, the more urgent to communicate because he imagined that Johnny was curious, eager to understand. He looked from Johnny to Columbine, walked distractedly in a tight circle tugging his fingers through his hair and eyed them thoughtfully, warily, all over again.

'Do you want to see?' he began nervously. 'If you are serious, truly serious . . . '

'See what?' Johnny asked directly.

'But perhaps not Columbine. She would ridicule, refuse to understand. I don't show people. Not yet.'

'Show what?'

He came close to Columbine, almost shouting: 'You wouldn't laugh, eh? You promise not to laugh! Not to despise!'

'Promise,' she whispered, a little shaken.

'Ha!'

He took himself off to a corner, hid his face and, in a mumble, communed with whichever gods he was accustomed to consulting. It was a long and furious debate. When he had finished he remained silent for a while, as if awed by the decision which had been taken. Then, without warning, he stepped briskly towards the door which led to the cellar.

'Follow me down,' he said. 'But be careful. It's a long way, and very steep.'

The descent was darkness, each step tested by a groping foot, until Kumans reached the bottom and flicked a switch. A dim light filtered up to meet them.

'An apparently stupid place for the controls,' their host laughed over his shoulder, 'but it deters snoopers.'

He waited for them, his eyes bright with excitement, and as they joined him below and entered the subterranean world he had created it was evident that their reaction only increased the intensity of his pleasure. Johnny found himself looking back up the steps to restore his sense of perspective. How could so vast a concourse – for here were streets running from some kind of a meeting place, the whole in bulbous, rounded, flowing forms of seamless concrete, not even the walkways entirely flat, the edges of buildings bulging into the open spaces – how could such a metropolis exist beneath the small square of Kumans's humble house?

But of course it could not! Now he realised (his first steps into the place showing him that this was no illusion but a fabricated reality) that the land must be undermined far beyond the property above.

Columbine took his hand, perhaps from uneasiness, as they followed Kumans into the heart of his heavily vaulted city. What was so eery about the experience? Was it the emptiness of the grey thoroughfares, so obviously designed to be busily populated? Their footsteps echoed. Partly that, but something else too. It was, he suddenly understood, the effect of the lighting which, though subdued, was produced by a vast array of concealed bulbs, so that not a single shadow was thrown, anywhere.

'Forget everything you've learned about architecture,' Kumans bubbled with an almost manic enthusiasm. 'The past is over. And Modernism? Yes, that too unless it dares to follow its pure instinct. Don't think of comparing this with anything. I know what the critics will say. Visceral, they'll call it. It's like walking inside your intestines! But who'd ever want to do that? (I'll tell you about my sewage disposal another time). These fake modernists all have a fatal hankering after the traditional. If I'd built it all square they'd liken it to cliff faces, which wouldn't be any better than comparing it with the Parthenon. This is new, it creates its own reality!'

They climbed a ramp and passed what looked like a row of cells with large round openings.

'You'd perhaps call them homes,' Kumans suggested with an unforced condescension, 'but think of them as spaces to perform whatever function seems appropriate. You might sleep there, or read, or feed.'

'Small,' Johnny ventured, 'for a family?'

'But there you go! Who said anything about families? We're looking beyond the present. Here we have everything for the needs of the people, and most of it's communal. Privacy is a bourgeois concept.'

He showed them where tracks ran in a deep channel for the communal transport. He pointed out alcoves for yet-to-be-devised machinery providing heat and light and a host of abstruse amenities. He led them along a street which ended at a wall of clay, a wheelbarrow at the foot of it with a spade and two familiar buckets.

'A harmony of forms. See how the whole concept is informed by the one spirit. Point and counterpoint. I've heard architecture described as frozen music. This is my symphony.'

'Unfinished,' said Johnny, with a little laugh.

'But its structure already clear. A mere hack could complete it.' He began to lead the way back. 'One day I shall show it to the world. Not when *it* is ready, but when the world is ready. At present? Intellect is invisible to the man who has none! I often feel that Man is something that is to be surpassed.'

He ran his finger along the smooth wall as he walked, thoroughly at one with his creation. Columbine disappeared into one of the small rooms. When they looked inside they saw that she had taken a scarlet ribbon from somewhere on her clothing, tied it into a small bow and deposited it in the centre of the floor.

'Pretty,' she said. 'A wreath of blood.'

Kumans's face clouded to see his vision besmirched, and it seemed for a moment that he would snatch it away. He only shrugged, however, and marched on.

'Why?'

Columbine's question careered along the concrete curves.

'Why *what*, in heaven's name?'

'All of it. Why?' She tugged at his sleeve. 'Something in your past . . . '

They had reached an area where there were groups of heavy conical structures with projecting sills low down to serve as seats. Kumans flung himself down on one of these, an interested expression on his face.

'What do you mean?'

'It's all inside,' she said, sitting close to him. 'Inner dreams escaping. From when you were a child? A fairy tale your mother told; a picture on the wall; a half understood book. I remember a story where dwarves lived underground forging gold coins from stones.'

Kumans gazed on her with wonder, as if she had turned a stone into gold herself. He drew Johnny down at his other side and sat for a moment with his arms around both their shoulders in an uncharacteristic display of warmth and openness. He seemed suffused with a strange innocence.

'You're a witch, Columbine, I always sensed it. You see where mortals are blind. Yes, I knew a story once – a foolish and fantastic story, but dangerously alluring for all that. I learned to reject its fake charm years ago, but I don't doubt that its images lie behind my work. Fortunately I've substituted reality for colourful fancy.'

He leapt to his feet and went on a little tour of his immediate environment, smiling contentedly upon it, touching it, as if to reaffirm his escape from that childish vision. Johnny had never seen him so relaxed.

'When I was very young,' Kumans said, 'I lived with my uncle and aunt in the country. My father would come to see me every so often, but he was an actor and always on the road. My mother? I never knew her. I understand that she was a beautiful blonde actress who for a brief spell captivated the hearts of audiences throughout Europe – but that's another fairy story, for another time.

'This Uncle Walter of mine was in every real sense my father. Indeed, since the two were identical twins the change of roles couldn't have been more complete! One day he took me into his study, closed the door, planted me in a chair and in earnest tones (because dear Uncle Walter could be rather pompous at times) began to tell me the family history. Perhaps I should call it the family mythology, but I'd spoil a good yarn if I tossed in all my cynical asides. Let me stress that Uncle Walter was the most honest man you could hope to meet and that he therefore believed every word of it. Shall I go on?'

He knew the answer but kept them waiting, jumping down to the tracks of his planned railway system so that he was hidden from their view and surprising them a little while later by climbing back up a ramp immediately behind them.

'My great grandfather came out of Asia. I ask you to imagine a small village under the mountains, with a river and a scattering of humble farmsteads. Primitive, but no doubt blissfully innocent. (There I go again! No more of this world-weariness, I promise you). A peasant community.

'He was, by all accounts, a remarkable man. He had visions. He was a poet. And the time came when he felt compelled to leave his family behind, wife and young children, and journey to a city far to the west. This is all in the mists of time and the exact nature of his quest isn't known, but it appears that he had a mission to purify the place, uplift it or whatever. (I watch my tongue, you notice!) He was an outstanding personality.

'Several years afterwards my grandfather, the only son of the family, set off in pursuit though armed with no clues whatsoever as to his father's whereabouts. He discovered a city of the most repugnant kind where brutality was the order of the day and which was ruled by a grimly repressive organisation called the Red Blade. But wait! He heard rumours that there was, somewhere, an ideal city inhabited by the good and true and that it was (take a deep breath!) *beneath* the hostile place in which he now found himself: a city underground! Being young and perhaps somewhat romantic . . . '

He checked himself once again, smiling, and sat on another of the concrete cones, some way distant, his voice lightly echoing.

'The story goes that he actually found this underground city, which was a splendid creation mimicking the glories of the world above while suffering none of its nastiness. A kind of urban paradise. His father had been there before him but had left, presumably to complete his mission among wicked and fallen mankind. (Sorry! I've a blind spot for that type of moralising.) His father had gone, so he followed, and – not to send you to sleep with an interminable account of all that happened – eventually the two were reunited.'

'But not in the underground city?' Johnny asked.

'No. The entrance he'd once used was sealed off and he never found it again.'

He fell silent for a few moments, and when he resumed there was a tinge of diffidence, perhaps embarrassment, in his voice.

'Now we reach the part of the story which thrusts my family to centre stage in a great and bloody drama. I see in the mind's eyes a tableau painting: "Grandfather Discovers His Destiny". He learns that the Red Blade and a rival organisation whose symbol is a bright blue eye have been at war, moral and often actual, for several decades. My great grandfather, the great seer, has been elevated to the leadership of the virtuous faction by popular acclaim. He is venerated, a man others will follow, and that aura of sainthood which surrounds him like a nimbus (another style of painting comes to mind now!) is held to shimmer around his son likewise. Despite himself, despite his fears and his feelings of inadequacy, my grandfather eventually adopts his father's mantle. When the Eye at last defeats the Blade he in effect inherits the city.'

He stared at them as if daring them to disbelieve, a finger all the while idly stroking the scar which ran down his cheek. Or was it their *belief* he was challenging?

'These civil wars go on for ever,' he continued. 'It's their nature. No sooner had the Eye achieved their victory than they were vigorously assailed all over again – the crimson tide, as one of my school history books had it (though in another context) forever ebbing and flowing. My grandfather had twin sons who were their mother's unwitting murderers: she died in childbirth. Fearing for their safety, because they too would become inheritors, he sent them away to a country in the west to be raised separately and anonymously. It's the fate of our family to move west each generation.

'My father lived with an elderly couple in a large city. Uncle Walter was brought up in a monastery, which accounts for a good deal – though I won't go into all that. They were both completely ignorant of their origins. On their fifteenth birthday each was given a broken piece of pottery and a slip of paper with an address on it. This part of the tale I can vouch for. I've heard my uncle recount it dozens of times with never a word out of place. For you, though, the briefest summary of it. The two lads at last met up and were given a letter from their father which had been deposited at a bank. This outlined the family history and urged them to do the decent thing. Moral duty and so forth.'

He laughed, rose and came towards them.

'Well, some vital ingredient in my ancestors' blood failed to come down to me! You wouldn't catch *me* responding to such an appeal. But we're not all the same . . . '

'They went?' Johnny asked. 'To inherit the city?'

'Ah, there was no telling whether there would be anything to inherit. Some people would have welcomed them, but others would have feared their influence. It would be a highly dangerous business. Meanwhile they learned from another source that, through some sort of trickery, and for suitably high-minded reasons, their father had gone into voluntary and permanent exile. He himself would not be there. Indeed, he was never seen again.'

'But did they try?'

'Did they try?' Kumans pondered. 'That, Johnny, is an arguable question. Uncle Walter tried, I'm sure of it. But my father? I suspect that I derive my moral frivolity from him.

'What seems to have happened (and my uncle was always vague about the details, which makes me believe that he was loyally shielding my father from criticism) is that the two of them agreed upon a plan of action. They were to approach the city from different directions, contacting different supposed friends of the Eye – there was an additional peril, as you may imagine, in being seen together. Uncle Walter travelled a long way east and actually secured a thick sheaf of family papers which had been rescued from a burning building during one of the city's frequent upheavals. (He gave them to me, much as I didn't want them. They're stashed away in one of the ventilation ducts down here – it seemed amusingly symbolic to put them underground!). Before reaching the city itself, however, he received a message from brother Jack, my scapegrace father, which persuaded him to pack his bags and return home. What was in that message I've never discovered, but I'm convinced that my uncle later felt himself to have been deceived.

'And that,' he concluded, sitting close to Johnny and putting a friendly hand on his thigh, 'is a long-winded way of answering Columbine's question about this underground city of mine. The grand idea was there, and I pay tribute to it. Otherwise, though, the two have nothing in common. Nothing! That other one, supposing it to have existed, was reactionary, an imitation. You were supposed to imagine yourself in the old quarter of a medieval city or sitting by the clear waters of a schloss. A false sky flickered with the moon and stars at night.'

'And perhaps still does?' queried Johnny, shrinking from the press of Kumans's fingers.

'Perhaps so. Who can say? But what meaning have night and day in a city underground? It's nonsense. New forms, new expectations for the new civilisation!'

He paused, his ears straining, and then they heard it, too – a strange roaring sound which at first had no obvious location. Only when they had divined that it came down the steps from the architect's house did they credit it with a human source. They stood together listening, and all three recognised it at the same instant as the fractured howling and baying of a mob. It was loud, but sufficiently distant to be outside the building. As they began to climb the steps there was the more distinctive, brittle sound of glass being smashed.

36 Flotsam

Larooning twisted his head helplessly to left and right, unable to catch the attention of his nearest companions who, their elbows lodged against his own, bore him along the street at a frantic, inelegant pace. They were like madmen. There was spittle on their lips. When he attempted to slow his pellmell advance, to wriggle free, there were more bodies behind, kicking feet, out-thrust hands propelling him ever forward. The sweat poured down his neck despite the chill of the night air. He cried out: it was but one more shout, quite lost in the uproar.

The riot swept through the city thoroughfares like a medieval dance of death. For its initiators it heralded a new age; for its victims it was a mere continuation of dismal reality. Each street erupted in a turmoil of screams and caterwauls, of wailing and the gnashing of teeth, of broken glass and crackling flames, all this to an unremitting chanted litany of hatred and abuse, of slogans as high-sounding as they were devoid of compassion and charity.

Why, Larooning asked himself, should it be his misfortune? Was it more than this? Did some malignant Fate? He had meant to heed stern advice and keep clear of trouble. It had been a yielding to impulse to venture onto the streets, and yet . . . yet he had only tentatively hovered on the fringes of the forbidden area. What had he been caught up in? And who was this violence and invective directed at?

The casual observer (should there be such a creature) might suspect that anybody, anything that could be easily injured or destroyed was a legitimate target for the arm-banded thugs who yelped their promises to clear the streets of 'foreign filth', 'decadent scum', 'wealthy parasites'. Could the old lady, white-haired and bleeding in the gutter, really have posed such a threat to public decency? Or the young boy, nursing a broken arm and howling for the protection of his missing mother: was he discernibly foreign in his pain and misery, or were his cries the cries of children everywhere. And the old man seated in the wreckage of his shop, head held in hands, encompassed by swathes of ruined suit fabric: had his trade really been at anyone's expense, or was success his only crime?

'I am a foreigner,' Larooning thought, dashed along like driftwood on a foaming current. 'But a visitor, which is surely different. I shall be safe.' He closed his mouth, nevertheless, and dropped his eyes.

So blind and lurching a progress! The riot funnelled, boiling, into the old quarter, its pressure intensifying as the space between the buildings contracted. Doors burst inwards at the press of the mob, offering new opportunities for wholesale desecration, irresistible opportunities, the ransackers invading with the eagerness of rampant colonists swarming over rich, virgin ground. Furniture was scattered and shattered, splintered and ripped and, finally, put to the torch.

Larooning was lifted over a threshold, his feet for a moment treading air, then suddenly released so that he stumbled forward, striking his shins on a low chair and crashing to the floor. The heel of a heavy boot crushed his fingers. A knee caught the back of his head. An ear was sprinkled with a liquid which, looking up, he found to be deep blue in colour. The looters were spilling the contents of a phalanx of bottles over the floor. The blue liquid was sweet. As he rose, he licked at the rivulet which ran across his chin. But these vicious moralists were not drinking. The empty bottles were hurled across the room, splintered glass raining upon the busy bobbing heads.

Paper was thrust into his hands, a long sheet covered with thin lines and minuscule writing. Other hands were ripping other sheets, making confetti of them, and anxious not to stand out from the rampaging crowd he tugged clumsily at his own. There was shredded paper everywhere. It was thrown from the smashed windows, to be caught in the rising heat of neighbouring fires and carried high aloft into the wintry sky.

Was it possible to escape? He edged towards the door but, at the very moment of his passing through, the interlopers had done with their business and surged outside. Larooning was wedged against the jamb, his chest painfully constricted. *Help me*, he wanted to cry. Someone kicked him from behind. There was a great heaving, a rage of battle-cries and undirected oaths, and then the flood of savage humanity was on the move again, he picked up and borne along by it.

Swirling smoke and choking brick dust filled the street. Oh, the terrible sound – an awful howling like the wild and aching misery of a thousand bedlams! Larooning groaned but could not hear his own despair. His feet when they touched ground were beaten against hard cobbles. On and on. Past small shops where earlier in the day crowds had queued for morsels of food and which perhaps now – their doors ripped away, their interiors charred – would never open again. Past the wreck of a once-fine motor car, its tyres slashed and ragged, its windscreen shattered, its running boards flapping. Past a dozen scenes of heartless brutality until the tumult spilled out of the old quarter into wider thoroughfares and Larooning, an insignificant piece of flotsam on that scummy tide, found himself carried closer and closer to its slower-moving marges and was at last beached, bruised and panting, on an ash heap.

37 Buried Dreams

The door slammed on Kumans before he had reached the top of the steps. When he turned the handle and pushed there was no movement at all. Something heavy was lying hard up against it.

'Open up!' he shouted vainly against the fury of the mob beyond it. 'Let me out!'

Down below, Johnny was dramatically massaging his injured leg, having contrived to trip and fall lest anything too unpleasant should be awaiting them above. Columbine bent over him, her fingers tracing patterns in his hair.

'We're trapped,' Kumans said.

For a while he continued to shout, but the sound seemed to lose itself in the vast echoing space behind him and scarce penetrated the door, let alone the unimaginable din on the other side. He came down the steps.

'Plenty of air,' he consoled himself. 'If it's not for too long.'

'Someone's bound to come sooner or later,' Johnny replied, strangely resigned.

The lights flickered ominously.

'In that box,' the architect indicated, 'you'll find candles. The cable's probably been damaged. We'd better . . . '

But before he had finished the sentence the lights flickered once more, dimmed, brightened for the briefest of moments and then failed completely, plunging them into a total subterranean darkness. Kumans groped his way to the box. There was a creaking, rustling and scratching, and then a sudden bright star lit a tiny fraction of their firmament.

'Divine!' squealed Columbine, waking to the possibilities of this improbable prison. 'More candles! More! We'll make a cathedral of it.'

The box, which held a large supply, yielded her enough to place candles at intervals throughout the embryo city. The other two watched as it became a place of bright, inviting hollows and mysterious shadows whose depths seemed limitless.

Kumans was rather taken with the transformation, more attracted by its faery unreality than he would have cared to admit. But to Johnny it was something far greater than attraction and far less easily defined. He stared around in wonder. Somewhere deep within his being, below the layers of cunning and cynicism with which he armed himself against the world, something was touched that was terrible in its beauty and fragility, something that had lain dormant since his earliest years when, as he curled up in his cot each night, Sophie would whisper stories to him through the wooden slats, stories that supplemented the meagre warmth of his blanket and drove away the pangs of his hunger. In Sophie's stories there was always a land beyond, a place where mothers were clear of speech and steady on their feet, where they smelt of lavender rather than schnapps, a place where fathers came cheerfully home from a day's work able to love and provide for their family, a place of small, snug cottages surrounded by an infinity of forest, a forest whose dark evil could never penetrate the magic of the hearth where logs glowed and crackled and sent showers of glittering sparks into the sooty hollow of the chimney . . .

He trembled. These dreams, the same dreams that Columbine had so recklessly woven into the fabric of her everyday existence, Johnny had buried for fear that they might hurt him – buried so deep that he himself had imagined them dead. But here they were, bursting into new life as heady spring bursts green from winter, and all he could do to express this unexpected resurrection was to take Columbine's hand and press it tightly in his own.

'Don't waste more candles,' Kumans broke in. 'We may need them later.'

'They are phantom spirits,' Columbine instructed him, 'and cannot die.'

She wandered trance-like up and down the flickering streets singing gently to herself, a song as gauzy and vaporous in its images as the intelligence which shaped it.

Was it madness to live so fully in the imagination? Johnny would normally have thought so, but now that he found himself so strangely transported he felt no mental torture or derangement but rather a profound and invigorating peace. It was, he recognised, not only the candle-lit allure of this cavern which had affected him: it was, even more, the peculiar story which the architect had told.

'Those family papers of yours are down here?' he asked falteringly. 'Can I see them?'

'Whatever for? They're simply tedious old documents which don't make a great deal of sense.'

Kumans was finally persuaded, however, that examining the archives might prove marginally more interesting for Johnny than staring at the wall, even if he himself preferred the latter course. Having fetched the papers and dumped them without ceremony at Johnny's feet, he returned to his own silent deliberations.

'Family secrets,' Columbine breathed rapturously. 'The warp and weft of the soul.'

Johnny looked down at the sheaf of yellowing parchment, a heavy bundle held by ribbons of an indeterminate colour which might once have been purple. He knelt and, his hands shaking, began to loosen the knots. They did not readily submit and he was absorbed by the task for several minutes until suddenly the ribbons fell away and he was able to lift a sheet to where the candlelight could fully illuminate its secrets.

> *No birds sing beneath*
> *the city's vaults;*
> *the eagle's wing cracks*
> *against stone*

'Poems!' cried Columbine, seizing the paper. And, indeed, there were several pages of them which Johnny was happy to give up to her. He next came to a weird sheet headed AN ACCOUNT OF THE BIRTH AND DEATH OF THE STAR MACHINE, which contained the details of a supposed device for creating an artificial sky. Then, in protective oilskin, there were two maps. One was of a city – not, he at once realised, his own - with a large red cross struck at its westernmost end. The other was on a larger scale, showing mountains, rivers and villages. One of these had been heavily encircled twice over.

'You've seen these?' Johnny asked Kumans. But the architect sat with his chin between his fists and appeared not to hear.

> *The lizard's tail strikes*
> *sparks of crimson*

Columbine recited, her voice reverberating:

> *cold crimson;*
> *the cockroach inherits,*
> *and the spider*

Johnny turned the pages of a letter, hurriedly, feeling that he should not read. This was in an erratic hand, whereas the sheets immediately beneath it were covered with a neat italicised script as if written with great deliberation. They gave a description of an isolated religious community, a simple life in which the brothers kept to a strict routine of prayer, gentle gardening and the tending of goats. Last of all, and in the same hand, there was a single page with a sketch map at the top and, beneath it, a series of notes and instructions. There were names and addresses and brief comments such as *Trebitch knows more* and *visit the crypt in Rat Alley*. Glancing quickly about him to check that he was not watched, Johnny folded this sheet in half and thrust it into an inside pocket.

Why had he done it? His motives were not clear even to himself. He only knew that the hidden document seemed to feed him strength, like a talisman. It had a power, no doubt. Would Columbine divine it? She came close to him and rested her sheaf of papers on his knee.

> *Wear me as your helmet*

she read with relish,

> *falling masonry will break*
> *across my back.*
> *Wear me as your spiked heel*
> *I will bite into ice for you.*

38 Vacancies

Deserted the streets when the mob had passed through them. Hard the black sky. Blinds shook shredded in the cold wind, rags on a forsaken corpse. There was blood on the cobbles.

Here by the dance hall deft shadows swirled in step, to the tune of the wind, a beat of cracked slate.

Black the sky and black the timbers where the fires had travelled. Sooty specks sank, spiralling, down. They stank of death.

There in the cafe a singer had strained, defying the babble. No melodies now along the stricken tables, the crippled chairs. Only an absence. The roof was a window, the window a door.

Broken heads, broken spirits. It was a time for private griefs. Away from the unforgiving streets a thousand secret tears were shed, a thousand reckless prayers were spilled. And on the death-delivering streets – an emptiness.

There was no singing, no dancing now, but a distant withdrawing clamour that grew fainter and fainter.

The pale young man was a shadow and his cloak was a darker shadow as he paced the hollowed-out streets. The cold wind smacked his face. The dark sky sought his darkness. His lips were the colour of blood. The young man contained a void where the two darknesses swarmed and fused.

39 Tell, Tell, Tell!

It was Sophie who rescued them. She came with the moon-faced boy and persuaded two strong men to tug away the heavy cupboard which had fallen against the door.

'Everything's gone,' she stated hopelessly as they emerged. 'Everything.'

The house had been sacked. The destruction was all but total, yet for Kumans the one shattering grief was the shredding of his blueprints. His jaw hung slack as he walked from room to room surveying the wreckage. The furniture, the glass, those things did not bother him: they were replaceable. But the plans, his precious plans . . .

He held the few remaining fragments in his hands, fragments which Columbine had silently gathered from the floor and given to him, and as he looked down at them sudden tears fell, blurring the thin blue lines as if even the fraction that remained must needs wash away.

'Why?' he asked distractedly.

Johnny, embarrassed, stood at the window looking out into the street. A few dim lights came back on. People who had barricaded themselves in now emerged to reckon the damage and help douse the fires. Others, less fortunate, lay where they had been stricken and wondered at their sins, that fate should have contrived to heap such calamity upon their heads, to launch such a plague upon their community. They wandered, numbed, trying to account for their families, friends and neighbours. He watched them sift through scorched interiors for what remained of their possessions.

'It started down by the canal,' Sophie said. 'They broke up a money-lender's shop and threw the old fellow in the water. Nobody dared fish him out and he drowned.'

The boy began to shake, his puffy white face twitching uncontrollably. She put out her arm and drew him close.

'It might have ended there, but the police turned up and did nothing – well, worse than nothing. They stood and shouted encouragement, by all accounts. After that there was no holding them. They took it into their heads to settle a few old scores.'

'The police did nothing . . . '

Johnny repeated it incredulously. Of course he had no love for the police, but he had always regarded them as a necessary evil. Without their control of the society he milked he could never ply his trade.

'The world's stood on its head,' Sophie added.

Now the boy whimpered and tried, desperately, to speak: 'I'm f . . . '

'You poor mite! Come to Sophie.'

' . . . frightened, Sophie.'

She stroked his hair and murmured against his ear.

'Poor lamb, he's seen bad things tonight. Our home's gone, Johnny. Everything. We got out and they burned it down, the whole block.' She spoke in Kumans's direction. 'Now we've nowhere to stay.'

The architect waved impatiently, acknowledging the inevitability of sheltering two more guests in what remained of his house. He had been standing, weeping and wordless, for several minutes, but now he allowed the papers to fall to the floor, dried his eyes with a sleeve and announced simply in a clear, firm voice: 'It all needed reworking anyway – new discoveries, new technology, new materials. It'll be even better next time.'

The courage of this brief speech moved Columbine greatly and she threw her arms about him, an embrace which he enthusiastically reciprocated, even to the point of placing his lips full upon hers. They stood toe to toe.

'What did I say?' Sophie laughed coarsely. 'The world's stood on its head.'

Upstairs the destruction was every bit as complete. Johnny found his possessions strewn over a large area. The sketch of the dark-haired young man lay, heavily creased, in a corner but even as he stooped to pick it up Kumans reached out and, with a grunt of surprise, added it to his own pile. Johnny, puzzled, allowed him to claim it.

Slowly he collected his things together. He came across the arm-band with its increasingly familiar markings. The newspaper cutting had been screwed into a tight ball and the recipe was torn in two, but everything survived. Sophie and the boy helped to restore order while Columbine arranged a collection of broken trinkets into a colourful, elaborate work of sculpture.

'Their life-forces ooze and glow,' she said.

Eventually they retreated downstairs, carrying their damaged trophies almost tenderly in their arms. Kumans seemed incapable of dealing with the chaos. It was Sophie who stuffed large cracks in the window panes with cloth to keep the cold draughts out; who busied herself in the kitchen to fetch coffee in chipped cups; who wrapped the trembling boy in a blanket and coaxed him into a noisy, troubled sleep. But perhaps all this activity was merely her way of keeping the horror at bay, for when at last she sat with the others on the thick carpet, cradling her drink, she began to breathe rapidly and her hands shook.

'I knew it would happen,' she said in little more than a whisper. 'I saw it.'

'Saw what?' Johnny asked.

'The blood! It was prophesied. An old lady I went to, a clairvoyant. She showed it to me.'

'Like a tick,' Columbine said dreamily, as if reciting, 'he will drink the blood of the city.'

'It was horrible!' Sophie began to cry. Johnny put a hand on hers. 'I saw the blood – and now it's happened. There are dead people out there on the streets. Our home gone . . . '

'Don't believe those old charlatans,' Johnny counselled her. 'They're just tricksters, Sophie. They don't know. We'll be all right.'

'They *do* know, Johnny! It's second sight. They can tell what's coming.'

Now it was Kumans's turn to speak softly, as if from memory: 'Stone,' he mouthed, the trace of a smile on his lips, 'dropped in well.'

'What's that?'

'A saying.'

'What saying? What does it mean?'

Kumans studied Johnny's agitated face with amused interest.

'It matters to you for some reason? It was something I learned when I first came to this country as a boy. The language was new to me, and my imagination seized upon odd phrases and sayings. You don't know it? Perhaps it was peculiar to my tutor. I was a restless, inquisitive pupil, always asking questions, and he would put me in my place with that saying. This is how it goes:

Stone dropped in well
clapper in bell,
the tongue of a gossip
will tell, tell, tell!

'It's unremarkable, I know – trite – but because of the circumstances in which I learned it I've never managed to dislodge it from my brain. It's what I always reply when people begin to pester.'

Johnny, understanding at once, wondered how he could have been so slow to realise. Under his nose! For confirmation he leant across to the architect's pile of tattered treasures and began to withdraw the charcoal sketch.

'What do you want with that?' Kumans asked. 'It's mine.'

'Are you sure?'

'Of course!' He took it from Johnny's fingers and held it up for their inspection. 'It's a portrait of my father.'

'I thought I'd lost it,' he continued. 'It must have been lining a drawer all the time.'

'Your father . . . '

'When young. It could, of course, equally well be my uncle but it wasn't, if you see what I mean. Not at all like me. I am my mother's son.'

'And you lost it?'

Johnny restrained the urgency he felt. He was playing the game again now: disguising his motives, manipulating the conversation, coaxing his victim into unwitting revelations. Kumans was wonderfully suggestible.

'I thought so, yes. At least, I actually suspected it stolen, ridiculous though it sounds. But that's another story.'

'An odd one, I should think,' laughed Johnny. 'Who'd steal a thing like that?'

'The kind of man,' Kumans replied, 'who would steal a shopping list or an old party invitation.'

'I don't understand.'

The architect returned the portrait to his pile, clearly debating with himself the wisdom of saying more. But Johnny knew that he would talk, and he waited.

'There was a time,' the flow at last resumed, 'when I would have dreaded to breathe a word of this. It's only because the danger has long since passed that I can talk about it at all. And because I'm with friends.'

He dropped his hand to Johnny's knee and was surprised to find the overture allowed.

'Not that I realised I was in danger at the time. How should I? Life seemed simple enough. I was studying for the architecture exams – hours and hours of material stresses and load-bearing calculations and surveying techniques. In the evenings I'd relax with sport of various kinds. Boxing chiefly, as I think I've told you. A normal existence.'

'But?'

'But all the time something sinister was going on.'

A gentle snore interrupted him. Columbine had curled herself up, foetus-like, on the carpet and was soundly, innocently asleep. Sophie sat between the two slumbering forms, her eyes glassy and distant.

'All the time I was being spied upon.'

Johnny shook his head, expressing utter amazement.

'Strange, eh? You find that hard to believe! Well, I shall convince you. Think back to what I told you of my grandfather and that city he came to inherit. It seems that despite his voluntary disappearance, despite his sons' failure to follow him there, the people of the place still regarded the family as – how shall I put it? – as an absent royalty. To love or hate, revere, despise, to petition or fear, depending on the point of view. And therefore, as the descendant, I was the target of all those attitudes and emotions. Quite unknowing! I learned later that some wished me dead, some would have given me the keys of the city, some only wanted the papers you saw down below.'

'They came looking for you?'

'One at first. Of course I had no idea. He was my fencing coach. He came to my flat two or three times a week and I got to know him well. I suspected nothing, not even when things began to disappear. How should I believe that this sober, more-or-less respectable gentleman would steal my humble tram tickets and recipes? When those trifles went missing I put it down to my own absent-mindedness.

'He was a little stupid, I think now. I suppose that he was charged with investigating me and that he thought of me as the sum of my parts! What he did with all the bits and pieces he took I can't begin to guess. Unfortunately for him he took too long about it. It was his undoing.'

Kumans glanced apprehensively about him, seeming relieved to find that Johnny was his only audience.

'Eventually, again unknown to me, another man appeared on the scene. His sworn enemy, as the writers of romance would say. The two of them came face to face in my presence – in my flat, indeed – and everything was revealed while the blades flashed.'

'Blades?'

'It was at the end of my fencing lesson. The newcomer took up an épée and they both set to. I was so young then! Imagine how shocked I was. It accounts for my idiotic behaviour . . . '

He seemed reluctant to admit his foolishness. Johnny kept silent, waiting.

'What I did,' admitted the architect with a short laugh, 'was to step between them. You can imagine the result! Here it is – this scar down my cheek. I *saw* the blood spurt out.

'Not that it matters,' he added philosophically. 'The skin wasn't very pretty just there, anyway.'

Columbine began to titter in her sleep, her throat trembling, and Sophie put out a hand to shake the spasm away.

'After that they concentrated on cutting one another. You never saw such a carving outside a butcher's shop!'

Johnny felt the sweat start on his forehead. When he closed his eyes there was nothing but a thick pulsating redness.

'I ran,' Kumans went on, 'and I went into hiding. That was another stupid thing to do. I emerged weeks later for a tournament at the Academy because I fancied my chances and couldn't keep away. I was changed for the fight and posing for a newspaper photographer when friends sent word that the police were after me.

'Well, think how it looked – my room splashed with blood, the body of the fencing master in a corner, another corpse down a side alley! I didn't wait for the bout, as you may guess. I fled. Disappeared. Changed my name (another family tradition) and apprenticed myself to an architect in another city. It was a couple of years before I had the courage to return, and only recently that I've begun to feel safe again.'

'And what was your name,' Johnny asked, already knowing the answer, 'before you became Boris Kumans?'

The architect leaned close.

'A confidence shared only with a bosom friend,' he whispered, stroking Johnny's thigh. 'Before the birth of Kumans I was Eric Alph.'

40 Betrayal

He was more than half way towards Mr Farg's house before he would admit the appalling truth to himself – that he was not going there at all. He fought against this truth like a saint with temptation. Of course he must go, to tell what he had discovered. Of course he was on his way to claim his large and hard-earned reward.

But he was not.

The first snowflakes had been indistinguishable from the flecks of grey and white ash that still lingered in the sky above the stricken sectors of the city. Now they fell more thickly. His boots kicked up flurries of the powdery whiteness, his indecision made manifest by a tangled line of tracks which went neither forward nor back.

At once the excuses, miserably unconvincing. It was late and Mr Farg always retired early: no, he would have welcomed being shaken awake to hear this news. The evidence was incomplete and therefore inconclusive: no, it was complete in the very detail that mattered, the identity of Eric Alph. To secure the papers themselves would be a potentially valuable ploy: yes, but that could be achieved later and was a separate issue.

He could not so much as begin to believe his own rationalisations.

There was no moon tonight, or stars. The streets were empty, as if the populace had imposed a curfew upon itself. He passed only a frail, consumptive lamplighter, leaning his ladder against the crossbar and climbing painfully towards the mantle to transform the eery snow-light into a pattern of sharp contrasts. Johnny, scarcely able to admit his own weakness, turned away from this splash of brightness into the unlit cobbled alleys of the old quarter where he could wander the labyrinth with no apparent destination at all.

Dark the alleys where the light never filtered. Shadows piled on shadows.

Was it loyalty to Kumans that checked him? The idea brought a curl to his lip. He disliked the architect: worse, the man made his flesh creep. He had never enjoyed a single minute of Kumans's company. That loathsome intimacy! It would be no betrayal to deliver him to his pursuers. No, not loyalty . . .

The old lamplighter's moist cough echoed through the deserted streets. The air was cold now. Johnny turned his coat collar up over his chin and sank his hands deep into his pockets. Snowflakes clung to the material yet melted to wetness the instant they touched the decorated arm-band which he had tugged over his sleeve as he left the house. Security. He stamped his feet for warmth.

A hungry darkness in the hollowed-out streets. A swarming darkness which threatened extinction. It breathed.

His brain commanded him to strike out immediately for Mr Farg's house, repeating the message over and again, but he could not obey it. He felt himself mysteriously, irresistibly manipulated, as if he had no will at all. He had never experienced such a sensation. His mind was allowed to function normally, but its power to influence his behaviour was utterly suppressed: there was another imperative. It was like – an image sprang up – like his mother forswearing drink for the hundredth time. There she was, lecturing him on its evils, assuring him that she would never again touch a drop, while her hand, at the very same moment, groped in the cupboard for another bottle. She meant what she said but was ruled by a stronger passion.

And what mastered Johnny? The admission was devastating to him, to his pride. To reject the opportunity of easy money (easy, at least, now that the work was done) for the ludicrous romance of a fairy tale! How could this be? He rebelled against the notion with a violence that brought tears of frustration to his eyes. He wanted nothing to do with Kumans's strange story. Why, Kumans himself had derided it! No, he wanted only to collect the money and run.

But he did not.

Two darknesses: the dark sky mingled with the darkness of the streets. There was no sound along the cobbles where the soft snow muffled a footfall. There was no movement save the swirling of darkness within darkness.

It was himself that he was betraying. He, who had always advocated seizing the main chance; who had scorned the idealistic and other-wordly; who had never known any man to put fancy dreams above his own pocket. What would the world make of his folly! It was, undeniably, utter folly.

A smell of burning. He stopped by the shell of a baker's shop. At his feet lay a charred board with the simple message scrawled across it: NO MORE BREAD TODAY. Did he hear a sob from somewhere deep within? It was too dark to see. He looked across the street and it was darker still.

Let me go, he pleaded with the delirium which tyrannised him.

Approaching a cramped meeting of ways where the alleys seemed to buffet one another in passing, he was aware of not being alone. He could see noone, but he felt the swirling darkness to be possessed, inhabited.

'Who's there?'

A pale face issuing from black folds; a large, ungainly figure stumbling forward calling his name – the two movements instantaneous, the collision heroic. Something bright and sharp skidded across the cobbles.

For a moment he could not move. He saw the shadows in crimson colours. He watched the pale young man, the pursuer, the exterminator, laid out dazed on the cold pavement. His cloak was separated from him and it was alive. It crawled and it shrieked and it sobbed like a malignant sprit, like a wickedness made flesh and lusting to prey on its creator.

'Black! black! black!'

Larooning, in a panic, threshed and lunged, brought his head out of the dense folds, stumbled and fell to his knees, while the other stirred, stretched and groped for his knife.

Johnny ran. He hurtled through the narrow streets with never a look behind, on and on, the night air burning ice against his throat, until he threw himself upon the architect's door. It would not budge.

'Kumans!' he cried. 'Let me in! Danger!'

He struggled with the handle, he beat upon the wood with his fists. It was only as he stood back to swing a kick that he saw the paper speared to the door with a nail.

41 Angel and Devil

In the centre of the sheet was a large, bold representation of the symbol which he wore on his armband. Above it, in thick capitals, were the words REQUISITIONED. FOREIGNERS. Below there were three indecipherable signatures.

Johnny snatched the paper from the door, rolled it up and pushed it inside his coat. Then, looking repeatedly over his shoulder, he hurried away. Somewhere behind him was a man with a knife. Somewhere else (it could be anywhere) were Sophie, Columbine and Kumans. He had never before felt lost and alone in his own city streets.

Refuge took the form of a night cafe which announced itself from a distance with wild celebratory singing. Inside, a seething horde of rough and ill-dressed men – a few accompanied by girls, most content with the company of their fellows – crowed and caroused, ate, sang, thumped the tables and congratulated themselves on a job well done. Their common bond was the band each wore high on his right arm, the band that Johnny was wearing and which ensured him a welcome within the sweaty confines of the place.

The counter, far beyond the clamouring heads and shoulders, was presided over by a gigantic plaster angel with heavy, spreading wings which, arching down in gilded pleats, formed two sturdy side pillars. Enfolded within them the proprietor was labouring mightily with his assistants to keep the press of customers supplied. A day that had seen ruination visited upon so many businesses had evidently proved highly successful for him. He lifted his eyes towards his protector from time to time as if in thanks, perhaps fearful that the angel might capriciously withdraw its favours. As for Johnny, only a miracle could have carried him through the dense malodorous throng as far as the bar itself.

'We showed 'em, eh!'

A rubicund face topped with dishevelled flaxen hair thrust itself forward, promiscuously intimate. Perhaps its owner mistakenly imagined that they had shared some act of destruction earlier in the day. Johnny smiled but, feeling the response inapposite, swiftly adopted a leer which in turn metamorphosed into a sneer. This was evidently correct, for almost immediately a jug of beer was thrust into his hand and the face distanced itself sufficiently for Johnny to raise the ceramic lip to his own, though the close-packed jostling company ensured that as much of the liquid spilled over his shirt as down his throat.

Now a new tune was struck up. It was an old folk song with words he had always regarded as feebly sentimental, but he sang them now with assumed relish, as if his very life depended on it. And perhaps it did. Fingers stroked his thigh as Kumans's had earlier, but he was unable to discern their owner in the crush of bodies and in any case felt the assault far preferable to a slit throat. He threw back his head and emptied the contents of the jug.

> *Hands to the plough, lads,*
> *For the work we've to do.*

We shan't mop our brow, lads,
We shan't question how lads,
We shan't cry Enow! lads,
Until we are through.

By what strange magic the jug was refilled he could not tell. He again emptied it with dispatch. The ugly celebration began to distance itself, weariness and hunger slowly exacted their payment and he drifted gratefully into a state of untroubled torpor.

'Didn't know you were one of us.'

It took some little while for him to focus, and more time again to shape the features into a face he recognised. It was the architect's underground workman who every day carried the buckets up and down, tipping the spoil into his cart outside the house. The two faced one another over a rough wooden table, though Johnny could not remember sitting down. The dank smell carried over the table.

'We've done for him, all right.'

'Done for who?'

'Mr Kumans. They didn't know he was a foreigner, but I did. When you work for people long enough you know. They put the notice on his door and he got out quick.'

'What would have happened to him?'

The workman shrugged.

'Anything. The house burned down. Him strung up. Who cares?' In a spirit of camaraderie he carried his jug to Johnny's and poured a stream of frothy beer into it. 'You don't care, I suppose?'

The cafe was much emptier now. It must be very late.

'Of course not,' Johnny replied, his wits not quite gone, 'but I've some unfinished business with Kumans. Could you find him for me?'

'Perhaps.'

'Get him to meet me at the station?' He reached out his jug and touched it against the other's. 'Tomorrow? For the cause?'

'Perhaps.'

He was asleep, his head on his arms, when he felt the pricking sensation against his leg. He twitched and changed his position but the irritation only increased. His eyes opened painfully, the surrounding skin swollen. There were only a few dim bulbs in the cafe, but outside the window the dark sky glimmered with the beginnings of the day. It seemed to flicker. That was snow. It was falling heavily. His leg hurt.

'Take some coffee, my friend.'

The voice spoke softly and was very near, the accent foreign. He turned to find the cloaked figure up close to him. The hand that held the knife was hidden to all but Johnny, and the smiling countenance, demonic though it was, could arouse no suspicions. Two cups of black coffee steamed on the table top.

'Drink, please. I should like you awake.'

The lips were red in the pale face. The young man withdrew the knife. His lips were like a wound.

'And then?' Johnny asked, the coffee rank and hot on his tongue.

'Drink!'

There were men taking early breakfasts, who paid no attention to anything but the greasy food on their plates. There was no-one whose eye he could catch. He had to finish his coffee and, all to soon, was forced to leave the shelter of the cafe for the world of whiteness outside, for streets which felt the more silent against the memory of wild, riotous clamour. The air struck cold, sharp as a blade. The snow swarmed upon them, large white flakes which stuck. Early risers emerged from the warrens of houses and apartments and padded, heads down, through the thick powder with never a glance at the pale young man and his pressed and despairing companion.

Red the lips of the pale young man against the snow. Black the cloak he shook free of the accumulated whiteness.

Angels' tears, Sophie used to call snow. But why were the angels crying? She never said and he had never dared to ask, fearing terrible revelations. Sophie's was a knowing melancholy. Now he thought of her visit to the clairvoyant and the vision of blood. Was this, then, true?

He trudged along, half a pace in front of his captor. If he had gone straight to Mr Farg with his information he would not now be at the mercy of this cold assassin. He cursed his foolishness over again. He had, in a moment of madness, ignored the guiding principle of his short lifetime, had forsaken brute self-interest for something he did not fully understand. Why should he care what happened to Kumans? He did *not* care. Truly he did not! Then why that fatal hesitation? Because for some reason he cared about Kumans's story. But why should he? What possessed him? He recalled how he had taken the sheet of paper with names, addresses and instructions, had slipped it into his pocket when they were trapped below ground.

They came upon men grouped round a brazier, their hands held palms forward to soak up the heat. Ordinary working men. He was accustomed to pitying the sheepish subservience of such as these, but now he would readily have joined their number, exchanging inconsequential quips and badinage, passing the long day like some semi-articulate animal but at least surviving it. He looked on them with longing as he passed, the absurd caps pulled over their foreheads, the wispy cigarettes stuck to their lips. Was there not, after all, a wisdom in their dull simplicity, their stupid lack of expectation?

He thought of the peasants on the mountain, equally stupid, and of his brief interlude at the Spa. Violence everywhere, and fear. It had all come about so rapidly, altering the contours of life like smothering snow.

It fell ever more thickly, obliterating. It seemed to seal everything off – his past life submerged and irretrievable, the future unreachable across the white and clinging drifts. He and the pale young man were alone in an eternal blood-chilling present: step after step but never moving on, nightmare figures destined to rehearse ugly floundering movements for ever amid the swirling flakes, drenched by angels' tears.

They entered a foul courtyard and Johnny was prodded towards an open doorway. Stairs climbed through air cold and fetid. They halted at a door that bore a crudely painted 27. The cloaked figure pushed it open and ushered him in.

The room was as chill as the stairwell and stank as badly. In a chair hard against the far wall sat the moon-faced boy, his hands clutching the seat so that the knuckles showed white. The puffy face was red with weeping.

'Haven't moved,' the knifeman said, 'have you?'

'N-n-n-no.'

'Such a good little boy.'

Johnny was forced on to a dirty straw pallet that lay in one corner of the room. He felt the knife's point against the back of his neck as his tormentor began to talk in his queerly hushed foreign voice.

'You and I are going to have a little talk, my friend. About a man called Alph.'

'Who?'

'Fool!'

A foot stamped on his back, crushing him to the bed, while the knife ran along his arm, opening the fabric of his coat and parting the surface of the skin in two white lips of flesh with a pink blush between. There was no flow of blood, so perfect was the control, so great the artistry. He heard himself whimper with fear and pain at the same time as the boy began to gurgle wordlessly.

'Silence!'

The foot shifted from his back to behind his head and pressed it into the filthy bedding. The man's strength was immense. Johnny tried to wriggle free but was powerless to do so. It was impossible to breathe. He began to grow faint. At last the foot released him and, gasping and sobbing, he turned his face towards his persecutor: 'All right.'

Now he was allowed to sit up on the straw mattress, still dazed and shaking. The other grinned at him.

'What little resistance! You value your life, I think. Tell me about Eric Alph.'

Johnny conjured up an image of Kumans's questing hands – it made betrayal the easier – and began to tell what he knew. He told it slowly, hopelessly wasting time, knowing that the knife had not yet finished its work. The young man with the cloak seemed in no hurry.

'And you,' he asked. 'What is your interest in this man?'

'Money, of course. The same as for you, I dare say.'

'Fool! What do you know of my purposes? Money! I have enough of that. You think the world motivated by such stuff, do you? I chase this man for others who have their own purposes – and they have nothing to do with money. But for myself . . . '

'You enjoy killing.'

'Ha!'

'The solicitor. Those peasants on the mountain. My friend Hans.'

Here the poor lad on his chair began to quiver uncontrollably, his eyes pitifully glazed with a lava-flow of hot tears.

'Yes, yes – the sport! Those delicious moments of utter knowing when the blade breaks through the black veil of the mystery!'

Suddenly excited, the eyes alive in the pale face, the scarlet lips twitching, he brought the knife to Johnny's throat.

'Where,' he demanded simply, 'is Kumans?'

'He's gone. I don't know where. Perhaps I could find him, lead you to him.'

The sharp edge was against his windpipe.

'I think not.'

Johnny, his eyes closed, his teeth clenched, heard a movement outside. The door swung open, bringing cold air and then the hunched, shambling figure of Rook. His persecutor scowled at the intrusion, turning in anger. No words were spoken, however – for Rook, rushing at him behind a spiked wooden pole, rammed the weapon with manic force into his victim's chest.

The cloaked man staggered backwards, the crude spear lodged in him, his eyes wide with horror. He began to career wildly about the room, turning and flailing the air with the knife he still gripped. As the spear struck against walls and furniture it sent further spasms of agony coursing through his body until, letting out the pitiable high-pitched whine of a stuck pig, he collapsed on the floor and his life flowed from him.

'Foreign scum!' Rook hissed. 'This is my room.'

He saw the arm-band and looked on Johnny with a sudden respect.

'I rescued you,' he said. 'Remember that. You tell the party that.'

'Of course.'

'Yes, you tell them,' Rook continued, shuffling about the room. He went over to the body in its pool of blood, stared at it for a moment, then opened the door and stepped outside, muttering to himself. 'Foreign filth in a man's own home. There's a new wind blowing . . .'

He was gone. The moon-faced boy, trembling on his chair, reached a hand into his pocket.

'D-didn't . . . sh-sh-show him, Johnny.'

'Show him what?'

He took a crumpled sheet of paper from the trembling fingers. It was tinted a delicate pastel blue and was faintly scented. The writing was meticulously rounded:

Dictated by Emanuel Farg and transcribed in his presence by Princeps Larooning.

Fresh and vital intelligence having transpired, your instant arrival is solicitously demanded. In the interim your dear sister keeps us fond company. Do come soon.

Beneath, the hand unmistakably Sophie's, was the single word *Please*!

42 Last Chance

' . . . nor should you so misconstrue my motives as for a moment to nurture the thought that I meant the remotest harm to this sweet girl. She has, will you not vouchsafe to your brother my dear, received in full the courtesies of the house.'

Sophie nodded dumbly, though her eyes told a different story. She sat upright in her chair, taut and frightened. Next to her, Larooning sprawled as if at ease with the world, but here, too, there was a deception: the truth was revealed in the havoc wreaked upon his facial flesh. Swollen ridges of raw tissue converged and crossed, the original features quite distorted, scarcely recognisable, less a human visage than the fiery mountains and deep craters of some red, volcanic wasteland. Johnny could not keep his glances away.

'No, the reason for my haste,' continued Mr Farg tirelessly, 'was the sanguinary unpleasantness visited upon our friend here, with all that it horripilantly implies for our own sheeny skins. May such a monster be assumed fastidious in his choice of victim? I think not, the more especially when he no longer has good reason to withhold his butchery. I mean, of course, when he has triumphantly discovered the present identity of the man he has so unremittingly pursued. I believe that you understand me?'

'I think so.'

'Which does demand the question, not preposterous in the circumstances, of why you chose to delay imparting the information our good friend here was seeking and for which he has been happy to pay a modest sum. Why, I ponder, does young Johnny not come beating upon my door? Is he – I search with great sensitivity for the *mot juste* – is he playing treacherous?'

'No!'

'No, no, clearly not. Perish the uncharitable thought! For what would it profit him? The money is here, after all. There must be a simple misunderstanding.'

He leant forward, took a Dresden figurine in the crook of his arm and pulled it softly towards him. There was a long silence. Johnny was aware that it was his last chance, that he dare not misplay his hand.

'I discovered only recently that Kumans was Alph,' he said at last, struggling to suppress the tremble in his voice. 'I had to be sure. I knew, too, that he held valuable documents, and I was determined to find them. Then the house was attacked by the mob and we had to get out.'

Mr Farg continued to fuss over his figurine. Larooning spoke mournfully.

'The mob saved me,' he said. 'He was cutting me to pieces. When they came up the street he fled.'

'And where,' asked their host, perhaps not caring to be upstaged, 'is this Kumans now?'

'On the run,' Johnny replied. 'But I think I can find him.'

'Think?'

'I know I can. It's already in hand. I'll have him here by nightfall – with the documents.'

He rose and took Sophie's hand, knowing on the instant that his old skills had not deserted him. He was in control. They would see that they needed him.

'If he's frightened he'll run. If I reach him first, before that madman with the knife, I'll get those papers out of him. Or Sophie will. He's besotted with her.'

He stared Mr Farg in the eye, challenging him.

'But I'd like a little more money for the danger we'll be in.'

His gaze was undeviating. The cheek of his demand must be seen as unquestioning self-confidence. He was a loyal worker, a professional who deserved his reward. No, more than that: he was the lynch-pin of the operation.

'Show him where there's money,' came the sudden verdict. 'For quick spending.'

Larooning led Johnny into the next room, where there were sacks piled against a wall. He opened one and saw that it was stuffed with notes.

'Help yourself!' called Mr Farg lugubriously. 'It's worth half what it bought you last week and will in all probability be worth half again by tonight. Untrustworthy as a baby's bottom.'

Johnny nevertheless brought two of the sacks with him, dragging them along the floor. Larooning, following, took him by the arm.

'Those documents,' he said, 'are vital for us. I don't know exactly what's in them, but there will somewhere be references to a hidden underground city – a city of myth. Look for those references. In the place I come from there are many who seek that city, some for good reasons and some for bad. My people, on the other hand, wish the city never to be found.'

'Why?'

'It's a story too long to tell here, ' Larooning replied. He looked away for a moment, distracted. 'Why is it, I ask myself, that I never have the time and the opportunity? For anything! Is it fate, perhaps? An unkind destiny?'

But then he pulled himself up, remembering the business in hand.

'There is an organisation called the Red Blade, which seeks to subjugate the people. It is opposed by a movement whose symbol is an ever-open eye of bright blue. According to myth there is a city of goodness and beauty beneath the ground. The Red Blade would like to invade it and destroy it. That madman with the cloak works on their behalf. The others wish to find strength from its existence.

'My colleagues, although they support the Eye in most things, fear that the hunt for the mythical city will deflect the good people from the work that has to be done in opposing the Blade. We want those papers discovered and destroyed. Let us, in the words of the great Wilderness Poet, have an end to dreams!'

'And Kumans?'

'He is the grandson of an illustrious man and might once have been the symbol of a new dawn. Perhaps he yet could. There are those even now – good men, too – who would welcome his return as a hereditary ruler. I despise all strong rulers! Should anyone attempt to spirit him back we will have to liquidate your Kumans, I regret to say.

'But I am interested only in the documents. We must find them – and destroy them!'

As he uttered this final phrase he flourished his arms in the air. With a brittle sound, several colourful figurines leapt from their resting places and toppled to the floor. Mr Farg uttered a sharp and anguished cry.

'My children!'

Johnny led Sophie down the stairs, pulling the sacks of money behind him. When they were outside in the street he reached inside his coat and tugged from it the notice which he had found affixed to the architect's door: REQUISITIONED. FOREIGNERS.

Having unrolled it, he reached towards Sophie's hat, pulled out the long silver pin and, striking as if with a dagger, impaled the paper against the woodwork.

43 Departures

Unexpectedly, incredibly, the station was wild with a milling throng of pushing, yelping, hysterical would-be passengers, all of them surging towards a single train with but half a dozen carriages which already had a cluster of faces at every window and desperate boarders stacked in every open doorway. The foreigners were trying to escape.

Johnny, holding the package to his chest, skirted the agitated crowds, trying to spot Kumans among their number. He saw an old man fall and be trampled by hectic feet; he saw a young girl, her hand torn from her mother's, weeping blindly among heedless strangers; he saw a delicate, emaciated woman beating her fists furiously against the backs of people who blocked her way to the nearest carriage.

He reached the end of the platform and began to retrace his steps. A whistle blew and the clamour increased. Steam gushed along the length of the train. A guard was trying to close one of the doors but the press of passengers inside was too great. He waved a flag in a vainglorious display of authority but still people tried to clamber aboard. The train was moving. The whistle blew again.

'Stand back!' sounded an official command. 'For your own safety . . . Another train in an hour's time.'

From the crowd there came an angry growl which grew slowly and ominously. The last carriage creaked away and the people at the platform's edge pushed backwards to avoid being flung onto the lines. Punches were thrown.

'Give us space, for God's sake!'

'Lift the children over!'

'Someone get the police – we'll all be crushed!'

Though the next train was an hour away the crowd showed no inclination to retreat. Indeed, more people were joining it all the time, struggling along with swollen suitcases which must contain all the essentials of life they could ever hope to keep. The noise grew louder and louder.

For a moment he was caught up in a small knot of new arrivals. A young man among their number, catching sight of the arm-band, curled his lip and carefully spat at his feet. He was at once whisked away by his companions who loudly made all kinds of excuses for such uncharacteristic behaviour (he was unwell, he had mistaken Johnny for someone else) and apologised in chorus with beseeching eyes. Johnny's reaction was to hurry away, stripping the band from his sleeve and pushing it into a pocket.

He found Kumans and Columbine in the bar, sitting close and silent. It was quiet inside after the disorder of the platform, and he heard his own voice brash, loud, uncomfortable: 'You have to get out!'

The architect smiled indulgently, but said nothing. Columbine shook her head with exaggerated solemnity.

'There is no escape,' she declared. 'The universe is enclosed.'

'Away from here,' Johnny continued, lowering his voice. 'You're in danger, Boris. I know.'

Kumans was pleasantly startled by the unaccustomed use of his first name.

'Because of my blood?' he asked. 'Because I'm a foreigner? Don't think I'm frightened by all that!'

Johnny dropped his package on the table.

'Because of this,' he said, still whispering. 'These are the documents from the basement. I've just been there. The door was open. Upstairs there were people tearing the place apart.'

'I've no use for those papers,' Kumans replied flatly.

'You're in danger because of your past,' Johnny persisted. 'Believe me! There are people who want these documents – who would kill for them.'

'The answer is obvious, then. Give them away. Burn them. Why bring them to me?'

Johnny, frustrated, looked about the room. Small groups of people were hunched over drinks and idly chatting. A few individuals sat behind newspapers and magazines.

'I think,' he said hesitantly, 'that you should go to that country you spoke of. Look for the underground city.'

'Senacherib!' Kumans's strange exclamation was accompanied by a display of teeth as in laughter. 'You warn me of danger and then ask me to leap into a snake pit? What a dear friend you are!'

Columbine reached out both her hands and captured one of Johnny's, fetching it to her lips.

'Snakes may dance,' she stated, 'but more often sting.'

'Some danger,' Johnny agreed, 'but many people would welcome you gladly. They want you back. And wouldn't it be . . . home?'

Now the architect laughed bitterly.

'What do I know of home?' he demanded. 'Nothing. The word is meaningless to me. It is, in any case, a limiting, bourgeois concept. Back to the womb! No, don't foist your fond fantasies on me.'

'*My* fantasies?'

'Of course! I've watched how you react to my diverting little story. The stuff of myth, isn't it? You can't resist it. It answers to some need of your own – a sense of belonging, perhaps, of security, family affection. Well, it's a tired and threadbare fantasy, and it's all yours. Don't try to implicate me!'

Johnny wanted to protest that this was nonsense, that all he wanted from life was enough cash for comfort, easy money and an easy life, but then he remembered his behaviour on the way to Mr Farg's and he said nothing. But surely it was nonsense . . . Kumans, meanwhile, had begun to raise his voice.

'What do we owe the past?' he challenged. 'Nothing. And our families? Nothing. Did we ask to be born? I recognise no allegiance to yesterday's fooleries.'

Columbine leant up close to him and, to Johnny's amazement, fussed at his hair and ran a finger down the scar on his cheek. The architect, for his part, allowed this intimacy as if it were commonplace, even inclining his head slightly towards her in a gesture of happy consent.

'Yesterday,' he continued, not at all deflected from his speechifying, 'is a word we should expunge from the vocabulary.'

'Don't we,' Johnny asked quietly, uncomfortably surprised to find the thought surfacing as he spoke it, 'have any duty to our families?'

And what sort of obligation to his own family had he honoured? The self accusation came immediately and justifiably to his mind. What had he and Sophie done to rescue their mother from her sodden decline? Who was he to put these preposterous questions? Why did he ask them?

'The world is born afresh every day,' Kumans declared. 'Every minute. This minute! There is no past, and even the present is eager to transform itself into the future. What does it matter if my father was a saint or a sadist, that I come from a line of poets or poltroons? They've had their present, which I refuse to recognise. We should bury the dead entire – all their thoughts and laws and institutions along with their bones!'

Among the group at the next table was a frail white-haired old man whose eyes nevertheless suggested intellectual vigour. Johnny watched how he responded to the architect's declamations, sitting forward alert and attentive. He seemed about to spring.

'Let us all deem ourselves orphans,' Kumans added with a satisfied laugh. 'No sins of the fathers to bother our heads with.'

'Nothing so tiresome as tradition, eh?' came the sudden retort from the white-haired spectator.

Kumans, surprised, took a little while to assess the spirit of the intervention. There was a tartness in the remark which required answering, but he was not a man to feel himself at a disadvantage in an argument.

'No tradition,' he replied after some seconds. 'Quite so.'

'And no inherited values?'

'None.'

Here the old man shook his head from what appeared to be exasperation.

'I'm an architect,' Kumans said. 'I use the materials which are available to me, and these may be the same as other men have used, but my creations derive from my own brain. Totally. I don't turn to past masters for inspiration. Does that make sense to you?'

'I laugh at your presumption,' said the old man simply. 'You flatter yourself.'

Kumans stood up, his face flushed: 'What do you know of it? You've never seen one of my buildings!'

'And yet I know that you deceive yourself.'

Now his companions sought to restrain their argumentative friend, plucking at his sleeve, patting him firmly on the shoulder: 'Enough! No point in starting a row. Drink up your beer.'

'My work is my own,' Kumans added, subsiding.

'If I may say so,' continued the other, 'complete originality is surely an impossibility. But the desire to overthrow the values of the past leads to what you see from the window over there. Brutality and victimisation. All kinds of unspeakable horrors.'

'I know nothing of that,' Kumans replied.

'A brutal trampling on all that a thousand years of civilisation have taught us to revere. This rush to the future which you're so proud of is nothing but an abominable denial of man's finer instincts. What an example to this young friend of yours here! No respect, decency, honour . . . '

Kumans banged a fist on the table: 'If you want to talk about violence,' he said hotly, 'then what you see out there is simply common humanity on the loose. It's the morality of the common man in all its ugly glory. If you think I advocate such a thing you're badly mistaken. What we need is not this dirty stampede but a revolution from above, led by men of vision!'

'The two are the same.'

This gnomic utterance seemed to bring the debate to a close, to the general relief. From the window the desperate jostlings on the platform could indeed be seen, but obscurely. Flurries of snow swept across the view. Anyone entering the bar performed a comical routine of foot-stamping and coat-slapping at the door, usually followed by a tossing of the head and a rubbing of the eyes.

'But let's be more specific,' said Kumans's tormentor, as if there had been no pause in the conversation whatsoever.

'No, no!' chorused his companions again. 'Enough, Old Tom! Give us a rest!'

'If your father also was an architect and had built some dwellings which later, after his death, proved dangerously below standard . . . '

'Oh, if!' smiled Kumans.

'. . . would you not, even though you had nothing to do with the designs, feel some sense of responsibility?'

'How should I?'

'Being your father's son. No moral obligation?'

'None at all! You speak with an ancient tongue, Methuselah. That's not the kind of talk that has any meaning these days. When you were young, perhaps . . . It's mere romance.'

'Ah yes, when I was young,' the old man said gently. 'There's much I could tell you of that. I had to make a decision between two different kinds of obligation, and I have never known whether what I did was right. But it would never have occurred to me to shrug off the very idea of obligation, as if the world had no meaning in it save what I invented on the spur of the moment.'

'So you suffered the most dreadful pangs of conscience,' mocked Kumans.

'Endlessly.'

'And for whose benefit? For mankind?'

'No, I chose differently. I chose for my own sons and their sons. It may have been a selfish act, but I chose for their freedom.'

'And you may depend,' lectured Kumans with a sneer, 'that they won't thank you for it. I know *I* shouldn't. Be eternally grateful to some ancient for a decision he took for his own good reasons years and years ago? As if that had any power to dictate how I should behave? The world's moved on, good sir!'

The old man looked upon the architect with such an expression of pity and contempt that his friends redoubled their efforts to draw him away, at last persuading him that there was nothing more usefully to be said. He put on coat and hat and made his way somewhat unsteadily to the door, standing in silence for some time before stooping to the handle and venturing, head down, into the white storm.

'Harmless,' allowed Kumans, reaching for his drink. 'He meant well enough, I dare say.'

Another train had arrived. The cries of the crowd rose so loud that they could be heard from deep within the bar. Fights were breaking out. The scene was all confusion, but it was evident that a group of arm-banded men, their faces hidden within large hooded garments, had advanced to the centre of the disturbances, and that heavy sticks were being wielded.

'And you wanted to send me out there,' Kumans said wonderingly.

Johnny brought two pieces of paper from his pocket.

'No, it's a different platform,' he said. 'For the east. I've already bought a ticket. And look – this is a safe address where Sophie's staying. I'll take Columbine there. You could write to us . . . '

But it was useless. Kumans waved away both slips of paper, while Columbine wrapped her arms about his neck.

'We're together now,' she said.

Johnny rose to his feet. He knew what was going to happen but was not yet ready to admit it to himself. He pulled on his overcoat and picked up the package of documents.

'I'll get you a seat on the train,' he said. 'If you change your mind come and find me.'

There was no reply. He left them elaborately entwined and pushed open the door. The cold struck against his face like a sharp blade. Within seconds his ears ached, his nose burned, his eyelids were caked with chill whiteness. A swift wind drove the snow towards him, a soft relentless hail, a vast flock of white birds.

The train for the east stood waiting at its platform. He thought what a long journey it had to make into regions that were mere names in fables. He touched the polished coachwork with a numbed finger as if to take some of the magic to himself. The windows were misted over, the train's occupants dark shadows behind the glass. Doors opened and closed. Kumans would not come.

He climbed into an empty carriage and deposited the package on the seat. It was as much as he could do. He sat next to it for a moment. The compartment glowed with burnished wood. The seats were richly upholstered, and there were finely stitched antimacassars with the railway company's motif embroidered upon them. Above his head was a webbing of strong cord for luggage, by his knee a small, lipped shelf for drinks. Along the corridor somewhere was a restaurant car where people would eat sumptuous meals and smoke long cigars as they were carried further and further east to wonderful places that could only be dreamed of.

Kumans would not come, he knew, but he nevertheless forced himself out of the comfort of the carriage and stood once more on the platform in the billowing snow squalls. A guard was loading the last of a collection of trunks into the goods van.

'Get inside,' he chided as he swung the door shut. 'You'll freeze.'

'I'm waiting for someone.'

'Well, they'll have to hurry. We leave in five minutes.'

Johnny walked up and down the platform, beating his arms against his sides for warmth. Yes, he knew what was going to happen. He allowed the idea a little glimpse of light before quickly smothering it again. It was unthinkable.

'Two minutes!' called the guard cheerily.

Could your life change in the space of a few weeks? He thought back to that first meeting with Mr Farg and rapidly recalled everything that had followed from it – Otto's death, other deaths, the fear of his own death, his time at the Spa, Kurt Cherfas, the peasants and the beautiful Hildegard, Boris Kumans and his strange story . . . Was it only the last of these which had touched his brain, or was it a fusion of them all which produced the intoxication?

A whistle blew and the guard reappeared with a flag. A spurt of steam signalled an anxiousness to be off. The time had come. He felt as if there were two demons dicing for possession of him, one which would have him reject the foolishness he was drawn to, the other urging him to do as he now did, striding forward to the carriage, pulling himself inside, slamming the door shut and sitting with the precious package, waiting for the train to start. He felt the carriage shudder. He heard the wheels creak. They were moving.

Did he do this for Kumans? That could not be. No, it was for himself, as if by taking upon himself Kumans's role he inserted himself into that other story, became part of that heady myth, was no longer bereft of a meaningful past, a context, a family history, but partook of the glory that fell like a golden mantle upon the shoulders of the sons of that great poet who had found the lost city, and upon the sons of their sons and all those who followed.

The train gathered speed. He wiped the glass with his sleeve: snow and more snow. Under the wooden awning at the far end of the platform stood the white-haired old gentleman, sheltering from the blizzard. He saw Johnny's face at the window and raised a hand in salute.